HILD

NICOLA GRIFFITH

BLACKFRIARS

BLACKFRIARS

First published in Great Britain in 2014 by Blackfriars

A CIP catalogue record for this book
is available from the British Library.

ISBN 978-0-349-13422-2
C Format ISBN 978-0-349-13424-6

Printed and bound in Great Britain by
Clays Ltd, St Ives plc

Papers used by Blackfriars are from well-managed forests
and other responsible sources.

MIX
Paper from
responsible sources
FSC
www.fsc.org   FSC® C104740

This imprint has no connection with The Order of Preachers (Dominicans)

Blackfriars
An imprint of
Little, Brown Book Group
100 Victoria Embankment
London EC4Y 0DY

An Hachette UK Company
www.hachette.co.uk

www.blackfriarsbooks.com

For Kelley, my warp and weft

Contents

✦

✛ BRITAIN IN THE SEVENTH CENTURY ✛

Iona

PICTLAND

DÁL RIATA

ANTONINE WALL

GODODDIN

NORTHUMBRIA

ALT CLUT

BERNICIA

Bebbanburg

Yeavering

Haltwhistle

HADRIAN'S WALL

Tinamutha/Arbeia

Corabrig

DERE STREET

Caer Luel

Broac

RHEGED

Catterick

Bay of the Beacon/Mulstanton

CRAVEN

DEIRA

Derventio

Isle of Vannin

ELMET

York

Goodmanham

Caer Loid

Sancton

Brough

Barton

LINDSEY

MON

Glannauc

Lindum

Deganwy

GWYNEDD

MERCIANS

ERMINE STREET

NORTH FOLK

NORTH GYRWE

SOUTH GYRWE

Deorham

Tomeworthig

EAST ANGLES

SOUTH FOLK

Rendlesham

Gipswic

EAST SAXONS

HWICCE

Lundenwic

Canterbury

WEST SAXONS

KENT

DYFNEINT

SOUTH SAXONS

Caer Uisc

0 Miles 50 100

0 Kilometers 100

© 2013 Jeffrey L. Ward

Northumbria
began as two adjacent
kingdoms, Deira and Bernicia

Bernicia

Ida

Æthelric Theoderic Adda others

Æthelfrith = Bebba
of Alt Clut

Theobald

Æthelfrith = Bebba
of Alt Clut

Eanfrith   others

Talorcan

Acha =

others

Æbbe   Oswald = niece of Beli
of Alt Clut

Oswiu

Eanflæd   Wuscfrea   the twins

Deira

Yffi

Ælla

Ælfric

Osric

Oswine

Æthelric

Cwenburh = Edwin = Æthelburh
of Mercia   of East Anglia

Eadfrith   Osfrith = *Clotrude
of Frankia

Yffi

*Onnen --- Hereric = Breguswith
of Elmet   of Kent

*Cian

Hild

Æthelric = Hereswith
of East Anglia

*Ælfwyn

Ealdwulf

=	married	
---	liaison	
*	fictional character	

1

✦

THE CHILD'S WORLD CHANGED late one afternoon, though she didn't know it. She lay at the edge of the hazel coppice, one cheek pressed to the moss that smelt of worm cast and the last of the sun, listening: to the wind in the elms, rushing away from the day, to the jackdaws changing their calls from "Outward! Outward!" to "Home now! Home!," to the rustle of the last frightened shrews scuttling under the layers of leaf fall before the owls began their hunt. From far away came the indignant honking of geese as the goosegirl herded them back inside the wattle fence, and the child knew, in the wordless way that three-year-olds reckon time, that soon Onnen would come and find her and Cian and hurry them back.

Onnen, some leftwise cousin of Ceredig king, always hurried, but the child, Hild, did not. She liked the rhythm of her days: time alone (Cian didn't count) and time by the fire listening to the murmur of British and Anglisc and even Irish. She liked time at the edges of things—the edge of the crowd, the edge of the pool, the edge of the wood—where all must pass but none quite belonged.

The jackdaw cries faded. The geese quieted. The wind cooled. She sat up. "Cian?"

Cian, sitting cross-legged as a seven-year-old could and Hild as yet could not, looked up from the hazel switch he was stripping.

"Where's Onnen?"

He swished his stick. "I shall hit a tree, as the Gododdin once swung at the wicked Bryneich." But the elms' sough and sigh was becoming a low roar in the rush of early evening, and she didn't care about wicked war bands, defeated in the long ago by her Anglisc forefathers.

"I want Onnen."

"She'll be along. Or perhaps I shall be the hero Morei, firing the furze, dying with red light flaring on the enamel of my armour, the rim of my shield."

"I want Hereswith!" If she couldn't have Onnen, she would have her sister.

"I could make a sword for you, too. You shall be Branwen."

"I don't want a sword. I want Onnen. I want Hereswith."

He sighed and stood. "We'll go now. If you're frightened."

She frowned. She wasn't frightened. She was three; she had her own shoes. Then she heard firm, tidy footsteps on the woodcutters' path, and she laughed. "Onnen!"

But even as Cian's mother came into view, Hild frowned again. Onnen was not hurrying. Indeed, Onnen took a moment to smooth her hair, and at that Hild and Cian stepped close together.

Onnen stopped before Hild.

"Your father is dead."

Hild looked at Cian. He would know what this meant.

"The prince is dead?" he said.

Onnen looked from one to the other. "You'll not be wanting to call him prince now."

Far away a settling jackdaw cawed once.

"Da is prince! He is!"

"He was." With a strong thumb, Onnen wiped a smear of dirt from Hild's cheekbone. "Little prickle, the lord Hereric was our prince, indeed. But he'll not be back. And your troubles are just begun."

Troubles. Hild knew of troubles from songs.

"We go to your lady mother—keep a quiet mouth and a bright mind, I know you're able. And Cian, bide by me. The highfolk won't need us in their business just now."

Cian swished at an imaginary foe. "Highfolk," he said, in the same tone he said *Feed the pigs!* when Onnen told him to, but he also rubbed the furrow under his nose with his knuckle, as he did when he was trying not to cry.

Hild put her arms around him. They didn't quite meet, but she squeezed as hard as she could. Trouble meant they had to listen, not fight.

And then they were wrapped about by Onnen's arms, Onnen's cloak,

Onnen's smell, wool and woman and toasted malt, and Hild knew she'd been brewing beer, and the afternoon was almost ordinary again.

"Us," Cian said, and hugged Hild hard. "We are us."

"We are us," Hild repeated, though she wasn't sure what he meant.

Cian nodded. He kept a protective arm around Hild but looked at his mother. "Was it a wound?"

"It was not, but the rest we'll chew on later, as we may. For now we get the bairn to her mam and stay away from the hall."

Caer Loid, at the heart of Elmet, wasn't much of a hall. Hild knew this because when they'd first arrived in the rain months ago, her mother had sniffed her sniff-that-was-a-sigh. Breguswith had done that often in their exile among the kingdoms of the wealh, always as a prelude to driving Onnen and her other women to organise the temporary stop into a reflection of home while she set out her cases of whorls and spindles and tucked her distaff in her belt. At these times, Hild and Hereswith must creep like mice, and the score of sworn warrior gesiths who remained would get more magnificent baldrics for their swords, gold thread in the tablet weave at cuff and hem, even embroidered work along the sleeves. They must look proud and bright and well provided for, that all would know who they were, where they came from, and to where they might still ascend in service of the lady Breguswith and Hereric, her lord, should-be king of Deira.

Hild recalled no sights or sounds of Deira, the standard against which all was compared, the long-left home. She had vague memories of sun on plums, others of a high place of lowing cattle and bitter wind, of ships and wagons and the crook of her father's arm as he rode, but she knew none of them were home, could be home. Æthelfrith Iding, Anglisc king of Bernicia, had driven them out before she and her sister were born. She recognised people who might be from that long-lost home when they galloped in on foundering horses or slipped through the enclosure fence during the dark of the moon. She knew them by their thick woven cloaks, their hanging hair and beards, and their Anglisc voices: words drumming like apples spilt over wooden boards, round, rich, stirring. Like her father's words, and her mother's, and her sister's. Utterly unlike Onnen's otter-swift British or the dark liquid gleam of Irish. Hild spoke each to each. Apples to apples, otter to otter, gleam to gleam, though only when her mother wasn't there. Never stoop to wealh speech, her mother said, not even British, not even with Onnen. Never trust wealh, especially those shaved priestly spies.

From the byre came the rolling whicker-whinny of horses getting to know each other. At least two new voices. Hild clutched harder at Onnen's hand and Onnen shook her slightly: *Quiet mouth, bright mind!*

The riders, two men, were with Ceredig king and the lady Breguswith in the hall. The room was smoky and hot, like all British dwellings—the peat in the great central pit was burning high, though it was not yet cold outside—but still the smell of travel, of horse, was clearly on the men, and their bright, checked cloaks were much muddied at hem and seat. Breguswith, distaff tucked under her left arm, rolling her fine-yarn spindle down her thigh with her right, stared absently at the fire, though Hild knew even as her mother's fingers were busy, busy, busy teasing out the yarn, testing its tension, her attention was focused on Ceredig king, who laughed and leaned from his stool and let firelight wink on the thick torc around his neck.

Onnen pushed Hild forward. The visitors, both slight, with magnificent moustaches and the air of brothers, turned.

"Ah," said the taller one in British. Strange British, from the west. "You have your father's hair."

Yffing chestnut, her mother called it. *And her outside one big prickliness like a chestnut, too,* said Onnen. *Or a hedgepig,* said her mother, and they would laugh. No one was laughing now but Ceredig, and it was his laugh-because-I-am-king laugh, the one for important visitors, to show ease in his own hall. *Everything a king does is a lie,* Onnen said.

And then the stranger looked beyond Hild. "And who's this?"

Hild twisted to look. Cian had followed her into the firelight, ready to snatch her back, as he'd done in spring, when the ram had charged as she got too near.

"He is nobody," said her mother, in Anglisc. "My woman's boy." And as she turned—with that long, careless grace that made men look, made the strangers look—Onnen put her arm around Cian and tugged him gently back into the shadow. But this visitor was quicker than most.

"Wait," he said. "You." He crooked his finger, and Onnen and Cian stepped back into the light. "Your name?"

"Onnen, lord."

"And this is your son?"

"He is, lord."

"And yourself, Onnen, you were born here?"

"Indeed, lord. Six and twenty years since." She stood a little prouder. "I am cousin to Ceredig king."

"You're all cousins in this benighted wood," said the second stranger, but he was already turning away and beckoning for the first to do likewise. And Hild understood that although her mother and Onnen had told nothing but the truth, the visitors had been fed an essential lie.

Quiet mouth, bright mind.

"Edwin Snakebeard will come to avenge Hereric Yffing's death," the stranger was saying to Ceredig.

"Of course he'll come. He'll come from the south with Rædwald's war band to claim Deira and lay his rival kinsman's death at my door. The excuse he's looked for. Or made."

Onnen tried to herd Hild away, but Hild rooted herself to the floor, the way puppies turned limp and heavy when she tried to pick them up.

Ceredig was still talking ". . . this hall is burnt about my head, will there be a place for me with the king of Gwynedd?"

The stranger shrugged: maybe yes, maybe no.

"So. I'll fight, then. As I must. And make for Cadfan of Gwynedd an excuse, in his turn, to swarm north with fire and sword against the Anglisc. But tell you, Marro, to Cadfan king, aye and young Cadwallon, that one day he'll have to face this serpent, this king-killer, in the open. Tell him that."

Marro said, "I will tell him."

Gwynedd, Hild thought. *Marro. Cadwallon.*

Her mother was looking at her. "Hild, go with Onnen now, to your sister. Comfort Hereswith for me." And Hild's mind closed seamlessly over the names as though they'd never been.

Hereswith was eight. She had their mother's hair, the colour of linden honey, and their mother's round, pretty face—usually. Tonight, when Onnen pulled aside the embroidered curtain, Hereswith fell on her, weeping, babbling in a mix of Anglisc and British: What would happen now? Where would they go? Had it hurt when their father died? Would they starve? Where was their mother?

Seeing Hereswith weep started a tickle deep in Hild's chest, and then her nose ran, and then she howled as Onnen unfastened her cyrtel and tucked her next to Hereswith on the horsehair and sweet-gale mattress, promised them warm milk, and stroked her chestnut hair. Her dead, dead da's hair.

Hild shut it out, imagined she could hear nothing but the wind in the elms, blowing where it would, a soft roar under the moon.

She woke to Hereswith's slow, steady breaths beside her and her mother's murmur above. She kept her eyes tightly closed.

". . . can't flee to Frankia, not with the storm season almost on us."

"The Hwicce might take us in," Onnen said. "They took Osric. And he's ætheling."

"Only a cousin. And soon enough he'll be riding to Deira to show Edwin Usurper his belly and kiss his ring."

"Like the whole isle."

"Like the whole isle." A faint click as Breguswith slipped her fine-work whorl off her spindle and laid it on the ivory-inlaid casket that held her treasures. "Ah, Onnen, Onnen. He was to be king. Not poisoned like a dog." And Hild knew they were talking now of her father.

"We are alone in this world," Onnen said.

Faint rattle as her mother unfastened her girdle and hung it carefully on the hook driven into the wall post for that purpose. Hild imagined the hanging things one by one: the knife in its woven sheath, the seeing crystal, the needle case, the fire steel and tinderbox, the purse with chalk and thread and spare hairpin . . .

She woke again when her mother said in her voice of iron, "We will go to Edwin. He has won."

Hild felt a light touch on her hair but willed herself still and copied Hereswith's breath: in and out, in and out. Her mother smelt of smoke and heather beer.

"As king his nieces will be valuable to him."

"Your dream?"

"My dream."

"She's so young—"

"She's Yffing. Needs must. She'll be ready. They both will. In their different ways." And then the touch of the hand on her hair was gone and Hild heard the faint tck of her mother unpinning her hair, followed by the two women moving about the room, and the hff of the rush light blown out.

Hereswith inched closer to Hild, whispered fiercely in her ear, "That stupid dream—the light of the world! Ha! That was when she still thought you might come out a boy!"

———

The next day Hild could eat nothing, waiting for this usurping uncle, this Edwin, to come. But no one came; it was a day like any other but for two things. First, when the time came to wash and then rinse all three children's hair, Onnen added oak gall to the rinse water for Cian's turn.

"You rinse mine with vinegar," Hild said, peering at the tub of black water, talking as much to distract herself from her misery as anything else. She hated the washing and rinsing of hair. No matter how she tried, there was always water down her neck. And no matter how warm the water was at the beginning, by the time it wormed between her shoulder blades, it was cold.

"And mine," Hereswith said. "For the smell and the shine, you said. Why can't we have oak gall, too?"

"Because it would make your pretty honey hair dark."

"Daddy called me honey. But not Hild. She doesn't have honey hair."

"What makes your hair and Hild's hair shine, and what makes Cian's shine is different. His hair is different."

But it wasn't, Hild thought, it wasn't. Her hair and Cian's were even the same colour. Or had been, before the oak gall.

And then, while they were shivering like wet rats, Inis, the king's man, came by. "You're wanted," he said to Onnen. "You and the boy both."

Onnen took all three of them, because wet unhappy children had a tendency to quarrel when unminded.

The middle fire in hall was burning bright, and Ceredig king wore his ceremonial wolfskin cloak and most splendid torc, though there was no one else there but two housefolk standing by the wall.

Onnen and the three children paused just inside the doorway.

"Come," the king said, and Onnen gathered Cian under one arm and Hereswith under the other, and approached. Hild walked alongside Cian, her hand in his belt, as she'd been taught. She was nervous because Onnen was nervous, but also curious.

"So, cousin, you've done a fine job by these young ones these years. But a boy needs a father."

"I don't know his father. I was prettier then, and not minded to keep track. As you yourself know. Cousin."

He smiled and turned away momentarily to bend and lift something from beneath his bench. Hild couldn't see what it was but Cian obviously could: the damp tunic stretched between his shoulder blades quivered as his heart began to hammer.

The king held out a small oak sword with a finely carved painted hilt and a little wicker shield. "Well, come here, boy."

Onnen let go of him, as did Hild, who thought he might topple where he stood, but after a moment he managed to walk to the king.

"You're a year yet from weapons training, but who knows where we'll all be a year from today. A boy needs a sword, and you've no father to give it. Hold out your left arm." The king slid the new shield straps—Hild could smell the stink of tanning still on the leather—up the boy's arm. "Grip the— Ah, you've the right of it already, I see." Cian's whole arm tightened as he squeezed the bar behind the boss of the little shield. "And now the other." The king put the sword hilt in his right hand. He smiled and said, looking at Onnen, "Don't stab your—those girls' eyes out, or your mother will have my hide." Then he turned away, and Hild realised to her astonishment that it was because Onnen was weeping.

"Come," Onnen said eventually, in a voice Hild hardly knew. "Come. Quick, quick. The king has spent enough time over three wet-headed children." And she gathered them to her and they left.

They walked in silence past the grain house, and suddenly Cian stopped, and shouted, and banged his shield with his sword. "I have a sword!"

"You have a shield," Onnen said. "Wherever you go."

A sword given to his hand by a king: a shield and a path.

Autumn blew, leaves fell, flames flickered, and in hall song turned to war. Hereswith refused to speak anything but Anglisc, and Breguswith—when she wasn't teaching Hild that while one jay was bad luck two meant not double but opposite—was at the side of Burgræd, her chief gesith, talking persuasively, talking, talking. Most of their other gesiths already slept and drank with Ceredig's men.

"Your lord is dead and your oath with him," Breguswith said to Burgræd one dark afternoon as Hild half drowsed at Onnen's hip, lulled by the repetitive twist-twirl of spinning. "He left only the girls, no æthelings whose honour you can fight for. And perhaps swearing your sword and honour to Ceredig now seems to you worthy. He is a king. But even as this peat burns Edwin retakes Deira. Before the frost he'll be secure and he'll turn to Elmet. He will crush it. Ceredig can no more stand against him than a leaf can defy winter." She leaned back, the very picture of ease and Anglisc wealth with her smooth honey hair, fine-draped dress, and gold winking at throat and wrist. "No doubt there will be much glorious death." She looked over at his stripling son playing knucklebones with Ceredig's men. "Though not Ceredig's."

Burgræd, a stocky man with grey streaks on either side of his mouth and one cheekbone higher than the other, ran a callused finger around the rim of his cup and said nothing.

"You will die for him, for you'll keep your oath. You're Anglisc. But would he die for you? How much is a wealh oath worth?"

She took his cup and poured him ale, and as she took up her own she glanced about the hall. Hild shut her eyes tightly. Even at three, she understood the danger of overhearing a hint that a king in his own hall was an oath-breaker: Never say the dangerous thing aloud.

They sipped. A servingman laid more peat on the fire; it hissed. When he had gone, her mother said, more softly than before, "Know this. We will leave this wood before Edwin king falls on Ceredig. We'll go to him in Deira. In time my daughters will rise high in Edwin's favour. You could rise with us. And you wouldn't be sworn to a gesith's oath. You could take it back anytime."

After Burgræd left, her mother bent down and whispered, "Quiet mouth, bright mind, little prickle."

For a while it seemed nothing would change. Cian wouldn't walk anywhere without his wooden sword and wicker shield, and he became tedious, issuing challenges to vicious branches or charging without notice at a shelf of mushrooms growing from a sickly birch. It made Hild's time at the edges of things less than easy. How could she be still and listen and watch when Cian's yell made the rooks croak and fly away or the deer bound into the undergrowth? How could she study an old dog fox who sat in the thin morning sunlight to comb his chest hair with his tongue, if he ducked into his run when Cian rolled and tumbled with invisible enemies in the leaves?

She helped Onnen collect eggs and was proud to break not a one, and tried to help gather hazelnuts with everyone else, though she had to be carried when the walking grew too much. She sat with Hereswith as her mother explained the sunwise and widdershins twist of spinning yarn and how by mixing the two you could make spin-patterned cloth. In the shadowy hall she listened to the cool clicking tiles of wealh bishops' Latin and to old Ywain, when he was well, play the harp. She liked the sound of the old man's voice as he warmed it to himself, then of the men setting aside their weapons, the thunk of heavy hilts laid down on the boards, and the bronze-and-gold sound of the strings. Hereswith said at home all Anglisc men took turns with the lyre, but Hild knew that was silly. How could warriors with their burst voices sing like Ywain? Besides, their real home had been overrun by Æthelfrith Iding's war band before Hereswith had been born, and now the Idings were being driven out in turn by Edwin.

And then Hild would remember her father was dead and now she never would have a home, and she would hum along with Ywain's heroic song and try to make her breastbone buzz the way she was sure Ywain's did when he sang "*Calan hyddrev, tymp dydd yn edwi / Cynhwrv yn ebyr, llyr yn llenwii: The beginning of October, the falling off of the day / Tumult in the river mouth, filling up the shore.*" Tumult in the river mouth, she sang to herself, tumult in the river mouth.

And at the next new moon as the wind whipped there was tumult in the dark: tumult as someone bundled Hild in a cloak and carried her, tumult as Cian and Hereswith, Onnen and Breguswith, the gesiths—so few!—and their slaves boarded a boat. Tumult during the days as they beat north in the driving rain, the sea roaring like the elms in autumn. Tumult then at the river mouth, and at the dock far up the wide, wide river.

Torches hissed and fluttered and Hild was more or less asleep when she was carried down the gangplank, but she still saw the rich trappings of the horses there, and the gleam of jewelled hilts and brooches clasped at cloak necks. And she woke fully when an apple voice, so firm and round as to be almost scented, said, "Lady Breguswith, Edwin king welcomes you home."

2

✦

IN SOME WAYS, Hild's new life was not so different. Her days, the court's days, were ones of constant movement from royal vill to royal vill: Bebbanburg in the lean months for the safety of the rock walls and the cold grey sea, and Yeavering at the end of spring, when the cattle ate sweet new grass and the milk flowed rich with fat. Then south to the old emperor's wall, to the small towns built of stone, and a day at Osric's great house in Tinamutha, and a boat down the coast to that wide river mouth, wide as a sea, and up the river to Brough in early summer, and then, sometimes, Sancton, and always to Goodmanham's slow river valley at summer's height—the rolling wolds crimson with flowers, the skeps heavy with honey, and the fields waving with grain. Then the twenty-mile journey to York, with its strong walls, its river roads for carrying the last of the sweet apples and the first of the pears, and its high towers in case of bitter war, winter war.

The king and his court spent a month here, a two-month there, eating their way through the local offerings, levying and taking tribute, listening to local troubles and rendering judgement.

"But why?" Hild said when they had to pack up and leave Sancton, again, just as she'd got to know the rooks in the beech spinney and the frogs by the south pond, and one particularly fine old hornbeam whose bent boughs even she could climb. She watched her mother and Onnen folding dresses and rolling hose, and threw her own box of treasures on the floor. "I don't want to!"

Her mother's irises, pale blue as forget-me-nots under unseasonable frost, tightened, though her voice stayed even. "You will pick those up."

"No."

"Very well. Then we'll leave you—"

"I'm the light of the world!"

"—and when we're gone the wolves will come, and the foxes, and the wights."

Hild wasn't afraid of foxes, perhaps not even of wolves, not in summer when they were well fed. But wights . . .

Her mother was nodding. "They will breathe on your face as you sleep and you will be trapped in a cold dream forever and ever and ever."

Hild picked up her box, began searching for her treasures—the wooden brooch Cian had carved and painted for her, the shark's tooth Hereswith had given to her last Yule, her magic pebble that fit just right in her hand. She frowned. The pebble seemed smaller than it had.

"But why?" she said.

"Why what?"

"Why do we move all the time?"

"It's how it is."

"But why?"

"Because otherwise we'd eat ourselves out of house and home."

Hild pondered that. "When Fa was ætheling, we didn't send all the gallopers first."

"An ætheling is one of many, a maybe-king," Breguswith said. "Your uncle is the one king. He travels with five hundred people. The king can't just pack a loaf and a sack of salt and head for the horizon. He must first send a message to his reeves: How was the harvest? How are the roads—and the wood supply? Where is the honey flowing, where are the royal women needed for the weaving, where do bandits need to be warned away, and where is the hunting good? Then he must gather food and other supplies for the journey. And then his galloper rides ahead—tells the vill steward to begin brewing beer, slaughtering cattle, strewing rushes. Only then may we travel."

"And when we get there," Onnen said, "we eat them out of house and home and move on."

Hild set her pebble aside. It was just a pebble. "But why can't we stay? Why can't Uncle Edwin have a home like everyone else?"

"The whole land is his home."

"Yes, but why?"

"He must be seen."

"Yes, but—"

"And he can't simply have a steward on each estate sending him tribute. Because a steward, unless reminded by the presence of the king, begins to think himself a thegn. He begins to see the land as his, to wonder why he shouldn't send only a portion of his food, his ale, his honey, to the king. The revolt always begins when the steward wants to be king. A lesson the Franks never seem to learn."

But Hild was no longer listening. She was playing with her special pinecone, remembering the tufty red squirrel she had frightened away the day she found it.

Every summer Edwin took war on the road with his war band, tenscore gesiths, sworn to death or glory, and their men, their horses and wagons, a few handfuls of shared women. They were always back before autumn, weighed down, depending on the war, with Anglisc arm rings and great gaudy brooches, British daggers with chased silver hilts—though the blades were no match for Anglisc or Frankish work—or strange heavy coin, and they would wind themselves about with boasts and intricate inlaid sword belts. And always by the end of summer there was a double handful more of big-voiced, hard-chested men glittering with gold. Not all were Anglisc, but they drank and shouted and boasted alike. Hild's mother told her to stay out of their way. "Our time is not yet come. For now we live like mice in the byre. Everyone knows we're here, but we're not worth attention. Quiet mouth, bright mind."

Breguswith taught her the gathering and drying of herbs, and began to spirit Hereswith away for mysterious lessons that, when her sister tried to share them with Hild, made no sense.

They were sitting with a tablet weave—the simple band weaving that would do for a border on a neck or cuff—and Hild was telling Hereswith about how swallows never came until the white butterflies born from colewort were outnumbered by the black-and-red jewel-winged kind.

"Beat the weft," Hereswith said.

"But I beat it just after I turned," Hild said. "It'll spoil the pattern."

"Do as I say. I'm older."

And Hild, because Hereswith had that sulky look that meant she was unhappy, tapped the cross threads down to lie more densely across the warp threads. She smiled tentatively at her sister, who said, "Ma says there are different ways to smile at people."

"How—"

Hereswith overrode her. "If the king notices me, I do this." She straightened her spine and smiled a proud, glad smile that shocked Hild. "Try it."

Hild shook her head.

"Try it."

"No. I'm not happy."

Hereswith laughed. "That doesn't matter! Well, never mind, I expect you're too young to understand." She turned the tablet.

Hild beat the weft. The pattern was already spoilt. She might as well please her sister.

Hereswith nodded. "Good. And this, too: If you think you're going to smile at a gesith's boast, you must let your hair fall to hide your face. Like this."

"I know that one!" Hild remembered her mother's words exactly—the light of the world must remember everything. She repeated them proudly: "Men are afraid women will laugh at them. Women are afraid men will kill them."

Hereswith blinked. Her face curdled. She leaned forward, punched Hild in the arm, and burst into tears. "I hate you!" She flung the tablet weave to the dirt and fled.

Hild picked up the weave, mystified. What was all that about? She would ask her mother. Or maybe not. Lately whenever she put a question to Breguswith she got answers that made no sense—if she got answers at all. "Where do swallows go in winter?" had merited a pause in the grinding of herbs, followed by a question in turn: "Winters are uneasy times. Why does the king hold feasts at Yule?"

"Because it makes people happy?"

"A king doesn't care if the folk are happy. He cares that they think him strong. Pass me the bitterwort."

Hild passed the bitterwort. She thought about winter, and home, and strength in one's own hall. "Oh," she said. "Stronger than anyone else. Like not having a steward who stays in the vill." It came out wrong, but she knew what she meant.

So did her mother; she always knew the words Hild couldn't find. She smiled but said only, "This root was pulled too early. Bitterwort is best harvested in autumn."

Hild grew taller. Her milk teeth loosened. Now she could cross her legs and balance on her hands, and she could name all the king's hounds and all his horses. She had worked her first perfect tablet weaving, and she remembered enough of the names of the heroes of Gododdin to argue with Cian when he named them as they fell under his wooden sword. Sometimes Hild worked alongside him, exercising with a rock in each hand, as boys who hoped to be king's gesiths must. Sometimes she swung a stick sword; she had learnt long since that it made him happy for her to pretend to be Branwen the Bold, just as it made her happy for him to be still when she was watching and listening. They remembered: *We are us.*

But she could climb now, and sometimes when Cian wanted to play hero and she did not, she ran to a tree—she had favourites in every place—and climbed up among the leaves and stayed silent as he called. And if Onnen wanted to wash her hair and the weather was foul, there was a roof-tree and its sloping rafters to clamber to. No one ever looked up, not even her mother. This was her secret. But she liked trees best. Hidden in the leafy canopy, sometimes she stayed so still and quiet even the birds forgot she was there.

Like today, a hot day for late spring, bright but sullen. It would rain later. Meanwhile, it was cooler inside the leafy hideaway of a pollarded ash drowsing by a woodcutter's trail. She settled comfortably against the fissured bark and watched dumpy little siffsaffs hop from their half-built nests among the nettles and peck about in the leaf rubbish for soft stuff to line the nest.

She sat there, breathing the cool leafy air, so still that a sparrow hawk, intent on the siffsaffs beneath, landed on a bough by her face and turned its marigold eyes to hers. They regarded each other for an age. It blinked, blinked again, then tipped forward from its hidden perch, flapped, and vanished into the trees on the other side of the trail.

The court left Sancton before the siffsaff eggs hatched. Hild hoped the sparrow hawk wouldn't eat them.

The summer's war had ended early and the household was at Goodmanham. Hild was six years old—tall, strong-faced (*All bone,* her mother said, *like your father*)—when one hot day her mother took Hereswith away and when she came back she wore a small girdle with various cases and boxes attached. She showed them to Hild one at a time. She was to get her own pin beater from Queen Cwenburh, the edgeless sword of some long-dead ætheling. She was to help the other women in the weaving hut. And wasn't this gilded needle the very picture of beauty? The queen's own cousin was to be her gemæcce: one to weave and weep with forever.

Hereswith looked happy, and Hild was glad for her—at last her sister had something of her own, something to compare to being dreamt of while in the womb. Then Hild grew even happier when she realised that all the women, including her mother and Onnen, would be so busy fussing over Hereswith that she and Cian might now find time to sneak away to the bottomland at the foot of the sacred hill south of the vill.

The bottomland, unlike most of the wolds, with its chalky soil, was dark and damp. Hild led them through an old wide dike full now of a tangle of oaks and holly and thorny crabapple, then over the bank mostly hidden by fern—Cian had to push the wooden sword through his belt, despite the imminent threat of marauding armies, and use his hands to scramble up— to the boggy dell with its quiet pool and the mossy boulder by the shallow end where the sun showed the muddy bottom. All she heard was a blackbird, far away, and the burble of the spring. She wondered where the water came from. She wondered this in British, the language of wild and secret places.

"I don't like this place," Cian said, and he spoke, too, in British, their preferred way when alone. "It smells of wood ælfs, and there's no room to swing a sword." He then proved himself a liar by pulling his sword free and lunging at an invisible opponent. It occurred to Hild that both Hereswith and Cian now had their paths. She had only her mother's dream. "I shall make you a sword," Cian said, "and we shall continue our fight in the gash." He pointed to the fallen alder which, from long experience of these matters, Hild understood to be, in his mind, the top of the banked war ditch.

She did not sigh, though she disliked the trench-warfare game. It meant the firing of the furze, which meant many pauses while Cian waved imaginary firebrands and tested the imaginary wind.

"Make me a spear instead, and you can be the hero Morei while I play the great oaf on the top poking at you and soon to be raven food."

That way she could stay on the water side and, during the brand-waving and wind-testing, she might study the pool and all the little things that came to its edges. Besides, he would have to go all the way back to the oaks for a long, strong limb.

While he was gone she settled back against her boulder and closed her eyes. If it were night she would smell the perfume of bog myrtle, which her mother called sweet gale. At night, wood mice would sit atop the fallen tree, wiping dew from their whiskers in the moonlight. At night, she might see the water sprites she was sure lived here. Meanwhile, she worried with her tongue at her front tooth, which hung by a thread.

Soon enough Cian had her spear. A fallen ash branch, thicker than her wrist, with a pronounced bend. Cian grinned and said, "Oh, I'll slaughter a score of you spear wielders! Close your eyes now!" and leapt away. Hild sang the agreed-upon three verses—*Adorned with his wreath the chief . . . adorned with his wreath the leader . . . adorned with his wreath the bright warrior*—then she parted a fern on the alder and peered down. Silent. Still.

A cream-striped caterpillar humped its slow way over the mossy bark. Hild picked it up and looked for a place to put it safely out of the way of the coming battle.

In the end she chose the base of the bird cherry at the rocky end of the pool. It was old, for a cherry, with that odd, gnarled look of such trees that weren't likely to reach the age of oaks and elms. With the haft of her bent spear she poked at the soil by the root. It was lighter and drier than the soil by the other end of the pool. She poked a little more. Her shoulder jostled her tooth.

"What are you doing?" Cian, standing on the fallen alder, looking sweaty and cross. "How can you abandon your post to dig?"

Hild, whose tooth hurt, spoke crossly in her turn. "How can you play the same game over and over?"

"It's not a game!" Cian's face pinked. His eyebrows, she saw, did not match his hair. "What are you doing that is so important?"

Hild, feeling perverse for no reason she could name but that she was sick of playing war, said, "I am digging with this stick."

"It's a *spear*."

"It's a stick." And she stroked deliberately at the great kink in the wood, then pushed the blunt tip into her palm and showed him: no blood.

He rubbed his lip with his knuckle. "When we fight as heroes, it's a spear."

Please, his eyes said, *please*.

And just like that she didn't want to hurt him anymore; she wasn't sure why she had, only that she, too, wanted to say, *Please, please*. She settled on her hams by the root she'd been poking at.

"I'm following the root to see if Eochaid the slave is right and there is a rainbow at the tip, or if my mother has the right of it, and at the centre is the root of the world tree and the one-eyed god."

"You're forever finding things out."

"I'm the light of the world."

"Finding out the how and the why of things is for gossips and priests," he said, not so much scornful as puzzled, not by the fact that she did it—she had always done it—but that they should be talking about it.

"Gossips and priests, yes, but also artisans and kings," she said. "And was Morei not familiar with the ways of fire?"

"True," Cian said, craning for a better view.

"And, indeed, heroes of old sometimes had need to bury their hoard."

He scrambled over the fallen tree and landed next to her. "I will help."

He found himself a stick—his sword was a sword only—and they dug, the sun warm on their backs.

"It goes ever down," he said after a while.

"We will dig more tomorrow."

He stood and stretched, said to the horizon, "And now will you be a hero with me and take the wall, shoulder to shoulder?"

"Am I to be Branwen again?" And she couldn't help the sigh in her voice.

"Be who you like," he said, ever the generous lord. "You choose."

"Owein," she said. "His sword was blue and gleaming, his spurs all of gold—"

"No, I am Owein. I am always Owein."

"Then I will be Gwvrling the Giant: He drank transparent wine, with a battle-taunting purpose; the reapers sang of war, of war with shining wing, the minstrels sang of war—" She spat out her tooth. It lay white and red on the turf at her feet. They stared at it.

Hild bent and picked it up. Her tooth, from her mouth.

"Soon you will grow another, and stronger."

She nodded.

"You must put it in your belt, or a sorcerer could steal it for a spell."

She pushed it into her sash.

"You are bleeding."

She wiped her mouth with her hand. A tiny, bright smear.

"Bright was the blood," she said, the next part of the verse of Gwvrling the Giant.

"And bright was the horn in the hall of Eiddin!" Cian said, relieved. He held out his digging stick. "Gwvrling must have a sword. Come!"

And they scrambled over the tree trunk and swung their swords at invisible foes together: Y rhag meiwedd, y rhag mawredd, y rhag madiedd—in the van are the warlike, in the van are the noble, in the van are the good.

As usual, after a while they found it more exciting to swing at each other, and, as usual, Hild got hit more often because Cian's reach was greater than hers, his sword longer, and he had a shield.

After one particularly hard smack at her shoulder, Hild jumped back. "Let us swap arms for a while."

She had never dared ask before, but today she had bled, like a real Yffing. Cian considered, then held out his sword for Hild's stick and slid the shield from his arm.

They leapt together again, and Hild found that taking a blow to a shield was a much finer thing than a blow to the ribs. She hacked with enthusiasm.

"Swap back now," Cian said, panting a little.

"Just a while longer."

"I want it. It's mine."

Hild didn't want to give them up, and the wanting turned her mind smooth and hard as a shield wall. "It is yours, absolutely and only yours, given from the hand of Ceredig king. No one of this earth could dispute it. I do not dispute it. I ask for your great favour, a hero's generosity."

Cian blinked.

"And as we fight you may think secretly to yourself, Those arms are mine, I have but to say the word and they are in my hand again, I have the power to take them back anytime, anytime."

He rose up on his toes, and back down, thinking. "Anytime?"

"Anytime."

"It is mine?"

"It is yours. That is your secret power." Holding secrets, her mother said, made a man feel mighty.

"Well, then. You may keep the shield for a time." He lifted his stick and charged. They battled for a while.

Once again, Hild stepped back. "Now here, back to you, are your sword and shield."

And he took them, returned her stick, and smiled. "These are mine. But you shall borrow them again. Tomorrow. Tomorrow when we come back to dig your hole."

She nodded.

"It's hot," he said.

They sat by the pool. Hild slid her stick in and out of the water. The cherry leaves whispered in a slight breeze.

"You like the water."

"I do." She laid the stick aside and watched a waterbug dimple the surface and skate across it.

"And you're not afraid of the sidsa?"

Her mother's word for sorcery or witchcraft, not the immanence, the wild magic of these hidden places—there was no Anglisc word for that. *Sprites live in rivers and springs, and are not to be meddled with*, Onnen said. "I'm not afraid." She was the light of the world. Besides, her mother said it was still water that was bad. She frowned slightly, as Breguswith did, and said, in Anglisc, "Still water is not to be trusted. It shines and it gleams, but is not what it seems."

They both giggled. *It shines and it gleams, but is not what it seems.*

"And yet it is so . . . magic," Hild said, in British. "Watch." And she slid her stick in again at an angle. "See how the water breaks it?"

"I do!"

"And yet when I pull it out, it is whole." She slid the stick in and out, in and out. Whole, broken, whole, broken. "What spirit breaks and re-makes? Or is it only a glamour? Now, listen." The cherry leaves whispered again, and again more strongly as air moved over them and the pool. "Feel the breath of it? Now look you down there. The mud seems rippled, does it not?"

"It does."

"Yet it is not."

"It is too. I can see it."

"Then put your hand to the bottom."

"The sprite will eat me if I disturb her magic."

"She will not. I will give her an offering." She drew her tooth from her sash and threw it into the pool. The soft silty mud closed over it and it was gone.

"You have given yourself to the sprite!"

"I have offered my tooth, of which I'll soon have more." But she touched her tongue to the raw place on her gum and hoped the new tooth wouldn't belong to the sprite, hoped it didn't mean she would drown one day when the sprite reclaimed what was hers. "Put your hand to the bottom."

He rolled up his shirt sleeve. Slid it gingerly into the water.

"Now lay your palm on the bottom. And tell me, is it rippled?"

"It is smooth." He patted the muddy bottom, sending up a swirl of brown. Hild had a sudden fear he would find her tooth and bring it out.

"Gently, gently. You may take your arm out now." She lifted her face to the sky. The wind had died once more. "The beast begins to sleep again, and so forgets to weave its spell. See you now, the sand is smooth in appearance as well as fact. It is only when the water sprite breathes that it casts its veil on our eyes."

Cian rubbed his arm dry on the turf, then on his tunic. "Tomorrow you shall show me more magic."

"Tomorrow I shall show you the great frog who swallowed the heart of a hægtes."

But the next day the Goodmanham steward declared it an auspicious time to harvest the rest of the flax—the base of the stems had turned yellow— and every able-bodied member of the community, young and old, was drafted, even the visiting thegns Wilgar and Trumwine. Men pulled the plants whole from the ground; housefolk, mostly wealh, gathered and tied the stems into bundles, then leaned them into stacks to dry. They laid cloth on the ground and shook the already dried bundles until seed rattled out; children carefully folded the cloth and carried it to the women who funnelled the tiny golden-brown seeds into jars and sent the cloth back to be laid again; at which point other wealh pulled the bundled stems through the coarse-toothed ripples set like arrowheads into posts to pull free the empty seedpods. It was thirsty, scratchy work; the children, highfolk and urchins alike, ran to and fro with jars of gruit—heather beer.

From the resinous scent of it, it was her mother's special batch, heavy with sweet gale, which Hild already knew would lead to loud laughter and the energy to work all day. Many of the women did not drink and sent her instead with empty jars to the river.

Her mother scooped out three fingers of salve, handed the pot to Hild, and warmed the greasy stuff between her palms. When she worked it into Wilgar's back, Hild thought he looked like a bristly black hog smeared with lard before going on the spit. She put the pot at the end of the bench out of the sun and watched her mother kneading the slablike muscles, pushing into his fat with her thumbs, running along lines of sinew like a saddlemaker pushing the needle through thick leather.

"Crops must have been good the last two years," Breguswith said to him as he groaned with pleasure. "You're plump as a prime bullock."

He agreed that the gods had been kind and the weather favourable. They talked for a while about the crop in his valley to the north and his farmers, and after a while she slapped him on the arm and handed him his warrior jacket.

Wilgar eased the jacket back on, squinting against the late-afternoon sun. He twisted this way and that. "It feels better." He sounded surprised.

"You'll do," Breguswith said.

They watched him head back to the hall and brace himself for Trumwine's punch in the shoulder in the doorway.

Breguswith said, "The man is getting fat," in the kind of voice that meant she was thinking more than she was saying.

Hild looked in the pot. "Will there be enough left for the women?"

Breguswith wiped her hands on her apron. "Do you see any women?"

There were only housefolk hurrying with yokes of beer buckets and platters of bread to the hall. She shook her head.

"Why you suppose that is?"

She pondered. "Because girls don't show off?"

Breguswith huffed in amusement, sat on the bench, and wiped now at her forearms. "You're not wholly wrong, but there's more. Men's arms are stronger than ours. That strength is their weakness. They forget—" A gust of laughter rolled from the hall. The drinking and boasting had begun. Breguswith stood. "I've things to see to. We'll talk another time. Watch women and men, put yourself inside them. Imagine what they're thinking. And remember what I've said."

Two days into the retting, the river was sluggish and the air still and heavy with the ret stink. Breguswith and Onnen were inside the undercroft of the great timber hall, sorting cloth into bales for merchants and bales for the household, and Hereswith and Mildburh were in the weaving hut tying weights to the warp on a piece of tabby. Hild was long since tired of watching women and men from the loft in the byre and under a bench in hall (the rooftree at Goodmanham was low, close enough to the fire pits to make her cough and choke the one time she had tried it). All they seemed to do was lie to each other; the women did it while giggling and the men while boasting. She had no idea what that had to do with strength.

So today she forgot about it and, with Cian, followed the king and his household—his advisers, the various bands of warrior gesiths and their war hounds and sight hounds, the priests and petitioners and housefolk—into the meadow. The dogs settled down in the shade of a stand of alders in the bend of the river, and Hild, with Cian behind her, cautiously held out a fist to Gwen, the huge scarred wolfhound bitch whom they fed sometimes, when they could, and who consequently allowed them to approach on occasion. Gwen sniffed, then lifted a lip at Brannoch, the leader—a boarhound, and mad, though not as mad as the brutalised war hounds—and after some grumbles he licked his chops and lowered his nose to his paws, and the children sat themselves slowly, and Hild dared to lean against Gwen's flank, and they all settled in to half doze and half listen to the run of the river, the whine of flies, the laughter of drunken fighting men, and the king's petitioner.

Edwin, a compact man with chestnut hair, a grey-threaded beard, and heavy rings on both arms, sat on his carved stool under the oak, his chief steward Coelgar at his ear and his advisers about him, with his chin on his fist and his eyes on the petitioner, a one-handed local thegn, rewarded with five hides by Æthelric Spear years past for service rendered as gesith, who complained that a local widow had set eel traps in the river: his river, his.

Æthelric Spear. Hild's grandfather. Hild paid closer attention.

Edwin had his face turned to the man, and smiled and nodded in the right places, but after a sentence or two his feet began to move this way and that on the turf. Hild plucked herself a blade of grass, sucked on the fat end, and pondered him. His gaze roved over his household: the priests—a bishop from the British west (spy of his foster-brother Cadwallon ap Cadfan, her mother said), a soft-voiced Irishman (bearing news of the Dál Fiatach and their hopes for the Isle of Vannin), Coifi, the ambitious young priest of the great temple, a woman who tended the well of Eilen (or tended first the needs of the scruffy local priest of Saint Elen, some would say)—the warrior gesiths (calling for more ale, more mead, "More white mead," "White mead, at this hour!" the houseman muttered as he broached a second cask and gestured for a wealh to remove the empty), the confidential adviser from Eorpwald, the sulky new king-to-be of the East Anglisc, and his two sons, the young æthelings Eadfrith and Osfrith (no daughter, no future peaceweaver as yet). Edwin's gaze moved from one to another and back again, head tilted. Hild had seen a dog look at his master that way when trying to guess which hand held the bone.

Gwen woke from some dream with a muffled bark and shook Hild off into the grass and scratched mightily, and stretched, and set the whole pack to shaking and stretching and scratching, and Hild after a moment tried it, too: the long stretch with both arms, then the legs, one at a time. It felt good. The push of her feet against the turf, the long line of her back. She did it again. Cian, next to her, copied her, limb for limb. Then he tried to scratch behind his ear with his right foot and fell over, giggling, and then, though she knew it was impossible, she had to try, too. They howled with laughter, and the dogs bayed and one, confused, snapped at another, and soon they were snarling and foaming and the warriors shouting and flinging arm rings as bets. One hound clamped another's muzzle between its teeth and, neck rigid, haunches bulging and shining with effort, hauled it, screaming and bleeding, across the turf, clods of dirt ripping free as both fought to push in different directions. Hild was glad when Domnach, the Irish dog boy, came running with whip and raw meat and beat the hounds into whining submission. She stared at the bloody trails gouged by both dogs.

The king used the distraction to send the petitioner away with a fine knife and no decision.

Hild was seven, in the stone undercroft of the palace at York, helping her mother count the tuns of honey. Her mother told her she would be seated at the high table for Modresniht, one of the twelve winter feasts.

"You're to sit by the king. The queen, too. If she's well. You're to talk to him." She counted on her fingers again. "That makes three dozen. Do you have the tally sticks?"

Hild held up the smooth, notched sticks. *You're to sit by the king. You, not We.* But she had learnt to say nothing until she understood. She would think about it later.

She loved the undercroft. It was vast and cool and mysterious, room after room, with water running along the southern wall in a sharp-edged gravel-bottomed channel. One room, with thick walls, no windows, and a stout, banded door, was full of treasure, but Edwin kept a man outside it at all times, even during feasts, and Hild had never seen the hoard of gold and garnets that Cian—one early evening, as they ate small wrinkled apples and hard cheese and fresh hazelnuts—assured her were heaped in piles on the tile floor. Hereswith had snorted and said Cian had never seen it, either. And then the two of them fell to throwing nutshells at each other and pulling each other's hair. They did that a lot now, since Cian had carelessly months ago boasted that his father was a real king, with a real kingdom, and Hereswith shouted back that Ceredig was the chief of a tiny *wealh* forest who, even now, was being hunted like a wounded boar through the wood he'd once called home for killing her father, and Hild's, who if he'd lived would one day have been overking of all the isle.

Hild had ignored them and concentrated on keeping a stick tucked under her arm like a distaff while she ate. Her mother could do anything with a spindle or a distaff in her hand, and Hereswith and Mildburh were already working on a diamond twill. She hated the idea of not knowing how to do something when it was time.

Besides, everything they said was wrong. Ceredig was not Cian's real father. And Hereric was an ætheling who had been poisoned in exile and no one cared anymore. Even the men who had come with them from Elmet were deserting them. Her mother was bitter, she knew, but she understood: How was a man to measure his worth without a noble lord to fight for and receive rings from? It was a fall to be a should-be king's gesith and then a mere fighting man hired to protect a woman and children. Eight had come with them from Elmet. Six now were oathed to Edwin: gesiths again. Only Burgræd and his stripling son were left, and Hild knew by the way the son stood stiff when Edwin was near that he was pulling away in secret.

Hild shivered. It was cool in the undercroft built under the redcrest palace, and shadowy, with pictures of old-fashioned people in robes painted on the walls—painted on the walls! The robes had a border dyed a purple her mother could not reproduce with her lichen. At the western end was a stone table and niches. An altar, Onnen said: whether to Mithras, to the Christ, or to the goddess of the spring, nobody knew. Hild resolved to bring an offering when her mother was busy.

Much of the palace was broken and patched with timber and thatch, but anyone could see it had once been magnificent. Edwin, it was said, planned to restore its former glory.

". . . and, little prickle, when you sit by the king, you must talk. You don't talk enough."

Quiet mouth, bright mind.

"Oh, this is cloudy." Breguswith dipped her finger in the honey, sniffed, and gestured to Hild to come close so that she could wipe her finger on her daughter's brown tabby sash. She pointed to the lid, leaning against the wall. "Pass me that." She banged the lid back on, fished chalk from the purse at her belt, scrawled a mark, and shook her head. "If Cwenburh would only . . . No matter. If we strain it well, it might do for mead. Help me roll it over there by the— Bend your legs, not your back."

A memory of stretching like a dog, the push of feet on turf and flash of teeth, flicked across her mind like a leaf on a gust of wind. She tried to catch it back but it was gone.

They moved on to the wheels of cheese. Breguswith slipped her knife clear of its sheath, paused. "I shall lend you my second-best brooch."

For Modresniht. "So I'm to be a princess again?" And Hereswith? But that was too many things to think about at once.

"You always were. Pull this tight." Breguswith sliced the outstretched cheese wrapper, resheathed her knife, and began to unwind.

"Not a mouse in the byre?" She took the linen wrappings as her mother unwound them. They smelt sour.

"That time is ending."

"Tell me your dream again." She needed to hear the familiar story. One more time.

Her mother considered, then nodded. "One night, in the days when my belly was as flat as a loom and your father was out hunting more than deer, I dreamt of a light, oh such a strange and beautiful light, and the light turned into a jewel—"

"What kind of jewel?" Hild felt four years old again.

"A great glittering gem."

"What colour?" She loved this part, loved the ritual of the broad, slow Anglisc, pouring like a river in its valley.

"Luscious as your lips."

"Yes, but what colour?"

"Like your skin with the sun beneath it, with a glow like a blushing pearl. Like a garnet shining through milk."

"A carnelian!"

"A carnelian. The best, biggest, brightest you ever beheld."

"As big as a king's token?"

"Bigger."

"As big as an overking's token?"

"Bigger."

"As big as a redcrest emperor's?"

"Bigger and brighter than the moon. It hung before me, then it sank into my belly, which swelled, and a voice said, 'Behold, the light that will shine on all the world!' And the light shone from my belly, brighter than the best beeswax tapers burning in their sconces of burnished bronze."

And then, in a more normal voice, "And the next day the midwife told me I was to have a child."

"And who was the child?"

"Hmmn," Breguswith said, just as she had when Hild was very little. "A baby goat?"

"No!"

"A lamb?"

"No!"

"A heckled little hedgepig?"

Hild chortled and her mother smiled. The smile, as usual, didn't last long.

"And so, little prickle, you will sit on Edwin's left hand and you will smile and talk as well as eat. You will make him notice. It is time to give your light to the world."

You. Your light. The shadows around her loomed longer and darker. She didn't know what her light was. "Will Hereswith be there?"

"I didn't dream of your sister."

"I want Hereswith!"

"Well. Well, perhaps. Yes, I don't see why not. Yes, indeed. Hereswith."

"And Onnen."

Breguswith laughed. "Oh, not Onnen. She's wealh."

"And Cian?"

"No. Now come, smell at that cloth and tell me—"

"But what will I do?"

"You will accept your wyrd. If Cwenburh isn't well . . . Ah, but who knows?"

Hild had no idea what the queen had to do with anything. Her wyrd. Light of the world.

"Come, tell me what you think of this cheese. Fit for a king or merely his pigs?"

Hild put her wyrd from her mind. "It's stinky."

"Indeed. But look, the rind is firm enough. And a good rinse in brine and a fresh wrapping and it may last a while longer. But it should have been rinsed and rewrapped long since. What is Cwenburh thinking?"

After the cheese they moved from the food room to the room of skeins of yarn and bolts of already woven cloth. One bolt, wrapped in plain un-dyed hemp, stood in the corner on its own. Breguswith pulled down the corner of the outer wrapper.

"Do you see this colour?" It was finely, tightly woven wool as lustrous as linen, a brilliant red. "Fit for a queen. But with your hair blue is better." She dismissed the roll. "I have the very thing. When we have it cut, I shall work a border with gold."

"Gold?"

"I have a ring in my chest. Wulf shall beat it thin for me and cut it. Your wrists and neck will outshine the queen."

"We have gold?"

"There is always a bit hidden away."

"I don't want our gold." That wasn't exactly what she meant but she didn't always know how to say gauzy but strong things in Anglisc.

"I dreamt of you, you are to be the light of the world. Of course you shall have gold. What is the matter with you?" Breguswith reached for two skeins of weld-yellow flax and tilted them towards the light, examining the yarn.

"Is it a good ring, and heavy?"

"What use would I have for lightweight trifles?"

"Then give the ring to Burgræd's son, have him swear on it."

"Burgræd?"

"His son."

Her mother put the yarn down. "His son, you say?"

Hild nodded. "Burgmod. He is . . . drifting."

"Towards the king?"

"I think so."

Breguswith's face stilled and her finger moved very slightly as she ran some calculation. "He is of an age," she said eventually. "But it will wait until the sixth night . . . Yes." Her smile was the kind of smile Hild had imagined on the water sprite's face as she pulled her down and drowned her. "Yes. You shall have your gold and Burgræd his."

"His son, Burgmod."

"Him and his son both. And Hereswith shall bring her gemæcce to Modresniht."

"Mildburh."

"Child, I know their names." She picked up the two skeins again. "Yes, it's time to declare ourselves. We shall make a striking group at the feast. Now, tell me whether and why we should choose the left-spun yarn or the right."

Hild, in fact, did not choose either. Her mother chose for her—armsful of both—and with Onnen wove a beautiful spin-patterned pale yellow underdress with wrist- and throat-work in blue and glittering real gold. Her long, rather old-fashioned—as was right for a child, light of the world or not—sleeveless jacket was as blue as the summer sky just after sunset, and fastened with a great wheel-like gilt-copper brooch whose rim was as large around as her closed fist, like a hand on her chest it was so heavy, for all that it was mostly copper.

Every time she swallowed, she gleamed. Every time she lifted a hand, she glittered. Every time she breathed, she glinted. She was breathing fast; her legs trembled; the glitter and gleam and glint became an endless shimmer.

She stood behind the hanging in the doorway between the kitchen corridor and the hall proper, thirty women and girls waiting beyond her. They did not talk to her. With Cwenburh still ill, she was to be cupbearer. "But Hereswith is older," she'd said when her mother prepared her, but her mother had taken Hild's face between her hands and said, "This is your wyrd."

Beyond, in the columned hall, the scop was finishing his praise of Edwin's vast holdings, the whiteness of his sheep, the richness of his soil: the necessary preamble to the introduction of the women of the household to begin the Modresniht feast. The hall had been quiet at first, less to listen to the scop than because everyone was hungover from yesterday's Yule feast. As the informal jars of heather beer began to empty and housefolk brought in the wooden platters of intricately woven and spiced breads with their little pots of fruit butters and jams and herb pastes, stomachs and heads settled and conversation began to rise like a tide. The scop's chant moved majestically from folk and fold to hearth and hall, wealth and wine, his rolling Anglisc now transmuted into the language of flame, and gold, and honour.

Hild's legs trembled. She stood as straight as she could.

"Soon now," her mother said.

Hild nodded but couldn't speak. What if she dropped the cup? Or spilled it? Or tripped? What if she took it to guests in the wrong order? The omens would be calamitous.

"Hold out your hands."

She obeyed.

"It's heavy," Breguswith said. She put the great cup in Hild's hands. Hild sagged. She had never held anything so weighty.

It was as wide around as her rib cage, not gilded bronze but pure gold, with silver and gold filigree, studded with garnet and beryl and blue enamel. It was empty.

Breguswith gestured to a houseman in a work tunic, who passed her a red-glazed jar. She unstoppered it. The stinging scent of white mead made Hild blink.

As Breguswith began to pour, a houseboy lifted the hanging cloth and a rush of housefolk carrying stoppered jars flowed around Hild and into the hall. "Hold still!" Breguswith said.

Hild did her best. The boy still held the curtain. The housefolk in hall were spreading out along the wall behind the benches, ready with their jars. The scop's voice rose.

The weight of the cup was unbearable. The noise was unbearable. The heat was unbearable.

Her mother was smoothing Hild's hair back from her forehead, tucking it securely behind her ears. She was saying something. ". . . since a maid without a girdle was cupbearer? Never, is my guess. It's a job for a queen but today, O my light, O my jewel, it is you. Today you are queen in this hall. You step first, with me just one step behind, and your sister and her gemæcce . . ."

She wanted Onnen. She wanted Cian. She wanted the queen to rise from her sickbed and take this cup from her.

". . . Edwin first, then the guest at his right, the guest at his left, then across the hall to his . . ."

She wanted her mother to have dreamt of Hereswith as jewel and light. She wanted the king to be dead, dead, dead so that someone else's closest female relative would do this.

Even over the din of conversation, the scop's voice rang with that triumphal note which, whether in Anglisc or British, meant it was time.

". . . here at your shoulder. But you step first, you step first. Step now, Hild."

From behind her she felt the women smoothing their dresses, checking their wrist cuffs, and flicking their veils one last time. The houseboy was looking at her. Her hands felt slippery on the gold. It was too heavy. Her hands were too small. She would drop it.

The boy stuck out his tongue. She blinked. He crossed his eyes.

"They'll get stuck," she said in British. He nearly dropped the curtain in surprise, and it was with a private smile she stepped into the hall.

It had been the principia of the Roman prefect, then the palace of the king of Ebrauc, and was now the feasting hall of Edwin, king of Deira and Bernicia. It was too big, too high, too hard. More stone than wood. Wealh. Really wealh, in a way Ceredig's smoky great house had not been.

It was not smoky here. She could feel the air stirring about her. She dare not look up from the cup in case she spilled, but she knew the roof would be too far up, in too much shadow, to see. Perhaps there were windows up there. But she wasn't cold.

Wood coals glowed in a series of pits down the centre of the room. You could lay a herd of cows on those coals, end to end. Torches roared and rushed in their brackets along the high second-storey wall (how had the housefolk lit those? ladders?) and matching torches burnt less vigorously along the inner colonnades, behind the benches where the men sat in two long—long, long—rows facing one another across the fire pit. The walls were draped with tapestries and smaller hangings brocaded in gold and stitched with jewels. The shadows gleamed.

In the centre of the right-hand row was Edwin's bench. He wore red. Four huge bands glittered on his left arm, three on his right. Royal bands. Every time he reached for bread, muscles in his neck and shoulder bunched and corded. Any one ring would, she knew, make her cup seem light. His sons, Eadfrith and Osfrith, sat on his right; Lilla, his chief gesith, on his left. As Hild approached slowly with her cup, Edwin looked at her and put down his bread. The scop played a dramatic chord on his lyre. Many turned to look and saw the girl in yellow and blue, carrying gold. Conversation dropped from deafening to loud.

Hild moved with as much grace as she could muster until she stood before Edwin and slightly to his left so that her back was not quite turned to the guests—British in Anglisc clothes—across the way.

"Edwin king," she said as loud as she could, and because her voice was higher than any other voice in hall it cut through the din and the hall quieted more. Now she could hear distinctly the hiss and roar of the torches. "My king," she said. And her carefully prepared speech fled. What could she say before so many that any would want to hear? "Great King. For you, a drink." And she held out the cup. She nearly lost her balance.

Edwin, smiling, stood, leaned over the table, and took the cup in one hand. "I will lighten it for you," he said, and took a great swallow. The gold at his temple and throat and arms, pinned to his chest and along his belt, winked. He handed it back. Hild took it carefully. Then she turned to the eldest ætheling, Eadfrith, who stood and drank, then to his brother, Osfrith. All around her, men began to stand. Her arms ached, but she held the cup out straight, as though it weighed nothing. She moved down the bench to the chief gesith, held it out.

"Ah, empty it for the maid, Lilla," Edwin said. "She can barely hold it."

The gesith laughed and swallowed once, twice, three times, then turned it upside down to show it empty. The crowd roared. Hild stood straighter. The weight of the brooch at her chest was terrible. She looked over at the houseman behind Edwin's chair.

"The cup is empty," she said.

He ran with his jar all the way down to the end of the bench and all the way back up to Hild, where he knelt and poured into the proffered cup. How did he do that without seeming to look?

She said clearly, using her stomach the way the great hounds belled when hunting, "Fill it high. Then bring your jar, in case our guests have a great thirst." She knew full well that now the guests would feel it necessary to empty the cup twice over, and then she would go back to Edwin and he would have to maintain Anglisc prowess and drink more than those British in Anglisc clothes. And wasn't that the point of a feast, to drink and sing? She remembered Ywain in Ceredig's hall saying, *Ah, if you make men drink they will sing, and if they sing, they are happy, and if they are happy, they throw gold to the harper and compliments to their guests.* And Onnen had told her who was among the guests.

She spilled not a drop, and when she got to the guest bench, she held the cup to the head guest, who stood, and his entourage with him. "Dunod ap Pabo," she said. "Drink and be welcome." Then, quietly, in British, as he took the cup, "If your lady wife were here, I would give to her greetings as a friend of Onnen, who is cousin to your wife's brother, Ceredig ap Gualloc, who was king in Elmet wood."

He paused, shot a startled look across the hall.

"Drink, my lord. And tell me, for Onnen, is he well?"

He sipped and swallowed, nodded slightly.

She switched back to Anglisc. "If you drink more the cup will be easier for me to hold and you will have my gratitude. And," in British again, "the housefolk have said that the mead from the hall jars is not of a strength of that first poured for the king. He will be amazed at your steady head." She grinned. "Though who knows who has paid which man to say what in the hope of foolishness?"

They took a moment, the grown man in clothes foreign to him and the young girl in splendour she could barely carry, and understood each other. He laughed.

"You are a strange little lass," he said in Anglisc, for all to hear.

"I am the light of the world," she said, clear and high, and the scop, always sensitive to dramatic possibility, drew an uncanny chord from his lyre, and at that moment a great gust of wind made the torches on the upper level gutter then flare.

The hall fell silent.

"I drink to you, little light!" He drained the cup, upended it, and the men beat their palms on the boards and the scop nodded to his whistle man and his drummer and they plucked a few measures of a lively air and, while the other women now moved to fill drinking horns along the benches, she could recross the hall without too many people paying attention.

But as she approached Edwin he gestured to a houseman, who ran down the benches, and up, and said, "The king desires that you sit with him for the feast if, being a little maid, you are not too tired. And he desires me to take the cup from you now, so that you may walk with ease to his bench. Your lady mother and sister may join also, should you wish it."

Hild looked at Edwin and nodded. "Yes. I thank the king. But my sister can carry the cup. The girl with honey hair and the green dress."

Another houseman ran to bring Breguswith to Edwin, and Hereswith to Hild, to take the cup. Hereswith, twelve years old, brilliant in beryl green, with a silvered-tin brooch at her breast, gave Hild a complicated look as she reached for the cup, but looked startled when she felt its weight. "Thunor!" she said. "That's heavy."

"Hold it tight," Hild said, and she was glad to have a sister to walk beside her down the hall. The housefolk watched them closely. The boy who had stuck his tongue out at her poked his head through the curtained doorway and the houseman standing there—the kitchen chief, Hild saw—shooed him back. The chief seemed tense.

Hild understood: He couldn't serve until the cupbearer sat. "Let's go faster," Hild said.

Breguswith timed her arrival at the head table to match theirs. Edwin stood, the æthelings and Lilla with him, and a fuss was made of seating them all: Hild, as cupbearer, to the king's immediate left, her mother and Hereswith and Mildburh between the princes.

The minute they sat, housefolk poured into the hall with roast pigs in apple-scented crackling and tubs of roasted vegetables and great wooden bowls of soup. At other tables, Hild saw, the men and their women shared the soup, passing the table bowl back and forth as they would a drinking horn, but at the king's bench, each guest was brought his or her own birchwood bowl.

Her mother gave her a meaningful smile—*Talk to the king!*—then turned to Osfrith. Hereswith looked at Eadfrith and nodded as though they had always sat side by side, and he said, "How do you, lady?" though his voice squeaked a little and his spotty skin reddened. The scop began a pleasant tune, with an endless feel to it, like spinning, and Hild understood she would be here a while. She wished her feet touched the floor.

The king lifted his bowl and slurped. He wiped his beard with a heavy-ringed hand, wiped his hand on the cloth running along the edge of the table, looked at Hild. His eyes were mostly blue around the pupil and mostly green around the edge. She lifted her own bowl; without her feet to steady her, it seemed heavier than it should. The soup smelt of parsnip and cream. The steam rising from it was hot. She blew on the soup, took a tiny sip, blew some more.

"A princess does not blow on her food in my hall," said the king, with a smile.

Hild nodded, then remembered she should talk. "Then what must I do? The soup is too hot, yet if I sit and wait, the whole will grow cold."

"An ætheling or a princess must never wait. Our food comes to the table just so." He clapped his hands twice, clap-clap, and lifted her bowl. A houseman appeared at his shoulder with a fresh bowl. "See? Try that. Yes, perfect. And if it gets cold you learn to clap"—clap-clap—"for another."

Another houseman appeared. Hild recognised him as a friend of Onnen's.

The king ignored him. "A king's table is always watched. They will have seen you blow; when you clap they understand your needs."

The houseman stood right there, while the king talked in his presence the way he wouldn't even talk before his dog unless he gave it a fondle of its ears. Then he drank his own soup again.

She tried not to see her mother's swift glance up the table. She swung her feet to and fro, thinking.

"I like your tunic, lord King."

He turned to her, puzzled.

"It is a very fine red." She tilted her head. "Though with our hair colour, blue is better." She couldn't interpret the look on his face. "I could help you pick the colour, next time."

"You could?"

"I could."

"Well I thank you for that, little maid."

"I am seven. Not so little as I was. Though I do wish my legs were longer and would reach the ground."

"By all means, let us fix that." Clap-clap. This time Hild watched. The houseman peeled himself from the wall and as he approached, another from farther along the room took his place. "Bring the maid a cushion."

When the man left on his errand, Hild said, "Do you not know my name, King? It is Hild."

"Hild," the king said. "You are a strange little maid."

"So Prince Dunod says."

"What do you know of Dunod ap Pabo?"

"That he would be sad for his wife if her brother were to be killed."

"He told you this?"

"No, King, but what sister wouldn't grieve for her brother, and what husband wouldn't hurl himself at the wind to try to keep his wife happy?"

Edwin leaned in. His pupils were expanding, drinking the blue centre from his eyes, until all was green and black. "You have seen this?"

"My king?"

He wrapped his huge hand around her right wrist. "Tell me true, now. You have seen Dunod ap Pabo go to war over the death of Ceredig ap Gualloc?"

Hild blinked.

Edwin shook her slightly, and it took Hild back to a time she couldn't quite remember, the day her world changed, when her father died, and she saw the grey snakes of hair in Edwin's beard and heard a voice: *Tell Cadfan that he or his son shall have to face this serpent one day.*

"Cadwallon," she whispered. Edwin let go as if scalded. "Cadfan's son. Your foster-brother. He will have to face you."

"Hild," he said. "Now I know that name. You are the one in the lady Breguswith's dream, the jewel who will light the way."

Hild nodded. His face looked very strange, so pale that his eyes seemed to shine and crawl like summer flies.

"You will light my way."

She nodded again. *Talk to the king.* "Yes, King. Though any light must have fuel to shine."

"Fuel, is it?" The colour began to come back to Edwin's face, and, along with it, a knowing look.

Hild felt encouraged. "Yes, King."

"And what do you ask from me as your . . . fuel?"

"You are king, and do king things. My sister learns to weave. My—that is Cian—my mother's . . . my mother's gemæcce's son, learns the sword. I want a path."

"A path? That is your price?"

Price? She was aware of a houseman approaching bearing her cushion, but dared not pause now. "I want to learn, to wander and ask and think and listen like . . . like a priest or a prince."

"Not gold?"

"Gold comes to priests and princes."

Edwin threw back his head and laughed. "So now we get to it. Gold." He stood, looked over at his scop. The scop's rippling music stopped, and he struck two peremptory chords. "Hear me!" the king shouted. "I have a challenge." Every warrior in the room came to attention. A feast challenge meant gold for the winner. "Though, as it is Modresniht, my challenge is for a maid."

Puzzlement. Settling back of the men, leaning forward of the women. Breguswith's eyes shone like blue glass.

Edwin stripped the lowest band on his left arm, wrapped both hands about it—they barely met around the circle—and lifted it over his head. It was soft yellow gold, thick as his thumb, worth a hundred cattle, two hundred, five hundred. He turned slowly, so it reflected light to the farthest ends of every bench. Then he threw it onto the table.

"Hild, princess and niece, jewel of Deira who will light our way in wisdom and prophecy, the gold is yours. To claim it, you must only fill our feasting cup to the brim, and carry it and the ring to our guest's table without spilling a drop, and then back again."

Hild stood, beckoned to a houseman, pointed to the cup. Her mother's eyes glowed so hot they might melt. Gold, acknowledgement of her status, and a path. All for one trip across the hall.

It was impossible. The cup and ring together weighed more than half of what she did.

"Hild," said her mother, and beat gently with the palm of her hand on the table as her daughter passed her. "Hild," said Hereswith as her sister walked by.

"Hild," said the women along the table, and then "Hild!" shouted one gesith, and now the drumming was like the surf at Bebbanburg, loud, unstoppable. "Hild. Hild. Hild." There wasn't a one among them who didn't want to see her win an ætheling's ransom from the king. She walked on the wave of sound the length of the tables and back up again until she stood before Edwin, on the other side of the board.

The arm ring winked hugely in the light. The white mead shimmered in its great cup. Her arms would not carry both.

Men's strength is their weakness— *A dog, snapping teeth*—

The houseman lifted the cup. Hild raised one hand: *Wait.*

Neck rigid, haunches bulging. Furrows in the turf. Stretching the line of her back. Bend your legs . . .

She looked at Edwin. "Edwin, King, I will carry your gold. I will carry it as a princess does, as a crown." And she bent her head—but also her legs.

When Edwin put the heavy ring on her head, Hild locked her knees and straightened one inch, two. It was like carrying the world. But she pushed with her feet and lifted and lifted until her spine was as straight as a plumb line and the weight poured through the muscles along her spine and in her thighs and calves and feet. She gestured to the houseman and turned to face Dunod and his folk. Then she accepted the cup.

This was for her path, for her freedom, for her life and family. To make her dead da proud. She was strong. She was royal. She would set her will. She would do this.

So she fixed her gaze on Dunod, on the glint of the gold around his throat, and she began. The drumming rose and, from the men, stamping and cheering. From the women, a ululation. And the sound swept her across the room, between the fire pits, to Dunod's table.

"Do drink it all, lord, if you will," she said, and he did, in one long draught, and his men shouted and he bellowed, "Hild! Light of the world!" and Hild took the cup back again and, again, was swept across the hall to Edwin's table. It seemed not so difficult to walk a clear path.

3

✦

THE QUEEN'S ROOM at Sancton smelt of blood and weeping and, perhaps, Hild thought, something else. She stood by the door hanging, watching, listening, while her mother and the king stood by the empty bed. Like the last time Cwenburh miscarried, her women had washed her and carried her away to a new apartment, so that when she woke she would not have to remember staring at the heroic embroidery of the white horse, or the blooming apple tree, or that knot in the pine cladding on the ceiling while she screamed and bled and pushed and wept: for a bladder-size sack of slimed slipperiness, for nothing.

"It would have been a girl, my king," said Breguswith. "It would have been your peaceweaver."

Edwin was trembling. "Her women assured me this time all was well."

"Yes, my king. They thought it was."

"They?"

Perhaps her mother hadn't seen Edwin's rage. Hild took a step into the room.

"Are you, lady, not one of them?"

Another step, and another until she stood by the small table at the head of the bed.

"Oh, no, my king," her mother said. "That is, yes, but you may recall I suggested to the queen after the last time that she wait, perhaps for a very long while."

"And you?" Edwin whirled on Hild, who was sniffing the queen's cup, and thinking. "Perhaps an eight-year-old may prove wiser than the collective mind of my entire household. Tell me your prophecy, O shining light!"

Hild put the cup down. She didn't understand why he was so angry. He didn't care much for his wife, and despite the court's cautious optimism of the last few weeks about the queen's pregnancy, no one could be surprised at this event, not after all the others. So it was something else.

"Uncle, your wife will bear no more babies." Not while Breguswith made her special heather beer and disguised the sweet gale with tansy.

"None?"

She shook her head.

"I need a peaceweaver!"

Hild said nothing.

"I need one. Over the water those cursed Idings are making their name with Eochaid's freckled brat, Domnall, who took a retinue to Meath and won some small squabble that they name a great battle, and today I find one of them has married a Pictish princess. A Pict! Now I have Idings feeling their oats at both ends of the Roman wall. Do you know what that means?"

"War."

He blinked. "You've seen this?"

Hild shook her head. There would be war, it was the way of the world. Young stags watched for the old to falter. The exiled Idings were feeling their strength, and Edwin had no daughters to marry into alliance with other Anglisc kings, and the Irish and Pictish might watch the old stag and think his antlers too heavy for his head. They might think it time to sweep down from the north and put the Idings as client kings on the throne. "Like the king stag, you must lift your head and show your tines."

"Well they are still sharp, by the gods. I have three hundred gesiths sworn to me til death. I give them treasure. I am greatly to be feared!"

"Yes, Uncle."

"I will take the Isle of Vannin."

"Yes, Uncle."

"You've seen this?"

Hild was used to his abrupt decisions and equally sudden reversals, but she could not get used to his insistence on visions. She looked at her mother, who gave her the look she had given on Modresniht more than a year ago— *Talk to the king!*—and gave the impression of stepping back a pace.

Hild tried to tell Edwin what she saw.

"The rooks in the west wood build their nests high in the elms. The squirrels skip past rowan berries without tasting."

He waited.

Hild did her best. "The rooks don't expect great winds; the squirrels know that other forage is plentiful yet." He didn't seem to understand. Her mother, at least, was nodding. Hild stepped back very slightly.

"My king," Breguswith said. "Our guiding light foresees that the winter weather will be a while. And with fine weather you might still take a ship to the Isle of Vannin, while Fiachnae mac Báetáin of the Dál nAriadne is drinking with the Ulaid in their moss-grown, fog-bound land."

"It is a risky plan."

"Yes, my king. But you are brave and your war band strong."

Edwin stared at the brightly woven blanket pulled over the bloodied mattress. Hild doubted he even saw its beautiful pattern, the poppy orange and calf-eye brown. But it didn't take the light of the world to prophesy that if the blanket were not washed very soon it would be ruined, fit only for housefolk, and a blanket like that took two women a winter to card, spin, dye, and weave. And if someone didn't take away the cup soon, someone else might work out what had happened.

"And no peaceweaver?" He was looking at Hild.

"No, Uncle."

"Will she die?"

She didn't believe her mother bore Cwenburh any ill will. "Perhaps not, if she tries no more children."

But two months later, as the court packed its wagons to move to York, where Edwin would consult with his lords on the matter of a winter war—a war that could have been fought and won by now if he hadn't changed his mind so often—Cwenburh told her cousin, Mildburh, that she was again with child. Mildburh told Hereswith, who told her mother and Hild.

Breguswith was scanning their apartment one last time—all was stowed in chests and bags; housefolk were dismantling the beds—when Edwin sent a boy to call Hild and her mother to his hall. They donned light wraps.

It was a cold, grey morning of wind and fitful rain. Oxen lowed as drovers herded them from their warm byre and began the long business of fitting yokes and checking harnesses. Rain drummed on the stretched leather of the waiting wagons. Coelgar and his men marked wagon beds with chalk as they were loaded.

The hall was dark and cool. The fires were out, the best hangings already taken down and rolled, and Edwin's great sword and spear lifted from their hooks above his chair. Indeed, housefolk stood about, clearly waiting to remove the chair itself. By him stood Coifi, bare-armed and bear-cloaked as usual. And Lilla and a young gesith—tall as a fifteen-year oak sapling—called Forthere, looking watchful. And the latest Christ bishop, one of the less common ones, who held rolls of pale leather to the light and stared and murmured—their god must be very strange. And even the ugly old woman children threw stones at, who made auguries from burnt pinecones and the flights of birds. Dunne, Hild had heard her called. The hall reeked of sacrifice oils and incenses.

"You told me she would bear no more children," the king said to them as they walked into the dim hall.

"Nor has she, my king," said Breguswith.

"Yet," said Coifi.

"Aye," said the old woman. "She seems strong as a mare."

"So she seemed at other times," Breguswith said.

Everyone looked at Hild, who said nothing.

"I want auguries," the king said. "I want the opinion of every god mouth in this hall, and I want it before I climb on that miserable wagon."

"My lord King, the gods require things done in the proper order and in the proper—"

"Today, Coifi. And we'll start with you."

"Now?"

"Now. Go find your bullock and knife." He looked around. "And you, Mother, what do you need?"

"Only the outdoors, and mayhap a fire."

Edwin stood, gestured to one of the hovering housefolk. "Bring a torch and some firewood, and my cloak while you're about it. And if you see the priest, tell him we'll be . . ." He looked at the old woman.

"By the undern daymark." The three tall elms south of the gate, where, from the well by the bread kitchen, their silhouette cut the horizon immediately below where the sun hung on a cloudless day in the quarter day before midday, undern. Today was not cloudless. Hild wondered if she should run and fetch her mother's heavy cloak and a hand muff. In this rain there could be no fire on the brow of the hill, so it would be a bird augury, and Hild knew there would be few rooks by those elms at this time of day. It would be a cold wait, and her mother's joints had been more painful than usual. But then they were all moving and there wasn't time.

Auguries and sacrifice: crude tools of toothless petitioners. Or so her mother said, even as she'd rehearsed Hild in every variation. But she said, over and over, there was no power like a sharp and subtle mind weaving others' hopes and fears and hungers into a dream they wanted to hear. Always know what they want to hear—not just what everyone knew they wanted to hear but what they didn't even dare name to themselves. Show them the pattern. Give them permission to do what they wanted all along.

What did Edwin want to hear?

By the time the king, swathed in a blue cloak (*With our hair colour, blue is better*), stood by the elms, almost forty people, including Coifi and his assistants—free of all edged iron, as befitted servants of the god—leading a calf, were assembled. Twenty or more were gesiths. They'd been bored at Sancton, nothing to do but play knucklebones, fight over women, and burnish their chain mail, and they loved a good prophecy. They stood about, smelling of iron and strong drink, spears resting on their shoulders, sword hilts jutting from the waist at their left hand, for the warrior gesith did not wear cloaks, except on a hard march. One was throwing his knife, a pretty jewelled thing, at the burr partway up the trunk of the closest elm, yanking it free, pacing, throwing. Soon there would be jeers, then boasts, then bets, then more ale, then a fight.

At least it had stopped raining.

A man, the head drover, trotted up the rise, fell to one knee in the wet grass, and spoke to the king. The king nodded, then shouted out to the old woman. "The wagons are ready, Mother. Will your gods speak?"

"I will call the gods to speak, if you lend me a war horn."

"A war horn? Very well." He gestured to Lilla, who handed him the great horn of the Yffings. He held it up for all to see. "Will this do?" The gold filigree around the rim and tip shone as yellow as the absent sun. "Mind now, Mother, even if the omens are the right ones, you don't get to keep this one." He handed it back to Lilla, who walked it over to the old woman.

She weighed it in her hands. "You are familiar, lords, with omens of black-winged birds." Hild, who had been watching the gesith with the dagger—it would be Cian's birthday soon and she was wondering where she could get him a pretty thing like that—focused on the old woman. Her mother straightened subtly. They didn't look at each other. Black-winged bird. Why not just say rook? "If the birds fly from the southwest during undern, it portends numerous offspring. If they fly overhead, the fulfilment of wishes."

Hild ran through the portents her mother had schooled her in. If the birds flew from the southeast during morgen, the first quarter of the day, the enemy will approach. From the east was more difficult: relatives coming, or battle to arise, or death by disease. During æfen, and on into sunset, if they flew in the southeast, treasure would come, and overhead meant the petitioner would obtain the advantages hoped for. Then there were the more ominous single-bird sightings, and the opposite meanings assigned to two birds. But now it was undern, the quarter day before the sun stood at its height, and they were interested in rooks, many rooks, flying from the southwest or overhead, because it was rooks that roosted in the undern elms and the elm wood beyond. What did Edwin want to hear? He wanted a peaceweaver, yes, but what else?

The old woman lifted the horn and blew a blast that surprised everyone. Below, in the fenced settlement, two warhorses screamed. War hounds bayed and other dogs barked. The gesiths all dropped spears to the ready. One, with a shield, brought it to the defence position. And then Hild understood. A war horn. Recognised by man and beast. Even crows and ravens. And crows and ravens nested to the south and east of Sancton, among the elm and oak on the other side of the river. Ravens knew war, knew the tasty morsels war offered. They would come.

They did, seven of them: big and black and bright, croaking up from the southwest, then flying overhead once and landing with audible thumps on the turf at the top of the hill.

"Seven black-winged birds from the southwest, that then flew overhead, my king. Seven, the luckiest number of all. Numerous offspring and the fulfilment of your wishes, King. Dunne says you shall have your peaceweaver."

"Well, Mother Dunne, you shall have your reward." Edwin looked for Coelgar, remembered he would be with the wagons. "Lilla here will see word is given for your winter comfort."

It was an undeniable omen. The old woman was clever. A war horn to call ravens. Hild would remember that.

The king, now in high good humour, looked at the Christ bishop. "And you, Anaoc?"

The Christ priests were mostly envoys from British kingdoms, come to talk to a rising king about trade and alliances and marriages. Anaoc was from the kingdom of the southwest wealh, or as they called it, Dyfneint, whose every other king seemed to be named Geraint.

"Christ and all his followers abjure *superstitiones*."

The king, still smiling, said, "Don't spit."

Anaoc swallowed. "My lord, we refuse divination, idolatry, and the swearing on the heads of beasts."

Superstitiones. Hild tried the word in her mouth. *Superstitiones.* It must be Latin.

"But it works, Anaoc."

"We have no quarrel with that, my lord. We who live in the light of Christ find *superstitiones* sinful not because they are not efficacious but because they are efficacious due to the intervention of demons."

"Demons."

"Servants of the devil, God's adversary."

Edwin scratched the snakes of his beard. "You're a bold man. Does this boldness mean your prince no longer wishes my help against the Gewisse?"

"No, my lord! That is, yes, my lord, our need is as urgent as ever. It is only that I cannot help you because my God will not speak through animals or other portents."

"Though your god's enemies will?"

Anaoc nodded unhappily.

"So the god saying through his birds that I will have more children speaks as the enemy of your god?"

Anaoc said nothing.

"Now this is very interesting, priest. Am I to believe, then, that your god does not wish me to have more children?"

One of the drunker gesiths spat. Hild doubted he'd even been listening, but Anaoc swallowed again and bent his head. "My lord, forgive me, I am but a mortal. My God does not make His wishes known to me."

"Then what use are you to man or beast?"

A gust of wind shook a spatter of raindrops from the daymark elms. Coifi's bullock lowed.

Edwin smiled. "We'll talk more of your Christ god and his enemies another time, priest. Coifi, the priest of Woden, has a calf whose innards wish to speak of our destiny."

Anaoc bowed and withdrew. When he thought no one was watching, he wiped his shaved forehead with his sleeve. The Dyfneint's petition would fail because Anaoc had failed; the kingdom would soon fall to the

Gewisse and its people be sold into slavery. Hild wondered if the priest's god would be a comfort to him then.

She turned her attention to Coifi, whose attendants had the bullock by the nostrils and who himself was beginning the slow one-handed drumbeat. Dum-dum, dum-dum, like a heartbeat—though, without the hard enclosure of the ritual place, the drum had no resonance, no menace.

The drum beat faster, like a heart speeding up. Away from the usual ceremonies it sounded thin and wrong. Perhaps it was because childbirth was a woman's issue, and Woden was leader of the Wild Hunt, carrier-off of the dead, god of gods, a man's god; even the elms they stood by were men's trees.

The nearest stand of ash was a good mile or so up the river. Hild had been there with Cian only a few days ago. It had been wet then, too, and Cian had been wondering aloud, again, who would sponsor him for his sword. The leaves would fall soon, he said, and it would be his birthday, and Hild's, and one day his fifteenth birthday would come and there would be no one to give him his sword. Hild had told him, again, that all would be well, she knew it would be, she just wasn't sure how.

The drum stopped. Coifi handed it to the young man behind him, raised his bare arms. "Woden! All father! Husband to Eorðe." Edwin leaned forward and Hild sensed her mother move slightly; she had realised something. But Hild didn't dare look at her. "Here stands your many times son, Edwin the son of Ælla, the son of Yffi, the son of Wuscfrea, the son of Wilgisl, the son of Westerfalca, the son of Sæfugl, the son of Sæbald, the son of Segegeat, the son of Swebdæg, the son of Sigegar, the son of Wædæg, the son of Woden, god of gods, and of his wife, Eorðe. He asks that you both guide my hand as I give to you a bullock, so that you may speak your wills in the matter of a peaceweaver for your son and his wife, Cwenburh."

He held out his hand to the assistant with the drum, who handed him the black knife.

At Goodmanham, and in the enclosure here at Sancton, Coifi had roofless temples floored in boards that were scrubbed white before every sacrifice. Hild wondered how the blood patterns would be read on the wet and already slippery grass.

The bullock knew something was up. Perhaps he smelt the blood awareness in the tightening attention of the gesiths. He bellowed and tried to kick out at Coifi's assistants but one managed to grab the bullock's tail and lift it, and the bullock stretched out his neck and lowered his head.

Coifi, slick as goose grease, slashed its throat with one diagonal backhand slice. Blood dropped like a red sheet from the open neck, like something in a mummer's play. It spattered and gurgled and just as the bullock's front legs buckled Coifi moved again, but this time Hild saw his muscles bunch and strain as he whipped the knife along the beast's underside. Its guts fell out.

They fell in one neat package, a good omen, though still attached by the intestine, and in some ugly turn of fate looked like nothing but a gigantic stillbirth, dangling its umbilical cord. Coifi cut the gut cord swiftly, but everyone had seen it.

"The blood, my king," he said, and pointed with the knife. His whole forearm was red-sleeved and glistening, but even as Hild watched wiry hairs on his arm sprang upright, like red worms after rain.

The king, like all of them, had difficulty moving his eyes from the obscene gut package to the edge of the blood moving sluggishly, as a cold snake might, downslope to the elms.

"Woden has spoken!" Coifi shouted. "He calls the blood to him. He accepts your sacrifice. You will have your peaceweaver." But without the enclosure his voice was trained for, his pronouncement sounded insubstantial, a cast skin rather than the snake itself.

No one said anything for a moment. The smell of blood was overwhelming, thick and sweet. The gesiths didn't like it, it reminded them of too many brothers fallen. Edwin was shaking his head. He didn't like it, either.

Clouds thickened and darkened overhead and birdsong changed. It was about to rain again.

Breguswith slung one side of her wrap over her shoulder and stepped forward, her hand touching the crystal seer stone on her belt. She gestured at the sack of entrails glistening by the gutted bullock. "This is the smell of the queen's bed."

Edwin said, "You have seen this?"

"Waking and sleeping." Dreams were the most powerful of all prophecies. "There will be no peaceweaver from this queen."

This queen.

Hild's stomach tightened down to a lump as hard as twice-baked bread. The smell was terrible and her mother would make it happen again, over and over. Couldn't they see?

She lifted her face to the sky. The clouds were as dense as the tight black wool of the upland sheep. She wished it would rain now.

"And you?" Edwin said to her, his eyes glimmering and green in the darkening morning. "You have seen this, too?"

Hild had a sudden hideous thought: What if everything that had ever died lay rotting where it fell? All the frozen birds, the misborn lambs, the leverets savaged by foxes. One stinking charnel pit. What if the world never came clean? "It will all wash away," Hild said desperately. It always had before. "It will rain, and the blood will wash away and the carcass will be taken away and all will be fresh and new." Wouldn't it?

Then a fat droplet burst against the back of her neck. She lifted her face to the rain, cold and clean.

Coifi looked at her. His eyes were black and blank, like a stoat's when it eyes a fledgling fallen from the nest, but then Breguswith pulled her mantle up over her head and her elbow broke the priest's line of sight. Though not Edwin's, not the gesiths', not Anaoc's. Her mother wanted them to remember what she'd said: *All will be fresh and new.* She had no idea why that was important and her heart was kicking like a hare. But she had been trained to show a still face so she raised her own mantle and looked back. Anaoc made that flickering hand gesture over face and chest that Christ priests made when they were afraid.

The drover reappeared, this time with Coelgar. As they spoke to the king, the drover shifted from foot to foot. Edwin listened and nodded and turned to his entourage.

"The wagons are miring themselves so rapidly they'll sink to meet the root of the one tree if we delay much longer. We will leave now." The look he directed at Coifi and Anaoc as they backed away respectfully was dissatisfaction. The gesiths ambled off as they pleased; they were the king's chosen, they had never needed to learn the obsequiousness of priests.

Edwin turned to her. "So you're a weather worker, too."

She started to shake her head but her mother put an arm around her shoulder and squeezed and said, "She is filled with a light she does not yet understand, my king."

"Though you do, of course." He laughed shortly. "Then ride in my wagon and we will discuss Cwenburh and her health and where to look for these new beginnings."

In the wagon her mother and uncle talked of marriage prospects. Hild listened as best she could, recognising the names of some Kentish princesses and East Anglisc æthelings and, to her surprise, Hereswith. That's what Edwin wanted: not just the alliance forged by a peaceweaver but a new wife, bringing her own, even more powerful bond to another kingdom. Coifi hadn't understood. Her mother had, and had plans . . . But Hild had had a fright and was now safe from the priests and with her mother. She didn't want to think about it. She fell asleep.

At York, Edwin's counsellors and thegns and gesiths agreed that the Isle of Vannin, midway between Ireland and the mainland, could and should be taken. The war band left just as the leaves began to turn. Cwenburh's belly grew during the two months before Yule, grew during the twelve days of feasting at the kingless court, grew as the royal women and their personal retainers—men like Burgræd and his now-strapping son, Burgmod—made their slow way by ship down the river to Brough and then transferred to bigger ships and sailed up the rocky coast of the northern sea to Bebbanburg. As the sea dashing against the fort's stone foundation turned from the cold, heavy waves of winter to the restless turbulence of spring, the queen's belly grew. It grew as news came that the cattle at Yeavering were swollen with calf and in the vales the bumblebees were out early and in large numbers and it would be a spring of plenty.

In the stone fastness Hild watched her mother, who, in Edwin's absence and Cwenburh's absorption in her belly, tightened her reins on the running of the household and laughed with the queen at her happiness. She seemed unperturbed by the queen's continuing good health. As the days lengthened, she spent time teaching Hereswith and Mildburh the intricate work of piled weaves. It must have been difficult, because it made Hereswith bad-tempered. In the evenings, with the light good for nothing but spinning and skeining, they joined the other women of the household in their gemæcce pairs, old woman with old, young with young, women who had woven and spun and carded together for years, through first blood and marriage and babies, who had minded each other's crawling toddlers and bound each other's scraped youngsters, and wept as each other's sons and daughters died of the lung wet, or at hunt, or giving birth to their own children—all while they spun, and carded and wove, sheared and scutched and sowed. Hereswith and Mildburh, Breguswith and Onnen, Cwenburh and Teneshild, old Burgen and Æffe. Onnen was the only wealh. Hild watched them, and the other not-yet-girdled girls—Cille and Leofe, who were already meant for each other, and half a dozen younger—and wondered when her mother might choose her gemæcce and who it might be. She was taller than all the unmatched girls, even the ones with breast buds, just as her mother was taller than the queen and Cian was unusually tall for a boy with a wealh mother. In the stories, tall and royal ran in the same breath.

It was usual that a highborn girl was paired with one who was slightly less so, that they might travel together when one married. In Hereswith and Mildburh's case, Mildburh might be the queen's cousin, but Hereswith was the highest ranking unmarried female blood relative of the king. She was the default peaceweaver. But perhaps not for long, not if Cwenburh brought her child to term and it was a girl.

Tonight, they were using beeswax tapers, a new luxury, because Ædilgith, recently returned with her gemæcce, Folcwyn, from the court of the East Angles, said that Rædwald's queen and daughters made magnificent embroideries by such light, and the court was the richer for it. And indeed, Hild thought, as she rewound Ædilgith's skein of blue-green wool while Ædilgith held—for Folcwyn was shaking with the ague, caught no doubt from the East Anglisc marsh they had passed on their way to the coast—the tapers cast a light as white and clean as moonlight. Though moonlight never wavered the way the taper light did when one of them flicked a veil back over a shoulder—Ædilgith said the East Anglisc wore their veils longer, too—or stood to rearrange her dress and then resettled on her stool or the cushioned travelling chests.

Ædilgith tapped the side of Hild's hand and motioned for her to pay attention to the tension on the yarn between them. "I like this colour."

"It's uneven," Hild said, thinking about the East Anglisc. Good enough only for housefolk.

Ædilgith glared at her. Hild glared back. After a moment Ædilgith decided to ignore the insult. "Folc thinks that if the year is as rich as it seems it could be, and trade is good and the king generous, we might buy indigo. Think of it. Weld and indigo would make a green bright as a grebe's feather."

"Like your eyes," Hild said, to be friends again. Ædilgith was notoriously vain about her eyes. Her most prized possession was a beryl ring, and Hild had overheard her tell Folcwyn that she wouldn't marry any man who couldn't give her beryls for her ears and green garnets for her veil band. Hild wondered who Hereswith might marry, then remembered that mention of her name in the king's wagon. Already it seemed a long time ago. Hereswith's bleeding had come more than a year since; it was past time, Onnen said, to find her a husband. But would she marry as peaceweaver to a victorious overking or as the gemæcce of the cousin of the queen by marriage of a defeated northern warlord? It all depended not only on Cwenburh but on the fight for the Isle of Vannin, and they'd had no word.

Hild did what she always did when she couldn't influence a thing; she stopped thinking about it.

Cwenburh was sitting quietly, leaning against Teneshild, who was laughing at Æffe, who was pointing at the newly whitewashed wall opposite the doorway. "Yes," Æffe was saying. "Coloured paint on the walls, like the undercroft in York. Anything you like. I saw it in Frankia, oh, long ago."

"A picture of anything?" Teneshild said.

"The queen had a picture of rutting couples which she kept covered by a tapestry except when she and her women would be undisturbed."

Now everyone was listening.

"Hung like stallions, they were."

"Sounds uncomfortable to me," Burgen said.

Several women shifted on their stools.

"Mind you, in my younger days I saw a man once who would have put old Thuddor the Yeavering bull to shame."

"Only saw?" Burgen said.

"Yes," Æffe said with such regret that they all laughed. "He was my brother's cowherd. He'd been rounding up the calves for gelding. It was a hot day. He didn't know I was there. He pulled off his tunic and just poured water all over himself." She grinned. "The water was very cold. He might have looked like Thuddor before he got wet but more like a freemartin after."

Off-colour jokes followed, until Burgen began a more serious talk about how to keep your cunny slick so you could take your man inside as many times as you wanted, no matter how big his stick. She had dismissed goose grease, pondered flaxseed oil, and was about to discuss the merits of Frankish walnut oil when Cwenburh straightened and said, "Have you ever seen a fountain?"

A few older, well-travelled women, who knew what a fountain was, smiled, expecting another joke.

Burgen obliged. "All husbands are fountains if you treat them right."

"No," the queen said. "A real fountain, built of stone. Have you seen one?" In the strange white wax light, she looked pale. "I've heard that there's one up by the great wall, at Caer Luel, a fountain that still works. That's the picture I'd like on my bedchamber wall."

"What's a fountain?" Leofe said.

"It's a white stone spout in a white stone courtyard from which water squirts like a whale's breath."

"Truly?" said Ædilgith.

"Oh, yes," said Æffe, "and then the whole thing bursts into song and flies away."

"No," said Cwenburh, "no, it's real. A Christ priest told me of it, once. He said in summer it was like standing by a waterfall, cool as a cave. Imagine, being cool as a cave in the middle of summer." She wiped her neck. She was sweating. In winter.

Hild looked around, saw her mother watching the queen intently.

"A fountain," Cwenburh said. "I would like a fountain. A picture of one at least, so that when I lie on my bed, when I lie on my bed . . ." And she bent suddenly in the middle like a hairpin.

Teneshild put a hand on Cwenburh's shoulder. "My queen?"

Cwenburh cried out, forlorn as a bird in a net.

Breguswith stood. "Lie her down, lie her down now. Loosen her girdle."

"It's the babe," Teneshild said.

"Yes, and too early. Hild, bring me my bundle. Ædilgith, go fetch cold water—cold, mind, for drinking—and you, ladies, if you will," this to Æffe and Burgen, "please gather the tapers so I can see, and send everyone away, and then ask the housefolk for hot water. Mildburh, Hereswith, stay with me. The queen will have need of a kinswoman at this hour. No," she said to Teneshild, who was lifting the curtain to Cwenburh's bed alcove, "there's no time for that. Onnen, help me."

There was no time for anything. No time for Ædilgith to return with water, no time for farewells, time only for one long wail and a great slow seep of blood and a sigh, and the queen was dead.

Hild regarded her mother as she closed the queen's eyes. Her mother's hair was no longer the same colour as Hereswith's. The rich honey shine was duller, as though dusted with ash, the way petals lose their brilliance before they shrivel and fall. But Hereswith was about to bloom. And thanks to her mother, when the time came she would take her place as peace-weaver.

Breguswith looked up, saw Hild watching her, and smiled. She didn't say anything, but Hild knew what she was thinking: Thanks to me your prophecy has now come true. The king will give us everything we have dreamt of.

Hild lay on her stomach in the loft of the new Yeavering byre, looking down through the platform timbers at the old tom who liked to curl up in the straw between the milch cows. The faggots of tree hay prickled through her underdress but she barely noticed. Part of her mind was on the tom—his left ear was missing in a line too clean to be from a cat fight—and part was daydreaming of the war trail. She was going with the king and his war band when summer turned from green to gold. She would see a fountain, deeds worthy of song. She might be the one they sang about. She was the light of the world. Everything she said became true.

The tom liked to clean himself before curling up. He always began with his balls. He reminded her of the old thegns who had once been gesiths but now lived on land given by the king. When they came to visit they scratched themselves in hall, and after too much mead bored the young gesiths with stories of how hard it had been in their day, swearing that, by Thunor, if they didn't have responsibilities at home, they'd stand with them in the shield wall and the youngsters would see a thing or two!

Perhaps she'd get to see a shield wall. Perhaps she would see patterns that no one else could. She might be worth a score of gesiths to a king who would listen . . .

The tom had cleaned his balls and his belly and was now working on his forepaws in that on-off, this-then-that way that meant he was falling asleep, when Hild heard her mother's low voice.

". . . can not. No. Anglisc ladies don't tread the war trail."

"But lowly wealh do?" Onnen. They were right beneath her. "For pity's sake, she's a child."

She couldn't see them; the gap between the timbers was in the wrong place. She inched to the edge of the platform then stopped. If they were facing her way they'd see her if she peered over. She flattened herself to the boards, willed her heart to stop its noisy banging, and listened hard.

". . . she's Yffing," her mother was saying.

"She's nine."

"Needs must." Rustle of straw, catch of fingernail on cloth. Her mother stepping forward to put her hand on Onnen's arm? "And Edwin was just through those territories on his way to Vannin. Most of them. They know his strength. They can't match it. They won't try. She'll be safe enough. And think: months under the eye of the king as the light of the world. Months!"

"And months for you out of the eye of the king to weave your schemes."

Silence. Hild knew that silence and wasn't surprised by her mother's cool tone. "Hereswith needs training. Here."

Here. Hild frowned.

"Please," her mother said, and Hild's heart squeezed. She had never heard her mother say *please.* "Keep her safe for me."

Onnen sighed. "And if I can't?"

"You will."

Hild tried to sort it out. Her mother wasn't coming. She was staying to train Hereswith. Her mother and Hereswith weren't coming.

". . . not like you," Onnen was saying. "Some of the choices I make— you won't like them."

"It wouldn't be the first time, would it?" And now her mother sounded weary, which frightened Hild even more.

Rustle, flick. The sound of women turning to go, making sure their wrist cuffs and veils were in order.

Wait, she thought. Wait. She didn't want to go on the war trail. She didn't want to be part of a song. She wanted to stay with her mother.

She rolled onto her back and stared at the rafters. It didn't matter. The king had already said yes, and when the king said yes, that was that. She was going, with or without her mother. *Yffing,* her mother had said. *Needs must.* And *Please.*

When she peered over the edge of the loft platform, the old tom was gone. If she never came back, would anyone miss him?

4

✦

IN DAYS PAST, when Morcant the Murderer was king of the Bryneich and
Hereric the ætheling expected to be king when his father died, and Edwin
was only the spare, the track to the coastal hill fort of Colud had seen more
than one ambush. And, indeed, as the war band—Lilla in front with the
great banner, then Edwin riding before three hundred gesiths and their
hounds, with Hild at his left hand and the æthelings Eadfrith and Osfrith
at his right—rode out of the late-afternoon sun towards the sea, Hild saw
that armed and mounted Bryneich awaited them. But the shields of the
men and their lord, Coledauc ap Morcant, whom men called prince, were
slung on their backs not their arms, and between them, instead of a hedge
of spears or a burning barrier, lay a heap of tribute.

It was a small heap, and painstakingly arranged to show all the gold on
the side facing the Anglisc and gleam in the westering sun. Similarly,
though the hill ponies of the Bryneich had been combed and their manes
plaited, though they glittered at mouth and headstall, their tail pieces were
plain, and when one stripling leaned forward to get a better look at the
Anglisc, the saddle revealed by his swinging cloak looked lumpy and forlorn, showing gaps where jewels and inlay had been gouged out. Hild
became aware of the height of her own gelding, the weight of her luxuri-
ous piled-weave cloak, and the great kneecap of a brooch pinned at her
left shoulder.

The brooch was new to her. Earlier that day, when the war band
had reined in to form up before riding out of the hills, Edwin had kneed

his chestnut in front of her grey and crooked a finger at Coelgar, who turned from some serious talk with the young æthelings and tossed something gleaming. Edwin caught it. It looked heavy. He leaned forward, pinned it to her cloak, and sat back. "Better," he said. It weighed three times the gilt-copper brooch that had seemed so massive and rich at that Modresniht not so very long ago. "Pin that other trinket out of sight. I can't have my niece looking like a beggar." He wheeled his horse. "Ride close to me."

And now a Bryneich, one with a harp slung on his back rather than a shield, stared at her, at her brooch, leaned to Coledauc and whispered, and Coledauc looked directly over the heap at Hild.

Hild straightened and looked right back.

Watch men and women, her mother had said, *put yourself inside them. Imagine what they're thinking.*

The little muscles around Coledauc's eyes tightened. He was weighing information.

Perhaps her mother had already paid for stories to be sung, and Coledauc was thinking: It must be true, for no king in his right mind would bring a child on the war trail. The childlike thing sitting on a cygnet-coloured gelding with a silvered saddle and wearing a brooch worth a son's ransom must be the princess niece with a reputation as a seer and sorceress. Dunod said she'd known of Ceredig.

Coledauc's mount stepped in place then tossed its head. His fist on the reins clenched briefly and Hild imagined him wanting to back away from her: Aiiee, look at those eyes! They were boring right into him. Could she read his heart?

She gave him her best fathomless look.

Without taking his gaze from her, Coledauc nodded to his bard, who bent from his mount to lift something from the heap to join the items already lying ready across his saddle bow. The bard now fixed his gaze on her—they must think she could cast spells—and Coledauc turned to Edwin. He closed his eyes briefly, then smiled, as men do when they're about to do something difficult but want to seem at ease, and walked his mount forward.

The tension in his shoulders and the ripple in his jaw shouted Usurper!, and when he spoke he shaped the Anglisc carefully, like a man mouthing something disgusting. Hild realised that every shape the man's body made refused the words, and that the bard was nodding along. The bard had made the speech.

". . . pleased to offer you a portion of the great Bryneich treasure so that we may continue to walk side by side in friendship . . ."

Hild watched his body and ignored the words.

Friendship! When the fathers of these Anglisc beasts had crushed his people, driven them from their rightful strongholds.

". . . and welcome you to our hall."

He braced himself, tightening down in his seat, waiting for the usurper to laugh in his face and dare him to do something about it. But Hild knew he knew there was nothing he could do. His men numbered only fifty, if you counted boys and grandfathers, and those mounted on hill ponies whose ears barely reached the Anglisc mounts' withers.

But Edwin nodded as if to a trusted right hand, made no mention of the pitiful nature of the tribute, and began a pleasant speech back about eternal friendship and valued counsel and allies against the wolves of the Irishmen and Picts who, as everyone knew, had no honour.

Coledauc, who had been slowly loosening, stiffened at that. Hild considered. Honour. Perhaps Coledauc thought Edwin was making sly reference to the shameful deeds of Morcant, his father. Perhaps the king was.

But the king's voice was smooth and Coledauc seemed to let go of his tension: If the Anglisc king spoke lies they were pleasant ones. And eventually he was done.

Coledauc beckoned to his bard. "In addition to this treasure from the Bryneich, my family wishes to offer more personal tokens of friendship. Accept, from our son, Cuncar"—three months old, Hild knew, probably blissfully sucking his toes by the hearth with his mother—"gifts for each of your own sons, and for your"—he cleared his throat—"your relative. The seer."

A gift. For the seer.

The wind from the hills was picking up, blowing Ilfetu's forelock this way and that. Hild leaned forward and brushed it out of his eyes. She felt every hair, distinct as flax.

On the beach, gulls squabbled. The bard was looking at her still. She kept her face as calm as the pool at Goodmanham as her thoughts boiled.

A gift. From a king. To her as the light of the world. What should she do?

Coledauc gave Eadfrith a sword. Eadfrith unhooked his own sheathed sword grandly and offered it in return, with a flourish and a smooth and princely speech. Except that Hild knew his sword had a great blue stone set in its pommel and cunning gold wires twisted about the lip of the red leather scabbard, and the sword he gave Coledauc was scabbarded in black, with a silver-gilt chape and red glass in the pommel.

He'd been expecting this.

Osfrith also gave and received a sword. His pimples burnt a deep and ugly red and he looked younger than his fifteen years as he began to stumble his way through a prepared speech.

Everyone knew their words but her. Why hadn't anyone prepared her? Did they think the light of the world would foresee it? She looked down at her brooch. Her uncle had foreseen it. But he'd said nothing. He hadn't been sure. And if he'd admitted he expected his niece to be gifted by Coledauc, and then she wasn't, he would have to take notice and assume insult. This way was better—for him. But she didn't know what to do.

Her mother would know. But her mother wasn't here, and Onnen was back with the other women, with Cian.

The brooch at her shoulder was a graceless thing, but massive. Worth more than anything this king was likely to give in return. And her uncle had told her to pin the gilt-copper brooch out of sight. Perhaps he meant that if they gave her a brooch or other jewellery of sufficiently low worth she should give them the gilt-copper wheel now pinned inside her cloak.

As Osfrith stumbled on, the wind twitched briefly and blew from the east, the fort, bringing the scent of roasting meat. Behind her, a horse stamped and tossed its head, setting others to the same with a great clinking of bits and harness jewels. A gesith coughed. They were getting restless. They wanted the feast they could all smell cooking.

Osfrith finished his speech and backed his horse into line.

A gull wheeled overhead, its underside lit to pink and gold. Gold. Gold was power. Power was safety. What should she do?

And then she saw what the bard handed Coledauc, and, as it had long ago with Cian by the pool, her mind turned smooth with want.

Hild leaned back from her half-eaten bread trencher and fingered her black-handled seax. It was a big blade, far bigger than any ten-year-old should wear by rights, a slaughter seax. But it was a gift from a king and to not wear it in his hall would be an insult. Though judging by Coledauc's pale lips when the bard had handed it to him, she thought perhaps the choice of gift would not have been his. But she'd kneed Ilfetu forward, unpinned her great gold kneecap of a brooch, held it to glint in the last of the sun, and proclaimed in a strong voice, in British, a thousand blessings upon Cuncar ap Coledauc and his house and their renewed friendship with the house of Yffing, which would last forever, in token of which she hoped they'd accept this trifle to remember her by. Then she'd said it less well in Anglisc, adding that the food smelt fine and they were all happy to go eat now. And the gesiths and Coledauc's men had roared and banged their shields, and it would have taken more than two kings to get between the warriors and their mead.

At their high bench the two kings huddled together as the first casks of ale—sweet brown wealh ale—were broached. When they broke and clasped arms, both looked well pleased with their discussions. It seemed they found it convenient to take Hild's proclamation as prophecy: a thousand blessings on Coledauc and his house and eternal friendship between Yffing and Bryneich. A prophecy sealed with a blade gift. So despite Onnen's pointed look as she poured Hild's mead, Hild had smiled and told her she would keep the blade and wear it. Anything else would risk the prophecy. And then she grinned at Cian, whom she'd made sure sat next to her.

Feasting and song followed, with very free drinking—Edwin's forces outnumbered those of the Bryneich prince so heavily that it was no dishonour to give tribute rather than battle, and hearts were high; no one would die that week—and more than one joke about a marriage in the future between Hild and the baby Cuncar, who had been brought out by his nurse briefly, and who to Hild looked remarkably like a sucking pig. Even the two packs of war dogs made a kind of peace and lay down together.

The seax was handsome, with a black horn hilt and a blade inlaid with patterns in a silver-and-copper mix, and hung edge-up in its supple black sheath suspended by two loops parallel to her belt, silver chape to her left. It had a battle edge with a very hard, sharp point. It could open a man's throat, or cut the twice-baked road bread, or joint a roast. That is, she was sure of the two last because she'd already tried it out, and had no doubt of the former.

Cian tried hard not to be jealous, and something of his look, or perhaps the fact that he was allowed to sit with Hild, and that she laughed as he made puppets of his mutton ribs and spoke for them, alerted one of the Bryneich lords, who whispered in the ear of his prince. They didn't know Cian was wealh like them, because he was tall, like the Anglisc, and he dressed like them and spoke like them—even Onnen spoke nothing but Anglisc among the untamed wealh—and during the toasts the prince had grandly given Cian an old but beautifully painted shield with an enamelled boss, and a sound little nut-coloured pony for his own, which he promptly named Acærn.

As the waning moon stood high and the boasting and singing surged and the flames roared, Hild slipped away to sit in the moon shadow of a tufted dune with the sheathed knife in her lap and listen to the night breeze in the grass, and think about nothing in particular.

She woke to the sound of a man and woman panting with each other, like overheated hounds, and then laughter. They talked. Hild recognised Eadfrith's voice, the elder ætheling, and then her own name. ". . . that knife?" the woman said. "A slaughter seax, for a maid!"

"Oh, she's no maid," Eadfrith said. "She's a hægtes in a cyrtel."

Then they stopped talking for a while. Later Eadfrith agreed to help the woman haul her share of the water from the stream to the fire, as long as no one would see him doing women's work, and if she agreed to dally further, later.

Long after they'd gone, Cian found her. She wouldn't speak to him. He left. Onnen came. She sat beside a wide-eyed Hild and wiped at her cheek with her thumb. "So you've heard what your own people say. Does it surprise you?"

Hild said nothing.

"Now, see, this is one reason they think you strange. Your eyes flash, but you never speak."

"I'm not a hægtes."

"No, no. Of course not."

"I'm not," Hild said. "I'm not a seer, either. I just notice things."

"If you don't want to be a prophet then stop prophesying. Or at least mix prophecy with some other talk. People know you're thinking, but they don't know what. It frightens them."

"Does it frighten you, too?"

Onnen's face was white and black in the moonlight, like a mummer's face smeared with ash. After a moment she said, "I caught you as you slipped from your mother. I taught you your first words."

It was neither yes nor no. But then Onnen folded Hild in her arms and that familiar sharp woman smell overlain by peat smoke. "Oh, my little prickle." And Hild breathed deep and wondered why her own mother never held her this way. "You're like a sharp bright piece broken from a star. Too sharp, too bright, sometimes, for your own good."

Two days later Hild was back on her gelding, Ilfetu, and Cian on Acærn, travelling west on the road by the wall with the dogs running back and forth alongside. Hild was mesmerised by that road, so straight and wide and hard, rounding up in the centre like the horizon. The gesiths had spent countless summers on such things, and the few women of the band were so busy foraging for figwort leaves in the hazelwood understorey and nettle leaves in the ditches, bog myrtle for their travelling mattresses, wild garlic for the stewpot, and birds' eggs for when game was thin on the ground, that they couldn't care less. Cian was lost in the endless tales of glory the gesiths told each other as they rode, so Hild was left to muse on her own of the people who would build such a thing and then leave. She tried to remember to talk to people sometimes, but she recalled that Eadfrith thought her a hægtes and could not think of anything to say.

On some days Hild rode beside Edwin. Mostly the king was happy. In his winter campaign, he had taken the Isle of Vannin from Fiachnae mac Báetáin for the loss of only one ship, and that mainly carrying horses; the isle's fort had surrendered immediately when they saw the size of Edwin's band. And now the Bryneich at their backs were sworn to eternal friendship. And so, mostly, he was content as they rode to point out—sometimes just to her, sometimes to his sons, who had heard it all before, but it never paid for even blood relatives to ignore the king—some valley where in years past he had driven a rival king's sheep, or the hilltop where he had fired a fort, or a lightning-blasted tree he remembered as an omen of a flood. But other times he would grow pensive at the sight of a flock of magpies shrieking in a field of spring barley, and he would pull at the stained leather of his reins until his mean-mouthed chestnut snorted and stopped, and demand that Hild tell him what the birds augured. She didn't like those days. Nothing pleased him. He would constantly shift in his saddle and finger his sword; his eyes would become green and shimmery; he would make Lilla ride close and keep his shield unslung. She hated having to give him omens. And then one day she thought of Cian laughing and telling stories with his mutton ribs, and she spoke as though she were one of the birds: that fat one, there; no, the one with the uneven tail, he is cross with his brother, there, the one with the worm in his beak, because they had a fight over who should have the thorn tree for the nest and his brother won. And, ha!, Edwin said, then the fat one is not king. And he laughed and called over the æthelings, and then Lintlaf and Blæcca, and had her tell more stories about the birds and their wives. The gesiths roared. And so some days she rode surrounded by beefy warriors laughing at her imaginary conversations—birds, clouds, mice, dogs, furze leaves—while on others the king frowned and demanded a prophecy, and she gave it: *The bird flies in from the south, as will your future wife, my king,* for Hild remembered that long-ago talk of Kent, and where else would he be seeking a bride? Or: *See how the thrush drops the snail on the stone? So will you crush Fiachnae mac Báetáin if he should rise again and creep forth from the Emerald Isle.* For everyone knew Fiachnae would rise again, it's what the Irish did, and mac Báetáin was cannier than most. As she watched the thrush beat its snail on the stone and saw its eyes like apple pips, she remembered Coifi's eyes as he had watched her in the rain by the daymark elms, as a stoat watches a fledgling. And she said to Onnen that night by the fire, "Onnen, when you steal eggs from the nest, where are the birds who laid them?" and Onnen said, "Off finding worms for breakfast, no doubt. Why?" And Hild, who was tired from talk talk talking, all the time talking, couldn't bring her thoughts from behind her eyes to her mouth. When she fell into sleep it was to evil dreams: Who protected the nest while the king was away finding worms? Who protected her mother and Hereswith? Old Burgræd and young Burgmod?

She missed them. Oh, not her mother's perpetual watching and thinking and manoeuvring for position, not her sister's talk of Mildburh and husbands, alternating with the silent superiority of a sister with a girdle for one without. No, she missed their smell. Here it was all horses and man sweat and the stink of the bushes in the morning, which she walked half a mile to avoid when she emptied her bladder. She missed the scent of weld growing in its pot, of cheese crumbling on a plate and fresh-baked bread.

Even the songs were different. On the road, between one settlement and another, as they swung along, sometimes on foot, their songs were not the heroic songs of the hall but coarse drinking songs that, when she understood them, she didn't like. She didn't like the way they made the men smell, the way they fingered under their tunics and looked at the hard, thin-faced camp women—strange women who spoke Anglisc and wore knives and strike-a-lights on their belts, but no distaffs, no spindles; women who darned and mended but never spun, never wove.

She befriended a one-eyed war dog by feeding him scraps and never teasing him the way the gesiths did, and by mastering her fear of him, most of the time. At night she curled with Onnen on her unrolled leather mattress with her cloak around her and her belt loosened but not removed—she could reach out and touch her seax—and listened to the long churr of the nightjars. She longed for the sound of girls' voices or a woman singing as she fed chickens. They were moving through wild country now, nothing but moor and road. Onnen said that she'd heard from one of the bony camp women that by the time the larks had sung their last for the summer and the figwort flowers in the little wooded valleys had turned white, they'd be in Caer Luel, and then, oh, the wonder and the glory! And Hild fell asleep that night thinking with a smile of old Æffe's scepticism about fountains and the young man of long ago hung like Thuddor the bull, and it was only later that the dreams turned to nightmares.

Crossing the Pennines was hard and cold; Hild learnt to use the slings the women used to bring down red squirrels and the occasional hare; she learnt to sit with them in silence, for the women didn't mind silence, as they cut up the tiny morsels to mix with dried peas in a pot.

Hild was almost as thin and flint-faced as Onnen's road friends the day they made camp by a rushing stream and Coelgar set every last man to searching for firewood. Hild went to find her uncle to ask him why. He was sitting on a tree stump overseeing the unfurling of his blue-and-red banner with the Deiran boar stitched in gold. The garnet eye, secured with silver thread, was loose, and Edwin was shouting good-natured orders at the two wealh holding the staffs and the woman with the needle and thread. He was in a good mood, for the only man he'd lost on the whole journey so far was Eadfrith's friend, a young fool who'd boasted about his horse one night after drinking too much and felt obliged to race it the next day and had fallen and broken his thigh.

"Why are we stopped?" Edwin said. "So that we may make fires, and eat hot food, and have light to clean our equipment by and warmth in which to sleep. So that the lookouts of Rhoedd of Rheged will see our fires and think us many hundreds strong. So that we have the leisure to sort through our baggage and choose our finest tunics and our brightest rings. And so that when we ride into Rhoedd's stronghold tomorrow, we will look sleek and rested and well fed, our armour well tended and our swords sharp. And he will smile and open the gates to Caer Luel and prepare his tribute." He laughed. "Oh, yes, in public he will smile. In private he will chew his moustaches. Last year his tribute was only ships to the Isle of Vannin, and he got them back safely, bar one. Plus sacksful of Irish gold and silver as his share of the booty. Rhoedd is the son of the brother of the son of a great man, and perhaps for a while he felt as big and fine as his grandsire, a real king. He might have got to thinking perhaps a king shouldn't pay tribute. Yet here we are. We outnumber his war band three to one. We're hard and blooded, bearing bright bitter blades." He laughed. "Even you." He scratched his beard, looked around at the hundreds of men, the boys, the women. "Rhoedd is prideful. It is easier on a man's pride to truckle to a great king than to a starveling. And so we preen."

Even the dogs were fitted with bright collars. Od the One-Eyed's was spiked bronze.

Cian was beside himself with excitement. Lintlaf had lent him a bottle of linseed oil to tend the straps of his new shield and the hooves of his pony. Hild found him cross-legged on a flat stone by a gesith fire. He was trying on and taking off and adjusting his straps, over and over again.

He saw Hild and said, "Perhaps he will speak to me!" His eyes shone in the firelight.

"Who?"

"Rhoedd, son of Rhun, who was brother of Owein!" Owein, Cian's hero, who had died at Catraeth. It was strange to hear his name surrounded by Anglisc words.

"We shall make sure of it." In the firelight Cian's hair was showing chestnut at the roots. Hild hoped Onnen would persuade him to rinse it before long. Though perhaps the time for that was past; Hereric had been dead seven years. Edwin was secure on his throne. Then she remembered the way he sometimes turned in his saddle and touched his sword, remembered the relief when the son of Morcant did not fight, and understood that a king never felt safe.

They stayed with Rhoedd for six days. Edwin, Hild learnt, was good at keeping his underking in countenance. He praised him lavishly, and toasted him heroically, and bade his own scop sing of Rhoedd's illustrious forebears, back to Urien. He sang only the warrior songs, though Hild knew much of the cycle was written to make men laugh. As old Ywain, the bard of Ceredig's hall in Elmet, had told her, a bard could sing anything of a man, that he is lazy, that he is stupid, that his word is no good, he could make all men assembled laugh at his subject—as long as he suggested that the man was the very god with the lasses, left them stunned and sighing and sated. Get them drunk, sing of their prowess between the thighs, and be showered with gold.

Even after all these years, Hild found it strange to hear those songs in Anglisc and accompanied on a flat, gut-stringed lyre.

In the crowded hall, Hild and Cian listened, rapt, as Rhoedd's bard Gwaednerth then took up the tale, singing in British of the men of Yr Hen Ogledd, the Old North. Tales of Coel Hen, who ruled the whole of the north from Ebrauc that was, the York of long ago, when its walls were whole and its paint undimmed and the smell of the redcrests with their olive oil and grey wheat bread lingered in every corner. But as an old man, when the Scotti came from Ireland, Coel overreached himself. Cunning as only old men are, he conceived a plan to foment war between the Picts and the Scots. With his chiefs and lords and sons he camped by the waters of the Coyle and set out to fight first one side and then the other, wearing each time the captured regalia of the enemy . . .

Firelight ran along the harp's bronze strings and the bard's voice rose and dropped, not unlike the fells to the east, making a twisting, hypnotic rhythm of poised and perfect words. He was younger than old Ywain, his voice as supple as a withy-wound chariot. He could send his words trilling into the roof corners or scuttling through the floor rushes. As he sang at first of Coel Hen's victories, of driving the Scots into the hills with shields flaming like bright wings in the sunlight, and of the evening's fine triumph and boasts and eating of the hero's portion, his voice was thrilling. Hild found herself thinking of her seax and how fine it might be to swing a sword whose blade ran like a river of silver in the moonlight, and whose battle cry made the enemy throw down his blade and crouch and shiver in the sedge, unmanned. But then the bard changed step, as suddenly as a horse reined in by its rider for a fence, and his voice became a hollow moan; his harp echoed as melancholy and strange as a song from Arawn, the otherworld. Now he told of the desperate Scotti, slowly starving in the hills, committing to one last desperate attack. On a moonless night—not unlike this night—the lords stripped their fine fish-scale armour, and their men their leather, hid their swords under the furze—not unlike the furze close by—and, knives clenched between their teeth, wormed through the heather to the camp by the waters. Coel's men were drenched and drunk with glory and gloat. They were warm and well fed and gleaming with gold—not unlike tonight, Hild thought: even the sentries had set their spears against the doorposts to sing. And the Scotti crawled closer, closer, faces smeared with dung and ash, hearts beating like the drums of their enemy, blood surging stronger than wine.

Hild found herself listening beyond the hall, beyond the crackle of the fire, beyond the thumping scratch of a dog under the trestle, half expecting to hear an unearthly shriek as the sentry's throat was cut.

Cian looked about uneasily. Lilla's lips were parted and his great ham hand kept reaching for his baldric then stopping as he remembered his sword, like everyone else's, leant upon his shield against the wall. He moved slightly closer to his king, whom he was sworn to protect with his life.

Hild saw that the bard was tapping his foot like a heartbeat, tapping *doom doom doom*—not unlike Coifi's attempt by the daymark elms, but Coifi had been trying to sway men in cold morning light, not men full of wealh beer and yellow mead and sitting in the flickering hearth light of a strange hall a hundred miles from home. She smiled and considered nudging Cian and pointing to the tapping foot but he was lost and wouldn't thank her for it.

Two days later, sitting in the middæg sun in the ruins of Broac, Brocavum that was, Cian was still lost in tales of Yr Hen Ogledd, this time of Ceneu and Gorbanian, the sons of Coel Hen, as told by Uinniau, Rhoedd's younger sister-son, who had ridden with them to the remains of the fort. Hild, settled on a grassy earthwork, hair tucked behind her ears, listened with only part of her attention; the rest was lost in the flash and colour of the beads around her wrist: another gift, this time from the infant princess Rhianmelldt, a strange, ravaged ælf of a child whose eyes slid side to side ceaselessly. Hild forgot about the princess's eyes when she saw the beads: seventy-three faceted carnelians.

She had fallen in love with the carnelians there and then. They were all different. In the light of the peat fires and wall torches of the hall, some had gleamed like the jewels of her mother's dream, garnets in milk; others were more like pearls in blood, or amber in wine. But in the sun, they burnt like a living legend, something forged by a god from a dragon's heart. They were strung on a cord of yellow silk braided with gold, fastened with a cunning interlocking gold clasp, the string long enough for a grown woman to wear around her neck and draped over her breast. Hild wore them wrapped four times around her left wrist. When the sun struck them, the toasted-bread colour of her skin, of the stone, of the gold and yellow silk was like a world she had never dreamt of.

She asked Uinniau where the beads came from—they had a redcrest look—and he beamed and said he could show her, if she liked, and Cian, too, and in fact it was most curious because it was just two summers ago, at old Broac, not far from the church named after a long-dead relative, Saint Uinniau. Had Hild heard of him? He was a very great saint. Would she like to see the church after they'd seen the fort?

And so she saddled Ilfetu, and Cian his Acærn, and Uinniau, small like many sons of wealh, climbed upon a mare far too big for him—he looked like a freckled apple perched on the saddle—and they trotted off. That is, Ilfetu and the mare trotted, Acærn had to break into a canter every now and again. Hild couldn't help but think how much better Cian would look on the mare and Uinniau on Acærn. But the life tree didn't always fruit as expected.

In the ruined fort, Uinniau was now talking in a singsong of Peredur ap Eliffer, beating on the sun-warmed turf with his hand, and Hild recognised the signs; any moment, he and Cian would leap up and start whanging at each other with sticks, and yelling, and trying to persuade her to play the to-be-vanquished enemy.

"I am going to the water's edge," she said, gesturing over to the bank where the hobbled horses cropped the grass near a stand of birches, and Cian nodded without taking his eyes off Uinniau.

Hild climbed the tallest birch. She settled in the saddle of a thick bough hanging over the water and thought of nothing in particular amongst the coin-size leaves whose undersides shimmered with water light.

A thin veil of cloud slid over the sun, turning the river from polished silver to dull pewter and the leaves back to matte green. A flash of brown in the reeds told her this would be a good place to find duck eggs in the spring.

From here, all that remained of the fort where they'd dug up the treasures and her beads were two turf banks. Once it had been home to half a hundred horse soldiers from far away. Perhaps their herds had cropped the same grass that Ilfetu nibbled now. She gazed down at the shoulders of her mare, the whorls of grey hair, the fly about to bite at the base of her tail.

She imagined the fort as it would have been in Uinniau's ten-times great-grandsire's lifetime: a square of tall wooden walls built of whole trees with their bark still on them and their tips sharpened, neat ditches and banks, a gate in the centre of every wall, the scent of fires cooking unimaginable food, and over everything the smell of horses, the sound of horses, the vibration of horses galloping away.

She always imagined them galloping away, leaving. That's what the redcrests had done; they'd left. They left behind their stone houses in Caer Luel and beautiful white fountains, their red-tile roofs and straight roads, their perfectly round red bowls with pictures of dogs hunting deer around the rim, their exact corners and glass cups. And now the marble statues had lost their paint and stood melancholy white streaked with moss; tiles had blown off in storms and been patched with reed; men built fire stands directly on the cracked and broken remnants of once-brilliant mosaics.

But the fountain still worked. It was a series of white stone bowls arranged on a white stone stem, like a flowering pinecone made of cold, smooth marble. The spout, taller than Hild, was a leaping fish—a porpoise, said the town reeve. He seemed to know a lot. So Hild had dragged him around the town for hours and made him explain how the water came through pipes, pushed by its own weight downhill, from the hills to the north, how the baths and the hypocaust worked, where the redcrest chief had lived. After she had sent the reeve on his way, bowing and scraping and walking backwards, she returned to the fountain. She sat on the lip of the lowest, widest bowl and dabbled her hand in the cold, clean water and lifted her face to the spray. She thought of Cwenburh and the slow seep of bright blood. Cwenburh should have seen a fountain before she died. But if she had lived that long, Hereswith might not be peaceweaver, and Hild might not be on this journey, might not have seen the glory of water squirting into the sky like a whale's breath.

Caer Luel was where she saw a Christ bishop snared by a spell, sitting at a bench holding a strange folded square of leather sewn from smaller pieces towards the light and murmuring. But when she pointed out the black-skirted bishop and asked if it was a ritual to do with light, Uinniau laughed and said he wasn't a bishop, he was just a priest, and he wasn't under a spell or making a spell, he was talking with a book. "Bishop Rhuel says a book is full of secret signs that tell a story. A god's story. It sounds as though it should be interesting, but it isn't. When he tried to say the story to me there were no heroes, no swords or galloping to battle. Just moony stuff about . . ." He frowned. "Well, I don't remember. It was boring. But his book was covered in gold and jewels. Not like that old thing the priest's reading. Perhaps because Rhuel was a bishop, an overpriest."

Book, she thought. Secret signs. And gold and jewels. Hereswith might like that. And then she wondered what Hereswith was learning from their mother, and she missed them both.

It grew colder. They travelled north to Alt Clut, to the great rock fortress in the river mouth ruled by Neithon and his son, Beli. She was excluded from the war councils of Edwin and his sons and chief gesith, for Neithon and his sons were superstitious in the way of Christ people, and they kept making the fluttering sign on their chests when they saw her. Christ people didn't hold with seers, and maids were not allowed in council. Unlike Rhoedd and the men of Rheged, the men of Alt Clut thought of themselves as equals to Edwin, allies, and he was unwilling to trespass upon their goodwill by insisting she be present. He told Hild this angrily, but he wasn't angry with her; he was puzzled by something. Being puzzled made him anxious. Being anxious made him angry.

Osfrith, the younger of the æthelings, would sometimes tell her what he knew of the councils but he never remembered very clearly, just shrugged cheerfully and said, *Well, it was boring—old men's talk of corn yields and signs and portents.* Hild was left to ask casual questions of the housefolk who carried the wine and built the fires for such meetings, to listen to songs— the Alt Clut seemed obsessed by tales of the Dál Riata to the north and west, of Aedan the Treacherous, who had died before Hild was even born, and of his son, now king, Eochaid Buide. Hild put together her informa- tion like a broken redcrest pavement and pondered the picture.

King Eochaid and his Dál Riata were enemies of the Irish Dál Fiatach. Everyone knew this. The Fiatach in turn were enemy to the Dál nAriadne whom Edwin and Rhoedd had beaten soundly on Vannin, and Eochaid was sheltering the Idings. Well and good: Edwin and Eochaid Buide of the Dál Riata were enemies. That was clear. Nothing puzzling about it. So what was bothering Edwin? Whatever it was, it was getting worse.

Now not only did Lilla accompany him everywhere, shield unslung, but Lintlaf, and Coelgar's son, Coelfrith, shadowed the æthelings. In addi- tion, instead of heading south then east to collect tribute from many, ending with the Gododdin, before joining the women at Yeavering, Edwin began a series of interminable meetings with his own men.

Edwin's temper grew fouler day by day. He had a woman whipped for spilling ale on his shoe. Eadfrith, only five years older than Cian, swung his new sword at a man at mead for calling him a stripling. He opened the space below the man's ribs the way the butcher at Yeavering split a side of beef with a cleaver. Hild saw the bloody gape, the flash of white bone and sliced liver, a bubble and then a spurt of red. The man died a day later howling with pain and fever, and Eadfrith had to give up his fine new sword as weregild.

Hild's dreams of birds stolen from their nests by stoats became so evil Onnen started to stuff her ears with tallow and threatened to find another sleeping place.

"He won't decide!" Osfrith said one day to Hild, who caught him strid- ing from the hall, his usually sunny face tight with displeasure. "Men will say he is afraid." He kicked idly at a piglet rooting at the base of a dead section of hedge that ran along the inside of the great ditch before the wall. The piglet, used to such treatment, ran, ears flapping, under the hedge before Osfrith's shoe connected. His pimples were fading and his jaw thickening. His shoe, once bright red, was now scuffed and mud brown. They had been on the road a long time.

Osfrith, cloakless like all the warrior gesiths, hunched a little and turned away from the wind coming off the river.

"So men will say he is afraid," Hild said. "Would men be telling the truth?"

"Thunor's breath!" He stared. "You are stranger than they say. Any man who says the king is afraid will have my sword to face." He laid his hand on his sword hilt—his battle sword, not one of the new ones he'd received as gifts over the summer.

"I am not a man," she said. "But nor do I say the king is afraid. I ask about those men who do say so, or might say so. Would they believe what they say?"

Osfrith looked baffled.

Hild sighed to herself. She needed Osfrith to sit a moment, to think. She considered. Boys and young men liked to eat. "Did the king feed you?"

Osfrith shook his head. The wind gusted hard and he hunched tighter.

"I know a woman in the kitchens. There's a warm fire and cold hare and bannock bread."

The bannock was nothing but crumbs, the hare splintered bones, and the pot of ale almost empty. Osfrith picked meat from between his teeth with a sliver of bone, looking more like an ætheling. "No," he said, "it's the boats that have Beli and his father muttering like old women."

"Boats?"

"Irish boats were seen crossing the North Channel from Ireland to the Dál Riata."

"When?"

"A month past. Or more. And many more than usual. More than enough for an army—"

An army.

"—but there's been no fires," he said, "no fighting, no stream of homeless south, no slaves for sale at the port. There's been no battle."

"Not here," said Hild, and her hands were cold with dread. *Where are the birds when we steal eggs from their nest?* Now she knew.

Grey sky, grey rock, grey water. Edwin sat on a boulder overhanging the great flat estuary, throwing stones. Eadfrith ætheling and a knot of the younger gesiths stood nearby, but not too close. It was clear by the set of the king's shoulders that he was best left alone.

Hild checked to be sure her mantle fell in deep folds, that the hair she'd had Onnen dress that morning was in place, that her pair of huge gilt brooches, Neithon's gift, were not crooked. She adjusted her carnelians for maximum flash and sparkle, and laid a hand on the hilt of her slaughter seax. She stood tall. She was the bringer of light. Let them call her hægtes if they must. If she didn't speak, her mother and Hereswith might die.

"King."

He ignored her. One of the gesiths shouted over, "He's in no mood for games, princess."

"King."

Another gesith detached himself from the knot. "Come away, little maid." Lintlaf. "Come away." He reached for her arm.

Hild drew herself up, fixed Lintlaf's brown eyes with her fathomless gaze, then sought and found Eadfrith's. In her seer's voice she said, "You know I am no maid. And I have a dream to tell the king."

That got Edwin's attention. He held his hand out to Lintlaf: stop. And jerked his chin at Hild: speak. His eyes crawled green and black as buzzflies on old meat.

Last time her mother had been there to explain. Last time the king had been in a good mood.

"King." The words, as they almost always did in Anglisc, caught in her throat like a bird bone or a mouthful of feathers. "The stoat steals fledglings from the nest when the birds are away catching worms."

No change in Edwin's expression. Why couldn't he see? Why could none of them see?

"King. We're the birds."

Now his face was stone. "I am not a bird."

"Boats," she said desperately. "I dreamt of boats." His whole face sharpened. "The stoat is coming in a boat. To the nest. My mother is there. And Hereswith."

"Your— Bebbanburg. You're talking of Bebbanburg?"

She nodded.

"And who is the stoat?" He was standing over her—when did that happen?

Her eyes were level with his throat apple. She raised them to meet his. "Fiachnae mac Báetáin. In a boat, going the long way around to take Bebbanburg."

Edwin, once free from trying to make sense of a puzzle as ungraspable as mist, and with a clear prophecy to hew to, marched his war band south at lightning speed, ignoring the coastal strongholds of Galloway and their expected tribute. As they passed Dumfries, he said to Hild, "I know to the ounce what I should have taken from them. You'd best not be wrong."

At the wall, they reloaded the pack ponies and Edwin detailed Eadfrith and Coelgar and twelve gesiths, including Coelfrith, to escort the treasure directly to the stronghold of York while the lightened war band rode for the port at Tinamutha and thence up the coast to Bebbanburg. Onnen gave Coelfrith a significant look as he mounted, and Hild knew she had reminded the steward's son that some of the treasure belonged directly to the princess Hild, that there would be an accounting.

Edwin watched the ponies disappearing in the direction of Broac and then turned to Hild. "The ride will be hard. You will keep up, if I have to tie you to your horse. You will tell me of every thought, every dream, every twitch of your eye or flight of birds. If you are right, you will be honoured beyond mortal ken. If you're wrong and we fail, I will strike off your head, feed your offal to my dogs, and bury your hægtes head by your buttocks in an unmarked hole."

Hild faced him, unflinching, because Edwin was like a dog: show fear and he would chase you down. But then she broke her gaze. To challenge an uneasy king before his men was to invite death.

Edwin raised his hand and shouted to the nearly three hundred gesiths remaining. "We ride in service to a dream from the gods. If our dreamer's horse fails, you will give her yours. If her food runs low, you will give your own. She will light our way. And now we ride."

A horse died—already tired, its leg plunged through a burrow and snapped—at Haltwhistle, and its rider was abandoned in a ramshackle farm holding with a thin woman and her husband, a witless farmer. No doubt the place would have a new master come spring.

The first snows settled in the folds of their thick cloaks as they passed Chesters. At Corabrig they found a farmer with a tall horse—a raw-boned roan, but fresh and eager—willing to part with it for a silver arm ring, and lots were drawn for a lithe, hardy rider to gallop for life itself all the way to Tinamutha to set in motion ships for Bebbanburg. Lintlaf won and light travel foods—twice-baked bread, dried berries, smoked meat—were offered from all sides.

As Lintlaf packed his saddlebags, the roan, a farm horse and confused by the press, danced and kicked but eventually Lintlaf boosted himself into the saddle. He was more excited than the horse, his lips red as carmine and eyes brilliant. He would ride for the king and glory!

Edwin kneed his chestnut close, clapped Lintlaf on the back, and slung his cloak back to show his royal arm rings. "If you've ships for half of us ready to sail when we arrive, you shall have one of these, and not the least." And Lintlaf rode into the east to wild cheering.

Every morning it was dark when they woke, dark as they struggled into the saddle, dark as they plodded along, walk, trot, walk, trot, on their tired mounts, dark even at midday when they stopped in the lee of a hill that seemed to touch a sky as heavy as the dark stones of the wall. The wind was relentless, blowing dry snow up and about them like sand, even on the leeward side of a hill. Hild looked at the hot spark and flicker of her carnelians and pretended they were coals. She couldn't remember the last time she'd been warm. Couldn't remember even when she'd eaten something hot. Her jaws were powerful from chewing fire-smoked meat and waybread dunked in freezing water. Ilfetu's ribs stood out like the strakes of a ship. Her dog, Od, was the only one of the pack that didn't look like a hound of Hel, a running skeleton with burning eyes. And they all watched her, all the time, and none came near—except, in the dark of night, and only briefly, Onnen and Cian. She had accepted the mantle of the uncanny and until the end of this journey it was her fate. It was her vision they marched to, into a future she had dreamt for them.

She rode a thin grey horse, a thin grey hound ran at the hem of her blue-grey cloak, and she sat tall, an enamel copy of a ten-year-old girl, hard and cold.

It was just past a large farmstead by a bridge, where they'd flung hacksilver at the farm wife and taken every last drop of her milk, all her just-cured bacon, a great wheel of cheese, and a barrel of strange-tasting ale, and still been hungry, that the rider from Tinamutha found them.

"Lord King," he gasped as he pulled up his foaming shaggy-maned pony. "Lord Osric sent me. He is besieged at Tinamutha. Your man got through, and there are boats aplenty, but no way of sailing them past Fiachnae's hordes at the river mouth."

The gesiths immediately began cursing, swearing vengeance and mighty deeds. The king looked shrewish and unhappy. Hild kicked Ilfetu until he shouldered the king's chestnut, which made the king look at her. "Bebbanburg?" she said.

Osric's messenger gave Hild a puzzled look. Who was this child? Then he saw her eyes and the huge seax at her waist. Perhaps she was an uncanny dwarf or a wall wight.

"What of Bebbanburg?" Edwin said to the man, as though Hild had not spoken.

"Fiachnae's main force besieges the rock. They have slaughtered all the cattle on the moors."

"How long ago?"

"A fortnight since. No more."

Edwin shifted in his saddle, and Hild recognised the movement; he didn't know what to do, and as a result wondered if he was being made a game of. She backed up Ilfetu, just in case.

A look passed between the king and Lilla, and the chief gesith took the messenger's reins in his beefy hand. At his nod, a handful of warriors loosened their swords in their sheaths. Edwin half shuttered his eyes. "Two weeks? And no boats in or out of Tinamutha?"

"No, lord." The messenger's mount picked up its rider's uncertainty. It snorted and tried to back up but its way was blocked.

"Then how did news reach your lord so fast if the way by sea is blocked?"

"My lord?"

"Dere Street is a fine road, but it's a hard ride south and west to it from Bebbanburg. And then along this road east to Tinamutha, and then back west to us."

"My lord?"

Edwin said, "We'll eat the horse," and turned away.

Lilla nodded to one of the gesiths, who drew his sword and swung at the messenger's neck where it met his shoulder. The man shrieked and spurted and fell off his horse, which tried to rear, and the dogs did the rest.

5

✦

MULSTAN, LORD OF MULSTANTON, wiped his beard, sent the cup down the table, and watched the strange maid. She was turning those blood beads of hers again, turn turn turn. At least she wasn't wearing that huge knife tonight. A maid the same age as his little Begu with a slaughter seax!

He'd made them all welcome, of course, the maid, her wealh woman and son, even that Irish tutor-priest, or hostage, or whatever he was. When your king arrives in a blood-splashed boat and departs in a hurry leaving behind a favoured kinswoman and her household for whom he demands hospitality, you give it. It doesn't matter that she's only ten. It matters that she's the subject of a prophecy and has the most direct and uncanny gaze of any maid you've ever seen, and that one wrong word to the king would mean being staked out for the ravens. So you give her your own bed and the highest place at table—for this was a country hall, after all, not much removed from its British roots, where women feasted along-side their men—and try as hard as you might to remember to show the boldness and generosity expected of an Anglisc thegn looking to gain fa-vour with a king whose fortunes were on the rise. Or who might be dead, depending. No, no, he was alive, for the trade boats were getting through and there'd been no reports of Anglisc slaughter from Bebbanburg.

He was old, near forty; his first wife and children had died in the great sickness before the maid was born, and when his first lord and king, Æthelfrith, died and he was released from his gesith's oath, he had declined exile north of the wall with the æthelings and had, instead, settled in to farm this once-rich land by the sea. When Edwin took the throne, he had charged Mulstan to oversee the safety of the small trading harbour and to take the tithe for the king of all goods that came and went across the sea. And eventually Mulstan was happy to marry the beautiful Enynny and build himself a good solid farmstead in the woods by the beck, just half a mile from the tideland estuary full of oysters and mussels rounding into Streanæshalch, the Bay of the Beacon, with its harbour that saw trade from Pictland and the North British, from Lindsey and the East Angles, and even the people of the North Way, whose narrow ships brought furs and amber across the North Sea and down along the chains of islands and along the coast of Pictland. Last year they'd had a Frisian ship creeping up from its more usual harbour at Gipswīc.

He swallowed more beer. Swefred was playing that song again, the one he liked about hearth and home. Couldn't play half as well as that odd Irish priest the maid brought but at least he could understand the words. None of that Irish caterwauling. Ah, he missed his wife. By Thunor, he missed both of them. Though this Onnen woman who'd come with the maid—

The maid had stopped fiddling with her beads and was looking at him. "My lord Mulstan."

He swallowed the wrong way and coughed. Had she read his thoughts about her wealh woman?

She waited patiently, which made him nervous. Royalty were rarely patient unless they were toying with you. At least she was talking now. For the first weeks she'd been mute and round-eyed as an owl. He'd seen gesiths with that look after their first shield wall.

"Who is the man who plies the withy beds?"

He wiped his beard. "I beg pardon?"

"The man. On the withy beds." She cocked her head slightly, as though listening to a voice only she could hear. "He has a dog."

"Black-and-white dog?" He slapped the board. "The willow man!" He immediately felt foolish. Of course the man in the willow withies was the willow man. "Irish," he said, trying not to look into her fathomless eyes. Seen too much, those eyes. "Man to an envoy taken hostage so long ago no one remembers." He'd never really thought about it before. Perhaps the envoy had died of sickness, perhaps he'd been freed but forgot to take his man with him. "But it's said the man found his way to the priest of the tiny British church by the ruined beacon tower on the cliff. Long time ago, that. Never been a priest up there in my time. No doubt the priest had him work in the willow withies. But that was years ago, and now the willow man's just the willow man. He doesn't say much."

Like you, little maid. But the willow man didn't say much because no one much understood him. He just planted and pruned and harvested white willow and brown willow and buff willow, softened and dried it, boiled it and stripped it, so that now a person could visit the willow man's bothy and exchange food or cloth or a copper pin for willow fit for any willow purpose and it was the finest for two days' walk. The willow man lived in a world where he talked to no British, for long years had taught him the pointlessness of it; a world where the Anglisc were wights—and perhaps to him they were.

That priest was giving him one of those lean and wicked smiles. Must have said that last bit aloud. Had to watch that.

He tipped his beer horn. Empty. Onnen filled it and smiled. Thunor bless the woman. "Anyway, the willow man communes only with his dog and his boles and poles and stools and rods. Though he's Irish, he seems harmless enough." Of course the maid's tutor-hostage, Fursey, was also Irish, some princely priest the king had taken in the bright clash at Tinamutha. Fruitless war, that. What was Fiachnae mac Báetáin, the king of the Ulaid, doing attacking his betters so far from home? And why had the king let such a little maid get mixed up in the blood and slaughter? "I hope the priest won't take that amiss."

Fursey rose and suggested smoothly that his lordship should pay no mind. For all knew that some Irish, especially the wicked Ui Neill, were known to be mad, to succumb to drink, to get too close to their horses and beat their dogs, and who could blame an Anglisc lord for not knowing the difference?

Hild, who had been living on this wild moor by the sea for some weeks now and, tutor or not, new friend Begu or not, was homesick and heartsick, listened but said nothing. More and more now she could tell the difference between what was real and what was a mix of memory and nightmare; more and more she felt sure that if she spoke she would be speaking to the living, not ghosts. Often now, Fursey's instruction on letters and Latin seemed like something of this world and not the next. But still the effort of deciding whether or not it was right to speak would bring the memories: the Irish rising like a tide, the slip and slide in the mud on the mouth of the Tine, the cries of *Osric, where is Osric?* answered by ever more howling

Irish. She felt the bruises still of the scramble into the boat, the fighting for space, the rock and tilt of the boat as an Irishman grabbed the gunwale with both hands . . .

She turned away from that memory. She would make friends with this willow man who also didn't like to talk.

She crouched in the grey-brown sedge on the edge of the rhyne and watched. It might be spring half a mile away, down in the valley along the beck, but here, high on the marshy moor by the sea, it was a harsh, colourless world. Here there was no greening blossom, no curve of burbling stream or round river rocks. The rhynes ran spear-straight into the horizon, the willow beds running between them, all under a tin-grey sky. Steel-coloured water lapped and slapped against the dirt banks, and the willow canes, not yet in leaf, rattled and shook like tally sticks.

She wished Begu could be there, but Begu had been careless about keeping warm in the rain and she had been breathed on by sidsa and her nose was dripping. Onnen—who somehow had taken over Mulstan's hall within a day of their arrival seven weeks ago—had ordered her to bed with a hot stone. So Hild had left her seax and belt with Begu, on the grounds that the willow man might be frightened by it, and wore her old sash instead. Then she had set out under the wide, scudding grey sky and found him here on the rhyne, the ditch between the withy beds, cutting white willow poles and stacking them in bundles, upright, in the water.

She had been watching the white-haired man and the black-and-white dog all morning. They were never apart. They knew she was there.

The willow man had looked at her sidelong once or twice and talked to his dog, whom he called Cú, or Dog, but more loudly than he would have if they'd been the only hot-blooded things on the moor.

The water slapped, the canes rattled, and man, girl, and dog all looked at the sky—clouds piling together, no longer tin but lead—then at one another. Hild, encouraged, stood, came closer—oh, her shoes were more mud cake than leather now—and pointed at the willow man, at his crinkly white hair, and said one of the Irish words she knew, "Bán."

And he laughed, showing a toothless mouth, then loosed a torrent of Irish at her. His accent was strange. She understood three words of it, ingen (maid), saxain (Anglisc), and occoras (hunger), and shook her head. "Mall," she said, "mall" (slow), and he said it all again. "Mall," she said again and furrowed her brow while lifting her eyebrows: Please. And Cú tilted his head and whined, and then Bán spoke one more time in a jumbled Anglisc-British-Irish mix, and Hild listened with her whole skin, the way she listened to rooks in the field or wind in the trees. She understood, she thought. He was asking her if she was hungry.

She sat in the mud—Onnen would scold her raw—offered a fist to Cú, the first dog she had allowed near her since she watched Od eat the guts of Osric's man, and repeated back to Bán as well as she could, with the words he had used, that she, the Anglisc maid, whose name was Hild, had hunger, a little, but that when she returned she would be very well provided for. And he nodded, but shook his fingers dismissively in that Irish way, just like Fursey, and tutted, and unfastened the sack at his waist and offered her half his cheese and a bite of onion, and a dip in the coarse grey salt collected in the seam of his sack.

When he waved the cheese Cú went painfully still and drooled and looked sad, as dogs do, and Hild and Bán laughed together and settled comfortably on the edge of the high bank between withy beds, where it was a little drier, and shared the cheese while Cú followed the movement of hand to mouth, and looked sadder and sadder. Both Hild and Bán were wise in the way of dogs, and they gave him none, and he stopped looking sad and instead went to sleep. And after, Bán let her climb into his flat-bottomed boat and coast up and down the rhyne with him while he used his little sharp knife to slide up along the grain of the growing willow rods, faster than she could see at first, and snick snick snick cut the little buds off the growing poles so they wouldn't come in crooked. Overhead the clouds scudded and darkened and closed tighter than a lid upon the world, and again they glanced, man, girl, and dog, at the sky, and Hild persuaded him to come to the kitchen at the hall of Mulstan.

At the door, it was Guenmon, not Onnen, who gave her muddy shoes a look, Guenmon who raised an eyebrow at Bán and then said to Hild, "Don't sit. Either of you. You're all over mud."

"He's my guest."

"Guest, is it? Well, Onnen would have my hair if she saw me feeding you in that state. And you dressed like that. Though it's nice to see you've taken off that sword-knife."

"I give him guest rights," she said, and she gave Guenmon the look she'd perfected in the months she'd been apart from her mother, months of having to demand the rights of prince and priest and light of the world while in the guise of a rangy, chestnut-haired girl with a strong-boned face. And Guenmon, as everyone did when faced with that swelling gaze, sighed and gave in. "There's some of my pasties, you know where they are, and I'll fetch ale. But you'll sit on the stoop til that mud dries, or Onnen—"

"Will have your hair, yes." Hild took off her shoes, pulled a stool close to the shelf, stood on it—carefully, for her hose feet were wet—and lifted down the basket with the napkin-wrapped pasties. She handed one to Bán, took one for herself. "Where is she?"

"With the little mistress." Guenmon set a poker to heat in the fire and then, despite her earlier words, took down two of the better copper cups and one wooden one, and from a walnut chest—she unlocked it with the latch-lifter that would usually hang on the belt of the lady of the hall— took a glazed clay pot of precious spice and added a pinch to each cup.

"Is she well?" Begu had looked miserable—dripping nose, sore throat, earache—but sturdy this morning. Being breathed on by sidsa could be a chancy business, yes, but usually only for infants and the very old.

"Nothing staying warm won't cure. But that Onnen does fuss . . ." She shook her head and poured ale from a jar into the cups, and Hild understood this to be a comment on Onnen's solicitousness for the lord's daughter, and by extension the widowed lord himself. The lord, too, had been extravagant in his courtesies to Onnen, and the people of the hall— servants and highfolk alike—looked on with those wry smiles that Hild had seen grown-ups exchange before at these times. Perhaps they would mate. She had wanted to talk to Cian about it last night but Cian was being unaccountably surly, and Begu was already tucked up in her very own linden-wood bed. Onnen had sniffed at that when they'd first arrived— a ten-year-old girl, daughter of a country thegn and a deposed British lordling's daughter, with her own bed and feather mattress! Wasteful, wasteful to build a whole miniature bed for a child—but had changed her tune quickly enough when Mulstan had made them all so welcome.

Hild understood and suspended judgement, as she had learnt to do in her strange position as the light of the world in a maid's clothes. And yet she was ten, only ten, her heft only that of her gaze and words and bearing, especially on days like this when she had set out in her plainest short cyrtel and hose and left all her fine stuff safe and dry in Begu's room.

So as Guenmon knocked the ashy scale from the glowing poker and plunged the hot tip into the first copper cup and sang a verse of a wealh song Hild didn't know while the drink heated, Hild munched on her mutton pasty—Guenmon had a way of adding tarragon and vinegar that gave it a wild, hilly tang—and was grateful for warmth and food and the possibility of a new friend, one who didn't belong here either.

Bán had finished his pasty and was looking about him. Cú was sitting quiet and well behaved, though there were suspicious-looking crumbs at his feet.

Guenmon handed out the ale. Bán sipped with caution, Hild with delight: mace and ginger! She watched the willow man lift his cup again, noted the calluses on his wrists, the suggestion of a thick scar around his throat as he swallowed. Mulstan didn't use collars for his wealh, but Bán had been in a slave yoke at some time. And his tunic was threadbare. Did he even have a cloak? It might be spring but on the moorland and beach there would be two months yet of cold wind.

"Good ale," she said, and Guenmon nodded as though such praise was her due.

"Ready yesterday, from the finest malting we've had this six-month or more, if I do say so myself."

"Might we spare a jar or so?"

Guenmon folded her arms.

"And perhaps we have some cloth set by for rags that we might piece for a cloak."

"And some sausage for the dog, while I'm about it?"

"Bán would no doubt be grateful," Hild said, with a smile for Bán, who had recognised the word *dog*. She really wanted to talk to him. "Where's Fursey?"

"Now how am I meant to know the whereabouts of that smooth-tongued, shave-pated Irish spy?"

And for a moment she sounded so like Breguswith that Hild missed her mother and sister fiercely.

Hild stood on the headland in the light mist of dawn with her toes hanging over the edge of the grassy east cliff. The edge of all things. Between day and night, between sky and earth, sea and land. The air smelt of iron and salt. Like Tinamutha. She rested her hand on her seax. No, not like Tinamutha: no stink of mud and marsh flats. No boats on fire. No armed men cutting their way towards her and the king. Just iron and salt. Her hand drifted from the seax. Behind her, behind the ruined stone beacon and the tumbledown wattle-and-thatch church, she heard cowbells. Their dull clank was almost tuneful, occasionally harmonious. She had never heard of such a thing, but now that she had, she wondered why every cow in the world didn't have a tuned bell around its neck.

As the mist began to dissolve she could see the dark, wet beach. Long-legged birds speared shellfish, and women with sacks collected coal and driftwood, dodging the surf that ran up over the sand like the froth in a milkmaid's pail. The sky showed as blue as twice-dyed linen. The sea was restless, glinting like napped flint. It, too, would turn blue if the sky stayed clear. Three ships were being loaded at the harbour on the mouth of the River Esk. Mulstan must be right. Her uncle must be winning. Though she didn't know why she'd had no word.

From the harbour, the river wound back through blossoming fruit trees and tangled copses choked with bramble. An arrowhead of black-barred geese flew out of the east, feathers rosy in the rising sun and yellow beaks tinted somewhere between marigold and pink—the same colour as Hild's carnelians that were now safely nestled in their carved ivory chest. Unless Begu had borrowed them again.

Hild turned to make sure. Begu was talking to the young son of the cowherd, one hand on the cow's back, one on her hip. No beads at either wrist. She patted the cow as she talked, one of the small black cows fa-voured in these parts, less milk animals than meat-makers. The goats were the milkers.

Begu looked a bit like a goat: a long, thin face with teeth grown every which way and wide-spaced eyes. Her hair was brown-blond, like a goat's, and always coming undone. She had a fondness for farm animals, as Hild liked creatures of the wild.

Except geese. They were landing on the beach and running, honking, wings spread, at women and sandpipers alike, until the beach cleared and the raucous things could pick the sand clean, and shit on everything, and leave still quarrelling. She hated geese, they made her anxious, she didn't know why.

"Hild!" Begu waved her over, bouncing in place she was so eager. She was always eager. "Cædmon says he has a book. A book!"

Hild walked back to them. "Where?"

The boy, Cædmon, blushed behind his freckles and shock of dark hair and muttered something.

"Don't be silly," Begu said to him. She looked directly at Hild. Her eyes were hazel. "He thinks you'll take it. You won't, will you?"

"The book is Mulstan's." This was his land, and Cædmon was his wealh. She waited. Eventually, Cædmon looked up through his ragged fringe. Cut with a knife. "What kind of book is it?"

He shrugged, looked out to the horizon.

"I wish to see it."

"It's not here." His voice was like the cowbells, soft-metalled and dull, but with music buried in it somewhere.

"Where is it?"

Another shrug.

"Where did it come from?" He shrugged again. "Where did it come from?"

"It was the priest's. He died. We buried him with his beads, but his wife took the book." Hild nodded. Books were precious, she was learning, especially the ones with gold and jewels. "Then she died. We buried her." He gestured at the creamy-blossomed blackthorn hedge around the oval graveyard. The gate had fallen down. "Da took the book. To keep it safe for the new priest, he said. But there is no new priest. And Da's forgotten about the book."

The cows were grazing close to the gap in the hedge. It was wicked to let such a place fall into ruin. "It's good land up here," she said. "Good grazing. Water. And you could see trouble coming for miles."

"Trouble?" Begu laughed her tumbling laugh. "There's no trouble up here!"

There was always trouble in the world. She thought of fighting at Tinamutha in the flaring torchlight by the dock with the Irish, and Osric's men strangely absent. The scramble for the ship. The gesiths for whom there was no room on the last boat forming a wall with the dogs on the quay, dying one by one as Edwin and his party fled.

Not here, she told herself. Not today.

"Still, it should be farmed. If no priest is coming, the land should be given to someone to steward."

"It's grazed," Begu said, patting Cædmon's cow.

"Yes, but are these the lord's cattle?"

"Yes. Mostly."

"How many?"

"Most."

Hild's mother and Coelgar both would have known exactly, and from them, Hild would have known. Accounts must be kept, obligations fostered. "Cows shouldn't graze by the dead. They shit on everything."

But Begu seemed immune to her reputation and just shrugged. "There's a hedge around the graveyard. Mostly."

Hild gave up and said to Cædmon, "What does the book look like?"

He made a frame in the air with his hands. Small.

"What colour is it?"

"Cow-shit brown." They all grinned.

"Can I see it?"

He squinted at the sun, handed his switch to Begu, and said in his careful Anglisc, "Watch the cows." He plunged down the scrubby hill towards the river.

"It is good land," Begu said, turning slowly and looking at the headland as though she'd never seen it before. "More than just grazing. Eel traps in the river. Hares on the edges of the woods. Mushrooms and mast in the woods. Cows, sheep, oysters, seagull eggs . . . Do you want to see the secret spring?"

"A spring?"

"Of course there's a spring." They started walking. "You thought there was just that pond? Huh."

"It's not a bad pond. You could put fish in it."

"Why? There's lots of fish out there." Begu waved in the direction of the sea.

Bebbanburg was by the sea. It could withstand the Irish because it had everything you could possibly need inside an unbreachable wall. But Begu was smiling at her and Hild couldn't think how to explain without making that smile falter.

"Here." Begu stopped by a stand of ferns, knelt, and used the cattle switch to move them to one side. Hild smelt mint. "It was Sirona's spring once, long ago."

Hild didn't know Sirona. She didn't know half the wealh gods of well and wall and wood.

It was a rocky pool as wide as the biggest soup cauldron at Bebbanburg. But deeper. A blade of grass turned slowly, sunwise, on the surface. A little horn cup stood on a shelf of rock among the ferns. Begu dipped it in the spring and poured a thin stream out to the spring and the goddess, then handed it to Hild. Hild sipped.

"It's so cold!" She sipped again. "It tastes good." Like fern and mint.

"It's the best water in the world, my mother said. We used to come here in summer when it was hot down below. She told me stories of how she came here as a lass."

Hild rolled the little horn cup between her hands. It felt old. She imagined Begu's mother, Enynny, and Enynny's mother, and her mother, and her mother before her, back into memory, sitting here by the ferns drinking the cold, minty water and talking quietly in British. So many. All gone into the mist. She felt a twist inside, a longing for a family and home that never was. "Do you miss her, your mother?"

"Yes. I think so. It was a long time ago. I was very little."

"I miss my mother."

"But you'll see her soon. You'll see. My fa says no one can take Bebbanburg." Hild didn't say anything. "What's she like?"

"Tall."

"You're tall."

"She's very tall. Taller than the king."

"Is he very small?"

"He's as tall as Mulstan."

"No! Then she must touch the sky!"

Hild laughed. "Nothing touches the sky. Except birds." It was easy to talk to Begu. Perhaps because she said such strange things, perhaps because Hild got the sense she never took people seriously.

Begu flung herself down on her back in the sun. "What do you suppose the sky feels like?"

Hild put the cup carefully back in its niche and lay down, too. The grass was damp. They looked up and up at the blue sky. "Like mist. Like a blue veil. Like a cobweb."

"Do you suppose it goes up and up forever? A world of blue?"

"And of black, at night." When things that weren't birds flew.

They were silent. The ferns whispered in the wind. Far away the sea hissed. Geese honked. Hild shivered.

"Perhaps geese are part of your wyrd."

Hild looked at her.

"What? You don't like them. I've marked that."

"They're loud and dirty."

"So are goats. They all taste good, though."

Hild turned back to the sky. She listened past the geese to the gulls crying in the distance. The sound seemed floatier up here, unlike the sharp piercing cries on the beach. The wind sounded different, too. No tall trees to rustle and shiver and speak. But then what was that rhythmic creaking?

"What's—" The creaking deepened, stopped, was followed by a loud bellow and a wrenching crash. She sat up.

"The cows!"

They ran.

A cow, tempted by the tender grass among the graves, had tried to push through the fallen gate in the blackthorn hedge and got stuck. It was still stuck; it was thrashing and bellowing, destroying the hedge and driving thorns deeper into its neck and the tender pink udder. Blossom lay on the grass like snow.

"Keep them together." Begu threw the switch to Hild and ran straight to the distressed cow.

Hild advanced on the cattle. "Sweff," she called softly, as cowherds did. "Sweff sweff." She walked slowly around them so they bunched together but not so tightly that they panicked. "Sweff sweff." They began to lower their heads. One bent to the grass and tore a mouthful. Another swished its tail. This wasn't so hard. It was not unlike reassuring dogs. She wondered what it was about the sweff sound, the shape or the fall, that the cows found so calming. "Swip," she said, in the same tone. The browsing cow lifted its head. "Swip swip swip," she said on a falling note. Eye rolls, a nervous snort. "Sweff sweff," she said, with the proper rise and fall. They relaxed, though not as much as before.

"What are you doing?" Cædmon, one hand still on the sapling he'd been using to haul himself up the steep slope, one holding something wrapped in sacking. "Why are—" He caught sight of the cow stuck in the hedge and swore. "Gast!"

With Begu talking to her, the cow had calmed but was now lowing piteously. Begu was pondering the thorns. Cædmon dropped the sacking bundle, knelt by her, and patted the cow on the neck. He glanced at Hild. "Look to the others."

"They're fine now you're here." They were: all grazing peacefully. She wanted to look at the book, see if she could puzzle out some words. "You should take her collar off."

Cædmon shook his head; he seemed as immune to her reputation as Begu. He pointed at the pierced udder. "This is what hurts most."

"Won't she kick when you pull the thorns?"

"She might. But we have to get every single one or in a few days she'll leak yellow and stink."

She wasn't a big cow, but she weighed more than all three children put together. Hild longed for Cian's old wicker shield or, better still, the one of sturdy wood and hide with the painted boss the Bryneich had given him last year. She took a deep breath and knelt. Down here the hooves looked huge and sharp, and they were covered in the shit the cow had loosed in her panic. She set the book aside. "Where should I begin?"

◆ 85 ◆

An hour later, by the foot of the daymark hill, Hild and Begu put down their burdens, the collar and its bell—for Cædmon said the cow would need salve round her neck, not a collar, and Hild wanted to look at the bell—and the sack-wrapped book, and did their best to tidy each other up. Hild unbraided Begu's left plait, and with the leather tie held in her teeth combed the hair through with her fingers, picking out thorns and blossom petals and bits of grass.

Begu tried wiping her shoes on the grass.

"It won't help," Hild said, replaiting.

"It might."

"It won't. They can probably smell us from here." She tied off the plait, unbound the other. "Keep still. There. Now you do mine."

"Yours are fine and tidy. I don't know how you keep them so."

"I have my fa's hair. Not soft like yours."

"I like how yours feels, wiry and strong. Like you."

No one had ever said that to her before.

"What's wrong? Are you worried about the cow shit? I won't let Guenmon shout at you."

Guenmon was a beginner compared to Onnen, but being protected, and by someone who only came up to her chin, was so novel to Hild that she had no idea how to respond.

Fursey pursed his lips and turned the little brown book over and over in his hands, then knocked the cover with his knuckles. His fine black robe gaped a little at the neck, showing more than usual of the splotch of spilt-wine birth stain that ran from his left shoulder to his jawbone. "Cowhide over wooden board. Home-tanned skin at that." He opened it, shut it, opened it again. "A breviarium psalterii. And in a terrible hand, something a peasant might write. Is this anything to do with that Irish serf you wanted me to speak to?"

"It belonged to a dead priest. What's a"—she paused to sound it out carefully—"breviarium psalterii?"

"A shortened kind of Psalter. Like this." He took his own book, bound in fine-grained black calfskin, from his waist pouch and opened it one-handed to show her. Psalms. He'd shown her them before. She nodded. Looked at the dead priest's Psalter in his other hand.

"But the letters are different." The letters were rounder and fatter, blacker. She held out her hand, and Fursey gave it to her. She hefted it, opened it again, peered at it. Fursey had been teaching her to read, but these letters were all run together; she couldn't tell one word from another. There were no dots and other marks over certain letters, the way there were in Fursey's book.

"It's old," he said. "Versio Ambrosiana. It was old before your dead priest took his vows."

Curled in the crook of the big lime by the beck she leafed through the book. The dappled light swam over the ink that was fading to brown. *In a terrible hand, something a peasant might write.* There were peasants who wrote? If her uncle found out it would irritate him, that a peasant could do something his seer could not. Yet.

It would irritate Eadfrith, too. Even as their boat had crossed from the muddy surge of the Tine to the chop and heave of the sea, and men out of their wits moaned and the less injured laughed at their hurts when they remembered they should and looked as though they'd be grateful for their mothers when they didn't, Eadfrith had been badgering his father about Fursey, who lay tied like a hog on the plank half deck between them.

Eadfrith kicked the priest on the thigh. "Why does she get him? Does she get the hostage price, too?"

Fursey, who was awake but gagged and so—uncharacteristically as she was to learn—silent, watched one then the other as if he was in hall at a scop's contest.

"She gets nothing but charge of an annoying god mouth who will explain the value of the book."

"But why can't I have him?"

"You didn't earn him."

"Nor did she."

"He's mine to dispose of as I please." Eadfrith said nothing, but drew his foot back again. "He's not yours to damage. Unless you want to buy him from me?"

Eadfrith hadn't done well in the fight—few had, it was more flight than fight—and had no bounty to show.

"No? Just as well. You've no need of books. You have a blade."

While father and maybe-heir measured each other's gaze, Fursey met Hild's, raised his eyebrows, and looked pointedly at her seax.

Edwin missed nothing. He leaned down and said in that pleasant we'll-eat-the-horse tone, "She might wear a blade but she also wears skirts, priest, like you. So she will learn. Teach her. But not about your Christ. There'll be others for that, in time." And to Hild, "While he eats at my expense, see you learn the full use of these books, if any."

In the crook of the lime tree by the beck Hild closed the book. Fursey was now eating—and drinking, always drinking—at Mulstan's expense, not her uncle's. The gift of kings, her mother said: to make others pay. Another saying of her mother's popped into her head: *Women make and men break.* She frowned. What about men in skirts, where did they fit? Skirt or sword, book or blade . . .

"It's a strange book," she said to Bán in Irish, and he said, "Is it?" in Anglisc, because Hild had decided that was best. With Fursey unwilling to translate, that was how they would learn the most, one from the other. She would speak Bán's tongue and he hers, so that when she left—for she would leave by summer, surely—when she was gone, he could talk to the folk at the hall. And she would know more of how Fursey's tricky Irish mind worked.

They were walking along a track raised between the rhynes. It was spring even here now, minty green leaves on everything, and the air full of the scent of blossom that in the valleys would already be tiny fruit. Assuming Osric's men had joined Edwin's, that their march up the coast had gone well, and that they had broken the host around Bebbanburg, the court would be moving to Yeavering, to the sweet green pastures and the constant wind on Goat Hill. But if they had, why was she still here? Why had no one come? Perhaps the Irish were still at sea. She reached for her seax but found her sash instead of her belt, and remembered she had lent it to Cian. *It's still mine,* she'd said, *but you may have the use of it, for a while. Only not when we play, because it is very sharp.*

As they walked, Cú would run into the meadowsweet, comfrey, and reeds that lined the banks, and sniff and scratch, and sometimes whine, and then Bán would go look and untangle the tall golden withies from one another so they would grow straight. The golden willow grew fastest, he said, but the black willow was best for baskets. He had to shape "basket" with his hands twice before he found the word, but although Hild knew what he was trying to say, she didn't interrupt. She had found that people, especially people who spoke a different tongue, would get anxious if they didn't get to have their say in their own way, even if they spoke in a long rush, hurrying to get their words out. Like the strange Psalter.

"The Psalms are all written together," she said. "No beginning and no end, all in one long rush. Fursey says it's to imitate the long breath of god."

"Father lord Fursey is a godly man," Bán said absently, in Irish, and then stopped to test the suppleness of the withy. "Not now," he said to himself. "Not yet." They walked on.

"But what I don't understand," she said, "is how, if it's the breath of god, it's a different breath to Fursey's little book. Fursey says there is only one god, but surely that's wrong."

"It is not. There is God, only God, and God lives in everything. In the air and in the earth, in the rhyne and the willow, in you and in me and in Cú. How can there be two when God dwells in everything?"

Hild was glad she was speaking in Irish, because in Anglisc gods lived in particular places. In Anglisc it made no sense to say god was everywhere. Gods were called Thunor and Eorðe and Sigel, and they lived in their own places, in oak, or a deep well, or the sun. She wished Fursey were allowed to talk to her of his god. "If your god lives in your dog, why don't you kneel before him?"

"Because God is in me, too."

Hild pondered that as they walked. The sun was warming her back. "Once I met a British Christ bishop, Anaoc. He said prophecy was demon work. Is his Christ the same as your Irish god, and Fursey's?"

"There is only one Christ."

"Then if his god is in everything, too, where do the demons live?"

Bán looked at her helplessly, then said, "The willow in the yard will be dry now. Will I show you how to strip the bark?"

In the kitchen garth that had become the children's place at the end of the afternoons once the kitchenfolk had taken the herbs they needed for cooking, Hild finally found a way to tell the story of dogs and gods and demons in Anglisc to Begu and Cian. She had no idea why it was so much harder for her to talk in Anglisc to anyone but Begu, it just was, though these last weeks she was learning how to let the words come. It helped if there was no weightiness behind them, no import; if they were only words with no life or death hanging in the balance.

While Cian hefted his exercise stones up and down, up and down, and Begu wove daises together, Hild finished her story, and Cian laughed. Hild was glad. He hadn't laughed for a week.

"Gods and demons in dogs and worms!" He dropped his stones and smoothed his hair back from his forehead—it was now entirely the same colour as Hild's and as long as any warrior's. Hild saw Begu looking at it and wondered if she would think Cian's hair felt nice, too. "So when I cast my line into the river and catch a fish," he said, "and the fish eats the worm, will the worm gods have to fight with the fish gods?"

"And when we eat the fish," Begu said, "will the gods inside us fight the gods inside the worm inside the fish?" Her plait was coming undone, again.

Hild said, "And will the demons then fight the other demons or band together against the gods like the Gododdin and the men of Rheged did against the Deivyr and Bryneich?"

And then of course having mentioned Cian's favourite song, which she did deliberately, nothing would do but that they reenact the drinking of the wine and mead of Morei, then the fighting in the fosse with a bold and mighty arm, and the falling, always the falling in the fosse, the funeral fosse. But once they'd all fallen, they wiggled like worms in a pile, then like worms possessed by demons, then like people and dogs and demons and gods all fighting it out, and laughed until the dust on their cheeks turned to mud with their tears, and Begu's hair was one big knot. And Hild, for a while, was not the bringer of light who predicted the death of a queen and the siege of a fortress, not the seer tasked with learning to read, but just a child.

6

✦

FURSEY, HOSTAGE TO THE KING and tutor to the light of the world, was fond of good wine and long conversations at meat about the wrongs of the world and how to right them, and in the course of things the long conversations naturally made him more thirsty. So Mulstan would call for the lyre more often than was usual, for Fursey, being Irish and highborn— the son of the daughter of the king of Connaught and baptised by Saint Brendan himself—respected the makers of music in hall before even his thirst for Mulstan's fine wine or the sound of his own voice. But tonight it was yet too early for the lyre.

"This truly is a royal wine," Fursey said to Onnen, who in Mulstan's hall, where she spoke only Anglisc and wore clothes like a lady, sat at the lord's table, not in his kitchen.

Onnen could only agree. *Iberian*, she'd told Hild the day before, as she had ladled up a cupful from one of the great jars fresh from the hold of an East Anglisc merchant. *As strong as good dirt and as rich as blood. Fit for an emperor.* But Hild had tasted it and spat, and would only drink it watered and sweetened with honey.

"Something Isidore himself might relish," Fursey said. "Though he would no doubt quote Jerome: Growing girls should avoid wine as poison lest, on account of the fervent heat of their time of life, they drink it and die." He smiled to himself, as if remembering some sunlit girl and her fervent heat. "Yes. A man's drink." He smiled again—but differently, as flat-lipped as an adder—at Onnen. "An expensive drink. Though, given that his lordship Mulstan has charge of all the trade in these parts, it's no doubt only proper that he take some of the wares for himself every now and again."

"He takes no more than his due as king's thegn."

"Naturally. For everything hereabouts is his due, is it not? And it would be a terrible thing to suggest that one's host takes more than is quite proper."

He looked her up and down, lingering on the magnificent chain of Byzantine and Roman medals draped over her breast that Mulstan had given her only last week.

Onnen's spine was very straight. Hild put down her copper cup and looked over at Cian. He had put down his cup, too, and his face was turning red. Hild had a sudden regret at giving him the use of her seax.

"What's the matter?" Begu whispered, but Hild shook her head.

"Oh, yes," mused Fursey, "he does like his treats and his wealh ways."

Fursey looked over at the red-faced Cian and smiled another of those snake smiles, and Hild saw the priest was drunk—just enough to let his devils out to play, as he might put it. Onnen saw it, too, and called to Cian.

"Cian, tell my lord Mulstan how you acquired your fine shield. Better yet, fetch it for him. My lord would like to see it." She looked at Mulstan, who looked up from his conversation with the East Anglisc merchant captain and said, "Yes, yes, bring your shield, boy."

Fursey watched him go then said in a voice pitched for Onnen's ears, "His hair is a most remarkable colour, is it not? And it is interesting that his mother is making up to the most powerful man on the south Deiran coast. A man once sworn to Æthelfrith the Ferocious and perhaps still to his sons. A man with gold, who could command many swords, should he call for them. And the king already weakened in his fight with the Dál nAriadne." He laughed, like the slither of silk. "No one expected Fiachnae to run around your king and storm Bebbanburg, did they? Or, oh yes, someone did. Your young charge here. Strange, that. And now here is Mulstan and that boy with the interestingly coloured hair, thrown together at an opportune time."

Onnen contemplated the eating knife balanced in her hand, four inches of rippled steel honed to a sliver, and then Fursey. "Priest, are you tired of life?"

Begu stared at her. She knew Onnen only as the woman her father liked and who was a stern weaving teacher. Hild, who had seen Onnen gut more living things than most warriors could begin to dream of, did not believe, quite, that she would cut the priest. She found Begu's hand and squeezed reassuringly.

"Not at all. The little maid's uncle, your king, hired me as tutor and I am teaching." Hild snorted inwardly. Hired. It was one way to describe being hauled from the bloodied mud on the south bank of the Tine and put to double use by a canny king. "If she's to guide kings she'll need subtlety, and all the Anglisc know is blade and blood and boast."

Hild said in Irish, "You have not met my mother."

He threw back his head and laughed, showing teeth and tongue stained dark with wine.

Onnen wiped her blade on the edge cloth, sheathed it, and stood. She leaned across Fursey and took the wine jar. "Our gracious host has been overly generous with his wine. You are not yourself."

He reached to grab it back.

"Must I explain to my lord that you are in drink?"

Fursey cursed and reached for a sword that was not there. Accusations of drunkenness to an Irish noble, no matter his priestly vows, were tantamount to accusations of faith-breaking, for the word or boast of a drunken man was not to be relied upon.

Onnen smiled and cradled the back of Hild's head briefly. "Learn well, little prickle. And you, Begu, it won't hurt you to pay attention, though you must talk to me or Guenmon after of what you think you've learnt, for I'd not trust this sotted priest as far as I could fling him. I'll send more wine when the lyre comes down from the wall."

The next day Hild and Cian and Begu climbed the headland together, Hild and Cian copying Begu's natural habit of grasping whatever shrubs or rocks came to hand to ease the strain on thigh and calf. The furze—gorse, Hild reminded herself, gorse—was in full flower. Hild had the Psalter, now carefully wrapped in a soft old cloth, tucked safely into her sash, and used both hands, but Begu seemed perfectly at ease swinging the cowbell with one hand and using only the other to climb. Cian, as usual, wore sword and shield and the slaughter seax. His hair was dressed back with goose grease like that of Mulstan's men. He looked the very picture of a warrior, though somewhat slight and beardless.

When they reached the top, the headland smelt of windblown grass and cows. The horizon was dusty with purple heather, and daisies starred the grass. There was no sign of Cædmon or cows.

"He'll be along," Begu said, "but perhaps not until middæg."

"A fort!" Cian said, pointing at the broken Roman signal tower, and he ran towards it, drawing his wooden sword. It wasn't the same sword Ceredig had given him, he'd outgrown that one long ago, and kept it in his kist. This was sized for a man, shaped oak with a square of painted stone Hild had found from a broken pavement in Caer Luel set into the carefully carved hilt, and bits of begged scrap metal hammered into the edges to give it heft. His scabbard was a real one, but old, discarded long ago by one of Mulstan's men, though now freshly relined with sheepskin and its wood cunningly painted to look jewelled and chased. Hild and Begu were working on a tablet weave to replace the fraying baldric.

Begu and Hild ran, too.

Cian climbed the low east wall, jumped inside, and popped up again, eyes shining. "You shall attack and I'll defend!" He unslung his shield.

"Aren't you old for games?" Cædmon, standing, rubbing his eyes. He'd fallen asleep inside the tower, waiting. He studied the odd sword for a moment. "Old for toys, too."

Cian, ready for battle, slammed his sword hilt on his shield. "This is no toy!" The painted stone fell out of the sword.

Cædmon folded his arms and was about to smile when Begu said, "It isn't a toy. Truly. My father just last night declared it a shield fit for an ealdorman. Didn't he, Hild?"

"He did. And it was given to him by a Bryneich lord in the presence of the king. I was there. And the knife he wears slit the arm of a man of the Dál nAriadne." Though she had been the one wielding it. "Begu and I are working on a baldric fit for a prince. And look, we have brought back your book."

"And bell." Begu, holding out the bell, looked about. "Where are the cows?"

"Having to do with the hall's freemartin. Da thinks Winty—"

"The one caught with thorns," Begu said to Hild.

"He thinks Winty might be in season and he wants to be sure before he begs the prize bull. Besides, I've not mended the hedge." He unfolded his arms, took the bell and then the book. After a moment Cian sheathed his sword and slung his shield onto his back, then stooped to search for the fallen stone.

Cædmon unwrapped the book. He opened it upside down. "What does it say?"

"God things. Prayers."

"Like songs?"

"Yes," Hild said, surprised. "Like songs."

He held the Psalter out. "Tell them to me."

Hild stared at the black letters. "They are in Latin."

"Then speak them to me in Anglisc. Here." He pointed with his thick finger. "Tell me that."

Hild remembered some of the words and could puzzle out others. She mouthed the Latin phrases to herself carefully, then thought about it. It would be easier in British, but then Begu wouldn't understand. "And I am needy and poor. God, hurry for me. You can help me and save me. Lord, don't dawdle."

"God sounds like Guenmon," Begu said. "Or your mam, Cian. Don't dawdle! Hurry up!"

"Or was that his lord, not his god talking?" Cian said, picking up his painted stone.

"Lord and god are the same in this book, Fursey says."

"A lord would never say don't dawdle," Cædmon said. He looked at Begu. "Would your da say that?"

"Not in hall. Up here he might."

"Then"—Cædmon squinched his face up, thinking—"then maybe he would say, 'And I am needy and poor. God, hasten for me. You are my help and saviour. O Lord, do not delay.'" He pointed again. "Tell me this bit."

Hild traced the words with her finger, muttered the Latin to herself, and tried again. "Praise Him, sun and moon. Praise Him, shiny stars. Praise the Lord, you kings of the land and everybody, princes and judges, here."

Everyone looked at Cædmon. He shook his head. "No." No? He had no idea how difficult it was to read. To read in another tongue. To turn that tongue into Anglisc. She would never again make a difficult thing look easy. For a moment she missed being the bringer of light and having people truckle to her.

"No," he said again. "Like this. 'Praise Him, sun and moon. Praise Him, all you stars of light. Praise Him, you kings of the earth and all you peoples, you princes and all you judges of the earth.' You have to say it like a hoof-beat. Like a song."

Cian and Begu nodded. After a moment, so did Hild.

"Keep the book a while. Come up here at times and tell it to me. Once I get the hedge mended."

The next morning Hild sought out Fursey and found him in hall eating oyster stew, drinking ale, and complaining to the young servingman about the size of the fire: ". . . so small it wouldn't keep a rat's arse warm, never mind a man about God's work, and why are you gawping like that, you dim-witted spawn of a toadstool? More wood for the fire. More wood!"

He was talking in Irish of course, something he did on those days when he was still suffering from the night before but not yet drunk again.

"Father Fursey," Hild said, also in Irish, for Anglisc at these times made him snappish. "Give you a good day. Might you be willing to talk to me, at all, about the worth of this priest's *breviarium psalterii*?"

Fursey snorted, slurped up another mouthful of oysters, chewed and swallowed, and scratched his birthmark. "It's worthless. A poor hand, and the text is corrupt, taken from an old, outmoded, and discredited translation of the Septuagint. And the old priest or, rather, someone who had gone before him made a personal and, might I add, eccentric selection of Psalms. Singularly without use or ornament." Another slurp, more chewing, a noisy swallow followed by shouting for more ale, which the servant only understood when Fursey shook the empty leather cup in his face. "However, as a palimpsest—though it would take work and some pumice, which no doubt my lord Mulstan could acquire, him being so good at that and, ah"—he rubbed his hand over his chin—"pumice would be so welcome. Now what was I . . . ? Worth. Yes. Well, as a palimpsest it could be worth as much as . . . Ach, give it to me." He flipped through the pages, counting, measuring with his hands against the scarred board of the table. "Hmmn. Perhaps the skin of two lambs or one particularly small calf."

"Thank you. Do you happen to know where Mulstan might be found?"

"I do so happen to know. And as soon as the misbegotten mushroom brings me more ale, I'll be finding him, for it seems himself has need of my skills."

"Perhaps you might be willing to name to me the place, so that I might find him and ask him a pressing question without taking up your most valuable time, and may god smile upon the rest of your day."

"Does God ever smile, except perhaps at His more extravagant jokes?"

Here he smiled mockingly, though whether at himself or the servingman refilling his ale cup, Hild could not tell. He took a long, long drink and shrugged. "Howsomever, Mulstan might be found at the dock house by and by, for there I'm to meet him and make record of some exotic shipment, but where he'll be til then, the hairy creature, I couldn't begin to say."

Guenmon could say, and she did, and a lot more besides. She told Hild that if she hurried Mulstan might be found at the smithy, probably with Onnen. "And if you see that great boy skulking about tell him I have an errand or two. Hanging about his mam's skirts like an unweaned calf . . ."

Fursey and Guenmon were both right, Hild saw, as she walked downstream beside the beck to the roaring furnace and stinking smoke of the smithy. Mulstan stood with Onnen just outside, out of range of the heat and sparks, watching whatever was happening within, while the smith's hammer rang in that steady bang-bing-bing rhythm of a man intent upon his work. Mulstan was indeed hairy: His bushy hair, held back by a great gold ring inset with tortoiseshell, glinted red-gold in the sun, and his arms were furred like a fox. And Cian was, in fact, hanging about, standing a few dozen strides from Mulstan and his mother, out of earshot, pretending to be absorbed in a twig he was stripping, the twig he threw into the beck when he saw her.

He came to meet her. They stopped by the lime whose branches shaded a backwater of the beck. Its leaves were now bigger than her palms. When she'd first arrived the branches had been bare.

"Guenmon wants you," she said.

Cian scowled.

"She has errands."

"I'm busy."

Hild said nothing.

"Look at them." His voice shook with outrage.

Onnen had a hand resting lightly on Mulstan's arm while he shouted something into the red-lit gloom for the smith; she was smiling.

"She's happy."

"She's my mam!"

Onnen liked Mulstan, Hild could tell. She also knew Onnen liked the way he ran his holdings, though it lacked the fine and sharp efficiency a woman would bring to the household. She liked his daughter and his servants and the ease his housefolk felt in hall. And she leaned in towards him as though she liked his smell. And Mulstan liked her; Hild saw the way his nostrils flared as Onnen laughed at something he said and patted his arm.

"They'll do what they'll do, whether you're here or not," she said. Indeed, she'd be surprised if they hadn't already done it. Cian knew that, too. They were both familiar enough with the ways of the hall at night, when a woman crossed to a man's bench and crept under his blanket, and breathing got furtive, then fast. They'd seen the dogs, and the sheep at Yeavering, in the breeding pen by the River Glen; they'd even helped the horse master help the stallion with his stick that was so long he didn't quite know where to put it.

Hild tried to imagine her own mother with a man with a stick so long he didn't know where to put it, and couldn't.

"Cian, come away. Come away now. We will do Guenmon's errands together."

She tugged on his belt, as she had when she was little, only now she did not have to reach up, and she realised that though he was tall, she would overtop him when they were both grown. She understood then that they were no longer quite children.

Something in her sudden stillness made him look down at her hand, and he nodded, and with one last look turned away with her down the path.

Once out of sight of the smithy, Hild stopped. "You go on. I must still speak to Mulstan. I'll catch you up. Go on, go on now."

She watched him walk down the path—whipping savagely with his sword at harebells by the way—then set about tidying her hair and smoothing her eyebrows. She tore a dock leaf from its stem and cleaned her shoes and straightened her sash. She missed her belt and seax.

Mulstan and Onnen looked up. Mulstan beamed through his beard. He looked like a grinning hedge. "Hild. Are you come to fetch me for something?"

Bang-bing-bing. Bang-bing-bing.

"No, my lord Mulstan."

"Is something amiss? Is Begu well?"

"All is well, my lord."

Both Onnen and Mulstan looked relieved.

Onnen smiled at him. "I'll leave you to it, my lord." She gave Hild a look, nodded at them both, and walked down the path—more slowly than usual and with a sway that Mulstan watched until she was out of sight.

He turned to Hild.

She tried to imagine how her mother might phrase a request that was not a request. "I'm come to ask a favour within your gift. Two favours. One for myself, and one in the name of my uncle, the king." It was the longest thing she'd ever said in front of him. He peered about, startled, half expecting to see a voice thrower standing behind her.

He scratched his neck. "The king? Has a messenger come?"

"No, my lord. I owe a debt to one of your people. Royal kin should not owe debts, especially in troubled times."

"No, no, I can quite see that," Mulstan said, puzzled, but willing to go along with the odd maid who spoke with strange pauses, like someone receiving messages from the little people under the hill. She was, after all, high, very high, in the king's favour. "To whom do you owe this debt?"

Bang-bing-bing, followed by a loud hiss as metal was plunged into the water trough.

Mulstan turned and peered into the smithy. "I do like the smell of quenching iron. Quite makes me feel like a young gesith with his first sword." The maid said nothing. "Yes. So. Now. Who did you say you owe a debt to?"

"One Cædmon by name."

"My cowherd's son?"

"Yes, my lord."

He frowned. "And what is the nature and amount of this . . . debt?"

"I have a book from Cædmon worth, by Fursey's estimate, one calf or two lambs, but I have neither to offer."

Ting-ting-ting: a smaller hammer. Whatever the smith was making it was not large, and it was almost done.

Mulstan smoothed his moustaches, perplexed. "How is it his book?"

"He saved it, when the old priest died. I thought to reward him for it."

Mulstan pondered that. "And Fursey thinks it worth a healthy calf or two lambs?" The man must be mad. But this was the king's niece, and one must tread carefully.

"He spoke of the skin of one calf or two lambs."

"Ah, then that's a different case." He looked reflectively at the clouds, started to peer into the smithy again, thought better of it. "Cædmon. Yes,

I know the boy. Dekke's son. Mother dead of the flux that came through here long since."

"The one that took Begu's mother?"

The little people under the hill were clearly well informed. But no, the maid spent time with Begu. No doubt they talked as maids did. "The very same. So. No mother. An older sister, Bote, a milkmaid who forages at times for the kitchen. He seems like a good lad. Wealh, of course. Still, if you feel you owe him a debt then, yes, I'll ask Guenmon what she suggests as good recompense. Perhaps a small pig, or a she-kid."

Another great hiss from the smithy, then silence.

"Would such satisfy your honour?"

"Yes. Thank you. I shall recommend your generosity to my uncle."

Her uncle the king. "Good, then. Good." He looked relieved. Hosting people of influence was a chancy business. Then he remembered she had said two favours. "And there was another thing?"

She nodded, but this time imagining what her mother might say was no help, for her mother would not agree. She stood mute.

Mulstan put a hand on her shoulder. She was strange, this maid, but still only a maid and friend to his Begu. "Is this truly a serious matter?"

Hild nodded.

"Then you and I will withdraw to that rock." He pointed to the boulder in the curve of the beck, worn smooth over the years, where the smith's customers often sat on sunny days. "I find it easier to say a thing, sometimes, if I have another thing to look at."

Mulstan sat with his knees wide apart and a great fox-furred hand on each massive thigh. Hild perched cautiously next to him. They watched the water. Insects darted to and fro.

"Are there fish?" she said.

"There are. And if we sit long enough, perhaps a trout will rise for a fly. And if we sit beyond that, perhaps a pike, a water wolf, will ease his way downstream from yonder backwater and find his dinner." They listened to the splash and gurgle. "Now then. Straight as a spear: Tell me."

"Cian, Onnen's son, is unhappy. A sword would make him happy. You could give him one."

Mulstan tipped his head back and studied the sky. The clouds were like puffs of wool, far away. "Cian is wealh."

Hild said nothing.

"Aye, and so is his mother, for all her Anglisc ways." He sighed and slid his seax along his belt to a more comfortable position. "He's young."

"He has no father." Silence. Hild ploughed on. "When he was six, Ceredig, king in Elmet, gave him a wooden sword."

"Ceredig?" He mused upon the implications of that, humming in his throat.

"And he has been gifted by lords of the north with shield and horse." An exaggeration perhaps, but the pony, Acærn, like Ilfetu, had not left Tinamutha, so Mulstan would never know. "He has had the esteem of royalty. But Ceredig is no longer king in Elmet, and Cian is here. And his mother."

The smith's hammer started up again, *ting-ting-ting*. More throaty musings from Mulstan, only this time Hild made out words. "Young ram . . . wants to charge at things . . . his mother . . . who knows what at . . . Ceredig, eh?" He cleared his throat. "Well. Well. Has the boy had instruction?"

"My mother's sworn man has shown him a little. He's travelled with the royal war band. He sleeps in hall with your men and exercises all the time. The sword is his path."

"You speak like a seer." He sounded disapproving.

"It is his path."

He knew the rumours. And she sounded so certain. But he hated this notion of meddling with wyrd.

"Please, lord. He is like a brother to me. I wish to see him happy."

"No doubt so would his mother. Well!" He slapped his thighs and stood. "I thank you for bringing this to my attention, little maid. I will think on it."

"Thank you, my lord, for listening. And for Cædmon's kid, or pig. Thank you on behalf of my uncle." The king.

Hild sat with Begu in hall to one side of the open door. Midafternoon sun poured into the hall, throwing shadows all one way along the floor. It shone on the carefully cleaned table where they sat, on the flat band of red-and-black tablet weave growing between them, and on the walrus ivory of the eight square tablets, each the size of a child's palm.

"Keep it taut," Begu said, for the third time.

Hild kept leaning forward to touch the ivory. The tablets she used at home were polished elm. Her mother's were antler horn. These looked like something you could eat, like wafers of creamy curd or slices of the meat of some gigantic nut.

Each tablet had a separate warp thread through the holes at its four corners. They were twisted a quarter or half turn after every pass of the weft shuttle, also of ivory, to make the pattern. Hild had seen her mother and Onnen weave a band in one afternoon while one also worked a spindle and distaff and the other threaded the weft shuttle back and forth rapidly, beating in the weft every few passes. But she and Begu were new at this, and they must constantly stop to remind the other of something: turn this tablet a half turn, keep that warp taut, beat in that weft. It was a simple pattern but strong, a march of red and black squares.

Guenmon came by with a cup of meat tea for each. The men had killed two oxen that morning for tomorrow's feast—Hild had heard the snarling and snapping of the bulldogs as they controlled the cattle for the butcher. The fresh bones were boiled with their tatters of meat in salted water to make a tasty drink thick with marrow. Guenmon had added a pinch of thyme and a hint of precious pepper.

"It smells like a dream," Begu said.

"Wait til you see the meat itself," Guenmon said. "Luscious and marbled through with fine white fat. The spring grass always does it. And there are to be three fat-tailed sheep, as well as all those waterfowl Mulstan will be bringing home in his net. Celfled has promised us a stitch of eels and a hind from her woods. And Cædmon's sister brought us sacks of the freshest greens. But so she should, given that plump little milk goat the lord gave her. And I tasted that batch of mead we made from the run honey. Onnen's the finest brewster I've met. Though I think I might be a better maltster." She saw that neither girl had an opinion on the matter. "Well, now, that's a fine bold pattern. For Cian is it?"

"It is."

"Red and black. So as not to show the dirt and the blood, I expect." Begu paled and paused. Guenmon tutted to herself. What did the girl think got spattered on such things? "Will it be ready for the feast?"

"I hope so," Hild said.

Now there was a maid who wouldn't be surprised by blood. "I'll leave you busy little gemæcces to it, then."

She smiled to herself at the sudden shyness that fell on the two girls as she walked away.

Gemæcce, Hild thought, staring at the pattern. She looked up, found Begu looking at her, blushed, looked down again. After a breath or two she looked up.

"Is it good?" Begu asked.

"Yes," Hild said. "Yes, it's good." And she sipped at her tea and scalded her mouth and spat and laughed. "Ow. Be sure to blow on it. At my uncle's table, no one blows on their food. You will have to learn to clap."

"You will teach me."

"Yes. At his table no one waits. The food arrives just right, or the housefolk are punished." The wealh are punished. And Begu was half wealh—though beyond Mulstanton by the Bay of the Beacon no one would know.

When the housefolk began putting out the fires in hall, Hild went to find Onnen. She walked to the beach, where the grass met sand, past the place where kitchen servants turned their vast spits in their outdoor kitchens while others built a long, long board on the sand for the food, and found her between the two towering piles of wood that would be lit that night— that is, one towering pile, and one fallen mess.

Onnen was shouting at a slave in Anglisc. "Did I not say, throw the faggots on the shadow side of the pile, the shadow side?"

The slave hung his head. He was nearly as old as Mulstan, but thin and knob-kneed and barefoot.

"And where is the shadow? Look at me. Where is the shadow?"

The slave pointed.

"Yes. And why didn't you throw the wood there, as I told you? Because you're lazy, witless, and ignorant. And now the whole thing is a disordered heap and must be built again. I should have you whipped." She saw Hild approaching from the wood path and walked to meet her with a step that was as quick as usual but not light.

"Will you really have him whipped?"

"I might."

Hild had never seen her threaten a slave with a whipping for such a little thing. "Are you . . . well?"

Onnen folded her arms. "I could cheerfully strangle you. I feel like a bee in a bottle. Mulstan is plotting something, I can feel it, and it's something to do with you, with what you said to him. What are you meddling with?"

"Cian needs his sword."

"Sweet gods! Cian is too young for his sword! Oh, he would get the benighted blade, all in good time, if you simply let things alone. Look,

look here." She tapped the brand-new iron hangers on her belt. "I have the keys. The rest would follow naturally, in time. Do you have any idea what you've done?"

Hild didn't know what to say. Love and bed games were one thing, keys another. Onnen might be a cousin of Ceredig king, but Ceredig was dead, and Breguswith, daughter of kings, might not want to let her go.

"My mother—"

"Aye, your mother. Well, I warned her my decisions wouldn't—" She made an impatient gesture. "I don't want Cian to be a man just yet. If he must ape his betters, he should at least wait until he's grown before he goes off to get killed. Think what would have happened at Tinamutha if he'd had a sword."

Red and black, blood and dirt. Her seax opening the Irishman's arm, skin and muscle gaping like a flower.

Onnen smoothed her dress and sighed. "I don't know what possessed you, but it's done. Tonight stay close. Stay with Cian, stay with me. For once, do as you're told. Now leave me alone to see to this mess. Unless you want to help?"

At the beach the tide was out, whispering to itself as it ran along the pebbly sand and put a pale frothy line along the deep blue near the horizon. As the sky darkened, people—perhaps two hundred, all Mulstan's fighting men and kin, the beekeepers and swineherds and milkmaids, the sailors and guests and visitors, sitting in the sandy grass as heedless on this one night as children—began to lean back and loosen their belts and girdles and sashes and pick at the mountains of food of every kind. The beef, marinated all morning in vinegar and imported olive oil, and roasted right there on the beach, the sheep, the hind, the songbirds, the eels, the chard and mallow and goosefoot, the sow thistle and cresses and coleworts, all flavoured with vinegar and dill and sage, savoury and pennyroyal, rosemary and rue.

Hild sucked the juices from her bread trencher and gnawed the soft insides from the crust. She sat a few paces down from Mulstan, who had his arm around Onnen. Cian and Begu had competed to see who could eat the most red carrots in the time it took Hild to drink a cup of sweet elderflower wine, and now both were smeared with herby, vinegary streaks, and as neither had thought to count their carrots they were contemplating another contest. But then Mulstan unwound his arm from Onnen, nodded to his scop to strike a chord—Hild recognised Swefred, Mulstan's chief sword man, drafted for the purpose—and stood.

It took a while for the quiet to spread down the boards, but eventually all that could be heard was the slish-run-whisper of the surf and a querulous child, soon shushed.

"We stand on the other side of another winter and at the beginning of a summer that all the signs point to as good beyond memory. We live on good land, by a rich sea. Our stock is healthy, our crops thrive, and our children are strong."

Hearty, if sleepy and well-fed, rumbles of approval all around.

Mulstan gestured to Onnen, who stood. "I have taken to wife this woman, Onnen, of the Elmetsætne, and she will help me husband this land and see the old snug in winter and the young fat in spring." He twined his hand in Onnen's and raised it, and again there were rumbles of approval, though not as many; this was old news. "And Onnen has a son."

Mulstan looked down the board at Cian and gestured for him to stand. Cian scrambled up, wiping his hands down the front of his tunic.

"I welcome Cian as Onnen's son and my fosterling." People craned to see Cian; the light was leaking away and the cooking fires were being put out, one by one. Mulstan turned to Swefred, who handed him a long, wrapped bundle. "A thegn's fosterling should have arms."

Cian quivered like a horse bitten by flies.

"Cian, fosterling, come receive your arms."

"Wipe your face," Begu hissed at him, and when he looked at her, blank as butter, she made a wiping gesture at her cheek. He lifted his hand as though he wasn't sure it belonged to him.

"This is your path, brother," Hild said. "It is come. Walk tall." Then, as he stood there, overwhelmed, she said as her own mother had long ago, "Walk now."

He did.

And he smiled. He smiled as he tripped over everyone's feet and knocked over their cups. He smiled as he took the bundle, smiled as he unwrapped the sword, as his mother touched his cheek and Mulstan enveloped him in a bear hug. He smiled wider as the last fires went out and the sea slished. Smiled as he lifted his blade and tried to see it in the sudden rush of dark.

Then the rising moon, which had been flat as a silvered plate, popped as round as a ball of cheese, and it was full night. Mulstan gave a great shout and the crowd echoed him. He knelt by the tiny pile of birch shavings and sheep's hair, and with his steel struck a spark, and blew, and a tiny curl of flame, like a dragonlet's tongue, licked at the salty night. The crowd roared. The flame built, and Swefred, arms full now of unlit brands, handed them one at a time to Mulstan, who plunged each into the flame until it caught, then handed the first to Onnen, and the crowd roared, then one to the smith, and they roared, to Celfled, to the tanner, and on. Behind Swefred, Guenmon gave out unlit torches to everyone within reach and they passed them from hand to hand, still dark. Each initial torchbearer began the walk to hearth or hall, hut or smithy, and along the way touched the torches to those as yet unlit, and rekindled the fire for another year.

And then the crowd roared again, and this time didn't stop, and Cian, holding his own torch now, turned, sword raised, as a ship, pale sail glimmering in the moonlight, drew close to the beach.

Hild reached for a seax that wasn't there, then found an eating knife with one hand and Begu's wrist with the other. She began to push her way through the crowd to Cian. *We are us.* They would die together. But then two men in the bows of the ship unfurled a standard, and after a moment's flapping in the unsteady night breeze, the linen cloth streamed clear. Moonlight gleamed on the gold stitching and a single garnet sewn at the eye: the royal boar. The king was returned.

Hild was explaining to Begu for the third time why she did not need to dismantle her linden-wood bed, that she would not require silverware, that there was no room on the boat for her pony, that, yes, she could and should bring her ivory tablets, when she became aware of Onnen watching from the doorway.

Hild had last seen that expression on her almost-mother's face in the hall of Ceredig king, when the two strange men had beckoned Cian into the light.

"What are you doing?" Onnen said.

"We're packing," said Begu. "And I had no idea it was such a difficult thing. Hild says I won't need my bed. She says I won't need any hangings. But I don't know. What do you think, Onnen?"

"You won't need to pack your bed."

"I won't? Well. If you say so. But—"

"You won't need to pack a thing. Hild, with me."

They walked into the sunlight and gusting wind but got only halfway down the steps before Onnen took Hild by the shoulders and brought them both to an awkward halt.

"What have you promised her?"

"I have told Begu she is to come with me." Hild looked up into Onnen's eyes. She had to squint against the sun. "We are to be gemæcce."

"Have you lost your mind?"

Hild touched the heavy hilt of her seax, given back just this morning by Cian, who, sword-proud, no longer needed it, and drew herself up. It was only because Onnen was on a higher step that she was taller. Only that.

Onnen laid her hand on her own knife and for a moment they both breathed harshly, then Onnen sighed. "Hild."

"We are to be gemæcce. Guenmon said so."

"Guenmon is a bleating ewe. Think."

"I have chosen."

Onnen shook her head. "Your mother will choose."

Silence.

She touched Hild on her shoulders gently, increased the pressure until Hild turned a little and they were both looking out over Mulstan's sunlit holding. "Begu is all Mulstan has. She must marry, so that when Mulstan dies, the cowherd and butcher, the shepherd and fisherfolk, the milkmaids and smith, have a lord, have safety, are not turned like slaves from their homes."

"I could get the king to give it to me."

"Are you so sure?"

"I am his bringer of light. He promised to reward me with riches beyond human ken."

Onnen smiled sadly. "And before how many of his lords did he swear this?"

Hild didn't say anything.

"Beware the ingratitude of kings."

Hild gripped the rail. The wood had not yet been smoothed after the winter but she squeezed it as hard as she could, because it was real.

"I'm sorry, little prickle. But you must leave on the king's ship, and Begu must stay."

"I'll be all alone," she said, and she hardly recognised her own voice for the wobble. "You'll be here, and Cian. Even Fursey . . . even Fursey . . ."

"You'll have your mother. And Hereswith."

"Hereswith will soon be peaceweaver elsewhere." And maybe her mother would go with her sister. And then it would only be Hild and the king, and her cloak of otherness.

She said her goodbyes in the warmth of the hall and received gifts one by one and handed them unseeing to Eadfrith's man. She walked alone into the rain, half mad with trying not to remember the soft warmth of Onnen's motherly breast and the smell of her clothes, trying not to think of the glint of firelight on Begu's escaping hair because then she'd remember it always, one more memory to torment her. She tried not to take deep, deep breaths of the scent of wind-whipped sea blending with rained-on cowgrass blowing down from the cliff, tried not to think of Cian, Cian woven through everything. *We are us.* Trying to shut it all out, keep it all away—

She walked up the gangplank while the ship creaked and rubbed against the wharf. The wood was slippery. Eadfrith, waiting impatiently at the top of the gangplank, called something to his man behind her. Hild paused at the top of the gangplank, looked into the bows, and found Fursey looking back at her.

She blinked.

Fursey. Whose ransom had been paid, who should be long gone on his way back to his people.

Eadfrith shouted again. Hild could make no sense of his words. She could make no sense of anything. The rain increased. Eadfrith's man stood behind her, saying something. Then Fursey was there, giving her a hand onto the deck. She turned for one last look, for she might never see Mulstan's holding again, but the bright yellow sail dropped between her and the little wharf.

Fursey said, "Come out of the rain," but Hild was so rigid with not crying that she couldn't move.

"You," she said. "Why?"

"I was free to travel anywhere, and I remembered to myself your thrust at dinner: that I had not met any Anglisc who knew more than blade and blood and boast because I had not met your mother."

"My mother."

"Yes." He smiled that smile.

The sailors shouted in rhythm and tugged on a hemp line that squealed a little as it ran over the wood, and the sail turned. It was a new sail, beautifully dyed and tightly woven, the work of ten women for a year. Beyond it, Mulstan's man threw the end of a rope to a man in the bows, and the prow of the ship swung out a little.

"Can you afford passage?"

"I might have given Eadfrith to understand you wished me still as your tutor."

She looked at him, at his sly eyes and stubbled tonsure. "Why?"

"You have a bright mind but lack subtlety. I could teach you. And life around Edwin will be interesting—oh, very, very interesting, if I'm any judge, which I am—for the next little while. And I've a mind to meet your mother."

?

❖

HILD WOKE TO THE SMELL OF WOOL. Goodmanham stank of it. The week had been full of the chaos of shearing, and Hild had taken her turn with most of the other women and girls. She climbed out of bed slowly. Her back ached—and the top of her thigh, where a wether had kicked her as she helped flip him onto his back. She had a barely scabbed cut, the shape of a cat's long pupil, on the back of her left wrist where the shears had clipped her. But yesterday had seen the last of the pitifully naked sheep whistled out of their pens and herded back to the hills by the black-and-white dogs.

A brief memory of rhynes and rattling willow tried to take shape in her head but she pushed it away.

She stretched, pulled on her blue overdress, the hem of which was now three fingers shorter than it should be. Hereswith yesterday, as she and Mildburh dressed—more finely than Hild, even though they would spend the morning in the dairy—had said that no Yffing should look so shabby. Had she turned into a savage away from her family? But she had not had the time to nag at Hild about it, not during shearing season when even the peaceweaver must work like a wealh; and Hild was bone weary, and heart weary, and she didn't care about her clothes.

She slung on her belt and settled her seax. The haft was newly wrapped with rough ray skin, one of Mulstan's parting gifts—the rest of the ray skin would make her popular with the gesiths, Fursey said; he was scratching his head over whom they should favour. Later today, she and her mother would meet with Coelgar to discuss Hild's treasure, which had gone to York from the wall, and to decide what equivalents from the Goodmanham hoard she should be awarded. Part of her personal treasure had been a bolt of silk given in Alt Clut, but Onnen had told her privately at the time that it was old and no doubt rotten in places.

Onnen had a better idea of what, exactly, had been on that packhorse, but Onnen was not here.

As she combed her hair with her fingers she turned, as was now her habit, to the north and east, the direction of the Bay of the Beacon, to Cian and Begu. She tucked her hair behind her ears. Perhaps Onnen combed Begu's hair now.

Today she would attend her mother in the main weaving hut. Post-shearing, when hands were soft and smooth with sheep grease, was when the most intricate patterns using the most delicate yarns were set up on the looms. She was the only ungirdled girl to work on the main loom, the only one tall enough. The only one with the pattern-making mind, her mother said. The only one without a gemæcce.

She refused to think about the beautifully carved but clumsily painted box on its shelf above her bed, the eight ivory wafers wrapped in violet linen.

Fursey happened to be lurking at the bottom of the hall steps. His skirts were clean, well cut, and very black; his forehead tonsure smooth and shining; his cross made of heavy gold. Not long after they arrived at Good-manham, Hild had seen a priest who had come about other business give him a freighted look, and she'd known, from watching her mother all these years, that later, when no one would see, there would be an exchange of information and a small, heavy purse.

"I'll walk with you," he said. Hild nodded. They both walked care-fully, with their skirts held high; it had been a dry month. The dust made Fursey sneeze. In the distance four men shouted and swore as they whipped the oxen hauling a freshly cut oak for the expanded temple enclosure Edwin had given Coifi leave to erect. One ox lifted its tail and squirted shit.

Fursey said, "May they have time to enjoy their heathen temple."

She wanted to know what he meant but in the game they played she lost points if she had to ask.

"I'd give them a year. Two at most."

She said nothing, hoping her silence would goad him into explaining.

Two wealh, edge-rolling a half-full barrel of stale urine towards the hut where the fleece would be washed later in the day, saw Fursey and straightened. As they passed, Fursey made a hand gesture, the one Hild now knew was a sign of Christ's cross. The darker wealh bowed. The urine stank. The barrel had been by the door of the hall for a month, gradually filling, but in the open air its sudden reek made Hild want to wipe the inside of her mouth with her sleeve.

They walked on. Fursey was still silent, still smiling when they reached the sunken weaving hut where today she would work with her mother. Her mother, who hadn't said a word when Hild came back without Onnen.

Hild stopped by the southwest corner of the low roof where the door, like a trapdoor, lay open. "You can't come inside," she said.

"Well, no. But you'll both be coming out soon enough."

"Not today. We've a deal of work."

"Oh, yes. Today. Today most definitely."

She paused with her palm on the first rung of the short elm ladder leading down to the weaving floor, but Fursey just smiled at her. She shook her head, not wanting to play his game today, swung herself onto the ladder, and climbed down.

The hut was small and square, with a beaten-earth floor and brightly coloured loom weights stacked by size on narrow shelves. The loom was in the northeast corner, flooded with light. Beside it stood her mother.

Breguswith blazed with triumph. She shivered with it. Her eyes flashed brighter than the blue-glazed loom weights, brighter than the lapis on her veil band, brighter than the hilt inlay on her edgeless Kentish sword, thrust through her belt, which she used as a weft beater.

"Rædwald is dead!"

Hild stood very still. Rædwald. Overking of all the Angles, who had helped Edwin kill Æthelfrith and drive the Idings into exile. Sulky Eorpwald, Rædwald's second son, who had been too young to fight at Edwin's side. Eorpwald, who would step into the kingship of the East Angles—but Edwin would inherit the mantle of overking, the most powerful Angle in Britain.

Hild saw immediately what this meant for them. "Hereswith," she said. Hereswith. So soon.

Her mother nodded. Hereswith was now an overking's peaceweaver. This was Breguswith's chance to build for the family power and kinship beyond Northumbria, beyond her own kin in Kent. They would need it.

All kings fell, even overkings; it was their nature. And Edwin had many enemies, not least of them his own kin—though no one spoke of Tinamutha and Bebbanburg, and cousin Osric's betrayal, not even Hild and her mother: *Never say the dangerous thing aloud.* Hereswith's marriage would give them a second power holding. But it meant she would leave.

"Eorpwald is married, of course, but he's weak. And when he topples, his sons will be too young for kingship. The power then would fall sideways to the sons of Eni."

Eni, Rædwald's dead brother. "Æthelric Short Leg," Hild said. The eldest, already subking and lord of the North Folk, who called him Ecgric. Hereswith and Æthelric. "How does she feel about marrying a man with the same name as granfa?" How does she feel about leaving her family? But it was always her wyrd.

"We'll find out. After the king has the news."

Mother and daughter considered each other. Different hair, different eyes, different hearts. Both tall enough that people whispered of etin blood. Both with bright, pattern-making minds.

Hild said, "When will she leave us? Or . . ." *Hereswith needs training.* Hereswith was the eldest, the best path to power. "Will you . . . will you go with her?"

"Oh, we'll all go. If I know Edwin. A royal progress. The king, the æthelings. All the royal family. Even Osric."

Especially Osric. You didn't leave powerful kin of questionable loyalty at your back. But who would stay in East Anglia?

Breguswith slid her beater up and down in her belt, thinking. "The overking must show his wealth, the loyalty of his men. Every belt buckle must be gold, every chape silver, every veil like gossamer. Shoes will be new, rings heavy, horses proud. We will shine. We must move swiftly. I've sent messages, and I have people whispering in Eorpwald king's ear and those of his ealdormen, but Eorpwald's mind is as shallow as a milk tray, easily swayed by gold closer to hand. Others will be bidding for Æthelric. Even though your sister is now the overking's peaceweaver, we must show our strength and make our persuasions in person."

Someone at the top of the ladder sneezed.

Breguswith smiled. "He may come, too." She raised her voice slightly. "Only tell him he must find more subtlety in his messengers. I had word of this one's coming long, aye long, before his arrival, and could have seen to it that his message never arrived."

Hild said nothing. She knew Fursey, knew the sound of his sneeze; that one had been deliberate. Her head was full.

"We'll finish setting up this pattern, but the weaving we'll leave to others. We must bend our minds to our plans."

But it was nearly middæg and the weaving hut was brimming with buttercup light when they tied off the last loom weight. Breguswith tested the tension of the warp. "We've been too long here. I don't know what's wrong with you today."

Hild nodded. She hadn't said a word for hours. Her mouth felt turned to stone. Hereswith. Hereswith and Begu and Cian and Onnen.

"You'll talk to Coelgar on your own. Or take that clever priest of yours. He likes to dicker. I must see the king."

Hild nodded again. She would be glad not to attend Edwin. She had her father's hair, more so every day. When her uncle was thinking of power and dynasty it was best not to come to his attention. And she had a lot to think about.

Already middæg. She had no time to find the hornbeam over the river, her preferred thinking perch. She made for the kitchen garth. At this time of day, the herbs would already have been snipped and the rhubarb pulled, and in the shadow of the south wall, overhung by the orchard apples and plums, it would be cool and quiet.

But when she got there, she found a young wealh with thick eyebrows and pretty black hair spreading manure from a loosely woven brown willow basket. The garden stank.

"You," she said, and the wealh dropped the basket and ran to where Hild stood by the gate. "You know Fursey the Christ priest?"

The wealh bobbed her head.

"Find him. Bring him."

When the wealh had gone, Hild moved to the bed of lavender, for the smell, and sat on the grass. Bees bumbled from bloom to bloom. Such clumsy creatures, always bumping into things. She followed the progress of one from the lavender to the foxgloves, which her mother said was good for the faint of heart. Would Hereswith quail? Or would she blaze with triumph like their mother and walk away without a backward glance? The king would never let Hild go, not now. Not until she was dead or of no more use.

The furry bee crawled inside the flower bell, emerged a moment later covered in gold, like a triumphant queen. She didn't want to think about queens. Its legs looked thicker, too. She stood and followed as it bumbled over to the pots of weld growing near the kitchen door. She knelt and waited for the bee to emerge.

Behind her, the gate creaked. Hild turned: the wealh, now looking pale. Hild realised she was kneeling in shit, and the wealh, wise in the ways of the world, knew she would most likely be blamed. But then the gate creaked again, and Hild dismissed the wealh from her thoughts.

Fursey walked carefully. She could smell the white mead from here.

He smiled at her expression. "It's a big day: Edwin, overking. It's important for a foreigner to drink the overking's health and life with enthusiasm, to show loyalty."

Hild just pointed at his cross, which hung twisted. While he fumbled with it, she went back to the lavender and sat. The bees were still bumbling about. Stupid bees. They were all stupid. Or maybe just her.

"You let my mother know what you're about," she said, in Irish, just in case. "On purpose. My mother knows this. And you two are deep in your game, and I am one of those bees, sent by the queen bee to buzz from hive to flower, not knowing what's really going on."

"Well," he said. "I'm surprised it took you so long." He settled comfortably on the path by her feet and smiled blandly. "So, now. You dragged me away from my mead for a pressing reason?"

Her thoughts tangled in her head. Hereswith. Her mother. Hereswith. She was so lonely. Edwin. Plots . . . After a helpless moment she told him instead about Coelgar and the negotiation planned for middæg.

Fursey nodded and, while clearly aware of her frustration, asked her sensible questions about the weight of dishes and their size, the lustre of the cloth Coelgar had carried off to York.

"And do you want treasure of like kind—a dish for a dish, a jewel for a jewel—or what the treasure represents?"

But Hild tugged some more at the knot in her head. "What did you mean, you're surprised it took me so long?"

Fursey glanced at the wealh, working her way up the lavender bed with her manure basket. "I'd recommend gold and hacksilver, and yes, some silk if they have it. Gold is well and good, but it's not subtle. Silk as a gift is subtle. And while you have fripperies for men—I've taken the liberty already of gifting Coelgar, the æthelings, your mother's men Burgræd and Burgmod, and young Lintlaf with your ray skins—you've not many for women."

The wealh began moving back down the bed on the other side.

"What I meant was what I said. You had many clues—Christ knows I laid them nicely in your path—but you were slow picking them up. These days there is no luxury to be slow. Events are moving from a trot to a canter. Soon they will gallop. You must have a firm hand on the reins. And you must learn to look ahead—"

"I always look ahead. I'm a seer."

"Take your mother. You spoke of her as a queen bee. That's because she thinks herself a queen."

"She should have been."

"But she is not. Remember that. The world is full of should-have would-have. As your poets say, 'Fate goes ever as it must.' You must, you must, learn to see the world as it is."

Hild was so sick of musts. She plucked a stalk of lavender and sniffed at it.

Fursey tapped her on the arm. "You'd rather smell lavender than shit. I understand. You're not yet eleven. Your father is dead. Your sister is leaving. Your, well, let us say your childhood companion has left already. The king fears you—oh, yes, he does. Listen now. It is true that a maid two years from her womanhood should not have to see the world as it is, but you're not a maid. No, I said listen now. You are a prophet and seer with the brightest mind in an age. Your blood is that of the man who should have been king and a woman who is half sister to the king of Kent and wants to be a queen. That's what the king and his lords see. And they will kill you, one day. If not Edwin, then the king who kills him."

She threw her lavender at the wall. A bee zuzzed in surprise and bumped into the apple budding on a bough overhanging the wall.

"Of course, they've already tried. But you know that."

She looked at him.

"Ah, now, that's better. And you know who, too. The king's cousin— your cousin—at the mouth of the Tine."

Hild's spine went rigid.

Fursey smiled. "No one can hear us. I walked the orchard before I came to find you. Always remember that: Scout the ground. The only person nearby is that slave. And even if she has the Irish, which I doubt, she isn't close enough. So let us speak of what the king will not: cousin Osric sitting athwart the Tine valley and its flow of trade from the whole north and east. The man who has almost as great a claim to Deira as your uncle, and near as many men."

She shook her head. *Never say the dangerous thing aloud.* Never.

Fursey waved to get the wealh's attention. He called, "If you're about finished with this lovely manure, the lady and I would appreciate a jug of beer." The wealh put down her manure basket and approached.

She bobbed her head. "Father?"

He repeated his request in Anglisc. She bobbed again, then glanced at Hild, who, after a moment, nodded. "But bring small beer." Before Fursey could protest she said, "Coelgar is a canny bargainer. I don't want you any drunker."

When the wicker gate slapped behind the wealh, Fursey said, "They treat you like a prince, so think like one. Your mother does. She's already planning. She'll wed your sister to the man who'll become king of the East Angles. Why?"

"So we'll have somewhere to run. When it's time."

He laughed. "Do you really think so little of your mother? No. Try again."

Hild went blank.

"Think. What do you know of Rædwald?"

"He's dead."

"And?"

"And he was rich."

"Ah. Good. And?"

"But I don't see what good it is to be rich if someone like my uncle with all his gesiths will come along and take it all away."

"What do you think pays for gesiths? Gold. And there's as much gold to be had from trade as from killing a man and taking his. More. Think. See the whole isle. Who controls the flow of trade?"

She hadn't thought about this before. "Osric?"

"He controls the trade that flows from the north to the Tine valley." From the Picts, the Gododdin, the Bernicians, the north Deirans. "But Rædwald, now Eorpwald, soon Æthelric, controls the Anglisc trade for all of the south, trade with Frankia, Rome, Iberia."

Suddenly she saw the whole east side of the isle as one strong warp, weighted by the overking, with the main pattern wefts flowing through Tinamutha and Gipswīc, lesser threads through Lindum and the Humber, and minor threads like the Bay of the Beacon. But cloth had more than one warp.

Fursey was nodding. "Now you begin to see. Who hates your uncle with a deep and abiding hatred?"

"Cadfan and his son Cadwallon."

"Why?"

Hild didn't see what that had to do with anything. "Because my uncle was foster-son to Cadfan, and he and Cadwallon quarrelled—"

"Ha! That old Cain and Abel story. No doubt they did quarrel, boys do, but this is a hatred of kings. The fight for wealth and power. For gold. Edwin is now overking of the Anglisc. All ports in the east bow to him. Just as all ports in the west bow to Cadfan. Dál Riata and Alt Clut, Rheged and the Irish—to reach the wines of the Franks, the priests of Rome, they must all bend the knee to Gwynedd."

Hild frowned. "Sometimes ships from Less Britain stop at Caer Uisc in Dyfneint."

"And Dyfneint bends the knee to Cadfan of Gwynedd."

It was true. "But my mother, and Hereswith—"

"Someone will be overking after your uncle. Your mother is plotting. With East Anglia in her pocket—"

"She'll gather the next weft. Osric?"

"Perhaps. But don't forget the Idings, also your cousins. Most of them."

Not Eanfrith, the eldest. His mother was Bebba of the Bryneich. But when she'd died Æthelfrith had taken Edwin's sister Acha to wife. Hild's aunt. *You're all cousins in this benighted wood.* She couldn't remember who'd said that.

A thought struck her. "And you. You're woven through the other warp."

He tilted his head and smiled slyly. "My king hates your king. But he also hates the other Irish kings and the Dál Riata, who are sheltering the younger Idings. So we might be on the same side. Or we might not. But the end of that song is not yet written. For just a little while, at least, I am your friend."

The gate creaked.

"Blessings upon you!" Fursey called to the wealh in Anglisc, while making the Christ sign at her with one hand and taking the beer with the other. Hild wished that she had let the wealh bring full beer, or even mead. Hereswith. Osric. *Hereswith* . . .

Fursey drank, sighed with pleasure, drank again, handed the jar to Hild, and stood. "And now we must go talk to a man about a dish."

After the long negotiation with Coelgar—though Fursey did most of it—it was a relief to step into the dairy shed. The windows and doors were hung with gauzy white cloth, which let in light and air but not flies. The smell of curdling milk coated the back of her throat. The floor, like the weaving hut's, was hard-packed dirt, almost black from a decade of milk spills.

She walked past the rows of benches holding lidded clay pots nested in straw where the warm skimmed milk was clabbering, down a step and through a heavy elm door to a cooler room, the creamery.

Mildburh had a two-handed grip on a butter churn and was pumping it up and down, up and down. Along her spine, her pink underdress had darkened to red. She turned at the waft of warm air through the door and smiled, but didn't stop churning. Hereswith, sleeves unpinned and hanging through her girdle, did not even look up. She was tilting one of the shallow square oak trays where the milk had lain since yesterday morning's milking for the cream to rise to the top. As the tray tilted to the bottom right corner, she leaned forward and laid her right forearm across the lip, pouring thin greyish skim milk in an expert stream from the corner into a brown pot and collecting cream in a thick lake against her arm. When the stream stopped she let the tray lie flat again and ran her forearm lightly along the edge to skim off the cream. Then she looked at Hild.

Hild hadn't set foot inside a dairy since she had left with the war band.

Hereswith looked deliberately at the empty churn in the corner, then back to Hild. "Does the king's seer, armed and dangerous, wish to sully her hands?"

Hild didn't know whether to stab her sister or kiss her. But that's what sisters were for.

She set the lid to one side and picked up the churn by one of its handles. She examined the carved tools hanging from the wall and selected a flat-bladed spatula. She carried both to Hereswith.

"I'll lift," she said. Hereswith frowned, but Hild wasn't smaller anymore. She picked up one end of the tray. It didn't weigh as much as she thought it would, and she tilted it too sharply. Hereswith slid the open churn under the tray just in time and used the scoop to guide the slipping cream.

Mildburh's churn paddle thumped up and down more slowly as her cream turned to butter.

Hild and Hereswith moved on to the next tray and then the next. They worked smoothly until all the trays were empty. Mildburh turned the butter out of her churn onto a granite slab set in an elm bench, and she began to shape it with wooden paddles.

While Hereswith wiped her arm and pinned her sleeves back on, Hild fetched a lump of grey salt for Mildburh and mortar and pestle to crush it in. She loved the gritty *crunch* and *thump* under her hand. It sounded like a cat eating a bird.

When they were done, Hereswith brought them a dipper of buttermilk and they drank. Hild wondered how many times they had shared buttermilk in the dairy and if they ever would again.

Hereswith wiped the flecks of butter from her chin and said to Hild, "You're stronger."

"I'm bigger."

Hereswith nodded, looked her over. "Taller than Mildburh."

"As tall as you."

It came out as a challenge, and two years ago it would have led to a fight, but after a moment Hereswith said only, "But not even half as filled out. You're as straight up and down as that ridiculous knife."

"It's a very useful knife."

"It's a very big knife," Mildburh said.

"I cut an Irishman with it."

Mildburh looked horrified and thrilled. "Did you kill him?"

"No. But he bled a lot. And shrieked."

"Men don't shriek," Hereswith said.

What did her sister know of such things?

"Was he trying to have his way with you?" Mildburh said.

Hild stared. The thought had never occurred to her.

Hereswith laughed. "No," she said to Mildburh, "he was probably just trying to steal the king's prophet. She's worth a king's ransom, they say. Even if she looks like a slave wealh in that dress."

Hild let that pass.

Mildburh slid her arm through Hereswith's and looked at Hild. "They say you saved us all at Bebbanburg with your seeing. Do you . . . see anything about our coming journey?"

Mildburh's eyes were muddy, honest blue, like bilberries. Hereswith's were as blue as their mother's, but without the cold blaze. No, Hild wanted to say. *I see nothing. Let's churn the cream and salt the butter and gossip about your husband-to-be.* But what could an ungirdled girl have to say about husbands? Except as threads in the great pattern woven by others. And what would they want to hear about travel and sleeping outside a hall?

They were still looking at her. She put her hand on her knife. "I see that you will travel safely." How could they not? They'd be travelling with twelvescore gesiths and an army of housefolk.

She cut through the byre on the way back from the dairy shed. It smelt of sun on hay and of horse more than cow. At this time of year, the household horses were in their outdoor corral and even the milch cows were at pasture. Two stalls, though, were occupied: a shaggy bay pony and a tall roan gelding. She looked automatically at their hooves and tails.

The roan was shod in dark, high-quality iron, the hooves oiled, the tail long and well brushed. A horse from a royal stable. It was eating single-mindedly but at her approach lifted its head and rolled its eye. She did not step too close. A horse used hard and often, but no cut marks where you might expect them. A beast valued by its rider. She studied the length and strength of its leg muscle: one of the heavy Frankish mixed breeds. The Oiscingas of Kent had Frankish tastes in horses and cloaks, religion and jewels. So it had been a man of Kent who had spoken to her mother before speaking to the king. How did Kent connect to the east warp or the west warp? She tucked that in the back of her mind to discuss with Fursey.

The pony was a calm, even-tempered mare with a curious eye. A typical priest mount: ridden, no doubt, by the man who supplied Fursey's information. She felt the skin between its forelegs. Cool and dry: stabled long since. The little pony snorted and when she patted its withers its skin wrinkled under her hand, and the feel of it took Hild back to a wintry day by the redcrests' wall, climbing onto Ilfetu's back just as the wind blew her cloak sideways, making the gelding's skin twitch. Hild leaned her head against the pony's neck, breathed that horse smell that reminded her of so many things, so many people. "Perhaps you are sister to Cian's Acærn," she whispered in British, the first time in months she had spoken that tongue. "Perhaps you will see him and Ilfetu on your travels. Tell him I miss, I miss . . ." Her throat closed. She straightened, said in Anglisc, "But no doubt Cian has a fine new horse now, to go with his fine sword and his foster-sister."

The court did not leave that month, nor the month after. They would be a great company, four hundred strong, and riders must be sent ahead. An overking travelling with his court did not sleep on the ground, did not go uncombed or eat squirrels and figwort in the lee of a wall. He did not break his teeth on more-grit-than-grain ceorl bread, or let the ribs of his horse show through from lack of oats. He did not ride with one fist on his sword and his helm to hand but confidently, in brilliant clothes, to be seen, knowing his guard had cleared the road for half a mile ahead and to each side. He must be the pip at the centre of an apple of perfect safety and unstinting bounty. He must be as close to a god as any but priests ever saw.

Eventually, as the boughs of plum trees began to sag under their own weight, as the cornfields turned gold, as the constant hum of honeybees dropped a tone and maggots fattened themselves on the soft ripe fruit of brambles, they rode out from Goodmanham in great splendour.

Edwin, Osric—whose stripling son, Oswine, and daughter, Osthryth, had been left in Bebbanburg with Coelgar, "for safety"—the æthelings, and Hild rode bare-armed, draped in blue and gold, horses glinting with gold at headstall, tail strap, and saddle. Their scabbard chapes were chased and gilded and their hilts winked with garnet and blue enamel.

Breguswith and Hereswith rode under a canopy held by two of Coelgar's men, with Burgmod and Burgræd riding behind, hands self-consciously on swords. Tomorrow the two women would ride in the wagons with Ædilgith and Folcwyn and the others, like coddled eggs, but today they rode on display. They wore marigold dresses with deep red borders and boots the colour of owl breasts, and as soft. Their ears and veil bands glinted with lapis and gold. Hereswith's horse, a dark bay gelding, even had blue beads braided into its mane. Beside them, Mildburh wore the colours of her kin, the dead queen Cwenburh, a spring green, but with her gemæcce's colours, marigold and red, in the tablet weave at wrist and neck.

The king's gesiths' belts and baldric buckles could each have rendered enough gold to buy a prize ram and two ewes. Osric's were scarcely less splendid, and even the men of the Deiran thegns Wilgar and Trumwine could have been the gesiths of lesser kings. Many rode still spattered across face and sword arm with the blood of the sacrificial bullock. Coifi would stay in Goodmanham, home of his god, praying for an easy journey brimming with good fortune. He had promised the new enclosure by the time they returned. Hild still hadn't asked Fursey what he'd meant by his remark about them only having a year or two to enjoy it. How did that fit into the great weave?

Fursey rode a creamy gelding. No priest pony for him. He rode now as a prince of Munster, with marten fur trimming his fine black robe and rings on his fingers—though being in skirts he carried no sword. And behind everything creaked the swaying wagons, pulled by oxen with white-painted horns. One wagon, the one with the gilded elm wheel hubs and the pliant willow bed covered with feather bolsters, Hereswith's wagon, had a pale, sueded covering painted with the Deiran boar's head in blood-red. Later, of course, that covering would be taken down and folded carefully until their triumphal entry into the vill of the king of the East Angles, and a plain brown leather awning raised in its stead. But even that leather was the finest cowhide, dyed in one batch to the colour of walnuts.

It took them nine days to travel from Goodmanham to Lindum, a prosperous wool-and-leather trading centre overflowing its crumbling Roman walls. The war band, taking it easy, could have done it in two—less if they'd been willing to abuse their horses—but the wagons were like houses on wheels and not to be hurried. They stayed only one night. The city reminded Hild of Caer Luel, though less ruined and more patched: thatching on the roofs where the tiles had fallen away, timber replacing broken stone lintels. The chief man, Cuelgils, called himself princeps. The walls of his great hall were painted like the fading pictures in the understorey of the hall at York.

"Princeps," Fursey had snorted, during the usual ceremonies. "I doubt he can even read." But he'd said it in Irish, just in case.

The milestone outside Lindum, beyond the city's tannery and wool-fulling stench, was made of pale grey stone, as thick as Hild's thigh and taller than a tall man on a horse. It was much taller than Fursey. Taller even than Lintlaf, the hero of the ride to Tinamutha and proud as Thunor of the new gold ring from the king, glinting at the hilt of his sword. But a hero needs to constantly burnish his deeds in the eyes of others, he must seek out opportunities to shine, and Lintlaf had appointed himself guardian to the strange maid and the prince-priest. The two reeked of wyrd. Something was bound to happen at some point, and his name would be gilded by songs of fresh prowess.

When they reined in by the stone, therefore, so did Lintlaf, and the column of wagons toiled on into the overcast afternoon.

When Fursey and Hild dismounted, Lintlaf sighed. He loosened his sword just in case, though the road hereabouts was well cleared of scrub and any possible hiding place for wild men and robbers.

While their horses stood patiently nose to nose, the maid and the Irish priest walked around the stone. The day was hot and bright as dirty water, with no sharp shadows, no clean wind. Perhaps the gods would fight later, throwing insult and thunderbolt at each other then weeping with rage until the ditches at either side of the road runnelled and gushed with their tears.

" 'Durobrivae something miles,' " the maid read to Fursey. She had to stand on her tiptoes to touch the wind-scoured numbers: LII. "The citizens of Lindum paid for this road. Is that right?"

"It is."

"But on the last one it said Emperor Caracalla restored the roads 'which had fallen into ruin and disuse through old age.' " The priest said nothing. "Fifty-two!" the maid said triumphantly. "Fifty-two miles to Durobrivae! What's Durobrivae?"

"The place fifty-two miles farther south on this road."

Which Lintlaf suspected meant he had no idea.

It was hot, and it seemed the stone would tell them nothing more. They walked back to where Lintlaf held their horses. He led the horses to a piece of stone—part of a broken wall of some redcrest building of long ago—which the priest used first to mount. As Lintlaf handed the maid her reins and she boosted herself into the saddle, he nodded at the milestone and said, "Are the runes favourable?"

"We'll be in Durobrivae in . . . nine days. If the gods give us good weather."

He looked at the sky and shook his head. "At least the rain will cut the dust."

The priest rinsed his mouth with beer and spat. "Even dust is better than mud."

"Too bad," Lintlaf said. Gloomy lot, priests, no matter who they prayed to.

They cantered along the soft side of the road, Fursey sneezing in the wagon dust, until they reached the front, where they settled in behind the æthelings. Edwin beckoned Hild forward.

"What did the stones tell you?"

"That it's the same distance to Durobrivae as we've travelled from Goodmanham."

"And did the stones tell you that the road is very good for a while, so that we'll do nine days' travel in eight?"

She shook her head.

"I travelled this road eight years ago."

Eight years ago. When he'd taken the throne that should have been her father's, her father who died poisoned like a dog.

Edwin's horse sidestepped. "Don't look at me like that." He had his thumb on his seax. Then he relaxed and laughed. "Eight years, eh, Lilla?"

Lilla said, "It rained then, too, my king."

"So it did. But this time we have servants, and this time we're in no hurry." And he shouted at Coelgar's young son, who was riding ahead with the standard-bearer. "Coelfrith! Send your men to find a place to stop." He sniffed the still air. "There's a river nearby. Bound to be a place to shelter and eat something hot before the weather gods start their games."

They stopped a mile farther on, where a well-used trackway showed many travellers before had turned off the road to the graceful curve of a river with two convenient hills, a mixed hazel and oak wood, and what might have been the ruins of a bridge from the bank to the little island midstream.

The gesiths had time for an hour's war play—they formed two shield walls and took turns pushing each other across the meadow and trying to stab at lower legs and feet with their leaf-bladed spears—and the housefolk to heat the porridge and roasted sheep and heather beer Cuelgils had given them in parting, before hissing rain turned their fires to ash and mud.

Some of the younger gesiths, half drunk, staged small group attacks with sword and shield. Like Hild, the older ones sought shelter. They knew from long experience that beer wears off by dark but clothes stay damp until morning, and wet blades and chain-link armour rust slowly and thoroughly if not sanded and regreased immediately.

Hild sat in her mother and sister's wagon while the rain drummed on the waxed canvas pegged tentlike over the oiled leather canopy. The rain was coming straight down, so Breguswith had left the doorway unlaced, for the air and light.

They sat on the padded floor, their backs against cushioned chests cunningly carpentered to hold a variety of objects safely as they travelled. Breguswith and Hereswith talked quietly of etiquette in the south and eastern Angle courts, with Mildburh occasionally adding her perspective on the Saxons. Ædilgith and Folcwyn embroidered the sleeves of a dress, though Folcwyn spent more time wiping her forehead and neck than plying her needle. Hild lay with her head on Hereswith's thigh, half listening, half drowsing, tolling through the carnelians around her wrist. She wondered what Ædilgith and Folcwyn thought about having to stay among the East Anglisc with Hereswith, and what Cian might be doing at the Bay of the Beacon.

Breguswith talked about ancestry. When she talked about her relatives, the Oiscingas of Kent, her Jutish accent broadened. Hild listened to the familiar chant. Her uncle Æthelberht, dead king of Kent. Her cousin Eadbald, now king of Kent. Æthelwald, her younger cousin, ætheling of Kent and prince of the West Kentishmen.

Hild tolled a bead, a big one, the one the colour of an old flame. Eadbald, uncle. She didn't bother with Æthelwald—he was sickly—and Eadbald already had two sons.

Ricula, Breguswith's aunt, married Sledd, of the East Saxons. Breguswith paused and looked at Hereswith, who chanted, "Sledd, father of Sabert, the father of Sæward, now dead, and Seaxred king."

"And Seaxbald," Mildburh said.

Hild tolled a little bead, the one with the brown occlusion like a drying wound. Seaxbald, cousin.

"They have a sister," Breguswith said to Hereswith. "Saewara. Now wife to Anna." Anna, Æthelric Short Leg's younger brother and heir. "You'll have a cousin at court."

Saewara, cousin. Enemy or friend?

The West Saxons, Breguswith went on, Cynegils and his three sons, were friendly enough with their eastern kin.

She sorted through her beads to find the asymmetrical one, deep angry red. Cynegils of the Gewisse. Then three reddish-orange beads for his sons. One had a chip. She named that one Cwichelm, the eldest. Bad-tempered, all of them, and greedy.

Lightning cracked. Young, drunken gesiths hooted. Hild knew they would be jabbing their spears at the sky, daring Thunor to fling one of his bolts at them. She'd seen Thunor answer such a taunt, last year, just south of the wall. Thunor did not like to be made game of.

Fursey would be with the older gesiths and thegns, gaming, drinking, picking their thoughts. She pondered the Frankish horses in the Goodmanham byre, the fact that her mother had the news of Rædwald's death before Edwin, before the king. Her mother was a daughter of kings, widow of a man who should have been king, mother of a future queen, cousin to every court in the land and not a few across the sea. And yet Fursey had had the news earlier still. How?

The rain surged. The wagon rocked slightly under the weight of water. The ropes thrummed. Breguswith's voice rose and fell.

They rode through a land washed clean and humming with plenty, Lintlaf frankly dozing in the saddle behind them. His mail smelt of rust.

Hild tolled through her beads for Fursey, explaining who was the biggest and most brightly coloured, and why.

"You have forgotten the most powerful of all." He leaned across her and tapped a small, fiery bead, almost yellow in the morning sun. "You forgot Christ."

"A god?" He wasn't supposed to talk about that.

"A decidedly worldly influence. The Frankish queen who married your uncle in Kent brought Romans with her. Not soldiers but priests. Bishops."

She shrugged. "The wealh have bishops." A mangy lot.

"Roman bishops are different. They're as much ealdormen as priests."

Hild scratched the back of her hand. After the rain, midges were swarming.

"These priestly reeves collect not for their king but for the bishop of Rome."

The bishop of Rome. A kind of priestly overking, then, but unacknowledged. She tried to imagine a system of ealdormen who were reeving for an overking no one knew about. "Why don't the kings kill the reeving priests?"

Fursey smiled.

"They're useful to him?"

"Very. They read."

They read.

The sense of the world shifting was so strong she swayed in the saddle. They read.

One man in Kent or East Anglia could write something and give it to a man, who could gallop until he and his horse were half dead, then pass it to another man, a stranger, who also could gallop, or board a ship, and pass it to another messenger, and another. The message would cross the island in a day. It wouldn't be garbled. It couldn't be intercepted and understood by any but priests. *Shave-pated spies.* Not just skirt on one side and sword on the other but book balanced against blade.

"Close your mouth, it will fill with flies." He looked enormously pleased with himself.

8

✦

THE GLORY THAT WAS THE VAST AND GLITTERING vill of Rendlesham
made Edwin very angry indeed. But he chewed his moustaches in private. In public—sitting at table with Eorpwald in the great and graceful
hall with the beautifully tiled Roman-style floor and painted walls, riding
past the golden cornfields to get to the king's forest flickering with game,
inspecting the vill's port two miles away at Woodbridge with its acres of
sail-making and rope-making yards—he smiled and smiled. His gesiths,
who had seen this smile before, turned their dread into boasts and picked
fights wherever they went; Breguswith was kept busy with willow bark
and comfrey, mint and lavender oil, malt vinegar and honey. Even old
Burgræd dislocated his knee in a wrestling match. Breguswith wrenched
it back into place without a word and slapped on a poultice of warmed oat-
meal. She did not offer him willow-bark tea or her more precious helle-
bore. She had no time for this foolishness: There were Kentish envoys,
public and not so public, with whom she would rather be conferring. She,
too, began to smoulder.

Hereswith was as tense as a dog before a fight. Æthelric, ætheling of
the East Angles and prince of the North Folk, who called him Ecgric,
would arrive that day from his hall at Deorham.

She drove Mildburh, Ædilgith, and Folcwyn to distraction changing
her mind: She wanted the lapis braided into her hair and sewn to her veil;
no, she wanted the garnets and pearls; no, the beryl and jet. Hild watched
her hurl a veil at Mildburh, and then, as it floated airily to the polished

board of the floor, snatch it back and tear it to pieces. Her sister wanted to cry, but she was a woman grown. No one must see her tears, not even her women, for fear of bringing shame on the family name. There was nothing Hild could do. This was Hereswith's wyrd; it had been since Cwenburh's death.

Fursey seemed untouched by the tensions of the rest of the Northumbrian party. He and Lintlaf had formed an unlikely friendship. One moment they would be laughing over a woman who dropped her basket of eggs when a crow lifted its wings and crak-crakked at her—a very bad omen, but only for the one so scolded—the next seeing who could skip a stone clear across the fishpond where the geese swam.

Hild found them annoying. They disturbed everything. One had to sit still and quiet to really see, really hear. She sent them to visit the temple Rædwald had built a decade before his death, and took herself off to the priests' meeting place at the edge of the beech coppice by the stream. She settled out of sight in the deep, dappled shade cast by an uncoppiced tree. Beeches were rare north of the Humber, and she loved the way they whispered in the wind, like women before they fell asleep.

The black-robed Christ priests had flocked like crows to the vill after Rædwald's death. They all worked for different kings, some with the crown shaved—Romans—some with the forehead shaved, but they all wanted Eorpwald to acknowledge the Christ god, all wanted to be allowed to start reeving among the East Angles in his name. Did the shaved foreheads have an overbishop, like the overbishop of Rome? When they rose one by one to speak to the group they spoke Latin, but from the smaller groups Hild heard Frankish, Irish, the comforting Jutish dialects of young Kentish priests, even, she thought, Greek. But no British.

Frankish was a strange, Latin-stained tongue. She understood perhaps one word in three. As always when trying to learn a new language, she opened her mind and let the sound wash through it.

An ant ran over her hand, and another. They shone in the sun like tiny drops of amber. When she was little she had crushed one creeping on a bench to find out what was inside it to make it glow like that. But it had left nothing but a dark smear on the wood. She ignored them.

A man was speaking intensely, passionately, with a strong accent, spattering words about him like molten glass. She closed her eyes. She didn't understand most of it—heresy, apostasy, Gehenna—but he seemed upset about something Eorpwald had done.

She was tired of listening to irritable people. She stood up and brushed the ants and dust from her skirts. She would go watch the goldsmiths. Eorpwald had two—and three armourers and two blacksmiths.

There were more than two dozen men and boys, and a handful of women, working in the bend of the River Deben. The air was busy with the rasp of files, the chink of chisels, and the shirring thump of the slurry tub. It smelt of charcoal and clay, hot metal and wax. Four guards in matching leather tunics stood beneath a huge elm. Sun glinted on the scabbard of her seax as she approached, and they straightened and lifted their spears. Then they saw it was only a maid and grounded their spears again. The two boys at the slurry tub paused in their shaking of the watery clay until a woman at the polishing bench shouted at them.

The chief goldsmith wore a thumb ring and a thick silver twist in his long hair, and his slave collar was a mere gesture, light as a lady's necklace. He was a Svear. A long-ago sword cut had laid open the left side of his jaw and knocked out all the teeth there. Hild picked her way between the workbenches and waited quietly by his place, careful not to come between him and the light. Eventually the Svear paused, blinked at her, then shouted something mushy and broken over his shoulder. A slave—his collar was heavy—grumbling in Irish, stepped from the heat and shadow of the furnace shelter, wiping his brow with his forearm. He took one look at the cut of her dress, the gold at wrist and waist, that huge seax, and rushed to fetch a little three-legged stool.

He dusted it with his hand, withdrew a pace, and cleared his throat.

"Would the little miss care for some water, at all? It being a hot day. And there being a spring close by." But he kept glancing back at his furnace.

"What's your name?"

"Finmail. Fin."

"Fin, you have something on the fire?"

"I do, mistress."

"Then see to it." She looked at the benches of enamellers, chasers, polishers. "I am not here."

Fin frowned.

"I am not," she said in Irish, and met his sky-blue gaze with her own. He bowed and retreated.

She turned to the Svear, spoke clearly and carefully. "I will watch, if I may."

He nodded and went back to his work, moulding something palm-size from wax.

At the next bench, a towheaded man rolled wax into little sticks and, with a knife heated in boiling water, cut their ends and fused them to another tiny wax sculpture.

A boy ran up with a heavy faggot of stripped ash twiglets, the kind of thing left after the cattle have eaten everything useful from their winter tree hay. He added it to the fire. The towheaded man put the wax model carefully on a wooden tray. A woman took the tray—again, carefully— and carried it to the slurry tub. At the tub, another woman was lifting out a slurry-coated net; she hung it on a line in the sun next to others. She checked two of the nets at the far end of the line, took them down, carried them to a bench where an old man with gentle hands coated the hard-slurried model in thicker clay, smoothing carefully until there was nothing but a ball of clay like a wasp's nest. The faggot boy carried the clay to one of the kilns.

Bellows squeezed and furnaces roared. Tiny hammers chink-chinked. The river flowed.

Two creamy white butterflies—the same colour as the Svear's wax— danced together around the tip of one guard's spear, while he half dozed.

Hild returned her attention to the goldsmithing. She had watched the bronze casters at Bebbanburg. This was different. It was like watching seasoned gesiths marching from three corners of a rough field to slot smoothly into a shield wall, or listening to a bard build a familiar song. The Svear didn't have to watch the furnace or mind the kiln, he didn't have to shake the slurry, he had only to think of pleasing shapes and build them in wax—smoothly, unhurriedly—so that a clay mould could emerge from the kiln and be filled with gold. She thought of women always having to break the flow of their spinning to catch a child back from the fire, or pause in the heckling of tow to bind a wound . . .

Hereswith, married, with a child. Her nephew or niece. But she might never meet them. She should give Hereswith something to remember her by, something beautiful, something precious.

The sun climbed higher. The Svear stood, grinned—the way his cheek gaped was hideous; her mother would have stitched that when it was still raw—and gestured for her to follow. She followed him from table to table. She watched the melted wax poured carefully from a clay mould and saved for later; gold poured into the hot mould; the mould set in sand to cool slowly; a raw gold cast, a buckle, getting its gold spines snipped off—always one slave watching another when they were handling naked gold—and polished, then engraved. Back to the enameller's table, where a man with a squint used the tiniest spoon Hild had ever seen to dip into various bowls of powder and tap the grains carefully into the minute compartments on a gold brooch, made by fusing fine gold wire to a flat gold surface.

"Red," said the Svear blurrily, pointing to one bowl. "Blue," pointing to another. They all looked white and cream and grey to Hild.

"How can you tell?"

He picked up a pinch and rubbed it between his fingertips. "Different." Which war had captured him? His right palm did not have the sword-callus stripe; his left knuckles were not flattened from blows through a shield boss. He touched his finger to his tongue. "Taste different, too." He held his finger out for her to try. Hild stuck out her tongue.

"Hild," Fursey said from behind. "What on God's green earth is so fascinating about watching yet another stinking savage make jewellery?"

Hild felt like a dragonfly batted to the dirt. She turned, angry. Then she took in Fursey's mottled face. "What's the matter?"

"Apostasy!"

That word again. She still didn't know what it meant. Eorpwald's guards might not know what it meant, either, but they didn't like the tone. They unslung their shields. Lintlaf came up on his toes.

Men with weapons: as predictable as dogs.

"Stand down," she said to Lintlaf.

"They are paid men," he said, with the sting and twist guaranteed to provoke anyone's temper. The guards levelled their spears.

"Doubtless you could take them even with your sword in your left hand," she said to Lintlaf. "But you will not."

No one moved.

Her thoughts came together, smooth as a shield wall: The fact they could check becomes the prophecy they must believe. She fixed her gaze on Lintlaf but spoke to all four men. "I have seen two lives dancing in the guise of butterflies about their spear blades; butterflies dancing with death. Lives waiting to be lost. I have seen it." In her side vision she caught one of the East Angles nodding: Butterflies, he had seen them. "But no blood will be spilt, no lives lost here today. I say so. You will both walk with me."

She nodded at the enameller, then to the Svear, and swept away, as her mother would have. They followed.

"Apostasy, heresy, evil!" Fursey hissed in Latin as they walked along the river, then sneezed, which made Hild want to smile, but she remembered Hereswith's punch on her shoulder and didn't. Which reminded her that she wanted to give her sister a gift.

Fursey was still spitting like a cat. She looked at Lintlaf for an explanation. He shrugged. "He went into the temple his usual sunny self—ha!—and came out like that."

It took two hundred strides or more for Fursey to calm himself enough to speak Anglisc. Even then, Hild couldn't make much sense of it.

"Stop," she said. "Two altars? One altar for the Christ, one for our gods? Why is that bad?"

And Fursey exploded again like a duck from its covey, this time his Latin peppered with Irish.

"I don't understand," Hild said. "Are we in danger?"

"Our immortal souls are in peril! Christ will strike down the apostates! He will—"

"I'm not an apostate. Am I? Good. Are you? Lintlaf, then? No? Then stop it. Answer me this instead. Did the East Angles ever fight the Svear?"

"What?"

"The East Angles. Did they fight the Svear?"

Fursey, speechless, turned away. She looked at Lintlaf.

"No," he said.

"Then how did Eorpwald, or Rædwald, capture Svearish slaves?"

Fursey, despite himself, said, "He probably bought them."

"You can buy slaves?"

"Certainly you can buy slaves."

Lintlaf said, "Coelfrith says that at Gipswīc, you can buy anything. Anything at all. It's Rædwald's great wīc. Eorpwald's now. Like a vill, but a port."

"Like Woodbridge."

Fursey snorted. "Like Woodbridge the way Mulstanton is like York."

Hild felt very rustic. It made her cross. And the fumes of the gold-working had made her head ache. "We shall visit Gipswīc. We shall buy a slave." A wedding gift for Hereswith. More practical than a gold brooch. Someone to help her sister when Hild could not.

"My apologies, lady," said Lintlaf. "But not today. Burgmod told me specially that you're to be there for Æthelric Short Leg's arrival."

The men—Yffing and Wuffing alike—were already at their board, and Eorpwald's womenfolk were being seated while the visiting women waited behind the hanging separating the women's quarters from the hall. Mildburh peered through a convenient gap between curtain and wall, and gave Hereswith, Hild, and Breguswith a running commentary.

"And now Æthelric Short Leg is standing," Mildburh said. "He's escorting the queen to her place. He does it so well. And now he's returning to his seat at Eorpwald's right hand. He doesn't limp." She giggled—a very annoying giggle, Hild thought, like a whinnying horse. But she had such a headache; everything was irritating her. "And his legs are the same length. And not short."

Mystifyingly, Hereswith blushed and looked at her mother.

"Saewara was right, then," Breguswith said, and Mildburh giggled again. Hild knew what that meant: It was something to do with what a man and a woman do in the dark. She pushed Mildburh out of the way so she could see.

Æthelric's hair was beautifully combed, as thick and lustrous as a beaver pelt, and caught back with a blue-enamelled gold ring. His arm rings were inlaid with garnet and more blue enamel. Like Anna, his brother, he had the dark hair and eyes and fine bones that hinted of a mother with west wealh blood somewhere in her family, though the muscle snaking around his wrists and cording at his neck and throat were anything but delicate. His quilted warrior jacket was the colour of old bronze, with marigold borders. His hose and boots were half a shade darker, the exact brown of his eyes.

Hild looked at Hereswith's hair, shining like corn and gold; at her overdress of red and marigold; at the ivory underdress embroidered in blue and gold and red, the ivory wool veil secured with gold and garnets. Her sister could not have complemented Æthelric's colours more closely if she'd tried, nor he hers. Even his enamel matched her eyes.

She put her eye back to the gap just in time to catch Saewara, as she took her place next to her husband, shoot a significant glance at the hanging behind which they stood.

Of course. Cousins. Her sister and gemæcce already had the beginnings of a kin web here in this foreign land. They wouldn't be all alone.

The king's scop struck a chord and the steward drew back the hanging with a flourish. The pipers piped and drummers drummed. Everyone stood. Even the flames seemed to roar as they entered.

Gold gleamed from every shadow, every hanging and dish, every arm and waist and veil. Jewels glittered at ears and throats and fingers. White wax tapers burnt like stars in silver holders down the middle of every board. Light sparked and shot and bounced from every fold and every corner. It hurt Hild's eyes.

The noise and heat and music were overwhelming. Food and drink poured into the hall.

A swan on a great silver platter, its feathers boiled clean and glued back on with honey. Wine like blood, and mead the colour of sunshine. A sea of jellied eels. Sturgeon in a lake of bilberry sauce. Pearl-white bread. And music, music from all sides of the hall and from the centre, all playing parts of the same song. It was like being inside a lyre, inside a drum, inside a pipe. Hild thought her head might burst.

Eorpwald's flat-faced queen carried the great cup from guest to guest, and one by one important men from different kin groups stood to toast. It seemed to Hild that Æthelric and his North Folk formed a distinct group, one of three: the North Folk; Eorpwald and his men; and another thegn, Ricberht, whose men seemed easier with the king's gesiths than Æthelric's. He looked Wuffing, but something about the bunch and flex of his shoulders, the aggressive jut of his chin, made her think perhaps he was from a lesser branch and easily offended. Like Osric? Her mother would know.

Edwin smiled at every toast, and drank and drank. Hild was offered the great cup, and again. White mead. She drank deep.

More food. More wine. Another gulp of the guest cup, and another. The world seemed as though she was peering at it through a hollow reed. She drank more of the white mead and it writhed down her gullet like a fiery snake. She drank again. The burning was something to hold on to as her headache threatened to engulf the world.

More food. More wine. Flames burning higher. Speeches. Songs. Long recitations of kin. Hereswith the daughter of Hereric, the son of Æthelric Spear, the son of Ælla, the son of Yffi, the son of Wuscfrea, the son of Wilgisl, the son of Westerfalca, the son of Sæfugl, the son of Sæbald, the son of Segegeat, the son of Swebdæg, the son of Sigegar, the son of Wædæg, the son of Woden.

Hereswith, she thought, sister of Hild. And she didn't even have a gift.

Guests stood one by one and pledged mighty gifts. And Hild, drinking again from the guest cup, saw her wavering face reflected on the surface of the white mead, like a face slipping over the sea, leaving, leaving, and then she understood: heresy, apostasy, dancing with death. Her mother was right: Eorpwald was weak, he couldn't even decide between gods. He would die. Æthelric would be king. But what Hild knew now, what her mother hadn't yet seen, was that Æthelric, too, would fall. He was self-satisfied, pleased with his vanity, and not deigning to work for the respect of other men. Hereswith would flee to her nearest family: her mother's kin across the sea.

Hild stood. She raised her arms. She was the bringer of light, seeker of patterns. She had just the gift for Hereswith, something to help her in the time to come: the truth.

Hild was lying down somewhere and every time she opened her eyes the world began to spin. She closed her eyes. Her mouth tasted of vomit.

"What possessed her?" Hereswith's voice. "What did she mean by it?"

"I don't know, child." Her mother.

"But why did . . ."

Hild's mind slipped off the table. When she came back Fursey was talking.

"Possessed her? No. She isn't possessed."

"She—"

"With respect, Lady Hereswith, although Eorpwald king has apostatised, using the word *possessed* where Romanists can hear you is not healthy."

"But—"

"Go back to the table, child," Breguswith said. "It's your feast. Don't let your sister's gift spoil it."

"Gift? She prophesied my—"

"Gift," Breguswith said firmly. "Your husband will be king. Your son will be king. You will live long and happily . . . overseas, with kin. Go back. Smile at your betrothed. Tell your uncle all is well."

The world was muffled for a time.

Someone slapped her right cheek. "Child. Wake up." A hand behind her head, tilting it. A cup against her lips. A vile smell. "Drink."

Hild squirmed weakly. But the hand was implacable. She drank.

A blink later she was on her side and vomiting violently.

The hand again, and then the cup. "Drink." This time it was water. "Rinse and spit. And open your eyes. You can hear me."

Hild opened her eyes: her mother, squatting by her head, a dull pewter cup in her hand.

"Good." Breguswith nodded at the wealh to take the bucket of vomit away. She put the cup back to Hild's lips. "Drink."

Hild swallowed the lukewarm water.

"Now this." Her glass-claw beaker.

"What is it?"

"Necessary. Now drink. Only a little."

It tasted like burning earth. Hild felt her face turn instantly red.

"Again."

"I'll be sick."

Breguswith laughed grimly. "You won't." Hild drank. "You will lie there for the count of fivescore. Then you will stand, wipe your face, check your dress, and walk with me back into the hall. You are a seer overwhelmed by vision, not a silly maid who can't hold her drink. You will not hide. You will not hang your head. You will smile. You will eat. You will make a show of drinking your wine. One more sip of this. Good. Now gather your wits."

Hild didn't remember much of the rest. Her muscles trembling. Her insides hot and tight. The hall swollen with light and heat. Rows of pale faces with staring eyes. Gold gleaming from deeper shadows, though darker now, grimmer, like the stuff of dragon hoards and monsters and exiles . . . Æthelric saying something to her of a burial—would she see it? Smiling and agreeing. Smiling and sipping, hanging on, hanging on.

They approached Rædwald's burial mound from the river at dawn.

Hild, on the first boat with Eorpwald and Edwin, smelt it before she saw it: the old, cold scent of deep, turned dirt; the smell of bones. Then bluffs on the eastern bank emerged from the mist. The mound loomed long, high, and oval against the horizon. Bare earth, easily twoscore ells long, longer than Edwin's great hall at Yeavering. The gilded stem and stern post of a ship reared from each end. Six ells high at least. The carved eyes, gilded and inset with glass, glimmered with an otherworldly light.

Æthelric Short Leg stood at the prow of the second boat, his chief gesith beside him. His eyes burnt like a wight's. He knew his fate: a warrior's fate, a king's. He would be ring-giver, hero, laid into the earth with his treasure like his uncle Rædwald; sung for on the river at dawn, in hall at night, on the road at noon. Remembered. Renowned. She had said so, before every Angle in hall.

The three boats cut silently through the clear water, then slowed. Slack tide, when the muscular surge of the water stops, is just gone, like a dying man's breath.

Water slapped the bank. Boats rocked.

Eorpwald said in a strong voice, "My father, who was king."

"Rædwald, who was king," Edwin said.

And Hild and Breguswith, and the gesiths of the north and the East Angles, and Æthelric and Hereswith, and Anna and Saewara murmured, "Rædwald." "King." "Lord."

The scop stroked his lyre and struck a pose. He plucked a chord and chanted:

Hold, earth, now your hero cannot
the treasure of kings!
Wrested from your dark
torn from your deep
by men
who laughed
laid it in swords
boasted and beat it
into cups.
Heroes who killed
each the other
for the glory
for the gleam
for the gold of kings.
For Rædwald, king.

"Rædwald, king," they said.

Now there is none
to burnish blade
to lift the golden cup.
For he is gone.
He is gone.

"He is gone."

So, too, goes
the fish-scale corselet
the ribs that moved it.
So goes

the one who hammered it.
So goes the horse
from the pasture
sun from sky
sea from shore.
So goes
the ship over the horizon.
So, too, it goes.

"So, too, it goes."

So it all goes. Hild shivered. She was cold and sick and poisoned to the bone. Her skin felt greasy and her teeth hurt.

Beside her, Edwin stirred. Rædwald the overking was dead and under the dirt. Now Edwin was overking. Hild could feel him swelling like bread.

Gipswīc, Rædwald's wīc, was as big as Rendlesham, bigger, and humming with the sting and salt of a port. There were king's men in their matching tunics and spears everywhere. And everywhere coins. Gold and silver, Roman, Frankish, Byzantine. And everything for sale.

Hild and Fursey and Lintlaf—who was vilely hungover and worried about his mare and her gaudy regalia, which they'd had to leave in the king's enclosure: *No droppings between the stalls,* the guards said, *princess or no, hero with a ringed sword or no*—had never seen anything like it. Fursey muttered to himself about the dangers of pride and usurping the glories of heaven, and nagged at the two sturdy wealh Eorpwald's steward had lent Hild to carry her small chests of hacksilver. Lintlaf assumed the dangerous-hero-with-a-quick-sword mien he adopted whenever he felt overwhelmed. Hild, at first wary of so many strangers, soon forgot her caution under the weight of sheer wonder. They wandered the waterfront—filled with ships, more ships than any of them had seen at any one time, and swarming with men in strange clothes and with skin of every colour (one was as black as wet charcoal)—stopping at random to finger merchandise, calling out to one another: *Touch this! Look at this! Smell this!*

Rhenish glass: cups and bowls and flasks. Wheel-thrown pottery, painted in every colour and pattern. Cloth. Wine. Swords—swords for *sale*—and armour. Jewels, with stones Hild had never seen, including great square diamonds, as grey as a Blodmonath sky. Perfume in tiny stoppered jars, and next to them even smaller jars—one the size of Hild's fingernail—

sealed with wax: poison. Lumps of incense wrapped in waxed linen in straw-lined baskets. Timber arranged in layered rows: oak and elm, poplar and birch; raw and seasoned. Bronze ewers. Frankish throwing axes. Pigs of lead and iron. Knives: too glorious to use, inlaid with gold and mother-of-pearl; or plain, with sturdy elm hilts; or shark's-tooth size with cunning sheaths, to be worn at wrist or ankle. One even fit neatly behind the great buckle of a belt—Lintlaf lingered a long time over that. A horn of some sea beast, twisted like rope. Ivory caskets. Cedar and sandalwood boxes lined with silk. Sandals with laces tipped with silver and blue glass. Belts. A six-stringed lyre inlaid with walnut and copper, and the beaver-skin bag to go with it. A set of four nested silver bowls from Byzantium, chased and engraved with lettering that Fursey, peering over her shoulder, said was Greek. But Hild barely heard him: Somewhere a man was calling in a peculiar cadence, and he sounded almost Anglisc. Almost. Instead of the rounded apple thump of Anglisc, these oddly shaped words rolled just a little wrong. Not apples, she thought. Pears. Heavy at the bottom, longer on the top.

She wandered away from Fursey, following the voice with the lopsided words, trying to make sense of them, and found herself in a ring of buyers watching an auction for a naked slave.

The Frisian auctioneer shouted, "For two scillings, done!," and pointed at a plump man with a grey streak in his hair and a much-worn purse. Then he bent his head to the youth standing next to Grey Streak. "And a fine bargain, may I say, my lord." The youth had a warrior jacket the same dark blue as Eorpwald's, the same pelt-like hair as Æthelric. An ætheling. Of what branch? No doubt he'd been at the feast three days ago. But she didn't want to think about that.

The Frisian gestured for the slave, a short-haired wealh youth with an ugly bruise along his left thigh and his hands manacled to a slave yoke, to get off the block. One of the Frisian's men prodded another to take his place. A girl. A pretty one with hair the colour of honey, like Hereswith, and about the same age.

Hild's lungs felt too big for her ribs. She turned away, willing herself to breathe. It was not Hereswith. It was not. Still turned, she saw another of the Frisian's men using a huge key to unlock the sold wealh's yoke, and the ætheling's steward taking charge of him, moving with the slave and two gesiths to the edge of the crowd where two men sat at a table behind two sets of scales—and a counting board. She had heard of such things. But then the steward and the slave blocked her view of it.

"This is a fine and healthy girl," shouted the Frisian. "See the plump muscles, the strong bones. Show your teeth, girl. Your teeth." The sound of a goad striking flesh. Hild turned back. The girl, with a fresh red stripe across the top of her arm, stood with bared teeth. "Very shapely. Turn for the lords, slave. See those dimples? A lot of sport there. Good hips for childbearing later—"

"Skinny ankles!" the man next to Hild shouted.

"Show your dugs, slave. Lift them up. Good milk machines, those. Good—"

Two squealing piglets ran, tails bouncing, across the auction floor, closely followed by a hobbling wealh woman, swearing with abandon. The crowd laughed. The Frisian laughed, too, but the curve of his mouth was not jolly. His selling rhythm was broken.

He began again and got as far as how the slave's hair alone could inflame a man, make him stiff as a spear, when the old wealh woman came back, a piglet tucked firmly under each arm, and the crowd applauded. He motioned her out of the way. She didn't move fast enough. The Frisian nodded at the man with the goad, who slashed at the woman's behind.

The woman shrieked and dropped one of the piglets, which ran into the good-humoured crowd, and the ætheling shouted to the Frisian, "You break her, you buy her." The crowd hooted. The ætheling grinned and stuck out his chest. "Plus, now you owe me for the sucking pig." The crowd laughed; their prince would take this foreigner down a peg or two. "Or," the princeling said, "I'll take a discount on the wealh."

The Frisian's hand twitched—Hild had seen Lilla's hand do the same when he overheard a veiled insult to his king in another man's hall—but he bowed. "My lord, Ælberht."

Ælberht waved his hand. "Deliver her to me. Same price as the other."

"My lord! This is valuable stock." The Frisian thwacked the slave's buttocks with the flat of his hand, a meaty sound. The man next to Hild breathed through his mouth. "Four scillings at least!"

"Frisian, I won't bargain."

"But my lord, a sucking pig is a penny, at most."

"Frisian—"

"No," Hild said. Her voice rang. Everyone turned.

She stepped forward just as Fursey arrived and snatched at her dress. He missed. She pitched her voice to the Frisian but kept her eyes on the ætheling. Now she knew why gesiths smiled in hall when they threw down their food with a shout, and stood.

The bones in her face felt light and tight. "Three scillings!" She didn't know how much a scilling was, exactly, but she had two chests of hacksilver and could always get more.

"She's mine," the ætheling said, and put his hand on his seax.

Hild put her hand on her own. "No."

The crowd *oohed* and stepped back a pace. Royal children with knives: better than a cockfight. The ætheling faced Hild.

Hild crouched, as she had seen gesiths do. The ætheling crouched in return, without thinking, as he had been trained.

Fursey hopped from foot to foot. "Stop," he hissed in Irish. "Think!"

She didn't want to think. She was sick of thinking. It never got her anywhere. Hereswith was this wealh woman's age, being sold by Edwin—in a finer marketplace, it was true, but still, sold like a sucking pig. Cian was gone. Onnen was gone. Hereswith was staying here in a strange land. And maybe her mother would stay with her. And one day Fursey would leave. What did it matter?

She drew her knife. "It will be sheathed in blood." There, it was said. Now no one but a kinsman could stop them without making her an oathbreaker. No more thinking. She began to circle.

The ætheling drew his blade and circled away. Hild studied his blade. It shimmered, oily as an eel. A good blade, with a good edge. Hers was better, and longer. So were her arms and legs. She overtopped him by three fingers. She shifted her knife to the blade-along-the-forearm grip gesiths favoured for serious knife fights, and felt light and free. She smiled.

The ætheling stumbled, and that was when Hild saw how dark his freckles were: He was pale with fright. He was just a little boy who had never drawn a knife for real, never faced the Dál nAriadne on the quay at Tinamutha, never thought his sister and mother dead and that he was all alone. This wasn't his fault.

The piglet burst from the crowd, trotters twinkling. Hild moved easily, like a mother scooping up her toddler as it runs gurgling towards the fire. The piglet squealed as she swung it up by its hind legs, then stopped when she swept her blade across its throat.

Blood pattered on hard-packed dirt.

She wiped her knife on her thigh. Sheathed in pig blood. It would do.

She looked around the circle of silent men. To the ætheling she said, "Two pennies for your pig," which was more than fair, and, to the Frisian, "Three scillings for the wealh." She thrust the dead pig at Fursey. "Pay them." The crowd parted silently and she strode through.

In Eorpwald's garth Breguswith looked at Fursey, then at the blood across the front of Hild's dress, then at the naked slave.

"Well. I hope she's good with stains. Put some clothes on her." She turned away, then back. "Priest, with me."

When they were gone, Hild turned to the wealh, who was tugging at her iron collar, trying to ease the chafing. "What's your name?"

"Gwladus."

Oo-la-doose. A west wealh name. Southwest. Dyfneint. Hild had witnessed Edwin's refusal of their man, Bishop Anaoc, and his plea for aid against the Gewisse, against war. Perhaps this woman was taken in that war. "When were you collared?"

"Last cider-making."

The Dyfneint were great cider-makers. It was a land of apples, so they said.

Gwladus tugged at her collar again. She looked nothing like Hereswith. She was at least two years older, half a hand shorter. Her eyes were grey-green, and her hair would be paler when washed. Her whole body would be paler. Her nipples were more pink than red.

Gwladus covered herself with her hands. "Lady, can I have clothes? Like the queen said?"

"She's not a queen. She's my mother."

In the kitchens, Gwladus, now in a plain tabby dress and with half a loaf in her hand, sat opposite the killer child, who said, "What skills have you?"

Gwladus chewed the bread and said nothing. Her chief skill wasn't likely to please this one.

"I could sell you back to the princeling, Ælberht."

Gwladus had heard worse threats. She tore another bite from the bread and thought. It was the best bread she had eaten for nearly a year, and Ælberht was probably also too young to appreciate her talents. She'd be best off here by the princess with the slaughter seax.

She tried to remember what she'd done the first week in the collar before she'd learnt her other skills. "I shovel shit." Then, in British, to herself, "Gwladus of the Dyfneint shovels shit!"

To her horror, the princess said, also in British, "In Dyfneint, there is no shit?"

Gwladus wanted to throw her ale in the proud little face. But the princess would kill her, dead as a sucking pig.

"And your family," the princess said, "what do they do?"

"My family are dead. Now."

"So, then. You are lucky to be shovelling shit."

It was true. Gwladus's shoulders dropped.

The princess nodded at Gwladus's collar. "Your neck is sore."

After a moment, Gwladus put down her bread. The killer child was her mistress. For now. "Yes, lady."

"Tell the kitchen you are to lave it with comfrey and slather it with goose grease. Then we'll see about getting you a lighter collar."

The doors to Eorpwald's hall stood open but gloom filled the corners. No firelight, no rushes, no tapers called forth the glint of gold and jewels. Edwin sat with Lilla, Osric, and Coelfrith at a bench opposite the door. They were playing taff and sipping ale, but every time a passing shadow darkened the doorway, Edwin looked up.

Hild sat quietly with her mother in the corner between the wall and the inset doorway, where someone entering might not think to look. There were no housefolk present.

Breguswith nodded and Hild turned one of the elm tablets. The vine pattern, sunset red and gold, was barely visible in the gloom, but men, her mother assured her, wouldn't think to wonder at that. Listen and draw no attention, she said. *Quiet mouth, bright mind.*

Hild listened to the muffled rattle of antler dice in their leather cup, the brighter spill onto the table, Osric's mutter of disgust, the click as he scooped them up again. He and her uncle looked nothing alike. Osric was more like a badger: thick, splayed fingers, sloping shoulders, black hair, and pointed teeth. She hated him. Hated him for the mud and blood of Tinamutha. She hoped her uncle would one day burn him out of his sett, stake him out as a warning to all his kind.

A man in priest skirts entered the hall. Breguswith nodded. Hild turned a tablet. Breguswith wove the shuttle through the warp, beat the weft, nodded. Hild turned the next tablet.

The priest stood before Edwin's bench and bent his head. Shaved at the crown: Romish. Edwin looked at him over the rim of his cup and Lilla gestured the priest forward. The priest raised his arms. Lilla ran practiced hands over the priest's forearms and ribs, around his waist, down his thighs and calves. Clearly the priest was used to this: He turned unbidden for Lilla to feel between his shoulders. He had the blackest hair Hild had ever seen and a dark shadow along his jaw.

She dropped her eyes to the tablet weave until he turned around again.

Edwin put down his cup. "You have a message for me?"

"I do, lord." A Jutish accent. Kent.

"Is it long?"

"No, lord."

"Then spit it out."

Hild leaned forward but at a frown from Breguswith leaned back again until the weave was taut. She turned a tablet.

"Father Paulinus bids Edwin king to remember his dream." Paulinus. A reeve for the bishop of Rome?

"Does he now. Does he indeed."

The men at the table did not even glance at one another. Clearly they knew of this dream.

"And does Eadbald king also bid me to remember?"

The priest hesitated. "My message comes from Father Paulinus."

Now there were swift looks between Edwin and his thegns. Edwin leaned back. "But we have been remiss to keep you standing and thirsty. Sit."

Breguswith rose, laid the weave in Hild's lap, and bent for the jar of wine and five cups on the floor behind her.

Hild busied herself with rolling the tablet weave while her mother moved gracefully from king to thegn to priest, pouring and smiling. She could still make men watch.

When she was done she settled at the farthest end of the bench with the wine jar, giving the impression that the only thing on her mind was the hope to give exact and prompt service.

"So," said Edwin, "from Paulinus. What of Mellitus?"

"Archbishop Mellitus went to Christ three months since. Our father now is Archbishop Justus."

"Justus? I don't remember him."

"He is a wise and holy arbiter, my lord."

"Of course he is. And does he, like Paulinus Crow, think it time to remember my dream?"

"I am not privy to the archbishop's thoughts, my lord." The priest drank. Hild heard his gulp.

"A little more?" Breguswith said in a very strong Jutish accent. "It's the finest Frankish grape." She smiled. The priest beamed back at his fellow countrywoman. "Though perhaps you are used to such things, spending time at Eadbald's court with the archbishop."

"Oh, no," the priest said. "Father Paulinus does not travel at the archbishop's side."

"But I bet he wishes he did, eh?" Osric said.

The priest put his cup down.

Breguswith smiled at Osric but Hild knew from the set of her shoulders that she was irritated by his clumsiness. Hild didn't like the way Osric smiled back.

Edwin smiled, too, but his smile wasn't meant to fool anybody. "Forgive our cousin, priest. What's your name?"

"Stephanus, lord. Stephanus the Black."

"Then drink up, Stephanus, and we will hear more from Father Paulinus."

Hild lay on her back in the pear orchard, arms behind her head, watching the leaves shiver in the breath of air that passed for wind in the flatlands of the East Anglisc. Where did wind come from? A great cave far to the north, her mother said, where everything was white, even the bears. From Arawn's realm, Onnen said, stirred by the hooves of the horses and hounds of Hel as they hunted high in the sky. Especially in autumn, when the leaves turned brown and began to fall. These leaves were still green, but not for much longer.

In Goodmanham, the harvest would be in. Coifi would have celebrated a much-reduced Woden's festival in a half-built enclosure. There would be no point going to a great deal of trouble celebrating the Yffings' god when there were no Yffings present. But when Edwin returned, it would be as overking. Next year's festival would be a thing of great pomp and ceremony. But Hereswith wouldn't be there. Hereswith would never be there again.

She stopped thinking about that and wondered instead how autumn might be in Mulstan's hall. Were Cian and Begu getting along? Did Cædmon still walk his cows on the cliffs above the bay? It seemed like a lifetime since she'd played in the kitchen garth, drunk Guenmon's beef tea, stood on the beach with an angry Onnen.

That made her lonelier than ever.

So she sifted through what she had just heard in Eorpwald's hall. Paulinus was colluding with Edwin behind his chief bishop's back. Edwin didn't like Paulinus. Osric was stupid, but Breguswith had smiled at him and he had smiled back. Sword and skirt, book and blade. She couldn't understand the pattern. She wished the pear trees were big enough to climb.

Gwladus, carrying a basket, bumped open the wicker gate with her hip. Hild sat up and brushed at her dress.

"I'll have to wash that, I suppose," Gwladus said in British.

"Anglisc, Gwladus."

"It's all over filth." She plunked the basket on the grass. Some kind of meat pie and a jar of ale.

"One of the vill wealh will do it." A flock of young swallows swooped over the trees and settled on the great hall's rooftrees, chattering. Where did they go in the winter? Did they fly south to the land of eternal sun or sleep, like squirrels, in some snug hole? Perhaps they nested in rows on the gables under the roof of the hall.

"Did your mam drop you on your head at birth?"

Hild blinked, then put her hand on her knife.

"There. Like that. Threatening to stab your own bodywoman. No one does that. If you're displeased, you have me whipped."

Hild frowned. "You want me to whip you?"

"No!" Gwladus leaned back and folded her arms.

Perhaps all wealh learnt to fold their arms that way.

Gwladus unfolded her arms. "Well?"

"Well, what?"

"Will I tell you some things?"

Hild nodded. The pie smelt good. Pigeon?

"Well, then. The vill wealh will not wash your dress because it's your dress and I attend your body now. I do it. No one else." Hild thought about it, then nodded. She reached for the pie. Gwladus didn't move.

Hild sighed and withdrew her hand. "Yes?"

"If you didn't want me for your person, why did you buy me?"

Because a slave can't leave me. But she couldn't say that.

"I'll tell you then, shall I? You're a seer. A seer's woman makes sure the seer wears clean clothes and eats fine food and gets a decent bed to sleep in. She makes sure the seer gets the white mead and the hero's portion and the bench by the fire, like the king himself. It's a seer's due. And do you know how the seer's woman does this?"

Hild shook her head, looking at the pie.

"She is seen to have the care and protection of the seer. She has respect. She has good clothes of her own, and good food and . . . and a bracelet! And pretty shoes. And a warm cloak, and a bedroll to herself. And the housefolk will see how she is valued by the seer, see that offending her is to offend the seer herself, that she must be given in to when she asks the baker for the first hot white loaf and the cook for the first hare pie. And she has, yes, she has pennies in her purse!"

"Pennies?"

"Just one or two, mind. For those times when a visiting stranger has news. So that the seer always has the news first, for a seer taken by surprise is a very sorry seer indeed."

Hild hadn't thought of it that way.

Gwladus flushed. "It needn't be pennies. It could be little trinkets, worthless things."

"What is the worth of a worthless thing?" Gwladus's flush spread. It was a pale bloom of a blush, quite unlike Hereswith's dark rush. Hild did not understand why she had thought them alike.

"I didn't mean to say you were a sorry seer, that you needed your visions bought and paid for. No doubt you are a good seer, a great seer. No doubt you've the keenest vision since, since . . ." Gwladus floundered.

Hild stood. She was taller than Gwladus. "Pennies, you said. You understand coins?"

Gwladus bobbed her head. "Yes, lady."

"You will teach me. Then we will go back to the wīc." She wanted to see that counting table.

"And you won't have me whipped?"

Hild touched her knife. "A seer's bodywoman is never whipped. A seer's bodywoman loses her nose, or her hand, or her life." The same punishment as a king's bodyman, or a chief priest's.

She had gone seax to seax with an ætheling. She understood why a king often threatened violence. It felt good, and it worked.

They all made the journey to the market again: Fursey, Hild, Lintlaf, the two bearers of the hacksilver, and Gwladus.

"Is it deliberate?" Fursey said as they rode along by a field of barleycorn stalks turning the colour of cured oak. Weeds showed bright green. "Child?"

"Um?"

He pointed to Hild's blue dress, knotted up to one side under her belt, showing a faint stain still. "Is it deliberate? A reminder to the market sellers that it would be as well to give you what you want, at your price, before you pull that pigsticker?"

"Gwladus suggested it."

"Did she?" He twisted in the saddle to look back at the wealh, who sat sideways across Lintlaf's saddlebow, gurgling with laughter. She had started their travel walking, with the other wealh. "She's a cunning thing." He turned back. "What other pearls of wisdom has she dropped in your ready ear?"

Hild shrugged.

"I still don't know what possessed you to buy such a vixen."

"I need someone of my own." Someone who had to put her first.

Fursey surprised her by agreeing. "Indeed. But have a care. This one's as pretty as a grass snake but much more dangerous. See how she's already charmed the oaf. Though, granted, he has no more brains than a bull calf."

"She says I was dropped on my head at birth."

Fursey shouted with laughter, and behind them Gwladus gurgled, and they rode into the wīc wreathed in mirth.

The counting table was grooved with vertical lines, eight long strokes beneath eight short ones. The grooves were inlaid in yellow enamel. The long ones each held four blue beads, the shorter a single red bead. The Frisian money changer slid the beads up and down as he counted and added coins for a merchant but moved too fast for Hild to follow.

Then it was their turn. One of Hild's chests of hacksilver was emptied and expertly weighed under the eye of a Frank holding an axe who, every time he moved to brush at his weeping left eye, made Lintlaf twitch. The money changer asked Hild what coins she wished in exchange, how much gold, how much silver.

She hefted a gold coin in her left hand. The same size around as a cherry but as heavy as a plum. Good yellow gold, with a picture of a Frankish king on one side and writing that made no sense on the other.

"If I took all in gold, how many would they be?" She hefted the satisfying weight one more time, then put it down.

"By weight, the silver is fifteen and a half pounds. That would make"—flick flick flick—"fivescore and eight gold scillings and three silver pennies."

She rolled one of the little pennies, no bigger around than a willow withy, between thumb and forefinger. "And if I changed half to scillings and half to pennies?"

Flick flick. "Fifty-four gold scillings and eighty-six-score and eight pennies. Less the eight for my service."

"Three," said Fursey. Hild picked up another gold coin, smaller, the same size as the silver penny but heavier. The Frank wiped at his eye. Lintlaf twitched. The lustre, like the sheen of run honey or parsnips cooked in butter, made her want to put it in her mouth; she put it down reluctantly. Fursey and the Frisian haggled for a while and settled on a fee of five pennies, with a promise of custom if they exchanged the second chest. Hild was dazed. Scores, hundreds of coins. And that was only one chest.

Coins were power of themselves. They didn't need a king uncle or an almost-queen mother or the strength of a seer's gaze. She could take a gold scilling or a silver penny and offer it anywhere in the wīc and everyone would understand its worth. And there would be no weighing of hacksilver or a gold ring, no haggling and accusations of inferior workmanship, just the weight of these Frankish and Roman and Byzantine coins.

She took two-thirds in gold scillings and one-third in silver pennies. The money changer counted the coins into small sueded sacks stamped with his mark. Fursey laid them in plump lines along the bottom of the chest. The two bearer wealh and Gwladus watched as if under a spell. Lintlaf watched the Frank. Fursey watched Hild. Hild told Fursey to set aside the short sack of four scillings and one sack of pennies and carry them himself. Now they would buy.

They were a strange procession. Word spread fast from the money changer's table. Hild was recognised: a tall maid with fathomless eyes, a very big knife, and the pig's blood still on her skirts. But they remembered she had paid, and paid well, for that pig. Every stall holder cried out as she passed and sent boys running alongside with lengths of cloth, or tiny glass bottles, or a basket of honey cakes.

Hild bought and bought until the wealh were staggering and even Fursey was carrying a sack of small items. Lintlaf kept his hands free for his sword, though Fursey noted that this would do him no good if he didn't keep his mind free of the sway of Gwladus's hips. Gwladus herself carried three bolts of cloth, finely woven but plain Kentish stuff in apple colours—green, russet, gold—shoes fit to her feet, and, most precious of all, a thin silver bracelet with a red glass stone.

One enterprising stall holder sent two piping boys to follow them and blow jaunty tunes until they would come see his wares. Hild remembered the stall: a green cloth laid over the table and cunning little steps built beneath to show a cascade of luxury geegaws. She stopped before a row of tiny matching red glass bottles with gilded stoppers. The stall holder encouraged her to smell the oils: rose, myrrh, sandalwood. She bought them for Hereswith, to remind her of Hild when she left to live with the North Folk with Æthelric. She bought lesser oils—rosemary, sage, lavender—for Mildburh and Ædilgith and Folcwyn. Then she saw an ivory comb carved with a goat and inlaid with gold and thought of Begu, scrambling like a goat up the hill, hair springing free of her braid. She would send it. She could. Writing and coin. She could send a message and gift to anyone, anywhere. She could watch and weave the pattern of the world. And all she had to do to earn the gifts to turn into coin was to see clearly, to see first.

She let Fursey negotiate prices while she looked over the rest of the items laid out on the green cloth. A silver hand mirror polished on one side and chased on the other, with an ivory handle, for Onnen. Gwladus suggested a small chest of unguents to go with it, "In case the lady is getting old and her face is changing."

Now she needed something for Cian.

They moved on to the weapons stall. Lintlaf's eye was caught by a small knife with a blue glass pommel and blue-tooled sheath strapped for the forearm. "Try it on," Hild said, and when Lintlaf did, and beamed and flexed his muscles to test the fit, she gestured for Fursey to pay. Lintlaf's lord and oath-keeper was Edwin, only he could give swords and hilt rings, but this knife was more ornament than a tool of death to be employed at the lord's word. Giving it was permissible.

"Last time there was a cunning buckle knife," she said to the stall holder.

"This, lady?" He held up the massive gilded bronze buckle but, perhaps mindful of her last marketplace performance with a blade, did not pass it to her.

"Show me."

He obliged by putting two fingers in clever looped handles and pulling free a wicked tooth of a blade three inches long.

Hild and Gwladus were halfway up the steps to the door to the women's quarters, carefully sheltering their burdens from the drizzle, when they heard Hereswith shouting. They looked at each other. Hild shrugged; they couldn't stand out here in the wet. They went in.

The housefolk—four of them, all tight-shouldered and tense—did not look up, but Mildburh and Hereswith turned. Mildburh was red-faced, unhappy. Hereswith's face was gelid and pale, like custard.

"And what unwelcome news do you bring this time?" Hereswith said. "Am I to die horribly in childbed?"

Hild had no idea how to respond.

"Oh, don't stand there like a carving. Come in and keep out the rain. Tell me, what dreadful news does Ma have now?"

"I brought these. For you." And she held out the silk-wrapped packet.

Hereswith took it, unwrapped the first fold, and burst into tears.

"But you don't even know what it is," Hild said, and to her consternation Hereswith wrapped her arms around her and wept harder. "What is it? Are you ill? What's the matter?" She motioned Gwladus forward. "Here, I brought you buttermilk, too. It's still cool from the dairy. Here." She put the cup in her sister's free hand. She didn't know what else to do. "And summer ale for Mildburh." It was Mildburh's favourite. *Always know what they like*, her mother said. *They will love you for it.*

And then Mildburh started crying, too.

"Please, stop," Hild said. "Please. Here." She sat on the bed and tugged gently at Hereswith's arm. "Sit. What's wrong?"

Hereswith wouldn't sit, but Mildburh did, clutching her ale.

Hereswith threw her buttermilk at a hanging of a hart hunt. It dripped solemnly.

"I'm to wed this Æthelric and follow him to the stinking fen that he calls home." Drip. "Where he already has a woman." Drip. "You didn't predict that, did you, little seer? A princess of the South Gyrwe. A woman and two children."

Drip. Drip. Drip.

Breguswith, hand wrapped around the pendant she wore, smiled, and said to Hild, "It isn't a fen. Not all of it. And of course the man already has a woman, he's a man isn't he? He's sworn to set the strumpet aside—sworn to me, and to Edwin, his overking."

Hild wondered how much that meant. A man was lord of his own hall, king or no. And it was as Eorpwald's brother, Æthelric ætheling of the South Folk, he had sworn to Edwin, not as Ecgric, lord of the North Folk. Ecgric prince—and ally of the South Gyrwe and East Wixna.

"Besides, the Gyrwe woman's given him only daughters. He's more in need of an heir than a peaceweaver. One son, or even the hope of one, from your sister and the woman will be forgotten. And Hereswith will have Ædilgith and Folcwyn with her, and six gesiths—hardly alone."

Breguswith let go of her pendant: the biggest garnet Hild had ever seen, cut like a seashell and set among slices of the same stone. The workmanship was as fine as the Svear's but by a different hand. Kentish.

Breguswith smiled. "Yes. A token of appreciation. Edwin is getting married. To Æthelburh." King Eadbald of Kent's sister, Breguswith's half niece. Hild's cousin. "She'll come north next summer. With a priest, Paulinus."

The afternoon of the day before they were to leave. In Hereswith's apartment Hild smiled at Mildburh. "The kitchen has saved the very last of the summer ale. I told them not to release it to anyone but you."

"I don't—"

"I asked them to make sticky cakes, too," Hild said. "With run honey and Frankish almonds." Gwladus had arranged that. She said it had cost two pennies.

Hereswith studied Hild, then turned to her gemæcce. "I like sticky cakes, Mil."

When they were alone, Hild looked about. The hanging was gone. Being carefully cleaned no doubt. She hoped Hereswith wasn't in a throwing mood today.

She didn't know what to say. Her sister, whose fierce whisper and poke were her earliest memory. Her sister.

She took Hereswith's hand. It was smaller than hers now and hard with rings.

"Perhaps you really will turn out to be a giant," Hereswith said, lightly enough, but her smile wobbled and Hild knew what she was thinking: I won't be there to see it.

"This is your wyrd," Hild said. "You'll be a queen. You'll have children." In pain, and blood, and sweat. "I'll come and see them."

But her voice sounded false, and neither of them quite believed it. Wyrd never flowed along expected paths. Hereswith might die in childbed, and Hild wouldn't know until Æthelric or Eorpwald thought to send a messenger. Even then it would be king to king: *The peaceweaver has died, what do you propose?*

"Learn to read," Hild said.

"Read? I don't—"

"Please." She should have thought of it before. But she had never left her sister before. "You must. Find a priest to teach you. Pretend you're interested in their god."

"What—"

"The Christ. Please. Learn to read. For me."

"Does it really mean so much to you?" Hereswith's eyes were so blue. Sister blue. "I'll always be your sister. I will come if you call. I swear it to you. Please." She saw that her hand was squeezing Hereswith's to purple.

Hereswith tugged Hild's hair, as she had when they were little, but gently. "I'll learn to read. But you must do something for me."

Hild nodded, swallowed, saw she was clutching too hard again, tried to loosen her grip but couldn't. Her sister's hand . . .

"Find people. People you know are on your side. Not that priest. Not a slave. Kings die, even overkings. Especially overkings. So find people."

Hild nodded again. Her tears dripped on their hands. Hereswith wiped them off, as briskly as she would wipe a baby's nose. And Hild couldn't bear it, couldn't stand to face the rest of her life without a sister at her side.

"You'll be well," Hereswith said. "I'll be well. I'm older, and I say so. And on your birth day, and mine, we'll drink a toast, each to the other, and one day we'll hold hands again."

They saw each other the next morning but though there were words, Hild didn't remember them, they were ritual, for the people: a stern lady of the North Folk bidding smooth travel and fair weather to her uncle the overking, her sister the king's seer, and her lady mother. The three women were gracious but remote, dry-eyed players in the royal mummery of Eorpwald and Edwin's grander farewell: the pledges of honour and allegiance between king and overking.

As they rode away, none of them blinked, no one's smile wavered. But in her head, Hild was already imagining her toast to Hereswith on her own birth day next month, and the simple message she would send on her sister's birth day in Œstremonath.

And when she had imagined every dot of ink and wrinkle of parchment, she began composing messages to Cian and Begu and Onnen.

9

✦

IN YEAVERING, AT ŒSTREMONATH, Hild stood in the doorway of the women's hall and faced the late-morning sun. She raised her cup of grass-rich buttermilk and drank to Hereswith, and felt, for a moment, the sun warm on Hereswith's back as her sister faced north by northwest and lifted a cup of mead to Hild. But she didn't send a message: There was no one to trust with the spoken words, no one but Fursey, and East Anglia was too far.

But she could send him to the Bay of the Beacon. And when spring turned to summer and travel was easier, she did.

And now they were back in Goodmanham, and it was almost Weod-monath again. Fursey should be back in a month. On the rough northern pasture, the lambs looked nearly as burly as their shorn mothers. In the valley and on the southern slopes, barley heavy with seed bent its whiskers towards the sun-beaten earth; the weeds stood out livid green against the dark gold grain. Children took turns banging sticks to drive away crows. The crows crak-crakked and rose like black smoke, then settled in the next field and watched with oily black eyes, or indulged in aerial shows with the jackdaws that lived in the elms. During æfen, while the urchins frightened each other with tales—of ghost crows, and giant crows, and breath-stealing crows—Coelgar's understewards pulled at their beards in frustration as the birds flitted quietly back to the grain and ate their fill.

A week before harvest, the children went out with wide baskets to pull the weeds, which they then fed to the goats. The milk began to taste strange, as it did every year at this time.

The wild taste fed Hild's restlessness. She climbed her favourite ash tree but couldn't see anything but pictures of Hereswith in childbed, screaming for her sister.

She strode the woods, wondering if Fursey had given Cian his belt-buckle knife, if he liked it. What if he laughed and thought it foolish? Begu would like her comb, surely. But Begu had such a flighty mind, always flitting from one thing to another. Who? she imagined Begu saying to Fursey. Hild? Oh, yes, she was here last year.

And Onnen. *Learn to read*, she'd told Fursey to tell her almost-mother. *You must learn to read.* But Onnen, she knew, would always think of her as the child squirming at the washtub as the cold water ran down her back, or the foolish girl who misled Begu about being gemæcce. She wouldn't listen.

Hild tramped the wolds, watching birds at the edges of things and gathering plants for her mother. Whatever she did she would find herself thinking of people who weren't there: *Surely Guenmon checked that Bán had a new cloak before winter*, or *Did Fursey remember to seek out Cú and give him a honey cake all for himself?* Once, she remembered she'd sent no message for Cædmon.

And then she was back to Hereswith, to the empty bed in her room and the constant listening for the pointed comment that never came.

And Hereswith's absence was not the only change.

Gwladus voiced strong opinions of what was and was not proper for Hild—she was worse than Onnen that way—and in the vill Hild found herself dressed more splendidly and fed more regularly. She shot up like one of the weeds in the barley field and grew tender breast buds.

Gwladus also grew. She had been eye-catching before but now her pale hair—paler than barley, paler than wheat, paler even than the bryony growing by the alders along the beck—gleamed, her skin grew smooth and tight, and she smelt like wild honey. Lintlaf and the other gesiths seemed mazed by her. For Hild this was useful. Gwladus listened to many conversations between men who forgot to take care, and she repeated them to Hild word for word: Cwichelm, eldest of the ambitious West Saxon brothers, was rumoured to intrigue with old Cadfan of Gwynedd. Young Cadwallon ap Cadfan was in Ireland. British and Irish priests had been seen everywhere—even with Cuelgils of Lindsey, even at Arbeia, Osric's house in Tinamutha—carrying messages back and forth.

At night, when Gwladus was asleep on her pallet on the floor, Hild lay in her wide bed—her mother was elsewhere again; she didn't want to think about that—and mulled the rumours and whispers, turning her carnelians, flicking the bright angry orange beads one way then another. Cwichelm. Sending embassies to all parts of the country—even the north. What was he planning? She mused on the words and beads for days but couldn't see the pattern. There was a piece missing.

Fursey would know more, but he wouldn't be back from Mulstanton for half a month.

Hild and her mother worked side by side in the still room. They stood hip to hip and shoulder to shoulder: Hild was now as tall as Breguswith. While her mother rinsed an ox horn with hot vinegar, Hild strained the onion and garlic mash, steeped in a copper bowl for nine days with wine and bull's gall, through a fine cloth. When the liquid was clear, Hild poured it carefully into the clean horn. Breguswith pushed in the wooden stopper and Hild warmed beeswax to seal it. In winter, when eyelids were red and angry, they'd dip a feather into the mixture and use it to paint a line along the eyelash roots to treat styes. Eye infections were always worse in winter when everyone crowded together and the fires smoked.

"Did you harvest that figwort you said you'd found?"

Hild shook her head, but carefully; she didn't want to spill the hot wax on the back of Breguswith's hand. "Tomorrow, or the day after."

That would be another morning of squeezing the orange sap into brass pots and warming it gently with honey. That mixture was good for pink eye, but it was best fresh.

Orange reminded Hild of Cwichelm. She told her mother of the rumours. "And the priests have been seen as far north as the Tine."

Breguswith started stripping the leaves from the ribwort Hild had brought in that morning. "The Irish are always plotting something. Always sending their priests hither and thither." She gave Hild a sideways look. "Not the only ones."

"Fursey carries my messages to Cian and Onnen." And Begu, but she had never told her mother about Begu. "He'll be back any day. When I send him out again, are there any words you'd like him to take to Onnen?"

"None I'd trust a priest with."

Hild realised her mother had deflected her somehow, as she always did.

While her mother chopped the ribwort, Hild dipped up sheep grease from the little pot on the shelf and rubbed it into her hand. This year there were so many housefolk at the vill, so many women arriving with the new folk, so many slaves given in tribute, that Hild, king's niece, king's seer, had not been called upon to help with shearing. If Hereswith were here, she wouldn't be needed in the dairy.

There were many new gesiths, too, so many—Anglisc and Saxon, Irish and Frankish, Svear and Pict—swearing oaths to the new overking, feasting and gorging and drinking themselves to a heroic stupor, that beef and mead were running low and Coelgar scowled at the number of boastful mouths to be fed day in, day out. Edwin had taken to counting his arm rings. He would have to start another war soon to maintain his gift-giving.

War. Cwichelm. Cadwallon. Cuelgils. Osric? When would Edwin feel strong enough to openly oppose his cousin? What if he left it too late?

A thought struck her. What if he was planning to use her as a peace-weaver? She looked at her mother, who shifted slightly but didn't acknowledge Hild's attention. What was she planning?

Hild hung her hose in her belt and dabbled her toes in the pool where she had once sat with Cian, where she had made her offering, long ago. It smelt green and cool and secret.

Goodmanham drowsed, but Hild was wide awake.

The pattern was changing, she could taste it, feel it in the different weight and heft of her body every morning, in the way her mother looked at her. One day, to suit some purpose of their own, her mother or her uncle would pluck her from her life and send her to live in a fen with a man she didn't know. In the world of skirt and sword, it was part of her wyrd. But not all her wyrd, and not yet. There was so much to learn, so much to know.

She stopped kicking and let the water re-form its smooth mirror. Her feet looked broken and badly set, like the stick she had shown Cian.

The bird cherry—so much fruit this year—whispered. The ripples on the pool's smooth sandy bottom lifted and shimmered. Sprite breath.

She didn't turn around.

"I know you're there. Help me. I offered you my tooth. Help me."

A cherry dropped to the grass. Dragonflies hummed.

The barley and wheat were cut and sheaved, the stooks drying, the hay baled, and Hild was looking for Fursey's return, when the lords and chiefs began to arrive for the overking's festival. Osric came first, with his great retinue, second only to the king's. Then Hunric and Wilstan, Tond-helm and Trumwine, Cealred and Rhond, each with a dozen lesser thegns. They greeted Edwin with respect. Harvest had been early and yields good, from the wide valleys to the wild uplands, the sea to the mountains. Clearly the gods favoured this one. Coifi, as chief priest of the chief god of the chief king of the Angles, smiled and grew as sleek and self-satisfied as a seal.

This was the fruition of his ambition. He had spent a year supervising the building of Woden's great enclosure, months boiling flax oil and wood tar and mixing them with pigment to make the vivid reds, whites, and blues to paint the wooden walls of the roofless one-storey corridor coiled like a snake around the great totem. His underpriests had coddled the white calf and the white sheep, had worked during the dark of the moon to ready the decoctions of the thung flowers, wolfsbane, and nightshade, and elixirs of certain berries and mushrooms. This was the pinnacle of their year: the ceremony of Edwin, overking, son of the son of the many-times son of Woden, god of the Yffings.

But change was coming. *I'd give them a year. Two at most.*

Hild wore green. The entire household wore green. They stood before the entrance of the enclosure as the sun began to set. Coifi, in white, stood in front of the doorway, flanked by two burning torches thrust deep in the turf; no cressets, for the god permitted no iron. He held an ancient birch bowl. Thin, eerie music—pipes and horns and drums—skirled about them with the evening breeze. The musicians were hidden at the heart of the enclosure; the music seemed to come from the sky. God music.

The gesiths were nervous. They were always nervous when they had to leave behind every blade, even their eating knives.

The king took the first sip from the priest's bowl. As he passed between the flames, onto the path they would all walk tonight, he seemed to be trembling. Perhaps it was the breeze catching his clothes. The music rose and fell. Coifi nodded to the æthelings, who walked side by side. Another pause, then Osric. Hild followed immediately behind with Osric's pale-skinned, dark-haired children. Little Osthryth took her hand. Hild looked down. Such a soft small hand.

She smiled up at Hild, and her milk teeth showed sharp and white as an ermine's.

Hild let go of Osthryth and took the bowl in both hands. She sipped the thin, bitter stuff and swallowed.

Her lips went numb, and then the drug was coursing through her, cold as a cataract. Her tendons tightened and flattened against her bones. She trembled as she walked alone between the flames.

The corridor was high-walled and lidded by nothing but a now-lurid sunset. The king and Osric had vanished, gone ahead around the curve, and Hild walked, alone—they all walked alone—along the inwardly spiralling path painted with tales, the characters from songs she had heard in hall all her life, songs of music and magic and might, of heroes and beginnings. The story of the Yffings. As she walked their eyes stared from cunningly painted knotholes in the elm, the prows of their ships gleamed along its ridged grain: the three ships of long ago, filled with land-hungry lords and their men in old-fashioned helmets and hammered armour. She shivered, standing between the narrow wooden walls—and shivered as her ship's keel ground up the pebbles and coarse sand of the beach in Thanet. Her throat bobbled as she leapt with her men from their ship, roaring. Ravens fought over broken bodies, Britons knelt bareheaded . . .

For a heartbeat she was Hild again. Huge, vivid scenes of great faces and blood-spattered swords, all outlined in black, loomed from the curving walls. Everything stank of wood tar. Then she was in the forest, running through the mist to the pounding beat beat beat of her heart, driving the sinews of her forefather as he howled and ran, tireless, through the ferns and brambles, leaping the stream, pounding through the heather, burning out the Britons, sweeping the ghosts of the slain to the hills, taking their gold.

Then she stood in the heart of the enclosure. A massive carved totem reached up and up into the now-inky night sky. A shadowy crowd thronged the space—not only her uncle and her mother, her cousins Oswine and Osthryth, but all those who had gone before: her father and his father, and his, and back to Wilfgisl the Wide and his father, Westerfalca, whose chestnut hair sprouted from their nostrils and the backs of their hands like burnished wire, back farther to Swebdæg and Sigegar, who had the same ermine-pale faces and sharp teeth as her cousins, to Wædæg and— embodied in the great totem—Woden himself.

A circle of torches caught and flared around the totem with a soft whump. The light and music swelled, rose to a point, and threw the attention of the living up and up where the great totem vanished into the well of the sky. It was built of three oak trunks cunningly laid end to end and carved and painted and gilded with the most magical totems of their people: the boar and the raven, the flame and the eagle, the lightning and the sea, and He Who Holds It All—god of weather and war, life and death, and the turning of the world, Woden himself, with his beard and hands wrapping around and around and around in a dizzying whorl. Clouds unfurled from the moon. God's eye drenched them in white light.

The gesiths sang. Hild thought she sang, too, but she also thought perhaps she was flying, like the soft indigo clouds far, far away. Then the torches were guttering, and the stars were out, wheeling, and the totem seemed like the axle around which the whole world turned.

A fortnight after most of the lords had left Goodmanham—though Osric lingered—Fursey dropped his bulging satchel on the grass by the stream and sat down next to Hild. "Your wealh woman said I'd find you here."

She nodded and split the daisy stem with her thumbnail.

"What, no 'Welcome home, my hero, was it a terrible hard journey? What news from Mulstanton?'"

"It's an easy journey down the coast and up the river. You probably slept and diced most of the way."

That was in fact exactly what Fursey had done. "Well. I took the liberty of directing your woman to the kitchens to bring us sustenance. And I told her if she brought small beer I would shrivel her soul." Hild plucked another daisy. "She was with that moony young gesith again."

Hild slotted the second daisy stem through the first. She was making a chain. His sisters used to do that. "It suits me to have it so."

Fursey looked at her more closely. "What's wrong, child?"

"I'm not a child. Not anymore."

"Stand up for me." After a moment, she did. "Ah. I see. Yes. You're as tall as that bird cherry there." And beginning to bud. A difficult time. The child's mother should be taking more care. She would flower soon. "And your lady mother? She is well?"

Hild sat again, arranging her skirts carefully. "She is becoming friendly with Osric."

"Ah," he said again.

She lifted her gaze to his. He'd seen the North Channel west of Manau swell and heave like that before the storm that killed his older brother. He looked away.

He pulled his satchel to him. "Then let's on to what I have from

Mulstanton. Cian sends his best love, wishes me to tell you he could take the hero Owein and Gwvrling the Giant one-handed, and thinks he is second only to God in the favour of everyone female."

"He didn't say that."

"No," Fursey said comfortably, "but he was thinking it."

"Is it true?"

Fursey laughed. "Of course it's not true! The boy is not yet seventeen. But he's fine and handsome, a proper warrior, and foster-son, only son, of a lord. He's tall, and will be taller when he gets his full growth, though not your height, I don't think, not quite, and the girls, well, the girls are beginning to notice."

"Does he notice back?"

"He does indeed. From the flirty little grins he thought were so private I believe he might have tumbled one of the dairymaids."

"Bote, Cædmon's sister?"

Fursey shook his fingers. "I couldn't say. But she's a pretty thing."

"And Cædmon?"

Fursey sniffed. "I had no occasion to talk to a cowherd."

"Onnen?"

"Ah, now there's a woman." Fursey scratched at his ankle. "She has Mulstan barking like a seal and fat as a hog."

"But is she well?"

"Oh, she's very well. More than well. And she bids you to visit. If your mother sees fit."

At the mention of her mother the child pulled the head off a daisy. He waited until she'd unthreaded it from the chain and picked another.

"I told her you would be pleased to think you were welcome, that you would find it a joy to visit, fate and family circumstances allowing. And that no doubt your lady mother felt the same." No jerk this time. She learnt control so fast. "At which point she snorted—most unbecoming for the lady of the household—and said"—he half closed his eyes—"'And no doubt, priest, the freemartin will give milk and the swallows fly north for winter,' and she asked about Hereswith, your sister. We spent some time worrying about her situation in the fens, with a man who already has a woman and two children."

"Girl children."

"Indeed. I pointed that out. And Onnen snorted at me again. Then when I ventured that on occasion a woman could sound very like a pig, I was struck by a memory of your little adventure at the wīc."

Hild flushed.

Fursey scratched at his ankle again, then took off his shoe—he did not wear sandals when travelling. Ridiculous footwear, all gap and space. "And speaking of your adventure, where is that wealh with my repast?"

Hild shrugged.

"A waste of three scillings," Fursey said. "Though no doubt the moony gesith would argue. She has him firmly under her, well, let us say thumb."

Hild picked a new daisy and split its stem.

"So. Onnen. I told her of your knife fight, and your purchase, and she told me, gravely, to tell you to have a care with the girl. She said wealh and Anglisc do not walk the same path or dream the same dreams. And she should know."

Hild wasn't listening. He wondered what paths she walked in her head.

"But you haven't asked of your little goat faced friend."

She looked up briefly. "She isn't goat-faced."

"Of course she isn't. Nor is she a chatterbox and a magpie—I do believe I saw her considering stealing my cross."

At least that brought a smile. But the smile was so careful it cut Fursey to the quick. How long had it been since the child laughed and played with others her age?

"Very well," he said. "I will concede on the goatish front. She is little, though."

"Is she, still?"

"Compared to you, and to Cian, yes. Compared to Onnen and that other harridan who is very near with the honey cakes—"

"Guenmon."

"The very same. Compared to them, she is well grown for a girl her age."

Hild looked down at her chest.

"As are you," Fursey said hastily. "As are you." Repeating the lie did not help. "Howsomever." He opened his satchel and rooted about until he found a linen-wrapped object half the size of his fist. "She sent you this."

Hild dropped the daisies and took it, hefted it in one hand then the other. She unwound the linen to reveal a hard slate-grey curl of a stone, like a frozen worm.

"A snakestone," Fursey said. "The local legend is of some harried god turning all the snakes into stone so that he could get some peace from the peasants' pitiful petitioning."

Hild stroked the tight stone coils with a fingertip.

"Begu also says to tell you she found a dragon in the cliff."

Hild lifted her eyebrows.

"The girl does like to imagine, yes. But this I saw for myself."

"Truly?"

"Truly. A great skull and wings, entombed in the cliff in another age and showing now where some of the cliff had tumbled into the sea. The wings must have been eight ells long! The thing was still mostly buried, so I couldn't pace it out. But the skull was"—he stretched his arms wide—"bigger than I could reach. And all of stone."

"Bones of stone . . ."

"And black as the devil's eyes."

Hild shivered.

"Think," he said. "It must have been a cataclysmic event: such a beast hurling itself into solid rock." Fursey fastened his satchel. "Begu, too, begs you to come visit. She says she misses you. She said to tell you someone called Winty birthed fine fat twins this spring."

He paused briefly, but Hild was walking her interior landscape again. Wherever it was, it seemed bleak.

"She also said she was very pleased with her comb, then she spoke of demons in worms and fish and dogs, and demons in hair and combs but became so wound about with her own mirth it was difficult to extract her meaning."

Hild seemed to pull herself back from wherever she had been. She smiled, but it was a disturbing, hard flexing of bone and muscle. "Winty is a cow. If I'm ever to keep Begu's messages straight she must learn to read. She must learn, Fursey."

"I mentioned a priest to Mulstan—the man is more hairy than ever— but he laughed and said, 'All in good time!' and clapped me on the back hard enough to make me spit out my meat."

"You must go again. You must make him understand."

"Must?"

"He has to understand. Cian and Begu must learn to read. They must all learn. Hereswith in East Anglia, too. But her need isn't so great."

"So great as whose?"

She ignored him. "Yes. You will go back. You will tell him that I order it so."

"And if I prefer not? If I choose to simply walk away one day and take a boat for Ireland?"

"I'll have you brought back. And whipped."

"Child—"

"I am not a child." Under the ferocity Fursey heard the howling loneliness. But ferocity was winning. "Priest or not, I will have you whipped if you try to leave. Who's to stop me, who in all the world? Only the king, and he gives me what I ask. So who is to stop me? No one."

"Then I tell you truly, you must learn to stop yourself."

Silence. A crow cawed, then another. She said, "That will be Gwladus with your food."

More silence.

"I'm sorry," she said.

"No, I don't think so. I don't know what's got into you, but I don't think you're sorry."

He held her gaze this time, though it made him sweat, and this time it was she who looked away. "Please," she said. "Go to Mulstan. They must learn to read. I have no one else."

He sighed. "I'll go. But first I'll take a fortnight's rest here."

"We leave for Brough in less than that—at the new moon. Æthelburh is coming."

"At the new moon, then."

"But it'll be raining by then."

"Nonetheless." The weather seemed to him set for fair, but even if it rained like Noah's flood he wanted time to talk to Gwladus, and to Lintlaf—if the idiot gesith could keep his brains out of his hose long enough to think. He must find out what the witch woman, the child's mother, was up to with Osric, he of the kingly ambitions. He'd heard talk. And this child would soon be living in very dangerous times indeed.

10

✦

THE DOCK AT BROUGH was almost invisible in the rain. It sheeted down, beating itself to froth on the huge wharf timbers, drumming on the roof of the great warehouse, irritating the party waiting beneath. Edwin overking was not used to sharing his presence with baled wool and sacks of grain. But Æthelburh's ship was due, and this was the only shelter.

A half-drowned river man was shown through the side door: He had seen the red sail! They'd be in, he reckoned, by the time he got his reward, begging your pardon.

On Coelgar's nod, Coelfrith gave the man half a silver penny. Edwin straightened his gold-crusted belt and the gold band on his forehead, which he'd taken to wearing on important occasions. Breguswith smoothed her skirts. Hild shrugged her shoulders to make sure her long mantle fell in perfect folds. She drew her hood up. The gesiths—in their most gaudy splendour, cloaks thrown back over their shoulders to show their hero-ringed arms—rolled their moustaches between their fingers so that they hung thick and manly, just so. Lilla nodded, and Forthere and a wiry red-haired man new to the household, a West Saxon by his brooch, hauled open the big warehouse doors. The æthelings and Osric and Oswine went first, walking in careful step at the corners of the great canopy that sheltered Hild and Breguswith. Edwin's betrothed was to be met and tended only by honoured family. Æthelburh had been only four when Breguswith left but, still, she and her daughter were blood kin.

There was little wind, just the gush and runnel of rain. Hild and her mother could barely see beyond their canopy.

Even in the rain, the scent of the river and its mudflats overwhelmed her: old and cold and wide. She wondered if Fursey's boat had crossed Æthelburh's wake downstream. Then ropes were being thrown and a gangplank slid out, and the gesiths behind her drew taut as a dozen armed men in red cloaks marched down the plank. Then came a cluster of black-clad priests, six or seven, hunched and hidden in their wet cowls. Then came Æthelburh, escorted by five women and Paulinus Crow.

Paulinus Crow. Bishop Paulinus. Tall, stooped, and black-haired, even at his age. Black-eyed, too, with the high-bridged nose she had seen on broken statues. "Want on legs," Gwladus said when she saw him. "Though for what, I don't know."

Hild did. She saw it for the first time the morning Paulinus and Stephanus stood with her in a cold room of the ruined Roman palace on the River Derwent, just a mile south of the ford.

It was the beginning of the moon of Winterfylleth, when the nights became longer than the days. Osric had finally departed for Arbeia. Hild hoped he had drowned at the mouth of the Tine. The rain had stopped days ago and the mornings had turned dry and crisp. Inside the ruined palace, sun as thin as whey seeped through the gaps under the eaves and washed over the mosaic floor. The priests looked pinched and cold, though Hild didn't feel the chill. Even inside a broken building it was warmer than up a tree or on the brow of a hill searching for figwort.

"Here, child," Paulinus said, and pointed with his bishop's jewelled crook at the picture by his foot: a fish and a cup pieced together of tiny green squares. "Christ's sign. Those who lived here were good God-fearing citizens."

Those who died here, Hild thought, looking at the axe marks on the fresco on the wall where someone had hacked out the iron lamp brackets, at the hollowed and charred circle where they had dug out the floor and tried to build a fire.

The Crow turned to Stephanus and dictated instructions in Latin about rededicating the building as a chapel to Saint John. Stephanus lifted the wooden board covered with wax that always hung from his belt and scribbled with a stylus. Hild gave no sign she understood any of it.

No one but her uncle knew that under Fursey's tutelage she could make her letters or that she understood Latin if it was spoken slowly—and even he seemed content to let her learn privately. Until she knew how these newcomers thought and what they wanted, she would keep it that way, keep her dice rattling in her cup. It was foolish to throw before all bets were on the table.

More Latin. More writing on the tablet. Rebuilding didn't make sense to her. If the priests wanted a place by the river, they should just tear these ruins down and start afresh.

"Why do you care about this broken place?"

"The people remember Rome. Old and mighty, it stands as a wise father to errant children." Breath whistled through his bony nose and his olive cheeks darkened. "Here Rome will rise again, shining like a beacon for those who have eyes. We will rebuild here and at Campodunum and at York, at Malton and along the wall, and the people will see Rome come again, and they will fear us and praise us. Even the kings of this isle will fear us and praise us. The faithful will flock to our standard."

He stood straight and stern, and Hild understood he wasn't seeing the overking's tufa but his own silk banner of a cross sewn with pearls, and himself standing at the head of a congregation of faithful, the chief Christ priest of the isle. His ambition was so naked she wondered why the king allowed it.

No doubt her uncle had his reasons. She thrust her hands in her pockets and turned her snakestone over and over. She found it helped her think.

Her uncle had to have reasons for such big changes. Six priests, a deacon—like the trader she had seen at Gipswīc, he had charcoal skin—and a bishop was more god people than the household had ever held. Coifi was unhappy. He wasn't the only one. The rhythms of the household had changed. The queen and her women, and the Kentish warriors—no longer king's gesiths but queen's men—who escorted her everywhere when the king did not, ate only fish on one day of the week. They went to a ceremony called Mass on another. Their housefolk brought different traditions: at the turn of the moon, turn all the silver. They liked watered wine with breakfast rather than small beer. Their clothes were different.

The king had to have a reason.

As she turned her stone and watched Stephanus make neat rows of letters on his wax, she wondered if that was it. Something to do with writing. But that's what he'd kept Fursey for, to teach her—though since she'd returned from the Bay of the Beacon her uncle had ignored her. Every-

thing a king does is a lie. She would watch and learn. Find out why Paulinus was taking such an interest in her, the king's niece, why he seemed to want to persuade her of his god.

Gwladus, on her way to the kitchens, told her Fursey was back. Hild ran all the way to the byre and got there in time to see him beating the dirt of travel from his skirts and a young byre hand lead his horse away. She shouted and laughed and surprised them both by hugging him.

"Christ's sweet smile, but you've grown again!" He held her at arm's length. "You seem well."

"Yes," she said, "I am, now that you're here." And it was true; she was glad, very glad, to see him. "Fursey, I'm sorry. For making you go. You were right, I wasn't sorry before, but I am now." He smiled again, pleased, but it didn't hide the tightness in his jaw, the worry and weariness. "What's wrong?"

"We'll talk in the byre," he said in Irish, and bent to his saddlebags.

"Let me." She slung them over her shoulder without effort.

The guest byre, recently rebuilt and stinking of raw timber, was full, but the other animals had been tended to long since. The only person about the place was the boy rubbing down Fursey's horse.

"Will we be sitting here now?" she said, and pointed to the hay bales along the wall opposite the stalls.

"Your fine dress—"

"This?" She regarded her beautifully embroidered overdress in dark blue. "I suppose it is fine, isn't it? But Gwladus insists, especially since the queen and her ladies arrived." She dropped the bags and sat. She brushed at the dust on her shoulder. "Well, sit before you fall. Say your piece then we'll find you food and clean clothes."

"It's not an easy message to deliver quick off the tongue."

Something horrible had happened to Cian or Begu. Or Onnen. She closed her eyes.

"Ach, no, no, they're all well." She blinked. "I'm tired to stupidity. My apologies. No, everyone is well. But Onnen bids me give you news. She reminds you that she is cousin to the wife of the lord of Craven—"

Hild nodded while her heart calmed down. Cousin to the sister of Ceredig of Elmet, Dwynai, who married Dunod ap Pabo of Craven, whom some called prince of that land—the first guest she had ever offered the cup to.

"—and messages are exchanged with kin often and often, especially in times of unrest."

Unrest. Hild fixed him with her gaze.

"Onnen, the lady of Mulstanton should I say, has word from her cousin Lady Dwynai that Cadfan of Gwynedd is not long for this world, may his soul find swift peace. And that his son, Cadwallon, wishes you dead."

"Me?" *Dead?*

"You and every root and branch of Edwin's kin."

"Yes, but I'm only—"

"Only? You are Edwin's bringer of light and seer. You saved Bebban-burg. You are his niece, his peaceweaver. Must we have this conversation again? There is no more only for you." He tapped her on the knee. "Listen, now. Cadwallon has boasted at mead that when he is king he will wipe the Yffings from the face of the earth. He has sworn it. To that end he is talking now to any lordling who will listen. He has talked to Cuelgils of Lindsey—"

The man who called himself princeps, who had fed them on their journey south, at Lindum.

"—and to Ciniod of the Picts."

"But Ciniod is sending a man to my uncle in friendship! Or so said the messenger in hall last night."

"Yes. No doubt Ciniod sends a man in friendship because, indeed, he refused Cadwallon's embassy."

"I don't—"

"But his fosterling did not."

"His . . ." Hild was momentarily at a loss. Then she remembered. "Eanfrith Iding."

"The same." The eldest son of Æthelfrith and his first wife, Bebba. Cin-iod's fosterling. Enemy.

"We had heard Eanfrith took a Pictish princess to wife."

"Indeed. And now they have a son, Talorcan."

The name said it all. Talorc, like Beli, was one of the names reserved for potential Pictish overkings.

She thought furiously. "Will Ciniod lend Eanfrith his war band?"

"Perhaps. Unofficially."

"But my uncle's war band is huge now, easily twice the size of any other. It would be madness. They couldn't hope to— Ah, but if Cuelgils . . ."

Fursey was nodding. "Yes. If Cadwallon persuades Lindsey, then the Saxons might throw in their bet, too—at which point Ciniod might see an opportunity, using Eanfrith as a puppet. Then your uncle would be caught between the hammer of the Picts and the anvil of the massed Saxons and Lindseymen and Welsh."

"Not just the Picts," said Hild.

If the Pictish war band rose and joined Gwynedd, Cadwallon and Eanfrith between them might also carry the men of the north, the Bryneich and Gododdin, who might bring Alt Clut. Even Rheged. It would be like watching the birth of a winter bourne: a trickle becomes a chattering stream then a roaring spate tumbling boulders before it, tearing out trees. Hundreds upon hundreds marching, singing their songs of wealh glory.

All would go down in red ruin.

But there was nothing she could do. Ciniod's mouthpiece, when he came, would smile and know nothing. Seer or not, no one would listen until there was something to point at. Something she could prove. She would have to wait until it began.

They wanted her dead . . .

On the east bank of the Derwent the day glittered with scent-of-winter sunshine. The women sat at their heckling benches, wooden boards set with dense clusters of iron spikes. In the distance Coelgar supervised the hammering and adzing of the snug new settlement rising alongside the shell of the broken Roman remains. The king was with the queen. The gesiths had taken the dogs hunting. The few housefolk not labouring with adzes were asleep and the place was quiet.

Hild sat with the women. Her mother had told her she'd been spending too much time alone—the rumours of hægtes and etin blood were starting again. Hild wasn't sure how sitting with a handful of tow before the spikes of what looked like an etin's comb would dispel those rumours.

Pulling the fibres through the spikes, over and over, until the tow was fined down to line, was normally hot and dusty work, but the Winterfylleth sun was as cool as glass and the air damp with the burly river and soon-to-fall leaves. Every now and again a light ruffle of wind brought the scent of pork roasting with wildling apples and damson—legacy of the Roman gardens—and Hild's mouth watered.

Over the last few days she had rarely lifted her hand from her seax and had eaten nothing not prepared by Gwladus. Then she had begun to wonder about even Gwladus. She started awake at the sound of footsteps, stood more than a sword's length from every gesith, and listened and listened and listened, until she thought her ears might start twitching like a cat's.

But no one popped from behind a mulberry bush with an axe, no one slipped poison in her beer, and even fear lost its grip after a while. Now, at the scent of pork and apples, she was hungry.

She sat with her mother, next to old Burgen and Æffe. Æffe was bundled in a scarf and a cloak, as was Burgen. Hild, after years of roaming the valleys and ridges, or sitting in the top of a tree in the moonlight, had long since hardened off. She was warm. She considered unpinning her sleeves and hanging them in her belt but decided not to: She would be the only one, and the muscles in her shoulders would just fuel the rumours.

Four of the queen's women sat at the next bench. Their chatter was flat with Jutish vowels; Breguswith's vowels sometimes flattened in sympathy. Beyond them were Teneshild, the old queen's gemæcce, and Ædilgith, whose gemæcce, Folcwyn, had died in childbirth last year—though some thought the ague more to blame—and with them the young pair girdled only the summer before last, Cille and Leofe. Leofe, who barely came to Hild's shoulder, was already big with Forthere's child.

"What are you shaking your head at?" her mother asked.

"Leofe. Forthere is so big and she's so small."

Old Æffe leaned forward and leered. "Not as big as I hear your sister's man is."

"Eh?" said Burgen.

Æffe repeated herself at a shout.

"Does she remember my advice about goose grease?" Burgen said. "Ask her. I did tell you young ones about goose grease, didn't I?"

Æffe shouted, "I can't ask her, you old fool, she's long gone, away in that infested swamp with her new man, Æthelric Short Leg." She cackled. "Short leg!"

But Burgen was getting anxious. "I did tell you?" she asked Hild. "I did, didn't I?"

"You did, Mother," Hild said. She gestured at Leofe with a handful of tow. "And clearly one at least listened."

"And you, young giant," Æffe said, "do you have your eye on a man yet? I see those pretty beads of yours. Some heroic gesith, eh?"

"No, Mother. These were a gift from the princess Rhianmelldt."

"Who?" Burgen looked about, fastened on the queen's women. "Which one is Rhianmelldt?"

Æffe started a shouted explanation of the genealogy of Rheged—though she was getting it wrong, forgetting that Urien was long dead—and Hild was reminded of Alt Clut and the songs of the men of the north, and wondered if, even now, they were sharpening their swords and boasting of who would kill the king and his uncanny niece.

Her mother was looking at her.

"Æffe is old. But she's not wrong. Unless I'm mistaken you'll be bleeding by summer. We should consider husbands."

Hild pulled her tow through the heckles. If she married and left court she would no longer be counted an Yffing.

"How do you find Oswine?"

Hild bent and brushed the rind dust from the hem of her skirts. Oswine, son of the treacherous badger Osric.

"He is handsome, don't you think?"

"No."

"His prospects are handsome," Breguswith said, softly now, as the old women shouted in the background. "How would you like to be married to Oswine, to be, say, lady of Elmet?"

Hild had a fleeting memory of jackdaws in the elms, a smoky hall. "I like Elmet," she said eventually. "But Ceredig king is said to be alive still, somewhere." And Oswine's father hadn't stopped Fiachnae mac Báetáin from trying to kill them. At some point, Edwin would either have to publicly forgive Osric the trouble at Tinamutha or kill him.

"At some point your uncle will make it worth someone's while to kill him."

Hild nodded, then realised her mother wasn't talking about Osric but Ceredig. With Ceredig gone, Elmet would get its own ealdorman—traditionally a royal kinsman. If Osric was still alive when Ceredig died, Elmet would go to him. "Would Osric step aside for his son?"

"What if he didn't need to?"

Hild pondered her mother. Breguswith's eyes were hard, bright blue, with none of that milky aging Hild saw in Æffe's and Burgen's eyes. Her fingers were beginning to thicken at the knuckles, yes, and her honey-gold hair looked dusty, but it was still thick, the skin at her throat was still firm, and her breasts full. She still bled every month. Bed games were one thing, keys another.

"Will you marry Osric?"

"Your uncle would not permit it." Her mother's voice was rich and round with secrets. Hild tried a trick she had learnt from Gwladus, and studied her mother through half-closed eyes while she lowered her head to her apparent task. Breguswith was smiling to herself.

Hild changed direction. "Would my uncle want me to marry Oswine?"

Her mother lowered her own eyes and said conversationally, "Your uncle won't live forever."

Hild's heart squeezed.

Breguswith nodded at Hild's hands: keep working. Hild pulled the tow through the heckles. Behind them, Burgen was cackling about something, and the other women were calling out good-natured insults. She leaned forward a little.

Breguswith's voice was very soft. "At Arbeia, a West Saxon has been indiscreet. You know something of this."

It wasn't a question. She should have expected her mother to know she knew.

"Osric doesn't understand his danger, though the danger is nigh. But a word in the right ear, a careful word, would break that egg before it hatches."

"I don't—"

"It will hatch soon."

"But—"

"Are you whispering about love?" Æffe shouted. "Of course you are. Empty-headed youngsters—look at that tow. You've heckled it to ruination."

When the moon was up, Gwladus brought Fursey to the byre.

"What is it that won't wait for me to finish my food? The last of the damson and fresh-killed pork. And I don't know where they found those apples but they were the sweetest . . ." Hild stepped forward so the moon caught her face, thin and pale. "Ach. Well, at least it's warm in here."

Gwladus turned to leave, but Fursey barred her way.

"Gwladus, my honey, bring us food. Bring us a lot of it. Your lady is all bone; her face looks sharp enough to cut cheese."

"It's not—"

"Be a lamb and don't talk. Run. Bring food—and mead, of course— and I'll absolve you of all that sin you've been gathering to yourself." He watched Gwladus pick her way across the yard, already beginning to glitter with frost, and turned back to Hild. "Now let us sit on the bales by that post." They sat. "What is it?"

She said nothing for a moment. Around them the horses, which had stirred when she came in, began to settle back to their dreams.

"Osric knows of Cadwallon's plot against Edwin. The plot that's begun."

"Begun?"

"In Lindsey. My mother told me."

"She told you. Why?"

"I don't know." She clenched her hands around her belt. He assumed she wished it were her mother's neck. He certainly did. "If Edwin finds Osric is plotting, he'll kill him."

"And if he doesn't find out, Cadwallon will eventually kill Osric, plot or no. He's Yffing, too."

"I know that!"

"Osric is stupid."

"Yes—"

"But your mother is not."

"She wants me to tell Edwin there's a plot, and stop it, and keep Osric out of it."

Fursey nodded. "She wants him alive and to herself."

Silence. She seemed to be staring at the post. Some stable hand or gesith, bored while waiting for his mount, had carved a stallion into the new wood. A stallion with improbable natural attributes.

"She wants me to take my knowledge to Edwin, clothed in portents. She wants me to start the war to keep that treacherous oaf safe. She is weaving a spider's web and I must rush about at her bidding. Again."

"Stopping the plot would save all the Yffings' lives. Including yours."

The child strangled her belt slowly with both hands. "That's just part of it. She's aiming for something . . . I can't . . . Why is she doing this? Why is she defending him? Osric's men could have killed me at Tina-mutha!"

"Strictly speaking they were Fiachnae mac Báetáin's men. As I was. Am." Ah, she'd forgotten that. Well, the child needed reminding sometimes.

"You're confusing me."

"It's a confusing world."

She pulled her seax, leapt, and stabbed the post with a vicious overhand thrust. The mare in the nearest stall swung her head around and huffed down her nose.

His heart thumped like a rabbit. She was so fast. And strong. The battle-hard tip had sunk three fingers deep into the elm.

"If she had just asked! But no. She pushes me into a corner where there's no choice."

"It's what women do: weave the web, pull the strings, herd into the corner. It's their only power. Unless they're seers." He was proud that his voice didn't shake.

The child massaged her hands.

"Your mother has built you a place where you can speak your word openly. Now she asks you to use that for her, and for yourself of course."

Outside someone, several someones, crunched over the frozen grass.

He turned. It was Gwladus, now wearing a cloak against the cold— and because the russet colour made her hair shine like sunlit water, he suspected—and two housemen he didn't know. The men stood behind Gwladus and flinched when Hild looked at them. They were afraid of the child. Fursey didn't know whether to pity her or be glad for her. Fear could always be used.

He raised his eyebrows at Gwladus.

"You said bring a lot. And this should be enough to buy me a forgiveness. Two of them. One now and one tomorrow, for the sins I'll gather tonight." She smiled to herself as she stroked her cloak, then noticed the seax stuck in the wood. She gestured for the housefolk to put down the trays. "We'll leave you to your business."

She swept out. The men almost trod on her cloak in their eagerness to get away from the hægtes.

Hild began to work her seax free while Fursey fussed with the food. "I'm not hungry," she said without looking up from her task, but her stomach growled.

"Of course not. But humour an old man and eat anyway. There's pork in its crackling. Damsons, oh so plump and running with juice. And what's this? Oh, blessings upon that girl. Horse mushrooms fried in pork grease. Hazelnut with the apples. Good sharp cheese. And, may she be thrice blessed, wine." He sniffed. "The Crow's special cache, unless I'm mistaken."

She sheathed her seax and sat. "She stole the Crow's wine?"

Was that a smile? He handed her a round of floured bread, a pot of chestnut paste—more fruit of Derwent's Roman past—and a birch cup with a silver rim. "We'd better drink up the evidence."

The moon was high and small by the time she sat back and sucked the fat from behind the last piece of crackling. Fursey finished the wine while she chewed on the skin.

"You look better."

She nodded, picked the last hazelnut from the tray and crunched it. "Tomorrow," she said. "I'll go to my uncle tomorrow, in the middle morning, with his counsellors about him."

"Kings can be dangerous when surprised."

The child pondered that. "I should talk to him privately first?"

He nodded. "Seek him all ravaged with dream. He'll call his counsellors and you can speak in more certain terms." And pray. Pray no one is clever enough to look beyond the child to her mother and the terrible ambition there.

Hild studied herself in the polished silver. "Wilder about the eyes," she said, and lowered the mirror for Gwladus to dab ash in quick sweeps beneath her eyes. This time the king wasn't puzzled and far from home. This time he was newly married and content. It would take every portent she could muster. And dreams were the most potent seeing of all.

"Wait," Gwladus said, "hold still," and she dipped a chewed twig in Hild's ewer of water and streaked the ash deftly. Once, twice. "Look at that," she said with great satisfaction.

Hild looked. She looked like a tear-streaked maid sleepless under the weight of unbearable knowledge. She smiled.

"Don't smile. It makes you look mad."

Hild looked at her.

"You could try trembling your bottom lip. Go on. Just try it."

Hild lifted the mirror and tried it. Gwladus was right. The tremble turned her from madwoman to frightened maid.

Gwladus arranged her hair to an artful tousle and draped her with a heavy crimson robe: the very picture of a seer of the royal blood who leaps from her loyal bed to warn her king.

She strode from the room, calling for Burgmod.

In his sleeping apartment, Edwin, beard uncombed, sat on a stool. He had thrown a cloak over his sleeping tunic—though it was not cold, for the king's fire never went out.

Hild stood, but not too close. Even frowsy and hardly awake enough to be wary, kings did not like those who loomed—even royal kin. Especially royal kin. Was the queen listening from the curtained bed? She must speak up, just in case.

She had dreamt of eagles, she said, like to the eagles of Gwynedd, nesting over Lindum, with one eaglet pushing its brother from the nest.

"Cadwallon!"

In her dream she had swooped through the air alongside a jackdaw that flew into a just-dyed red cloth hanging by the Lindum gate and stained its beak scarlet.

He frowned.

"A common bird tangling with royal crimson, King. In Lindum."

"Cuelgils! That jumped-up ceorl. Intriguing with Cadwallon."

Hild bowed.

"Go on, go on."

And then she had woken, to hear that the vill's newest bull calf, "the same liver brown as the Lindsey Bull, lord King," had died, and some swore they had seen boar tracks around the pen.

This last was true, the death at least; Gwladus had told her.

Edwin turned his head and shouted, "Forthere!" The huge gesith stuck his head around the door. Hild caught sight of Burgmod beyond him, scratching at the back of his neck, tilting his helmet forward over his nose. "Is the new bull calf dead?"

"Bull calf, King?"

"Bull calf. Born yesterday. Is it dead or isn't it? Find out."

Housefolk, alerted to the king's early waking, hurried to bring hot water, breads, breakfast beer. One man slid the cloak from the king's shoulders and folded it while another unlaced his shirt. His chest hair glinted here and there with grey. A puckered and twisted spear scar ran along his left ribs.

His scowl was hidden briefly as his bodyman dropped a new tunic over his head.

No one offered Hild anything.

When his warrior jacket was fastened Edwin looked considerably more alert. His bodyman was combing his beard when Forthere stuck his head through the doorway again.

"It died, King. The freemartin born with it, too."

Edwin pushed his man away and looked at Hild. "The freemartin?"

"It signifies nothing."

He gave her a sly look.

"The bull calf is the one that matters, lord King. The calf the colour of the Lindsey Bull."

"Unless you're wrong."

"Have I ever been wrong?"

"So Cadwallon allies with Cuelgils to raise Lindsey." He stared at the fire, calculating. "Yet no armies have marched from Gwynedd."

"Not yet."

"It is winter."

His meaning was clear: If he took the war band to Lindsey in this weather and found nothing, he would have no spoil to share among his gesiths. He would have to gift them from his personal hoard. He would take his losses out of her hide.

"The armies of Gwynedd will come to Lindsey in spring. If Cuelgils still rules."

The long silence was broken only by the crackle of flames taking hold of the new wood on the fire. Edwin was looking at her.

"How old are you now?"

"Eleven, King."

"You want me to go haring off to Lindsey on the dreams of a maid of eleven years . . ." It was not a question, and in any case Hild had no answer. She simply stood. "So when I swoop upon Lindsey and slaughter them all, how will I know if you were right or not?"

Hild had no idea. "You will know." And now her life hung on her mother's information.

A maid of eleven years. A child.

Facing a formal summons to the king's hall, a woman girdled and veiled would have bolstered her breasts and painted around her eyes, cinched her girdle tight to accentuate her hips and the symbols of her rank hanging about them: the keys and crystal and weft beater.

Very well.

Hild unpinned her sleeves to show arms tan and tight as a stripling's, wore a light cloak in royal blue flung back from her shoulders gesith-style, and tucked her hair behind her ears, to remind them of a fighting man with greased-back hair.

When she was escorted by Lintlaf and Coelfrith into the hall she stopped four paces from Edwin's great chair, rather than the usual three, to stand in the shaft of winter light so that her hair blazed more chestnut even than the king's. She stood tall—she overtopped all but Forthere now—with her hand on her seax, and let rich royal certainty invade her every word: Cuelgils was a traitor. Remember Bebbanburg. Remember treachery.

"We will take Lindsey," Edwin said, and not one voice dissented.

This time there were no wagons, no women, no bags packed with finery for show. There were two hundred gesiths wearing their metal wealth, with their mounts and remounts, a hundred war hounds, a hundred servants on their own mounts, a smith-armourer, and fifty packhorses. This time they ate in the saddle and slept rolled in blankets, and the outriders had orders to kill anyone—Angle or wealh, man, woman, or child—who saw them. It drizzled steadily; they rode robed in tiny jewels of rain. They crossed into Lindsey on the second day.

Everything was mud. Horses foundered. Hild, being light, was easier on her mount than most, but even so, when they reached the shallow valley of the River Trent, she felt Cygnet trembling under her, just as her own thighs trembled and her wrists ached.

The river gleamed dully, like pewter. Patches of linden woods formed misty thickets along the banks. Clearly the outriders had missed someone: the Lindseymen had had warning enough to throw down trees on the west bank of the river, branches facing the road, and to form their shield wall on the east bank.

The Northumbrians laughed. The shield wall was only twenty shields wide and three deep and the clutter thrown in their path was light; the Lindseymen had had time to cut only small trees.

Edwin ordered a halt—long enough to wipe faces and eat a handful of twice-baked road bread—while fifty gesiths and the wealh dismounted to clear the road and collar the dogs in their war harnesses. The outriders rejoined them from the woods.

The horses and wealh did the work while the fifty gesiths formed an arrow shield facing the woods. No arrows flew. Lilla and the king exchanged looks.

The horses stamped and steamed, and the unoccupied gesiths laughed and talked in great booming voices, though some were pale. All made the motions of eating, though few actually chewed and swallowed. Many threw their bread to the dogs. The dogs fought over it. In the hissing rain the noise was sudden and violent.

Hild gnawed her bread. Her mouth was drier than summer straw. But she chewed stolidly and managed to swallow one mouthful. She raised her arm to toss the rest to the dogs, then thought better of it. Some were bleeding already, seeping red under the rain, standing in pink puddles.

Hild drank from the flask of small beer at her saddlebow and forced herself to chew and swallow again. She felt strange, as though it were someone else who lifted the bread, who chewed and swallowed, who carefully unfastened the flap of her saddlebag and put away the bread. Someone else who loosened her seax in its sheath, someone else who studied the fallen leaf rubbish and thought it beautiful.

A man put his hand on Cygnet's neck. Lintlaf, on foot. "The king wants you to stay on this side with the wealh and the horses," he said. Hild nodded. Most of the gesiths were dismounting. "Don't try to fight. It's not like a knife fight. You don't know . . . Forthere and his men will guard you." She nodded again. "Forthere is angry."

Forthere was. As Lintlaf and the rest of the war band checked their weapons and the dogs sat in a dreadful, eager silence, Forthere wrenched his horse's head this way and that, and shouted at the wealh to stop their Thunor-cursed hand-waving and get behind those trees with all the horses, all, mind, or he would lop off the left leg of any lackadaisical lily-livered limpknob.

Hild kneed Cygnet into his path. "Are you angry with your horse, Forthere?" She nodded at the great rope of drool that hung from its bit.

"You . . ." His face worked. But she was the seer who had saved Bebbanburg; she was the king's niece. She was the reason they were here.

She nodded. "Me." She understood his anger. Forthere, giant Forthere, was used to being in the van, running under the banner or stalwart behind a shield, not being left behind to guard the baggage. "Nonetheless, have a care for your horse."

He loosened the rein a little. "Stay behind the wealh, behind the horses, behind me. You lose so much as an eyelash and the king will have my ears." He lifted his huge ham hand, stuck two fingers in his mouth, and whistled. A gesith looked up. Forthere waved him over. "This is Eamer." It was the whip-muscled redhead Hild had noticed at Brough, now on a thin black gelding. "You will stick to him like honey on bread," Forthere told her, and then, to Eamer, "Everywhere she goes, you go. Even to piss. You, her, til the Lindseymen are dead."

The king's drummer began the beat. Both men went rigid for a moment, like hounds pointing, as the gesiths formed up in two bands. Forthere shook himself, gathered his reins.

Hild's scalp tightened. A battle, shield wall to shield wall. Linden wood to linden wood. She imagined meeting a man the size of Forthere, huge with battle rage, stinking with it; dogs dripping and snarling at her legs, her arms. Sharp swords cleaving down, splintering shields, crushing skulls, slicing off faces. Men sworn to follow their lord or die. Victory or death, no middle ground. They sang so they didn't piss themselves.

Forthere cantered off, already shouting.

"Lady," Eamer said, and backed up his mount to allow Cygnet past in the direction of the horse picket among the linden trees.

The two bands of gesiths were now shin-deep in the river, the dogs already swimming. She was glad she had no choice but to hide among the trees, hide from the blood and the rage, the striving to kill. She kneed Cygnet forward.

The drumbeat stopped. Hild twisted in her saddle. The gesiths were halfway across and up to their chests, and the drummer held his drum high above his head. The gesiths sang, to give themselves heart, and one group swung upstream from the Lindseymen, one downstream.

The picket lines were strung between trees. Hild slid from her horse, and the instant her foot touched the ground all sound of the river and the gesiths' singing disappeared. Gone, as though sliced through with a knife. She blinked. Pulled herself back in the saddle: the singing rising to a roar, like logs rolling off a wagon.

"Lady."

She got down again. The sound vanished. "The sound . . ."

"A sound shadow," Eamer said. "Cupped by a god's hand. Or so they say. But I like to hear what's happening." He unstrapped his spear and slung his linden shield before dismounting.

She loosened Cygnet's girth and handed the reins to a wealh, and listened again: nothing but the murmur of the wealh, Forthere's shouted command to the ten gesiths at the edge of the copse, and the dripping in the trees. She sat on the mossy top of a limestone rock shaped like a giant mushroom cap. A sword fern grew at its base. She tipped her head back and studied the bare branches of the linden tree above. If she stood to her full height she might just touch it.

Sword fern, shield tree, and a maid whose name meant battle. Yet she was shivering.

A horse stamped. Hild and the wealh jumped. Forthere's gesiths laughed.

The rain seemed to be easing. A few birds called from the trees. Hild pushed her hood back, trying to hear them better. She didn't recognise their call.

"How long will it take?"

Eamer leaned his spear against the rock, took off his helmet, and scratched his head. "When fools are in charge, wise men make no predictions."

"Fools?"

He put his helmet back on, took up his spear again. "Does war interest you, lady?"

Hild had never been asked a question by a gesith before. She looked at him afresh, at his Gewisse brooch. "It does today."

"Then the Lindseymen should have laid trees on the far side of the bank, where we would have to climb them already tired from the crossing, heavy with water and slippery with mud. Or they could have hidden bowmen on this side to pick off those who cleared the path. They are fools."

Hild pondered that. "Why are they so few?"

"Likely most are at Lindum, to guard the gold. If—" He broke off, slid his shield from his back onto his arm. "Down. Get down. Behind the rock."

An arrow chunked into his shield. She stared at it. Another hissed into the fern by her feet, and then she was scrambling to her feet, leaping, up, up, up into the tree. She balanced on a slippery smooth bough, arms wrapped around the trunk, heart banging like a drum.

She peered down at the clearing. Everything moved like flies stuck in honey.

Eamer brushed the arrow from his shield with his spear shaft. The broken arrow spun away, lazy as dandelion seed, and landed in the moss on the boulder, directly beneath Hild. Fletched with goose feathers.

Sword fern, shield tree, goose feathers. *Part of your wyrd.*

A horse screamed and others whinnied, and whinnied again farther away. Men shouted. The sound was wavery and unreal. Hild stared at the goose feathers glistening tawny and white on the bright green of the mossy boulder.

More arrows hissed from the woods. Men fell.

Lindseymen poured into the clearing. Forthere shouted, "Shields!" and the Northumbrians—the ones not lying on the green ground with arrows standing from their chests—locked shields, and the Lindseymen, running and leaping over the fallen, parted around them like water. Forthere shouted, "Break!" and then they were all running, gesiths chasing Lindseymen. To her end of the clearing.

"Death!" Eamer bellowed, and with a clang of iron that shook the tree, he slammed his shield at one Lindseyman's head and his spear at another's.

A Lindseyman in a round leather helmet took Eamer's spear under his jaw and the blade burst through his cheek. Eamer shook the man like a dead rat on a stick. Then, cursing, he flung spear and man down and drew his sword. Lindseymen, pursued by gesiths, poured around the boulder. Hild, shrieking like a gutted horse, half fell, half leapt from the tree, seax flashing.

Someone slammed into her, then another picked her up and threw her back down behind the rock.

Wealh were catching the horses the Lindseymen had loosed and killing the ones they had hamstrung. Forthere was asking her anxiously, loudly, if she was all right. Hild wiped the blood off her face with a wet dock leaf and nodded. It wasn't her blood. It was the blood of those who had fought over her like mad beasts while she lay stunned.

A while later, she didn't know how long, it was Eamer nodding while Forthere shouted. From this distance she saw Forthere had a dent in his helm, over his ear. Eamer wasn't listening; he had his foot on the dead Lindseyman's face and was trying to pull his spear free. Forthere kept shouting nonetheless. ". . . with her, like a burr. Like a burr. Woden's beard, it was her they were after. The maid." Eamer's spear pulled loose with a grating suck. "The king wants her over on the east bank. Get her there safe if you value your ears."

Threescore men lay twisted and burst open on the grass. A handful, Edwin's men, were laid tidily at the side of the field, covered with their cloaks and shields, swords at their sides. A dozen or so of the Lindseymen stirred and moaned and called for water. No one paid attention. The sound scraped at her bones. She focused between Cygnet's ears as her mare and Eamer's gelding picked their way delicately across the trampled, slimy expanse to the leather tent where the king's banner poles were driven deep in the dirt.

The gesiths had found the Lindseymen's beer. One of them, with a finger newly gone and blood all over his leg and teeth, was laughing and pissing in a dead man's mouth.

The thought of going alone into the king's tent full of men who had just killed other men made her feel dizzy. She told herself that Eamer, too, had just killed, but still her voice wobbled when she said to him, "Stay out here."

Just inside the tent, the king, unhelmed, stood with his naked sword in one hand, point resting on the floor, and a goblet in his other. Lilla, still helmed, red with gore, stood under the tent peak, where two short-haired men were bound to the centre pole. One of Lilla's men stood against the tent wall, deliberately seeing nothing, saying nothing. The tent reeked.

Edwin was smiling. Blood clotted the mail around his elbow. "It's a clear road to Lindum now, if we're swift, and we lost only eleven men."

"Eleven men on this side, King," Lilla said.

Edwin ignored him and said to Hild, "You were right." He pointed with his chin at the bound men. "Welshmen."

Both men were sagging in their ropes. One had been so badly beaten his mother wouldn't recognise him. The right side of the one closest to her was sopping with blood from a wound Hild couldn't see. Probably in his armpit. She knew from songs that was a good place to stab a man in armour. But this man wasn't armoured. He wore a checked cloak.

Hild knew him. The memory was sudden and sharp: the elm wood, the geese in the distance, this man standing with his brother in Ceredig's hall. *You have your father's hair*, and, later, *Edwin Snakebeard will come*.

Gwynedd. Marro. Cadwallon.

She wished she could run upstairs to bed with Hereswith, wished Onnen would be there to comb her hair. She made herself step closer. She nodded at the unconscious, beaten man and asked Lilla, "Will he die of his wounds?"

"No. Though he'll never be pretty."

Hild turned to Edwin. "Edwin king. Uncle. These are Cadfan's own men." She saw his twitch of surprise, which he covered with a lift of his goblet. "The bloody one will die. The beaten one can't talk. Or not soon. Give him to me, and the first will talk before he dies."

Edwin's eyes flashed green. "We don't have time for spells and sacrifice."

"No."

Silence. "Oh, very well." He waved his goblet as though the matter were of no account and stepped to the door flap to speak to Coelgar.

Hild turned back to the blood-soaked man. He was watching her. She said swiftly in British, which she knew Lilla barely understood, "I still have my father's hair, and my uncle's. And the serpent has come to you. No, say nothing. You have no time. Marro, you are dying." Marro stirred at the use of his name. "You are dying, but your brother"—and now he jerked in his ropes; she had guessed right—"your brother will live, I'll see to it, if you tell me true. Cadfan king is dying, yes or no?"

"Who are you?" It was little more than a whisper, but the same voice from long ago.

"I am the king's light."

He blinked as though he couldn't see well. "Are you real?"

She reached out and touched her thumb to his forehead. "Tell me now, is Cadfan dying?"

"Yes."

"And Cadwallon will be king."

"He is king now in all but name."

"And he plots with whom?"

A long silence. "You are not a man. Are you a demon?"

"I am the king's light." King's light. King's trembling leaf who hid up a tree. "Who does Cadwallon plot with?"

"You will keep my brother safe, demon, you swear it?"

"I swear it. Who?"

"Eanfrith Iding. Cuelgils princeps. Neithon of Alt Clut. Eochaid Buide of the Dál—"

"You lie," Hild said. "Alt Clut and Dál Riata would never ally."

"Enough gold will make for the strange—" He coughed. His tunic glistened as fresh blood seeped from his wound. His hose were soaked and sagging. ". . . strangest bedfellows."

"Cadwallon doesn't have that much gold."

"Edwin overking does, even when split among seven lords." His voice was a faint rattle and sigh, like a stirring in the willow rhynes.

"Seven?"

His eyes closed. She shook him gently.

"You said seven lords. Who else? Marro, who else?"

She wasn't sure but she thought perhaps the strange sound he made was a laugh. "You know. So close to you. Also Dunod . . ."

"Dunod of Craven?" He sighed, and this time the sigh went on and on. His eyes stayed open. "Marro?"

She blew on his eyes. He did not blink.

She stepped back. "He's dead," she said to Lilla. "Tie the other to a horse. When we have horses. Keep him safe."

Coelgar lifted the door flap for the king to leave and the moans of Lindseymen filled the tent. Edwin said over his shoulder to Hild, "With me." Lilla caught the eye of his man by the tent wall, gestured to the Welshman, and joined the king.

Eamer fell in behind them.

As they walked, Edwin and Coelgar talked of horses and supplies, and Lilla wiped at the gore on his mail, succeeding only in smearing it. The noise of the suffering Lindseymen was terrible, much louder than before. No one but Hild seemed to notice.

She said to Eamer, "Why don't they kill them?"

Eamer shrugged. "It's wealh work, and the wealh are on the other side of the river. Wealh work. Or women's work."

It was not like slitting the throat of a sucking pig. The pig had not looked into her eyes.

After the first one, the thrashing and choking and mess, Hild wiped her hands on the grass and asked Eamer to find her a spear, a short one. He brought her one broken halfway down the shaft. The pale ash was warm. She stooped to the second man, curled on his side with his leg almost off at the knee, and said, "Lie still now, and it will be quick." She tugged off his helmet and felt with her thumb for the soft spot at the base of his skull, set the point of the broken spear, and killed him with one leaning thrust.

It was not unlike sticking a skewer in a roast to see if it was done. The same pop as the skin broke, then a good push through the meat gripping the iron. The juices that leaked were red, though, not clear, and the smell was quite different: shit and rust and mud.

Around her men cried out louder, some asking to be next, some saying that, for pity's sake, it was a broken leg, only a broken leg, if she would just bind it, and bring water . . .

Hild moved in a bubble of quiet, her own sound shadow, but after the third man she found a knot of gesiths following her. She ignored them, knelt by the fourth man, and struggled with his helmet. He moaned, like a man in his sleep, but Hild thought he was probably too far gone to feel much. It was difficult to tell; half his face was missing. Behind her, the gesiths spoke in hushed voices.

She knew . . . she knew the Welshman's name . . . knew they were brothers . . . had foreseen everything . . . she'd vanished from sight . . . fell from the sky like an eagle . . . wouldn't die even when a score, twoscore, threescore Lindseymen attacked from ambush . . . hadn't she saved them at Bebbanburg? . . . she had the true sight . . .

At the edge of the field a man shrieked; a sow rooted in his belly. "Eamer, please. Kill him."

"Lady, I must stay at your—"

"Please."

But it was another gesith who drew his sword, ran to the edge of the field, and brought his blade down hard, once, twice, three times, and threw a clod of dirt at the sow. She ran off, hoinking in outrage, but didn't go far.

The gesith ran back. "He's dead, lady."

"Thank you."

Another gesith drew his sword, and another. They looked at her, as though for permission. "I thank you, too." They moved off through the strewn field, swords rising and falling. Killing at a seer's bidding was fit work for gesiths.

Hild bent over and vomited stinging bile, then, through her weeping, killed the man at her feet.

They left their wounded with a handful of wealh to care for them and to strip the dead enemy of arms and armour, and rode hard for Lindum. Hild's eyes would not stop leaking. Lilla dropped back through the ranks long enough to give her his flask. Mead. "Drinking helps."

Sometime later her eyes dried. Not long after that, the horses dropped to a walk and the message came back: The king wants the maid. Hild and her shadow, Eamer, cantered forward. Others cantered behind her: the gesiths from the field. Nine, all told.

The gesiths they passed sang a cheerful, ugly song. One in four rode with poles topped by the brutalised heads of Lindseymen. They did not look human. Hild pretended they were not.

Lilla put his hand on his sword as they approached, and Hild nodded at Eamer, who made a *Hold* gesture to her followers, and stayed with them while she approached the king.

"We near Lindum," Edwin said. "What will we find?"

Leathers creaked as those close by leaned in to listen. Her mind was empty of everything but the feel of iron gritting through muscle and cartilage. She shook her head.

His eyes swarmed green and black. "You are a seer. You will tell your king."

Hild stared at him, her mind as smooth as wax.

He kicked his horse, then reined it in savagely. "You knew the men in the tent. You couldn't, but you did. And you witched them so they talked to you, Lilla said. Now you've witched my own men so they follow you like puppies. So tell me, or, by Woden, I'll throw you in the river with your tongue and toes in a bag around your neck."

He would do it. She had seen enough that day to know he would. Who would stop him?

With a white hiss, the world began to turn. The ground seemed a long, long way off. She clung to her saddle horn. If she fell now, he would kill her. She must hold on.

She held on.

It didn't matter that she had nothing in her stomach, that she had pushed a spear into four men and snuffed their lives like guttering candles. It didn't matter that she was an ungirdled girl in an army of men who would piss in a dead man's mouth and leave another holding his own insides because to help was women's work.

I am the light, she thought. I am not a maid. I am the light. Cold as a sword. I will show no weakness.

She stepped to one side of her feelings, like stepping out of her clothes. She did not hurt. She had no need to eat, no mortal concern with life. She could breathe easily.

She lifted her head.

"Edwin king, seven lords are arrayed against you." Seven, a number brimming with wyrd. "I do not know every name. Yet."

He assessed her, then turned to Coelgar. "Keep the men moving at a walk. Lilla, with me. No," he said to Eamer, and then to the pack of gesiths who had followed, "you hounds will stay." To Hild he said, "Come."

"You're lying," he said when their horses were fifty paces down the trail. "Oh, not about the names you've given me: Cadwallon with Cuelgils and Eanfrith, Neithon, and Eochaid—the gold he must have promised for that unnatural pairing! Even Dunod. No, they're true enough. But you're not telling me something." He tapped his teeth with his thumbnail, thinking. "The trap was for you on the west bank. A score of men. For you. Why?"

"Ransom?"

"Look at you. What are you worth as a niece?"

As a peaceweaver, more than an ætheling. But Hild did not bother to say so.

"You shouldn't have let the Welshman die before he gave up the last name."

"Men die, Uncle."

"And that's something you can't do, eh? Shine your light beyond death."

From the strange, cold distance in which she had placed herself, Hild wondered what he would do if she said she could see into the realm of the dead. He would believe her. They all believed her, no matter what she said.

She heard again Marro's whisper. *You know. So close.* She did know, or could guess, the seventh name: Osric. He was an Yffing, a man in his prime, with an almost-grown heir. If Edwin died tomorrow half the kingdom would side with Osric against the young æthelings. But to betray Osric was to betray Breguswith.

"Well," Edwin said, "we'll have the truth of it from Cuelgils himself soon enough."

They took Lindum before æfen. Lindum, city of tanners and fullers, stinking for generations of stale urine and skin turning to leather, stinking now of blood.

Edwin and his counsellors, each with his own man, sat at the scarred marble table that had belonged to Cuelgils. Hild, who had brought Lintlaf—for Forthere had reclaimed Eamer, and she didn't even know the names of her hounds—sat a little apart. No one knew if she was in favour or not. Beyond the painted walls, gesiths hooted as they played kickball with the heads of Cuelgils's sons. They were small heads. The head of Cuelgils himself was being washed, its hair carefully dried and moustaches combed, to be mounted on a gilded pike.

Edwin was relaxed and smiling. Cuelgils was dead in the fight, a pity, but he had Lindsey and its gold. A lot of gold. Enough gold to buy his way past any northern conspiracy. On his forefinger he wore a new ring, a massive garnet.

He threw a great golden collar, probably Irish work, to Coelgar, "Wisest of counsellors," who bowed his head. An arm ring inset with silver and enamel to Lilla, "Bravest of men." A cuff to Blæcca, "Most loyal thegn," and on around the table, until everyone was looking at Hild.

Edwin extracted a small, heavy cup from the hoard. Polished silver from Byzantium, inlaid with gold: a lewd figure of a woman on one side and a stately queen on the other. Both women wore the same face. Edwin weighed it for a moment, then set it on the table with a click and pushed it to Hild. "For Hild, seer, prophet, and most favoured niece, on her birth day."

Hild had forgotten. She was twelve years old.

11

✦

THE WEATHER TURNED. The first leaves fell. In Goodmanham, Marro's brother woke and died of the black vomit the same day. Hild hadn't even learnt his name. Breguswith left for Arbeia the next day. She would return for Yule.

The court moved to York. Æthelburh's people gradually took over the household: James the Deacon, the dark-skinned music master, took administration. Eormenfrith, her trade master, suggested the women embroider hangings he could exchange for a variety of goods from the continent. Paulinus, her adviser and priest, stayed at the king's side, offering counsel, always accompanied by Stephanus. The queen herself became the woman that women went to with complaints, though her healing, Gwladus said, was as much a thing of prayer as of poultice.

Hild moved numbly in a cold world: the maid who killed, the maid who felt nothing. The maid with no mother or sister or friend, and a king uncle who had no more use of her for now. The maid with her own unsworn comitatus, nine gesith hounds who, when they had nothing better to do, tried to follow and protect her while pretending they were doing no such thing. Hild roamed the vale and its thicket of woods, collecting herbs and watching the world slow down, fade, and tidy itself away for winter. All but the peregrines.

She loved peregrines in winter: solitary, fierce, and dangerous, their cries clean and bright as a blade. She followed one male for three days, sleeping in the crisp understorey of the oak wood, huddled by a broken wall of a long-ago farmstead, wading, careless of the cold, along the pebbled bed of the beck he washed in every day. Her raggle-taggle band of gesiths tried to follow, but she shinned up a giant rowan, still dense with leaves, and watched them march past. Later she turned to watching otters on the Fosse, upstream of the walls. There she crouched in the reeds, ignoring the mud, unmindful of the wind rattling the stems, and watched their sleek brown play, their casual killing.

Cadwallon wanted to kill her. He wanted to hook her out of her stream and crunch her spine because she was an Yffing, and then go back to doing king things. Her king uncle didn't trust her. She didn't trust her mother. Her mother was with Osric the treacherous in Arbeia.

At night she dreamt of the Lindseyman crying out, *It's only a broken leg, for pity's sake . . .* and sometimes it was herself lying there broken, pleading. Sometimes the figure with the spear was Edwin, sometimes her mother, who wept, as she had wept, but showed no pity, as she had shown none.

As the weather worsened and the last of the leaves fell, she roamed the half-ruined wings of the old redcrest fort within a fort. One afternoon she ran into Paulinus—trailed by Stephanus—who ignored her wild hair and mud-smeared dress and served her a political smile and the information that he was surveying the wing for the queen. She wanted the royal ladies to have their own suites—including, of course, the lady Hild. Whom he hoped to call on soon in order to discuss the glories of Christ the Lord.

"Not my lord," she said. "My lord is the king. My uncle."

His smile didn't waver but Hild heard the false note when he turned to Stephanus and said in Latin, "Note that many of these bricks are crumbling."

Stephanus obediently pressed his stylus to the wax. Hild saw that what he wrote was *Of course the bricks are crumbling!* and she snorted.

Paulinus fixed her with his black eyes, and Hild knew she had made a mistake.

The next day, Hild stood by the queen, who had summoned her, in the centre of the echoing great hall of York. They watched as James the Deacon prepared to lead his tiny choir, four lay brothers selected because "they sing like cherubim, cherubim," for the queen.

James's face, up close, was the colour of charred alder. She wondered why Stephanus was called "the Black," but James was not. He had coarse grey hair fizzing around his tonsure and eyes like jet beads. But his mien was not dark. He laughed a lot and spoke Anglisc with a bubbling Latin accent though he had admitted, cheerfully, that when it came to music and administration he had the soul of a torturer. According to Gwladus he had certainly tormented the housefolk that morning. "Take down all the hangings, all. And sweep out the rushes, every one. No, I don't care that the king has said it is never to be moved. Talk to the queen. No, no cushions! No hangings! Get rid of them. All, I say. We are to have real music, music for the praise of God and the pleasure of the queen, for which I want this basilica as bare as a bone." And in response to their pleas the queen had sent word to the household: Do as he asks, it's just for today, and it will be a good excuse to clean the old cave.

The hall—*basilica*—without the fires, without the hangings, looked alien and old, and was as cold as death. Everyone in it stood wreathed about by their own breath. The queen wore a mantle tipped with beaver fur, the same sleek rich brown as her hair. Her great beaded gold necklace and cross gleamed at her throat. Hild stood cloakless, impervious to the chill. It fed the legend—the maid who felt nothing.

She knew why she was here, and she had let Gwladus see to it that she was clean, tidy, and heavily jewelled, but she was in no hurry to begin. She could outwait a hawk in the wild. She could certainly outwait any queen from the south. Indifference was her cloak and shield.

While James fussed with placing his choirmen, she pondered the floor. This was the first time it had been swept bare in perhaps a generation. She scuffed at the crusted dirt with her toe, trying to tell what kind of stone it was. She was aware of the brothers straightening, James the Deacon tapping time, their heartbeat of focus, but she didn't look up. Perhaps it was limestone.

The music, when it came, with a rush, a gush of voice seeking its note, ripped away her indifference and tore through her as sudden and shocking as snowmelt.

She forgot the floor. Forgot the queen. She felt hot, then cold, then nothing at all, like a bubble rising through water, then floating, then lifting free.

It was cool music, inhuman, the song stars might sing. Endless, pouring, pure. Were it water, it would turn any bird that drank it white.

The music soared. Hild soared with it.

The queen, standing with Hild in the centre of the hall, where James had insisted the fire pit be covered by a board, reached and took Hild's hand.

At some point the men stopped singing but for a moment the music soared on under the rafters. When even that faded, the queen squeezed and let go. Hild's hand tingled and remembered what she hadn't felt: a cold hand, smaller than her own, smooth but not soft.

Æthelburh brushed at Hild's cheek, at her tears, and Hild caught the queen's scent—some kind of flower, one Hild didn't know. She filled with a sudden gaping hunger for the scent of her sister, for Begu or Cian, for Onnen, even for her mother.

She wiped her face with her sleeve, aware now of the texture of the linen, the cold on her cheeks.

James walked to them, sandals slapping on the bare stone. He walked with a light step, as quick as Onnen's. "You liked it!" he said.

"Yes," said Æthelburh.

"It will get better, of course," James said. "Once we plaster those rafters and hang some doors instead of that pernicious cloth. And you," he said to Hild. "You liked it."

She nodded. But she didn't know how to say it had made her heart feel the way she imagined a gull might, hanging over a swell held by only the wind. That it had made her forget the stink of the insides of Lindseymen. That it had reminded her of the wordless, untouchable patterns she sensed when she counted the petals on a daisy or watched ripples on a pond.

She tried. "I liked . . . I liked the way it climbed, up and over on itself."

He beamed.

The queen patted him lightly on the arm, a dismissal, then she and Hild assessed each other.

The queen was pregnant, though no one was supposed to know. Gwladus, who had befriended Arddun, the wealh who attended the queen's gemæcce, told Hild that there had been no blood on the queen's sheets since the wedding night, that the king must be as fertile as old Thuddor: done the deed the first month of their coupling. You wouldn't know to look at her: planed face, polished hair, and thin wrists.

"They say you feel nothing," the queen said. "But that's not true, is it? Though clearly you don't feel the cold."

Hild waited.

"Paulinus says you know your letters. I never heard of a person who knows her letters but doesn't know Christ."

Silence.

"My gesiths say you are a sorceress. Or perhaps hægtes. They say you can fly. I wish I could fly. The music is as close as I come to it."

For a moment, Hild was cycling, soaring endlessly again with the song.

The queen reached up and brushed her new tears away. "You will speak."

"What's the flower you smell of?"

Æthelburh blinked, then laughed. "Jessamine, a precious oil from the East. A gift from my brother, who had it from our mother's people in Frankia. I will give you a little."

Hild did not protest. Her mother had trained her to accept every advantage: to smell like the queen would be a mark of great favour, one people would notice without knowing it.

"And you, you will walk with me every day. We are cousins but you may call me aunt. You will talk to me. We will get to know each other."

They walked along the river—upstream, away from the landing's shout and stink and the fretful reeve's men, who often turned to the queen now that Coelgar, seconded by Blæcca, was so busy taking the reins in Lindum on Edwin's behalf—with Lintlaf and Bassus, the queen's red-cloaked captain, following ten paces behind.

"We have nine women working now on the embroidery for Clothar king," Æthelburh said. "It'll be finished by Yule."

A skein of greylag geese took flight just beyond the trees at the curve of the river. "Nine?"

Æthelburh nodded. "Teneshild is a skilful hand. And Æffe. And Burgen might be deaf but her eyes are good and she knows how to make the colours dance."

And with their sly comments, Burgen and Æffe would soon have the Kentishwomen and the Northumbrians gossiping together like old gesiths on the war trail. "You're clever."

"I am queen." Æthelburh laid her hand on her stomach. For those who knew to look, she was beginning to show. "The question is, what are you? A maid without a mother."

"I have a mother. Your aunt."

"Yes." There was a world of complication in that one word. "You really don't feel the cold, do you? Like my brothers. Perhaps you will teach me that trick."

Hild couldn't imagine this queen in her beaver furs riding rough over half the north, starving and harried, thrusting spears into the brains of the enemy.

"I miss my brothers. Perhaps you miss your sister."

"Your cousin."

"My cousin. But she's with the East Angles now, and you are here."

Hild couldn't disagree.

"You prophesied her doom."

"Not hers. Æthelric's."

"Paulinus would say a woman's doom is her husband's."

"Why?"

The queen, startled, laughed. "It probably comforts him to think so." They walked quietly for a while. "You learnt your letters from the Irish priest, Fursey."

Hild nodded.

"You will introduce him to me. You will not speak of it to anyone."

Hild glanced at her.

"You must learn to speak those thoughts of yours sometimes, child, or those who watch—like those gesith hounds of yours—will decide for themselves what you think, who you are, whose side you're on. For there are sides. Though I don't know which is yours."

If Hild thought of sides, she thought of plots, of her mother, of Lindsey, its blood, its stink, and the world began to dissolve in a white hiss so that she wanted to step from her body and become the marble maid again. She breathed slowly, carefully. She was in York, by the river, with the queen, her cousin. Or aunt. Who had offered her a gift of perfume. Who was trying to be her friend. Maybe.

She would offer a gift in return, and an answer of sorts. "I shall sew with your women."

"Thank you. We'd be glad to have you."

It hadn't occurred to Hild that they might not be. She pretended to watch a pair of swans gliding by.

"And your mother, do you think she would sew with us? When she returns?"

Hild thought of the old queen dying in a pool of blood and the world began to turn cold around the edges.

"Never mind. We'll leave that for another time."

She introduced Fursey to Æthelburh, but what discussion they had Fursey didn't share.

The ice came early. An illness swept the city, racking old and young alike with wet coughs. The fingers and toes of wealh and then even of royal Anglisc grew red and shiny with chilblains. Hild offered the parsley in her pots for the royal table, but suggested privately to the queen that she might not want to eat it, in her condition. The queen declared that all, even wealh, would get cheese as well as barley bread or oats for breakfast.

Hild sewed with the queen's women in the morning, when the light was good. In the afternoon twilight she walked along the river, and at night she listened to the music with one ear and to the gesiths as they boasted and drank, and the thegns who manoeuvred for favour, with the other. The men drank gallons of beer and as much white mead as the women of the household could freeze out overnight from the yellow mead poured into the special tall barrels—all men but Paulinus Crow, who drank sparingly of the wine Æthelburh provided. Hild suspected that James the Deacon—who did not eat in hall but with his boys—was not sparing. James and Fursey had become friends, though Hild did not know if it was a natural affinity or at the direction of the queen.

For a while, she enjoyed a life in which she behaved exactly as she should: a royal maid with no secrets. She sat at her place of high honour on the bench, often near the æthelings Eadfrith and Osfrith, who were now men with no time for a maid, and sipped her mead. She let the ebb and flow of the hall wash over her, much as she sometimes sat behind bracken at the edge of a clearing or by reeds at the edge of a pool. Life, death, change, they happened most at the edges of things: where forest meets clearing, air meets water. A spider has only to spin at the edge of a puddle to catch the fly that dives to drink. A shrew has only to watch in turn for the spider. For the fly must come to the edge to drink, and the spider must follow the fly. *Fate goes ever as it must.*

Yule approached. Breguswith returned from Arbeia, followed a day later by Osric.

In Hild's room, mother and daughter regarded each other silently. "You've grown," Breguswith said. "Your woman is taking good care of you."

"I've told her to make up a bed for you next to mine." Despite her best intentions, Hild's voice rose in a question.

But Breguswith merely nodded.

That night, Hild didn't sleep well. The next night, her mother didn't come to bed. Hild made no effort to find out where she spent her time.

The high men of the isle gathered to seek favour and pay homage to Edwin and his new queen. Every evening, arriving at the beat of a drum or the ripple of a lyre, a handful of brightly cloaked men, wearing enough gold to dazzle a jay, would swing into the hall and bend their proud heads to the high table. Bryneich from the north, with their short hair, red mouths, and enamelled brooches, under Coledauc king—who bowed to Hild and gave best wishes from Prince Morcant. The piglet, Hild remembered. Men from Rheged, under Rhoedd the Lesser, Rhoedd's sister-son and little Uinniau's older brother, styling himself prince and bearing gifts from Rhoedd for the king and queen—and a beautiful double pin inlaid with garnet from the princess Rhianmelldt for the princess Hild. Coelgar, returned from Lindsey, with half a dozen Lindsey thegns at his back and a kinglike bearing. And Dunod, lord of Craven, whom some called king.

The hall hushed when Dunod was announced.

He and his retinue—twenty strong, defiance in their bearing, and wearing knives just a little too long for manners—strode along the benches, careless of their cloaks near the fire pit, and dropped, to a man, on one knee before Edwin. The room hummed; all knew what Cadfan's man had told the hægtes about traitors. Dunod laid a heavy casket on the floor before him. Edwin leaned back, pretending to sniff at the mead in his goblet, but Hild saw the green glitter of his eyes.

"Edwin king!" Dunod said in a strong voice, and the hum dropped— even the housefolk paused. "Edwin king, foul lies have been visited upon my honour. I am your loyal man." He lifted the casket; the man on either side put a hand on the lid. "I bring you a gift." They flung the lid back with a crash. "Ceredig of Elmet."

Even Edwin leaned forward.

The head was unrecognisable. It was the colour of the underside of a mushroom, the eyes sunken. Dark purple lips were pulled back in a snarl from black gums and long yellowing teeth. The hair was red-streaked grey, and a golden torc circled a stringy neck.

No one spoke.

Then Edwin looked down the table at Breguswith, who sat by Osric. "Cousin, is this Ceredig?"

Breguswith stood, leaned forward on both hands for a better view, and after a moment said, "It's his torc. And it's his hair as it might be after ten years."

Edwin gestured for her to sit. He tapped his great ring—the garnet carved now with his boar—against his cup, thinking. "Dunod. We accept your loyalty, and we thank you for the torc." He gestured, smiling, for Coelfrith to find places for the new guests, pleased with himself: not admitting it was Ceredig, not admitting the favour, but accepting the gift. "No," he said to Coelfrith's man, who bent to the casket. "Leave it there. We wish to enjoy it."

Hild watched her mother from the corner of her eye. She seemed to have swelled and hardened. Dunod had declared for Edwin. But if Edwin accepted Ceredig's death, Elmet now lay in Edwin's gift. Twelfth night was the traditional time for such things.

The morning of twelfth night, over a breakfast of hot spiced bread and mulled cider, the queen gave all her women gifts. Hild's was a tiny vial of jessamine oil.

At a formal feast, kin sat in strict order of precedence. Hild was seated to the right of the æthelings on the king's right. Breguswith sat to her right rather than with Osric. When Hild took her place, her mother's nostrils flared. "You've been busy while I was away. Good." But then Edwin and Æthelburh entered. "We'll speak of this later."

The king and queen and Coelgar held hands over the great war horn of the Yffings, which sat on a beautiful square of calfskin, dyed blue, and a hank of white wool—symbols of the leather and wool goods of Lindum—and swore Lindsey to Coelgar as ealdorman.

The king and queen swore to be generous, just, and vengeful of his honour, as need occasioned. "By our breath we swear this, by our blood we swear this, by our lives we swear this." And Coelgar swore to be loyal and true to his king, and to be just to his people in turn. "May every river hide its face from me, may my food fall to dust and my kin turn their backs if I be false."

And then the roasted meat from the sacrifice was carried in, the ritual cup drunk, and the feast begun in earnest.

Osric, sitting to the king's left with a face like curdling milk, shouted for more white mead. Breguswith saw Hild watching him. "His day will come, little prickle. Our day. Coelgar might have Lindsey but Elmet is the key. And soon Edwin will see that he must lean on kin."

12

✦

THE DERWENT coursed steely and dark under a scudding sky. Every now and again the sun broke through and shone on a daffodil, early bumblebee, or dangling catkin. Hild walked along the bank with Æthelburh, stepping around puddles so their just-healed chilblains did not get wet and flare again. Bassus and Lintlaf followed behind at a discreet distance.

The queen walked very slowly and, despite her best efforts, with a waddle. She was due to drop anytime. She was frowning.

The queen's first embroidery had been greeted with such pleasure and confident covetous words from Æthelburh's trade master that fourteen women were now working on three others. That morning Burgen had declared, louder than a honking goose, that the queen was obviously carrying a girl. She'd never seen such a clear case in her life—and they had to admit she'd had a long and full life. Well, hadn't she? Indeed, several women murmured. Oh, be quiet you old fool, Æffe said, we've all had interesting lives, even the roof-brushing young barehead, there. No, Burgen said, loud enough to override her gemæcce, it was clear: The queen was carrying a girl. You'd only to look at her. Carrying high like that, and nipples pink as a maid's. Why, probably even bareheaded and ungirdled Hild had nipples darker than that. And look at the width of the queen's hips . . .

"It isn't a girl," Æthelburh said to Hild. "It isn't."

Hild didn't see why she was worried about it. Her uncle would be pleased to have a peaceweaver—then he could keep Hild as seer. "He already has sons."

"Not my sons," Æthelburh said. "Let's stop here." She indicated a fallen poplar. Four months ago, Hild would have sat immediately, but she had learnt from watching the queen. So while Lintlaf stripped off his warrior jacket and hurried towards them she examined the fine-downed shoots and unfurling leaves on the poplar. It must have fallen in the recent storm.

Æthelburh smiled at Lintlaf as he laid his jacket on the knurled trunk then withdrew.

"He looks ready to die for you," Hild said as she helped Æthelburh lower herself gently.

"Even though I lumber like a pregnant sow?"

She knew better than to agree. She sat next to the queen, picked at the heavy burr under her thigh. She wondered why poplars had so many.

"Hild. Does your mother speak to you of women's things?"

"No." In the distance a pair of shovelbill ducks rose in a tight flurry of feathers. She wondered what had disturbed them.

"Are you ready for your veil band? A blind man can see you'll need it soon."

Hild watched the ducks as they settled back to their eggs. Probably not otter. Perhaps nothing. Nesting ducks could be unpredictable.

"Yet you're not wearing bindings. Does your mother even have a girdle prepared? A weft beater?"

Hild had no idea. She didn't want to think about her mother.

"You have no sister here. Your mother, well, she's busy. You need a gemæcce."

Hild remembered working on Cian's tablet weave with Begu, the shadows in Mulstan's hall all falling one way in the stream of sunlight.

"Hild?"

Hild shook her head. The memory of Begu was hers.

"Child, you need a gemæcce. Would you like me to choose one?"

"No!"

"Ah. So you've made your choice. Is she so very unsuitable? No? My dear, I can't help you if I don't know. And unlike you're reputed to be able to, I can't read minds."

"I can't read minds."

"No. But there are those who say you can." She nodded down the path to where Lintlaf was scratching his back against an oak tree and Bassus was cleaning his fingernails with a knife. "I warned you that if you didn't speak for yourself others would speak for you. And they are doing so. It's dangerous. You must learn to listen to me. But for now, I'm telling you, you must have a veil band and girdle prepared and a gemæcce chosen soon. Very soon. If neither you nor Breguswith take care of it, I will. I'm your aunt."

Cousin, Hild thought. But perhaps it might be a fine thing for the queen to be her aunt. "She wants me to marry Oswine and have Osthryth as gemæcce. My mother."

The queen didn't quite hide her surprise at this burst of confidence. "This doesn't please you?"

"They look like pointy-faced ermine."

Æthelburh laughed—then went white around the lips. She put her hands on her belly and, after a moment, said, "He's impatient." The pinched look eased. "Help me up."

Hild hauled the queen to her feet. Lintlaf hurried to retrieve his jacket while Bassus remained to guard the path. As they passed Bassus, the queen went white again and leaned for a moment against the oak tree.

"He wants to come into the world very soon." She panted. "So much wants to happen soon. Too soon. Think on what I've said." She pushed back against the tree, straightened, and took Hild's arm. "Look at all these oak apples. Remind me of it when we get back. Stephanus will be grateful for them, for his ink."

When they got back, Hild forgot about oak apples. Fursey stood by the gate, grinning. But it wasn't Fursey Hild saw, it was the two who stood beside him: Cian and Begu.

Hild stopped so abruptly that the queen, still leaning on her arm, slewed to one side.

Begu wore a veil band. A veil band and girdle. She was a woman grown. And Cian stood like a young gesith, a thegn's foster-son: tall, muscled, a hint of moustaches, cloak thrown back from his shoulders, hair greased, sword hilt tall over his left shoulder.

Bassus thought so, too. He stepped in front of his queen and put a hand on his sword. Cian crouched.

"No!" Hild said. "They're friends." And, heedless of manners, she abandoned the queen and ran to Cian, and the world filled with hugs and questions and the abrupt, bright laughter of relief and friends well met.

———

Hild, Begu, and Cian sat on the freshly ground limestone flags of the strange, bare, high-ceilinged room that was to be the Derventio chapel. Under the Crow's supervision men had cut a row of windows high along the length of the eastern wall. There were no shutters. Everything but those pale, gritty flags had been mudded, plastered, and limed.

"The air stings my tongue," Begu said, and tipped back her head to look at the ceiling. "A god is going to live here?"

"The Christ," Hild said.

"It's a cheerless space for a god," Cian said. He leaned back on his hands, turning this way and that. His scabbard chape scraped the floor and the sleeves of his warrior jacket rose a little. Hild saw the tip of a new scar snaking over his forearm. "Cold, too."

Hild, stung, said, "There will be silver and jewels, silk hangings, and gilded carvings to put old King Coel to shame once the walls dry. And the Crow will send to Frankia for glass for the windows!"

"Glass? In a wall?" Begu said, and Cian shook his head. Who had heard of such a thing.

Hild felt reproved, caught in a childish need to show off. Cian was a young warrior, a thegn's foster-son. Begu was a girdled woman, the thegn's marriageable heir. Hild might be touch-the-ceiling tall, the seer who saved Bebbanburg and predicted the fall of Lindsey, but she was still, officially, a child. It seemed another lifetime since they had rolled in the kitchen garth at Mulstanton, shrieking with laughter about gods and worms, and dogs and demons.

The silence lengthened.

"I like the queen," Begu said. A wisp of hair was escaping her forehead band. She noticed Hild looking. "I use your comb every day."

Hild touched her pocket. "I carry your snakestone."

"I hoped you'd like it. Cian practically sleeps in his belt buckle."

"I do not!" His flush emphasised the new strength of his jaw, the thickening bone of his brow. He jumped to his feet. "I hear singing. They've broached a new cask. I'm going to drink."

They watched him leave. The muscles wrapping his knees were bigger, too.

"He doesn't like to be teased anymore," Begu said.

He never had, Hild thought. Perhaps they weren't so changed after all. But Begu, Begu sitting there in her veil band and girdle, amber and gold glinting at her ears.

"What are you staring at?"

"Your veil band. It's . . ." It's a veil band. A woman's veil band. "It's lovely."

"Onnen made it for me. She made one for you, too. I brought it with me. And a girdle. Just in case your ma didn't remember to. Though she said I wasn't to say that. Oh."

They looked at each other for a long moment, then Hild laughed. "I'm glad, so very glad you've come."

Begu laughed, too, that shimmery, silvery laugh Hild would always associate with light along a wet beach and the smell of the sea, and took her hand. "I said I'd come. I said we'd use those tablets. Onnen would have come herself—she's very agitated for you, but that's Cian's to talk about, I don't know what's going on, no one tells me anything—but she couldn't."

Hild had forgotten how Begu's thoughts flocked like starlings, flicking this way then that. It took her a moment to sort through what Begu had said. "Onnen's ill?"

Begu stared. "Didn't I tell you? No, perhaps I didn't. But your veil band— Oh, it's so pretty! It's the exact colour of—"

"Begu, tell me what? What's the matter with Onnen?"

"Why, nothing."

"Then—" Hild took a breath, let it go. "Tell me how she is."

"She's well. She's cross that she can't come. She nagged and nagged and nagged Cian: Make that lass understand, mind, make her understand. Oh, she's like a bee in a bottle, and big as a house. Fa is happy, though. He thinks it will be twins. Just like Winty. Though of course he doesn't know Winty really. Did I tell you about Winty?"

"Onnen is with child?"

Begu looked surprised. "Well, of course. I just said so. She's due any day."

Hild took another breath. This was just how Begu was. She would talk to Cian about Onnen and her message. "You liked the queen, you said."

"She seems nice. But what was she doing out and about with those gesiths? She could birth if a bird sang suddenly. Any time. Maybe even today. You can always tell when they waddle like that and go white about the lips. The baby's dropped. And what's that perfume you smell of?" She lifted Hild's hand, sniffed her wrist. "You smell like her."

Hild was getting back the habit of plucking the meaning from the flying words. "Jessamine. It's a flower oil. And she is nice. For a queen." But Hild didn't want to talk about the queen. "What colour's my veil band?"

"Oh, it's beautiful. It's like that colour between moss and the sea. To match your eyes. Onnen spent all winter on it. And your girdle! She nagged and nagged at Fa until he gave her the stones." She frowned, which made her look just like a goat pondering whether to eat a thistle, and tilted her head, listening. The gesiths were singing more loudly. "Do you suppose Cian is getting drunk? I promised Onnen I'd look out for him. She said I was to remind him to keep his sword in his scabbard, that here he's just a man with a blade, and a young one at that, not the lord's son."

Hild had no idea how Begu could protect Cian from quarrelsome, bloody-handed gesiths. She stood. "We'll go make sure he's all right."

When they left the chapel, they paused and blinked in the cold wind, then started across the rough grass—Hild could already see a path between the serving door of the hall and the chapel, where the grass had been flatted by housefolks' feet—towards the singing.

By the good-natured sound of it, they were not yet very drunk:

Do your ears hang low,
Can you swing them to and fro?
Can you tie them in a knot
Can you tie them in a bow?
Can you throw them o'er your shoulder
Like a limp and Lindsey soldier?
Do your ears hang low?

"It makes no sense," Begu said. "No one's ears are that long."
"They're not singing about ears."
"Oh."

The gesiths, ten of them, had dragged two benches outside and leaned them against the south wall at the east end of the hall. It was a favourite spot for the younger men and their dogs to lounge: sheltered from the wind that had been blowing cold from the northwest these last few days and bright with midmorning sun. Also close enough to call out to the housefolk passing and repassing and demand food and ale. Two, the black-haired brothers Berhtred and Berhtnoth, were bare-chested and just sheathing swords after a demonstration bout.

Berhtred wiped his chest with his jacket and straddled the bench facing Cian. "And that, young chestnut, is how we did it at Lindum." Then he deliberately took the wooden bowl sitting before Cian and drank from it.

Hild clamped her hand on Begu's shoulder, and Begu turned to look at her. But Begu hadn't seen these men killing Lindseymen and thinking it of no more account than the slaughter of geese.

The men—her hounds; she saw Gwrast, the young Bryneich lord, and his cousin Cynan; Wilfram, son of Wilgar; Lintlaf; Eadric the Brown and his friend Grimhun; and Coelwyn, Coelfrith's much younger brother; though not Eamer the Gewisse, who hadn't exchanged so much as a word with her since Lindsey—sat back and waited to see how Cian would respond.

Cian reached for the ale jar, refilled the bowl, and gestured for Berhtred to drink again. "I honour you for it."

Berhtred's lip curled: The stripling was a coward.

"Indeed," Cian went on, "I heard the Lindseymen were so fearsome that even a maid killed half a dozen."

He knew what she'd done at Lindum.

Berhtred flushed dull red. Lintlaf leapt to his feet. "You insult the lady Hild!"

"No." Cian deliberately took back the bowl of ale and sipped. "I believe I'm insulting the Lindseymen."

Grimhun hooted and hurled a chunk of bread at Coelwyn.

Cian grinned at Lintlaf. "Perhaps you will honour me with a bout." He turned to Berhtred. "After I've crossed swords with Berhtred. Unless, sir"—another grin, this time exaggerated for effect—"you feel the need to rest here in the sun to warm your old bones."

More hooting, catcalling, and thrown objects. Now they understood the shape of things.

Berhtred looked at Lintlaf. "What do you think? Me or you?"

Lintlaf waved one dismissive hand, and sat. "I'll take the winner."

"This ring on Lintlaf," Berhtnoth said, slapping a chunk of gold and topaz on the bench, which earned him a reproachful look from his brother.

"I'll take that bet," Cian said. "But only if I try your brother first. No shields."

No, Hild wanted to shout, you're too young! But they were all young.

Cian stood, unbuckled his belt—Hild recognised the gold tongue and garnet eyes—and saw the girls.

"Come and watch!" he shouted. "I'm going to show them how we do it in Mulstanton!"

He's drunk, Hild thought. But, no: His eyes were brilliant, his cheeks hectic, but it was joy. This was what he'd been looking for all his life, to be a gesith and do as gesiths do, and here he was, at the hall of the over-king of the Anglisc, about to test his mettle against the king's own.

"It's for fun," she said to Begu. "They won't hurt him."

"Of course not," Begu said. "He won't let them. He'll beat those silly boys."

Those silly boys had disembowelled men and played kickball with children's heads.

"Come on, let's sit and watch!"

The gesiths greeted them cheerfully and made room on the sunniest bench. Betting and drinking and rude comments resumed.

Cian stripped off his jacket and threw it to Begu, who folded it lumpily. Hild took it, refolded it, set the package on her knee. It was a blue so dark it was almost black, embroidered in gold and green about the shoulder seams and hem by a hand Hild would recognise anywhere. She imagined Onnen working over it, dreading sending her son away. As it warmed in the sun, it released Cian's familiar scent, overlain with the tang of iron and copper—a man's smell.

Cian drew his sword with that slithering ring that set her heart pound-ing. "Not for blood!" Cian shouted, and tossed the sheath aside.

They circled in the sun. Hild recognised Cian's familiar stance, left foot leading, at an angle to his opponent, right foot and arm back, sword held back and high. She imagined how hard it was to hold a sword like that. Several gesiths shook their heads: without a shield his left side was ex-posed. Hild's heart squeezed. Was he trying to prove something to her, because Begu had teased him?

It was a risky stance, one that relied entirely on timing and joint strength: shoulder, elbow, wrist. And reach. Like Hild, he had the reach. He had the muscle, too, whippy rather than plump, veins like worms coiled around his wrist.

The scar she had noticed in the chapel showed ruched and red. About a year old. An ugly wound. A spear?

Berhtred chose the usual stance: right foot and right arm forward, sword held low. He was a badger of a man, thick body, short arms and legs, built for wrestling, for pushing with a shield at close quarters.

Perhaps Cian wasn't being foolish after all.

"Hai!" said Cian, and feinted, a fast jab with the point. Berhtred swung his blade up, like a horizontal bar, expecting a hard clash of iron, but Cian's blade was already back, waiting, and Berhtred met air, and teetered very slightly.

The Cian Hild had known, the Cian with the wooden sword and wicker shield, dreaming of Owein, would have yelled and hurled himself into the attack. This Cian, the one with corded muscles and a half smile, simply kept circling. Then, when Berhtred had the slanting morning sun in his eyes, Cian thrust.

Once for the feint with the tip, which Berhtred expected and so raised his sword only partway, then back and once more forward in a full stepping lunge, right foot leading now, and blade snaking over Berhtred's in a wrapping leftwise twist that flung Berhtred's sword up and away and into the grass. Cian stood with the tip of his sword against a curl of black chest hair while his opponent blinked, then he grinned and lifted the sword away in salute.

"My fa taught him that," Begu said. The gesiths hooted and slapped the bench. "He said it takes a strong, supple wrist. He says not one man in a hundred can do it leftwise like that. He says rightwise, sunwise, is easy but widdershins is special. Though most gesiths think it bad luck. And in a real battle it would get you killed."

Hild hardly heard her. Cian, her Cian, had disarmed a king's gesith, blooded in the battle of Lindum, without a scratch or a bruise or even breaking a sweat.

"I'll take that ring," Cian said to Lintlaf, voice vibrant with his own power. "Or we could go for double or nothing, you and me."

"I'll take that bet. With shield and spear."

Hild stood. Most of the friendly blood she'd seen spilled had been in spear games. A sharp leaf of iron at the end of a long pole of ash was not easy to control. "Cian, come away with us. Your foster-sister is lonely."

"You lied!" Begu said, when the three of them were out of earshot. The gesiths were singing again.

"Yes. I want to talk to Cian. It's easier if his guts are inside his skin."

Cian gave her a lazy smile. "He wouldn't have touched me."

Hild ignored him. She didn't know how to deal with this confident young lord. She focused on Begu.

"I know, I know. You want me to go away so you can talk to Cian."

"Ask for Gwladus. My bodywoman. She's probably in the kitchens."

When she was out of earshot, Hild turned to Cian. "You have a message."

"Mam said you were to take care. She said I was to watch you like a hawk. She said not to trust anyone, no one at all. She's heard rumours."

"What rumours?"

"I don't know. All I know is she doesn't trust you to anyone but me, and I'm to stick to you like honey on bread."

"Even here, in the vill?"

"Especially. She said especially when you think you're safe. She said your whole family should look behind them. But she reckons your mam can look after herself and your uncle has his gesiths."

"I have men, too."

"Truly yours?"

She thought about that. "They saved my life, near Lindum. Or Eamer did. The red-haired man. But they're the king's gesiths."

Cian nodded. "Their will is not their own. They have given their oath."

He said oath with the same breathy reverence he had once used to speak of the hero Owein.

Hild studied him. He blushed. He would have to lose that habit if he didn't want to be teased, though the girls no doubt would like it. She wondered how long it would take Gwladus to snare him, and how she could persuade him and Lintlaf not to fight.

"You want to swear to the king." He tucked his head down like an ox trying to refuse the yoke and said nothing. "So what would you do if the king orders me dead?"

"It's not the king who wants you dead."

"Not today."

They were both quiet. The gesiths were singing again. "About the king. I could never— I wouldn't—"

She said to him in British, "An Anglisc oath is like water. It pours into every part of you, every crevice. You can't hold any piece apart from it."

The sword was his path, and what better road to walk than the king's?

His eyes glistened. He rubbed his upper lip with his knuckle. Eventually he said in British, rusty from disuse, "I am not Anglisc."

She grinned fiercely. Cian. Hers. But he kept rubbing his lip. She said, still in British, "Cian, I will not ask an oath. The oath is yours, like your wooden sword of long ago. But perhaps, for now, you will loan it to me, unspoken, and you may ask its return at any time, because it is yours."

He smiled. The smile wobbled a little, but it was there. "Any time?"

"Any time." He remembered. She touched his arm, the scar, and said, now in Anglisc, "A spear, like Owein?"

He shook his head. A tear flew loose, he brushed it away. "A boar."

"Fearsome, no doubt?"

The queen's quarters in Derventio were large and bright. Like the chapel, the ceiling and walls were plastered and whitewashed. Like the chapel, the room was cool. The queen, as wide as an ox, found warmth unbearable. Hild didn't mind, but Begu stood with her arms wrapped around herself, and Wilnoð, the queen's gemæcce, sitting with Arddun by the empty brazier sorting embroidery threads, wore a heavy overdress. Unlike the chapel, though, the queen's room had a bed draped with rich blankets—striped and with chevrons in yellow and a red so dark it was almost black—where Æthelburh rested, and a finely woven rug imported from the East via Frankia covered the wide elm floorboards.

The queen looked up from the worked fabrics she had asked Begu to show her and nodded at Hild's bare arms. "You're the only woman who doesn't huddle and shiver and give me reproachful looks."

Hild nodded, wondering why they were there. Begu watched the queen anxiously.

"My husband"—she never called him the king—"tells me these rooms are as welcoming as an empty barn, though a barn is warmer. I told him I'll paint and hang as soon as the walls are properly dry."

Still sorting thread, Wilnoð said, "Not if the chapel dries first. Paulinus Crow will hog the painters and gilders for himself."

"For the greater glory of God," Æthelburh said, but Hild could read neither her tone nor her expression. "And speaking of God," she said to Hild and Begu, "I hope you will both attend chapel with us in the morning. James has been working on a special Mass for Easter. The music, he assures me, would make an angel weep and hens fly. The feast will begin in hall immediately afterwards."

Hild nodded again. She was curious about the Christ ritual.

"Good." The queen smiled and stroked the veil band and girdle Begu had brought to show her. "This is fine work. Yours?"

"Oh, no," said Begu. "That is, yes. Onnen—my father's new, that is, my— Anyway, Onnen helped."

Hild opened her mouth to say *Onnen is my mother's*— But her mother's what?

"And the embroidery on your veil band?" the queen asked.

"All mine. Mostly."

"Come here, let me look." Begu knelt by the bed. Æthelburh examined the band closely, then ran her fingertips over the violet-and-blue stitching. "Nicely done."

She sat up straight, arranged her blankets to her satisfaction, and stroked the raised nap while she studied both girls, back and forth. Her attention settled on Begu.

"You are of good family." Her voice now was strong and formal, and Hild's blood began to beat hard in her chest and stomach. "Tell me, your father and—Onnen?—would want you to stay?"

"I think so. Onnen sent me. She told me to stay close."

"And you would like that, to stay close to the lady Hild?"

"Oh, yes!"

Æthelburh turned to Hild, who understood now some of what Cian must have felt that night on the beach when Mulstan unwrapped the sword. "And your mother, the lady Breguswith?"

Hild tried to swallow and speak at the same time. "Yes." She sounded like a strangling toad. Begu giggled nervously. Hild swallowed again, took a slow breath. "My mother and Onnen know each other well."

"And this would please you?"

"Yes!"

Æthelburh winced, and Hild thought for one horrible moment that she had bellowed, but then the queen put a hand on her belly and took two deep breaths. After a moment her pinched look faded. She smiled. "Then it shall be so."

She smiled at Wilnoð, who smiled back fondly, and stood, holding a basket.

"Begu, you are welcome in my house in your own right and as the gemæcce of Hild, niece of the king. And the queen."

Hild didn't dare look at her gemæcce—gemæcce!—but Begu's hand stole into hers. Hild squeezed it.

"To seal the bargain I have a gift." The queen motioned for Begu to stand and for Hild to come forward.

She lifted items from Wilnoð's basket one by one and held them up to the light. An ivory spindle each, and distaffs in two lengths. Shears, made of iron and inlaid with fantastical beasts in silver. "The smith swears they are harts, though they look very like foxes to me." One gold thimble each. Two packets of the finest needles Hild had ever seen, and astonishingly bright. "And for you, Hild, when it's time to wear your girdle, this." A deep-dyed blue leather purse, its ivory lid held by three yellow-gold hinges, each inlaid with garnet. Hild longed to hold it to her face and smell the new-leather scent, test its suppleness. "To put inside it—" The queen's hand, feeling about in the basket, clenched in a fist and her face tightened. Wilnoð laid a professional hand on her belly.

"You may not make tomorrow's Mass, my lady." She handed the basket to Begu. "Off you go. My lady needs rest. No, hush now. Tomorrow will be soon enough for thanks."

Outside, they turned to each other but the courtyard was too busy. Hild looked at the sky. The clouds were little and white; it was unlikely to rain.

"I'll show you a secret place," Hild said.

She led Begu to the track worn long, long ago between the Roman villa and the ford. Part of it was overgrown, green and mysterious, a tube through woods coppiced generations ago, then run wild, and now gradually being reclaimed.

Every now and again Begu remembered what was in the basket and stopped swinging, stopped chattering, and looked solemn, but then she would notice something—"Look, the hedgepigs are awake already!"—and point and forget.

After a while they left the main track for a rougher, more spidery path. A woodcutter's trail. They jumped over a rivulet, running busy and brown.

There were eleven ash boles in a circle, all cut early in the season. The woodcutters wouldn't be back for years. In the centre, leaf mould had collected in a soft heap. Hild sat. Begu sat next to her. They spread their skirts to overlap and laid the queen's gifts on the cloth one by one then held hands and gazed at their treasure.

The breeze was now soft and light, the sun warm. The woods smelt of green living things. The rivulet bibble-babbled. A nearby wren tut-tutted. Greenfinches sang their creaky mating songs. Hild wanted to laugh and shout and be still all at the same time.

"I feel like my insides just filled with sunshine."

Begu nodded. "I could burst." She squeezed Hild's hand.

Hild squeezed back.

They gazed some more at their treasure. "I like the thimbles best," Begu said. She let go of Hild's hand and slid a thimble onto her middle finger, then the other onto her pointing finger. "I expect they're too small for you," she said hopefully.

Hild flopped down on her back and laughed. Begu, her jackdaw, her gemæcce.

The weather changed overnight. On Easter morning clouds smoked and twisted across a low sky and those who had to be away from a fire hurried between buildings pulling their clothes close against the cold, wilful wind.

The queen did make it to the Mass, though the king did not. Hild noticed that no men attended but the queen's Jutes, the priests and choristers, and a few housefolk in tunics painstakingly cleaned for the occasion and spattered about the shoulders with the first fat raindrops—no Anglisc men but Cian.

Cian glared at Hild, but Paulinus, in his cope stiff with jewels and gold thread, had seen him and smiled, and now Cian was duty bound to stay.

Hild ignored him. Her belly ached, strange and heavy, and she felt a little sick. Perhaps it was all the incense smoking in the brass censers two priests swung from chains.

The music made Hild forget her belly. Voices soared overhead. Outside rain runnelled and gushed over the tile roof.

Paulinus's sonorous Latin brought her back to earth. The ache in her belly returned. She concentrated on shifting her weight unobtrusively from one foot to the other. She wished she could sit down, but only the queen, looking pale, had a three-legged stool.

The Mass droned on. Rain beat on the roof. A wealh woman coughed carefully, persistently.

Music soared again, Paulinus walked in state back up the aisle, preceded by the smoking censers. The wealh woman's coughing rose to a crescendo. The queen stood, swayed, and Wilnoð and her other women hustled her away. Begu, with a glance back at Hild, who nodded, went with them.

Outside, under the dripping eaves, Stephanus spoke to Cian: The bishop would have words with the young lord at the feast, if the young lord was willing. Cian bowed and suggested that not only was he more than willing, he was honoured. Hild breathed deeply of the damp but fresh air and wondered when he'd learnt to lie like a thegn. Stephanus hurried away, holding his skirts above the wet. Cian scowled after him and wiped his rain-wet forearms against his tunic.

"Well," said Fursey, and they turned. "Stephanus seems as pleased as a black cockerel. If I were an expert on the matter, which I am, I'd say the Roman bishop anticipates his first gesith baptism."

"I'm not a gesith—"

"Yet," said Hild.

"—and I've no wish to be a priest!"

"I imagine not," Fursey said, smiling. "Luckily, baptism does not make you one. Though indeed"—his smile broadened—"it does make you exceedingly wet."

They followed him, mystified, to the hall for the feast.

Forthere stood watchful at the door while guests removed their weapons and leaned them against the east wall. Cian set his sword next to a sword-and-dirk pair with silver fine work: Pictish. Ciniod's emissary come at last. Hild laid her seax near an old British blade with a magnificent yellow pommel stone, probably Dyfneint, which meant Geraint had sent yet another petitioner. At least he hadn't made the mistake of sending a bishop again. She wondered what had happened to Anaoc. As she refastened her belt she scanned the row of weapons for evidence of Dyfneint's enemy, the Gewisse, but Cian and Fursey were already moving towards a knot of drinking gesiths. She hurried to catch up.

She felt queasy again, and the strange ache low in her belly was back.

The feast proper had not yet begun. The king's scop—a new one, the East Anglian who had sung the lament for Rædwald—supervised musicians with pipes and lyres; housefolk were still laying out bread trenchers and bowls and cups. Women moved from torch to torch with burning tapers. In the centre, all along the fire pits, men clasped forearms, or bowed, or punched shoulders in greeting. The largest knot stood around the king. The thin Dyfneint emissary in a scarlet cloak—the Dyfneint loved their Roman ways—stood by Paulinus, who had removed the jewelled cope but whose black was relieved by an emperor-purple silk sash wound about his middle. Stephanus hovered respectfully; even James the Deacon was there. The Dyfneint glared at the yellow-haired man with luxuriant moustaches talking in confidential tones to the king; Gewisse, the most powerful of the West Saxons, loved their whiskers.

The king's group made a good show of being absorbed in one another's conversation, but every time the king laughed, or sighed, or turned slightly to hold out his cup to a houseman for a refill, they noticed, and their stance or expression or volume subtly matched his.

None wore a blade, not so much as an eating knife, but Lilla stood always by the king's elbow, and Eamer and even Lintlaf were nearby and drinking sparingly. Eamer and the other Gewisse appeared not to notice one another. Perhaps it was that Eamer no longer considered himself Gewisse: A gesith's oath took precedence over all else. There again, Eamer didn't acknowledge her, either. She wondered why. He had seemed to like her well enough in Lindsey, though perhaps she had misread him.

At one end of the fire pit, Osric stood with Breguswith and the brothers Berhtnoth and Berhtred. Osric didn't lean in to Breguswith the way Mulstan had Onnen but slung his arm around her mother's waist. Her mother smiled and laughed and gave Osric smouldering eyes but, like a cat with a stranger, faced more away than towards him. They drank freely, as did Eadfrith and Osfrith, looking very much the young princes. Oswine stood nearby, clearly wishing to stand with his cousins the æthelings rather than with his father but uncertain of his welcome.

Cian was tense. A feast day was a time for great boasts, heroic deeds, offers, and oath-taking, and Edwin was overking, the best lord a gesith could hope for. Cian, a thegn's foster-son, wanted to make an impression.

Hild said to Fursey, "Give Cian your drink. He needs courage. He's going to talk to the Crow."

"I am?" Cian said.

"You said you would. Forget the king for now. Drink that. Good. Now another." She caught Stephanus's eye, as warning, then took Cian by the elbow and steered him towards Paulinus. Stephanus leaned and murmured something in his bishop's ear. Paulinus turned, smiling.

"Call him lord bishop," Hild whispered, and pushed him very slightly.

"Ah. Our Mass-going warrior," Paulinus said, and held out his hand.

Cian inclined his head but perhaps didn't know the amethyst ring was to be kissed. "My lord Bishop."

The muscles around Paulinus's eyes tightened briefly. "Yes. Well." He ran the tip of his ringed finger around the rim of his blue glass wine cup. "Stephanus tells me of your interest in the faith, young . . . Cian of Mulstanton, by the Bay of the Beacon."

"My lord Bishop. Yes. That is, the music was, the music is very fine."

"Yes. I brought Deacon James here especially to uplift souls to the greater glory of God."

"Most foresighted of you, Bishop," Hild said.

Paulinus focused on her, then looked back at Cian, and again at Hild. "You are cousins perhaps?"

Hild stilled. For a moment she had forgotten how dangerous it was to stand side by side with Cian, how a stranger would see their height, their hair, their solemn faces.

Cian laughed and shook his head. "Though we played together like fox kits for the years of our childhood."

Paulinus's hooded eyes gave away nothing, but Hild worried. The Crow was not stupid.

Her belly ached.

The crowd rippled. "No," the king said loudly—for the second time, Hild realised. "No, my lord Ceadda. I won't be badgered in my own hall." He turned deliberately from the West Saxon, looked over to Hild's group, waved at the Dyfneint. "Lord Dywel, come speak to me of Geraint king's proposal. In fact, all of you there, my lord Bishop, yes, and your priests, and Niece, come here and speak to me of things suitable for a feast day."

The scop stroked his lyre. Coelfrith looked up, caught the signal from the kitchen master by the hanging, and nodded to the king. Edwin smiled. "Saved by the food. Come. We'll feast."

He gestured at the table behind Hild's party and took a step towards them.

The world went mad.

Hild caught a wink of light. Lilla, two paces behind the king, bellowed and threw himself at Edwin and Eamer, and blood spurted in a short red arc.

Everything slowed down, sound stretched.

Torchlight glittered on rings, jewelled collars, a dripping blade. Flash. Flash.

Hild couldn't take it in, could only watch while a rivulet of blood wormed over the floor rushes and soaked into her shoe. Blood, in the king's hall.

Then the smell hit her and the world snapped back to the right speed. She crouched and her hand dropped to a seax that wasn't there.

Then Forthere knocked her aside, and Cian, and around her men reached for swords that weren't there and froze for a moment. Shouting, bellowing, a howling shriek, another knife flash, another.

Edwin rolled up from the floor, blood dripping from his upper arm, white-faced with pain, with Cian shielding him, wild-eyed, a tiny blade sprouting between his knuckles, gleaming garnet red. And blood, so much blood, spreading in a thick pool from Forthere, whose throat gaped. Lilla, cradling his own guts as though they were a small glistening dog. And

Eamer, still holding the long thin knife. An assassin's knife. Eamer didn't move.

Cian reached behind him to make sure the king was safe. "To me!" he shouted. "To the king!"

And then the hubbub broke against them: shouting, men running for their swords, the king with blood running down his arm, swaying.

Cian, and men armed with swords now, were backing slowly from the room, blades pointing everyway, like the spines of a hedgepig. Cian's belt-buckle blade looked tiny and vicious, like a red viper's tooth.

The Gewisse was gone. Fursey was gone.

Flames flickered quietly in Hild and Begu's chamber, glinting on the silver thread of the single hanging. Begu wrung out the cloth over the slop bowl and dipped it again in the copper bowl of warm water. She wiped Hild's neck carefully. Hild sat like a statue.

"How did you get it on your neck?"

"I don't know." Her tongue felt heavy.

"There's some on your shoe, too. Ooof, it's soaked through to your hose. Your best blue hose, too. And splashed on your skirt." She rinsed and wrung and wiped again.

Begu beckoned Gwladus from the shadow by the alcove. "We need cold water—something to soak these clothes. And more rags. And food." She looked at Hild. "You look peaky. I expect it's the shock. Though perhaps you're hungry. I know I didn't get fed while the queen birthed." Hild said nothing. She felt nothing. "Bring a lot," Begu said to Gwladus, "a lot of everything."

Gwladus left.

"Take it all off," Begu said to Hild. "Every scrap."

Hild stood and stripped, hands cold and clumsy, and Begu washed her head to toe, firm, soothing strokes. "Oh. You have a little cut here, on your shin."

Hild looked at it. It seemed very far away. Not her leg.

"Does it hurt? Well, it's nothing much." Begu mopped at it. Hild felt a distant tingle. Begu seemed to mop at it for a long time, then she wrapped a rag around it and tied it. "There, now."

Now Hild felt cold, cold to her marrow, cold as marble. Everything smelt of blood, as though she was drowning in it.

Begu murmured on and dried Hild as she would a newborn calf, then helped her into a clean, long-sleeved bedshift. "Let's get you warm." She helped Hild into bed, then covered her and stroked the hair from her face. "Stay there while I tidy this away."

Begu began to examine each piece of clothing for blood, folding and smoothing the unmarked things.

"I'll tell you about the baby, shall I?"

"Cian . . ."

"I'm sure Cian's fine. He's a hero. Lie quietly now."

The king would be half mad with fear. She should be there. But she couldn't seem to move.

Begu talked about the way the queen's women had fussed. "Anyone would think they'd never seen a baby born before. And the queen. She looks so quiet, but she swore like a gesith! Mind, they always do . . ."

Cian. She should be there.

". . . Eanflæd, she's called."

Eanflæd. The new peaceweaver, born in blood. They were all born in blood.

"I worried for a bit that she'd reject the little thing. But then she— Well, what's this?"

Hild opened her eyes. Begu was frowning over Hild's drawers. She touched a fingertip to the red stain. "It's still wet." She looked up. "It's yours."

Hild didn't understand.

"Does your belly ache?"

Hild put a hand on her belly.

Begu beamed. "You're a woman! Though you've picked a fine night for it: the king half dead, the queen with a new daughter, everything in uproar."

Hild rested her hand on her belly. A woman. Then she realised what Begu had said. "The king's half dead?"

Begu waved aside the king's health. She shook Hild's drawers. "You're a woman!"

Gwladus came in, followed by two kitchenfolk carrying a massive tray and two buckets of water. Begu waved the drawers again and said, "We'll need more rags, and raspberry-leaf tea!"

Gwladus sighed, told the kitchenfolk where to put their burdens, and turned to leave with them.

"Wait." Hild sat up. "Find out how the king is, and Cian."

"And bring mead. We'll have a feast! Up, up, you," she said to Hild.

"You're looking a lot better. It takes people that way sometimes I suppose. That and the shock. Nothing a bit of food won't cure. Come on. Get dressed."

"Cian—"

"Stop fussing about Cian. He can take care of himself. He saved the king's life. They'll make him a hero. Besides, you can't help him from that bed, can you?"

Hild couldn't argue with that.

"That's right. No, no. Proper clothes. You're a woman now. Your finest gown, with the underdress and shoes Onnen sent that will match your veil band. Make sure you line your drawers." She handed Hild a clean rag, showed her how to fold it. "I'll just do this."

So Hild dressed for the first time as a woman to the sound of Begu dipping and wringing, and visions of Cian dead at a half-mad king's hand.

"Don't forget your necklace, that thick gold one." Hild found the heavy necklace, put it on, moving like someone under water. Was this what it meant to be a woman? No one had ever told her about the thick tongue and the strange distance. She lifted the girdle Begu had brought from Onnen, let it dangle from one hand.

"It's like a toothache in your belly, isn't it?" Begu nodded at Hild's other hand curled protectively over her stomach. "The tea will help with that. And mead. Besides, the ache'll be gone tomorrow. Here, give me that." She took the girdle from Hild. "I can't put it on until you stop clutching yourself. There. Too tight?"

Hild shook her head.

"It's a pity your good hose are in the bucket. Still, no one will see. Besides, if that cut reopens you'd only bleed on them again. Keep still." She rummaged in the sueded leather purse hanging from her own girdle and took out the comb Hild had given her. "We'll comb you out nicely before we try the veil band. No, no, you'll have to sit on the bed. It's like trying to comb the top of a tree!"

Hild sat blankly while Begu combed, working methodically from the ends to the crown. When the tangles were dealt with, Begu lifted Hild's hair, bunching it close to the scalp, then stroked the comb through it vigorously, as though brushing out a horse's tail.

"I swear, your hair's the exact same colour as Cian's. You could be twins."

Begu let go of the hair and let it fall over her forearm, then carefully slid her arm away so it fell thick and straight between Hild's shoulder blades.

"There. No, keep *still*." She pushed the veil band carefully over Hild's forehead.

Modresniht, Edwin putting the heavy arm ring on her head like a crown. Her path.

"—ever is the matter? Oh, shush, shush, it's all right." Begu wrapped her arms around Hild. "It's all right. It happens to everyone. You'll like it soon, I promise."

Hild shook her head. Her ears fluttered as though filled with butterflies.

"Put your head down. Down. There now." Begu stroked her back. "There now."

"Take it off."

"Your band? But—"

"Take it off!"

Begu lifted it off carefully. Hild breathed. Begu nodded to herself. "That's better. You went as white as milk." She felt carefully around the embroidered, jewelled band. "I can't feel anything sticking out."

"That's not it."

"What is, then?"

"It's all different. Everything."

"Well of course it is."

"You don't understand." They came for her in Lindsey. They came for the king in his own hall. Cian, her Cian, killed a man. She should have stayed. How would she be the light of the world feeling like this?

"Of course I do. It happened to me not long since." She flapped her hand at Hild's worry. "In a fortnight you won't even remember how it was to be a child. Besides"—she took Hild's hand—"it's happened. There's nothing to be done. And I'm here. Your gemæcce."

"But—"

"No buts. No nothing. It is as it is. How does that new scop's song go?"

"Fate goes ever as it must."

"Just so. Cian's a man now. A hero. You're a woman. So are you ready to try again, with the band?"

Fate goes ever as it must. Hild bent her head, to all of it.

This time when the circle pressed on her head, she was ready. I'm not a child in hall, she told herself. We're none of us children.

"Stand up. Now put this on." Begu handed her the purse the queen had given her. "And your seax. There." Begu's face stilled. Her hands dropped into her lap. She smiled: slow, surprised, proud. "Your mother will never tell you what to do again." Again that smile. "Wait there."

She stood, poured drinking water into the clothes bucket until it brimmed and trembled.

"Now come and see. No, wait. I forgot. I have a present for you." She jumped on the bed, stood carefully, and felt along the shelf for the twin of the clumsily painted box she'd given Hild. "Here." Earrings. Moss agate strung on gold wire. "Keep still. Oh. Oh, yes. They match your eyes exactly. And this." She tucked an ivory distaff through the girdle, a match to the one at her own waist, then jumped off the bed. "Now come and look." Hild came and stood next to her. "You look like a queen."

Hild looked down at her reflection. A tall, obdurate woman gazed back. Blue-green veil band embroidered with gold-and-silver thread, sewn with lapis and agate and beryl. Agate swinging from each ear. Heavy yellow gold resting between her breasts. Dyed-blue girdle. A matching purse with ivory lid. Distaff.

She reeked of power: richly dressed, strong-boned, uncanny. She laid her hand on her seax and gave herself a long look. Begu was right. No one would be fool enough to get in the way of this woman. She looked like a pale and unearthly queen.

"You could order flame to leap back into the log and it would," Begu said.

Hild smiled, feeling the power of it. The smile turned the unearthly queen to a haggard and bony youth playing dress-up. She stepped back, startled.

Gwladus burst in. "Ha," she said, and put a massive tray on the table. "Scrying for your fortunes? Well, here's some news for you. Lilla is dead as a doornail. The king's roaring like a bear stuck with a pin but is said to be breathing easy now. They say tomorrow he'll be none the worse for wear than that scratch on his arm. Arddun said the witch, that is, begging your pardon, the lady Breguswith, sniffed the blade and thought the poison poor work."

"Poison?" Begu looked at Hild.

Poison.

"What?" said Gwladus.

"Tell me of the poison."

"He couldn't talk, Lintlaf said. Tongue sticking out like a dead thing. And he was dizzy and cold. His heart kicked. But he's fine now. As I said."

Poison. "I'm fine," she said to Begu. If it was Eamer's blade that nicked her shin, it was poor work indeed. "Go on."

"The bishop is telling everyone God saved the king. The king is shouting for his army and vowing fit to turn black in the face. He's shouting at the bishop that if the Christ will give him bloody victory over the West Saxons, he, the king, will give his new daughter for baptism to the Christ. The bishop is shouting at his priests to pray for victory. The captains are shouting for their men—and at each other, for both Lilla and Forthere are dead and no one knows who's in charge. Lintlaf just shakes his head and the brothers Berht scowl like black dogs. The queen is shouting at her women to shut the king up or he'll wake the baby. The baby is crying. The baby's name will be Eanflæd. Her hair is black and her eyes blue. And she's a pair of lungs on her. Pink and plump and loud as a sow."

"Cian?"

"He's fine, Lintlaf says. He's under guard til tomorrow when everyone's calmed down—but guarded by your dogs, who think he's a hero."

She gauged the impact of her news, nodded in satisfaction, then whipped the cloth off the tray, and began to point. "I brought the white mead, and sweet pastries, and an underbelt for the rags. There's so much shouting that no one cares what leaves the kitchen tonight."

"See?" Begu said. "There's nothing you can do. He's fine. You're fine. Now we celebrate."

They feasted and drank, fierce swallows to themselves as gemæcce, to Æthelburh and Eanflæd, to the king for surviving, to Gwladus for the feast, to Arddun for the news, to Cian.

"He'll get a ring for this night's work, Lintlaf says," Gwladus said. By now it seemed natural that their wealh should be sitting on the bed with them, sipping from a walnut cup with a silver rim. "A young gesith who saved the king. It's like one of the old songs."

"Cian saved the king!" Begu said. She jumped off the bed and danced about with her mead. "Cian saved the king!"

For some reason they all found this funny.

More drinking, more toasts, then they were kneeling by the brimming water bucket watching as Gwladus blew out all the tapers and lit a twist of hemp fibre floating in a dish of tallow.

After the white wax light, bright as moonlight, the broad flame flaring and dying in the rough clay dish felt like something from the beginning of the world. The water gleamed, ochre and black.

"Look, you," Gwladus said. "Look into the water and tell us what you see."

"Yes," said Begu, "oh yes! Do seer magic."

Hild looked down at the water, at herself, a woman. A woman who knows. Standing like a queen. Light of the world. Queen of the world.

"I could be a queen," she said.

"Is that what you see? Is that your wyrd?"

Hild looked deeper, letting her mind sink into the glimmer and shadow, as she might in the wood, looking at the leaves, or lying on her back watching the clouds, letting the thoughts come, letting the things she already knew arrange themselves in a pattern, a story that others might call a prophecy.

"Is that your wyrd?" Begu said again.

"No." There was no world in which she would be queen to another's king. Eanflæd would be peaceweaver. She was the light of the world.

"And what about Cian?"

"Shh," Gwladus said, "she's seeing."

Cian. Gwladus was right. He would swear an oath to the king, swear to lay his life down for the king's honour. He would be a hero with a ringed sword. And more, for Lilla was dead, and Forthere, and Edwin wouldn't know whom to trust, and Cian had proved his loyalty. Edwin . . . She shook her head.

"What? What are you seeing now? What's she seeing now?"

"Hush," said Gwladus, and to Hild, in British, "Drink this. Ah, and another sip. Now look you, look deeper."

And with the mead burning in her gullet, Hild felt all-wise, all-seeing, all-powerful.

She looked in the water, watched the rippling faces of her companions. Rustic little Begu, who knew nothing of the world. Gwladus, a wealh of the Dyfneint, who just wanted to go home. And perhaps she would. A Gewisse had tried to kill the king, a Gewisse who had forsworn himself.

"The king will hunt Gewisse. There will be war with the West Saxons." Enemies of the Dyfneint. But they knew that.

"Will Lintlaf fight the West Saxons alongside the king?"

"Yes," Hild said, in British. He was a gesith. What else would he do? "He will kill many Saxons."

"Will he come home to me safe?"

"Home . . ." If the war went well—and of course it would, Edwin's war band was huge—perhaps he would choose to hold the land he took from the West Saxons, the land they had taken lately from the Dyfneint. And if Lintlaf did well . . . "The king will take the Dyfneint land. Lintlaf, if he chooses, could hold some of it in the king's name."

"Dyfneint land, Lintlaf? He could take me home?"

"What?" said Begu. "What? What are you saying?"

Hild looked up from the water. The wealh's eyes glistened. It was so easy to change a life. "He could."

Gwladus shrieked, hugged Begu. "I'm going home! I'm going home!"

"My turn, my turn," Begu said. "See what's for me."

Hild smiled, looked in the water. That was even easier. Begu would marry and teach her children the name of every horse, cow, and goat on the land. But no, wait. Wait. Begu was now her gemæcce; she must follow Hild. But where would Hild go?

The foot of her hose, swollen with trapped air, rose from the depth of the pail, turned, and sank again, like a whale diving deep in the cold waters of the North Sea. Down and down and down into the dark . . .

She shivered. Begu's fate was wedded to her own. She should have thought of that. Begu had no idea of Hild's life; Hild should have explained. But it was too late. The queen herself had made them gemæcce; it couldn't be undone. Begu's life would never be simple again.

Why had the queen done it? The queen . . . The queen who had brought Paulinus, the Christ bishop . . . The Christ to whom the king was vowing to give the queen's child for victory in battle. A Christian peaceweaver . . .

The wick floating in its fat flared yellow, and Hild remembered the road to Rendlesham, Fursey tapping the small fiery bead. *You have forgotten the most powerful of all.*

The yellow bead, blazing with light, next to the other beads: the one for Cynegils of the West Saxons, a deep angry red, and the reddish-orange beads for his three sons. One with a chip. Chipped. Chafing at his father. Oh.

"Cwichelm!" she said. "It was Cwichelm, prince of the Gewisse. He sent Eamer."

She couldn't remember the name of the other Saxon at the feast. Ceadda? He had not looked at Eamer but he must have passed some signal. Why hadn't she seen it? Why hadn't she been looking? Because she'd had Fursey at her elbow and Cian in her thoughts. Her mother would be angry. Her mother . . . Did she have anything to do with this? No: The chaos after assassination was not something she could control, and Breguswith liked control. Osric? She thought about the way his body showed his thoughts: No, he'd been as surprised as anyone. And where was Fursey?

"Hild, what about me?" Begu said. "What about my future—our future? Will we be happy? Will I?"

The wick flared again and spat. The Christ. Cwichelm. Fursey. Everything was changing, and she couldn't see the pattern. It wasn't easy anymore. The ache in her belly was making her feel sick.

The silver rim of Gwladus's cup pressed against her bottom lip. "Drink."

She swallowed. She wanted to lie down. But now her head was full of pictures: Edwin, looking wildly about him, blood dripping from his arm: Whom to trust, whom to trust? And she was glad, then, oh so very glad, that Eamer was not one of her hounds. She saw Edwin sitting on his great chair, eyes darting, making and unmaking decisions all spring and into summer until his advisers despaired and began to listen to the promises of other kings and princes. So many other kings: Anglisc, British, and Saxon, Irish, Pictish, and Scots. So much fear and greed, so many whispers: a foster-brother in Gwynedd, hard-faced nephews in exile with Picts and Scots, and Osric his black-haired cousin plotting in Arbeia. The clash of swords.

"Black hair and chestnut," she said, watching the pattern of light and shadow twine and shimmer on the surface of the water.

Her hose rose again, like a dead and bloated whale.

She leaned closer. "So much blood."

"Don't touch it!" Begu caught her with her face so close to the water she could have flicked out her tongue and touched it. "It will spill and break the spell."

"It smells," she whispered.

"Well, yes. It's full of your dirty clothes."

Hild blinked. Clothes. Dirty water. Just dirty water. She straightened, then reached out and flicked the surface with her fingertip. The trembling water spilled down the side of the bucket. Hild stood, said to Gwladus, "When you've cleaned that up, bring me raspberry tea."

Her belly did not ache the next day but her head did, and her skin smelt different, like a stranger's.

Gwladus brought food and news that, according to Lintlaf, Cian was still whole, and according to Arddun, the queen and the baby were doing well. Hild sent her to make sure Cian had been fed, and she and Begu were sipping small beer and munching stickily on warm bread and honey when the curtain parted and Breguswith swept in.

"There you are. The king wants—" She stopped. "Well." There was more in that one word than in the whole of a scop's song. "What a lovely veil band." For a moment—so briefly Hild wondered if she'd imagined it—her mother's face seemed to thicken and pucker, like the skin on warmed milk, but then it smoothed to its usual unreadable expression. "A very fine purse, too. Kentish work, if I don't mistake." She stared deliberately at the spindle in Hild's girdle, then at its match in Begu's.

Hild brushed crumbs carefully from her skirts. *Your mother will never tell you what to do again.* She stood. She was taller than Breguswith. "What does my uncle want?" *My* uncle, not yours.

"Your meddling priest has found the West Saxon, Ceadda, the Gewisse who ran."

"And the king wants me to question him?"

Breguswith smiled, a bright spark of eyes and teeth, like a flint striking steel. "Sadly, the king killed him before he could speak. He would have killed your priest, too, if he hadn't run like a hare. If he's any sense, he'll keep running. However, word of your vision, black hair fighting chestnut hair, and your naming of Cwichelm, has run wild through the kitchen and reached Edwin. He is . . . anxious."

Breguswith turned to Begu. "You must be the girl from Mulstanton. I thought you'd be better dressed."

Begu tilted her head and studied Hild's mother with one eye, then the other. "You must be Hild's mother. I thought you'd be taller."

Hild had a horrible urge to giggle. Instead, she took her gemæcce's hand. "Perhaps the queen would like to see you."

Begu turned that bird gaze on Hild, considering. Eventually she nodded. Hild and her mother were silent as Begu collected her things and left.

"You stupid girl!" Breguswith said. She sounded like a hissing swan. "Cwichelm! What if you're wrong?"

Hild sat down. "I'm not." She ate a piece of cheese.

Her mother sat, too. "How do you know?"

Hild stopped chewing, surprised. She swallowed. "I'm the light of the world."

"Yes, yes. Light of the world, the king's seer. But he's going to ask you what you saw, and how. So what will you tell him?"

"I looked in the water."

"A sacred pool, I hope?" Hild shook her head. "A silver bowl under the full moon? A pool you found while following an eagle? No. No, you stupid child. A tub full of dirty clothes! I heard as much from the kitchen. Does a wash bucket fill the listener with awe? Do filthy garments inspire fear of the otherworldly message and she who bears it? No. It inspires only thoughts of dirt, of human stink. Human. Human lies and trickery, the treachery of plots and assassins with poisoned knives."

"It was only a game."

"At the king's vill, the king's seer's words are weighed like poison, or like pearls. Nothing you say is a game."

Hild glared at her shoes. It wasn't her fault that the housefolk were spreading rumours. It was just a game.

"No, little prickle. Now is not the time to curl up and wait for the hunter to go away. The king will kill you or Cian if you so much as look at him sideways. Look at me." She tipped Hild's chin up until she lifted her gaze. "Think."

Hild wanted to snatch at her mother's hand and bite it. But her mother was right. Edwin was mad with pain, mad with fear. She pushed her mother's hand aside, but gently. "What was the poison on Eamer's blade?"

"Something akin to wolfsbane. Brewed by an incompetent." That sparking smile again: If she'd made it, the king would be dead. "I gave the king a cold tea of foxglove. He's well. In his body at least." She dismissed his health, much as Begu had, with a wave. "Tell me about your vision. Leave nothing out."

Hild listened to her heartbeat: steady. Her breathing: smooth. She didn't need foxglove tea. "It wasn't a vision." Breguswith quelled her with a look. "Vision. Yes." She told her mother of the clothes, the blood, the water.

"Ah." Breguswith leaned back, thinking. "The blood of a king and the first blood of a virgin seer mixed with water drawn cold from the well under moonlight. Yes. Very good. Your wealh and that— Your gemæcce. They will both swear to it?"

"Her name is Begu."

"I know her name. It was a foolish—" She mastered herself. "Done is done. For now we must be quick. We can recast your seeing so it reeks of sidsa: king, virgin, blood, well water under the moon. And it was witnessed. Well and good. But how will you answer to the charge that Eamer, the assassin, was your man?"

"What? No! Near Lindsey he was set to guard me—"

"Who gave that order?"

"Forthere. Who had his orders from Lilla. Who had them from the king."

"He was not one of your hounds?"

"No. Never. I'd wondered why. I thought he liked me—"

"Perhaps he did. If he knew his fate it was an act of kindness to ignore you. Now tell me the story of your vision again, as you will tell the king."

Her mother took her through her story, step by step, shaping it, sharpening it.

"It will do. But be careful, child. Above all, you must soothe his vanity. You must make him feel strong and in control. Make him feel like a king."

———

In hall, Hild wished she had her mother with her. The king seemed barely to be listening to her story. He could not keep still. A muscle by his eye and one at the corner of his mouth fluttered and twitched. He sat in his great chair on the dais with a bloody sword across his knee and a seax in his left hand. Every now and again he lifted the seax hand and blotted his forehead with his forearm. His great garnet shone hot red, the bandage on his upper arm was bulky and clumsily tied. Not Breguswith's work. His gaze flicked this way and that, probing the shadows. Paulinus stood at his left hand, his bony forehead like old wax and his eyes glittering. Stephanus sat at the foot of the dais at a tilted wooden contraption: some kind of writing table piled with wax tablets. Everyone was there—every man: Osric the badger, the æthelings, Coelfrith, the brothers Berht—unwashed, unshaven, unrested, muscles coiled, ready to leap on any moving shadow and crush it. Cian, swordless and beltless, knelt in one corner, wrists tied back to his ankles. The right side of his face was dark and swollen. Blood, his own by the looks of it, matted his hair. He looked bewildered and very young. Being a hero wasn't like in the songs.

Tondhelm held Hild's wrists behind her and shook her slightly to encourage her to continue. "Eamer was set by Forthere to guard me, at Lindsey."

"Forthere who is dead," the king said. He twisted in his chair to peer behind him, then back at Hild. "And Eamer saved you at Lindsey yet tried to kill me, his king. Why?"

There were none of the usual murmurs of a hall audience. No one wanted to be heard; no one wanted to be noticed. Fear lay over them all: fear of the king, fear of the young hægtes, fear of Saxons in the shadows and the fates of men being spun by otherworldly hands. Nothing like the songs. Songs . . .

"Because Cwichelm, his lord, told him nothing of me. Because I am not important. Whereas you, lord, are overking. King of all the Angles."

"Soon to be king of the Saxons." He spoke flatly, for his gesiths and counsellors and all those who, having seen his blood, smelt it, might plot against him. He leaned forward. "So tell me how it is that this stranger"—

he pointed his smeared sword at Cian—"came to be in my hall with a serpent-tooth knife?"

She drew herself up. *Like a hoofbeat, like a song.*

"Say a wolf cub's tooth, my king. It is a small blade, but honest. Like the man who bears it." She was glad that Cian was not whole and uninjured and standing beside her with the height and hair of their father. "His mother, one Onnen, was bodywoman to my own mother. We played together as children. But children grow. Onnen knew my time as a woman approached. She sent Cian with gifts." She touched her veil band and earrings. Her mother had made her wear every piece of good jewellery she possessed, and hang every mark of womanly rank from the girdle given by the queen—she had even lent her own seeing crystal. "The buckle blade was a gift from me. From my hand to his. Into his hand to protect your life."

"Indeed." He rested his chin on his fist. "And how did you know he would need it?"

She touched the crystal hanging at her left hip. "I am your seer."

"Cwichelm, you say." He gestured for Tondhelm to let her go. He stared at his seax then sheathed it. He scratched his beard, thinking. "He tried to kill me."

"Yes, lord King." She wanted to rub her wrists but didn't dare. Anything could irritate Edwin, anything bring the swing of the sword.

"And you claim you stopped him."

"Lord—"

He lifted his hand. "Yet Paulinus here says it was the Christ's will that I be saved."

"Perhaps it was Christ's will that I be born to see your path and guide others to keep you safe."

Paulinus Crow stared at her. Hild stared back.

"The bishop of Christ and the handmaid of wyrd," Edwin said. "Which should I believe?"

"You have promised me your daughter for baptism, my lord," Paulinus said.

"I have promised her if you can promise your Christ will give me victory. Can you? Or will you witter like that fool bishop of the Dyfneint who told me all prophecy is the work of demons?"

"Not all prophecy, my lord."

"And you have seen my victory?"

"I have prayed. I have asked for the aid of our Lord Jesus Christ and all His saints and angels."

"Pity you didn't ask yesterday." He ran a finger up and down the clotted channel of his sword, sniffed it, wiped his hand on his thigh. He lifted the sword. "Come closer."

The black-clad figure stepped forward.

"Closer." Edwin touched the point of his sword to the bishop's throat, just below the throat apple.

Hild admired the Crow's courage, and his self-possession. He wore clean robes and had shaved. The apple in his throat did not bobble.

"Will you take a wager?" Edwin said.

"Name the terms, my lord."

"My daughter against your life. Victory against the Saxons and you shall baptise her. If not . . ." He smiled and pushed, gently.

"I accept the wager."

A growl of approval ran through the hall. They liked a brave man. They liked a betting man.

"Tondhelm!" The whole hall jumped. Edwin lifted the sword away and held it out hilt-first to his thegn. "Clean this and put it away. And bring food. I'm as hungry as a goat. And cut him loose." Hild along with everyone else followed his gaze to Cian. "And someone find that tooth of a blade and his belt. He'll need a blade to swear on."

Hild backed away slowly.

"And, Niece." She froze. "Find that priest of yours and bring him to me."

Outside, she leaned against the doorpost and threw up her breakfast while Cian swore his life to the king.

Hild forgot about the salve she held and watched Cian spar with Berhtnoth, shield to shield, his moves simple and deft, like a poem: never lunging, never off-balance, always over his feet, always behind his shield.

Behind them, Coelfrith, as attentive to detail as his father, oversaw the grooms bringing horses in batches from the pasture for his examination. The war band would be moving fast. He ran a hand over fetlocks and face, approved each mount with a nod just like his father's. Every single mount must carry its gesith forty miles a day into Saxon territory and still have the strength for a hard gallop away if the battle went badly.

The gesiths paid no attention; the horses were not their concern.

Berhtnoth began to pant, though Cian did not. Not long after that,

Cian banged Berhtnoth's shield to one side, stepped away when Berhtnoth lunged, and ran his padded sword along the gap between Berhtnoth's cheek flap and mailed shoulder. Berhtnoth was dead.

They stepped apart and a wealh ran to take their shields and helmets, and the two gesiths slapped each other on the back and laughed over each stroke while the wealh ran back with cold well water.

The king was nowhere about. She stepped from the shadow of the wall.

Cian saw her and walked over, water spilling from the jar into the grass. His leathers reeked of sweat and his mail of grease and iron.

"You're very good," Hild said.

"I am." He grinned and wiped his face. The left side was still greenish-yellow. "I'm a king's gesith! I'm going to war! All those days fighting in the furze with sticks. And then Mulstan—oh, he's a strong shield fighter! He beat me so many times, just banging me aside, not even breaking a sweat. 'Hoard your strength!' he'd say, and wallop me on the head. 'Mind your feet and hoard your strength! The loser in a shield fight is the one whose legs start to tremble first.' And soon—" He broke off. "What's wrong?"

Hild shook her head. He was going to war. He didn't need her burden: a missing Fursey to find and nightmares of a suspicious king. Besides, soon she wouldn't have to worry about the king's mood.

"Where's Begu?"

"With the queen and the baby."

Cian made that face men made when women mentioned babies, and drank more water.

"Cian."

He wiped his mouth.

Come home safe. Don't be a hero. Stay away from the king. But he was a king's gesith. She might as well tell rain not to fall. "Remember Mulstan's lessons. Wash your wounds well." She hefted the waxed sausage of salve she'd prepared, then held it out. "And send a message when you can."

13

✦

BEGU'S HAIR STRAYED FROM UNDER HER VEIL BAND and she muttered to herself as she folded dresses and rolled hose. Her muttering became peevish. The war band had been gone a fortnight.

"Gwladus will do that," Hild said.

"Gwladus is busy doing the work of all the men who left with the gesiths. I'm doing this."

Hild doubted Gwladus would ever do men's work, but she said nothing. She leaned against the doorpost, remembering Mulstanton, Begu wondering out loud whether she would need her bed.

Begu carefully stowed their ivory treasure boxes in the carved trunk that would ride under their direct supervision. "I don't even see why we have to leave the Derwent. Eanflæd is still so tiny!"

Hild shrugged. "It's how it is."

"Why can't we at least wait until the war band comes back?"

They wouldn't all come back; they never did. And this time Cian was with them.

"I wouldn't move a lamb at that age, never mind a princess!"

Hild nodded.

"What's Sancton like? Is it near the sea?"

"No. But Brough, where we'll go later, is on a river as wide as the sea, and sometimes if you're at the dock early enough you can go out on a boat that will go to the sea and be back in time for dinner."

"But not at Sancton."

"No."

"I miss the gulls."

Hild stroked the back of Begu's arm. "I'm sorry we have no home."

Begu said without turning, "Moving is stupid!"

Her hair smelt of the resiny pine they used to ward off moths. Hild didn't know what to say.

"Oh, just go away and let me finish this in peace. I think the queen wants to talk to you about something."

At the door of the queen's apartment, Hild put her finger to her lips for a moment and old Wulfhere, who had taken a spear behind the knee at some long-ago Kentish battle, nodded and said nothing.

She watched Wilnoð and the queen, who sat on stools with a tablet weave between them. Every now and again Wilnoð tapped the foot of the painted and gilded cradle and kept it rocking.

After a moment Hild cleared her throat. Wilnoð looked up. "Good," she said. "You can take the queen out for a brisk walk. Accept no excuse." The queen began to shake her head. "The babe's asleep, Æthelburh. She won't melt if you let her out of your sight. Go for a walk."

The string-thin paths of early spring were wider now, wide enough for the queen and Hild to walk abreast. The soft green tapestry of the woods was stitched with the bright gleam of birdcall, too many birds to name.

They walked silently. It was clear the queen's thoughts were elsewhere. Or she was trying to find a way to say something.

They'd been walking now for a while. The queen seemed to have forgotten that they should pause for Wulfhere to catch up but Hild felt no obligation to remind her.

They heard the creak-crash of a deer deep in the woods, followed by a sudden hammering nearby. Æthelburh clutched at her cross.

"It's a woodpecker," Hild said.

"Not a wood sprite?"

Hild shook her head. The hammering, loud—a big woodpecker— came closer. "If we keep still it might fly this— There." A red plumb-bob shape flicked across the trail in the characteristic rise-and-dip path. It would be heading for the big oak by the clearing. Woodpeckers liked that one; she had seen the plates of bark there the other day; the tree must be infested. Perhaps it would fall in the next big storm, be nothing but broken wood when they came back to the Derwent. Once again, Hild was struck with longing to have a home, year-round, where she could watch and learn a wood, a stream, a hillside in snow and fog and sun, in wind and rain, in summer and winter. Begu was right. Moving all the time was stupid.

"Begu misses the sound of gulls," she said. "She misses her home. I never had one. Do you miss yours?"

Æthelburh stroked her cross. "When Eanflæd fell asleep last night I listened for the sound of the wheat. In the Kentish summer it rattles and hisses in the breeze. Everywhere. Wherever you look, from every vill: golden wheat waving like the sea."

Hild felt she should offer the queen something, as a comfort. If it were up to her she would climb the ash and watch the badgers, this was just the kind of weather that badgers liked: warm sun to drag out their bedding to air. But she doubted the queen would want to climb a tree and, besides, badgers reminded her of Osric.

"Do you want to go see the rookery?"

"I would be happy to watch the rooks with you."

Hild led them onto another, barely discernible path and the scent changed from summery open green to something cooler and loamier. Apart from that once with Begu, on the day they became gemæcce, she was the only one who walked this way. After a week with no rain the rivulet ran clear and quiet, and instead of the vivid primroses of spring, its narrow banks bloomed with blue cornflowers and a spill of delicate creamy yellow petals, over which no butterflies flittered. Bitterwort. An antidote for several poisons, and good for fevers and fatigue. Her mother was always looking for it but the root was the best part and it wouldn't be ready until autumn, when they wouldn't be here.

After a little while, the small, densely packed ash and elder gave way to a clearing and, beyond that, a stand of tall elms. The ground beneath the rookery was white with bird shit. The kah-kah of young birds, recently fledged but still wanting to be by their parents, echoed through the trees.

They sat quietly on a rock, beyond the patch of shit. The breeze was soft and warm. They watched the birds.

"They look like crows," Æthelburh said.

"They're young. They'll lose those face feathers in autumn and look like rooks. At least, that's what happens at Goodmanham and York."

Æthelburh's face, pale and plump for a week or two after the birth, was beginning to plane down again. Her eyes were half closed.

Hild lost herself for a while in the gossiping to-and-fro of the young birds. The breeze changed slightly, coming now from the south as well as the west. Coming from where Cian was. Perhaps he was fighting. Perhaps he was hurt. Gradually she became aware that Æthelburh, no longer sleepy, was watching her.

"You look like that when you listen to music," she said. "You watch everything, don't you? Why?"

"It's peaceful. I learn things."

Æthelburh untied her braid and began combing through it with her fingers. "What things?"

"That rooks—dogs, cats, people—do some kinds of things depending on how old they are. Like those young rooks. In autumn they'll lose their face feathers, and they'll start playing—flying for the fun of it, only they're not doing it for the fun of it, they're proving they're good enough for the rookery, that they can stay. Like gesiths with their boasting and fighting. And rooks are like jackdaws—like people. They have families. They talk. They don't like change. There's an ash spinney a mile away where they like to go pluck the twigs for their nest. Always the same place; one patch is almost bare of twigs. But they're just twigs, why fly all that way? I don't know. But that's what they do."

Æthelburh untangled a burr from her hair and flicked it away. "And what do dogs and cats do?"

"Dogs own space and cats own time."

Æthelburh's hands paused for a moment, then resumed their comb-and-pick.

"The cats share the barn and the byre. All of them. But you've seen the big ginger tom with the torn ear?" For a moment she couldn't remember which vill he belonged to. It didn't matter. "He gets to sit on the hay bale by the door at middæg. The two grey queens curl up there at æfen. The tom wouldn't go there in the evening, and the queens wouldn't go there at middæg. But a dog in hall or the kennel likes his own corner, morning, noon, and night. That's his corner, no one else's."

"And people?"

"Kings travel from place to place like a cat but want to own those places like a dog. It's why there are wars."

The queen blinked. "And the queen?"

"The queen . . ." She was realising she'd just compared Æthelburh's husband to a dog. "The queen is like a new bird in the colony. She finds new grubs, builds new nests as her price for belonging." Hild tilted her head back, in the direction of the vill.

"Derventio was Paulinus's idea. A lot of things are Paulinus's idea."

Ah. She waited.

"Like Eanflæd's baptism. It was agreed as part of the marriage settlement—any girl would be mine to baptise—but the timing . . . That's Paulinus."

Some hint was moving, eellike, just out of Hild's reach. "Have you had news?"

"No. But it will come. The king, my husband, will be victorious. He'll return laden with gold and glory to Sancton, where Eanflæd will be baptised as my husband's tribute to God, the first Yffing."

It didn't need a seer to foretell that. An Anglisc overking with a huge war band against a rabble of petty Saxon lords, all calling themselves king. The only question was how long it would take to subdue them, and who Edwin would install as his underking.

"Don't you see, child, what I'm telling you? When we get to Sancton, Eanflæd will be baptised. She will need powerful sisters and brothers in baptism. I had thought of asking you, but you're Yffing. Blood kin. My husband will not allow any greater tribute than an infant. You can't be baptised until he is. And he won't take baptism yet—though when he does, all must follow. Do you understand what I'm saying? Those who go first will find themselves in positions of favour. It happened in my father's court."

"But as you say, I'm blood kin."

"Your mother is not. Nor your . . . your gemæcce's foster-brother. You might mention it to them."

In the half-light of the byre, Hild smoothed her girdle self-consciously.

"It suits you," Fursey said. While his voice was as light as ever it sounded a little scratched, a little hollow, and she had not missed the way the bones of his wrist stuck out, the hole in his boot, and the small tear in his skirts. He smelt of dust, not horse. He had walked.

"What happened to your mount? We're leaving for Sancton tomorrow. You nearly missed us. Why did you run? Why were you away so long?"

"I shouldn't have come back at all."

Hild just waited.

Fursey laughed. "Oh, you've learnt a vast great deal since Tinamutha. I'll miss you."

I'll miss you. Sometimes if you ignored things they went away. "Eanflæd is to be baptised."

He raised his eyebrows, which only emphasised how drawn his face seemed. "You've heard already? I thought I'd outpaced that news."

"News?"

"Your king is proceeding in triumph to Sancton with most of the war band, claiming the death of five Saxon kings—if a kingdom is a stony field and a muddy stream. Though sadly Cwichelm and Cynegils are not among the dead. They're still running, pursued by threescore of the war band under Eadfrith. And, no, I've no news of Cian."

He'd be fine. He would. "How soon will they be in Sancton?"

"Six days from now perhaps. They have wounded."

Not Cian. Cian would be fine. "The queen said a strange thing."

"Yes?" He sounded so very tired.

"She said my mother, and Cian, should take baptism."

"Did she now?"

"She said it would give them power and influence." Fursey nodded. "But why would she want my mother to have that? I don't think she likes her."

"She does like you." He smiled, but tiredly. "And you're both blood. She's trying to protect you."

From the king. From Paulinus. From Cadwallon and all the conspirators who wanted her dead for no other reason than she was an Yffing.

"Child, I'm weary to the bone and I must leave again soon enough, so—"

"You can ride with me to Sancton. As we travel you can tell me about baptism."

"I'll tell you everything you could possibly wish to know about the holy rite of baptism, but I won't be going to Sancton."

Silence.

He said, more gently, "I must leave. For good. Your king can't trust me."

"I don't understand. You didn't do anything wrong. I can explain—"

"My king is dead. Fiachnae mac Báetáin, king of the Dál nAriadne, was slain by Fiachnae mac Demmáin of the Dál Fiatach. At Lethet Midind. Three of the Idings fought at my king's side."

Idings. The friend of my enemy is my enemy.

Hild stood. "I'll find you a horse."

"Oh, sit, for pity's sake. I've a night's grace. As long as I'm not seen."

One night. "I'll send at least for food."

"I would like that. Have your three-scilling wealh bring it for me. She knows how to keep her mouth shut. And I'd like to see her wicked face one more time before I trudge my weary way into the unknown."

"I won't be long."

When she got back, Fursey was curled on the straw, asleep. His face twitched as he dreamt; a gold fleck of straw glinted by his nostril. Priest, prince of Munster. A shabby man without a king. Without a home. Fursey. Who had taught her her letters.

He stirred when she sat on the bale next to his.

"Gwladus is bringing cold mutton, bread, and cheese."

He scratched his stubbled tonsure.

"You need a shave."

"What I really need is a drink."

"Gwladus is bringing heather beer—everything else is packed."

His lip curled, but his scorn was halfhearted.

"Fursey?" He looked at her. "What will you do?"

"Drink the jar dry."

"No, I mean—"

"I know what you mean, child." He rubbed his chin. It made a dry scritching. "I'll leave tomorrow. I've a fancy to see your sister again. She'd welcome me, do you think?"

"My sister? Hereswith?"

"You have another?"

"No. I mean, yes. Oh, yes." Of course she'd welcome him. He was Fursey.

"And she needs to learn to read. Once the overking's daughter is named for Christ, it won't be long before Paulinus is forcing the whole island to dip their heads and kiss his ring. Hereswith will need advice."

Fursey and Hereswith. Hereswith and Fursey. If she knew where he was, if she could write to him, he wouldn't be gone. And she could write to her sister. They wouldn't be lost to her.

Gwladus brought the food. Fursey was too tired to do more than smile, and Gwladus seemed to catch his mood. She put the tray on the ground, nodded, and left.

Hild sat down next to him. "Tell me about baptism."

He talked as he ate. Hild was content to watch, to try to carve the picture of him on her mind.

Baptism, he said, a lamb bone in his hand, was getting your sins washed away.

"What's a sin?"

"It's . . . well now, it's a kind of stepping from the path. A wrongdoing." At Hild's blank look he said, "An oath-breaking against God."

"A sinner is a nithing?" Cian wouldn't want to be thought of as a nithing.

Fursey drank more deeply of his beer, clearly wishing he had not embarked on an explanation.

Another thought occurred to Hild. "But if you haven't taken an oath to the Christ, how can you break it? How can you have sins?"

"We're all born sinners. All born with a stain on our soul."

"A stain?" Like a birthmark?

"Some more than others. Perhaps that's why the queen suggests—" He shook his head. "Ah, but don't worry about it. Paulinus will explain everything to you long before your own baptism."

"I don't like Paulinus."

"No one does but Paulinus."

"If I get baptised, I want you to do it."

Fursey paused, cup halfway to his mouth. "You don't want me to baptise you, child—hush, now. You had best get used to being called child. It's what priests do with their flock because we represent God on earth, and you are God's children."

"So are you."

"Don't interrupt. Paulinus won't take kindly to being interrupted. Listen to me now. When the time comes to be baptised, let Paulinus do it. He's a bishop, perhaps to be an overbishop. And baptism is like . . ." He drank his beer, wiped his mouth, refilled his cup, considered. He switched to Irish. "Baptism is very much like a sword in this way: that the man whose hands the sword or the soul passes through adds his lustre. Just as an overking's sword is more noble than a thegn's, a bishop's blessing is more holy than a priest's, which in turn is better than a deacon's. It's the way of the world, which is to say, the way of men—who, being created in God's image, reflect His intentions for the world."

"You were baptised by Brendan himself, so why aren't you a bishop?"

"Well, now, perhaps I will be. Just not today, and not here."

A little after dawn the next day, she walked with him as he led his mare down the path to the daymark elms. They stopped.

"Well," he said, and hitched at his belt.

Hild didn't know what to say.

"This time it will be long and long before we meet again."

Her throat closed.

"Well," he said once more, and he looked small and tired and she couldn't bear it. She opened her arms and hugged him, hard. He patted her back. Patted her again. "Child, I can't breathe."

She let go. It was like letting go of the world.

His eyes glistened. "Help me up now."

She made a stirrup for him. His shin was dirty. It would be dirtier before the end of his travel. Such a long way to go. All alone.

She heaved.

He looked down at her. "Goodbye, now, Hild, daughter of Yffings. Fare well."

Yffings didn't weep. But she watched him, watched the path until even the dust of his passing had fallen.

In the predawn light, thin and grey as skimmed milk, mist rose from the river, cool and smelling of secrets. A bittern boomed from the marshy plash downriver but fell silent at the approach of thirty people, eleven in white wool robes—twelve if you counted little Eanflæd, fast asleep in her swaddling and snug in the queen's arms. Ducks rose in a flurry of wings and honked into the distance. Something splashed hurriedly into the water, out of sight.

Stephanus led the procession, swinging a brass censer. It kept going out. It was out now, but no one mentioned it. Getting to the baptism place on the river was the important thing, not stopping to fuss with burning Frankish resins. Few of them knew what to expect, but they all knew rivers flow with sidsa, especially near dawn. The air trembled with it, like the skin of a colt standing still but longing to run, run, run over the rich new grass.

James the Deacon led his six-man choir in a low spoken chant. One of them, the straw-haired youth with the freckles, kept stumbling over the words. Everyone ignored that, too.

Someone's belly rumbled. Berhtnoth nudged Berhtred and whispered. Berhtred hitched at a sword belt that wasn't there, then wrapped his arms tightly around his wool-draped middle. Their hair, like Cian's, glistened. Everyone was hungry. Paulinus had insisted that those to be baptised not eat in order that their bodies be empty and pure enough to receive the grace of the Holy Spirit, and the queen had suggested that the whole party forgo food.

Cian, like Breguswith, like the four members of James's choir, like Burgmod and Eadric the Brown, Grimhun and the brothers Berht, had been persuaded of the political advantages of baptism. Hild and Edwin's other kin—the æthelings, Osric, and Oswine and Osthryth—must follow Edwin's example, and Edwin, before making a decision, wanted to see with his own eyes what happened when some finger of Christ's spirit took up residence in a body.

Hild walked with Begu behind the candidates in white: all treading carefully, unwilling in the strange mist-wrapped half-light to break a twig in passing; they didn't want to attract the attention of any ghosts, holy or otherwise. Fursey had been a little vague about the Holy Ghost; Hild thought perhaps it was some kind of godly cousin, an otherworldly ealdorman of the Christ. She wondered if she would see it. The morning was certainly uncanny enough.

Begu leaned in to whisper, "Eanflæd wouldn't be sleeping like that if she was hungry."

Hild said nothing. She didn't want to talk. Fursey had told her that today would be the feast of Pentecost, which commemorated tiny tongues of flame dancing on saints' heads. She wanted to see that. No wonder they did this by a river. She hoped Cian wouldn't get burnt.

She had warned him about the flames. He had wetted his head as a precaution. The brothers Berht had followed his lead.

She hadn't cried when Fursey left. Yet now, as they trod solemnly towards Sancton's river for this Christ mystery, she found she had to swallow and blink fiercely and try not to listen for his mocking Irish voice that made everything seem less important, less frightening.

At the great curve in the river where the north bank was low and the current slow, a swath of reeds, recently cut, was laid in a green path over the mud to the water. Paulinus, resplendent in his jewelled cope and carrying his gilded shepherd's crook in his left hand, stopped and raised both hands. Stephanus stopped swinging and clanking. James quieted his chant.

Hild and her mother raised their heads, alert to the pattern. They were about to meet their new god.

There was no sound now but the river.

Paulinus cried out, a great shout in Latin. Another great shout, something about eternal life and the seal of God, and Stephanus, James, and the choir all shouted in unison.

The river poured.

"Then the eleven disciples went away into Galilee," he shouted in Anglisc, "into a mountain where Jesus had appointed them. And when they saw him, they worshipped him: but some doubted. And Jesus came and spoke unto them, saying, All power is given unto me in heaven and in earth. Go ye therefore, and teach all nations, baptising them in the name of the Father, and of the Son, and of the Holy Ghost: Teaching them to observe all things whatsoever I have commanded you: and, lo, I am with you always, even unto the end of the world. Amen."

"Amen," said the priest and the choir and Æthelburh.

Paulinus shouted some more, and his normally waxy face began to flush as he warmed to his theme. He spoke too fast, and his accent was too strange for Hild to follow every word, but he seemed to be talking to someone called Satan. He sounded like a herald provoking an opposing army, taunting them with their imminent defeat, boasting of his champion's skills and the worthlessness of his enemy.

Paulinus's cheeks grew mottled. He waved his crook. Hild wondered if it was a good idea to provoke an uncanny enemy when the sun was not quite risen. She glanced to her left, to the north and east—she wasn't the only one—but there was no sign of Satan and his army in the shadowed woods.

The sky began to pale in earnest; a blackbird sang, then stopped abruptly.

Paulinus stopped, too. He smiled and gestured to Æthelburh—who glanced at Edwin and took his left arm with her right—and then to Stephanus, who came forward with a white-and-gold stole and laid it around his neck. Hild found herself, along with everyone else, leaning forward.

Paulinus and Stephanus waded thigh deep into the river and turned. The king and queen followed.

The spot was carefully chosen. The water was not still—for that would be dangerous; sprites liked quiet water—nor was it swift enough to sweep a mother off her feet. Even so, and even with her husband to steady her, Æthelburh stopped when the river lapped at her knees.

For a moment, Hild thought Paulinus would refuse to step closer, but Stephanus stepped first and the Crow had no choice but to follow. Stephanus uncapped one of the tiny silver pots at his waist and held it out.

If Satan were to come, it would be soon. Hild longed for her seax, or even Cian's hidden buckle knife.

"Face west," Paulinus said. The king and queen turned cautiously to face upstream. Paulinus dipped his thumb in the pot. It glistened a little. He traced a cross on baby Eanflæd's forehead. She opened her eyes and made a questioning sound. Stephanus stowed the pot in his belt and brought out a different one.

"Do you, Æthelburh, on behalf of your daughter, renounce Satan and all his works?"

Hild tensed. She was so aware of the position of her mother and Cian and Begu that she could feel them like firelight on her skin.

"I do," Æthelburh said in a clear, strong voice.

"Face east," Paulinus said, as a king would speak to a wealh.

Edwin narrowed his eyes but the Crow did not blink. Edwin turned. The river pushed at the back of their knees.

Paulinus bent and scooped a double handful of water. "In the name of the Father"—he dribbled water on Eanflæd's head—"and the—"

The rest was lost in the baby's piercing shrieks.

The gesiths all crouched—Hild very nearly did—then straightened. The shrieks seemed to break the spell: It was just a river before dawn, with people getting wet. Hild saw her mother's shoulders drop at the same time as she herself realised this was not unlike one of Coifi's blessings—and they had never met Woden.

Paulinus trickled more water and raised his voice, though no one could tell what he was saying. He wiped at the struggling child's head with his stole, then dipped his thumb in the second pot and touched her head, then nose, then breast. The outraged shrieks grew louder. Paulinus, unmoved, signed the cross in the air over father, mother, and daughter just as light broke over the river.

"Oh, you should have seen it!" Begu said later to Gwladus. "The baby never shut up, and the Crow scowled at James, and James nodded at his choir to sing, but they started on different notes and it sounded like the cows at Mulstanton when they haven't been milked! And then James waded into the river at the head of the others to be baptised, and he bumped into the king. They nearly went down, *splosh*. Wonder if the Christ would have saved them then? If the king'd had a sword at least one priest would be headless now. But the big surprise was Cian. The queen stood for his godmother! Took even the Crow by surprise."

It had taken them all by surprise, especially Hild. She didn't know much about baptism, but she knew royal favour.

"Cian's mouth dropped so wide I thought he'd drown when Stephanus and James dipped him backwards in the river. They did it three times. Once for the Father, once for the Son, and once for the Holy Ghost. But the sun was up by then so we didn't see any ghosts. Not that they might not all be ghosts by next week. You should have heard their teeth chattering on the way back!"

She was exaggerating. The sun had been high as they walked along the river, the choir singing and censer swinging. It had glinted on the wet hair of the gesiths and Breguswith—who had not been forcibly bent backwards like the men, but held at an angle while Paulinus dribbled water on the crown of her head.

Hild had walked next to her mother. Breguswith didn't seem any different, apart from being wet, but she was not inclined to talk—she had always had a fine sense of occasion, and Hild had told her what Fursey had said, that she was supposed to be filled with grace, washed clean, serene; Breguswith was determined to play the part. Hild then walked with Cian. He didn't talk, either. He hadn't talked much since his return from fighting the Saxons with what looked like a bite mark along his jaw. "The shield wall is like being thrown into a pit with boars and blood," he'd said. "A striving of mud, and muscle, and madness." And he had refused to say more. The bite was healing. Perhaps baptism would wash him clean of the things he had done.

Hild stayed at his side, content to walk in silence and watch a covey of mallards, all drakes, green heads sparkling in the sun as they dove and preened and made their own kind of baptism.

14

✦

EADFRITH THE ELDEST ÆTHELING continued to pursue the Saxons south and west. Osric returned to Arbeia, but Breguswith stayed. Since her baptism, she and the queen had reached some kind of understanding whose shape Hild was still trying to fathom. The queen's good word spread: Her mother was once again the woman that women went to with their pains and troubles. The baptism had changed the spin pattern of the whole cloth. Edwin paid more attention to Paulinus and less to Hild. It wouldn't last long—the king would change his mind, it's what he did—and meanwhile, he was no longer concerned that Hild bring him Fursey. What was one homeless, hunted priest with a wrongly shaved head to him?

Cadfan died and Cadwallon became king of Gwynedd. Edwin brooded, then married Osfrith, his second son, to Clotrude, second daughter of Clothar, king of the Christian Franks. He would draw more Romish weft to his warp. Let Cadwallon eat that.

Osfrith seemed stunned by marriage. Gwladus reported to Hild that, according to Arddun, Osfrith and Clotrude screamed like stuck pigs every night. The gesiths, including the handful of Franks who had accompanied Clotrude, teased the ætheling without mercy. The Franks wore crosses, very like those worn by the newly baptised Anglisc: squat, heavy things, easily mistaken for the hammers the majority of gesiths still wore. Most gesith crosses were bronze. Some silvered copper. Cian's was gold.

Hild and Cian took to walking along the river at the end of the day when they might go unnoticed. He wore both his sword, with its gold hilt ring from Hild's uncle the king, and his cross, a gift from his godmother the queen, with the same mix of pride and wariness.

Larks crisscrossed the deepening sky as they walked west along the river's inside bend, where the flow was sluggish and water bugs dimpled the surface. Hild walked with her skirts kilted up. It was the first hot day of the year, and there was no one to see but Cian.

"I wish we were by the bird cherry at Goodmanham," she said. "There always seemed to be a breath of wind there."

"Breath of the tree sprites, you said."

"You believed me."

"I did."

"You believed me, too, about the frog who swallowed the heart of a hægtes."

"I did not."

"You did." The birdsong was fading. Crickets chirred in their place. "Did you ever believe I was a hægtes?" He didn't say anything and she couldn't read his face in the gathering twilight. "I don't mind."

He stopped, took her arm, a hard grip just below her elbow. "Yes, you do." His voice was rough as a blacksmith's file, his eyes a deeper blue than the sky. "We all care, we always care, what they say of us."

He let go. They walked on. She rubbed her arm.

"You are not a hægtes."

She walked with her chin up, not understanding why her eyes were suddenly brimming.

"You know the gesiths sing songs about you?"

"I've heard them." She fell behind a moment and surreptitiously blotted her cheek with her shoulder.

"Not all of them." Now there was a smile in his voice, an encouragement, the kind of tone he'd use to gentle a horse before changing gait. "In their songs you might be a hægtes, but you're *their* hægtes. You're the seer who saved Bebbanburg and revealed a conspiracy of kings. Who falls from trees to kill a dozen Lindseymen with one blow. And offers to gut irritating æthelings who get in your way."

"They know about that?"

"They know the song. Coelwyn wrote it. He got the story from Lintlaf. There's a chorus that's very catchy: *I swear I'll gut you, like a leveret, and fling your parts to feed the royal dogs.*"

"A *leveret?*"

"Sometimes he sings *sucking pig*, for the funny version."

The funny version.

They walked for a while. Soft shadows pooled between the trees. Soon bats would swoop in place of larks. Dusk. The in-between time, when ælfs might watch quietly from behind the hawthorn, and it was easy to talk, even in Anglisc. "The ætheling was called Ælberht."

Cian simply nodded.

"I meant to kill him. I could have. But he was afraid. He looked in my eyes and was afraid."

"Men are, when it comes to it."

"He wasn't a man. Don't you see? That's the point. He was just a boy." The trees were denser here, growing almost to the edge of the river. He wouldn't be able to see her face. "But in three years he'll have a sword and know how to use it, and I won't. He'll be no taller than me, no faster, no more royal, but he'll have a sword and I won't. And if he angers me and I draw my seax in earnest he'll just lay his hand on his sword hilt and I'll have to bend my head."

"Not if I'm there. Or the brothers Berht. Or Grimhun or—"

"But you're sworn to the king, not to me."

The ring on his hilt tinked dully as he fiddled with it.

"Teach me."

The creak and scritch of tree frogs rose suddenly, and just as suddenly fell. Swords were man magic. It would be his death if he was caught, ringed sword or no. They would nail him to a tree, pull his lungs through his back ribs, and spread them like wings.

Eventually he said, "You don't know what it's like. You don't want to."

They were clear of the trees. A fan of cloud in the west reflected the last rose-gold light. She touched his arm. "Stop. Please."

He stopped, turned, faced her, back to the horizon. His face was in shadow. He could be a wight, risen from a barrow, glinting with gold. But she could smell him, she could hear the creak of his belt as he breathed.

"I was at Lindum. I don't want to be a gesith. I want to know how to beat a man with a sword. Perhaps with an axe." Women cut wood sometimes. It might be thought odd to walk about with an axe thrust through her girdle, but it was not forbidden. "One on one, sword against axe, could I do it?"

"No."

"You brought a message from Onnen: to watch my back. Help me. If not an axe, then what?"

After a moment he said, "A club."

"A club? Against a sword?"

"Swords aren't magic."

"That's not what you used to think." She remembered his singsong recitations about his imaginary sword: snakesteel blooded in battle, bitter blade, widow-maker, defender of honour and boast, winner of glory. Of course they were magic. Just not for her.

He ignored her. "Show me your wrists."

She held out her arms.

He circled a wrist with each hand. "Big, for a woman. Now make fists." He tightened his grip. "Spread your fingers."

It hurt but she forced her fingers wide.

"Good." He let go. "You need strong wrists for a club. But they already call you hægtes. How would you explain a club in your belt?"

"I wouldn't carry it all the time."

"A weapon's no use if it's not to hand. A gesith is always ready."

"I'm not a gesith." She pondered. "How about a staff? They're every-where. The handle of a rake, a spade, a broom—"

"Or a crooked tree limb by a pool?"

She laughed. "We are us!"

He sighed. "We are us."

The midges were breeding and biting when Eadfrith brought back the re-mainder of the war band. Cwichelm and Cynegils had escaped.

Hild, alerted by a message from Begu, who'd had it from the queen, was sitting in the shadow by the hall's western door by the time Eadfrith, filthy and stinking of horse and worse, arrived and took a seat at the board with Edwin, his counsellors, the glazed-looking Osfrith, and Paulinus. Hild laid her left arm carefully on her lap, palm up, to hide the scabbed slice along her left forearm where the tip of Cian's sword had caught her. The great bruise on her shin was covered by her dress. Her mother, by the queen, gave her a look. Hild wondered if she'd winced.

Gesiths—Cian among them—lounged nearby pretending to dice and drink.

"The West Saxons had help," Eadfrith said. "From Penda." He paused to strip the meat from a cold pork rib with his teeth. His normally pale hair—like Osfrith, he had inherited the gilt hair of his mother—was dark with sweat and dull with dust. "I left Tondhelm to treat with the Dyfneint, with a score of swords at his back. I told him to help them rebuild Caer Uisc. We can't have the Mercians and West Saxons"—he paused to drink and the hall was so quiet Hild heard his every gulp—"can't have them joining forces without argument. Not now, not with Cadwallon king."

"No," Edwin said. He pushed a loaf at his son. "What's the mood?"

"Cadwallon, they say, is eager for a fight."

"We'll make him bend the knee." Edwin scratched his chin. He gestured at Stephanus to make a note, and said to Eadfrith, "In a fortnight, once you're rested, you'll take the war band to Gwynedd."

Eadfrith glanced at Osfrith, clean and well fed, then at his father.

Edwin leaned forward. "That's my word."

Hild breathed softly. Since the attempt on his life, Edwin couldn't abide being questioned, even sideways. He trusted no one. Lesser folk would be whipped around a tree for such insolence. The gesiths paid attention to their dice.

But then Edwin laughed and tossed another loaf at Eadfrith, who caught it without thinking. "Of course it must be you. You're the eldest. Besides, your brother's still mazed with marriage." He raised his hand so the garnet glinted blood-red. "You'll wear my token and speak with my voice."

Breguswith looked thoughtful. Hild wished she could talk to Fursey. She had no idea what path her mother's thoughts might be taking.

Just inside the elm wood west of Sancton, in a glade where dragonflies glinted like enamelled pins as they swept the air clean of midges, where just a week ago Hild had seen a young fox play-stalking a hare and the leaves smelt of afternoon sun and unstirred dust, Cian swung hard and two-handed at Hild's neck. Hild met his blade with her staff, met it at the right angle with the right speed so that oak and steel rang and sprang apart. Cian lifted his left hand, palm out, sheathed his sword, and reached for the new shield leaning against a gnarled crabapple.

While he attended to the business of adjusting his straps, Hild sighted down her staff to make sure the sword hadn't weakened it. It was unmarked. She was getting better at judging the angle to swat aside the flat of the blade. She wiped her forehead with her forearm and hitched her kilted shift tighter. There was no wind. There had been little rain for a fortnight. The glade sweltered.

A wood pigeon called from deeper in the trees. A flick of red caught her eye as a robin redbreast hopped on the fallen trunk nearby. She had seen him here before. Sometimes he pretended to study the clump of blue speedwell by the mouldering roots or to peck for ants on the flaking bark, but Hild thought he just liked to know what was going on.

She twirled the staff in her hand, enjoying the heft and balance. She liked oak best, it was hard and sure, solid as an ox's shoulder under her hand. Ash was more plentiful—broken and discarded spears, or green poles cut from one of the coppices found near every royal vill—and whippy, which had its advantages. Birch was soft wood, and light, almost useless. Elm wasn't much better—softer than oak, less whippy than ash. But if she had to, she could fight with a staff made of anything, whether smoothed and seasoned heartwood or a knobbed bough recently fallen.

She preferred something her own height and as thick as a boar spear, but she had practiced with axe handles, with split-lathe poles and a lumpy cudgel made of blackthorn root. Wood was everywhere, as common as air; she always had a weapon to hand. She practiced with Cian every day and often when she was alone. The exercises came easily: She had spent time every day of her childhood stamping and swinging alongside Cian and his wooden sword. In addition to her tree-climbing calluses she now had a knot against the inside of both middle fingers. She had distinct muscles along both forearms that danced when she rippled her fingers, and shoulders as wide as a stripling. She knew the strength and speed needed to send a man's sword flying, to crack his neck, to sweep his feet from under him or punch out a rib. She knew the play of muscle from its anchor on the ribs, across the front of her chest, and running up over her collarbone like a rope over the lip of a well. She knew the knack of using her fingers and the muscles in her forearms to lift the tip of the staff just a little, until it balanced itself, as one dairy bucket on a yoke balances the other. She knew pain. But she'd had worse falling out of trees. Pain was just pain. She healed quick as a young dog.

Now, with a full-length oak staff, a moment's warning to get distance, and an opponent without a shield, she might not lose.

Shields, though. Shields were a problem.

Cian had a new one, painted with his colours: the red and black of that first baldric Hild and Begu had made at Mulstanton. Fine red leather around the rim. With the spoils of his fighting against the West Saxons he had persuaded the smith to add a layer of gleaming tin to the iron boss and two silvered fish mounts, one on either side. He breathed on it now and rubbed it with the hem of his tunic.

"Very pretty," Hild called, and edged east a little, so that when he looked up from his strap and buckle the sun was in his eyes. "But while you *hurred* and polished, I stole the sun."

He just smiled his crooked smile, slid a hand through the straps, and swung the shield up. Reflected sunlight leapt from the boss and dazzled her. She jumped to one side but he was too fast. He ran at her, knocked the staff away with his shield, and walloped her across her left hip with the flat of his blade. She went down—but rolled efficiently to her feet, remembering to avoid the fallen tree, blinking furiously, trying to see, testing her weight on her left leg. It held. He'd pulled his blow, again, and outwitted her, again.

They circled each other warily. Hild kept her gaze very slightly unfocused and spread wide, as she did in the woods, to see change: the unmoving shadow, the flick of a fox ear against wind-bent grass, the hunching back ready for the spring. With Cian it was the trick he had of moving the point of his sword a finger's width to the right before he moved his feet. While she watched, she let her own feet find their way; she knew every root, every rut and hare scrape, every fallen bough in this glade.

"So will you ask to go with Eadfrith to Gwynedd?"

"Why?" He feinted with his shield but Hild didn't blink.

"Because you're a gesith and there might be glory."

"Glory," he said. The healing bite on his jaw darkened very slightly; he leapt in the air, sword high, but Hild wasn't there when he landed.

They were both breathing harder now.

"What's wrong with glory?" She shifted her grip slightly, watching, watching. His new shield seemed heavier than his old one. She could find a way to use that. "You're a sworn gesith."

"Sworn to the king, not his son," he said.

Hild stabbed with the end of her staff at his face and, fast as a tiddler squirting from its nest, again at his knee. She almost got him. "You're slow with your pretty new shield."

"It's yew."

Hild nodded. Denser, springier, harder than lime. Good for a shield wall. Good against axes and thrusting spears. She feinted. He feinted. They circled. The robin flew off, offended.

"Besides," Cian said, "there won't be fighting. You heard the king. It will be all talk talk talk. That's why he's sending Eadfrith. Cadwallon will bend the knee."

"He might not." Those warps were not yet ready to be woven into the same tapestry.

He didn't respond. She blinked hard and shook her head, as though she had something in her eye. But he knew her too well and didn't take the bait. She would have to distract him some other way.

"Cadwallon hates Edwin king."

"He's always hated the king. What does it matter? You know the songs: Cadwallon's word turns corners no one else can see. He'll smile and bow while we're there, and lead an army when we're not looking. But it's just Gwynedd."

"Just Gwynedd? Land of heroes! Remember Gwyrys: Bull of the host, oppressor of the battle of princes."

"We're all Anglisc now." His attention never wavered.

"You had your first sword from Ceredig of Elmet!"

"He's dead. To be wealh is to be dead or a slave."

"Cadwallon is a king. Not a slave, not dead."

He shrugged. He made it look easy, despite the sword, despite the shield. Wouldn't he ever get tired?

"Do you remember those little streams in the dell at Goodmanham?"

"No."

"Yes, you do. By the boggy place, where the hægtes frog lived."

He smiled. "I didn't believe you."

"You did."

"Did not."

"Did."

They both laughed, but didn't stop circling.

"Besides, they weren't streams," he said, "they were trickles. Not much bigger than the sweat running down your face."

Now she wanted to wipe her face with her shoulder. Oh, he was clever. "Trickles, then. Little, harmless—on their own. But if they joined together, they'd cut through that soft bank in a week." She tried a lunge followed by a swift uppercut. Nearly. "Penda's Mercian trickle has already joined the Saxon trickle of Cwichelm and Cynegils—"

"And if Gwynedd joins them they'll wash us all away. Yes." He lifted his sword high and back, and his shield over his body. "But they won't join Mercia."

Hild retreated, unsure of his intent. "They might. Because Cadwallon hates Edwin king."

Cian advanced. "Aye, he hates like a wealh." Cut. "And like a wealh he won't say so to an Anglisc face." Cut. Backhand cut. "And any vow he makes will be a worthless wealh vow." Thrust.

He sounded hard, bored, careless. A stranger. And he kept coming. She swung hard, right, left, but the shield was always there and the oak and painted yew thumped dully.

His lips skinned back. The vein in his neck throbbed. He swung hard, at her ribs, edge-on. She only just deflected it. He kept coming. She backed away.

"Cian . . ."

He wasn't listening. She swung at his head, at his legs, even at his wrist. But it was a big shield, and he didn't seem tired at all.

He came on like the tide, relentless, eyes hard and blank as blue slate. She stabbed, she swung, she stepped back and back.

Her back was against a tree. Nowhere to go. He raised his sword.

The world slowed. A dragonfly glinted to her left. She could see each back-and-forth of its see-through wings, as though the air they beat was as thick as honey.

He was so close: sweat inching its way over the great vein in his neck; his tunic dark with it, and his hair. Did her hair, too, turn that shade, dark wet chestnut, at the temple? He smelt as tangy as new cheese.

"I win," he said, and the world turned again with its usual speed. He grinned and lowered his shield. "You looked as though you expected to wake in the hall of Woden."

She laughed, harsh and metallic with relief. She wanted to shout and hug him but settled for pushing herself off the tree with a writhe of her spine and giving him a friendly thump across his rump with her staff.

They sat by the river, by the smooth slope of an otter slide and a fallen alder rotting into pinkish punk. She dabbled her feet in the water. He sat cross-legged, whittling a fist-size lump of pale fawn birch.

She breathed the rich scent of the dark water, the reeds, the glossy mud.

She said, "I thought you'd gone mad." He didn't say anything, the way only he could: an easy silence, no hurry to know. "The things you said, your face."

He looked up. "We were fighting."

"What you said about wealh. Did you mean it?"

"We were fighting." He turned the nub of wood in his hands. It was the beginnings of a duck.

"It sounded true."

"I'd say I wanted to fuck your mother if it would make you blink." Now it was her turn to say nothing while he whittled. Perhaps she wasn't as good at it as he was: He cut too deep.

He sighed and threw the birch in the river.

"Perhaps I did mean it." He sheathed his knife. "In the shield wall I must be one of many, one of the same. Anglisc, not wealh. To the man on my right my mother is the lady of Mulstanton; to the man on my left, I'm a thegn's foster-son. We're all king's gesith."

"Don't hate her," she said. "She's your mother."

He threw a pebble into the river.

"Is her word worthless? Was Ceredig's? He gave you your sword—"

"A wooden sword."

"—as he would any prince of the blood at that age. A sword from the hand of a king."

"A prince of the blood . . ." He aimed to sound careless. "Yet my mother never spoke of it."

They had grown up closer than most brothers and sisters, played together naked as eels. He would know if she lied outright.

"She didn't need to: He gave you the sword."

"But not in public."

"Does it need to be witnessed for it to be real here?" She tapped his breastbone with two fingers. It made a round sound, like a drum. A strong sound. She leaned back on her hands. "You had your first sword direct from the hand of a king, and your mother was a royal cousin. Royal, of the blood of Coel Hen. The same blood as Cadwallon. Go with Eadfrith to Gwynedd. Look your royal cousin in the eye. See again a king in a king's hall—a king from a line ancient when my people were over the sea. And when Eadfrith—or Osfrith if he's not so married by then—is sent to Craven to take it from Dunod, go there, too. Meet your people—the warriors, the kings, the bards at their harps."

"Perhaps I will." He threw another pebble. "But it will still be all talk talk talk. They're even sending priests. Priests don't fight."

Hild shook her head. "Paulinus is a Roman bishop. Fursey says wealh bishops and Roman bishops are like cats and dogs. The one will always hiss and the other bark. The wealh bishops will never kiss the Crow's Roman ring, not even if Cadwallon bends the knee to the king. Paulinus wants Cadwallon to fight and die. Otherwise he can't be overbishop of the isle, to Edwin's overking." Kings picked the chief priest who then picked the underpriests. It was how it had always been. The name of the god didn't matter.

Cian considered that. "So no matter what presents Edwin sends or what pretty words Eadfrith speaks, Paulinus will spoil it all by flinging insults about like a dog shaking off the rain?"

Hild nodded. "Cats and dogs. They won't be able to help it."

He pulled a plate of bark from the alder and drew his knife. "I'm still not sure I want to go to Gwynedd. Eadfrith . . . worries me."

She remembered the Eadfrith of long ago, nuzzling a girl in the heather, laughing, telling her Hild was a hægtes in a cyrtel. She had never liked him.

He turned the bark this way and that in the light. "Eadfrith's like the king."

"The king has won all his battles."

"But he has a dint in his arse from sitting so much on the fence."

"He does jump, in the end." But she wondered about her mother's thoughtful look.

"But will Eadfrith?"

"Um?" She thought about it. "It depends how many men the king sends."

He tossed the bark into the river. It floated away like a tiny raft. He sheathed his knife. "Lintlaf thinks the Gwynedd war band is fourscore."

Triple the enemy number was usually held to be the right number for overwhelming force: a guarantee of Cadwallon bending the knee. But twelvescore was a lot of men to send just for a talk, especially when the West Saxons and Mercians were allied, Elmet unsecured, and the harvest due.

She fished her carnelians from her purse and wrapped them around her wrist. "Still, you should go. Meet your people." She let the beads flash in the sun and grinned. "Besides, you might get presents."

Five days later Edwin sent Eadfrith west with Paulinus and four priests, sixscore gesiths, and Cian. Osfrith went back to making Clotrude squeal every night—and during the day, too, Gwladus said, and in this heat!— Edwin to brooding like a moulting hawk in his hall, and Æthelburh and James the Deacon to conferring about music.

"I don't know what she sees in it," Begu said to Hild as they counted the skeins of yarn from Elmet that Breguswith had asked them to sort. "Eighteen, nineteen, twenty. That makes threescore of the red. It's nothing you can hum." She pulled a soft sack closer and peered dubiously at the green skeins inside. "And this is nothing we can use." She lifted a badly dyed hank of wool to the light. "More yellow than green."

Hild was thinking about the king. Dint in his arse indeed. Sixscore against fourscore. A bold war leader certain of his men might force a battle at those odds. But if Eadfrith did not no one would call him craven out loud. Not in enemy territory. Cian would be angry. But at least he'd be safe.

"They should be whipped."

"Um?"

"The Elmetsætne. They should be whipped."

At least it was Anglisc people she wanted to whip this time. "Give it to me." Hild pulled a thread from the skein and rolled it between forefinger and thumb. Poor stuff: short-fibred, coarse, and uneven. Not even worth redyeing. She would tell her mother. Her mother would tell the king that he was being fed worthless goods as tribute from the leaderless Anglisc of Elmet. Edwin would brood further and build elaborate stories in his head about why he had not yet brought Elmet firmly into the Northumbrian fold. "Put everything back in the sacks," she said. "Gwladus will carry it— Where is Gwladus?"

"Spitting in Lintlaf's mead, I expect."

Lintlaf had returned from the West Saxon campaign with a fistful of gold and the news that he'd turned down an offer of Dyfneint land, *Because why would I want to live so far from all the action, with no one to talk to but wealh?* And when he pulled Gwladus onto his lap she had not resisted—she was a slave, what choice did she have?—but later Begu had seen her spit in the cup she filled for Lintlaf and hand it to him, smiling.

Hild went to find her mother. She told her of the wool.

Breguswith listened, nodding.

"You're not surprised," Hild said.

"They have no lord. No one to protect them or watch for them in bad times. So they protect themselves and hoard their best against the day, yet know they should send the king something so he'll leave them alone. Meanwhile, he tells himself they'll come to him of their own accord." She smiled. "So let's not worry the king with this just yet. Let's wait for news from Gwynedd. Why take an unnecessary risk? No. Always approach kings with answers, not questions."

In bed that night, Hild listened with half an ear while Begu wondered aloud if Wilnoð, the queen's gemæcce, might be pregnant. "It would explain the handfasting to Bassus in such a hurry."

Hild, still thinking about her mother, said, "Listen to everything the queen says."

"You already told me that."

"I mean it."

"You didn't mean it before?"

Hild closed her eyes. How did Begu always make simple things seem so slippery?

"I need information."

"Why?"

"My mother is . . . She's planning something. Making up a pattern to weave all the threads into, to tell a story. I want to know if it's based on anything real. Listen carefully for anything about the north. Or the king's sons. Please?"

Begu made an indistinct noise: She was falling asleep. She fell into sleep like a stone into a well. She always had, even in her little linden-wood bed in Mulstanton. There was no stopping her once she started to drop.

Hild talked anyway. Of Osric—he would be back from Arbeia at the mouth of the Tine once the harvest was in and the season's last trade goods shipped—and how she wished her mother hadn't taken his part. She didn't understand why her mother was doing it. Their bodies didn't lean towards each other the way Onnen's and Mulstan's did, or Lintlaf's and Gwladus's had. And Edwin didn't trust him. It was just a matter of time. Then she wondered about Fursey: Was he in East Anglia with Hereswith yet? Would he like it there? She missed him—she missed the gleam of his wit, she missed his information. Where would she get information now? And Onnen: Had she had her baby? Was it a boy or a girl? Would it look like Onnen or Mulstan, or maybe Cian . . .

The moon rose. Begu snored gently.

In the weaving huts at Goodmanham the women worked in two sets of two. For days, the weather was perfect: steady sun and a light breeze from the northwest smelling of wildflowers and ripening corn. Hild, decent in veil band and girdle, strong hands disguised with rings, sometimes worked with her mother setting up loom patterns, but often with Begu and the queen and Wilnoð, relaxing in the back-and-forth of conversation about nothing in particular as they lifted the warps, shot the shuttle, and beat the weft. There were advantages to being ignored by the king.

Hild studied Wilnoð. She looked as plump as a winter wren. Begu was right.

The infant Eanflæd lay on her stomach on a striped cloth by Æthelburh's feet, wriggling about, sometimes lifting herself onto her hands and being surprised by the late-afternoon sunlight slanting through the open roof door, sometimes stretching her hands in the direction of the hanging loom weights and cooing. Whenever Æthelburh or Wilnoð spoke, Eanflæd looked at them and beamed gummily. Her hair and eyelashes were fine and sooty, darker even than Æthelburh's. Very like those of Cygnet, Hild's mare.

Hild stood and stretched. Her fingertips brushed the thatch.

The queen said to Wilnoð, "Look at that. Like a young oak. I doubt even Bassus could reach so high."

"Oh, he could. If he jumped." They laughed at the very idea of red-cloaked Bassus so risking his dignity.

"Cian could," Begu said. "I think."

Perhaps Hild only imagined the queen and Wilnoð deliberately not looking at each other.

But then Begu was talking about Eanflæd—she'd be teething soon, no doubt, look how she was drooling, and she bet that Hild's fine carnelian beads would never be safe again, the baby would always be wanting to stuff them in her mouth. From there they talked of the best smooth stones for a baby to gum—Æthelburh claimed to have had an agate circle to chew as a child, "The very colour of your eyes," she told Hild—and what herbs worked best when the endless wailing and bleeding gums began. They had reached a discussion of fennel when Hild felt the vibration of hoof-beats, a horse ridden at speed. Then they all heard it, followed by the messenger's shout: "*News for the king! News from Gwynedd!*"

The hall didn't have the light of the weaving hut but it was too hot for torches. Edwin sat in his great chair, his gesiths ranged about him, Coel-frith at his right hand, and the tufa looming behind him in the shadow and half-light.

He was livid.

Hild glanced at the messenger, sitting on a bench out of the way, trying to eat while the scop pestered him with questions. She would have to wait her turn for news of Cian.

Everyone was there, waiting to hear Edwin's pronouncement: the gesiths, James the Deacon, Coifi and one of his underpriests, a visiting emissary from Rheged, even dazed-looking Osfrith. On the women's benches on the left side sat the queen and her ladies, including Breguswith and Begu, most giving a decent appearance of spinning.

Edwin stood.

"Am I not the overking of the Angles?" No one was foolish enough to speak. "It was a simple enough message. Acknowledge me overking and keep your miserable mountain fastness. Hard to misunderstand." He looked around the assembly, settled on the emissary from Rheged. "Wouldn't you say?"

The emissary, there only to deliver the news of the death of Rhoedd the Lesser, said carefully, "Perhaps Cadwallon king did not misunderstand, lord."

"Don't name that nithing king in my hall!" Edwin roared. "Soon he'll be king of nothing! He will kneel at my feet in shackles and watch as I burn his hall and use his women and sell his children as slaves. I'll hack off his limbs and stake them at the four corners of his land. I'll salt his fields. I'll tear out the tongues of those who speak his name. I spit on him!"

He spat on the rushes before him. One by one, every man in hall hawked and spat.

Hild refilled James the Deacon's cup with Rhenish wine. "I imagine the bishop's anger was almost as great as the king's," she said. *Worse,* the messenger had told her. He'd also told her that Cian had sent her a message: He had a bold new cloak from his kin. Hild had given the messenger a ring pulled from her thumb and tucked away the news to ponder later.

James nodded, sipped. "The letter was in Stephanus's hand, of course, so it was smooth and bold as usual—a lovely hand that man has, lovely. If he sang half as well as he wrote . . . No, no. No more for me. Oh, very well, just a little."

"So Paulinus was angry."

"Incandescent. He said to make sure that by the time he got back every single wealh priest was to be gone from Goodmanham. Even that pathetic wisp up by the well."

"The priest of Saint Elen?"

"Even so. And then we must rid the entire kingdom, he said. Rip them out, root and branch. All spies, he said. But I doubt most of them can even read, never mind write secret messages to a king they've never seen. And how I'm supposed to do it all in two days I don't know." He shook his head, setting his grey curls abounce. He pushed his cup aside with regret and tapped the brown-bound book on the bench. "Now. Where did we get to yesterday?"

"James, son of Zebedee and brother of John."

James beamed. "Most beloved of Christ."

"Yes," Hild said. She liked hearing James's stories. She liked his accent, hot and spicy as mulled wine. Even his Latin, when he spoke it: such a different Latin to Fursey's.

"I visited his shrine you know. In Iberia. Gold, gold everywhere, studded with gems of every colour. More gems than stars in the sky. And, oh, the singing there. Like the angelic host. It makes me weep to think of it."

She refilled his cup. "Did James like music?"

"Of course he liked music! He was the brother of the beloved of Christ! His soul was as fine as silk, and as pure. He lived in a country full of sun and wine and fine food. Until the wicked Herod Agrippa struck off his head with a sword. Is that all kings can think of, swords?"

Then he was off, talking of swords and how they should all be thrown in the sea, that life should be love and music, a heaven on earth of angels and sunshine, of wine flowing like water, and kings of ancient and settled lineage whose people were all happy, all obedient to their church, and of priests who tended their flock and didn't worry about kings and armies and imaginary spies!

Gwladus caught her as she was leaving the deacon's rooms. "Herself wants you to eat with her in hall." She handed Hild a ring—a yellow stone, big and gaudy, though not as heavy as it looked—to replace the one the messenger now wore. Hild slid it onto her thumb. "Hold still," Gwladus said. She adjusted Hild's veil band. "Osric is back. With Oswine."

Hild sighed.

"Shall I say I couldn't find you?"

Hild shook her head. "Go find Begu. Tell her Cian's safe and will be back the day after tomorrow."

Gwladus nodded, and Hild knew the news that the men were returning in two days would be sold around the kitchen: a bannock cake here, a cup of milk there.

Hild sat with her mother and Osric and Oswine at a corner of the table. At the other end of the hall, gesiths sang something maudlin about hearth and hall. When Osric touched her mother's hand, Hild kept her spine straight and her expression pleasant. It wouldn't fool her mother but Osric wouldn't know how much she longed to take her seax to his throat, to open it as she had opened that man's forearm on the dock at Tinamutha. Instead, she twisted the new ring round and round, as any bored young maid might. It was slightly too big. It wasn't nearly as fine as the one she'd given the messenger.

Oswine was paying more attention to the gesiths' end of the hall, clearly longing to be one of them. Hild reminded herself to talk to him when no one might overhear.

"When is Eadfrith due back?" Osric said, not bothering to lower his voice: Grimhun, on the lyre, had clumsy hands, which only encouraged the other gesiths to sing louder to drown out the sour notes.

"Tomorrow," Hild and her mother said together. They looked at each other.

"I had it from James, from Paulinus," Hild said.

"From the queen herself," said Breguswith.

"Then soon we'll move on Elmet," Osric said.

Hild and her mother nodded: of course. If Gwynedd and Mercia joined forces, Elmet would be the only buffer between the allied army and Northumbria, more important than ever. Edwin must secure it.

"He must garrison Elmet and name me as ealdorman." Osric slapped the board with both hands. "And don't even think about counselling me to more patience!" One or two gesiths glanced over. He leant forward. "I waited when he took Deira and Bernicia. I waited when he gave Lindsey to that soft-handed reeve. I'm Yffing. I have men, a strong son, healthy daughters. Elmet is mine by right. And I'm tired of waiting."

Hild saw that he would not listen to her mother on this. So, clearly, did her mother: She did that thing women do that Hild didn't yet understand. From one moment to the next her body turned pliant and soft: willow rather than oak.

"Yes, my lord, it should. And you should not wait. But overkings don't take kindly to being pushed. So let me be the one. I have just the weight to tip the balance. That wool," she said to Hild. She turned back to Osric. "Elmet shorted the wool tribute."

It took him a moment—so slow!—but then he smiled. Short tribute was an insult. No king could ignore an insult. The smile widened his face and slitted his eyes, and with his sharp bright teeth glittering in the torchlight he looked less like a badger than a broad-headed stoat smelling the hens.

Breguswith smiled back and Hild was certain her mother pressed her knee to Osric's under the board. "News best delivered by a woman who doesn't stand to profit from it. Delivered to the queen, who will drop it in the king's ear at the right moment. Be ready."

But Elmet was not Lindsey, peopled by a rich trading nation of soft-handed merchants, and Edwin was a man of greater cunning and ambition than his cousin. He would gather Elmet to Northumbria with care, to hold for life: not only his but his heirs', and theirs in turn. He would build a kingdom to last longer than song itself.

The moon waned and waxed and waned again, and the Winterfylleth moon was past the quarter when Coelfrith began to supervise the loading of the king's wagons.

It was strange weather: a leaf turn earlier than anyone remembered followed by blue skies and biting cold. The leaves should have blazed in the sun, but they hung dully, like dead brown hands. Strangest of all was the wind. The wealh loading the wagons were chased by whippets of wind that blew one way then another, no rhyme or reason.

Wight weather, said the kitchen wealh. From the warm side of the kitchen doorway's leather curtain, they watched the maid, sleeveless and with that staff she often had by her, lift her face just as a silent rush of shiny, black-edged clouds swarmed like silverfish across the sky. They shook their heads: The long-dead kings of Elmet and the Old North were stirring and planning mischief for Edwin Snakebeard.

Snakebeard knew it, agreed the baker and the cook—who stood, as befitted their rank, at the front, with a view of the goings-on. "For one thing," said the baker, a man with thinning sandy hair and burns on his wiry forearms, "they're yoking oxen—young oxen, mind—to the wagons for the trip out, but taking extra horses for the trip back. That means sacrifices. And he's taking twoscore gesiths—but no women." The maid didn't count.

"You don't need a war band to fight dead men," said the cook, which astonished almost everyone, for the cook was not one to talk much, except with her hands. "Just the maid and her four pets."

"Five," piped up the basting boy, who'd had it from Arddun's nephew, the message runner. "The brothers Berht, Eadric the Brown, Grimhun, and Cian Boldcloak."

"Boldcloak's not the maid's pet!" said the baker's lass with scorn, for the basting boy was newly arrived from the west and sorely ignorant. "I had it from Gwladus, the maid's bodywoman. The maid and Boldcloak grew up together, like brother and sister!" The cook and the baker exchanged looks, but the lass didn't notice, seeing only the chance to humiliate the new boy with her superior knowledge. "Don't you know the song, how she gave him a secret knife and he used it to save the king's life?"

A groom led out a string of horses: gesith mounts, with glittering headstalls and tooled leather girths.

"The pets going are all baptised," the baker said. "The Crow's hand, no doubt. And he's taking five priests. Five. Elmet wood is full of wights."

Behind him everyone crossed themselves deliciously.

"The maid's from Elmet, long ago," said the baker's lass.

"I heard she's half hægtes," said the basting boy. "Or half etin!"

The lass snorted. "She's twice royal so twice as tall! Everyone knows that."

"What about Boldcloak, then?" said the boy. "He's tall."

At which point the cook slapped the back of his head with her meaty hand, the baker's lass took the opportunity to elbow him in the ribs, and the undercook said, "At least Lintlaf will get a rest, poor man." Knowing looks were exchanged. Gwladus, who of course went where the maid went, had expressed a certain unhappiness at the young gesith's inclusion, so he was staying behind and, for a while, he would be free of grit in his gruel, beetles in his bedcloak.

"The Loides won't," said the baker. Osric's men were all to take whips, which didn't bode well for the wealth of Elmet.

They watched Coelfrith's underreeve, a half wealh called Pyr, instructing the yardfolk to handle the sacks more carefully. As he walked away, the foreman flipped his fingers at Pyr's back, and the yardfolk threw the sacks with renewed force.

"That's a month's worth of twice-baked bread," said the baker. "And mead. More mead than even twoscore gesiths could drink in a fortnight. There'll be feasting with the sacrifice."

"Aye," said the cook. "But feasting with who? Sacrifice to what? It's a strange party. Strange weather. Strange days."

As Hild had known it would, the rain started when the king's party had made it barely a mile down the road from Goodmanham and hadn't stopped even for a heartbeat since. She didn't care. This felt like the first time on the war trail but better. This time she rode next to Cian—who wore his new cloak of red-and-black checks, densely woven from the little Gwynedd sheep that had run the West Welsh mountains since the time of the redcrests—with her four gesiths behind. Back on the second wagon, it was Gwladus, not Onnen, who rode with everything Hild could possibly need for a fortnight on the road. For once she didn't have to sleep on hard ground, rolled in her cloak and hand on her seax. She didn't have to share a bed with her mother or dream bitter dreams. She didn't even spend every moment in dread of the king: He and Paulinus were wrapped in some plan on which they had not asked her counsel. Though she could guess what it was. Edwin wanted to win the Anglisc Elmetsætne without bloodshed; he wanted to be acknowledged rightful heir, not murdering usurper. Paulinus wanted to see every wealh priest driven into the river. Clearly the king had a use for her or she wouldn't be here, but for now she was happy.

Usually wagons followed the old Roman road to Aberford and Berewith, where Ceredig, after Hereric's death, had marched with his Loides to meet Edwin's invading Anglisc, before fleeing to his ill-fated refuge in Craven. But after a conference with Paulinus, Edwin had ordered the party to strike west on the wood road to Caer Loid Coit, Ceredig's hall at the heart of Elmet by the great River Aire.

The endless rain had turned what had been little more than a track into a sucking mess of mud and wheel-clogging leaves. Drivers cursed, oxen heaved, axles creaked—and two broke, but they were surrounded by the elm wood; axles were easy to replace.

The elm wood woke something in Hild. She found herself breathing faster, pausing mid-word and listening past the drip of rain and snort of men and beasts. Perhaps it was that no children ran alongside the horse, shouting, begging for an apple, a lump of bread, a meat pasty; no anxious local lords or their ladies were sent to ensure royal comfort.

They saw no wealh—no Loides, Hild reminded herself. By the time the royal party crossed a faint track to a settlement in the trees, its inhabitants had long since vanished, along with their pigs and dogs and iron cook pots. They did see Anglisc. Three times they crossed great clearings centred on sturdy homesteads, too modest to be called halls, flanked by outbuildings, with firewood neatly stacked, goats tethered, pigs penned, and watchful farmer and sons leaning on their spears, nodding at the tufa, which seemed boastful and tawdry in this dripping wood.

The first time they passed such a farm, Paulinus motioned to his priests and turned his horse from the path, obviously preparing to go make them kneel to their God. But Edwin shook his head. The second time, they'd heard the bleating of sheep but seen no sign of the animals. "Lord King, they're hiding their riches," the Crow said, but again Edwin gestured for him to stay with the wagons.

"They're Anglisc, and proud. We'll bring them to heel, but not yet."

At their next stop—another wagon mired in the mud—Edwin sent for Cian. Hild came with him.

"That's a fine cloak, boy."

"A gift from Gwynedd, my king."

"A wealh cloak, bright and bold."

"Yes, my king," Cian said.

"It wouldn't hurt if you rode a little ahead of the wagons. Make sure you and your bright and bold wealh cloak are seen. Keep the maid at your side."

Hild and Cian broke through the trees at the crest of the rise and looked down at Caer Loid Coit.

She remembered—as much from dream and song as from life—a grassy slope with a well-tended wide way leading to a massive blackthorn hedge and timber gate, around which some king of the long ago had thrown up a flinty earthwork and ditch, which in turn had gradually softened and greened over the generations. Then, the gates had stood open during the day; blue peat smoke seeped from the eaves of the mixed-timber and stone hall, and people went about their lives: the goosegirl with her hazel switch, the milkmaid—such red hands; she hadn't remembered that for years—the old man with the leather apron who sharpened sickles in summer, butcher knives in autumn. She smelt the ghosts of toasting malt, sour mash, and, from the orchards to the north and west, apples. Past the apples and plums had stood the tiny stone church whose scruffy priest and his wife made the worst bannock cakes in all Elmet but who were always ready to smooth disputes between folk not mighty enough to be judged by the king. To the south and east of the enclosure, the hazel wood, ash coppice, and the elm wood full of jackdaws. Behind everything, the Aire, wide and slow. On the far bank, clothing the rise in gold and bronze—up and up, as far as one could see—the great forest of mixed oak and elm that gave the country its name.

The river was still there, and beyond it the oak and elm—the canopy thinner than it should be, with this early autumn—but there was no smoke, no people, no sound but the drip of rain and the pour of the river.

Cian's mount stamped and sidestepped. Cygnet settled for turning her head against Hild's slack rein and rolling her eye, trying to see what was upsetting her rider.

Ceredig's royal enclosure lay dark and broken and forlorn: the gate torn down, the roofs fallen in, the coppice overstood. Scrub broke the once hard-packed dirt of corral and path, and bare saplings poked through the collapsing wattle of the goose pen. A buzzard wheeled at the crest of the far ridge, its belly flashing pale against the dark cloud. It called twice, *kee-wik kee-wik*, cut across the river, soared over the tangle of branches that had once been carefully tended rows of apples and plums, and vanished.

Hooves thumped up the rise behind them: Edwin, Paulinus, the tufa bearer, Coelfrith, Osric.

"So," Edwin said, and the Anglisc word was lumpy and alien to Hild. "We'll tear it down and build a better one."

They tore it down: every stone, every gate, every leaning timber on the near side of the river.

Edwin's men and the Crow's priests strode into the trees, to the wealh houses with their just-returned pigs and unsuspecting owners, rounded up every able-bodied man, woman, and child, and drove them, clutching what they had in the way of billhooks and mattocks and mallets, to the ruined enclosure. Over the next fortnight, as the sun broke free of the clouds and the early autumn retrod its steps to a threadbare copy of late summer, Osric, with an eye to his own likes, supervised the cutting of every tree but one within five hundred paces of the ditch—every tall elm, every wide oak, sending up clouds of cawing rooks and jackdaws—even the orchard, though with patient snedding many of the trees could have been brought back. Paulinus insisted that the tiny church be pulled apart, stone by stone, though the wealh had to be encouraged with ox goads for that. The font and altar stone, finely carved, he put on a cart.

It was seeing the thorn hedge torn up and burnt that made Cian rub his lip with his knuckle and turn away. Hild swapped her staff to her left hand and reached past his cloak with her right and tugged his belt, as she had long ago, and they walked to the river.

"Those roots were planted in the days of Coel Hen," he said in British.

"They grew strong in the days of Eliffer of the Great Retinue," she said, in the rhythm of the dirge.

"And were mighty when the princes Gwyrgi and Peredur were born." *Amen*, a priest would have said. *Woe!*, a bard.

Cian said, "My people."

By the river, gesiths were throwing stones at the roots of the lone willow where one had spied a fish shadow. Chub or perch, she knew. She felt, suddenly, a memory of hot sun on her bare back as she and Cian squatted by the ditch, fishing for tadpoles under Onnen's keen eye, though perhaps that, too, was part of some song she had made her own.

They turned and walked south along the bank. After a while they were among the elms. She remembered moss on her cheek, a stream of jackdaws crying *Home now! Home!*, the faint honk of geese. Something inside her threatened to break and spill.

"My people," Cian said again. "Food for wolves, food for the ravens."

She shook her head, trying to catch and pin the memory she knew was her own.

"They're not dead?"

She shook her head again, and her memory eeled into the dappled shadows thrown by dreams and song.

"Then where are they?"

He was thinking of the men of the Old North, princes with their fish-scale mail and bright swords and mead-soaked voices. The glorious, arrogant dead. Not the flea-ridden, filth-caked Loides being whipped by Osric. She wanted to explain, but she couldn't let go of the memory swimming now into the deep—and, in following it, was three again. She lifted the edge of his new cloak—the one that could have been the twin of the one worn by Cadfan's messenger, Marro, had it not been red and black—and shook it.

He didn't understand at first, but she pointed at the Loides and kept shaking it. Then he did.

"Those are not my people!" he said in Anglisc, and the memory dived away, deeper than she could follow.

She breathed carefully, as though unused to air. "Then whose are they?"

The Loides sat in small groups around their tiny fires, hunched in what rough cloth they had been able to snatch up when the Crow's men herded them to the river.

Hild squatted by a woman who reminded her of someone—Guenmon maybe, someone sensible—and gestured for Gwladus to come forward with the basket. "Bread," she said in British to the woman. "And hard cheese. You'll see it's shared?"

The woman looked at her. "I will. Your name, lady?"

"Hild."

The woman nodded. "So tall. Like your da."

"You knew him?"

The woman laughed. Hild was astonished by that laugh. It wasn't bitter, not the laugh of a woman torn from her home and driven like a goat, but a laugh like spring, the laugh of a young girl. "Know the Anglisc king-in-exile!" Two other Loides looked up, though they were so hunched and dirty and the firelight so wavering that Hild knew that they were human only by their smell. "No, chickie, I used to watch him ride out past my geese, in his fine byrnie and thick blue cloak, and once he smiled at me, and I smiled at him, saucy-like, and dreamt in my foolish dreams that he might one day climb off his horse and say, *Lweriadd, here's a pretty for you, and a kiss.*"

"You're the goosegirl!"

"Aye, once upon a time."

"I never knew your name."

Gwladus snorted. Lweriadd. A lofty name for someone wrapped in sacking: Lweriadd, daughter of Belenos the sun god; Lweriadd, mother of Beli Mawr.

"Lweriadd of the Loides, enjoy your bread and cheese."

"We'll need more. And blankets. Or at least the time and tools to build a shelter." She stabbed her thumb up at the gauzy clouds dimming the waxing moon: thin but dark, dark blue—the kind of blue any woman would kill to get from her dyes—a blue that meant more rain. "Tell that to the whipping thegn."

"I'll see you get them. If you don't, ask for me or for Gwladus here."

"Or for that fine lordling in the British cloak you walk about with?"

Wealh, even tired and hungry wealh—especially tired and hungry wealh—noticed everything. Hild nodded. "Cian, son of Onnen."

"Ah."

While the Loides toiled by the Aire, Edwin sat with his counsellors beneath the one great oak left standing. Beneath it, his men had built a rough shelter: a reed roof, one solid wall behind him, and painted leather curtains to each side. His tufa stood at his right hand, his scop on the left, and about a brazier his travelling court. Most perched on three-legged stools—if their body servants had thought to bring one; some stood.

Edwin said to Osric, "Take the men out to every farm and hamlet in Elmet. Tell the Anglisc to send men who can speak for them, to be here at the full moon."

"They'll be here." He patted the whip in his belt. "If they like their skin." His men laughed.

"They're Anglisc, cousin, not wealh. Persuasion will work well enough. Promise them mead. I doubt they have anything at home but ale and milk. Mead and meat."

"And song," Hild said. Her stool was padded with a brown-and-marigold cushion.

The scop preened.

Edwin dismissed Osric with a pleasant smile and turned to Coelfrith. "Pyr will sort the feast. I need you to ride out on another task."

The highfolk of Elmet and their spearmen would be his first shield wall, his buffer, should Gwynedd join with Mercia. But highfolk were only the crop of a land. To know the land itself, you had to know the fields the crop sprang from. You had to know the ways and byways of lesser folk.

When Coelfrith bowed and left, Hild followed him. He was only a dozen years Hild's senior but lately his face was settling into worry lines like those of his father before he'd been named ealdorman of Lindsey.

"You'll need men for this task who'll behave," she said. "I know who'd suit. You'll need guides; I'll find them. But I come with you."

Coelfrith agreed. "Dawn."

Hild went to find Lweriadd. She found her with a young girl and a stripling with a bruised arm, rolling a chunk of trimmed elm trunk to the foundation ditch of the new hall.

"The king requires a survey of Elmet: its strong places, sound and broken, and its husbandland, farmed and fallow."

Lweriadd straightened. "Why should I care what he wants?"

The young girl spat. The stripling picked a splinter from the pad of his thumb, but Hild could tell from the cant of his head that he was listening. His chin had a look of Lweriadd and the bruise was very like those made by an ox goad.

"The king is not Osric Whiphand. And we are the king's. We need folk we may trust to guide us."

"We?"

"I ask it. Hild, daughter of Hereric, friend to the last king of the Loides. And Cian Boldcloak, who had his first sword from the hand of Ceredig king." She nodded at the stripling. "And perhaps the guide may find less trouble while guiding than in the rolling of logs."

They assembled at dawn in the white river mist: Coelfrith, Hild, Cian, Eadric, Grimhun, who had an eye for fortification, if no hand for the lyre, and the brothers Berht, who held torches that stained the mist an eerie red. Gwladus would stay by the river, Hild's eyes and ears while she was gone.

With a swirl of mist, the stripling appeared, wearing a piece of patched cloak tied to his shoulders by an assortment of yarns and with nothing at his rope belt but a fist-size sack. The bruise on his arm had darkened from red to purple. He stood by Hild's knee and touched a fist to his chest.

"Morud ap Addoc."

She said to Coelfrith, "This is Morud son of Addoc, a man of the Loides commended to me." She arranged her cloak and said to Morud in British, "You know what we want to see?"

That cant of the head. "The hard edges first, no doubt. Berewith and Aberford."

"Berewith," she said.

Morud trotted away, leaving them to follow in whatever order they chose.

At Berewith Grimhun shook his head without getting off his horse. "One good rain and water would run gushing through the wall, there, and soon your fort would be knee deep in mud."

Berhtnoth tucked one foot up on his mount's withers and scratched his left buttock. "So why did their king come here, then, if it's so useless?"

Hild was watching Morud. "Tell us the story now, Morud ap Addoc, as we ride to Aberford. Tell us of the last of Ceredig king in Elmet. Was he fleeing?"

"He was not! He marched with his war band, proud and fair . . ."

Hild smiled to herself. They would all get dreamy-eyed and gesith-like now, for a while, lost in the just-so sparkle of setting sun on gilded armour, the brave snap and ripple of banners, the proud step of the horse. The marching through moonlight. The Anglisc didn't even understand the words, but they knew the rhythm. And Cian, though he knew the song, would be lost for hours.

Ceredig had never made it to his last stand at Aberford. That was not his wyrd.

Grimhun fell in love with Aberford, the deep and narrow beck, the straight road with its sturdy bridge. "Look at that!" he said. "There's no crossing it except by the bridge. And those walls! How high is that bank? It must rise eight paces. There's even . . . yes." He pointed at a narrow trench. "Just waiting for a stockade. Though they didn't have time." He scrambled down from his horse, which promptly began to crop the grass. "Banks, dikes, beck, a stone road . . ." He bent and cut the turf, ripped up a clod, crumbled the dirt between his fingers. "I could build with this." He wiped his seax absently on his tunic, saying to Coelfrith, "With a score of men I could make this place tighter than a Lindsey maid's—" He turned red and sheathed his seax without looking at Hild. "I could make it tight."

Coelfrith dismounted, dug up his own clod. Sniffed his fingers. Hild could smell it from her mount: good dirt, rich, well drained. "How long would you need?"

"Good enough to delay an army? A month. Full moon after next, say."

"And how fast could you make it strong enough to fight off a band of mead-mad farmers?" In case Edwin couldn't win them with sweet words and strong drink.

"We'd need axes, shovels, rope—"

"I can have them here the day after tomorrow."

Grimhun turned slowly, squinting. "And men?"

"I'll bring them with the tools."

"I'll need a dozen, well fed." Coelfrith nodded. "Seven days from to-day, then."

They ate sitting on their cloaks on the south slope of Becca Bank.

"I'm happier out of that wood," Berhtnoth said. "Drip drip drip."

"It isn't always like that," Cian said.

"No," said Berhtred. "Sometimes it snows."

Cian threw a clod at his head.

They talked of the unusual weather: the early leaf fall, this unexpected sun.

"The first thing we'll need is a shelter," said Grimhun. "It won't be warm when the sun goes down, and I know you're all as soft as girls."

Morud glanced at Hild, but she was used to the gesiths forgetting she was a woman unless it suited her for them to remember.

Later, she and Coelfrith walked east along the north bank of the fast-flowing beck, their shadows falling long before them. The ridge of Becca Bank, half a league long, followed the water. The ditch was rock-cut in places, and the rock had been used to buttress the north slope of the bank. They scrambled to the top of the rise.

He pointed to the south bank and another dike, almost as long, following the water at about fifty paces. "It's a funnel."

"Like a fish weir," she said. Any invading army leaving the road to head west into the heart of the kingdom would be hemmed in, caught between the two lines, and slaughtered.

She squatted and laid her hand on the stone, staring down at the rushing water. An unsuspecting war band would startle when the spears flew. They would try to cross the beck to escape. They would drown. If Ceredig had marched half a day earlier, had had time to get to Aberford, even without the stockade. If Edwin hadn't stolen the march. If her father hadn't been poisoned like a dog.

Their fire burnt small and hot. A white, bright moon showed the picket line and the pale gleam of Cygnet's shoulder as she shifted.

Grimhun was telling the tale of the seafarer from the lost land of the west. He couldn't play the lyre, but he had a fine voice for the chant: the cry of a lonely gull, the slap of the water against the rudderless boat drifting, drifting in the mist. The brothers Berht took the verses of the seals. Coelfrith stared into the fire, face set in his habitual worried frown. Eadric dozed. Morud listened—Hild was sure he understood Anglisc well—and Cian whittled, pausing every now and again to tilt the wood to the fire or the moon.

Hild watched the delicate flex of his wrist. His rings glittered. The hairs on his fingers glowed like bronze wire one minute, silver the next. This way and that. He seemed to be taking unusual care with his little knife, flick, flick, pare. The wood was dense and twisted, a root of some kind, an old one. The shavings looked black.

The day dawned cool, with mare's tails glowing pink in the not-yet-risen sun. Coelfrith and Eadric rode back to Caer Loid. Before they were out of sight Hild was calling Morud and Cian to her.

To the north and west, between the heartland of Elmet and the River Wharfe, lay the Whinmoor. Lonely land, said Morud, populated only by hare and partridge and peregrine, and the kind of wild men whom no one took in.

So they rode south and east, along the low-lying limestone escarpment that formed the eastern boundary of the Loid. The soil was well drained and loamy, crisscrossed with springs and becks and streams. Rich land. Everywhere on the gentle green slopes they saw sheep, like drifts of dirty cloud, but every flock was whistled away long before they reached hailing distance: The wink of sun on their rings and bits and hilts was visible for miles.

At the first Anglisc farm they accepted the farmer's offer of ale and bread. Cian talked to the man and his son—a boy of five or six whose eyes stretched at the sight of Cian's mail shirt and sword. When the woman of the house and her daughter brought out three leather cups, Hild motioned for a startled Morud to accept. They ate under a huge elm at the south end of a little coppice. Cian thanked their hosts—Ceadwulf and his wife, Saxfryth—and told them that Edwin king was by the Aire, rebuilding Ceredig's hall, and would welcome them there on the night of the full moon.

"A feast!" the boy said.

"A feast," Cian said. "With meat and mead and scop's song."

"Though I doubt the king's ale can match this brew," said Hild with a smile for the wife. In truth it was thin stuff, but the wife blushed prettily at praise from a woman wearing royal blue and more gold than she'd dreamt of in all the world. "And that's a fine twill, beautifully dyed."

Saxfryth smoothed her overdress proudly. "Nothing like yours, lady."

Indeed, Hild's dress was the rich, summer-afternoon-sky blue of royalty, a spin-patterned diamond twill, with neck and hems worked in scarlet and gold. She watched Saxfryth glance from the clothes to the glitter of their tethered horses' headstalls, to their finger rings and the tiny agates sewn onto her veil band, and slowly understand the depth of the wealth before her. She grew rigid on her three-legged stool.

"Saxfryth. Look at me." The woman lifted her head slowly. "I am Hild, daughter of Hereric." Hild slid the yellow-stone ring from her little finger and held it out.

"Lady!"

"Take it." The woman did. "Try it." It fit the ring finger of her right hand. She moved it slightly, to catch the sun, then folded the hand in her lap, with the other curled around it protectively.

"Your men will come to Caer Loid Coit. Every man with a spear will come before the full moon. You will show that token and I will see that Edwin king knows of the hospitality offered today to his niece and seer."

They rode, through a light shirr of rain, over five or six hides of cleared land surrounded by oak and elm. Two milch goats and a kid, stripping the weeds by the track, lifted their heads but did not pause in their endless side-slide chew. A bull—full-muscled, dark brown, sleek as a seal in the rain—glared from his own stone-walled pasture, beyond which stood a large sty with a half-filled water trough cut from elm. The pigs would be grubbing in the wood for early mast.

They began to see people: the men tall, the women rounded, and everywhere wealh and Anglisc working side by side, wearing the same competent tabby weave with good strong leather belts and sturdy shoes. The rain was so light most hadn't bothered with their hoods. The place reeked of peace and prosperity.

Morud led the way across a little stone bridge of finely cut limestone, Roman work. They passed a deep track leading into the wood—clearly more than a woodcutter's path—and after a moment's thought Hild called Morud to her. "Run up that track. Find the priest or his wife. Tell them to fade into the wood for a fortnight or two, never mind the rain, and to take anything they value with them. They should bury the altar stone if they hope to come back."

Not even the Crow would break his Christ's holy stone, but he would drag it away and then the Loid priest would have nothing to come back to and no livelihood.

At Aberford two days later, the rain was coming down like rods of glass from an iron lid of a sky, and it was Cian and Hild who were gathering their reins to ride back to the king, and Coelfrith, drenched, standing by her knee. This time there was more than a score of men clearing the ditches and refacing the banks—even some boys carrying water and a handful of women relighting cooking fires under rough shelters.

"I'll tell the king you'll be back by the full moon," she said.

"Before." He pulled his cloak tight and peered east through the rain.

"Coelfrith."

"Um?"

"Leave the locals to their work. They have my token. They have wool to card and grain to thresh, pigs to feed and wood to gather."

"The king needs Aberford to—"

"The king wants the Elmetsætne to come gently, horses to the outstretched hand. Leave them to their work."

She nodded to Morud, crouched under one of the shelters out of the worst of the rain. He flipped up his hood—she wasn't sure when he'd acquired it—and stepped into the downpour. Cygnet snorted. Hild patted her neck. She said to Coelfrith, "Don't worry so much. Grimhun can do as he promised. I'll tell the king you have Aberford well in hand."

As they rode west the rain eased. By the time they crossed Brid's Dike the sky was torn into rags of blue and grey and darker grey, light grey tatters flying one way, dark another, and the sun bursting out like a child jumping from behind a tree and running away again. Hild threw her heavy cloak back from her shoulders. The world smelt like a just-ploughed field: rich, mysterious, waiting. She wanted to shout, or gallop, or set Cygnet at a wall.

A great cloud of birds rose violently from the wood tangling the low hills just to the north of their path. Cygnet pointed her ears, and Hild suddenly, fiercely, wanted to know what hawk they rose from, and what land lay beneath them.

Morud followed her gaze skyward. "It'll be raining again by the time we get to Caer Loid."

"Yes. But we're not going to Caer Loid." She pointed at the swirling birds—rooks, jays rising like smoke, and a puff of finches, catching the brief sunlight and gleaming like seeds flung from a thresher's basket—and laughed. "We're going there!" She kicked Cygnet into a gallop and after a moment she heard Cian galloping after her, and Morud running, and they were all laughing.

At the trees she slowed to a canter and bent low to Cygnet's neck. Oak, ash, hawthorn, wild cherry, all growing in a tangle. Then a hornbeam, twisting low across a beck, and Hild kicked Cygnet lightly and lifted up, over, down, and on. Cygnet's hooves drummed fast and steady, like Hild's heart.

The drumming softened—the ground grew wet—and they burst into a little valley by a pollarded oak, thick and gnarled, and Hild reined Cygnet in. She walked her slowly around the oak while she blew.

It was an ancient pollard, as old as anything Hild had seen. As old as the one tree that connected the fates of the three realms. It reeked of wyrd. Her wyrd.

She looked north along a winding system of beck and bog and pond. Now that she was looking, she saw the thick, even growth of old willow coppice and what might, under the moss and fern, have been the straight edge of a deliberate channel at an angle to the beck.

Cian's gelding trotted from the trees, Morud loping comfortably beside him.

"I'll bet that was once a millrace," she said, pointing. Someone's home, once.

"Here?" Cian said. "Why? It's a bog."

"It wasn't always," said Morud. "Or so they say." Hild gestured for him to go on. "They say that in the long ago, before even Coel Hen was king, when the redcrests owned the valley, it rained in the summers, it rained in the autumn, it rained through the winter. And the people grumbled but it wasn't their land to leave. There was nowhere to go that other redcrests didn't own. And the water rose. The fields turned to bog and the sheep retreated up the hills. The hooves of kine rotted, but there was no field left to plough, so they killed the kine. Ducks took the place of sheep, and heron the hawk. Then the redcrests left, and so did the people, looking for a place less wet."

"Those birds weren't rising from a heron. And look." Hild pointed at the oak, where fern grew all about its roots. "And there." She pointed along the banks of the beck, east and west, where saplings and nettles grew close to the water—"And up there"—to a pond, what perhaps had been a millmere. "The water is leaving."

Cian slid from the saddle. His feet squelched. "There's a lot still here." His Anglisc sounded alien alongside the rush and runnel of the beck.

"It's the rainiest season for years."

"It's a bog."

The sun poured sudden and beechnut yellow into the valley. Spiderwebs glistened. A fish plopped. She knew there would be crayfish and frogs, newts and loach, mallards in the spring, and heron and kingfisher, and, on the hills north of the wooded mene, hare and hawk. To the south, a ridge ran alongside a crooked arm of the beck, and she imagined standing there, peregrines tilting on the wind overhead. She imagined standing there last month, swifts pouring overhead on their way south to the sun, and then in May, when they returned. She wanted to see the beck in spring, the frogs' eggs grow tails, then legs, then leap onto the bank. She wanted to see the acorns grow as well as fall, wanted to see the pigs get fat, wanted it all, wanted it here.

"It's beautiful," said Hild, "and I will have it."

At Caer Loid the weather turned dry and crisp and the farmers began to arrive for the king's feast. A man and two sons, all with spears, the man with a sturdy linden shield and a seax with a worked-leather sheath. Ceadwulf and two ceorls, with his wife, Saxfryth, wearing Hild's ring, and their son. From the steading Hild had warned to hide their priest, four men—one shorter and slighter than the others—all carrying spears. Two brothers armed with axes, with the kind of finger rings and cloak brooches unlikely to have been earned through farming.

Coelfrith, back only two days earlier, was kept busy every moment the sun shone. He would have preferred Pyr to handle the new arrivals but Pyr was half wealh, and who knew what the prideful newcomers might take as an insult, so he put Pyr in charge of the hunting parties and other provisioning details, and toured the growing encampment, listening. This farmer wanted a space in the bend of the river, but his neighbour had taken it—his neighbour who owed him a ram and hadn't paid. That red-faced man pointed to a bruised boy: This starveling wealh had stolen two loaves and what were they to eat now? What was the king going to do about that? And many, many demanded to speak to the king: It was why they were here; it was their right.

Hild walked with Coelfrith, watching, learning, sometimes staying for a quiet word, sometimes sending Morud—who seemed to have attached himself to her—back with a message for the farmer to come to her wagon later. She conferred with Coelfrith over which man might be invited to break bread with the king; which might be best seen with others in a group; which to be ignored. And everywhere, the Crow's priests, accompanied by Osric's men, questioned the farmers, taking the information to the Crow and Stephanus, who wrote and wrote and wrote.

At night, Cian took a keg of ale, and Eadric or another hound, to the fires of the new arrivals and compared weapons, and drank and boasted and learnt things that Hild might not. Hild herself, accompanied by Gwladus, talked to Lweriadd; to Morud's wary sister, Sintiadd; to Saxfryth. She left them ale or cheese. Occasionally they gave her a cloth full of elderberries or mushrooms or wildling apples.

In the morning, she and Cian broke bread in the cold clear sunlight, sitting on their little stools by the wagon.

Cian tore another chunk from his loaf and caught up more of the paste from the beautifully turned elm bowl on the table Gwladus had thought to bring with their stools.

"What is this? Is there more?"

"Just what you see. Saxfryth brought it for me, as a thank-you, she said. She wanted most particularly for the young gesith with the bold cloak to know that it was her recipe: the first puffballs sliced and fried in goose grease then chopped and packed in butter. When I tell her you liked it she'll want you to visit, and she'll push out her chest like a pouter pigeon and twirl her new ring so it gleams in the firelight, and tell you how very tall you are, how long your sword, and so very sharp!"

Gwladus, bringing more bread and a pot of honey, snorted.

They ate steadily. "There's two bandits in from the Whinmoor," he said.

"The ones with the axes?"

"The same. I told Coelfrith. He says it's the king's order to leave every man his weapon until the feast tonight."

Hild wondered who would be the unlucky gesith honoured with the duty of standing watch over the blades away from all the drinking and boasting.

"I saw a sword that might have come over with your forefathers: a hilt looking like cheese squeezed in a man's fist." Hild knew what he meant; she'd seen swords like that hanging in the firelight, brought down when the scop sang of times past: a ridged hilt, sometimes bound with wire, always with a name and a list of dead kings to its credit.

"I saw a Loid with an inlaid spear today," she said. "A dot and a cross on the blade." Ceredig's mark.

Cian looked up from his bread and honey. "A king's man?"

"His son, maybe. If you want to ask him, he's with the Anglisc of that rich steading west of Saxfryth's. They're camped south of the orchard—or what was the orchard."

At the noon meal, Hild saw Cian sitting with the Loid at a fire of fragrant applewood stumps, listening, nodding, whittling away at his root, while the man mimed thrusting and slamming with his shield. Behind them, slave wealh watched over by Osric's men worked on the king's new hall.

Tenscore men and not a few women settled down under a moon bright and white as polished chalk. The air was still and sharp, the river slow. Bonfires roared between the people and the wood, driving the dark back, keeping the wights under the trees.

They had listened to the scop's stirring songs of hearth and hall, gold and honour, and the fate of man. They had drunk jar after jar of spiced ale, and eaten the oxen that had pulled their wagons from Goodmanham. The first beef most of them had eaten in years. Good red meat that made them feel like heroes.

The king rose, gleaming with gold, and to many of the men there—full of more beer and food, aye, and better, than they'd had in an age—he seemed a song made flesh, a hero of old, a king worth listening to. And while the king's men passed among the crowd with mead—mead! the drink of warriors!—the scop declaimed the king's lineage: Edwin the son of Ælla, the son of Yffi, the son of Wuscfrea, the son of Wilgisl, the son of Westerfalca, the son of Sæfugl, the son of Sæbald, the son of Segegeat, the son of Swebdæg, the son of Sigegar, the son of Wædæg, the son of Woden. A son of kings, and he stood among them like an equal. The scent of mead made them glad. Their hearts beat high.

Edwin said in a great voice, "I have never lost a battle. I have two strong sons, with many more to come. Kings—Briton, Saxon, Angle—bend the knee before me. Like the men of Lindsey, you may now look to me as lord. I swear to keep your larders full, your pasture free from marauding Mercians, your fields unburnt by the savage men of Gwynedd. I stand between you and harm. To you I extend the cloak of the king's justice, the king's vengeance, the king's protection. In return I ask no more than before. Indeed, I will ask less, no more than any man can bear. But you must give it, in full and with goodwill. And your neighbours will be responsible for you and you for your neighbours. Your tithe weights must be fair, your cloth fine, your kine healthy. Smell the mead, now, men of Elmet. It is a gift from your king. Will you take it?" He lifted his great jewelled cup, a cup, surely, like one a god might drink from. "Men of Elmet, will you drink with me? Will you swear your oath?"

With a roar like a host, they shouted *Yea!* and *Aye!* and *Edwin king!* They drank, and drank again, and the scop and his drummers and whistle men set up a merry tune.

The bonfires burnt low and men drew into groups around smaller fires. The gesiths had their own fires near the wagons, and many farmers were already sleeping, but perhaps half a hundred lingered, unwilling to end the night. Someone was plinking on an old lyre, playing the tune of a bawdy song that he kept getting wrong.

Hild sat with Gwladus, half asleep, wrapped in her cloak, half aware of murmured Anglisc on her right, British on her left. Cian was nearby, she thought, and Morud, but she was not sure where. She drifted, dreaming of the ridge over the valley, the beck, the pond. That pollarded oak at the head of the mene was hollow . . .

Gradually she became aware of a conversation, an Anglisc man saying, "'I'll ask less,' he said. But that black-haired priest kept asking, 'How *many* sheep? How *many* milch cows? How *many* pigs?' The gleam in his eyes didn't promise *less*."

"He'll keep us safe," a younger voice said. "He said so." Hild knew that kind of voice: a stripling, ready to run to war for glory and gold, the kind of voice that ended torn out on a muddy, bloody field. "You, wealh, bring me more ale."

The sudden silence was as sharp as salt. Hild opened her eyes. The young Angle with the glory voice looked just as she'd imagined: unkempt blond hair, downy moustaches, flushed face, muscled like a young bullock. The man he faced was a little older, a hand's-breadth shorter: the Loid who had carried the spear of a king's man. But all weapons were under guard for the night, by order of the king, and farmers didn't wear the jewels of a gesith, and the young Angle didn't know that this Loid was his own man.

Two Angles got up and stood behind the Loid—farmers from the same steading. They had hands on their eating knives.

And then Cian was there, sheathing his whittling knife, squatting easy by the fire, smiling, beer jar swinging from one hand. The Anglisc gold at his throat and on his hands gleamed, the red checks of his bold Welsh cloak glowed.

He said, "Once upon a time, if there was such a time, an Anglisc farmer built his steading alongside a Loid. The Loid owned a hen, a fine hen, that laid one egg every morning as the sun came up. Every morning the Loid's wife would carry the egg from the coop to the kitchen to break into his beer for breakfast. One day, she looked in the coop and there was no egg. But then she saw into the Angle's garth and there was her foolish hen, sitting on her egg."

"You said it was a fine hen," called someone from the crowd.

"It was the finest hen that ever clucked, though being a hen, it was not very bright, and thought an egg was a great achievement no matter on whose land it was laid." He took a pull of the ale. "So the wife fetched her husband, the Loid, and he began to step over the ditch to fetch the hen when the Angliscman steps out of his hall, sees the hen, and picks up the egg. The Loid shouted, 'That's my egg!' but the Anglisc shouted back, 'It was laid on my land!'

"They shouted at each other—for they'd not had breakfast and were testy—and finally the Loid said, 'My people have a way of solving disputes,' and the Anglisc said, 'Good, then tell me what it is because I fancy this egg while it's still warm.' So the Loid said, 'I kick you in the balls and count how many times I can sing the bread song before you manage to get back up. Then you kick me in the balls and see how long it takes me to get up. Whoever gets up quicker wins the egg.'

"The Anglisc, being brave and strong, agreed to this. So the Loid went to find his boots, his best boots, with the reinforced lace holes, and put them on, and hopped over the ditch. 'Are you ready?' he called, and the Anglisc stood with his feet wide and his jaw set, and the Loid ran at him like a cart horse and kicked the Anglisc as hard as he could in the balls. The Anglisc fell to the ground clutching himself, gasping then howling then cursing in agony, while the Loid sang the bread song a score and twice. Eventually the Anglisc stood up and said, 'Now it's my turn to kick you.'"

Cian put the jar down and leaned back on his hands. The crowd leaned forward.

"And then the Loid tucked his hen under his arm, stepped back smartly, and said, 'Keep the fucking egg!'"

The crowd roared and Cian handed the beer to the Loid, who drank and passed it to the Angle, and shouted, "Someone give me that lyre!" and someone else shouted, "Sing the bread song!" and they laughed some more.

Hild motioned for Gwladus and Morud. "Bring more food, and wood for the fire. Tell Coelfrith I said so."

The next day, as a stream of important Anglisc, those with six or more spears to their name, swore their oaths to the king before witnesses—who included, at the Crow's suggestion, for he had been baptised, Cian Boldcloak—Hild accepted a trickle of lesser folk, Anglisc and Loid, who came to her in ones and twos.

Lweriadd brought Morud. "Lady, has he served you well?"

"He has."

"Then it would please me for you to take him with you when you leave."

Morud then knelt, put Hild's hand to his forehead, and swore the threefold oath: to keep faith until the sky fell on his head, until the earth opened and swallowed him, until the seas rose and drowned him. He was standing behind her stool on one side, and Gwladus on the other, when Saxfryth approached with her young son.

Saxfryth held out Hild's ring. Hild folded the woman's hand around it. "A gift."

Saxfryth's smile was brilliant but almost immediately extinguished by indecision and anxious looks at her son.

Hild sighed to herself. "I don't know your boy's name."

"Ceadwin, lady."

"A strong name for a strong lad."

"He is strong, lady, very strong for his age."

"How many winters has he?"

"Five, lady."

"In two years he'll be old enough to foster."

"Yes, lady."

"Does he have brothers?"

"Not yet, lady."

"When he does, or when he is seven, whichever is sooner, you may send him to me, if you wish."

"Lady!" She looked as though she might fly apart with joy, but instead pulled the boy to her and hugged him so hard he began to struggle. Eventually she recovered her wits enough to pick up her skirts in one hand and take the boy's little fist in the other and hurry away, stopping every stride or two to turn and say thank you.

"Her husband won't thank you," Gwladus said as they watched her go. "You wait, she'll kill that man this winter trying to get another son."

"Anglisc, Gwladus. Morud needs the practice. From now on, Anglisc, both of you, until we leave this place. And Morud, you will do as Gwladus tells you." She sat back on her stool, watching the now-distant figures of Saxfryth and the boy. "Five. Really. What am I, a wet nurse?"

"Here comes one," Morud said in otter-splash but understandable Anglisc.

"Another," said Hild. "Here comes another."

This time it was the young man with the ancient sword.

He was too young and tightly strung for any greeting. He simply drew his sword, knelt, and offered it to her, hilt-first over his forearm. "I am Oeric, lady, and I would serve you."

She touched his hand. He looked up. Brown eyes, tight and anxious. Fading pimples. Strong bone at brow and jaw. Older than Cian by a year or so, but not as tall. But then few were.

His brown tunic, restitched with sleeves and padded in an approximation of a warrior jacket, was faded and patched. He would never be able to afford the mail shirt to wear over it. A knuckle on his right hand looked as though it had been crushed at some point but he'd had no difficulty handling the sword. The blade, as Cian had said, was ancient. Perhaps his father's father's grandfather's. Part of its edge, near the point, was missing and the wire inset in the grip black with age. The blade itself, though, was lovingly polished of hammer-folded snakesteel.

"Your sword, it has a name?"

"Clifer," he said. Claw. But he didn't offer a lineage, and Hild wondered if he'd found it somewhere or taken it from a dead man.

"How would you serve me, Oeric?"

He blinked. "Lady?"

"How would you serve me?"

"I have a sword . . ."

Hild nodded. A sword. What use did she have for a sword? "Are you hungry?" Of course he was hungry. He was a stripling. He could eat an ox and still have room for a sheep and a score of loaves. "Morud here will bring you a stool and Gwladus will find us something to eat and you will tell me of your family."

"My mother is dead—"

"But first you will get off your knees." She must ask Gwladus to find a mat or a fur to put before her stool so these people didn't have to get down on the muddy grass.

He scrambled to his feet.

"And put the sword away before someone gets the wrong idea."

He sheathed it—not with the unthinking ease of a gesith but with more skill than she'd expected.

Morud came back with a stool and placed it with ceremony opposite Hild. Clearly he also made some kind of face at Oeric, who glared at him.

Hild pointed to the stool. Oeric sat. He perched gingerly on the padded embroidered cushioning but relaxed quickly enough when no god flung a thunderbolt at him for soiling such fine work with his farm clothes.

Adaptable, at least. "You were telling me of your family."

His father was Grim, son of Grim the Elder. His mother dead these six years. When his mother's sister's husband had gone away one day and not come back, the widowed Grim had married her. Grim had three more sons now and a daughter. He farmed a hide south of the Aire, mixed land, some barley, some oats. Pigs, of course, they couldn't get by without the pigs, who ate their bodyweight in mast every autumn, and two milch cows. Their horse, though, had died this spring when the grass came so late. The cows' milk had been late, too. Perhaps without Oeric to feed they might have enough for a colt next spring.

"Perhaps your father could swap Clifer for a mare in foal."

"Clifer is mine! From my mother's father, who had no sons."

Gwladus brought a tray with bread, bowls of barley stew with beef shreds, and the beautiful cup Edwin had given Hild in Lindsey. The cup was half filled with mead. She gave Hild one bowl of stew, Oeric another. Oeric took a spoon from his pouch, remembered to check that Hild had a spoon, and waited for her to take the first mouthful. Manners and restraint. Hild had seen worse at Edwin's board. She took a taste so that Oeric could begin. It needed more salt. "Does your father know you're here?"

Oeric swallowed hastily. "I am of age!"

Hild gestured for him to keep eating. She applied herself to her own bowl. "Why?" she said, when half her stew was gone. "Why me? Why not swear to the king?"

"Would he have me?" They both knew the answer. Oeric had a sword but no mount, no mail, no men. "They say you're powerful. That you see a man's wyrd. That you've used that seax."

Hild studied him. "And you would swear an oath?" An Anglisc oath, from a man with a sword.

"I would."

It wasn't usual. But neither was she. And this boy with his old, broken sword wouldn't threaten her uncle.

She stood, and gestured for him to do likewise. She put her hand on his chest. "I am the king's seer. I shine light on the way. I look into men's hearts. Is your heart free to make an oath, Oeric son of Grim?"

"It is."

His heart beat high but steady, and he met her gaze—blushing but not looking away.

She picked up the cup. "Oeric, son of Grim, I, Hild, daughter of Hereric Yffing and Breguswith Oiscinga, do swear on my oath, on this mead by this river under this tree, that I will be as your lord. I will protect you, feed you, defend your name and person while you are true."

She took a sip and passed the cup to Oeric. He took it with both hands, shaking slightly, and she remembered the weight of Edwin's feast cup that Modresniht long ago.

He raised the cup to her. "I, Oeric, son of Grim, swear on my oath, on this mead by this river under this tree, that I will be your man. I will protect you, obey you, defend your name and person as long as I breathe."

He sipped the mead. Smiled tremulously.

"Finish it," Hild said. He was going to need it.

The king's new thegns sent to their farmsteads for tools and men, and the great clearing by the Aire rang with hammers and adzes and clattered with lathes. The king's hall rose.

The days grew colder and the nights colder still. Hild missed the warmth of Begu sleeping by her.

They woke to hedges salted with frost that didn't melt until noon. The king rode out with Osric Whiphand, Paulinus Crow, Coelfrith Steward, and Cian Boldcloak to tour the land of his new thegns and inspect the fortifications at Aberford. While they were gone, Stephanus paired priests and parties of gesiths and sent them north and south and east and west to root out any wealh with a tonsure and drive them from Elmet. "None must remain," he said. "They are spies."

Hild persuaded Pyr that none would think him soft if the Loid workers were fed and sheltered, for a healthy Loid worked faster. And besides, she spoke for the king when she said that in Elmet now there were no more Anglisc, no more Loid, there were only Elmetsætne. She set Morud to making sure all grumbles reached the right ears.

More people, Loid and Anglisc, straggled in and sought her out, some to swear to her, some just to see for themselves the tall maid who called them all Elmetsætne. The daughter of a hægtes and an ætheling, some said—no, a wood ælf and a princess, said others—though that didn't stop them wanting to touch her hem or catch up a fallen hair for luck. Farmers, coppicers, a dairymaid. A quiet man with a bow and a huge silent dog. Half a dozen ragged children, slings thrust through their twisted grass belts, who looked to have been living on their wits for a season. And one man, Rhin, older and footsore, whose tunic was too small and worn in places that didn't suit his body, a man who didn't take his hood off—he begged her pardon, he said, with a glance at Morud, who ignored him, but his ears were aching in the cold.

Hild sent the man with Morud to Oeric, for a meal at least, and said to Gwladus, "Do you trust him?"

Gwladus said, "He has the look of a man more used to skirts."

Hild nodded. She should send him on his way. But he might prove useful. "Find out what you can. Ask Morud."

That night she called Oeric to her wagon. She sat wrapped in a wolf fur on the step, and studied him. Perhaps it was that he was getting fed regularly, perhaps that he now had a ring on his pointing finger, her token, but he looked older, more solid.

"I gave you that ring so that you could do my bidding without hindrance. Why is Gwladus telling me some of my people are hungry?"

"We have food for eight days, lady. And some of these beggars are Loid who will move on."

"When the king returns, we'll be leaving. I doubt it will be eight days.

But even if we stayed a month, I gave orders that all my people were to be well fed and well clothed. All. Take heed. In my service there are no Deirans, no Bernicians, no Loid or Anglisc, no Dyfneint or Elmetsætne. In my household there are only my people." Her household. Yes. "Gwladus will speak in my name in the world of servants. You will speak in my name to freemen. You are mine, as are all those sworn to my service." Her people.

The king came back from his tour. Cian came to Hild's wagon, carrying his saddlebag over one shoulder, and accepted the cup of hot spiced wine Gwladus brought him outside.

Morud brought him a stool, set it by Hild's.

Cian dropped his bag and sat. He unhooked his scabbard, propped it next to him against the wagon. "We leave for York in the morning."

"All of us?"

He glanced at Oeric, who stood a discreet three paces out of earshot. "Stephanus and his priests will stay, as will Pyr and two understewards, a score of gesiths, and those men Grimhun has at Aberford." He glanced at Oeric again. Oeric gave him a bland look.

"How is Grimhun?"

"Happy as— Why is that boy with the old sword here?"

"Oeric? He's . . ." She beckoned him. "Cian Boldcloak, king's gesith, this is Oeric, son of Grim, my sworn man."

The two eyed each other, but Cian's height, the cut of his clothes, his sword and jewels clearly overmatched Oeric's. Oeric inclined his head. Hild waved him away.

Cian sat. "He's sworn to you? He's coming to York?"

"Him and more than a dozen others."

"You have a *household*?"

"Will you help me?"

"Help you do what? Feed them? I'm a king's gesith, not a landed thegn."

"Just . . . help me. You and the brothers Berht could train Oeric, enough so he'd be more help than hindrance in a fight." Then she remembered the brothers Berht were with Grimhun at Aberford, for now.

He drank off his ale and held out his cup for a refill. Gwladus took it. "Have you told the king?"

"Not yet."

"Tell him." He took the refilled cup from Gwladus, with a nod of thanks. "The lady's a rare one, eh?"

"Yes, lord," she said. "Will you want stew? Some of the new . . . household have an odd notion of king's property and it seems some hares wandered into a snare and then somehow got dropped in a pot." She turned to Hild. "Should I bring three bowls?" She tilted her head slightly in Oeric's direction.

"Yes. No, wait. Bring enough for everyone. Put up a board. We'll eat together, this one night, the household. Tell Oeric and Morud to help."

When they'd left, Cian cleared his throat, drank more ale, rubbed his lip with his knuckle. Eventually he bent and lifted his bag to his lap.

"I made something."

He untied the bag, lifted out a lump wrapped in sacking. Hefted it. Held it out.

Hild took the bundle, unwrapped it. Dark wood gleamed in the firelight.

Travelling cups, three of them. Tiny things, fitting one inside the other: small, smaller, smallest. Old wood, black with age. Carefully cut with the grain, smooth as a girl's shoulder and as warm to the touch.

"I cut them from the root of the great thorn hedge. The biggest will hold two fingers of white mead."

She put them back together. They felt dense and weighty in her palm. She turned them, it, over and over in her hands. Old in the days of Eliffer of the Great Retinue . . . "Oh." Carved under the base was a tiny hedgepig, prickles out.

"Look at the others."

She slid them free again. On the smaller one, the hedgepig's prickles were drawn in; on the smallest one, the hedgepig lay curled in sleep.

"One for you, one for me, one for Begu," he said. "So we may drink to home wherever we are."

Edwin sat on his chair under the oak, warming his hands over a brazier while Coelfrith stood patiently nearby. He seemed in high good humour.

"Clotrude is with child. My son is having a son!"

"May he be strong and lucky."

"Of course he'll be lucky."

Hild bowed her head. An ætheling was always lucky. At first. "My lord . . ." She wasn't sure how to say it. "My lord, there will be extra people returning with us to York."

His hands slowed. "Extra? How many?"

"Fewer than a dozen." So far.

Edwin turned to Coelfrith, who said, "Lord King, if we're to make the journey tomorrow as you wish, with a dozen extra mouths the food might not stretch. As it is, by the time we reach York the horses will be skin and bone and our porridge gritty with the end of the sack."

"We can feed ourselves," Hild said.

"You can?" Edwin leaned back, hands on the arms of his chair, his eyes on Hild. "Hear that, Coelfrith? Perhaps I should put our seer in charge of provisioning. No doubt her seer sight would show the deer in the wood and the fish under the bank."

"Or you could send Osric and his men directly back to Tinamutha instead of him going back through York." It would keep him away from her mother.

The king waved away her suggestion. He looked her up and down, then smiled. "You may bring your people. But not a mouthful of our supplies, not a sip, not a bite, not for you nor any of your people. Still want them?"

"Yes, Uncle."

"It's uncle now, is it? Ha!" He pounded the arm of his chair and laughed. "Coelfrith, bring my niece a stool, bring us a jar of mead, and either sit yourself or go pack something. And when you're fetching the mead, get the Crow in here." He stretched his boots to the brazier. "I'll be glad to get back to four walls and a roof. So tell me, Niece, before that black-skirted crow gets here, how do you see Elmet?"

"Uncle?"

"The saddle's barely off my horse and you appear to be acquiring a household. Why? What have you seen?"

"I have seen, as you have, Uncle, enough to gladden any heart. Take Aberford."

"I believe I have. Twice."

"Yes, Uncle. But it's more than a fort. It's surrounded by good sheep land. There's water, a road—a path right to the Humber. Remember Eorpwald's gold workshops? An overking could build folds and weaving huts by the score there, make cloaks for trade. Ship them to Coelgar at Lindsey. It would be the biggest exchange for wool in the land. The Frisians would come, and the Franks."

He leaned down and pulled off one boot, scratched at his ankle. "Why Lindsey? Why let Coelgar's people have a piece of it? If Eorpwald can build a wīc for trade, so can I."

"Where?"

"York. That was your mother's idea." He put his boot back on, wriggled his feet, stretched again. "What else should I know?"

Her mother's idea. "There are bandits on the Whinmoor, trees for any purpose you could name south of the river, and good cattle country beyond that." A wīc. At York. Another weft in the great weave. "But the land's half empty. The people . . . They hide. They don't trust each other. They'd work if they felt safe. If they knew they had the king's goodwill."

"That's why I brought them here."

"That's why you brought the Anglisc."

The weir sounded suddenly loud.

She was in it now. "Elmet is . . . underused. It could grow rich." Which means the king would grow rich. "But only if people work. Only if they know that the land they clear, the hall they build, and the corn they sow will be safe. That no one will be fighting. That they aren't Anglisc taking from Loid or Loid taking back from Anglisc."

"It seems you've already spoken for me on that, or so Coelfrith hears from Pyr: no more Anglisc, no more Loid, only Elmetsætne."

He sounded more curious than angry. But you could never tell with a king.

"Uncle, lord King, they need to know they can't take from each other, and that whoever the king names as their lord won't take from them, either." Osric and his whips. "The first two years are all work, and the winters will be hard. Why risk that, if someone will just come along and take it once the land is giving crops?" She paused. "But if you tell them protection with no tithe for three years, they'll do it. In five years, your tithes will double." A longer pause. He was still listening. "Tell them the king's niece will do it, too."

"She will?"

"Uncle, I've seen a place. Such a place! Two leagues north and west. A great ridge, overlooking a wooded mene. A valley with bog and beck and bramble. Somewhat wet, yes. But, oh, what it could be. What it once was. Fish and krebs, herbs and honey, a millstream, corn growing round about . . . It will be a land of lard and cream, of beef and strayberries and songbird pie!"

"You will show me this place."

"I will, my king. Though it's not on the way to York. And it's . . . wet, just now."

"People?"

"None that I saw. One of the Elmetsætne told me they all left in the long ago, when it grew wet."

"Wet, you keep saying. It sounds like a bog. You're daughter of an ætheling of Deira and a princess of Kent. Niece and seer to the overking. It wouldn't be seemly for you to live in a bog."

"I wouldn't live there."

"No, because you're my seer. But you want it. Tithe free. With my sworn men here and at Aberford ready to protect it. For nothing. Because it will be an example to my would-be thegns."

"I . . . Yes."

"A birth day gift worth a bit more than that cup I gave you last year."

"Then . . ."

"Then the mene wood is yours. But in exchange it'll be your task, along with Coelfrith, to apportion Elmet to would-be thegns. Make sure they all understand this Elmetsætne notion of yours."

She bowed. A king's bargain. He gave her something worthless to him in return for something from her he wanted very much. But, there again, so did she.

"And tell Stephanus. He has some notion of writing it all down, scratch scratch scratch. Strange men, these Christlings. Ah, Paulinus. Come sit. We were just talking about bogs."

"Bogs, my lord?"

"Bogs." He turned back to Hild. "Describe it to Stephanus. To a limit of thirty hides. With no tithe for . . . five years."

"Thank you, Uncle." The whole valley!

"Only yours, mind. Everyone else gets three years. You have someone to run it?"

"I . . . Yes, Uncle."

"Good. I need you by my side. And now you should go pack your things."

When her people gathered at the board for their last meal in Elmet, Hild drew aside the man with the hood.

"Rhin. Tell me, yes or no. Are you the priest I sent Morud to warn, near Aberford?"

He met her gaze steadily—his eyes were big and red-brown, surrounded by fatigue-stained pits like those of a goshawk—but said nothing.

"That was a fine steading, a rich, strong holding where men of all kinds got along. If I said I need a man to help me make that happen in another place, a man who can read, what would you say?"

After a long pause, he nodded once, slowly.

"Let me tell you of the place, particularly of the pollarded oak at the head of the valley. Hollow, and dry . . ."

15

✦

IN YORK, the first day of Blodmonath dawned unseasonably mild. High, bright clouds coated the sky as evenly as egg foam. Larks and starlings gathered in flocks on the stubbled fields on either side of the Fosse and every now and again lifted in rushes for the south. To the north, just beyond the louring yew woods, darker rain clouds drifted towards the walls of the inner fort, threatening the rebuilding.

The wīc would grow in the fork of the Ouse and Fosse between the fort and the outer wall. The span of outer wall between Dere Street and the Ouse had long ago fallen into ruin. Edwin had cleared the rubble, re-dug the ditches, and drained the land. His two new Frankish stonemasons, rebuilding the walls of the inner fort, were notoriously finicky about the damp and the temperature of the strange sandy mud they mixed to stick the stone together. They worked slowly. Edwin fretted. To defend a wīc a fort must be strong. They'd have to make do with a hedge to protect the northeast end of the wīc field.

Hild rose without waking Begu or Gwladus. She wanted to see the laying of the great hedge.

What seemed to Hild to be half the women and men of the vale of York worked in the field that would be the wīc. Children ran about with jars. No one seemed to care about the possibility of rain. They were happy to carry their billhooks and hand axes and knives to the scrubby flatland and work for good portions of food and beer while their children herded their pigs in the wood south of the river to fatten on the early mast fall.

This year there would be enough for every pig. There would be bacon and ham and sausage to feed every family all winter. There would be plenty of pork fat to soothe chilblains and fry the mushrooms soon to sprout in the east pasture and along the ditches of the west fields. One or two old women muttered now and again, and shook their heads—such mildness was uncanny, and trouble would come of it—but old women always said such things.

Coelfrith's woodsmen had already laid out the hedge lines, driving in elm stakes every two feet and marking scrubby trees for saving with splashes of ochre. The strong young men and strapping women grubbed up all the other bushes and saplings. Old men chopped the torn brush into manageable pieces for later. Younger women and unmarried girls cut wands of hazel, and nursing mothers and old women plaited the hazel into great open weaves.

The woodsmen set to work on plashing the marked trees. They lopped a branch here, a branch there—Hild tried to spot the pattern for their choice, but they worked too fast—and with a casual flick of the axe cut the tree almost through at the base and bent it over to weave between the stakes.

The dark, shaped saplings lay all one way like a cat's just-licked fur. "They point away from the river," she said to Detlin, the chief of the leathery little men with the hand axes.

He spoke without pausing. "Sap only flows uphill. Point 'em downhill and they'll die. Just as they will if these splits don't have time to close up before the frost shoves its fingers into the wood. So I'll thank you to step aside, lady."

Hild stepped to one side but didn't stop watching as he cut and bent hawthorn, sloe, hazel, blackthorn, ash, and the occasional rowan.

"It'll be pretty in spring," she said. The thorn blossom would look like snow. In summer there would be sloes for the birds. Bright red rowan berries in autumn and winter.

"Rowan's for luck," he said unexpectedly.

Hild nodded. The uneasy weather had them all thinking of luck.

Detlin moved up the marked line. Hild stayed where she was, enjoying the scent of cut wood and torn earth. The combination was as rich and tangy as brine. Another rush of birds poured overhead, flying before the clouds, moving south. Perhaps they'd fly over the East Anglian fens. Perhaps Hereswith would see them. And Fursey. Perhaps it would remind her sister of the need to build a nesting place overseas.

By the time the rain reached them, the hedge was laid in an elegant line, the woven hazel binders laid over the pleachers, and Detlin sawing the stakes off neatly just above the binders.

It was beautiful: The bare hedge glistened thick and sinewy as a dark snake with the white-sliced stake tops like a dotted pattern along its back.

Hild joined the rest of the women, who, along with the old men, were tidying away the loppings, chopping them and bundling them with the grubbed up brush.

The drizzle came and went, a pulsing rhythm of damp that no one much minded, but they wanted to be done before the heavier clouds to the north and east arrived. They began to hurry. Hild helped an old woman and her broad-shouldered daughter tie a bundle of brush. One whippy thorn branch ran over her forearm.

"Gast!" Right over the still-pink scar left by Cian's sword.

The old woman grinned toothily. "Watch the thorns, missy."

Hild pressed the arm against her hip, to stop it stinging.

"Your fine dress, too," said the daughter. Her mother cackled.

Hild wore her oldest overdress, too short by a hand's width, but still no doubt finer than anything the old woman had ever seen. Gwladus wouldn't be happy with the new stain. She thought Hild should look like a queen even when shearing sheep. *Why try to look like a farmwife? You're taller than any two of them end to end. They all know who you are.*

The old woman, looking behind Hild, stopped cackling. "Eorðe's tits. Just what we need." Hild turned: Coifi and two of his priests, wearing their white and green, walking towards the new hedge with great ceremony and deliberation.

They all looked at Coelfrith, who looked at the brush, at the approaching storm cloud, at the priests, and sighed. He motioned everyone to stop and step back to let the priests pass.

The daughter wiped the rain off her face with a meaty forearm and grabbed a jar from one of the runners.

By the westmost root of the hedge, near the road, Coifi used an ox's shoulder bone to dig a hole, in which he put a rowan branch and a bird—a wren, Hild thought, but couldn't tell from where she stood—and then the bone. His priests pushed dirt over bone, bird, and branch, and Coifi poured mead on the mound. Then he raised his arms and began to sing a prayer to Woden, for luck and blessing.

"Wish they'd put aside those fancy cloaks and do more than sing," the daughter said.

Her mother huffed. "Have you ever seen a priest work?"

"The Crow's priests are just the same," Hild said, and the daughter passed her the jar. Ale, old and sour, but Hild was thirsty.

The rain picked up. Coifi sang faster.

As soon as the priests were mincing back to the road and thence to the safety of the walls, the women got back to work. The dirt was turning to mud, and the wood was slippery and cold; there was a lot to be done before dark.

Men threw the brush into carts. One was heading for the byres, tree hay for the cattle, the other for half a mile beyond the little river, the east fields and newly coppiced ash grove, to make thorny barriers against browsing deer and strayed goats. Hild and the women followed the field cart.

The daughter spat when they reached the outer field: The old brush barrier, settled and dense, still needed tearing out. A long, hard job, and dark was coming.

They sat on the edge of the ditch to gather their strength. A flock of blackbirds fell out of the sky from the east. One landed heavily, just one hop from half an ear of fallen barley, but it seemed stunned, too tired to move. More birds struggled in: redwings and fieldfares, all young or female, all exhausted. Fleeing weather, Hild thought, or even battling it over the North Sea. So that's what the larks and starlings had been trying to get ahead of: a big storm or a sudden plummet in temperature. Either promised trouble for the new hedge and half-built tower. She stood.

"Leaving the rest to us, then?" the old woman said. "Creeping off to a hot bath and a warm fire?"

Hild grinned. "And don't forget the bread dripping with grease, a sizzling slice of beef off the spit, and dried fruit with honey." No one liked to be lied to. "I'll send you something."

"I'd love a bit of roast," the woman said, and looked old and tired and used. "Never had that."

"Tell them it's for Linnet and her mother," Linnet said.

"I'll tell them it's for everyone," Hild said. "But I'll tell my woman you're to get the hero's portion. A gift of the king himself." They looked sceptical, but she knew once they saw it, they'd sing the praises of the king and his seer for a year. "But it might be some little while."

"I don't doubt we'll still be here. Better send torches, too."

"I will. First though, I've to tell the king weather is coming."

"Weather's here," Linnet said, pretending to wring out her dress.

"Something more. Worse."

"When?"

"Not tomorrow. But soon. Maybe tomorrow night, or noon the next day."

"Bad?"

"Stay indoors if you can."

"And the pigs?"

"Keep them close until you know the shape of it."

There were plenty of torches fluttering and roaring under the leather awning the king had put up over his half-built tower—but the only men visible were gesiths bundled in cloaks against the wet. The Frankish masons had downed tools again. Hild decided to find Gwladus first. Her uncle would be irritable, not in a mood to listen to a dirty ragamuffin trying to tell him something he didn't want to hear. She would have to look every inch the seer.

Hild stood to one side of the king's hearth, glad of the heat on her tired legs.

"So," said the king, "you've come. I've sent messages all day."

"Yes, Uncle."

"Where were you?"

"Watching the hedge-laying." She accepted a cup of wine from Wilnoð, and smiled her thanks at the queen.

"At least that's up," Edwin said. "Or so Coelfrith tells me."

She sipped, and nodded. "It's beautiful."

"Beautiful, ugly, who cares. It's done. It's the wall I care about now."

"That's why I'm here."

"Good. Do something about those masons. If they're not moaning about the sand, they're complaining about the damp or fussing about the mallets. The wrong size, they say, the wrong weight, the wrong balance. Mallets!"

"They'll work tomorrow because there'll be no working for anyone soon. Bad weather is coming."

Pine resin spat in the hearth.

"You've seen this?"

"The birds told me. Bitter cold, or fierce wind, or a hurtle of hail, I couldn't say. But it's bad, and it's coming."

Edwin swore and kicked his chair. "I want that tower up by Yule!"

Hild reached past her mother and Begu for the breast of mutton cooling in its own fat. She tore the top layer of skin away with her teeth and juice dripped on her overdress. Gwladus sighed—but quietly, Breguswith had a heavy hand—and passed Hild a torn loaf to soak up the worst of it.

Oeric stood by the door, relaxed enough to have set aside his sword, but not willing to sit with Hild with others present. Hild wondered what was wrong with his face, then realised he was trying to grow a beard.

Breguswith was talking. ". . . just hen birds, you say?"

Hild nodded.

"And tired? What about the chaffinches? No matter, we'll have one of your people set a watch for the cock birds on higher ground tomorrow. Do any of them know enough to tell the difference? You need to train one of your swelling household in birds."

"I can go myself if it comes to it," Hild said. She would take Cian and Oeric. They could get in some practice away from prying eyes.

They discussed birds and clouds and other weather portents. Begu chipped in with a story about a magpie attacking a hen, or so she'd heard, she'd been very little, but she remembered her mother's woman, Guenmon, saying—Guenmon, Hild remembered Guenmon, didn't she?—saying it was because the magpie knew there'd be nothing left with the cold snap coming . . .

When Breguswith left—no doubt to find Osric—Hild held out her wrist for Gwladus to unfasten the carnelians. "Did you and Morud take that food to the east field?"

She nodded. "Though I could have done with Oeric's manly strong arm to help."

Oeric, staring stolidly ahead, blushed the colour of the coals. Hild reminded herself to have a word with him about not stooping to Gwladus's lure. Lintlaf could kill him without breaking stride.

The sky was again high and white and the afternoon even warmer than the day before. At the east field, there was no sign of the flocks of exhausted redwings and fieldfares. She wondered if she had imagined the whole thing. Even Linnet and her mother, standing stiffly by the old grey matting of brush they'd piled to one side to be dragged to the walls and chopped into kindling chunks for the bread ovens, were calling her lady and giving her yes and no answers. Perhaps it was her gold, perhaps it was the presence of Cian and Oeric, though they were behaving like boys, throwing stones at a bare white branch poking from the brush.

She shaded her eyes against the high white brightness and studied the fields. Nothing but the tidy stubble, looking picked cleaner than the day before.

But as she turned to go she heard the rippling whistle, Per-r-r-r-rit, of a snow bunting—a month early—and hoped Detlin had driven the fence stakes extra deep.

The moon rose, a thin sliver. The torches by the wall roared. The Frankish masons shouted at their men to hurry. Another layer of carefully shaped stone rose above the foundation. It didn't match the Roman work: different stone, different style.

Hild gestured to the chief mason, a burly, big-bellied man with no moustaches, his hair white with stone dust, who trotted over, a Christ amulet bouncing on his chest.

"Will it be wet or cold we should worry over?" he said.

"Both."

"Both! Christ protect us! The king will be unhappy. The mortar is very difficult. If it's to be wet, it's one mixture, for cold, another."

"Both," she said. "Cold. Then wind. Then bitter cold. Cold enough to break iron. The first cold will come tonight. Tie everything down, and get the Crow to pray."

"How long will it blow? Will it be wet?"

She stared at him. "Why don't you ask your Crow to ask your Christ?"

He went back to his men. In the odd flare and pool of torchlight she watched him wave his arms, exhorting them to greater effort, pointing to her, telling them she could visit terrible consequences upon them if they didn't give their best. Then they all crossed themselves.

Two chaffinches huddled together on top of a heap of stone. Young birds by their colour. Their first winter.

The wind died. The pour of the rivers in the distance seemed muffled.

Something ghosted by her, flickering palely through the torchlight, then there was just one finch on the wall.

An owl, noiseless as a feathered cloud, glided away in the moonlight, a songbird in its left foot. *Fate goes ever as it must.*

The rain puddles of the day before turned hard and milky white. Frost loosened the last leaves clinging to the oak and elm in the west forest. They dropped silently, startling the pigs rooting through the leaf mould for nuts. The masons, bundled in hoods and wraps, directed men to pack the walls in straw and tie everything down twice.

The king sent word for people to gather in hall. The queen opened her bower to her women and Hild. The king, trusted gesiths, and queen's men, including Cian and Bassus and Lintlaf, disposed themselves about the bench in front of the hall side of the bower curtain. Helping Begu settle their bedding next to her mother's reminded Hild of the early days, when Edwin's household had been small enough to sleep together in one hall.

After noon, the wind began to pick up, sliding like a filleting knife between wool and skin. Black-bellied clouds sailed over the horizon from the north and east.

The gale ripped the last acorns from the branches, wrenched the branches from the trees, and tore the trees out at the root. Pigs, and a woodcutter and his family, died, crushed.

Then came the hail, angling over the fields, beating birds and foxes to death, thrashing the river to froth. Women and men who had to walk from the hall to the kitchens, or who emptied night soil on middens, came back battered and bloodied. After that, no one left. The hail turned to rain, then snow. The wind died then picked up. Two thrushes flew into the great hall and fluttered around under the rafters until they found a place to hide from sight. The next morning they woke half the hall with cheerful— but loud, so very loud—song. A gesith threw a beer mug at the great crossbeams, but it was still half full and splashed another, who rose with a roar, eating knife in hand, and stabbed the man next to him before he was fully awake.

Breguswith and Hild, wrapped in otherworldliness, left the queen's bower to stride through the midden that the hall had already become and tend the man's wound. Hild held his skin together while her mother sewed as impersonally as she would a torn shift.

It lasted three days. In hall, men drank, women whispered, and the scop sang himself hoarse.

The hall stank: No one wanted the door open. Drunk men wouldn't go outside to expose their most tender parts to the weather. They pissed in corners. Many vomited and came back for more mead. Mead and song drove away the fear of famine, fear of homelessness, fear of the dark. The pain in their throats from shouting their own names, boasting of battles, affirming their ancestors—who had lived in the dim distant past and got through this, aye worse than this, who laughed in the teeth of a gale—made them feel human, alive. The sting of mead on raw throat made them feel brave. The stink of the piss and the gnawed bones and their unwashed muscle made them know their animal strength. Piss on the weather! Fuck the winter!

They rutted behind benches, arm-wrestled between torches, and laughed at their burns, lost themselves in the sight and sound and smell of people like them, their people. Them. They were all one.

By the third day they were maudlin. By the third night, resigned to their wyrd. What would be, was. This was the way it was because this was how it would be. They were threads in fate's great weave, snowflakes in the gale of the world.

Hild, wrapped in two cloaks, stood by the crushed byre and sipped the cold, brilliant air carefully, afraid it might give her lung crackle. Men were hauling away timbers. The butcher was directing his man to bring an axe; nothing else would cut through the frozen carcass of the milch cow—and then they'd have to get moving on the pigs in their pen. But he spoke quietly, and the men stepped softly, afraid of the eerie quiet: The rivers had frozen.

Then Oeric was by her elbow to tell her some woman by the name of Linnet would like a word, and Linnet herself was bowing and bobbing and promising her anything the lady would name, anything, for, thanks to her warning, her boy was still alive—still cheeking her, Eorðe bless him. Her boy and their pigs, while their neighbour's girl was dead, stiff as a smoked fish, and the man of the house weeping and silent and both pigs missing. But she was all right, her mother, too. Her mother sent all thanks, though she did want to know how in Eorðe's name they would feed their pigs, with the whole forest floor littered with fallen tree stuff, the acorns buried knee-deep . . .

Then the Frankish mason was asking if the lady had a moment to be so kind as to tell him when it might be warm enough to get back to work on the wall . . .

"Oeric," she said. "Find Coelfrith's man. Tell him the rivers will flow again by moonrise. Tell him that unless the king wants his fine wall standing around a city of the dead he must send men to help clear the forest for the pigs. Besides, the remaining cows will need the fodder—half the hay was lost with the byre. Tell him today, understand? Not tomorrow. Then bring Cian to me. Tell him to bring any who'll listen. And bring Begu, and Gwladus and my bundle."

She turned to Linnet.

"I'm glad you and yours are well. The king's men will set to work on the forest. I'll come to your neighbour. We'll walk by the hedge and see how it does."

Within days, the byre was mostly rebuilt, a new milch cow installed—Hild wondered what farmer now wore a silver ring while he suffered the scolding of his wife—and the scop had a new song. The gesiths went back to drinking—the mead was unspoilt—and wrestling, heedless of Coelfrith's men who rode out, grim-faced, to the steadings round about and of the constant refusal of beggared farmers at the king's kitchens.

The hedge had survived. Hild suggested to Coelfrith that Detlin be sent a present—a sturdy knife, say, with a copper inlay, something he could boast about—so word of the king's generosity to good craftsmen would spread. It was one way to counter the rumours of disaster spread by starving men turned away by their lord.

Edwin didn't care about his reputation among the lowly, and Paulinus encouraged him.

"What does their opinion matter?" he said. "They aren't baptised. If any want to test my lord King's rumoured weakness, they'll meet a wall as implacable as nightfall, bristling with half a thousand spears."

The new tower began to rise again. The mason swore on his son's head that the king would have it, aye, and a rebuilt east wall by Yule.

Yule, the queen said, would be the most magnificent ever seen in York. She had Bassus select men to accompany him on the hunt: venison, she said, and boar, swan and blackbird pie, enough to make the undercroft burst at the seams.

Meanwhile, she and James set about rehearsing music in hall, and once again the place was stripped of all its soft furnishings while the choir sang. The scop sulked. The queen laughed at him, and said she and the lady Breguswith were planning the most magnificent new tapestry for the east wall, to hang behind the king's table, and he should make a song about that.

Breguswith looked to her store of herbs. Hild saw that these were heavy on the comfrey and garlic and other wound-care medicines but said nothing. The seas were now closed to trade, which meant Osric would come down from Arbeia for Yule. She'd winkle out her mother's secrets soon enough. There could be no war in this weather. Meanwhile, she had secrets of her own.

She wrote a letter to Rhin and sent it with Morud. "If he's not about, put it in the hollow oak and come back."

Morud came back with a reply: Rhin had ten and seven men and women with him now, and six children, and had cleared two fields. The goats and pigs were doing well. The cold had not found its way to the mene wood. "And he says, lady, that he has dug out the millrace and found the old mill-stone, but thinks the building of a new mill to bear the weight of that stone might be beyond him."

Morud watched her sort yarn but made no move to leave.

"What else?"

"It's said that Stephanus"—he looked around for a place to spit, thought better of it—"Stephanus, on orders of the Crow, is now beating priests before driving them off."

"What else?"

"I didn't meet all of Rhin's new men. My guess is one or two of them will be wearing hoods for a while."

At least Rhin was being careful.

Later she walked to the west wall, listening absently to the birds: thrush, sparrow, winter wrens, and tits with song so high she could barely hear it, in the distance a quarrel between resident rooks and a flock of winter incomers. Beyond that the steady, reassuring roar of the rivers. Clouds slid by in layers of grey and white: no sun, but no rain, either. A good day.

The mason could advise her about the mill. A mill would be a fine thing, a steady source of income for her household in years to come. A hen for a sack of meal. A milch goat for three of flour. She had no idea how many farms were growing corn round about, though perhaps more would if there was a mill.

Paulinus was there, looming over the chief Frank: a hole in the light, a hole in life, next to the white-dusted mason. His mate was mixing mortar on a board with a paddle, *slush-scrape-slough*, pretending not to hear anything. Hild stepped quietly to one side of a pile of stone and elm timbers, out of sight, and watched Paulinus. Paulinus, beater of priests, spurner of beggars.

"No, my lord Bishop," the Frank was saying. "I would, but I daren't. You'll have to find help for your church elsewhere. The king wants his wall by Christ Mass."

"God looks kindly on those who help His servants."

"Yes, my lord. And I would. But it's the Anglisc king's word."

"The Anglisc Hel is a dark, cold hole, I'm told," Paulinus said. He was thinner, if that was possible, formidable in his black robes, with the massive amethyst weighting his left hand. In the winter light, its purple glimmer was otherworldly. "But the hell you will go to if you thwart God's will is not cold. You will burn. Have you ever watched a pig roast? First, the stink of singed hair. Then the eyes melt. The skin bubbles. The fat runs into the coals and the flames burn higher, higher, higher. Imagine if the pig, by some blessing or damnation, still breathed."

The mason began to sweat.

"Imagine." *Slush-scrape-slough.* "Breathing your own fat turned to smoke with lungs that scar and crackle. For eternity, mason. Eternity. Weigh that against a day, perhaps two, of advice for a new building dedicated to the greater glory of God, the God who saw us all safely through this terrible time."

Hild stepped into the Crow's line of sight. "A time your god didn't see fit to warn you of," she said.

His eyes glittered like jet. "My God has no truck with demons."

Hild nodded at the mason to get back to work. He looked from one to the other, the bent Crow with the power of damnation and the young giant with the uncanny eyes and the ear of the king, and chose his mate and the mortar.

Hild met the Crow's gaze. Beater of priests, spurner of beggars. He didn't move, but the cross on his chest rose and fell, rose and fell.

In the stripped great hall Hild had barely finished telling the king about the Crow's attempt to frighten the masons before Edwin turned to Coelfrith. "Bring the bishop. Now." He glared at James the Deacon, who was about to launch his choir into another round of endless practice. James herded his boys out of the hall.

Edwin and Hild had nothing to say to each other. The king chewed at a callus on his thumb and Hild merely stood, still as a heron waiting for a fish.

Paulinus arrived, attended by two priests, and Edwin didn't bother with courtesies.

"Bishop, this will stop. I've Penda and Cadwallon circling like wolves. I need men. I get men by showering them with gold. I need gold at hand, gold I'll take from trade. For trade I need a wīc. A safe wīc. I need walls. I need towers on those walls. Until that stone is laid, my masons will do nothing else. Nothing. Do you understand?"

Paulinus focused his black eyes on Hild. "My lord, this is not a conversation for women."

"She's not a woman," Edwin said with half-shuttered eyes. "She's my seer."

"Christ admits of no seers."

Hild said, "He has prophets."

Edwin waved her to silence. "Priest, you forget that this is my hall, and the Christ is not yet my god."

Hild had heard that tone before. She still dreamt it: *We'll eat the horse.* The Crow heard it, inclined his head, and backed up, step by step, until he reached the door, turned, and hurried away.

Edwin turned to Hild. "That man and his god are useful to me. Don't annoy him unnecessarily."

In the ash coppice, Cian and Hild fought in light rain. Hild's legs were splashed with mud. Cian had a bruise swelling on his sword arm. She still hadn't found a way to defeat his shield.

They talked in bursts as they swung and parried.

"Coifi's offered the Crow use of his carpenters," she said. "And some prime timber for the building of a new church." On church, she lunged for his right knee.

He deflected her staff into the turf. "Seems only a month ago he was plotting to smother the Crow in his sleep."

"I doubt the Crow sleeps." She slipped slightly in the mud but distracted Cian with a low sweep at his ankles. He jumped back. They circled each other. "Coifi is a worm but he's not stupid. Everyone knows the king will take baptism at Easter, and then what use will it be to be a high priest of Woden?"

"High priest of sheepherders and cheese-makers."

Begu, hair already braided for bed, knelt on the bed behind Hild and combed her hair. "It feels like an age since I've done this."

"Gwladus does a good job."

"Not as good as me."

Hild closed her eyes, enjoying the steady rhythmic tugging, the crackle of flame, the wool-and-weld smell of Begu, her chatter.

She talked of Wilnoð's growing belly, Bassus's foolish grin, the queen's lessons about Christ—they were spending less time on letters than Hild, more on women's things, the rhythm of blessings and baptism, of when a woman was deemed clean and when she had to avoid sacraments. So much to learn before Easter . . .

". . . Eanflæd is eight months old now and chewing the queen to tatters. She'll give her out to nurse soon enough. Not before time. The king needs a son."

"The king has two," Hild said, half asleep.

"A proper son, Wilnoð says, one born to a Christian marriage. You should come and see how we're getting on with the tapestry. Your mother set up the weave. She was boasting of you today as we worked. The pattern-making mind of the world, she said."

"Mmmn."

"We miss you."

"I'm right here."

"You know what I mean."

"I miss weaving with you, too." And she did, a little.

"No, I don't think you do. But it's not your wyrd. I know that. Ha, here's a knot Gwladus missed."

Snow arrived two days before Yule, along with Osric, who brought with him a larger retinue than usual. Hild watched them dismounting, greeting king's gesiths: the usual unsubtle testing and jeering. If they were to fight Edwin, Osric's men knew nothing of it. No, the retinue was to impress the other thegns. He wanted Elmet. As she left the stables she had to stand aside for a herd of fat pigs being driven up Ermine Street and through the southeast gate. A gift from Stephanus in Elmet, the herder called to her when she asked. Coelfrith would be happy.

That evening she was brooding over Osric when Morud came to her with a gaunt man wearing nothing but grey rags tied together with twine.

"From the lea west of Caer Loid," Morud said. Then, in British, "Tell the lady what you told me."

The gaunt man looked at Hild sideways but didn't dare speak. Morud elbowed him aside. "Aunt Lweriadd said they took our pannage. The Roman priests. 'King's pigs only in the king's wood,' they said. But without pigs what will we eat?"

Hild thought of Stephanus, well fed, writing his careful letters with columns of numbers for Paulinus. Osric would be an even more demanding master. She said, "You will go to my wood." Her voice was harsh; the Loid cowered. She took a breath, said more softly, in British, "First, you will go to the kitchens and eat. Morud will take you."

Fighting with Stephanus meant fighting with Paulinus, which Edwin had forbidden. But how many men could her mene wood support?

Hild walked with Æthelburh along the north bank of the great river, trailed by Bassus—much heftier than he had been, and wearing a new red cloak, Wilnoð's work—and Oeric, with his wisp of beard, new war hat, and steel-ringed leather tunic.

"My husband keeps his plans for Elmet close," the queen said. "But you know why he's letting Paulinus drive the wealh priest from the countryside."

"Spies, yes."

"And for the friendship of the bishop of Rome. An alliance that was foretold before he was king."

"Paulinus told me Christians don't believe in prophecy."

The queen kicked a little stone into the river. "Not in prophecy by women."

They said nothing for a while.

"Perhaps I will give you a Yule gift," the queen said. "Perhaps my husband will give me all those pigs and perhaps I will give them to you and you may herd them to your wood for slaughter."

"Thank you." Coelfrith would be unhappy, but she didn't care.

Behind them the two men were talking about how to pad a war hat properly.

"Will there be war in spring?" Æthelburh said.

"No." Cadwallon needed to consolidate his new kingdom. Penda was still reining in the West Saxons. "At least not here. Not in spring."

16

✦

BEBBANBURG IN SOLMONATH. A cruel month of blue sky and bitter wind. To the east: the sea, colder than a hægtes's heart. To the west: fields under a blanket of snow, broken only by the tracks of the king's messengers.

The king hated Bebbanburg, hated being perched on a hill of rock with its face to the north and flank to the sea. Sea food, he said, was for seals, and high places for wealh and eagles. He liked green rolling hills, gentle valleys, and wide river mouths, good Anglisc dirt under his boots. But no matter how many messengers he sent to ask, the north wall at York was not quite finished nor the west ditch redug, and the end of winter was when starving wolves made desperate forays. Bebbanburg, a fort within a fort on a lump of rock sticking up from a beach, was impregnable. The beach was top-and-tailed by rocks but for a sandy hithe overlooked by a fortified tower on the outer stockade—a massive timber box-parapet. The inner fort had one entrance, tunnelled out of the rock and raised in steps leading to the great gate of the inner stockade. This enclosed the halls, shrine, and well in an area as big as a good-size field. The outer wall protected enough wiry grass for a couple of goats and space enough for work-shops and a byre.

Near the end of the month, the king declared they weren't to call it Bebbanburg anymore. Bebba had been the first wife of Æthelfrith and he would no longer abide reminder of those nithing Idings. They would call it Stānburg, because that was what it was, a fort on stone. Edwin was king;

they called it Stānburg. But among themselves the wealh went on calling it Din Guaïroï, as they had since the long ago, and the Anglisc, after a few days, forgot and called it variously Bebbanburg, which infuriated the king—who twice had to be persuaded by his counsellors not to kill a forgetful gesith—or Cwenburg, for Edwin's dead wife, which irritated the queen.

Hild thought perhaps she and Begu were the only ones who liked the place.

Begu enjoyed the closeness. She didn't mind the people-upon-kine crowding, she didn't even mind the food: oysters and mussels, pork—salted pork, pork in goose grease, dried pork—and bread. She liked the gossip all day in the queen's hall. She loved falling asleep to the sound of the sea.

Hild liked the songs and stories at night: the same songs she'd heard at this time of year every year, but different in hall and in the byre, in the huddled farmstead over the fields and in the overcrowded kitchens where the cook and the baker struggled to feed an overking's household from a petty king's fireplaces. During the day, she liked escaping on her own along the snow-dusted beaches and into the unbroken whiteness of the fields. Sometimes she rode Cygnet and sometimes she took Cian, but mostly she walked on her own.

She didn't remember the first time she had spent Solmonath in the burg, though it had been a time when Edwin was newly king, his household much smaller. But the rhythms were the same: The king paced his small hall like a trapped wildcat, demanding information his counsellors did not have. His counsellors vowed to send out another messenger—to York, to the north, to Lindsey, to Rheged, to Elmet—and to post another lookout on the stockade's western tower with his eyes fixed on the overland path. They even watched from the seaward tower, though only a fool or a god would attempt a voyage at this time of year.

Osric had returned to Arbeia after Yule, dissatisfied but mollified by Edwin's declaration that his dear cousin didn't need to come with the other thegns in spring—he, Edwin, would come to Osric. Breguswith stayed, but Hild had no idea what her mother thought of all this. Though she seemed pensive. Hild watched anxiously for what herbs she might call for, but it was just the usual remedies for this time of year, for pink eye and lung crackle. They were well stocked, and the Crow was always at the king's side—priests in black robes seemed to skulk everywhere in the thronging shadows of the short days—and Hild had little to do.

The household stewed in its own juice and kegs of mead and winter ale, and gossip and rumour flowed into the gap: The Idings were marching with the Dál Riata—no, the Picts. Cadwallon had allied with Rheged, and the men of the north would stream down the beach in the dead of night. Penda had already taken Lindsey and was even now burning Elmet.

Quarrels, love, hate, alliances, and whispers flared and died and flared again, and every night men fell asleep longing for colewort or nettle leaves or even a pint of cow's milk—and a time when blue sky promised warm air and not killing frost. Teeth loosened, belts tightened, tempers frayed.

Slate sea on one side, white field on the other, beach scattered with rock to the north and south. At night, Hild listened to the seals moan.

One evening she stood with Cian on the wooden walkway at the highest corner of the stockade and watched the sun setting over the white fields like a winter apple, small and shrunken, staining the snow with its tired juice. The air smelt of iron and brine.

"The weather's changing," she said.

"It will never change. It will be like this forever. We will grow old and die and be forgotten, and the foxes will gnaw at our bones."

He always got like that after spending too much time indoors. "Come with me tomorrow."

"Where?"

"There's a farm two leagues west."

"Two leagues over the snow and two leagues back? With Hel and the frost giants ready to take us if we turn an ankle in a badger hole?"

"The weather will change."

"It hasn't changed yet."

But the next day, just after noon, Hild pointed out puffy little clouds sailing in from the south and west, very white, followed by larger ones, greyer. "The snow is melting inland."

"But not here," Cian said.

"Not yet."

The field, ringed by bare trees, was silent but for the crackle of their breath—no robins, no wrens, no sparrows—and beneath that the faint whisper and rustle of snow melting. The crest of the field showed patches of brown ridge but the low point where they stood was unbroken snow. At their feet lay a dead wood pigeon. What was left of it looked thin.

Hild pointed to the odd, knobby prints on either side. "Peregrine kill. That's where its talons dug in the snow. There's where its wings touched when it mantled."

"A hawk made this mess?"

"Then a fox, then a crow," she said, pointing. "They're all hungry."

Cian pulled his bold cloak more tightly about him, and they walked on. Not far from the farm Hild thought she saw a stoat—blotched, like the field, with brown—but didn't bother to point it out. She wondered what it could be eating with most of the birds gone, the hedgepigs and squirrels asleep, and peregrines and owls, foxes and crows fighting over the rest.

Their shadows were slanting by the time they reached the farm.

"Look," he said. Mixed with the brown melt ridges she saw a very faint hint of green: the tips of winter colewort. Hild swallowed and wiped her mouth. Soon. Two weeks or three.

Hild came to the farm most years but this year she was greeted not by the old man but a child, sitting on a greasy fur in the sun by the hut's low door, half naked, hair matted, jamming a pebble in its tiny-toothed mouth.

"Aurgh!" it said.

A man burst through the door brandishing a hatchet.

"Peace," Hild said, empty hands out. "Ulf, he's fine."

"I'm not Ulf," said the man, lowering the axe. Indeed, he wasn't. He was too young. "I'm Rath. Rathlaf. My father has gone on."

"I'll miss him," she said. "And my friend, Cian Boldcloak, will miss him, too. He has heard how strong and clever he was, how canny a husbandman. We'll drink to his memory."

Cian—who had never heard of Ulf or his son, Rath—nodded agreement and swept back his cloak to show the two bottles hanging by straps from his shoulder.

The hut stank of people and goat and leaf litter crushed and soiled all winter, and something else, something rank that Hild couldn't place. Rath's wife, Cille, produced a round of stale gritty bread, a pinch of precious salt, and two elm bowls.

Hild shook her head and took the beautifully carved travel cups from her belt. She unstopped the white mead, filled the smallest cup for Cille, the medium cup for Rath, and the largest for her to share with Cian. Cille looked terrified of such beauty.

"To Ulf, the finest farmer on the coast, father of Rath, who lives on in . . ." She looked at the child.

"Hathlaf. Hath."

"Hath, a fine and sturdy farmer-to-be."

They drank.

"Good luck on this house," Cian said, and they drank again.

"To spring," said Rath.

The fire burnt high and clean. They ate the bread with salt, and drank, and studied one another.

Rath was about Cian's age but already with an eyetooth missing and the knuckles of his right hand beginning to thicken. In eight years he would be stooped, in twelve bent, and in fifteen dead—and Hath's knuckles beginning to swell and his back to bend.

When the bread was gone they talked: of the lung crackle that had taken Ulf, the hornbeam crop and how it made their pork taste like earth, of the colewort poking up on the ridge of the field. Hild and Rath agreed that they would have to trust to luck that no new frost killed its tender leaves. Cille—her voice was reedy as a pipe—said they might swap some colewort for a milch cow next month. "The lordling looks surprised," she said, "and I would be, too, but it's not just for colewort. Though people are famished for greens before the hedgerows sprout, I can tell you. Famished. No, they owe us for the seal meat, and the doctoring."

So then there was nothing for it but to hear about the terrible winter storm that had brought the seals out of their way when Rath was gathering wood from the beach, and how he'd killed a bull seal, killed it dead, if you please, with his knife, and then dragged it up onto the dune grass out of the reach of the tide and walked all the way down to Heah and Din's croft—did they know Din and his wife? No? Well they had a lovely daughter, Gode, just lovely, she was surprised the tale of her beauty hadn't spread far and wide, yes, even as far as Din Guaïroï itself, even to the king! What did young men think about these days . . .

At which point Rath took over and talked in his slow—and ever slower—voice: of the king, and the harvest, and the milch cow, and his son, and the weather. Hild saw it slowly dawn on Cian that they would be spending the night in this seal-stinking hut, and she was amused. But she wanted to hear everything they had to say. This was why she'd told Cian to bring two bottles of mead.

The boy fell asleep in a heap and Cille tucked him in a wrap in a nest by the fire where she could see him. The fire burnt down and Rath added wood—driftwood: the flames spat blue and green—and the fire burnt down again. High then low, high then low.

Soon they were telling stories. A selkie tale first, from Cille, one they'd all heard before, but told as though true, as though it had happened to her and just yesterday. Then Cian told the story he'd told to Loid and Angle. ". . . keep the fucking egg!" And they all laughed until they wept. And in the moment of silence when they were done they heard, from far away, in the cold dark hills, an unearthly caterwauling.

Rath put more wood on the fire and told the tale of Cait Sith, the uncanny black wildcat killed, so they say, in times past in the byre of this very farm but still walking the night—aye, and the day, too, when ill luck was abroad—for the cat had been no cat but a hægtes trying her luck with stealing a milch cow for her very own. As she lay gushing out her blood on the straw, she had turned back and sworn with her dying breath that she would return, one bright noon when the tragedy was to befall the farm, and she would have her revenge. And sometimes you could hear her in the night, yowling for the blood of the farmers who had taken her land, yowling . . .

The wind turned raw and wet. "Just like it is before spring at Mulstanton," Begu shouted happily, hair blowing every which way, as they roamed the beach. To the south, past the rocks, in the dunes, stood the carved posts of the graveyard. Bebba lay there, it was said, and other queens, Anglisc and British, including Cwenburh. It was ill luck to linger by the dead, so they walked—they ran, they skipped, they laughed, their dresses kilted up like they were children, bags of bread and beer bouncing, noses streaming—north, to the islands.

In summer it would be a short row from one sandy beach to another, but the water was still too rough. They did, however, find a rocky causeway to scramble over to one of the bigger islands. It was deserted but for a little heap of ruined huts.

On the east beach, they couldn't hear themselves think: It was seal season, and seals of all colours, white, grey, brindled, black, brown, lay hauled up on the sand barking and moaning. They smelt bigger, like cattle long in the rain.

"They look like shaggy horses," Begu said. "The same colours, same whorling of hair. Fur. But their eyes are not the same."

They were not. Hild stared into the eyes of one seal, which stared back: black pools, otherworldly eyes.

Begu sat down on the rough grass of the dune. "Tell me that selkie tale again."

So Hild did, and then they ate their bread and drank their beer and watched the guillemots and puffins, counted the water rail, dropped their jaws at a sea eagle falling between sky and water like a bolt of lightning.

"Will we have a home one day by the sea?"

Hild took her hand. "Yes." They would have many homes. But that was for later. For now, her face ached with the cold and the wind and happiness.

The wind died down, and Hild and Cian took to riding out along the beach with the hounds and Oeric. Cian would give Oeric an exercise, and Grimhun—or the brothers Berht, or Gwrast and his cousin Cynan, or Eadric the Brown, or Coelwyn—would hoot and laugh and fall to arguing, with demonstrations, that it wouldn't work, couldn't possibly be of any use, but here's a better way, and Hild and Cian would edge away unobtrusively to find a spot where they could talk and practice alone. The gesiths were used to this. They would nod and wink but say nothing. Hild ignored them and thought Cian didn't notice. She doubted it would occur to him what the gesiths might be thinking—at least not in terms of her. She'd seen him eyeing the lasses of Bebbanburg, and she knew he slipped away now and again to the crofter to the southwest with large breasts and big feet.

Once they rode out to the cot of Heah and Din and their daughter, Gode—Cian noticed her, Hild saw, and indeed she was supple-handed and fresh as the morning, with a neck pale as milk and a mouth like the promise of summer plums, and young, only a year or two older than Hild, a leaf newly unfurled—and on the way back Hild, unaccountably cross, finally found a way to beat a gesith with a shield.

They had stopped by a stream guarded by a wind-thrawn oak, and Hild attacked Cian furiously, thinking of neck and mouth and supple, supple hands. Cian, with shield and sword, fought back with equal fury, driving her back and back until her back foot was against a root of the tree. No, she thought, this time I will not flinch, I will not lose, and she punched at his face with the end of her staff, threw it up into the tangled branches, and pulled herself up after it. The stream roared, in full spate. The tree creaked a little under her shoes.

Cian shouted, "Come down!"

"Come make me!"

He sheathed his sword, threw his shield aside, and jumped for the branch Hild was standing on. She moved to the other side of the trunk.

He scrambled up, clumsy in his war boots, panting, cursing, then stopped. The heel of Hild's staff was a foot from his nose. He was defenceless.

"I worked out how to beat you."

"But I don't have my shield!"

"That's right. How to win against a gesith with a shield: Make him drop his shield."

"No, no, no. What if there isn't a tree?"

"Let's see," she said, and dropped lightly to the ground.

She walked with her staff away from the tree and waited near the stream. Cian dropped more heavily, picked up his shield, and they did it all again: him driving, driving, driving her back to the stream.

She jumped in, half waded, half swam to the other side, climbed out. Cian stayed where he was.

"What if there's no stream?"

"Come over and we'll find out."

"My armour!"

"Yes. A pity. It'll take a lot of work to polish it."

"As a favour to me. How can I persuade you?"

Hild wrung out her hair, thinking. "When the harp comes around to-night, sing for me. Sing the song of Branwen."

"Done."

She waded back across, shivering, walked past him, then turned, so that he was between her and the stream. "Now come at me fast, for I'm freezing."

And, again, he drove her back and back and back, and she waited until he smiled in anticipation, and then she turned and ran.

He ran after her, but he was wearing armour, and war boots, and his shield was heavy. He fell farther behind. She turned and waggled her hand at him.

"You're cheating!"

"Indeed I am."

"I'll never catch you, unless . . ." And he dropped his shield and burst out laughing, and they were still laughing, off and on, when they got back to Bebbanburg, and if anyone thought it strange that the seer should find being cold and wet funny, no one mentioned it.

As the weather improved, messages began to come in from all over the isle. Two, from Rheged and from Alt Clut, said the same thing: Eochaid Buide of the Dál Riata was sending an army to aid the Cenél Cruithen against Fiachnae mac Demmáin of the Dál Fiatach, and chief among the Dál Riatan war band were Idings—though the man from Rheged thought two, Oswald and Osric, called the Burnt, while the messenger from Alt Clut thought three, Oswald, Osric the Burnt, and the young Osbald.

In hall the men argued: Wilgar pointed out that everyone knew Oswald didn't like any of his brothers, except his little half brother, Oswiu; the messages were clearly false. No, said Coifi, it was clear Eochaid was aiming this spear at the heart of the northern Anglisc, that he couldn't lose: If the Idings fought well, they would attract followers to lead in a swoop upon the Anglisc throne; if they fought badly, they would die. Perhaps, said Paulinus, but the real message was that the men of the north were feeling their strength, and they had on their side Christ, the one true God—even if served by wrongheaded wealh priests. At which point all eyes turned to the king.

Hild, watching silently, as befitted a seer, saw that this speech was prepared, for Edwin nodded at his scop, who struck a chord, and the men quieted.

"The bishop Paulinus is right. He has counselled me well on Elmet and other matters. He brings the promise of the friendship of the greatest priest in middle-earth, the bishop of Rome. It seems to me good that we consider what he says. For that reason I will send messages to Sancton and Derwent, to Goodmanham and Brough, to Lindum and Elmet, and ask my thegns to meet at Yeavering. There we will have it out about this Christ god and we will see if it is good, and if it is, I will accept baptism from the hands of Paulinus in York on Easter Day. Paulinus, who through his foresight has driven out the priestly spies of the men of the north."

Uproar.

Hild, though, listening past the noise, found no surprise. Edwin had been laying the groundwork since his marriage to the queen. His daughter had been baptised, and a dozen gesiths, and no harm had come of it. Indeed, Elmet was now theirs and with no wealh priests sending their uncanny messages north or west. The word would go out. Men would show up with their kine and their arguments next month as the grass greened and the milk began to flow. They thought this god of no more account than the others.

Morud came to find her. "Lady, the queen wants you."

Oeric escorted her back to the women's quarters, where she found the queen and Wilnoð, and her mother and Begu and Gwladus waiting.

The queen handed her a package. It was small and lumpy. "A man came. He said he'd had it from a man wearing East Anglisc buckles. He said it was for the lady Hild, sister to Hereswith."

Hild's heart squeezed. She found Begu holding one arm and Gwladus the other, and was glad of it. *Gwladus smells different*, she thought vaguely. Her mother gave her a stern look: *You are Yffing!*

The queen was still talking, but Hild concentrated on taking a breath, then another, while Wilnoð, herself as big as a hut now, brought her a stool.

She sat, turned the package over. Waxed linen, sealed. She didn't recognise the seal, which looked like some kind of duck. She broke it.

Inside was another wrapped lump, the size of a plover's egg, and a letter. She unrolled it. The letters were clumsily formed and the words badly spelt:

> Dearest sister. Æthelric my husband has not put aside his woman.
> Fursey is here and sends greetings. He says my letters will improve
> with practice. I am to take baptism. Here, too, is Æthelric's half
> brother Sigebert, visiting from Frankia. He already is baptised. I
> send you a lump of Frank's incense. I am with child. H.

There was no date. She read it again.

"What does it say?" Begu said.

Hild gave her the letter.

Begu frowned. "Yes, but what does it say?"

Æthelburh gave Eanflæd to Arddun, plucked the letter from Begu's hand, and read it aloud.

Fursey. Sigebert. Frankincense. With child.

Someone put a hand on her shoulder. Hild looked up: Gwladus, with a cup of mulled ale. Hild sipped gratefully while Æthelburh read the letter again.

"Is that the incense?" Begu said. "I want to see."

Obediently, Hild unwrapped it. The astonishing smell filled the room. Hereswith, she thought. Hereswith forming her letters under the eye of Fursey. Both safe. And making friends with the Franks, making sure of a refuge.

"Worth more than gold I should think," Wilnoð said, then clutched at her belly and gasped: The baby was kicking.

The women fussed.

Hild sipped again at her ale. Hereswith. Perhaps as big as Wilnoð. Sitting in a swamp. Perhaps she'd already had the child. Perhaps Hild was an aunt.

Wilnoð gasped again.

Perhaps Hereswith had died in childbirth, as Cwenburh had in these very chambers, in a great sigh of blood.

Hild woke from a dream of Gwladus standing in a pool of blood, an Gwladus the wrong size, the wrong smell.

"Shhh," said Begu, "it's just a dream." She stroked Hild's head. "Just a dream."

Hild clung to her.

"What's wrong? What is it?"

"Hereswith's having a child."

"Well, that's true," Begu said. "But people have babies all the time."

"They die all the time, too."

Begu kissed her forehead. "You dreamt that?"

Hild shook her head. "Talk to me," Hild said. "Anything. Please."

Begu sat up, reached over Hild, and pulled open the curtain. The banked light of the fire was enough to show Gwladus already sitting up on her pallet and yawning.

"Light a rush," Begu whispered. "Bring some milk. No, not milk, I forgot, some small beer and come talk to us. The lady Hild has had a bad dream. No no, not a *dream* dream, just a dream."

They set the rush in its bowl on the shelf at the foot of the bed, and Begu lifted the cover and told Gwladus to get in.

"My feet are cold," Gwladus said.

"Hild won't mind. She burns like a forge. It'll take her mind off things, anyway."

So Hild found herself warming her bodywoman's cold feet with her warm hands while Begu talked about this and that.

". . . why's she still breast-feeding Princess Eanflæd? She's ten months old."

Hild massaged Gwladus's ankles, stroking the strong bone on the inside, thinking of the place to press to bring a birth more quickly.

"Maybe she doesn't want another just yet," Gwladus said. "Maybe she doesn't want pawing at, and swelling, and nothing to look forward to but a growing ache in her back and the thing in her belly eating her from the inside."

And then Hild understood. Gwladus was with child.

Hild leaned into the buffeting wind on the top of Ad Gefrin. She opened her mouth and let the wind whip her breath away. She loved it up here with the goats, loved the scudding clouds, the sun and shadow chasing each other over bent and silvered grass. From here she couldn't hear the lowing of the little cattle the British lords drove in as tribute; she couldn't hear the constant shuffle of hooves in the enclosure where ponies, smelling spring and the promise of green grass, pushed for room at the fence. Up here there was just the whistle of the wind, the occasional dull clank of a goat bell, the cry of a hawk circling, tilting, sliding down the air.

She liked Bebbanburg, but here she could see for miles. Here she could think.

Change was coming, and it wasn't just spring, wasn't just the first milk of the year, or stallions flaring their nostrils when the mares walked by, or little throstles pecking at the backs of the goats to carry away the soft hair for their nests. It wasn't just the hammer and shout of the king's new talking stage rising west of the great hall.

The thegns thought they understood. Oh, they would talk for two days, yes, the tide of conversation ebbing and flowing, but they knew the story of Edwin's dream at the court of King Æthelberht long ago, and why should they deny him? What was one more god? Gods were like the flotsam that washed up with the waves, always coming and going, and those big enough to remain gradually were worn away by wind and water and time. But the thing must be talked about, beards tugged, and the last of the year's mead drunk.

The thegns were wrong. The Christ and his priests were different. They were a storm that would change everything. *They read.* They would sweep the beach clean. But not of her. That was not her wyrd.

When the thegns understood their Witganmot wasn't to be at the big oak, or even in hall over mead, but at the new talking stage, they muttered. It was Romish, not Anglisc. It wasn't right. But then Coifi announced he had blessed a new totem to stand witness to their pledges. And wasn't a totem better even than an oak?

Hild listened to the newly arrived thegns as they inspected the talking stage. It looked like a wedge of cheese, Tondhelm said, though higher at the edge than the point. He stood with two others on the stage at the wedge's tip, careful not to brush against the still-drying paint on Coifi's Woden totem. Tomorrow they'd sit with other listeners in rows rising to the back. The thing reeked of new wood. Hunric, a thegn from near Goodmanham who had ridden in with many men, said that there would be splinters in all their arses by moonrise the next night.

That night, after the main feasting, the queen withdrew from the great hall with her women and those who had ridden with their men to the Witganmot. Breguswith and Begu went with them to the women's hall, but Hild stayed awhile with Oeric at her elbow. The men got down to the serious business of drinking. Cian and her hounds drank as mightily as the rest, or seemed to, though she suspected several were pacing themselves for the wrestling and boasting to come.

There was much gossip among the thegns, who had less to prove than the young gesiths: who had brought the most cattle for the king, who wore the most gold, who had a new wife, a new son. The scop sang songs of their ancestry, flattering them outrageously, his boy scooping up armlets and finger rings and sparkling daggers as the progressively drunk thegns sought to outdo each other in generosity.

Hild noticed that Hunric threw his smallest ring, and boasted merely that he had brought the most cattle, which was true, and that his son would beat anyone else's son at anything—once he was grown. Given that his son still ran bare-legged with a wooden knife, this was a safe boast, one no one would remember in a dozen years. A canny man. Edwin, she saw, had raised his cup to Hunric and Hunric toasted him in return. Hild knew what Hunric didn't: that the king was only amused by those he thought little of.

Faces grew redder and drinking competitions sprang up at every bench. Bets were laid. Soon they would start boasting about their horses, and the scop's man—traditionally the keeper of the boasts—would set up the racing for the morning. Meanwhile, the scop's praise grew more extravagant. The thegns roared: The scop was teasing Tondhelm about a brain as small as his ear finger and a prick bigger than his arm.

She picked her way through the raucous men—who were too worried about what other men might be thinking of them to bother with a woman—to Cian, who was telling some involved story about the little sheep of Gwynedd and why the men of that land were also small.

He grinned at her when he was finished. "I'm leaving now for the women's hall," she said. "I'll send Oeric back. Take him under your wing. Don't let him make any boasts he can't keep. And if you're planning to ride Acærn to riches tomorrow, don't drink too much more of that."

To which he just grinned again and offered her his cup, and she grinned back and sipped.

The women's hall, if anything, was even bawdier than the men's. Veils were askew and sleeves tucked in belts. Arddun and Gwladus could barely keep up with filling the cups, and Hunric's wife, inarticulate with mead, was shaking a broken-stringed lyre as though it were a choking baby.

Breguswith was deep in conversation with two women Hild didn't know, and Begu was whistling like a cowherd. Hild sat next to her on one of the queen's prettily embroidered cushions and took off her shoes.

"Stop thinking," Gwladus said. "You'll frighten everyone and spoil the party. Drink this." Hild sipped: stinging white mead, made from . . . She sipped again . . . heather honey. Part of some thegn's tribute or a gift? She looked up, saw Breguswith looking at her, then back at the women she was in conversation with. Hild made a note to herself to make friends with whoever that was.

"Stop it," Gwladus said, but then had to fill another cup.

Hild sipped absently, then heard her name. "Hild knows that song. We sang it together at Mulstanton. Don't you?"

Hild nodded.

"How does the tune go? The one Cædmon sings to Winty."

So Hild sang the jaunty tune about running free in green, green grass, and Begu joined her, and someone restrung the lyre and plinked the tune.

Gwladus refilled her cup. "Better," she said. "But the queen says you must drink this down in one, then smile, then drink another."

Hild doubted Æthelburh had said any such thing. She looked up, but couldn't even see the queen.

"Oh, for earth's sake," Gwladus said, and took Hild's face between her hands. "Look at me." Hild found herself looking straight down Gwladus's bodice. Gwladus tilted her chin until their eyes met. "Listen to me. Truly: Arddun told me that the queen has ordered that anyone sober enough to walk a straight line tonight will be put in the corner and covered with honey. So drink, look stupid. Better still, be stupid. Look at your mother." Breguswith's cheeks were now cherry red, her sleeves undone. "She knows when to let go. You should, too."

And, later, when the women were kilting up their dresses and setting loose their hair to dance, Hild did, too, and a little while after that she even forgot to think about what she was doing.

Hild squinted in the morning light, glad of the keen wind and low clouds. She didn't think it would rain. She stood with the other women, pale but tidy, at the north end of the horse path. At least they merely had to cheer while the men rode their horses against one another.

In the first race, one gesith had to vomit from his saddle before he could drink the race toast. He was better off than his race mate, though, who fell off at the first bend and broke his collarbone. Edwin gave the winner a dagger.

More racing, more accidents, more wagers, more straining and shouting and falling in the mud.

Gold, boast, blood, sweat: The crowd shook off its lethargy and grew cheerful.

The only grumbles came when the midday feast—roast ox and heather beer, on benches set under a canopy of branch and reeds—was delayed for the Crow to give thanks to his Christ. Christ wasn't their god, some muttered, not yet. But most didn't care. They were happy to eat. They planned to doze on full stomachs for most of the Witganmot and rouse themselves sufficiently to vote as their chief men directed.

Hild watched the looks and nods travel up and down the benches— the king and the Crow, Hunric and Coelfrith, Coifi and Tondhelm—and knew Paulinus would be pleased.

The king and his chief men—the æthelings, Coelfrith, Paulinus, Coifi— sat on a bench at the back of the speaking platform. The men of the kingdom sat in the tiers rising before them. The women sat at ground level to one side, out of the thegns' direct line of sight; they did not have a voice in the Witganmot. Begu sat next to Hild, nibbling on the bread she'd tucked in her pouch at breakfast. She chattered about this and that as one by one the men—wearing their finest, groaning with gold, moustaches carefully greased—stood and swore their oath to their king, named the tribute they had brought, and numbered the spears they could rally at the king's word. Many of them got very florid: They liked the sound of their own voices, liked the regard of their fellows.

Many of the women were frank in their assessment of the men, gossiping about which would make a good husband, which good sport. Hild mostly listened to the birds. ". . . Trum something, I forget what," Begu said. She was pointing at the man now standing, wearing rich brown embroidered with gold. "Isn't that a lovely colour? Like a polished acorn— like Cian's horse. Oh, I was so pleased that he beat Lintlaf today. I bet one of my combs on the race. No, no, not the comb you gave me! I'd never part with that. But anyway I won, so now I have two extra combs, I'll give you one . . ."

Hild listened to the *hweet* of a siffsaff somewhere over the rise and thought perhaps later she'd walk to the west of Ad Gefrin where last year she'd found a throstle's nest with eight eggs—eight!—bright with their red blotches. But it was probably too early for eggs.

The king's feet were dancing this way and that, but even the king had to listen when men spoke at Witganmot. Eventually, though, the speeches came to an end, and then the king stood, walked to the front of the platform and the totem, and made his own speech, full of praise for the strength of his men, the wealth of their tithe, the generosities he would visit upon them during the next year in reward for their loyalty. He named a man here, a man there, sometimes joking, sometimes flattering, pleasing everyone with his notice. Then he said he would stop, for there was a fine feast in the making, and once they had made their weighty pronouncement on his question, they could eat until dawn. But for now, he would let the Romish high priest, Bishop Paulinus, speak. Paulinus had words from his god. The god had also spoken to the king in a dream at the court of Æthelberht—they all knew that story, he wouldn't repeat it here—but they were to understand that Paulinus spoke as with the king's mouth: His words were the king's words.

The thegns roared and thumped their benches.

Paulinus took the king's place. His white robe, embroidered in crimson and yellow, shimmered. The cloth-of-gold stole around his neck must have weighed more than a sucking pig, and the gold-headed crook in his left hand blazed with jewels. When he raised his right hand, his ring flashed like Earendal, the dawn star.

The thegns sat back, enjoying the display of wealth and power, expecting a short, rousing speech about wealth and wyrd, the king's protection and the Christ god's cunning, the promise of good weather and better luck, of alliances and strength of arms and honour, larded with flattery.

The Crow began well enough, speaking loudly and clearly, careful of his accent: the bishop of Rome held the king of the Anglisc in high regard, and his power and favour would shine upon the isle as a mark of his blessing and the blessings of God. The Franks would honour them, and the Frisians, and the people of Rome. Their cattle would grow fat, the corn tall, and gesiths would flock to the tufa to make one nation under God. Everyone would know the name of their king, of the Yffings, of Northumbria! They had but to accept Christ as their God, and all those who were in agreement with him would be cleansed in the Fount of Life.

The thegns nodded and murmured among themselves. Fine promises, exactly what you wanted from a god.

Begu whispered to Hild, "We'll be going into the feast early." Indeed, one thegn was already standing to make his agreement.

But Paulinus wasn't finished. He fixed them with his glittering eye—so dark, so foreign—and began to admonish them about Satan, about driving out the wealh priests as his spies, about obeying the will of the one true God, who spoke only through His bishop in Rome. Their king willed it! Their king demanded it! Their new God commanded it!

The thegn next to the one who had stood shouted: Who was this god to command a king? To command thegns in good standing?

Paulinus overrode him in a torrent of words. They had no choice but to obey! If they obeyed their God's commandments, He would deliver them from their earthly troubles, save them from the everlasting doom of the wicked, and give them a place in His eternal kingdom forever. But they must obey. They must bow their heads.

The rumble of disgruntled thegns drowned out the Crow's now thickly accented last words.

Bargaining? They were used to that. Persuasion? Yes, of course. Bribes and promises? Naturally. But commands to submit? They didn't even know this god. What had he done for them? Had there been a battle the god had won for them, a crop he had brought home with unexpected bounty? Yet the priest wanted them to *obey*. Was he mad?

It was Coifi who stepped in. He sprang onto the platform and strode forward, holding out his arms so his leaf-green cloak billowed. "Hear me! Hear me!"

He stepped in front of Paulinus.

"You know me!"

They couldn't disagree.

"I am the chief priest of the chief god."

Even more unarguable.

"Look at me!"

"You just get uglier!" Tondhelm shouted. Laughter.

"Am I rich?"

Frowns.

"I ask you, am I rich? I am not. Why? Because my god is not as powerful as the Christ god!"

Begu whispered, "Why would he say that? Why—"

"Woden's shrine is made of wood. Painted wood. But in Rome they stain glass like jewels, they build of stone like the giants of old, they cover their ceilings in gold!"

Gold.

"Woden is a great god, a fine god, but there is a new god, more mighty still. His altars are spreading. The men who have been to Kent, to East Anglia, have seen how rich their kings are, how generous to their thegns. I have seen it." He pointed to Coelfrith, to Osric, to the others sitting behind him on the bench. "They have seen it."

"I have seen it!" Coelfrith shouted.

"Gesiths who took the Christ's blessing do well for themselves," Coifi said. "They have rings on their swords, jewels at their belts, horses swifter than the wind."

"Does he mean Cian?" Begu whispered. "I think he does. Cian! And you said this was going to be boring!"

"The Christ god will make us richer than the Franks! I tell you truly. It is our wyrd."

Behind him, Coelfrith was stretching his eyes at someone in the front tier: now, now.

A man leapt to his feet. Hunric. "Edwin king! I say the chief priest of the chief god is the one to know! If any man can. For what can men know? Our understanding is like that of a sparrow flying through the king's hall at Yule. Outside it's all howling darkness and rain, inside it's a warm hearth and music. The sparrow flies in one door, into light and laughter. Then out the other door, back into the dark. And that moment for the sparrow is like our moment in middle-earth. Because, like the bird, we know nothing of what came before now or what'll happen after."

"I know what comes after this!" Tondhelm shouted. "Food!"

"The food's not going anywhere," Hunric shouted back. "I say that if the priests are right, and they were right in the king's dream long ago, when he was just an exiled ætheling—and look at him now! our king! overking!—then men aren't on middle-earth for long. We're like that sparrow, mazed by a moment of comfort. Well, if the priests say they can teach us the before and the promise of the after, then I say we listen!"

Other thegns were standing to speak, and Hild knew they'd be there all afternoon.

"Hunric's sparrow is a very stupid sparrow," she said to Begu. "Birds always know where they're going!"

"Don't be silly," Begu said. "It's not about the bird. It's about people who don't know where the bird is from or where it's flying to. I think."

"Then the people are stupid. I know where all the birds around here nest."

"You're getting peevish," Begu said. "Are you hungry? Eat this bread."

She got more peevish when, at the door of the great hall, Gwladus, waiting with Morud, told her the feast was delayed: The king wanted her in his small room with the other counsellors. She handed Hild a lump of cheese. "Eat this. You might be a while. Two messengers came, with three letters."

"The deacon talked to them while you were all out there listening to the windbags," Morud said. "Something's up. The deacon looked right peaky."

Hild arrived in the small room just as one of the messengers—they were both priests with the Roman tonsure—unrolled the letter. Others were still arriving—no sign of Paulinus—and she took a place next to James. Morud was right. James looked a little damp around the hairline, and his complexion was tinged with ash.

The priest began to read in Latin in that peculiar, weighty voice that Hild realised was common to those used to waiting for an echo from stone walls.

"To the illustrious Edwin, king of Anglisc: from Boniface, bishop, servant of the servants of God . . ."

King of Anglisc, not all the Anglisc.

The second priest translated, in a voice of brass, better suited to the hangings and corners of a king's hall.

"The words of man can never express the power of the supreme Divinity . . ."

In this at least, Boniface, the bishop of Rome, was just like a scop. *The words of man can never express* . . . But he was going to try, and at length, by the look of that letter.

Clearly Edwin had just reached the same conclusion. He leaned back in his great chair, tufa at his right hand, Coelfrith at his left, looking bored and mildly irritable. No doubt he was hungry, too.

Paulinus arrived finally, looking slitty-eyed as a cat who'd killed a pigeon. Three letters.

". . . Divine Majesty who alone created and established the heaven and the earth, the sea . . .

"To Him are subject all imperial power and authority, for it is by Him that kingship is conferred."

The king put his chin on his fist.

". . . our Redeemer in His mercy has brought light to our excellent son Eadbald and the nations subject to him . . ."

Our excellent son Eadbald. Boniface was putting himself on a par with the god, and a Jutish king on a lower bench.

". . . your gracious queen and true partner . . ."

The queen wasn't there, Hild realised. Three letters.

". . . affectionately urge Your Majesties to renounce idol-worship, reject the mummery of temples and the deceitful flattery of omens, and believe in God, the Father Almighty, and in His Son, Jesus Christ, and in the Holy Spirit. This faith will free you from Satan's bondage . . ."

The king flushed dull red but the reader ploughed on, oblivious.

". . . cannot understand how people can be so deluded as to worship as god objects to which they themselves have given the likeness of a body . . ."

The translator faltered momentarily, then steadied.

"Accept the message of the Christian teachers and the Gospel that they proclaim. Believe in God, the Father Almighty . . .

"We impart to you the blessing of your protector, blessed Peter, prince of the Apostles. With it we send you a tunic with a golden ornament, and a cloak from Ancyra, asking Your Majesty to accept these gifts with the same goodwill as that with which we send them."

The Anglisc translation continued for a moment, followed by silence.

Everyone looked at the king. "So. I'm in some wight called Satan's bondage but this princeling priest, Peter, will protect me. Did I hear that right?"

The translator swallowed.

"This Romish bishop thinks himself my foster-father, and tells me if

I'm a good boy, I can be almost as good as his son Eadbald. Are you sure you got those words right?"

The priest swallowed again and couldn't speak.

"Eadbald is my wife's brother. The Kentish king, king of the Jutes. A small people, who owe their grace and favour to the Franks. I, on the other hand, am Edwin, overking of all the Anglisc. So, priest, are you sure you got those words exactly right?"

Paulinus took a half step forward. "If my lord King—"

"Shut up." Edwin hadn't taken his eyes off the translator. "So not only am I in bondage to a wight, beholden to a mere prince, and striving to be as good as a Jutish king, I'm to be grateful for a tunic, which is the mark and favour from a godlike bishop. You'd better show me this tunic, then, this most marvellous tunic for which I will be happy to acknowledge my fealty to a priest in Rome."

The translator, white-faced, didn't move. It was Paulinus who strode forward, took the package, unfastened it, and went to one knee before Edwin's chair.

Edwin took the tunic, shook it out, held it up to the light.

It was purple, with a silklike lustre and sheen.

"It drapes beautifully," Edwin said. "Don't you think?"

Dead silence.

Edwin smiled at the messengers. "There's going to be a reply."

Hild poured wine for James and for herself. They both drank fast. She re-filled their cups. They drank again.

"By Christ I thought he'd kill them," James said.

They drank more.

"No, by God, I thought he'd kill the bishop."

Edwin couldn't kill Paulinus. He planned to trot him out to all the great houses of the north on the grand progress to York for Easter. "The king likes a brave man."

"Well, I was quaking like a jellyfish. But I'm a mere deacon. A lesser mortal than a bishop. Though indeed he's now practically an archbishop."

"That's what his letter said?"

"Oh, yes. He gets a pallium the day the Anglisc come to Christ. He can feel it on his shoulders. Then he won't have to bend the knee to Arch-bishop Justus in Kent."

What would the Mercians think of that? And Cadwallon? An over-bishop in the court of the overking tilted the balance. The threads of trade and tithe and obligation were about to run through Edwin.

While Frisians had always traded directly with the Angles of the east and the Saxons in London, Franks mostly went through the Jutish Kentishmen. Justus, the overbishop in Kent, Paulinus's overbishop, reported directly to the bishop of Rome. It had always made Edwin unhappy. An overking's priest should not be lower than a lesser king's priest.

But soon Paulinus would be overbishop in his own right, reporting directly to the bishop of Rome. And Frankish trade would come through the new wīc at York. More gold meant more gesiths, which meant more victories and more gold again.

And Paulinus's priests had already tightened their grip on Elmet, cutting off information to the north, to the Idings.

While Gwladus combed Hild's hair, Begu told Hild about the pope's letter to the queen. She couldn't remember much about it, only that it mentioned something about becoming one flesh with the king, once he accepted Christ. "But they did that already. Or does the pope person think Eanflæd fell from the sky? Or, oh, maybe that's what the queen's been waiting for, before she weans Eanflæd. Eorðe knows, if she wants a son she should be getting started. But the presents were nice, a silver mirror—it's like looking in a pond!—and a gold-and-ivory comb. You'll do my hair after hers?" This to Gwladus. Then, to Hild, "Not as nice as the one you gave me, of course, but it's heavy. Very heavy. Which is silly when you think about it, because who wants a comb so heavy you can't use it? I suppose now we've had the Witganmot, we'll be packing up again. When do we go to Mulstanton?"

"After Osric's house, at Arbeia."

"How long will we be at Arbeia?"

"Not long."

"You don't like it there, do you? I can hear it in your voice."

She hadn't been back since she and the king and three dozen gesiths had escaped with their lives. "I have to go. But you don't. My mother is thinking of taking a boat from Tinamutha to the bay as soon as we arrive."

"Not staying with Osric?"

"She has things to sort out with Onnen. You could go with her."

Begu's face lit like a candle. "Oh! Home! And Cian could come, too. Couldn't he?"

"If you persuade the queen to persuade the king to give permission."

"But what about you?"

"I'm the king's seer. But we won't be at Arbeia long. The king would kill Osric, else. And, besides, I'll have Gwladus."

17

✦

THE MOUTH OF THE GREAT RIVER seemed like another country in another time.

Arbeia was an ancient house, built with stone and plaster and slate. Two hundred years of Anglisc occupation had added wooden wings with thatched roofs and new doorways knocked in two sides, but its bones resisted change. Even the bakehouse was stone, and a stone colonnade ran along the south wall. The walls were high: a stronghold built by the same redcrests who raised the great wall, to oversee all the trade of the north. Ironstone and silver, pearls and pelts, wheat and wool: Goods from Anglisc farmland, from the kings of the north, Rheged and Alt Clut and Gododdin, all flowed into and along the river or down the coast. Tinamutha was the best port north of the Humber.

A man is lord of his own hall, and Hild hated Osric's hall, hated the men who lounged in its oddly sized rooms—Roman rooms, Osric said proudly—the men with bright blades, whose eyes turned first to Osric and only then to the king. She found herself looking at the forearm of every man she met, looking for that curling scar she had put there with her slaughter seax on that nightmarish flight so many years ago.

At night she dreamt, again and again, of the hand gripping the gunwale, the curve of muscle, the tendons standing out. Over and over she drew her blade along that curve, over and over the skin opened like a flower and she looked at his arm and saw a blossom of meat, red bone, yellow fat, blue vein, plump muscle, before the blood welled up and poured over the memory, blotting it out.

As the king's seer she should have stayed in those small rooms and watched those men, listening and weighing, judging their interest as Edwin and Paulinus talked to them of the Christ and the bishop of Rome, and the righteousness of a strong shield arm and preferential trade. But she couldn't settle. She felt restless and trapped. She thought of Hereswith: *Æthelric my husband has not put aside his woman . . . I am with child.* She had sent a note with her mother, who, on the way to Mulstanton, would find someone heading south: *Flatter Sigebert. And get better at your letters, or have Fursey set them down for you!* She needed a window onto what was happening down there.

So instead of sitting in strange cold rooms ignoring her own fear and the sideways looks of Osric's men, she roamed the estuary, drowning her dreams in the flight of birds, endless flocks of them—goose and redshank, oystercatcher and tern, lapwing and plover, and, for two days, settling drifts of heron and egret. They lifted on the third day at dawn and left the mudflats desolate, flat and ugly and stinking. Did Hereswith's swamp smell like this?

She walked down to the harbour, watched men and some women bringing in their catch of cod and haddock, mackerel and herring while the gulls wheeled and shrieked and squabbled, and offshore the heads of seals bobbed up and down as they swam. She wondered how that would feel, to swim naked through the heavy, cold water. To navigate the simple currents of brine, not politics.

That night she dreamt of seawater coursing over her glistening skin, of flying underwater and over it, and woke in the glimmer of dawn with a shivering yearning, delicious and unnameable. Gwladus, sleeping at the foot of Hild's bed, didn't stir. Hild watched for a while. The curve of her cheek, the top of her shoulder where her shift had slipped, had the bloom and sheen of just-risen cream ready to be licked.

She followed Gwladus's form under the blanket, the flare of waist to hip. The child didn't show. Pennyroyal and sweet gale, that's what she'd recommend. Parsley in a pinch. But she hadn't seen any yet, this far north, and they weren't herbs she carried for wound care.

The next night Hild joined the king at mead with his host and their sons and thegns and counsellors. The only woman. She stared at them, still half dreaming of birds lifting, seals diving. One of Osric's thegns touched his amulet and made a sign.

Edwin threw a duck bone at the man's head. "You don't like my seer? You're in good company. My pet bishop doesn't like her, either. He tells me he half expects her to dissolve and disappear in a shriek of oily smoke when she's baptised at Easter."

Osfrith, sitting next to Hild, and well used to her, laughed, and others laughed cautiously along with him. It struck Hild that the younger ætheling was now seen as a man to be laughed along with, a man in his own right, no longer just a stripling prince. Since his marriage he had found his way. He was becoming the king's man of business, negotiating affairs of trade with other kings and chieftains the way his brother, Eadfrith, negotiated affairs of state.

But as men laughed she saw the discontent in Edwin's eyes: like the nights he smiled with Eorpwald at Rendlesham. She remembered Begu telling her of the pope's letter to the queen. *One flesh with the king, once he accepted Christ.* The æthelings might be useful but an overking could not abide a rival. The letter from the pope, backed by Paulinus once he was chief priest of the Angles, might be enough to blunt his rivals' tines. Rivalry, the disease of kings.

Hild became aware of Paulinus's unwinking gaze. His nose was more bladelike than usual, the muscles around his mouth set and hard. He was angry, no doubt as much for being referred to as a pet, and for disclosure of his thoughts, as for her presence. Righteous anger, the disease of bishops.

The sound of mead, poured into the silver cup next to her hand by a pretty servingwoman—not as pretty as Gwladus—seemed unnaturally loud. The woman's hand was shaking. Hild motioned *Enough*; if the woman spilt anything at the overking's table, she'd be whipped. Being surrounded by the stink of fear, the disease of seers.

She picked up the cup. They all watched. She turned it in her hand. Rivalry, anger, fear.

"I have one very like this," she said. "A gift from our generous overking. For Lindum." She smiled at them over the rim.

They looked away. They'd all heard of the seer's deeds at Lindum.

Edwin laughed. "Perhaps I should have given her something for Bebbanburg." The room stiffened—like estuary mud drying in the sun, Hild thought, a sucking bog under the cracking skin, treacherous.

Bebbanburg. Osric always denied that he had betrayed them to the Irish, and Edwin, at the time not wholly secure, had deemed it prudent to accept his word. Osric was Yffing, with a claim to be king and the men to back it up. With the Irish swarming, and the æthelings not quite of age, the king had needed his cousin. But now Osric was just another rival.

She sipped her mead. Fine, very fine. She sipped again, rolled it around her mouth, swallowed. "Good mead," she said to Osric, but pitched to be heard at the farthest tables. "Made from southern honey. No, farther away than that, a land of blossoming walnut groves and poppies." Obvious, now that she thought about it. "You didn't tell us you were trading with the Franks, cousin."

Silence rippled outwards.

Edwin looked at her, nodding. His eyes were ordinary, not black in the middle and banded with swarming green. He wasn't surprised. He'd just been waiting for her to declare it openly. She nodded back and raised her cup, as though she had known for a week and had waited for the proper moment. But her heart thumped. So obvious but she had nearly missed it. She had nearly missed it.

Edwin smiled at Osric, showing too many teeth. "The Franks, kinsman?" He shaped kinsman with particular edge. They all heard the threat: Being kin will only take you so far. He sipped his Frankish mead. "I'll take my cut of that trade when we reach York for the baptism. And no doubt the bishop here will put in a word with his god once you donate an equal sum to the glory and beautification of his new church."

Osric had been king of his hall at Tinamutha, but here, by the Bay of the Beacon, Mulstan was king of his.

He was on his feet, cup in hand, making one of his rambling but heartfelt speeches welcoming the king and his household to his humble abode. The abode the king's niece had seen fit to grace just a few short years ago, which visit brought his dear wife and lady, Onnen, to him . . .

Hild found it eerie to see all the people in her life drawn together: Onnen, with Mulstan on her right, and Cian and Begu to her left. The king, without his usual coterie—Paulinus, Osric, and the æthelings had all headed straight to York from Arbeia—to Mulstan's right. Hild had chosen to sit on the left side, with Onnen's people, including her mother.

Breguswith and Onnen had reached some understanding. Begu had given her the news breathlessly that afternoon, jumbled in with news of Cædmon and Winty—that is, Winty's calf's calf, who looked just the same, even to the golden tips of her ears—and Guenmon. She thought

Guenmon and Gwladus would take to each other very well. And wait til Hild saw Onnen's twins! Plump as geese and only a little less toothless. Oh, but Hild didn't like geese. Plump as, as . . . pigeons! But Bán, Bán she was very sorry to say, had, according to Onnen, died just that winter of the horrible cough that swept through the people around the bay. And his dog, well, that was very sad. His dog had died just a moon before Bán himself . . .

"Why such a long face?" her mother asked as Mulstan wound up his speech and called for Swefred to *Play that song, you know the one.* "Not what you remember?"

"It's just the same. We're even eating Celfled's eels. Swefred will now sing the tale of the wight who haunts the wrack, and glare suspiciously at anyone who praises him too much."

"But?"

"But there are people missing."

"Yes." She laid a hand briefly on Hild's cheek, which startled Hild so much she nearly knocked her cup over. "There are always people missing. And sometimes I see their ghosts." She looked briefly at Cian, who was laughing at something Begu had said, and, in his polished mail, with long chestnut hair falling about his shoulders, looking every inch the foster-prince of the hall. His eye gleamed, his muscles shone like greased piglets, his bones were as strong as oak. He was the tallest man in the room and shone the brightest. A young god.

It was the closest they had ever come to speaking of it. "Are you . . . Do you mind?" Hild said.

"If I do, it's not the son or his mother I blame. Not any more." Another roar of laughter from down the table. "Even his laugh is the same."

And Hild had a sudden memory of her father tossing her in the air, laughing, but she didn't trust it. "Did he toss Hereswith in the air to make her laugh?"

Breguswith nodded. "He liked to see her hair fly about and shine in the sun. But Hereswith didn't like it. It made her cry."

"I miss her."

Breguswith nodded again. It was the most they had agreed on in years. "But she's well enough where she is. Dream of a son for her tonight, and maybe Eorðe will hear."

"Shouldn't you be praying to the Christ?"

"Ah," her mother said, and smiled. "I forgot."

Fursey wouldn't have trusted that smile, but Fursey wasn't there. Besides, his remedy would have been the same. "Let's persuade Onnen to give us some of the Gaulish wine Mulstan always has put by. Then let's drink. A lot. To those who are missing."

That night, Hild dreamt she crouched in the reeds by the spear-straight rhyne. Tin-grey clouds scudded overhead and willows rattled. In their boat, Bán and his dog Cú glided along the bank, Bán's little knife on the willow, *snick-snick-snick*, flashing in the watery light. Hild rose, waved. Bán smiled, and Cú's tongue lolled in a dog laugh.

Hild and Cian walked along the path by the smith's beck. Dark lingered under the trees and long slanting shadows fell over the water, where bats still swooped. The river smelt of night, but the early-spring grass along the path, pale green in the growing light, smelt of morning, fresh and sharp as new-forged iron.

Spotted woodpeckers, half a dozen, swooped into the wych elms, and all started hammering at once.

"They do that every spring," he said. He stopped. "Like a gang of tree cutters."

The birds fell silent, then one tapped, fell silent, another tapped, fell silent, another.

"More like Witganmot," she said.

"But shorter!" they said together, and laughed.

They walked some more.

"After you left, I came here a lot," he said. "I missed you showing me things, making them magic. So I decided to find them myself. Like this." He reached up into the newly fledged birch and pulled down a handful of tiny leaves, pale as a new kitten's eyes. He popped some in his mouth, offered the rest to her. "They taste like sorrel."

They walked on to the smithy, where the fire wasn't yet quite hot and the smith was happy to talk steel and edge with the thegn's foster-son. He kept looking at Hild's seax as he talked, and eventually she took pity on him, drew it, and offered it hilt-first over her forearm.

"Beautiful," he said. "Northern work, that. I'll just put a fresh edge on it, shall I?"

On the way back, kingfishers hunted where the bats had been, and morning held full sway.

Cian sighed.

"You'll miss it so much?"

He didn't say anything, then he shook himself. "We've three more days. Begu will want to show you every last cow."

"Winty's calf's calf."

"And I want you to see me spar with Mulstan. He's a wily old bull. I bet you couldn't get him to drop his shield."

"I bet I could." And she pushed him, and he pushed her back, and he slung his arm over her shoulder and she rested her hand on his belt and they walked that way, close together, all the way back to the hall.

Onnen, who was berating a houseman about cobwebs she had found in some dark corner, broke off when they entered.

"Mam, is Mulstan about? I want Hild to watch us cross swords."

"He's walking Celfled's son along the bounds."

"I thought they'd sorted that."

Onnen folded her arms. "You know Celfled. Nothing's ever sorted." She nodded to the houseman to be on his way, then said to Hild, "Guenmon made some of those pasties you like. You and I will take them up the south cliff, to the beacon." It wasn't a suggestion.

Hild insisted that they all go. Onnen was wise to her ways, though, and knew how to deal with that. She handed the girl little Onstan and picked up Mulfryth herself.

Little of course wasn't the right word. Each twin weighed more than a spring lamb.

As Hild had intended, Cian, carrying the sack of Guenmon's pasties— which he kept shifting from one side to the other—the chattering Begu, and Breguswith moved ahead of them up the steep cliff path, pulling themselves up using the stunted, still-leafless saplings along the path.

As Onnen and Hild fell farther behind and Begu's chatter faded, the only sound was the wind in the furze and the grass and the thistles and, a long way down, the steady roll and crash of the incoming tide.

Hild, with her long, strong legs and young lungs scrambled faster. Onnen climbed as fast as she could. By the time she got to the top, she was breathing hard. Hild reached down one-handed and hauled her up.

The girl still had manners, at least. She might look longingly at the church weathering into the dirt and the repaired thorn hedge but she stayed with Onnen while the older woman caught her breath. The others, Begu in the lead, were already halfway to the old beacon tower, which looked to have lost a few more stones since she last climbed this way.

They stood side by side, facing south and east, away from the wind, looking half out to sea, half at the figures in the distance. Begu had stopped and now seemed to be shrieking and laughing and pointing at something. The air smelt of salt.

Hild shifted Onstan to her other arm. He stayed fast asleep, thumb in his mouth. "He's big for his age," she said.

"Mulfryth's bigger. She takes after her father. Sadly, she also has his nose."

Hild leaned over to peer at Mulfryth's little face. Her eyes flicked open. Pale brown, almost amber, and fierce. "Hawks," Hild said. "Begu said they were like geese. But they're not."

"They're my centre now, these two." Onnen reached over and tucked Onstan's blanket more securely beneath his chin. "Begu's no longer my responsibility. She's yours."

"Yes."

The wind shifted, and Onnen thought she heard the clank of cowbells.

She'd said many hard things to the girl over the years, but this might end up being the hardest. The girl was too young to understand the depth of it, but she had to understand the importance.

She nodded to where, in the distance, Cian was shifting his sack yet again. "He always did hate carrying anything that wasn't a sword."

The girl nodded.

"You two are very close," Onnen said.

The girl glanced at her. "Yes."

Onnen wanted to hug her, smooth her hair, make it better. She hardened her heart. "You can't have him."

The girl frowned. "What—"

"You don't understand. But you will. For now, take heed."

The girl's gaze fastened on hers: clear, clever, stubborn. But Cian was her son.

"You can't have him. And you can't tell him why. Keeping him ignorant keeps him safe. Whatever he knows always did shine out of him. Like a beacon." Now the girl's eyes changed. That part at least she understood.

Below, waves rolled in long easy lines onto the beach. The girl, watching them, said, "I've never told him. I never will." A black-headed gull wheeled overhead, crying. She lifted her face to follow it. "But my mother says gossip flows into gaps."

"She's not wrong." That was the problem. Mother and daughter were both so rarely wrong they thought they never could be. "Yes. I'll start telling the stories again, the story of Cian taking the sword from Ceredig. I'll tell Guenmon. She already knows, but I'll remind her. And what Guenmon knows, all the wealh will know. Including the visitors. Then the king will know."

"He already knows that one. I told him."

"But this way, he'll know that everyone else knows. And the story will crowd out any other that might arise. And being thought as Ceredig's son, now that Elmet is wholly Edwin's, makes Cian useful to him. Useful men stay alive."

Hild found her way to the kitchen, and thanked Guenmon for the pasties.

Guenmon said, "Was there something wrong with them?"

"No. I liked them."

"Well, no need to sound surprised."

"It's not . . ." But she had no idea how to explain the puzzling conversation she'd just had with Onnen. "I'm glad you remembered I like tarragon."

"Well of course I remember. Reach me down one of those cups, now." Hild did. "I remember when you had to stand on a stool, too. Now don't go away. I want a word with you."

Another word. Hild hoped she would at least understand this one. She watched as Guenmon measured and ground spices, tipped them into two copper cups.

"Now." Guenmon handed Hild a cup of spiced wine. "It's about your bodywoman."

"Gwladus? Why? Where is she?"

"Poorly. I gave her something to drink."

"What—"

"What you should have given her a fortnight ago."

"She's—"

"Not anymore."

"Did it, was it—"

"The baby doesn't matter. It would only have been a slave, anyway. But it hurts to lose them. It hurts." Guenmon looked lightless for a moment, then huffed, impatient. "It's done. But you're to see it doesn't happen again. That lass is yours. Protect her."

For the next two days, Gwladus, pale and slow moving, was in the care of Guenmon; Begu happy to renew her acquaintance with the cows and goats; Cian showing off his ringed sword to the young men of the hall; and Breguswith and Onnen lost for hours gathering herbs and talking of old times, or sitting in the sun weaving quietly together, each with a twin at her side. The king was busy with Mulstan, discussing trade and sailing weather and the new wīc at York. No one needed a seer.

Hild was glad to escape the responsibilities she didn't quite understand and roam the moor.

She watched a goshawk rolling and diving over the gorse and heather, crying like a gull. She didn't see a mate; perhaps he soared and swooped for joy. She hiked along the cliff's edge, paused to listen to the rock pipits building their nest in a crevice and watch the male feed beetles to his mate. The eggs would come soon.

When she thought at all, she thought in British, the language of the high places, of wild and wary and watchful things. A language of resistance and elliptical thoughts.

She climbed the paths morning and evening, breathing the salt-sharp air, watching the slow spring dusk tighten around the shore like an adder and the sea turn to jet. She was glad to be alone, to be free, to be high above the world, where she could see everything coming. She had people to protect.

On the last afternoon she walked four miles north along the shore, over sand and shingle and long beach grass. By one rill, where low tangled hawthorn and gorse grew among the long sea grass, she found a row of tiny wrens and mouse pups spiked on thorns: the work of the wariangle, the butcher-bird.

She walked half a mile inland, checking blackthorn hedges, but the only nest she found was abandoned. By it were thorns hung with two caterpillars and a bee: the work of their young. All gone now, master and apprentice, flown to warmer climes. Like kings, they ravaged then moved on, leaving their trophies hanging from battlements, drying to husks, proclaiming, *My land, my law.*

Hild stood at the aft rail with Breguswith, watching the world slide by and the wake unfurl. The Humber was mushroom brown, still thick with spring silt. On the north bank, as they moved west and inland, the mud-flats became wolds, undulating folds of green grass dotted with flinty-coloured sheep and tiny white puffs of lambs.

"A lot of lambs this year," her mother said. "And their dams with good thick wool after the cold winter."

Hild nodded, idly pondering the wake, the little curls of dirty cream constantly being born and dying along the edge of the deep trough they cut through the water. There was a pattern there but she hadn't the words to describe it.

"I talked to Onnen about Aberford and the York wīc. She'll watch for the good wool that comes down from the north, from Tinamutha. Aberford will make a good place for collecting, sorting, and spinning in winter, as you said. Though I think somewhere along these banks, too, might be handy."

Hild liked listening to her mother planning to build, rather than destroy or take. It felt as comforting as a larder full of food with only a month til spring. It made her feel safe; that their web, their weft and warp, was wide and strong.

"And between the York wīc and Lindum port we can reach the Frisians and Franks ourselves. We won't have to go through Gipswīc with sulky Eorpwald taking his cut. Tinamutha and the Bay of the Beacon will feed trade with the men of the north, even west across to Rheged and east over the North Sea."

On the bank a woman, dress kilted to her waist, threw something in her bark basket and shaded her eyes to watch them glide by. "Not the Irish, though."

Breguswith shook her head. "Nor the Scots. Gwynedd still has that trade. And a fine, lordly gesith to trumpet their wares." She nodded to where Cian, bold cloak thrown back from his shoulders, was leaning with Lintlaf against the rails midships and passing comments on the folk, mostly women, working in the bows. Lintlaf offered him the jar of beer he was drinking. Cian shook his head. "We must make him a good Anglisc cloak that he likes better."

"I like his cloak," Hild said. "It suits him."

"Something in blue. The blue that the women of Northumbria make better than any in the world."

"But not royal blue."

"No."

The water slished. The sail rippled.

"No doubt the king will soon be putting Cadwallon and Gwynedd in their place," Breguswith said. "And, meanwhile, there's always Dyfneint."

"Do you know anyone in Dyfneint?"

Breguswith shook her head.

"Nor do I," Hild said, watching the way Lintlaf watched Gwladus, who stood over Morud, bossing him with close to her usual vigour on the proper way to scrub a pot. "But I know who does."

It was evening by the time the ship docked on the south bank of the Ouse. Ropes were thrown, gangplanks dropped fore and aft, and people disembarked with the usual din of near disaster and swift efficiency that Hild had come to associate with the meeting of ship and land. The deck swarmed with men, all shouting, all carrying things. The ship, now seized tightly to the dock, felt stiff and lifeless underfoot.

The king and most of his retinue were already forming up on the muddy landing near the bridge. Horses milled. Hild stood by the fore gangplank, looked about for Gwladus, thought she saw the flash of her pale hair among the heave of men unstepping the mast. There, midships, pressed back against the larboard rail . . .

"No," said Hild, and a man turned, thinking she was talking to him. "Lady?"

She picked up a batten. "Out of my way."

Then she stood before Lintlaf and Gwladus. Lintlaf, hand still white and tight around Gwladus's arm, turned, face slack with drink.

Hild said, "Gwladus. You will take my bag to shore. Now."

Lintlaf stood there, mazed as an ox just herded from the byre. Hild tapped his hand with the end of her batten.

He blinked, let go. Gwladus rubbed her arm, glared at him.

"Bitch," Lintlaf said. His breath was sour with ale.

Gwladus spat at him. He raised his hand.

Hild drew his gaze with her batten. "Don't touch her."

He put his hand on his seax.

She hefted the batten: good, weathered oak. "I'll break your arm."

"She's wealh."

She set her feet. "She's mine."

His face puckered like a purse with a pulled string. "So. The freemartin has finally learnt what it's all for."

She hefted the batten again. "You will not touch her."

He considered, spat, took his hand from his seax. "She's soiled, spoiled, and sullen. You're welcome to her."

He pushed himself from the rail and walked with care to the gangplank.

Gwladus slid her hand around Hild's waist and whispered in her ear, "Thank you, lady." Then she stepped away. "Where's your bag?"

"My bag?" For a moment, she had no idea what Gwladus was talking about. She still felt that warm whisper in her ear. She gripped the rail. Had someone untied the ship?

"There it is," Gwladus said, and left Hild standing with batten in one hand, rail in the other.

It was strange to be back in York only a few weeks after Bebbanburg and Yeavering. The new women's wing was ready, a row of rooms running at a right angle from the hall. The apartment Hild shared with Begu was three small rooms: a bedroom with a curtained doorway to the chamber where Gwladus and others slept, which had a stout door to the next, in which slept Morud and a guard, often Oeric. At the mouth of the corridor, the queen's men stood guard over the whole wing: the queen's suite, Clotrude's, Breguswith's.

Like Osric's house at Arbeia, its bones were stone and brick, but it was rebuilt with elm and oak and pine and hung with tapestry and embroideries. Their bed was big, with a padded bench at the foot, and a little table against the northwest wall under the high window—shuttered now, but not proof against the smell of yeast and rising dough and, in the mornings, baking bread from the giant ovens to the east. There were specially built shelves, faced with polished slate, for lamps.

A taper burnt there now, lighting their supper.

Begu leaned forward for her ale, and a curl of hair dabbled in her lamb stew. Hild reached over and lifted it out without comment.

"How am I supposed to keep it out of things if we can't bind it for the ritual? And what if it's windy in the morning?"

It would be windy. It was Œstremonath. "The walls should shelter the church well enough." The church was only a frame and roof in the principia courtyard.

Begu sucked the hair clean and tucked it back into its braid. "Here, eat some more. Who knows how long we'll have to go hungry tomorrow."

The baptism of a king would involve more ceremony than that of an infant. A king, two æthelings, Hild and Begu, Osric and Oswine and little Osthryth, Coelfrith, Coifi, and two dozen assorted thegns and gesiths, including Oeric.

Hild ate some of the stew.

"I hope I get all the words right," Begu said.

"You'll be fine."

"He seems like such a solemn god. And fussy. Now, look, you've eaten the last of the stew." She twisted on her stool. "Gwladus!" Gwladus put her head through the curtain. "Oh, for Eorðe's sake. What do I keep telling you? Don't pop your head in and out like a woodpecker from its hole. Someone will bite it off. Try to behave." She lifted her bowl. Gwladus nodded and vanished. "Why can't she learn? I should have her whipped."

Gwladus did it because she got to lean forward and show her breasts. Showing off her best points was a habit that had saved her life more than once. And she did have good points.

"They don't seem to like jokes," Begu said. "Now what's that look for? The Christians. They don't like jokes. I don't think their god does, either. I asked the queen for a funny story about the Christ, like the one about Ing tricking Herthe with the acorns, and she had to think for a while, and then told me about two villages called Sodom and Gomorrah and God-the-Father turning someone's wife into salt, which wasn't funny, and a horrible story about a man called Abram who was supposed to kill his son just because this God-the-Father said so. Not even any bargaining. Just obedience, like a wealh. Imagine! Imagine what Edwin king would say to Thunor if he suggested he kill Eadfrith or Osfrith just because. Which reminds me, Clotrude is very near, your ma thinks so, too. And she thinks it's a son."

Hild nodded, wondering about Hereswith. *I am with child.* The letter had only come two months ago but who knew when it was sent?

"What will I do if I get the words wrong tomorrow?"

"You won't," Hild said. "All you have to do is say your name. You know your name. And then swear against their demon Satan and for the Christ."

"And his father, and the holy breath—or is it flame? That bit never makes sense."

"No." She didn't like to think about it. James talked about a Holy Fire, a cleansing fire. Perhaps it meant being cleansed of the memory of the grit and slide of blade into spine. One quick sear, he'd said, and done, like a cauterising iron. But he had never tended a cauterised wound. Most swelled, turned angry, and leaked stinking pus. But her mother would have mentioned pain. But perhaps her mother hadn't killed as many people as she had. She put it from her mind, scraped the bowl clean, and licked her fingers. The lamb tasted good this year.

"And I don't understand why the Christ, or whichever one it is, is so squeamish. No blood in the church. No woman with her monthly bleeding. It makes no sense."

James hadn't thought to mention that to Hild. Perhaps they didn't think a hægtes bled.

"And wearing white. What god likes plain old white and no jewels?"

"It's so those priests can see if you're bleeding," Gwladus said, putting the bowl of stew on the table, along with a wedge of crumbly new white cheese and fresh watercress.

"What would they do if you are?" Begu said.

"No doubt nail you to the door, like the Christ," Gwladus said. "And jam a hat of thorns on your head." She laid her hand, brief and light as a drift of hawthorn blossom, on Hild's head.

Begu didn't notice. "You'd think their god was a slave, the way he let himself be treated." She ladled herself some stew. The curtain swished behind Gwladus. "Your bleeding's due soon, isn't it?"

"Not tomorrow."

"Better wear a rag just in case, or it's a hat of thorns for you." She paused, spoon over her bowl. "Do you suppose we'll feel any different? I asked Cian if he felt different, afterwards. He said he felt . . . better. But he wouldn't tell me how."

No, thought Hild, because then he'd have to explain what he'd felt bad about, and neither of them wanted Begu to know what they did in war.

"Then I asked your mam, and she put on her meek-as-milk face and said it made her a better person, but the queen was listening, so you know how much that means."

Hild nodded. Saying what made the people in power think well of her was as much a habit for Breguswith as showing her curves was for Gwladus.

"Do you think it odd that we'll be swearing fealty to a god, like a gesith to his king?" When Hild didn't say anything, Begu sighed. "Now what are you thinking about?"

"Um? Oh. My mother. And Gwladus. How they're not so different."

To Hild's astonishment, Begu just nodded. She picked up her knife. "Let's eat some of this lovely cheese. Let's eat a lot of it. It'll be a long morning." She paused, cheese in hand. "What do you suppose the body of a god tastes like?"

"It's bread. Like the bread Coifi buried at the root of the hedge."

"But bread dipped in god juice. I expect it tastes like the air from a forge, buttered."

Buttered?

". . . cheese, then you can tell me about this Uinniau who's coming from Rheged to witness for the king."

Uinniau, prince of Rheged, sister-son of Rhoedd king, stood by the font. He was older than Cian, and though he had done some growing, he still was not tall. He still was freckled. His eyes still were the clear hazel Hild remembered. But he was no longer the boy who had bounced like an apple on the back of his too-large mare on the way from Caer Luel to Broac. He was there to stand in for his uncle as British witness to the baptism of Edwin, overking of the Anglisc. He wore the air of power the role lent him.

The font was the beautifully carved stone Paulinus had taken from Elmet, now mortared over the old well in the principia courtyard and bright with gilding and fresh red and blue paint. The font took up the north corner of what would become the church but was now merely a freshly sawn timber frame and a roof, open to the air. Beyond the brick of the principia, wind twisted the clouds this way and that, sometimes tearing them open and loosing flurries of cold rain, sometimes driving the sky clean for a moment and making way for a brief flood of daffodil-yellow sun. When the sun shone for more than a few heartbeats, it raised a strong smell of the dung with which the gardens north and west of the principia had been manured that morning.

Uinniau—and the priests, and the baptismal candidates and their sponsors—stayed dry and relatively sheltered. The crowd spilling into the courtyard was not so lucky. They didn't seem to mind. They'd all enjoyed the big Easter breakfast the queen had ordered for anyone within the walls who asked. Anyone who wasn't about to be baptised.

Hild tried not to think about her empty belly or how tired she was of standing. The morning had started with singing in hall, then a procession—led by Stephanus with the great cross, James with the choir, priests with censers, Paulinus with his crook, then the white-robed candidates, then their sponsors—cutting smoothly through the crowd to the church. Then the great Easter Mass began, complete with special blessings of a giant candle—thick around as a gesith's thigh and nearly as tall as Hild, carved and gilded—and the water in the well, or font.

At the very dawn of creation your Spirit breathed on the waters, making them wellsprings of all holiness . . .

Two priests swung censers over the font. Wind whipped the heavy smoke into the women's side of the royal party. Wilnoð coughed. She tried to stifle it, but that just made her eyes water. At least it covered the smell of dung.

Paulinus began the proclamation of the word of God. Begu, in the second rank of white-clad candidates and short enough to be half hidden, frankly leaned on Hild and shut her eyes. Hild, always visible, always watched, settled an attentive look on her face and drifted away into the music still cycling through her head. Cool, clear, endless as sky. Perhaps it would help with any cleansing burn to come.

Begu stirred and Hild came back to the moment. Stephanus was passing along the rows of candidates, touching a glistening thumb to each forehead.

. . . oil of catechumens . . . liberation from sin and its instigator, the devil . . .

She had to bend slightly for Stephanus to reach her forehead. His touch was light and quick. The oil didn't seem to smell of anything.

. . . profession of faith . . .

And the world slowed, for this was the oath.

All around her, she felt chests rise and lungs fill, ready to give voice to the words they had learnt. Then she would be baptised and god's flame would burn her, or not.

Paulinus's gaze fastened on her.

He, at least, hoped for her to burn. She breathed deep. She was Anglisc. She would not burn. She would endure and hold true to her oath. An oath, a bond, a boast. A truth, a guide, a promise. To three gods in one. To the pattern. For even gods were part of the pattern, even three-part gods. The pattern was in everything. Of everything. Over everything.

"God the Father," she said. God the pattern. "God the Son, God the Holy Spirit . . ."

All around her, words took shape and rolled from their mouths, high-pitched and low, harsh and smooth, loud and soft. They spoke together, oathed together, breathed together. Her kith, her kin, her king. Her people.

Her heart beat with it, her tears fell with it, her spirit soared with it. Here, now, they were building a great pattern, she could feel it, and she would trace its shape one day: that was her wyrd, and *fate goes ever as it must*. Today she was swearing to it, swearing here, with her people.

She watched the king bend to the font and the water poured three times on his head in the name of the Father, the Son, and the Holy Ghost. He flinched but didn't burn. Paulinus welcomed him to God with a kiss on the cheek and a great gold-and-garnet cross to hang about his neck, then turned to her.

She met his gaze, agate to jet. She would not flinch, not even if the water turned to a river of fire. She stepped forward, bent her head, and set her will.

The water was cold, like ice, like flame, and she clamped her muscle to her bone so hard that she felt turned to stone. The world faltered then resumed and the queen was kissing her cheek, welcoming her to God, and she wasn't burnt.

She hardly felt the queen fastening a cross around her neck or leading her from the font. Watched through a daze as Paulinus poured the water three times over Begu's head, anointed her on forehead, breast, and both palms, and Breguswith came forward to kiss her cheek.

White-clad back after white-clad back bent over the font. After the king and his family came his counsellors. Coifi and his priests. Rank after rank of gesiths joining Christ, now their god, god of Yffings.

When Paulinus turned from the font to the crowd and raised both arms—his arms were very thin Hild saw, very dark against the cream and gold of his robes—time began to flow in its proper course. The Crow cried out in a great voice that they had put on Christ, they had risen with Christ, and they would share the glory of Christ. The air under the roof bulged with choir song and the crowd cheered. She was baptised to Christ—their name for the pattern, her path, her wyrd. She was still herself.

Uinniau smiled at her and winked.

The hall heaved. Every freeman and woman within miles, all wearing their best, squeezed behind long tables; Oeric sat in his white robe with two lesser priests of Woden—no, not priests, not anymore—and several gesiths. Every servingman and woman was pressed into service; even Gwladus, even Morud. The hall roared with conversation, and despite the raw weather, it was hot. The thick slippery scent of the oil on her hands, the chrism of olive and balsam, stuck in her throat. Hild wiped her hands surreptitiously on the board cloth, but it didn't make much difference to the smell.

She ran her finger around the collar of her robe, as though it itched, but it was the gold chain around her neck she felt. It was thinner than she was used to, a woman's chain but bearing a massive gold cross. The great garnets flanked by pearls running down the centre looked like the bloodied froth that flew back in ropes from the bit of a hard-driven horse and the chain cut into her neck. But she couldn't take it off, and she couldn't look uncomfortable in it; it was the Christ's symbol and half the people were still wondering if she would vanish with a wail and a puff of smoke.

Begu reached over and lifted the cross as though admiring it. "Better?" She hefted it. "It must weigh half a pound. Not very practical though. That great big knuckle of a thing will catch on everything. Still." She weighed it again admiringly. "You should hold it yourself every now and again. It looks pious, and it'll save your neck until we can get you a thicker chain." She let it go. "Go on."

Hild cradled the cross in her right hand. Christian.

Begu lifted her own cross—silver gilt, from Breguswith—and leaned in to Hild. "What does the writing say?"

" 'In Christ's hands.' "

"Sounds like the kind of thing you'd say before running into a burning byre. Not that I'd ever run into a burning byre. You'd have to be mad. But that's what it sounds like. Are we really supposed to long for death and a seat at Christ's right hand? Well, I'd be on the left. Maybe you'd be on the right. Christ might look at your seax and your bare arms and get confused."

Hild smiled. Begu was still most definitely Begu. "I'm sure he'd sort it out. James says Christ is all-knowing and all-powerful. He could put me in both places at once if he wanted."

"Or maybe all three, or, no, six! At the right and the left of the Father *and* the Son *and* the Holy Ghost. Though . . . a ghost . . ." She frowned. "What would a ghost look like in heaven?"

Hild tried to imagine a ghost sitting in the golden light of heaven. Ghosts grew from the thin grey mist of hollow hills, the damp and drizzle of dusk, the breath of the dead. They drifted and glimmered along boundary ditches on moonless nights . . .

"Are all the men of Rheged Christians?"

Hild blinked.

"Well?"

Hild followed her gaze to the other end of the king's board, where Uinniau was seating himself after a toast to the king.

"Why didn't you tell me he was so handsome?"

"I didn't think of it. I didn't notice."

"Well, he's noticing you."

Uinniau was smiling in their direction and raising his cup. Hild raised her own.

"And people are noticing him noticing." Begu nodded at Cian, at the second bench. "He used to scowl just like that when his ma first cast her lot with Fa." Begu giggled at her foster-brother and stuck out her tongue.

The world sharpened suddenly, as brilliant and bright as when she got rain in her eye. She saw everything: a lick of Cian's hair curled in front of his right ear; Breguswith sitting with her back to Osric, talking instead to the queen; the queen— "The queen's breasts are bound."

"Haven't you been listening to a word I've said? She's given Eanflæd to nurse. Now that the king's baptised, she'll get to work giving him a son. Or maybe she already has. He's certainly looking pleased with himself."

Edwin was leaning back, chin on one hand, smiling, eyes half lidded, listening to Osfrith and Clotrude exchange some witticism. It was a look Hild recognised: a cat watching a stunned mouse, in no hurry to kill. Who was his smile for?

"Ah, now, you've smeared mint sauce on your sleeve," Begu said. "Never mind, we'll have to dye everything anyway if they're to be of any use. What a waste and fuss for a bit of water and a few words. Though at least we didn't have to blunder about in a muddy river. Oh, oh, he's looking at me." She tucked her braid behind her ear, untucked it, and turned carrot red.

Hild was on her feet before her thoughts caught up with her body and she realised Begu meant Uinniau. *Uinniau* was looking. Not the king. The king barely knew Begu existed.

The air in her lungs evaporated in a puff that she turned to a laugh, and she sat down. Breathed. Smiled.

Begu glared at her. "It's not funny."

She smoothed Begu's hair. Her hand trembled. "Sshh, sshh. Your hair is fine. You look lovely. White is a good colour for you. You look like . . . like apple blossom."

Begu allowed herself to be offered a morsel of lamb. Hild smiled some more and breathed. Behind her smile, her thoughts whirred like a pole lathe, back and forth, shaving away the layers. As she let Morud refill her cup, as she commented on the food, as she chatted about the best way to dye already woven cloth, she studied the table.

Paulinus was standing by a torch-lit pillar with Stephanus, who had arrived the day before from Elmet, almost unnoticed in the press of representatives from neighbouring kingdoms. Hild thought she'd even spotted a man from Craven, though not Dunod himself. For once, Stephanus was not taking notes. For once, Paulinus had drunk more than a single cup of wine: Edwin's baptism was the beginning of his triumph. And Edwin still needed him. So, the king's smile was not for Paulinus.

Her mother was still talking to the queen, who listened intently. Hild couldn't think of any reason why Edwin would go for her now. Not her mother.

Next to her mother, Oswine stabbed sullenly at his trencher with his eating knife. But he was an unimportant piece in the game. Osthryth, with her white robe and pointy teeth, looked more like an ermine than ever. She was even less important than her brother, unless Edwin needed to appease some king with a marriage.

No. Edwin didn't need to appease anyone today. He was baptised. His plans were in place.

Next to Oswine, Osric sat like a bulldog in a white robe. His little brown eyes alternately tracked Breguswith—she was ignoring him steadfastly—and the king. The king, pretending to be unaware of his kinsman's regard, gestured to Coelfrith, said something in his ear, and leaned back again. Coelfrith left the table quietly. Osric watched him, watched the reeve's nod to the scop on the way out, and the scop's answering nod, and straightened. His shoulders went back—the hound waiting to be tossed the heart of the kill. Hild caught the glint of Edwin's teeth before he hid his widening smile with a forced yawn and covered both with his hand.

Osric.

Now the pattern was clear: her mother, not staying with Osric at Arbeia; her mother, ignoring him now; her mother, getting baptised early, growing close to the queen, reweaving Onnen into her plans. Her mother, changing sides, so gradually, so carefully that even Hild hadn't noticed. She had understood, long before Hild, that Edwin was ready to topple his cousin.

At the doorway, Coelfrith, carrying a three-legged table and followed by two of his men—one carrying something brick-shaped, wrapped in closely woven embroidered linen, another with a long, finely carved birch box—made a brief eddy as he entered.

Osric stroked his moustaches with that pleased look men wear when they expect acclaim. Edwin stood.

The scop played a dramatic chord.

Edwin took his time catching the gaze of all his people: the beady black of the Crow, Uinniau's open hazel, Breguswith's bright, bright blue, Coifi's clay brown, the æthelings' blue-grey, the black-brown of Osthryth and Oswine and Osric.

Edwin, king of Deira and Bernicia, of all Northumbria, overking of the Angles, lord of the north, and most powerful man on the isle, smiled and raised his cup to Osric, who inclined his head and swelled with pleasure. Edwin gestured for him to stand.

This was how it would be for her, she realised, when Edwin king decided he no longer needed a seer. She would stand, plump and fed and brushed like a sacrificial cow, with gilded horns and a ribbon around her neck, too stupid to know she was being led to slaughter.

Edwin poured the white mead with his own hand and held out the cup to Osric.

Hild wanted to throw bread at his head. *Think! It should be poured by the queen!* But the queen watched impassively, and Hild kept her face and hands still. Osric took the cup.

"Our kingdom is growing. We are strong. Yet we need strong men on our right hand to guide the farmers of our borderlands, strong men to crush the vermin who whisper of other kings in other lands, to smash those who skulk like stray dogs in search of the weak and yap at their betters from behind trees."

The scop must have come up with that.

"My counsellors and wise men say to me: Lord King, the Christ might now be on our side, but the priests tell us their god, our god, helps those who help themselves. And they say, 'Lord King, our people need a strong man to look up to. It is time,' they tell me, 'to appoint ealdormen, to seat men as princes. Known men, trusted men. Strong men. Kinsmen. Men to protect the people and command the respect of all.'" He smiled at Osric over the rim of his cup. "They said this to me at Yule, and I said, 'Be patient.' They said this to me again, yesternight, and I said, 'But tell me what kinsman will be willing to leave his fine and comfortable house to take up this burden? Who will fight in the king's name to bring fallow land under the plough, to open dark forests to the light?'"

Around the hall men were nodding. They saw, they thought they saw, where the king was heading. Elmet, they whispered to their less sharp neighbours, the king will give his cousin Elmet.

But she knew her uncle. And the fruits of Elmet did not sit in long birch boxes or heavy brick shapes.

"'Who?' I asked them. 'You have sons,' they said—"

Osric paled.

"—but: 'No,' I said. 'I have other plans for my sons. And I know just the man I need.'"

Osric flushed.

Edwin's smile widened. So many teeth. "And so, Lord Osric, kinsman, are you willing to leave the lands known to your kith and kin since time out of mind to take up this honour on behalf of your king?"

"Cousin," Osric said. "My king." His voice shook with sincerity: ealdorman of Elmet! More or less a king. He would give anything. "I am willing." His men drummed on the board.

"Then, Lord Osric, Osric Yffing . . ." The hall breathed, one great lung, in and out, in and out. This would be something to tell their grandchildren: They were there when the Kingdom of Elmet became part of Northumbria forever. The scops would sing of this. "I name you Lord and Ealdorman of Craven."

Hild wondered how the scop would sing of the two smiles. The king's spreading like melting lard in a pan, wider and wider. The ealdorman's widening, jerking, spreading tremulously, wiped out, gone. Even his lips went pale.

She imagined the roaring in his ears.

". . . yesterday of Dunod's death . . . our shield against the treachery of the men of the north . . . friendship with the loyal men of Rheged as reaffirmed by Prince Uinniau . . ."

His legs would be shaking, the world turning black at its edges, but he had to stay upright. His eyes seemed even smaller than before, confused, like a badger driven from its sett and facing a ring of torches.

Then Æthelburh was standing by her husband, and Coelfrith placed the small oak table, carved and inlaid with Edwin's boar's-head blazon in red gold, before the king and queen. Coelfrith's men laid the small covered brick and the long box on the boar's head. Coelfrith lifted the embroidered cloth to reveal a pig of iron, spotted with rust, despite the glistening grease. Hild could smell it from where she stood: raw iron, the smell of delving and hammering and stoking. He lifted the lid on the birch box: a whole salmon, dried and smoked. The smells of autumn: rust and smoke and hunger. Autumn and the ending of Osric's hopes.

"Priest," Edwin said, and Coifi jerked and swayed but did not, quite, step forward. Paulinus did. He lifted the embroidered cloth in both hands and waited. Osric stumbled out from behind his bench to take the oath he could not refuse.

Paulinus put Osric's right hand on the box. Edwin and Æthelburh laid theirs on top, and the Crow draped the cloth over all.

Paulinus spoke for a long time: of sacred trust; loyalty to the king, beloved of Christ; of the people of Craven. Long enough for Osric to begin to understand what he had been tricked into. The king was taking his house, his family's house. Edwin the Deceiver was sending him, loyal subject and kinsman, once-and-no-more ætheling of Deira, to the godforsaken wilds of Craven, land of leaping salmon and the stink of pig iron. A land jammed up against the base of the western mountain spine, full of streams rushing down ironstone hills, full of shivering birch and shaking wealh, a land so worthless that no one had bothered to take it away from Dunod.

Long enough, too, for Coifi's face to mirror his sudden, bitter understanding of his new place: no longer chief priest of the chief god but a simple man without a sword. A man with nothing.

Uinniau hung upside down from the low limb of an apple tree, laughing up at Hild. It was the only apple tree inside the new wooden walls around what would be the wīc on the west side of the big river.

Cian sat on the grass with his back to them. Begu was on the riverbank, making a flower chain from dandelions. Oeric had been pressed into holding them for her.

Uinniau laughed again. "I'm stuck."

Hild reached down. "Swing a bit and give me your hand." He swung, she caught his hand and hauled. He came up. Hild dropped down next to him. They sat facing each other, astride the bough. Uinniau had blossom in his hair.

Hild picked some of it off, rolled the tiny petals idly between her fingers.

He pointed to the mound of dirt growing in the fork of the rivers. "It won't be a very big tower."

"Tall enough to shoot fire arrows onto the deck of a ship."

"What about chains across the river?"

Hild blinked. And when she didn't say anything he tilted his head back and looked at her down his nose with all the arrogance of a prince.

"It's been a long time since Broac. I'm short, not a child."

She sighed. "You're right. I'm sorry."

He waved the apology away. "You and I, we should be friends. One day, perhaps, if I'm . . . Well. Perhaps those days will never come again to Rheged and the north." He shrugged, the kind of shrug that went with songs of the Old North: an elegy for what once was great. "Your uncle is making himself a name," he said. "He's like Arthur come again."

She flicked the rolled-up petal at him. "No, he isn't."

He grinned. "Some people like flattery."

"Not me."

He peered down at Cian, out at Begu and Oeric, at his hands. Finally he looked at her. "So we'll speak truth, you and I?"

She thought about it. She liked the feel of him. He was clever, but straight-grained. Sound as an oak staff. She nodded.

"What will happen to Osric?"

"He'll go to Craven and brood in his upland hall, plotting to take back Arbeia from Osfrith and Clotrude, pouring his bitterness into Oswine's ear and filling him with twisty dreams of being king of all Deira." She stripped a leaf from the branch overhead, turned it this way and that. "Just like, I imagine, Eanfrith in Pictland, and the other Idings with the Dál Riata."

"Such dreams are not for you?"

"It's not my wyrd. Besides, they're hopeless." Speaking straight felt different. She found she liked it.

"Perhaps not if you . . . they had allies." She threw the leaf at him. He watched it flutter down, then shrugged. "Will they, Osric and Oswine, try to ally with the Idings in secret?"

"Why would the Idings keep it secret?"

Uinniau nodded. The middle Idings had a claim to Deira through Acha Yffing, Edwin's sister, as well as to Bernicia through their father, Æthelfrith Iding. If they had Osric Yffing on their side, they would shout it out and march.

"It's more likely Osric would try to ally with Eanfrith." The eldest Iding, son of Bebba. "Osric would take Deira, Eanfrith Bernicia. But my uncle will be watching for that."

"Cadwallon would be a surer bet as an ally," he said. "Or Penda."

"Not even Osric would trust Cadwallon. Not even for an hour. As for Penda . . ."

"No one knows him."

She nodded. "They say he's clever."

"They say you're clever, that you see into men's hearts." His hazel eyes shone with something. Perhaps it was the reflection of new leaves. She hoped so. "Hild. I—"

"How's Rhianmelldt?"

"Rhianmelldt? She's . . . no better."

Hild thought of the fey child she had met in Caer Luel, that ravaged ælf.

"Hild, please. Listen to me."

For a moment, she was tempted to push him out of the tree. She didn't want to hear his moony words. He was going to spoil it all. But she was Hild, king's seer and light of the world. She didn't push princes out of apple trees. She motioned for him to speak.

"The lady Begu. Does she like me?"

A bee bumped into her hand. Hild waved it away, and it sizzled crossly against the trunk for a heartbeat or two before it found a way around.

"I think she does," he said. "But you know her best. Would she . . ." He turned the same carrot colour Begu had at the feast. "I'm a man of Rheged. But sister-son to the king. Only, who should I . . . I don't . . ."

It was interesting how people lost their words when they liked someone. As though it drained their senses.

"Please, say something."

Hild pointed down.

Begu stood at the base of the tree with a chain of dandelions around her head, like a crown, like a princess. She stood on her tiptoes and held another out to Uinniau. "I made one for you."

They walked along the new hedge: Uinniau and Begu in their circlets of golden dandelion, laughing and talking—though, as far as Hild could tell, about nothing very much—followed by Cian and Hild, and, a few paces back, Oeric.

The sky was busy with birds—siffsaffs and blackcaps, nuthatches and greenfinches—and the river was at slack tide, quieter than usual, smelling of spring: mud, ducks on their nests of twigs, caterpillars, the fresh sawn smell of the beaver dam, newly moved earth where shoots pushed through to the light. More bumblebees buzzed and bumped over the hedge's freshly leafed hazel and the pink-and-white snow of blackthorn and hawthorn blossom.

Cian was a thundercloud.

"Look at the thorns," he said loudly. Uinniau and Begu turned. "That one's the size of my thumb." He waved at the road disappearing arrow-straight to the northwest and Rheged. "By summer it'll take an army with axes to break through."

"Rheged is not your enemy."

Cian gave him a look that would scorch iron. "No," he said, meaning, *Not today.* "But there are men north of Rheged. And if they got a mad notion to march down Dere Street to the wīc, they'd get a nasty surprise."

"None would be fool enough to try surprise. Your king—"

"The overking."

"The overking has told the world how strong his new wīc is. Besides, the men of Rheged keep their ears close to the ground. And Rhoedd king sends his assurance to Northumbria that Rheged, and beyond us Alt Clut, is with you."

"Oh, indeed." Cian clapped the young prince on the back—harder than necessary, Hild thought. A reminder that, while Uinniau was a princeling, Cian topped him by a head, that he was a thegn's—an Anglisc thegn's—foster-son, and that Uinniau was walking with his foster-sister.

Begu rolled her eyes at Hild, but her lips were full and her cheeks flushed and she skipped along like a new-born kid.

Begu sighed again and kicked at the covers for good measure. Hild, emerging from a half dream—of swimming naked as a seal, water coursing over her skin, between her legs—propped herself up on her elbow. The waning moon lit the room enough to see that her gemæcce's face had that stubborn set Hild knew well, the my-fa-the-thegn-will-make-you-give-that-to-me look. "What?"

"Rhianmelldt."

"What about her?"

"Whoever marries her could be king-in-waiting of Rheged."

"So?"

"And who wouldn't want to be king of Rheged? Even if it means taking a woman to wife whose mind is at a slant."

Hild waited.

"Uinny says she sometimes hears voices and bangs her head on the wall."

Hild nodded.

"They say she was pretty once."

"She was pretty when I met her."

"Perhaps she bangs her face, too. But some princeling will marry her anyway, and then he'll have to fight Uinny to be king-in-waiting."

Hild knew where this was going, but questions would only send Begu's thoughts flying in all directions.

Begu fixed her eyes on the strange smooth ceiling over their bed. "To be king, he would have to marry well. Very well. A thegn's daughter won't do."

"He didn't say that."

Begu turned to face Hild. Her breath was fresh with the elm seeds she'd been eating lately, ever since she gave Uinniau his circlet of dandelions. "He didn't have to. People look at him and see a child."

Hild couldn't disagree.

"He'd need to marry someone formidable. Someone like you." Begu flopped on her back again. "No, he didn't say that, either. There's no point. After all, you'll marry someone much more important."

She couldn't disagree with that, either. So she stroked Begu's forehead, smoothing back her hair. "Does Uinniau want so badly to be a king?"

Begu laughed, but it was a soft laugh, quite grown-up, and it made Hild long to hold her and shield her from the world.

"If you don't want to be a queen, all will be well. Think. Uinniau didn't grow up to be heir. That was his brother. I don't think he wants it. And once Rhianmelldt marries her king-in-waiting, Uinniau can please himself. He can marry you."

"But Rhianmelldt's a child. She won't marry for years. Years! You don't know what it's like!" Begu reached for Hild's hand, laid it on her belly. "Here. That's where I feel it. It's like . . . It makes me feel wild as the autumn and nervous as a kitten, and the world is big and new. I smell everything, I hear everything, and inside I feel . . ." Under her hand, Hild felt Begu's blood beating, thump-thump, thump-thump, like an Irish drum. "It's like, I feel like a leaf on a river pouring over a fall—I'm being hurried along, then sucked under. I look at his arms and his shoulders and I'm drowning. I want to lick them, I want to gnaw at them like a teething puppy. No, not like a puppy, like a wolf. I want to tear him apart, eat him up. You can't stop teeth from growing. I can't wait years."

"You don't have to wait to marry for that." She imagined bodies in the dark. The panting. Hægtes in a cyrtel . . .

"But I want to be by him forever. I want to hear his silly laugh—he sounds like a sheep, have you noticed?—at night. I want to watch him split wood, stack flax, practice spear and shield. Oh, I love to watch his skin move on his bones when he swings a sword with Cian. And his smell. He smells like a young colt, new and bright. What does Cian smell like?"

"Hot iron. Sometimes copper. And salt." Hild lifted her hand from Begu's belly. "We can watch them tomorrow, if you like."

"And maybe you'll think of a way for Rhianmelldt to marry someone soon?"

"Maybe," Hild said, but she couldn't think of any man her uncle would approve of.

She forgot about her dream of swimming, set aside the nameless yearning, and thought about Rheged. Who could her uncle offer to Rhoedd, which of his kinsmen could he control? Three days ago, she would have suggested Oswine, but after yesterday, that would be madness. Who could Edwin trust, who would both suit a British kingdom and be thought great enough for Rhoedd's daughter?

18

✦

IN YORK, the days warmed and opened. Bluebells began to dot the west woods. Crabapple blossomed. The first larks flew at dusk. Along the little river, kingfishers caught newts and water beetles, and on the big river when Hild walked with her mother and the queen—talking, as always, of wool and trade—she saw the tiny paw prints of otter kits.

On the morning that she heard the first cuckoo—so early!—Uinniau went back to Rheged. He left with many promises to return, and Begu nailed a smile on her face and wept in private; for a few days she didn't have the heart even to threaten Gwladus with a whipping. Hild wondered if this might be partly due to the change in Gwladus: always to hand, always ready with just what Hild wanted—hot bread, cold water, soothing brushstrokes.

Stitchwort blossomed in white spatters along the riverbanks and figwort grew yellow beneath the great hedge. The world filled with the liquid melody of thrush song, and tits hung upside down from every bush.

Hild's restlessness rose like the tide. At night she lay still while Begu stroked herself, jerked, and shuddered: Thinking of Uinniau, no doubt. While Begu slept Hild lay awake, hungry and restless and savage. During the day she beat at Cian so ferociously he refused to play again until the bruising on his ribs healed. Hild's gesiths noticed that they didn't slip off together and were particularly kind to her, which made her cross. Worse, Oeric then began to behave like a farmer who had won a prize cow, fussing over her, smiling at her. If she didn't do something, he'd be patting her and putting a bell around her neck. She pondered sending him away to Elmet to see how Rhin and the mene wood were coming along. The peregrines would have brought off a brood. She'd like to see that. And what about the mill wheel? Rhin would be too busy to worry about sending messages.

The whole world seemed to be busy. Far away, Hereswith with child—or already a mother—and Fursey teaching her her letters. Also far away now, Osfrith and Clotrude—swollen with her own child—up in Arbeia rebuilding webs of trade and influence, knitting the Franks and Frisians into the Northumbrian web. Here, Breguswith and Æthelburh planning a new wool trade, something akin to Eorpwald's goldsmithing trade: shearing, spinning, weaving, dyeing, sewing. Sheep to cloak, Breguswith liked to say. Osric, shorn of influence, in Craven. And Eadfrith, the elder ætheling, all over the isle, talking to the Britons of Rheged and Gododdin, the Mercians, and all manner of Saxon.

So many people doing so many things, except Hild.

Even James was busy, taking up some of the administrative burden of Elmet. Though, as he pointed out, that province was running smoothly now, thanks to Hild's idea that the king shouldn't demand tithes from new farmers. Really nothing Coelfrith's man, Pyr, couldn't run. All he had to do for now was keep track of who was clearing forest and breaking ground where, and keep the bigger landowners assured of the king's benevolence. "Which mostly involves feeding them slabs of bccf once a month. And mead. The number of mead barrels he's getting through is iniquitous!"

Paulinus Crow was busy: He could practically taste the white pallium of overbishop, James said, and was building a web of his own priests to shuttle information back and forth. Lindsey was coming along very satisfactorily, so much so that James thought the bishop would soon be pushing for the king to lean on the apostatised Eorpwald in East Anglia. Paulinus would love to baptise him and appoint an underbishop of the East Angles— make himself the overbishop of all the Angles. Let Justus keep the Kentishmen, and welcome. All in the interests of the king, of course.

The king himself spent his days with Coelfrith and bundles of tally sticks, pondering his wīc, what he could funnel through it, what he could charge. Counting, counting, counting, rearranging possibilities, shouting at Coelfrith when he didn't like the answers. They should have moved to Derventio a fortnight ago, but the king, obsessed with his wīc, would have none of it.

Hild wanted to talk to the king about Rheged: Rhianmelldt might not be capable of weaving peace, now or later, but Rheged didn't need that, it needed protection. And though Rhianmelldt wasn't old enough to marry she could be spoken for. If Northumbria didn't pluck her, someone else would. Mercia or Gwynedd could give Rhoedd what he craved: a strong enough alliance to leave Rheged safe from violent annexation and obliteration when he died.

In the kitchen garth claimed from the rubble at the north corner of the great hall buildings, Hild flicked a caterpillar off a colewort leaf. Caterpillars. Soon there would be butterflies and moths. She'd never seen such things in York. For her York meant stone, brick, winter skies. This greening felt all wrong. They should be at Derventio by now—she missed her secret spinney; she missed the rooks—and then Goodmanham. It would be summer before they knew it, yet here they were, still in the city of stone.

She straightened, twirled her staff slowly, thinking.

"Morud." He levered himself to his feet. "Run to the kitchen. Find Gwladus and tell her to meet me in my rooms. I want to dress for the king. Oh, and tell the kitchen the colewort is ripe, though they'll have to hurry to beat the caterpillars to it."

Gwladus came to Hild's apartment in time to help with her hair. She told Hild the king was in a bad temper. "Flung the tally sticks at Coelfrith's head and told him to get out, get out. Then he flung his trencher at the wall hanging and swore he'd have the cook's breasts for a coin purse if she couldn't stop burning the lamb, and he was sick to death of lamb, anyway, fed up to the back teeth. Well, lucky him, I say. Today might not be a good day for whatever you had in mind. Even the Crow thought better of going in."

Hild turned. Gwladus adjusted her brushstrokes deftly. "The Crow? What did he want?"

"Arddun says he's been pestering the queen to pester the king to send Coifi to Woden's enclosure at Goodmanham to tear it down."

Hild closed her eyes and leaned back. She loved the firm pressure of Gwladus's hand on her crown, the steady strokes of the brush, and the scent of dried lavender and spicy tansy rising from her skirts. She pondered the enclosure. It had to happen. It should happen soon. "Where's Coifi now?"

"They say he spends time in the church. I don't know why: howling empty space."

The church, still only uprights and a roof, was empty but for Coifi. The ex-priest of Woden, wearing a brown tunic and hose—he had thin legs, she realised—stood with his hand on the great stone basin mortared over the well, staring at the painted stone. Hild stood by what would become the main doorway and watched him. He seemed unaware of her—of anything. She doubted he even saw the bright colours under his hand.

She had never liked him much, but she felt for him. The king no longer had use for him. That would be her lot, one day.

She bumped her staff on the doorpost, as though by accident, and stepped under the roof.

He said, without turning, "Do you feel it?"

"Feel what?"

"Nothing." He turned. "I feel nothing. Is there a god here?"

"The priests say he's omnipresent." She joined him by the font.

"Then why build him a house?"

She didn't have an answer. James hadn't had one, either.

"They haven't even carved the doorposts," he said. "What kind of god is expected to visit a house no better than a wealh's hut? Even the king's horses have better posts to look at."

"Paulinus will tear it down. He'll persuade the king to build a hall-size church of stone."

He stroked the limestone font. "Cold stone. What kind of god is this Christ?"

"Ours, now."

Silence. "The king refused to see me today."

"He is . . . busy."

"He'll always be busy for me now, won't he?"

"Yes." She heard the faint clash and stamp of gesiths in the yard. He heard it, too. His face twisted: He had exchanged sword for skirt long ago; it was too late. And he had no land, no wife. "Where will you go?"

"Who would have me? The Crow took everything. For his church, he said." He looked about the rough empty space. "The king smiled and watched."

That was how kings were. If you were of no use, you didn't exist. "If you could go anywhere, if I got you something to go with, where would you go?"

He thought about it. "Craven."

Two displaced men under one roof. Hild turned it over in her mind, looked at its underside, its corners. She imagined the bitterness, the endless stories told over mead and smoking fires, the constant gnawing on the bones of *what if*. It wouldn't be a happy hall, but she couldn't see anything coming of it. Osric was much reduced and a priest without a god was nothing. "I know how you could please the king and win the goodwill of the Crow, and you'll leave riding a king's stallion, wearing the rich clothes of a gesith and bearing arms. And your name will last forever."

It was delicate work, like guiding a team of nervous cart horses along an overgrown track, but not difficult. It was a matter of holding the right tension on the reins and nudging each in turn to take a step, to make promises that would be to their advantage, and then hold them abreast so that each thought the other was taking most of the strain.

Coifi would formally desecrate Woden's temple, and leave—if he left equipped like a thegn, including a little silver in his purse and a wealh to tend him all the way to Craven. Paulinus would make no argument—if the king agreed to be present and witness the final humiliation and repudiation of the old gods, then acknowledge Paulinus chief priest and bishop of all the Angles. The king in turn would agree to witness and proclaim and provide the gear for Coifi—if it would get both priests off his back and give him the time and space to think about his new wīc.

Coifi further agreed to persuade Osric to invite Paulinus to Craven for baptisms. Paulinus agreed to return one or two of the items appropriated from Coifi. Edwin agreed that the chief church of the new god would be grand enough to honour His glory.

It was stitch-by-stitch work, following a plain pattern. Child's play. It made her restless and impatient.

She brought her latest proposal to the king and Paulinus in hall. They were going back and forth about just how much honour the new god required—not only stone, the Crow said, but marble, and tile, and glass— when Gwladus glided to Hild's side and whispered in her ear.

The warm breath, the swirl of tansy and lavender, the words triggered a surge of something wild she couldn't name. She trembled, like a horse sliced free of its traces. *Kings can be dangerous when surprised.* She didn't care. This, this was what she was born for. She was the light of the world.

She stood to her full height.

"An omen, lord King. An omen!" The click and rattle of knucklebones from the gesith's corner stopped.

King and bishop both faced her. The king's eyes slowly blackened, then swarmed around the rims with green, and Hild, with absolute certainty, knew what he was thinking: Omens were wyrd-hammers, risky and unpredictable; they could swing in any direction.

But she felt reckless with power; it foamed through her. She knew he would let her speak.

After a moment, he nodded.

She looked down at Paulinus. Less like a crow than a dusty black beetle. She could destroy him with a word.

"My lord Bishop's book refers often to the Christ as the Lamb of God."

His eyes glittered. "He has many names."

"But Lamb of God is one."

"Yes."

"And all would acknowledge that the raven is Woden's bird."

Nods from every corner of the hall.

"All birds are Christ's birds!" Paulinus said, but no one paid attention. The raven was Woden's bird, always had been, always would be, his messenger of life and death and war.

"Attend!" She felt taller than an oak, taller than an elm. They would sing songs of the king's seer, the queen of wyrd. "My king. Lord Bishop. Even as we stood here and weighed the honour due the Christ, a raven swooped on the fold and took a new lamb."

Dead silence. Then the hiss of whispers up and down the hall.

"What, then, does it mean, Lord Bishop?"

His cheeks darkened. She knew what he was thinking: that she was about to drive him to the wall, wreck all his plans. And she could. She felt so sure, so clear. But that wouldn't suit her uncle's purpose. There was another way.

"What it means, my lord Bishop, is that Woden's bird is desperate. He is thin, he is hungry. The lamb is plump and new. The raven seized his chance." She hefted the weight of her words. "Did he steal the ewe? No. Why? He hadn't the strength. The raven, Woden's bird, took the lamb, because the lamb is small, because it is new on the fold." She spiked her words, impaling them along her battlement one by one by one. "This is not Woden's message."

The words hung there, a declaration, a taunt: *You can't stop me!*

"This is a message from Christ!" Her voice rang. "Christ, our new god. He shouts to us: Fight for me now!"

The whispers swelled to a roar. *Fight!* This the gesiths understood. But at the centre of the hall silence pooled around the three tall glittering figures: Paulinus wondering why Hild had turned the battle like that, what her deeper game might be. Edwin working out how much new control this might give him over the Crow. And Hild feeling stranded and appalled as the surge of certainty ebbed. Recklessness killed seers as surely as it killed gesiths.

A small party rode through the grey afternoon, along the river that led to Goodmanham. They passed the alders where once, long ago, child Hild and Cian had dozed against the scarred flank of the bitch, Gwen, while the king, sitting on a stool in the shade, heard the case of a man and a widow, and his gesiths horrified the servers with demands for white mead.

Hild smiled, then remembered that Edwin was now far too grand for stools in the grass, Cian was one of the gesiths, and old Gwen was dead.

When they passed the daymark elms, the clouds uncoiled from about the sun, birds wove their song through the trees, and the air smelt of ripening flax, growing corn, and thick-fleeced sheep being gathered to the fold.

The horses slowed to a walk. Sun glittered on the crosses hung on every breast. Gold, glinting with garnet for Edwin, garnet and pearl for Hild. A massive pectoral of gold and amethyst for Paulinus. Plain gold for Cian, from his godmother, the queen. Silver for Stephanus. Copper, silvered and gilded, for Coifi, a good match for his rich red-and-gold warrior jacket—Coelfrith's, hastily altered—and grey stallion, Edwin's third-best. His new sword hung well enough in its travelling scabbard at his back, but he held his throwing spear awkwardly. The gesiths—many of them Hild's hounds—wore crosses of bronze or silvered tin, though more than a few seemed to be wearing two leather thongs around their necks. Their crosses might hang on the outside, for all to see, but she guessed Woden's spear or Thunor's hammer lay against their skin. What the Christ didn't see wouldn't hurt him. And they were gesiths—used to a battle swinging from victory to disaster and back again in the time it took to roar and shove and slip in the mud. They liked to have a fallback.

Even the scop wore a beautifully carved elm cross bound and tipped with silver. Something about the graceful lines made Hild look at Cian and wonder if he'd made it. He seemed lost in another world. Probably dreaming of some long-ago glory. She touched her belt purse where the three thorn-root travel cups nestled with her strike-a-light, tinder, and spoon, and longed to run with him to their little pool by the bird cherry and dip a toast from the spring and talk. Things between them had been strained since Uinniau left. She wasn't sure why. It unsettled her, and she was unsettled enough, wondering what reckless taunter of fate had come to live inside her skin lately.

Edwin raised his hand. They reined in a hundred paces from the great carved posts of the enclosure.

They dismounted. Edwin nodded for Coifi, Paulinus, Hild, and the scop to join him. Paulinus took his great golden crook from Stephanus, the scop slung his lyre bag over his shoulder, and Coifi's spear dragged along the grass for a moment before he balanced the weight. Hild simply handed Cygnet's reins to Oeric and stood: the pattern's witness.

A wood pigeon called from the ash stand on one side of the entrance, another answered from the oak.

The king made his speech about strong new gods supplanting tired old ones, how those gathered here were about to witness the new god of the Angles casting down the old, the foreshadowing of Anglisc triumph. He told them that the bishop of the Christ would now bless the chief priest of the chief of the old gods, claim him for the new god.

When Coifi went on one knee before Paulinus and the bishop began his own speech, she unfocused her eyes and used her side vision, as she did in the woods to catch the pattern. A score of gesiths standing by their horses. Half with hands on their crosses. Many with hands on their sword hilts—or, rather, on then off, with fearful glances at the enclosure. Woden forbade edged weapons anywhere near his totem. They were uncomfortably close. And Woden, god of war and the wild hunt, god of chaos and uncertainty, pain and death, was unpredictable. This could all be a trick. Some glanced at the sky, alert for bird omens. Some watched the priests as they ploughed on with their parts. Some watched her, she realised, though all except Cian pretended not to.

Paulinus was lifting his arms, finishing his exhortation—iron, stallion, the crumbling of pagan gods!—and raising his face to heaven. Coifi stood.

More gesiths were looking at her now. Coifi wasn't moving.

She turned to Coifi. Poor Coifi. A lifetime in one throw.

She held out her hand. "I'll help you."

Hild nodded for Oeric to hold Coifi's spear—he'd trip over it, otherwise—and put his right hand on the withers of the king's third-best stallion. She took his left hand, put it on her shoulder and bent to make a stirrup. He put his foot in it and she heaved and threw him into the saddle. She gave him the reins, made sure he had them in hand, then nodded for Oeric to give him the spear. She turned the horse's head to face the enclosure.

"There's no hurry," she said. "Start at a walk."

But Coifi, in a panic, kicked harder than he meant, and within a breath was thundering full gallop at the entry posts. Hild gripped her seax and braced herself.

Five spear lengths from the opening, Coifi gave a thin screech and flung the spear into the enclosure.

The stallion, trained to within an inch of its life, knew that a thrown spear meant he should swerve away from the expected reply, and he did.

Priest and horse moved smoothly to the left and the spear, the edged iron, flew into the god's heart.

Every armed man, even the king, flinched. Hild closed her eyes but there was no flash of light, no last thunderbolt.

The grey stallion came thundering back, white-eyed, Coifi clinging to the saddle horn.

It was the scop who recovered his wits first. "Behold!" he shouted. "Woden is crushed. Christ is God!"

It was a victory cry the gesiths understood. They banged spears on shields and cheered. Hild let go of her seax and flexed her hand to get the blood moving again.

Edwin laughed and clapped the bishop on the back. "Now we persuade Eorpwald to Christ. Then we'll see who the bishop of Rome calls king of the isle!" Lintlaf brought him his horse.

When the king was mounted, Hild saw Lintlaf fish up something hanging from the string around his neck and toss it aside. She stared at it. God in the nettles.

"Lady." Oeric, with Cygnet. Horses were wheeling, galloping away.

"Take her back to the vill."

"Lady?"

"I'll walk. A god needs a farewell from somebody. I'll be there for supper."

When she was alone, she stepped between the entry posts. The spear lay at an angle across the beaten-earth walkway. She picked it up and propped it against the tall wall boards.

The enclosure smelt of weathered wood and soil being moved aside by growing things. The paint, so vivid a year ago, was faded. Many of the thick black outlines were still clear but the bright colours were turning to wood and mud. She walked the spiral corridor, running her hand along the painted horizon—sea, beach, dunes, woods, moors—the journey of her people from over the sea. The story of the Anglisc, woven with Woden back to the dawn of their songs.

Ships. Fire. Bright swords. Kin and kine. Woods and wold. Hearth and home. Where was Christ in this? Christ didn't fight. Christ didn't farm.

The totem was taller than she remembered. She walked around the base. Waves, cliffs, a ship's prow, cut sharp and deep and clear. Cut from wood, not cold stone.

Christ was a carpenter. Why did his priests build with stone?

She followed the rising line of the carving. A cliff, a tall pole with a boar banner flying. Flying banner blending with a tracery of oak branches. Birds flying with acorns in their beaks. Up and up. Windblown leaves. Wild geese. Clouds. Mare's tails. The horses of the wild hunt. Manes and tails becoming the beard, the beard leading to the chin. Up and up. The mouth. Eyes, gigantic but knowable. The eyes of a god who laughed, who lusted, who drank, who threw knucklebones and lost his temper. Up and up. The helmet crested with the boar. Totem and token of the Yffings. And all would warp and wear and weather into the earth as though it had never been.

She stood alone at the empty heart of a gone god, staff in the crook of her arm, one hand on her seax and the other on her cross. She would not wear and weather. She was Yffing. She would be totem and token for her people, the light of the world.

The next day, Goodmanham still seethed with the controlled chaos of the arrival of the king's party. Late in the morning Hild left Begu and Gwladus to organise their things and sought out her mother. She wanted to talk about the mad Rhianmelldt, to bring Rheged into Northumbria so that their land would stretch from the North Sea to the Irish Sea, and so that Begu could be happy.

Breguswith stood with Æthelburh in the middle of the flax fields, pointing. The queen was shaking her head, gesturing vaguely south.

Hild hesitated. It was best to approach royalty with answers, not questions. But then the queen saw her and waved, and it was too late. Hild waved back and walked towards them.

The flax came to her hip, as high as it would get, though the seed balls were still small and green. Little tunnelled paths ran through the crop. Voles. If her mother and the queen hadn't scared them away, there would be a hawk or two soaring over the field.

They greeted her with smiles. "Perhaps you'll give us your opinion," the queen said.

Her mother said, "We're of two minds. Risk or reward one way, steady surety the other."

Æthelburh cut a stalk of flax with her belt knife and rolled the stem back and forth between her palms. She offered it to Hild.

Hild bent and sniffed. "The fibre's ripe. But the seed isn't." They nodded. That much was obvious. "So. Oil or linen?"

"Trading for oil is expensive," Breguswith said.

"But so is good linen," said the queen. "And if we harvest now, we'll have softer, finer yarn."

"The sun came early this year," Hild said. She closed her eyes, imagined herself as a hawk, high above the field. Imagined the field just south of here, the one next to that, and the next and the next, south all the way to the narrow sea. Summer was always earlier in the south. She opened her eyes. "The Kentish and East Anglisc flax harvest will be an abundance of oil, and a scarcity of fine linen."

The two older women smiled at each other. "Linen, then," the queen said. "We'll break the news to Coelfrith. He'll argue."

"But the king will take your side," Breguswith said comfortably, and they both laughed in that womanly way that Hild didn't understand but that reminded her of the new Begu. They turned to go.

"Help me," she blurted. They both looked back, surprised. She plunged on. "Rhianmelldt of Rheged needs a husband."

"Rhianmelldt? But she's young," Æthelburh said, frowning. "Isn't she?"

Breguswith nodded, watching Hild. "But Begu isn't."

"Begu wants to marry Uinniau," Hild said. "He can't marry until Rheged's settled. Rheged won't be settled until Rhianmelldt marries a strong man. We want, my uncle wants, that man to be our ally."

"We need to find this strong man, one of ours, and offer him to Rhoedd for his daughter?"

"There'd be no hurry, but for Begu," Breguswith said.

Æthelburh smiled. "I have just the man."

Hild and Breguswith looked at her blankly.

Æthelburh looked pleased. "He's young. He's handsome. He's brave: He has a ringed sword. He's respected by Britons and Anglisc alike." She laughed, delighted with herself. "Oh, oh, he fits like a fist in a glove! He's a Christian, baptised by soon-to-be Archbishop Paulinus. You haven't guessed? He saved the king's life." Now she looked exasperated. "He's my godson. Boldcloak himself!"

"Cian?" Hild said, bewildered. Cian?

"They say he's the son of Ceredig king, yet he saved the Anglisc over-king's life and is sworn to him. He's perfect!"

In the sheepfold, Hild held the fat white ewe against her while Breguswith rubbed the fleece at its flank between her fingers, ran her palm over its shoulder, nodded to herself, then felt its front legs, neck, and belly. She frowned and tried its back legs, tugging enough for the ewe to bleat. She shook her head. Hild set the struggling ewe back on its feet and let it go. "The breech wool is worse than I thought. But the back and flank is thick. Thick and soft and good enough for a king."

"What are we going to do about Cian?"

"The front wool might not be fine enough for the Franks, but it will do well enough for the Frisians. Now let's try one of the brownlings."

Hild caught one of the little grey-brown ewes and hauled it up and back until it balanced on its hind hooves and its eyes rolled in panic. She pulled back a little more until it gave up and let go, and its slotted eyes went blank.

Her mother knelt and began running her hands over its neck. "You should have talked to me first," she said.

"Yes. But—"

"It's not like you."

"No. But—"

"This is very soft," Breguswith said, "very fine. But delicate. We'll have to try different bleaches." She stood up. Hild let the ewe go. "Why did you speak before thinking?"

"It's—"

"This isn't the first time, is it?"

Hild looked at her feet.

"I need to know. But bring me that yearling first."

And so while her mother ran her hands over the bleating lamb, Hild stared at the tight black hairs at the tufts of its ears and tried to tell her mother of the restlessness that rose like the tide, the formless longings, the dreams, the sleeplessness, the strange distance of the world, the urge to play with danger, to touch something she couldn't reach. "It's like . . . like climbing a great ash tree, higher and higher, and the boughs are bending, and I'm reaching, reaching for something, and part of me knows the bough will break, but I don't care. I want it. I just don't know what it is."

"And now Cian might end up in Rheged."

"Yes. We—"

"But not today. Today we need to sort you. You're a danger to yourself and others." She looked up. "Have you started touching yourself?"

Like Begu, under the covers.

"Next time you feel . . . restless, try it. It will help you sleep. But that won't work for long. You need a person to anchor you. Someone whose smell and touch will keep your feet on the ground, stop you from climbing until you fall, or from running off a cliff." She stood up.

"A person?"

Breguswith wiped her hands. "Someone no one will notice. Someone no one will believe."

The yearling bleated and struggled.

"You can let him go now." Hild did. He trotted over to a ewe and butted her anxiously on the flank. The ewe ignored him. Breguswith held her apron out for Hild to wipe her hands. "People can always tell who you've chosen, but if it's someone they can dismiss, they won't dismiss you. Do you understand?"

"No."

"If they're not your equal, if they don't matter, you will be seen to be you, still." She looked at Hild and sighed. Hild felt stupid. "Look around you. Pay attention to people. Like Lintlaf with your bodywoman and now Wilnoð's. Or Cian with that red-handed dairymaid at Bebbanburg—no one thought anything of it. But if he took up with one of the queen's women, everyone would gossip because it matters. Like it mattered to the people of the bay about Mulstan and Onnen."

"She's wealh."

"Don't be dense. She was the seer's companion, cousin of Ceredig king. Just as Cian is rumoured to be his son. Your bodywoman, now, she's no one important. Do you see?"

Hild felt as anxious and bewildered as the yearling.

"Also, make sure they're clean. Shall I find someone for you? No? Well, don't get yourself with child. Do everything but that. You know what I mean. If not, talk to your bodywoman. The king will have no use for a swollen seer, and you'll be more interested in your belly than anything else in the world. Oh, yes, even you. So anything but that. And don't attract the attention of priests. Why Christ or his priests should care what we do with each other, I don't know. But they like to meddle. So be careful. And should you slip, come to me immediately. Just remember, no one who matters."

"You chose Osric," Hild said.

"Osric was a mistake."

They listened to the sheep tearing grass. "What was he like?"

Her mother sighed, then smiled a slow, regretful, entirely human smile that made Hild like her. "When no one was watching? Biddable."

Biddable. She could see how that might be good. But what would she bid her person to do, exactly? She had seen people, in hall, in the byre. She had watched from the trees and through cracks in the wall. But not up close, not properly, just movement, blank eyes, flushed faces. She'd seen animals.

"Help me with this gate." They opened the fold, shooed the sheep out. They watched them flow like woolly clouds over the grass. "One thing. Whatever you do, make sure it's not your gemæcce: When these things go wrong, and they always do, you'll need her to be on your side, the one constant. And you'll need to find someone for her, now Uinniau's gone. I'd suggest you buy her a slave. In Kent you can buy gelded ones."

Hild stared.

"No? Perhaps not. Filthy Frankish custom. But she's the seer's gemæcce. She matters because of that. Because of you." She put a hand on Hild's shoulder. "Be careful."

Careful. Always being watched, always spied on. "I'm so tired of being careful."

"We all get tired of being careful." She cupped Hild's cheek. Her hand was soft with sheep grease. "But it will never change. It will never stop." She dropped her hand. "I'm sorry for it."

A breeze lifted the corner of her veil. Hild wanted to smooth it for her, but her mother hated to be fussed over. "Don't you ever want to . . . just walk away?" She waved her hand at the elms on the crest of the hill and the rolling wolds beyond.

"I could have," Breguswith said. "When your father died. I didn't matter. But your sister mattered, matters still, though it's out of my hands now. And you mattered—and will until this king is dead and gone, and his successor after him, and even the one after that. You can never walk away. They'll always find you. You matter for your blood. And your mind."

"Which you made."

"To keep you safe."

Your mother has built you a place where you can speak your word openly.

"So be careful, child. Delay finding a person until you must—because once you've shared yourself with another, touching yourself isn't enough. But find someone for your gemæcce soon."

Hild began to look, for Begu. She began to look through Begu's eyes. When she sat at the board, she noted where Begu's gaze lingered, what made her breath catch, her eyes cut sideways, or her hand pause halfway to her mouth. As the days warmed, and men stripped to the waist to wrestle, women cast off their sleeves and wore lighter cloth. Hild learnt to notice her gemæcce's nipples stiffen and push out the front of her dress when the gesiths wrestled, the way she shifted on the bench and demanded food from a passing wealh, or beer: something to mask how often she swallowed, how her eyes fixed on the men's hands grabbing a thigh, wrapping arms around another's waist, or slapping each other's arses when they stood.

She began to anticipate what might provoke Begu's flush and swallow: the roll of long muscle under sheened skin, the tightening and hardening of a tendon at the back of a man's knee as he strained against a hold, the glisten of a red mouth at the lip of a drinking horn, the interesting roll and jostle in a man's hose when he scratched at himself.

And now, at night, after Begu jerked and shivered and fell asleep, it was Hild's turn. Her restlessness receded.

Begu's did not.

Hild told Oeric to watch for likely men for their household. "Strong men," she said. "And young."

"Strong, lady?"

"Strong. And clean. With sweet breath. Men who laugh."

"Gwladus will know," he said.

The old bird cherry was still alive, though one limb was bare and dead. Cian leaned against the mossy boulder by the little pool and Hild, barefoot and with her underdress still kilted up after fighting, lay on her stomach stroking the still water, sending rolls of ripples this way and that. A water spider slipped and slid then climbed a leaf and waved its front legs in her direction. Hild rested her hand on the surface, pressing slightly as it rocked.

It was like resting her hand on Begu's stomach: soft, elastic, delicate, fascinating. She slid her hand in to the wrist. In. Out. Her arm broke and magically healed, broke and healed. Cian smiled, and she knew he was remembering the magic stick, the tooth.

Butterflies flitted around the bird cherry, white among the almond-scented white blossom.

"I think there are more flowers than last year," he said. "Perhaps it will bloom forever."

"It belongs here. Like us."

It felt like a moment out of time, endless. The grass was pleasantly prickly against her thighs and arms. She stretched, wriggled, laughed: happy.

He shifted slightly and turned away, and Hild became aware that she wore only an underdress, kilted tight between her legs. She sat up.

He picked up a fallen twig, studied the dark oval leaves.

"Cian." He stilled but didn't look at her. "Would you go to Rheged? If the queen wanted you to?"

"Rheged? Why? I'm sworn to the king."

"If he asked you."

"He's my lord. But by choice . . . There's no glory in Rheged." Now he looked at her.

"No, I've seen no visions of glory, no songs of war and blood and gold. But if the queen mentions Rheged or the princess Rhianmelldt, who is quite mad, tell me."

"Why would she?"

She shook her head.

He threw the twig at her. She batted it out of the air. "Why would she?"

She scooped water at him. He jerked back, banged his elbow on the boulder, swore. She jumped up, legs flexed.

He stared. "Your legs are strong," he said eventually. "You should learn to wrestle."

She looked down at her thighs, paler than her arms, paler than his.

He swallowed. "I could teach you," he said, and his voice was tighter than it had been, rougher. Her skin tightened and shivered, like a horse when a fly lands on its withers.

"Let's run," she said, and did, not caring what branches tore at her, just running, running, running.

Cian and the other gesiths left for York two days later with the king. Edwin was eager to oversee the first season's trading at his wīc. He wanted Hild and her mother to stay at Goodmanham to oversee the making of cloth for that trade. Paulinus and Stephanus were with the East Angles at Rendlesham: Paulinus to baptise young Eorpwald and appoint an underbishop before Justus could, and Stephanus to negotiate with Eorpwald's steward over the Frankish trade. Hild considered suggesting to Stephanus that he invite Hereswith to add her voice. She might have if it had been Osfrith, but Osfrith was in Arbeia, consolidating the north trade, pulling it east along the river valley to starve the route down the west sea coast through Gwynedd. Tightening the great weave. Besides, he didn't want to leave Clotrude, who, by all accounts, was as big as a hut.

The queen spent half a week in Goodmanham talking to Breguswith and then took her nurse and little Eanflæd and followed the king to York. The cloth trade was important but getting a son by the king mattered more.

With none to gainsay her, Breguswith ran Goodmanham with a rod of iron: Her weaving sword was always in her hand, and she was free with the flat of it if any man or woman didn't hurry to obey. Without anyone to please, she no longer bent and swayed. No longer willow but oak.

Hild had helped work out how the new wool trade would run, but even she was astonished at its efficiency. Sheep sheared in every royal vill, from the Tine valley to Pickering to the wolds to Elmet. Fleece sorted and sent by grade to rows of huts in Aberford, or Flexburg by the Humber, or Derventio. Armies of women to separate out the staples, to mix soapwort, urine, and pennyroyal to wash out the grease. Children to lay the washed wool in the sun to dry, to watch and turn it and to drive off the birds who liked to steal it. Men to barrel and cart oil and grease to the vills to make the fibre more manageable for the first finger-combing and sorting. Smiths hammering out double-rowed combs and woodworkers shaping wooden handles, for women to comb out wool in the new way, the better way, a comb in each hand. Carpenters to build the stools and tables. Bakers to bake the bread so the wool workers could work. Lathe workers to turn the spindles and distaffs—the long and the short—and, everywhere, women and men making spindle whorls and loom weights of clay and lead and stone, of every shape and size and heft.

It was a constant, endless river of work just to make the clothes for a household—cloaks and tunics, shirts and hose, veils and dresses and underdresses and hoods and caps—in addition to blankets, wall hangings, bandages, sacks, saddle cloths, wipes, shrouds, breech cloths. And now

Breguswith wanted enough fine wool—the very best, silky, long-fibred wool—to weave cloaks of the size, quality, and quantity to trade for precious goods from the Franks: jessamine, myrrh, poppy paste, garnets, gold, walnut and olive oil, silk. Coelfrith's men were even now talking to the Franks and Frisians at York, agreeing on colours, sizes, seasons; spitting and shaking hands.

More sheep sheared. More wool spun. More yarn dyed. More cloth woven. More cloth cut and sewn and embroidered. More weld cultivated and vats built. More wood cut and burnt. More, more, more.

The days grew longer, the nights warmer. The barley began to turn gold.

Breguswith was everywhere, touching everything, assessing, organising, nudging, anticipating. She had noted with Hild that this year at Goodmanham the fleece was thick, and so she sent the undersmith to the fold where he set up a portable forge to heat and hammer and sharpen the shears every night. Yet the shearing rate was still too slow.

She took Hild with her, and they sat on the sunny hillside and watched the shearers sweat and struggle with the heavy fleeces, and the waiting sheep, penned too long, grow restless and kick, and refuse to keep still, which in turn made everything take twice as long.

Hild watched the flexing muscles of the strapping young women and men, streaming with sweat, and said, "Begu could help here. She's good with animals. I've seen her keep a cow with a gashed udder calm."

Her mother followed her gaze to one particular man with a curl to his rich brown hair and a light in his eyes. After a moment she nodded. "But find out his name and his family."

Hild did: Berenic. Two sisters, a mother, an aunt, no wife, no children. Even-tempered and kind, though with a fondness for beer.

So then Begu spent her days at the fold. Soon after that Oeric was riding with messages to Aberford and Derventio, and Morud was drafted to fetch and carry for the household, to groom a horse, or cut wood, or help dig another pit.

"At least you've left me Gwladus," she said to her mother, who smiled tiredly and said, "Not for long."

And, indeed, when it was time to pull weeds from the barley fields, Hild told her bodywoman she would have to help somewhere. "The dairy," Gwladus said. And Hild smiled. Of course: cool, easy on the hands, access to food.

With the king, queen, reeve, and scop at York, along with Cian and the other gesiths, the hall was quiet, talk more a tired murmur than a thing of fire and song and boast.

One night, as they sat outside, lit and warmed by the setting sun, and ate pottage and drank week-old beer, everyone looked worn and dusty but content. Happy, even.

Hild leaned back on her bench and refilled her cup. Gwladus would have done it, but Gwladus was refilling her own bowl with the stew of barley and greens and slivers of mutton. Conversation hummed around her, someone laughed, but gently.

Happy, she thought again, though it was more than that. They weren't afraid. No drunken fighting and boasting. No gesiths pulling wealh onto their laps or persuading the dogs to fight. No thundering horses or sudden deadly silence as the king smiled that smile at someone. No Woden priests with their omens or Christ priests frowning and chastising. She'd even seen her mother deigning to talk to Gwladus. Was this what it was to live an ordinary life? Orderly, peaceful, calm. Work, yes, endless as rain, but also warmth and plenty and safety.

Even Mulstanton hadn't been like this. There she had been worrying about Bebbanburg, about her mother and Hereswith, about what might happen.

But here she was, and this was how it would be for the whole summer. Four months. More. In one place, with no one watching her.

The first night Begu didn't return from the fold, Hild didn't quite sleep— just planed over the surface of sleep and missed her. Twice, Gwladus brought her milk. The second time she rearranged the pillows, and took Begu's away.

The world turned, ripened, grew hotter and heavier. The days lengthened and stretched, thinning at each end to a kind of timeless blue twilight in which nightjars churred and moths fluttered.

Hild slept less and less. She fell into a waking dream and on clear nights walked for miles on the wold and in the woods.

The woods were thick with sound: hedgepigs and badgers in the understorey, the swoop of a bat and yip of a fox, the splash of an otter sliding into the water, the hoot of an owl. An endless song of life around her, eating, crying, dying, breathing, breeding.

She began to feel her own rhythm. Between her bleeding days, at the waxing of the moon, her senses opened like a night lily. For two nights she would feel the ruffle of the air against her face when a bat took a moth, taste the sweet sting of honey in the air near a full hive. Just by smell she knew when Breguswith had washed her hair, when Gwladus had walked through the byre, when Morud had stolen a loaf of fresh bread. Her skin felt denser, more alive, her bones stronger, her belly heavy.

She felt her mother and Gwladus watching her, just as everyone else watched the fields, watching the barley turn gold, the heads bend, the whiskers touch the dirt.

On the night before the harvest, Hild lay naked by the pool. In the moonlight the grass looked like straw, each stem sharp and distinct. She could smell herself: rich, sleek, ready. She put her arms behind her head, watched a stoat creep headfirst like a squirrel down the cherry tree. Then it leapt, and a sudden furious struggle erupted by the hollow alder. The ferns shook. Something ran away, squeaking.

"Soon," she told the stoat. "Soon."

She returned to the vill with the sun, sleeves neatly pinned and girdle tied, to find everyone awake and fed and binding their hair in cloth, preparing for the field work of harvest. A boy tootled on a pipe, and a woman banged her hand drum once, twice, ready to beat out a rhythm. Hild joined her mother at the head of the procession of people and hand carts full of food and sickles.

"No," Breguswith said. "Stay. Take charge."

Hild had no idea what the handful of wealh left behind—a groom, a cook, the swineherd—might need of her, but she nodded. Perhaps her mother was expecting messages.

With a great drumming and piping and shrieking of children, the procession moved out. The sound receded slowly, and quiet settled over the vill.

Hild sat on the south bench, facing the sun, and listened. The caw of crows in the distance, following the people. A brief hiss of wind in the grass. A fluttering butterfly. This was what it would be like after a contagion, or if the king were dead, the people fled, the Idings on the march. She remembered the farmsteads of Elmet, the missing pigs, the doused fires. But then she heard the groom whistling from the byre, a snort and whicker as he mucked out a stall, and saw the blue smoke seeping from the kitchen eaves. Swallows swooped up under the eave and out again. Blue tits, robins, chaffinches began to sing. Hild leaned back, eyes half closed, listening. Her vill.

She woke from a dream of stoat, all long sinuous muscle. It was hot. Milk, that's what she needed, a long cool drink of buttermilk.

She unpinned her sleeves as she walked—no one here but wealh—and tucked them in her girdle.

In the kitchen it was even hotter. The milk crock was not in its usual place.

"They took it to the field," the cook said. "But there's a bit of beer set by. Or there'll be some in the dairy if they've made the butter."

It was a relief to step into the dairy shed, to feel the black, hard-packed dirt under her bare feet.

She walked past the rows of clabbering pots, down a step and to the heavy door of the creamery.

A woman whose name Hild didn't know turned at the waft of warm air and was so startled to see Hild that her churning rhythm faltered.

Gwladus, underdress unpinned and hanging from her belt, was tilting a milk tray. Her bare skin gleamed. She saw Hild and nodded. As the tray tilted to the bottom right corner, she leaned forward and laid her right forearm across the lip. Muscles, small and busy as baby mice, swelled and stretched. Her breast, plumped against her biceps, was much paler than her arm, creamy, but not like the milk—creamy like the inside of a hazelnut.

Gwladus poured the thin greyish skim milk in an expert stream from the corner of the tray into a brown crock. Cream collected in a lake against her arm and breast. When the stream stopped she let the tray lie flat again. She straightened. Followed Hild's gaze down to her cream-dabbed nipple, then looked back to Hild.

The churning paddle thumped up and down.

"I was thirsty," Hild said.

Gwladus nodded at the woman churning butter. "Hwl will be done soon." Then she lifted her forearm and licked along the bone.

Something inside Hild squeezed and dropped. Gwladus nodded at the empty churn in the corner.

"If you help, the butter'll be done that much sooner. But you should hang your overdress and sleeves."

Hild turned away, pulled her sleeves from her girdle, hung them by the apron on the wall, unfastened her girdle, hung that, pulled her dress over her head.

Heat. Slipping cream. Gleaming skin. Lift. Tilt. Pour.

Hwl's thumping began to slow as her cream turned to butter.

Then the trays were empty. Hwl turned the butter out and began to shape it, squeezing out the last trickles of buttermilk.

Gwladus wiped her arm and breast with a cloth and repinned her underdress. Hwl ground salt. Hild listened to the gritty crunch and thump. Like a stoat eating a bird.

Then it was done. Gwladus brought them a dipper of buttermilk, passed it to Hild, who drank and drank again. It didn't quench her thirst. She passed it to Gwladus.

Gwladus dipped and drank, wiped the flecks of butter from her chin with her forearm and said, without taking her eyes off Hild, "Hwl, the lady Hild needs to lie down. Pour some of that milk in a jar."

She took Hild's clothes from the peg and slung them over her shoulder. She took the jar of milk in one hand, opened the door with the other. "Come on, now, we're letting the warmth in."

The sun was high and fat. The air seemed perfectly still.

Gwladus put the flat of her hand on the small of Hild's back, as you would a person who was old or ill, and Hild's mind went white.

Gwladus guided her, opening doors, nodding cheerfully at the groom who was carrying a saddle from the byre, closing the door to Hild's chambers, dropping the latch.

She draped Hild's clothes on a stool, put the jar on the table by the bed, and said, "Sit."

Hild sat on the bed. Gwladus knelt by her feet and unfastened the shoes and slipped them off. Then she stood and lifted off the cross on its chain, unfastened the shoulders of Hild's underdress. It fell around her hips. "Stand."

Hild stood. Gwladus whisked the underdress away, then her drawers, as she did every night.

But it wasn't night.

"Lie down."

"It's not time."

"Lady, it's past time. And you'll be better lying down."

Hild lay on the bed. Gwladus sat by her hip.

"Have you ever kissed anyone? Boldcloak? Your gemæcce?"

Hild shook her head.

"Well, perhaps they were frightened of kissing the king's seer. But I'm not. I know what you need."

Gwladus smiled, that rich slow curve that blotted out everything but right here, right now, then leaned in and kissed her.

Her lips were soft. Like plums, like rain.

Gwladus put her hand on Hild's thigh and stroked as though Hild were a restive horse: gently, firmly. Down the big muscles, up the long tight muscle on the inside. Not soothing but . . . She didn't know what it was.

Stroking, stroking: down along the big muscle on the outside, up along the soft skin inside. Down. Up. Up more. "There," Gwladus said, "there now." And Hild wondering if this was how Cygnet felt to be encouraged for the jump. Her heart felt as big as a horse's, her nostrils wide, her neck straining, but not quite wild, not quite yet. "There," said Gwladus again, and ran her palm over Hild's wiry hair to her belly. "Yes," she said, and rested there, cupping the soft, rounded belly, and then moved down a little, and a little more, and her hand became the centre of Hild's world. "Oh, yes, my dear." She kissed Hild again, and Hild opened her legs.

It was nothing like when she did it for herself. It built like James's music, like the thunder of a running herd, then burst out, like the sudden slide of cream, like a sleeve pulled inside out, and she wanted to laugh and shout and weep, but instead clutched at Gwladus as she juddered and shuddered and clenched.

Gwladus said, "There now. Better than buttermilk?"

Hild nodded, but couldn't say anything. Soft, shocking echoes lapped at her bones and squeezed her insides. Gwladus kept stroking her belly and the echoes began to run into one another, like ripples on a pond, and then slowly calmed. She said, "I'm still thirsty," and laughed for no reason.

Hild and Begu walked through the tall grass by the bend in the river. The moon was full and high. Hild held Begu's hand, because Begu hadn't been walking this path for years and at night the world was different. Smells, sounds, shapes loomed from the shadow and were gone, moonlight turned the shadows sharp and steep. It was a bleached world of bone and stone and tin where magic walked.

They came to the alders. One had fallen a year or two ago at an angle to the water. They sat, facing upstream. The water rippled and splashed. Something shook its feathers in the reeds and settled down.

"How are the sheep?"

"Still stupid." Begu giggled.

"And the shepherd?"

Begu sighed, but Hild heard the smile in it. "He's sweeter than the ram." Another giggle, and the kick and scuff of her shoes on the bark. "And he takes longer over his business."

"Why should he hurry? He has only one to tend."

"And then, too, I tend him in return."

"You do?"

Begu sighed again, this time so heavily that Hild felt the heave of her ribs. "It's like watching a little lamb at suck. He goes all soft and dreamy. He cries, sometimes. And his stick and balls go all little. I can hold them in my hand, like a sleeping mouse."

Hild wasn't sure what to say to that. She watched the alders stir in a breeze that didn't reach the ground, the black tracery of leaves shiver against the moon. She looked for the silhouette of the nightjar she knew lived in the trees but didn't see it.

"If I hold them long enough, and kiss him on his ear or his neck, they stir again. It's like watching a pea swell in water. Or a dog when it licks itself. It grows twice as big, three times."

"How big?" A ram didn't grow very big. A cat had nothing to speak of. A horse, though . . .

"As long as my hand?" They stared at her hand, silvery in the moonlight. "Yes, about that. And very thick." She made a circle with her finger and thumb.

Something plopped in the water.

"I find I want to give him presents. Nothing much, nothing dangerous, your mother warned me about the disapproval of priests, though there aren't any at the fold. But it's best if no word reaches Rheged, just in case. But a present—something, a linen undershirt or a better hood. Something to wear against his skin when I'm gone."

"We're here another month at least."

"But I might want to stop visiting the fold before then."

"Stop?"

Begu shrugged: a strange, writhing movement in the moonlight, uncanny. After a while she said, "Gwladus has a new bracelet."

Now it was Hild's turn to scuffle her feet. "It's not as heavy as it looks." Another plop from the water. "She keeps talking about a new dress, too. Do you think that would be all right?"

"She's always been above herself. It might be all right. As long as every-one gets better clothes."

"You, too?"

"Me especially! And jewels, and new shoes. But mainly clothes. What better way to show the quality and worth of our cloth?"

They grinned at each other, teeth flashing like polished tin in the light.

Hild jumped off the log. "I'll show you jewels. More beautiful than anything you've ever seen. Come on, it's not far."

At the river's edge, the moonlight was brighter. Hild found the over-hang where the fern and thung flowers and primroses grew, the stick of ash poking from the water. She pulled it out carefully.

It glistened with fish eggs, perfect as the most delicate pearls on the queen's veil. They shimmered with moonlit glamour, droplets of dreams.

Hild slid the stick back in the water. They watched the river for a while.

The moon moved higher, drew itself tighter and brighter. Then there it was: true night. That moment when the world seems to stop and wait and the air both stills and quickens, thick with tree breath and the listening of small animals. Foxes were abroad now, and badgers, and uncanny things.

"That smell, it reminds me of something," Begu said. "Beef tea. The way Guenmon makes it, with thyme and pepper."

Hild opened her mouth, breathed through her nose, lifting her tongue and letting the air run across the roof of her mouth. At this time of night, anything was possible.

"You look like a slitty-eyed cat when you do that."

"It tells me things."

"What things?"

"I can smell . . . bats. Not here, but close."

Begu sniffed, shook her head.

"Sharp, but musty. Like lye and old leather." A moth fluttered over the reflection of the moon on the water. She spoke quietly in the still, scented air. "When bats are hunting, a moth will fold its wings and fall as though caught in a sudden frost. I've seen it. The moths fall down, lie on the turf like dead leaves, and when the bats have passed, they fly away again."

They held hands. The river poured. The trees whispered. Hild thought she could already hear the difference in the leaves, stiffer than a month ago, though in the daylight the colour was just the same.

The air changed. Once again, it was just a beautiful night.

Begu stirred. "Oeric. He won't be happy when he comes back and sees how it is."

Hild shrugged.

"And then there's Cian."

Hild didn't say anything.

"We're like the moths," Begu said. "The priests and Uinniau and Cian are like bats. When we go back to York, we'll have to stop, lie down, for a while."

The barley was in the barn, the wheat cut, the sheep back on the wolds. Wagons creaked away, laden with sacks of fleece, to Sancton, to Derventio, to Flexburg, to Aberford.

Begu came down from the fold. She slept in Hild's bed again. She made sure she was not in the room in the afternoons. But she watched Gwladus carefully for a while. Gwladus behaved respectfully, and even Begu had to admit that Hild was better taken care of than ever.

Oeric returned.

When he reported to Hild and Begu on the mene wood, he stood stiff as a board and shot Hild wounded looks. Gwladus, who served them, was particularly careful to behave like a wealh slave in a room of wellborn Anglisc—Hild wondered how long that would last—but Oeric looked daggers until Hild nodded for her to leave.

When he had finished his report—the mene thrived, Loid and Anglisc were in accord—and had, in his turn, left, Begu said, "Was I that bad?"

"Not that bad."

"At least Gwladus is acting well."

And Gwladus was. In public, she never once overstepped her role. In private, the one time Hild had tried to give back, Gwladus had put her hand on Hild's and stopped her. "No, lady."

"But you let Lintlaf."

Gwladus stilled, like a mouse under a cat's paw. "Of course, lady. As it pleases you." Her eyes stayed open, but she could have been dead. Even her skin felt different: lumpen as a flitch of bacon.

Hild stopped. "Why?"

Gwladus said nothing.

Hild felt as though she'd bitten an apple and swallowed, then seen half a worm in the white fruit. She sat up. "Pass my dress."

While Gwladus dressed her, she stared at nothing, moving her arms when told, thinking. Gwladus had liked it, she was sure. She had felt

Gwladus's blood beating, heard her breath come faster, seen her nipples rise and pebble, smelt the sharp tang and glisten between her legs. So why?

That night she lay awake next to Begu. Berenic cried sometimes, Begu had said, and his eyes went soft. But Berenic was not a slave, and Berenic would stay on the wold.

The next afternoon, before she lay on the bed, Hild gave Gwladus a small purse of coins. She said, "I won't do it again," and later tried not to see Gwladus watching her when she came around her hand.

After that, some afternoons Hild stayed away from her room. But she always ended up going back.

The days were rich and fine and sweet. Most mornings Hild spent with her mother and Begu, tallying, discussing weaving patterns, trying the hand and drape of different cloths, trying cloak sizes. Begu had many good ideas about what people might like for next year. Hild could see ways to set up the pattern on the loom.

Hild walked the hills in the golden time before dusk, senses wide open but no longer restless. One evening she was moved to tears by the blaze of crimson, gold, and green of the wold, moving at the centre of a vast pattern that she knew she would never have the words to explain. The pattern watched over her from the face of every leaf and every tiny flower of furze. She felt sure and safe.

Word came from Arbeia: Clotrude and Osfrith had a fine, strong son and named him Yffi.

At the name, Hild, Breguswith, and Begu looked at one another. Yffi was a king's name, an heir's name. Æthelburh had better hurry.

King's messengers came from York, but never with anything they most wanted to know. Nothing about who the king would choose for Rheged. Nothing of the wīc. Nothing of Penda or Cwichelm or Cadwallon. Nothing from Cian. Breguswith's own messengers brought her samples of the cloth that came off the looms, along with tallies of the quantity. The quality was good. She forwarded the news to the king and Coelfrith in York.

Hild had a letter from James: Paulinus had converted Eorpwald king to the faith, Christ be praised, though it meant more work for James. The king had disbursed more monies for the church at York. They would all be stunned and amazed by its appointments, though he imagined she herself might not get to see it for some time: Paulinus, rather than consolidating his new flock, was now aiming to round up the people of Lindsey. But ealdorman Coelgar was a stubborner man than Eorpwald, and he knew the king's aims, the king's goals that lay behind the bishop's actions. He would not be as easy to persuade. No doubt the king would require the lady Hild's thoughts on the matter.

19

✦

HILD RODE WITH HER MOTHER and Begu, accompanied by Gwladus and Oeric and Morud, to York.

In the glow of the setting sun, Cian seemed brighter, denser, his eyes more blue. He laughed when he saw them, swung Begu off her horse and kissed her cheek, bowed to Breguswith, and grinned at Hild. "I've learnt a new song of Branwen!" He slapped Oeric on the shoulder, and told him four months among the women had put fat on him and that they'd need to work it off.

Gwladus bobbed her head to Hild and said that, if the lady pleased, she'd take Morud and go straight to their apartment, make sure all was in order. Hild nodded.

Cian watched her go. "Is she quite well?"

"What do you mean?"

"If the lady pleases? And not a bit of cheek. Did you give her a whipping?"

Begu poked him in the ribs. "Four months among women has made us all shy. Now tell me how you've been without us."

There was no formal feast, just friends sitting in small groups at the board, but after a quiet summer the flash of gold and snap of dogs, the laughter and shouts were sharp and loud. The meat was good, though, and the mead, and Cian entertained them with stories of horse races and hunting parties and the king rubbing his hands over the new wīc.

"You won't see much of it tomorrow. We're riding out early."

After a while he cleared his throat. "Now I'll sing of Branwen. Not the warrior maid. The other one." He launched into a song of Branwen, daughter of Lyr, who died of grief. His voice throbbed with emotion, the kind he usually saved for glorious death in battle. Hild wondered if he'd fallen in love with one of his red-handed dairymaids. She closed her eyes, belly full of meat and mead, content between her mother and Begu, and drifted.

Later, in their apartments, Gwladus told them the queen had been unwell; Arddun thought she might be with child.

The queen and her women, including Begu, removed to Derventio. The king and a small group of advisers—including Hild and her mother—rode to Lindsey to talk to Coelgar about Christ and wool.

Miles from the city of Lindum, on the edge of the thick stink of its tanning and fulling, Paulinus asked the king for a word.

Hild watched the conversation from her horse. Her mother reined in next to her. "You've been out of his eye too long."

Hild nodded without taking her gaze from them. She knew what Paulinus was saying: Beginnings were delicate times, and the king's seer, despite her prominent gold cross, made Christ-fearing men nervous.

"You'll have to wait for your moment."

Hild rested her hand on her seax and wondered what kind of moment. Meanwhile she would wait.

So as the king and his archbishop spoke to the great men of Lindum, while her mother negotiated with Coelgar and his reeve Blæcca by the fire in Coelgar's hall east and south of the city, Hild walked Coelgar's fields. The vill was safe enough to wander without Oeric, and Cian was dallying with some girl, the daughter of Coelgar's bread maker. Not that Cian would have offered to accompany her. He had been acting strangely since the morning they left York: ignoring her, avoiding even Gwladus. Hild did not understand it, but she had done without him for four months over the summer, and he would recover himself at some point. She just hoped it would be soon. She was tired of waiting, always waiting. And she missed fighting.

After nine days she knew the fields so well she could name every clod and stone along their edges. Today, drifting rain blurred the air over the low, tidy furrows and the air smelt dark and rich. She left her hood down, letting the rain cling to her hair, wanting to hear while her body walked and her mind wandered. On rainy afternoons, did the bread maker's daughter let Cian pleasure her, let Cian see her vulnerable and soft and hold her afterwards while she cried? Or was it only men who cried? Begu hadn't said. She couldn't imagine Gwladus crying, even if—

That lump of dirty flint by the hedge, it hadn't been there yesterday. She slowed. It was a partridge, hunched against discovery.

Rooks and jackdaws croaked and squabbled beyond the brow of the hill, fieldfares and finches hopped back and forth on the worm-rich soil: there were no hawks about. It was hiding from her.

"Don't be frightened," she said. It made no sign it had heard. Stupid bird. She glared at it. "What have I ever done to you?"

The bird's fear made her angry. She picked up a stone. She could kill it. Kill them all: Paulinus, Coelgar, Cian's woman.

But it was just a bird. It hadn't done anything to her. She let the stone fall and turned back the way she'd come, towards the river.

A hare, sitting in a furrow, almond eyes shining black in the rain light, regarded her. She regarded it. The pale fluff at the tips of its long ears stirred in a breeze Hild couldn't feel. Then it bolted. Bold hare! Brave hare! Hild gave a great shout and ran after it, knowing she wouldn't catch it, just wanting to run as it ran, muscles bunching, feet kicking against the loamy dirt, not hiding. It lolloped under the roots of the hedge and she heard a sifting splash, like a sack of grain going into the river. She ran around to a gap in the hedge and got to the bank in time to see the hare swimming like a furious small dog to the other side, where it leapt up the bank and ran, tail flashing this way and that. Then gone.

Her heart beat high. The hedge seemed outlined in crystal. The air was like beer. She held her arms out and turned, taking in sky, water, fields, hedges, the low, tidy, orderly land. She laughed. It was good to be in a field in the rain. Then she sat on a stone and fished a piece of cheese from the purse at her belt.

She was struck by it. A product of a well-run world in the palm of her hand. Deep yellow. Aged from summer milk squeezed from cows fed on rich green grass. She bit into it: fatty and sharp.

The stone she sat on had probably been hauled from the field generations ago and moved, season by season, in frost heaves and spring washes, closer to the river. This was Lindsey, never left to run wild for a generation.

Not like Elmet. She imagined sitting in her mene wood with her children, her children's children. Perhaps it would look as tidy and prosperous.

The sheep here weren't all that they'd hoped for, though, according to her mother. Too small. They could breed some of the larger ewes with some Deira rams. Coelgar would be only too happy to oblige her mother; he'd always felt kindly towards her.

Hild thought back. Perhaps it had been more than kindly—before Osric.

She popped the last of the cheese into her mouth and savoured it. If only Coelgar liked her as much as he liked her mother. He treated her with extreme courtesy, yes, but that was a mask for his discomfort. He wouldn't be alone with her, not since the tent in the field at Lindum.

She would have to think of a way to befriend ealdorman Coelgar. She would have to remember that those who weren't used to her, or who hadn't been around her for a while, saw the legend first: twice royal, twice uncanny. Wielder of wyrd, dealer of death, the king's seer.

She stood, checked the far bank just in case the hare had returned, then headed back for the vill.

A column of rooks and jackdaws rose, cawing, from the field over the rise. A hawk. She hoped the partridge was hiding.

But when she reached the brow of the hill, she saw it wasn't a hawk. It was a column of men riding furiously for the vill, the king's tufa gleaming at its head.

Hild got to the vill just as the king leapt from his horse. He saw her and strode over. His muscles were tight with more than the ride.

He yanked a sheet of parchment from his saddlebag, waved it in her face. He was holding it upside down.

"Who the fuck is Ricberht?"

"Uncle?"

"Some nithing called Ricberht has killed Eorpwald and set himself up as king of the East Angles! All those messages, all those gifts, for nothing. And no warning, not one single word, from my seer. Well?"

Ricberht. A lesser Wuffing. Surrounded by his men at Hereswith's betrothal feast, laughing with Eorpwald while Æthelric preened—

Hild was saved from having to answer by the arrival of more riders: Paulinus and his priests.

Edwin whirled. "And you're no better! Some god, who can't even protect a king I need." He threw the letter in the mud and stalked into the hall.

Hild bent to the parchment. The words were dissolving in the rain.

Stephanus darted through the riders, mud spattering his sandalled feet. She let him have it.

The next day rain fell unceasingly. Endless, wind-whipped rain. The men crowded into the hall smelt like a pack of wet dogs. Better than the smell outside, where the wind was bringing the stink of tanneries from Lindum. The hall was thick with damp and smoke and the king's rage.

Hild, who had been up half the night with her mother, met the men's regard steadily. Cian was the only one not looking at her.

She wore royal blue, her arms bare and her hair tucked behind her ears, gesith-style. In the firelight gold glinted from her ears and throat, arms and fingers. Her cross gleamed on her breast and carnelians winked at her wrist. The silver of her belt ends shimmered. She rested her hand on her seax and stood tall. Unlike Paulinus, she was both skirt and sword. The saviour of Lindum and, before that, Bebbanburg. Let them not forget it.

"My king, Eorpwald Sulkmouth was used to the summer mead of Woden. His thegns were used to it. Christ belief, though, is a foreign wine, a heady wine, and Eorpwald Sulkmouth was foolish. He drank too fast. He lost his senses."

Here and there, a gesith nodded. They all knew the perils of heady foreign wines. Paulinus, standing on the king's right, leaned on his jewelled shepherd's crook and watched her carefully.

"My king, you're wise. You understood the value of persuading your thegns first, letting them taste, letting them judge the strength of your pour. And, my king, you are rich. You are known as generous. You felt no need to pour all at once to win approval. You could advise men to begin slowly, and it was like a father speaking to his son: kindly and wise, not rushed, not hasty in the hope of avoiding the name of niggard."

Now Edwin was nodding: He was a wise king, and generous, and rich. Paulinus stared at her, unwinking. In this hall, with his black hair and eyes, he looked like a foreign shadow. His skin drank in the Anglisc light.

"A drunken man, my king, gives away too much too fast to the wrong people. And so it was with Eorpwald. He gave too much too fast to his new priests. The king had no wise adviser to temper his generosity." No one like her, skirt and sword. Book and blade. "The king's thegns were bewildered."

Coelgar was now looking speculatively at Paulinus.

"The thegns rose up. They swore to Ricberht, who swore to shun the Christ." She looked around the room and smiled. "Who here hasn't sworn to never drink again?"

Laughter.

"But, my lord King, like all of us, Ricberht will one day no doubt be persuaded to sip of this foreign wine anew. And, failing that, his thegns might listen to suggestions for another king. Sigebert, they say, is safe in Frankia. Where we have many friends." And her mother's relatives, her sister's, her own. "And much new trade."

"Meanwhile," Edwin said, "the East Angles are not bending the knee, and this Ricberht, they say"—ironic smile—"has friends in Mercia."

"Yes, my king." She had no idea if that was true, but it was best not to contradict one's king in public. "However, my sister's husband, Æthelric, is still prince of the North Folk." They would have heard otherwise. "He will hold the fens against the men of Mercia and the West Saxons. We will regain Rendlesham and, meanwhile, my sister's husband will guard the border. Lindsey is safe."

"You're sure?"

"I am." Hereswith would persuade Æthelric. Hereswith and Fursey. Between them they would remind him of Hild's prophecy: He would be king. "Meanwhile, my king, we must in future make sure that any kings whom we seek to turn to Christ are supported with wise advisers."

Coelgar nodded, and Hild turned deliberately to him. As ealdorman in his own hall, he did not need the king's permission to speak.

"She's right, my lord. I don't hold with this hurry." He looked over at Paulinus. "I hear they killed your underbishop. Put his head on the altar."

"Bishop Thrythnoth is in heaven. He was much loved by God and has been gathered to His bosom."

"Well," said Coelgar, "I'm not in a hurry to be loved that way by any god."

Gesiths laughed, black-clad priests crossed themselves, and Paulinus said nothing.

"My dear Coelgar," Edwin said, "I'll make sure that with you, Paulinus takes all the time you need. I'll make sure he stays here all winter if necessary. Is that all right with you, Paulinus?"

Paulinus had no choice but to bow.

Coelgar said, "Let's eat," and housefolk poured into the hall to move benches.

The king crooked his finger to Hild and waved Paulinus away. While everything rearranged itself around them, turning them momentarily into a private island, he tapped his ring on the arm of his chair. Hild wondered how that ring might feel. All that power. No more *waiting*.

He leaned forward. "I don't like surprises. I don't want any more. Do whatever you have to." They both glanced at Paulinus, who clearly wished he could hear what they were saying. "What he doesn't know, he won't hector me for. If the wyrd needs a little help"—he tapped the thick gold band around his left arm—"let me know."

"Yes, Uncle."

"Wear that cross outside your clothes. And no . . . distractions." She didn't want to think what he meant by that. "About Rendlesham. Work out with your mother how to make up for the loss of trade." He moved restlessly in his chair. "We'll be here another fortnight now. May the Christ bend Eorpwald Sulkmouth over a heavenly bench and fuck him!" He slammed both hands on the chair. "Someone bring me a drink!"

In York, birds were eating the last of the hornbeam nuts, the hazelnuts had been gathered, and the ash between the north pasture and the east fields pollarded. Everywhere smoke rose into the hard blue sky: fragrant ash from the hearth, keeping them warm; applewood smouldering under butchered pig, turning it to bacon; thorn-brush coals roasting hazelnuts.

Cian one day started talking to Hild again, though there were odd moments of silence, quick looks that she couldn't read, and every time she considered asking him, she found she couldn't. Their friendship grew back, like tree bark growing over a wound. But they did not fight anymore. "It's different now," was all he said. And, again, Hild couldn't bring herself to ask him why. She sparred sometimes with Oeric, but it wasn't the same.

She helped her mother persuade the queen that, even tucked up in Derventio with a swollen belly, she and her women could make embroideries more efficiently; talk Osfrith into squeezing his thegns just a little harder; and make sure the dyeing and fulling of cloth didn't slow despite the fading light. Then she turned her mind to keeping abreast of news from everywhere. The priests had had a network before Paulinus unravelled it. Hild would reweave it, to her own purpose.

In the woodland south of the site cleared for the wīc, Hild had to reassure two thin and owl-eyed charcoal burners that she wasn't a wraith from the long ago; she was looking for the hut of a woman called Linnet. Here, see, she was bringing Linnet and her old mother a sack of hazelnuts. Charcoal burners were often strange; not getting enough sleep for weeks led to a tendency to visions. And a gesith-tall maid draped in gold was not something you saw every day. She gave them a handful of nuts, and the earthiness of the little brown nuggets seemed to persuade them. They pointed her to a narrow path. Her boots crunched on the fallen leaves.

At the hut, Hild knocked on the doorpost.

Linnet's mother opened the door.

"It's you, then."

Hild agreed it was.

"And what's that?"

"Don't be rude," Linnet said, moving her mother aside. She leaned through the door, peered behind Hild, and frowned. "You're on your own, lady?"

"As you see." Hild shifted her sack to both hands and held it out. "Hazelnuts. I have more than I can use."

"Tuh," said Linnet's mother. "Doesn't everyone, this year?"

Linnet took the sack.

"They're from my own land in Elmet. Fresh and fresh. Elmet's—"

A pig squealed from behind the hut, a bubbling jagged shriek that reminded Hild of Lindum, the fallen wailing and begging, the sow rooting in the Lindsey man's belly.

"What are they doing to the poor thing?"

"It's my sons. They're young and don't yet have the hang of it. But, as Mam says, they have to learn sometime. Will you come in?"

Cian sat cross-legged on his folded cloak by the hearth, whittling hard white hornbeam. He hummed tunelessly, concentrating on the wood. His fingers worked. Firelight glinted red-gold in his hair. His throat apple moved as he hummed. His clothes smelt of the crisp green-apple smoke of burning birch from the hearth of Wen, the young widow with the freckles, who shaved the priests and those of the king's men who liked smooth chins.

"What are you making?"

He smiled and held it out: a horse. "Du likes horses." Du was Wen's toddler. Before she could stop it, Hild was imagining Wen stropping her razors on the velvety skin of birch-bracket fungus, Cian leaning back, head on her breast, Wen holding his chin with one hand, holding the razor against his throat with the other. They were both naked.

She poured mead. Gwladus was in the other room, brushing the mud out of her cloak. *If you must keep visiting these hovels*, she'd said, *at least try not to tread in the pig shit.*

"Will you paint it?"

"Um? I hadn't thought to." He drew his knife carefully down the tail, and again, blew away the shavings, hummed some more.

"Rhin sent twoscore sacks of nuts and a flitch of bacon from the mene wood. I sent a score and the bacon back. I would have sent everything but Morud tells me they truly have more nuts than they can use. So does everyone this year. Except the squirrels." The squirrels were almost frantic. And the newly arrived rooks were building low to the ground. "It won't be an easy winter."

Cian examined his horse. "Is it ever?" He set the horse on the hearth. In the flickering light, it seemed to be trotting. It stood perfectly, as his animals always did.

"It's beautiful," she said.

He looked at her. "It's just a horse." She looked away, sipped at her mead. He leaned back on his hands. "So how's the rest of the mene? Still wet?"

"Rhin tells me he has twoscore and six souls under his charge. He says the harvest was good. There's more land under the plough—and it's draining well. He says, too, that the crayfish from the beck are tasty and go well with pepper. If he could but get some."

He laughed. His lips were very red. "The poor man, suffering crayfish without pepper. I might send him a sack. When is Morud going back?"

"He's already there. I sent him out again with the nuts and bacon. Though perhaps he stopped to talk to his aunt. Lweriadd sends her best love to Lord Boldcloak, by the bye."

He nodded. Nothing out of the ordinary now in being called lord and Boldcloak. Cian, king of Rheged. It could happen. At least the queen was still in Derventio. No doubt she'd make it to York for Yule, but perhaps by then she would be more concerned with her belly than with marrying her godson to poor mad Rhianmelldt.

Someone entered the other room; she heard voices. If it was important, Gwladus would let them in.

Cian stretched, turned the horse the other way. "Perhaps next time Rhin will send us salmon."

"Do you remember the story you used to tell about the salmon of Elmet? Tell me again."

He poured himself more mead, sipped, put his cup down, and opened his hands. "Once upon a time, if there was such a time, nine hazel trees grew around a pool. Now, these trees were sacred trees, and the pool a sacred pool, and in the pool lived a throng, a rush, a river of salmon. Every year the hazel trees dropped their nuts in the pool. Every year the salmon rose up and ate the nuts. These nuts, as everyone knows, were creamy and fat not only with goodness but with wisdom. The fish ate the nuts and grew wise in their turn, and as they grew wiser they grew more spots. One day—"

"Lady." Gwladus stood at the curtain. "The boy is back. He has news from his aunt, news the king doesn't yet have."

Hild nodded. Gwladus lifted the curtain and Morud burst in and dropped to one knee. He was trembling with excitement. Or perhaps exhaustion. He must have run half the way from Elmet. Hild stifled her answering longing to run, to match staff to blade, to command with her own voice instead of others'.

Morud poured out the news from the British priest web, three main points.

Oswald Iding, his brother Osric the Burnt, and the Dál Riata under the prince Domnall Brecc had won great renown at the battle of Ard Corann across the North Channel in Ireland. They'd killed Fiachnae mac Demmáin of the Dál Fiatach. Domnall Brecc, the son of Eochaid, king of the Dál Riata north of Alt Clut, had declared the Idings brothers and heroes, high among Dál Riatans.

The men of Alt Clut had now sent an envoy to the Dál Riata, undisputed lords of the Scots and Irish. Hild remembered her first war trail, the way the men of Alt Clut had crossed themselves and not let her join their councils. The king sitting on the rock of Alt Clut, Hild standing tall and prophesying of Bebbanburg.

Rhoedd of Rheged was rumoured to be considering an offer for his daughter, though no one knew whose. Whoever married Rhianmelldt would one day sit by the fountain in Caer Luel, her fountain, while he laid plans to rally the men of the north . . .

She stood, and Gwladus was draping her newly brushed cloak, before Morud had quite finished. Hild gulped her mead, held it out to be refilled, gulped again. The king wouldn't like any of her news. "Find Oeric," she told Gwladus. "Find my mother. Be ready for anything when I get back." She looked at Cian. "Anything."

She wondered how it felt to be Cian, or to be an Iding, and fight for a place with muscle and bone, not just words. Fiachnae mac Demmáin dead. She remembered cutting open his man's arm. But she couldn't remember why it had upset her so.

When she got back they were all waiting: her mother, Begu, Oeric, Morud, Gwladus . . . No, not all. Not Cian. Hadn't he understood? Of course he had.

Gwladus took her cloak, shot a look at Oeric that Hild didn't understand, and brought her a cup of mulled wine. Hild sat opposite her mother. Sipped.

Eventually Breguswith said, "Well, you're not dead."

"I might be by next summer." She sipped some more. "I had to promise him a son."

Breguswith's spine went rigid.

"Don't," Hild said. "I didn't have a choice."

Her mother looked at her. There was always a choice. But in a fight you risked all on an opening; you didn't think about what happened if you missed. "I told him the bad news, told him it was going to be a bad winter in other ways, too—"

"How do—"

"It will. If you stopped thinking about wool for an hour, you'd see it. So I told him that. And the Crow started talking about witches bringing misfortune. The king . . . you know how he is." First the half-lidded look, then the widening eyes, the black pupils swelling like ink dropped in water, swallowing the blue centres, leaving the outer pleats of his eyes green and glistening, swarming like flies looking for something to eat, someone to hurt to make himself feel strong and safe. "So I told him it would be a hard winter, yes, but that he was strong and canny and his land rich, that the gods would grant him a son, a fine strong son, born into a Christian marriage, one blessed by the pope. A pope who, with the conversion of so many people, would be happy to call him king of all the Anglisc, happy to call him so to the Franks and the Jutes, happy to bless his heir. Heir to the overkingship of all the Anglisc. So what, in the end, would it matter about the men of the north and who they called brother and hero if he, Edwin king, could call on all the Anglisc?"

A boy. And healthy. Two risks, not one. But it was done.

She finished her wine, held the cup out for more. "Is there any bread? I'm starved."

Oeric cleared his throat. "There's more news, lady."

Hild stared. "More?"

"It's not urgent," Gwladus said.

"How do we know?" Oeric said. "It's a letter."

Hild held out her hand. Red wax, a goose. "It's from Hereswith." She broke it, read quickly. "She has a daughter, fine and strong."

"When?" Breguswith said. "What colour are her eyes?"

Hild held out the letter, then remembered her mother couldn't read. "It doesn't say." She smoothed the letter, so no one would see her hand trembling. Her mother couldn't read. Her mother hadn't noticed the signs of a bad winter. Cian wasn't even there. Hereswith was far away, and Fursey. She had taken a double risk and there was no one to help her.

"Well, what does it say?" Begu asked.

Hereswith's writing had improved. "The baby came just before midsummer."

"Late," Begu said.

Hild nodded, reading one thing, thinking another. "Æthelric is holding the fen, though he won't challenge Ricberht." *He is happy to cower in our stinking fen and play prince to the North Folk and stallion to his pagan woman.* She'd been right. She must tell Hereswith to watch what she wrote. Not everyone who could read was on their side . . . "Father Fursey sends his love and prayers."

Breguswith looked at her, and her thoughts were plain to everyone in the room: They'd have to be powerful prayers if the prediction about a son didn't come true.

"But for now," Begu said, "you're a grandmother. And Hild's an aunt." She smiled. "An aunt! What's her name?"

Hild shook her head. "She's didn't say. She's not very used to writing letters." She turned to Oeric. "Bring me ink. And get ready for a long ride. You're taking letters to Hereswith and to her priest, Fursey. Take two men, a pair of spare mounts each. I'll want replies faster than fast. Morud, you'll rest. I'll need your eyes in half a dozen places." Rhin had at least one wealh priest hiding with him. One of them could reshave his forehead and get up to Rheged, with Morud, and take the lie of the land. With the Idings ascendant, no man of the north would talk to Edwin's Anglisc now, priest or gesith. And now was not the time to stop being right.

20

✦

WINTER WAS HARSH: wind and snow, then, just as the snowdrops were poking free of the dirt, silence and cracking cold from skies as blue and hard as enamel. Sunlight glittered on ice-cased twigs. Fawns in the wood starved and foxes ran thinner than weasels. In York, folk like Linnet hunched against the cold alongside their byre animals, glad of the warm stink, glad of the dung to burn—while it lasted—eyeing the tree hay, and weighing the coming choice between staying warm and letting the kine starve.

Hild and her mother made sure Æthelburh always had tempting treats to hand; they needed her child to be healthy.

Towards the end of their stay at Bebbanburg, spring came at last. It began to warm. In the valleys, barley shoots poked through the dirt. Folk straightened and began to smile.

Then came the rain. Endless rain, beating the shoots back into the earth, flattening the early flowers, drowning the hum and bumble of bees. Cattle found hillocks where they could, or rotted where they stood. Cloth mildewed and flour mouldered. Rivers rose, and rose again, til herons roosted on roofs and ducks on styles. Pastures turned to mud and roads to slipways. And still it rained.

Everywhere there was unrest. From Tinamutha, Osfrith sent word of blood and mud-soaked raids by young Gododdin. Hild wondered if Coledauc pondered taking his Bryneich to join them. She rested her hand on her seax: Would he risk breaking her prophecy of friendship?

Men murmured: Wights walked the world under the uncanny sky, and moonless nights sent bats and birds mad; nets strung in the usual alleys caught only air. Wildcats and wolves came down from the hills and out from the weald and slunk into farmsteads at night. Eagles snatched sheep from the hillside in what passed for daylight. The king offered a bounty on wolfskins and eagle wings, but bowmen complained of slack strings and warped arrows, and spearmen threw awry.

Christ, folk whispered, was an unchancy god.

They were at Yeavering when Oeric returned with a letter from Fursey, so circumspect as to be brow-furrowing. *Your niece is a Noble Joy.* It took Hild several reads to determine he meant her name was Æthelwyn. *S brings incense of the kind your sister enjoys to drive vermin from the room.* That was easier: Sigebert had pledged allegiance to the Franks in return for arms and men. Edwin wouldn't like that. *Your humble correspondent bids you to remember the road to Lindum and our conversation about the brightest bead of all. He is everywhere.*

She turned her beads half the night, thinking about that. The little yellow bead, the brightest of all: Christ. He wasn't talking of the priests—that would be like explaining that the sun rose in the east. What did he mean? She fell asleep holding the beads and dreamt of damp. They all dreamt of damp. The weather was more like autumn than early summer. Rain-lashed seas heaved. Shipping was uncertain. Trade fell.

They moved to Derventio. Edwin fumed in his splendid mosaic-floored hall, guarded at every entrance by a pair of gesiths. Gesiths did not make good guards: guarding wasn't fighting. Lintlaf told them they'd have real fighting soon enough, and made sure the men changed places four times a day.

Æthelburh, swollen as a drowned ewe and not due for another two months, prayed in her splendid gilt and vermilion-painted chapel. James's choir sang bravely, but their song seemed to reach only as far as the high roof then fell back to earth, unheard. Hild, seer and prophet, repeated that the king's son would be strong and healthy. But she made no promise about the rain. The king shouted at her. Men muttered as she passed. Women drew aside their skirts.

Morud brought news of worried men in Rheged and a desperate message from Uinniau: Rhoedd was beset by envoys from the north—Dál Riata and Alt Clut—husbandmen driven from their farms by bad weather and a cattle murrain. He would have to make an alliance soon. Hild still had no one to suggest to Edwin for Rhianmelldt.

She slid her seax in and out of its sheath, thinking, then jammed it home and picked up her staff. Good oak, solid. She hefted it, balanced it in her hands, wondered how it would be to fight Idings. Then she rested it in the crook of her arm and smoothed her hair. The Idings weren't here, and she had news to take to Edwin in his hall.

Paulinus was there, with Stephanus. Edwin heard her out in silence and then began to rant. With no wheat and no barley harvest likely, he'd had to trade with the queen's brother in Kent for grain. He'd raised the tithe at his York wīc and Tinamutha. He'd pressed Mulstan for greater revenue from the Bay of the Beacon. He'd sent word to Coelgar in Lindsey, to their cousin Osric in Craven hiding in his birch-clad hills and iron-rich streams, and to Pyr in Elmet: They must be stern; their king needed what could be spared, and more. But what did he get back? Whining, nothing but whining and news of more problems. He wanted to hear some useful suggestions for a change from his so-called counsellors.

Paulinus stepped forward and suggested the king might force the Gododdin and the men of Rheged to pay higher tribute because they didn't worship Christ through the right priests.

Edwin screamed at him and stabbed the table to tatters: Had his nithing, criminal god stolen his brains in the night? Did he not understand that, in Gaul, Sigebert was kissing the ring of the Franks for aid against the East Angles? The Franks! What was he, Edwin: fried tripe? You'd think so the way the Gododdin were becoming so bold. And now Rheged was mulling an alliance with the Dál Riata. On top of that, Cadwallon was readying Gwynedd for war, and Penda marching his Mercians to meet the West Saxons. He'd win. And then anything could happen, anything, and it was the priests' job to pray to their mighty god and bring some fine weather and a good end to the queen's term. And failing that, he should shut his mouth or by the gods he, the king, would pull his bishop's guts through his belly button and nail them to a tree. And the bishop of Rome could shove that up his arse and shit around it.

"At least Coifi knew his place!" he shouted at his retreating bishop, and followed it with a hurled bowl, which clipped Stephanus on the back of the head.

Hild watched the elm bowl roll in a tight circle on its silver rim, then settle upside down. She knew how it felt: round and round, everyone watching. She longed to throw something: at Paulinus, at Cian, at the king. Or stab something. Anything but stand calm and still and wait, always wait for things over which she had no control but had predicted boldly. A son. And healthy. But no one would know for a month or two.

"Wooden-headed, skirt-wearing lily-livers. Someone bring me another drink. And you," he said to Hild, "tell me something good."

Even if she had something good to offer, he wasn't in the mood to hear it. What he wanted was to shout and stab. After a moment she said, "Coifi was no better. But he at least isn't here."

"Ha. Tell me something I don't know. I wish Osric joy of him. And speaking of our cousin, is the Gododdin folly his doing? It was once his job to keep them quiet."

"Once," Hild said.

"Maybe he's meddling, sending men to stir them up."

She said nothing. Her uncle saw plots under every bench but it didn't make him wrong. Besides, Osric was a fool. Those who bet on the behaviour of fools lost.

Edwin's eyes glittered. "He could be plotting with any of them: Cadwallon, Penda, Dál Riata, Gododdin, Rheged. Any of them. All of them."

"We need a spy in his hall, someone in his counsel."

"I've a better idea. I'll take his son."

Pointy-toothed Oswine. She turned that in her mind. War was coming, it didn't take a seer to foresee that. They needed Craven's iron ore, its willing men. "Cloak it as an honour. Send an honourable man to say . . ." She saw it, sudden and complete. "To tell Osric that Oswine is to be groomed for a great task. To win renown and position."

"It better not cost me money."

"Rheged," Hild said. "Rhoedd needs to marry off Rhianmelldt. Why not to Oswine?"

"Are you quite mad?"

She saw the opening. She could twist the sword up and away. "Rheged can't stand alone anymore. It must choose a protector. Let it be Northumbria. Oswine isn't Osric, he wasn't raised to believe Deira was his. Rheged will seem a plum. Much better than Craven. Bring him here, smother him in gold and flattery, and he'll be yours. So will Rheged." The vision trembled before her, like a drop of rain on an outstretched fingertip, brilliant, beautiful, perfect.

"Oswine, king of Rheged?"

"Ealdorman of Rheged. Your man." Couldn't he see? Northumbria from sea to shining sea. "Think of the ports. Northumbria from coast to coast. Cadwallon will be cut off from the north Britons."

She imagined the tufa, the boar banner, cracking in the wind, the weight of the red ring.

She took a breath, dropped her shoulders, smoothed the impatience from her voice.

"Bring Oswine here, Uncle. And Prince Uinniau. They can make friends under your eye, sword brothers, sworn to you. And Uinniau would be a hostage for Rhoedd's good behaviour. They would both come, if you sent the right man."

"Eadfrith Sweet Tongue is with his brother, bringing the Gododdin to heel."

"Not Eadfrith. A man the wealh might trust."

"And who might this totem of trust be?"

"Cian Boldcloak."

A midsummer with no sun. Hild felt wrapped in cloud, suffocated, as though the air were wool. She sat with the king's counsellors, listening but not speaking, tolling her beads, lingering on the yellow. *Christ, the most important of all. He is everywhere.* She was missing something. And the queen swelled every day.

She longed to clear her head, stride the moors above Mulstanton, lean into the wind on the cliff by the Bay of the Beacon. She envied Cian riding in Craven with his gesiths, one of many, free to laugh, to shout, to sing. To do, not be stared at and whispered over. Not waiting for the sun, not waiting for the queen to give birth.

A message came from Rhin: Bandits were preying on the people of Elmet. Saxfryth. Lweriadd. Her people. Her Elmet.

"Where's the king?" she asked Gwladus.

"Hunched in his hall like a moulting hawk, I expect." She already had out Hild's favourite earrings, the moss agate and pearl, suitable for delivering bad news to a king. "Keep still or they'll end up hanging off your nose."

Hild moved her head, impatient. She wished she hadn't sent Cian to Craven. She needed him for this.

"Keep still."

She was tired of being *still*. She batted Gwladus's hand away. No, she wouldn't wait. Why should she? What could Cian do that she could not? "Put those away. Give me my staff instead."

At the east doorway, Lintlaf saw her coming, folded his arms, and leaned against the doorpost.

The chief gesith glittered; he was growing rich. For most people, a nod to his gesiths to step aside cost something pretty, something precious. He was just another kind of bandit, one who had gripped Gwladus's wrist hard enough to leave marks.

She met his gaze, then looked him up and down. He had too much weight on one leg. One swing at his knees would have him on the floor before he'd even unfolded his arms. Neither of his gesiths was paying attention: She was the king's niece, and she didn't even have a sword.

Cian was better than any of them, and she didn't always lose against him. They wouldn't get their blades free before her staff heel took them in the face. Yes. Long sweep to the knees. *Snap* of heel to one mouth, *snap* of tip to another. Scatter-patter of teeth. Sharp warmth of blood. Flipping the end of her stave up with her left hand, legs bent. Both hands pulling the length down in a whistling overhead arc. The splitting *crack* of oak on knee-cap. Then kneeling, and the seax to Lintlaf's balls. The smell of shit.

Should I make a prophecy about spilt yolk and no sons, Lintlaf? No gesith would gallop to war with a doom on his head.

She smiled a creamy smile.

Lintlaf stepped aside.

Edwin was brooding in the shadows at the end of his hall, alone but for a few housemen standing against the wall. A small fire burnt, but the air was damp. She relayed Rhin's message.

He stared at her for a long moment after she'd finished. "Bandits? What do I care about a few bandits on the Whinmoor?"

"They're becoming bold. Farmers fear for their lives and livestock."

"Am I nursemaid to the world? I'm sick of men holding out their hands and bleating." He slapped the board. His cup jumped. "A man must hold his own steading."

"At least send men to Pyr at Caer Loid."

He lifted the cup. A houseman glided over, filled it, and faded back against the wall. "I'm spread thinner than a miser's butter. Who should I send? My sons are in the north. Coelfrith's with the Crow in York. I've Idings in the north plotting with Scots at one end of the far wall and Picts at the other. Rheged and the Bryneich rumbling below that. In the west Cadwallon's gathering an army. Nithing!" He slapped the board again. Wine slopped. "Baying at our arse from the middle of the isle, we've Penda and his Mercians. In the south and east—"

"Send me."

Silence. "You?"

"Me, and twelve gesiths."

"For bandits?" He picked up his cup, eyed her over the rim. "It would be . . . messy."

"Needs must."

"Well, well." They faced each other, gazes locked. Yffing to Yffing. He sipped, swallowed, put his cup down with a decisive click. "Six gesiths."

"Eight, and your token to show Pyr in Caer Loid."

"My token." He flexed his hand—open, closed—studying her, watching her watch his ring. He opened his fist. Smiled. Nodded once. "Six. And my token. Though you'd better not have to use it." He pulled the great carved garnet off his pointing finger, and leaned forward. "You'll ride straight for the Whinmoor. No meddling with Pyr's work."

She held out her hand. "Yes." He dropped it in her palm. She hefted it. She slid it onto her thumb and made a fist.

"King's fist."

She felt rather than saw the ripple of attention run through the housemen standing along the wall. King's fist.

"It suits you, Niece. But I'll want it back." He sat back, then swore and turned his arm to look at his elbow. His jacket was sodden with wine. "Someone clean up this mess!" Two housemen leapt to obey. "That goes for you, too, Niece. Clean it up."

In the queen's guardroom, Bassus frowned—not at the king's niece, the king's fist, but at her question. What did she want with bandits?

He waved the houseman out and threw a log on the fire himself. She poured them both wine, unbidden. She wore the Yffing token. She didn't need anyone's permission.

Bandits.

"I hunted them in Kent, when Eadbald was ætheling." He immediately felt foolish. The girl—not girl, king's fist—wouldn't care who'd been ætheling. He lifted his cup and sniffed it. Iberian. His favourite. The same colour as her ring. "It's hard and filthy work. I wouldn't wish it on my worst enemy."

The log caught, setting shadows dancing along the wall and the Yffing token glinting blood-red. He wished his words back: She was the king's fist. It didn't do to use the word enemy in the same room.

"I'll show you the scar they gave me?"

She nodded, and he thumped his wine cup on the board and his right foot on the bench. He took off his belt, unfastened the tie under his jacket, and peeled down his hose. The scar along his shin was the size of a grass snake, thick and twisting, blueish-white and sunken in the middle, pink at the edges. It hadn't healed fast, and the infection had taken some of the bone with it.

"Worse than anything I took in a shield wall. Not made with good clean steel. An iron-edged spade," he said. "Filthy thing. Still aches sometimes, when it rains."

"I'll send you something for it."

"Thank you, lady." It wouldn't do to refuse.

He pulled his hose up again, tied them carefully, rearranged his jacket. He picked up his belt. Paused. "They fight with teeth and hands, slings and stones, sickles and spades. They turn on you, even when they've a hole torn right through the belly. Like mindless rats, never knowing when they're beaten. You should hunt them like rats, with nets and clubs, or dogs and a ring of bowmen. Or poison. Kill them all."

"Not all, surely."

"All, lady. And their young." She'd killed at Lindum, so they said. But you didn't understand bandits until you'd had one turn under your heel like a broken-backed snake. "Some say bandits are good men fallen on hard times. And perhaps some begin that way. But they become savages."

He ran his belt through his hands, half listening to the clink of gold fastenings won in his time as king's gesith.

"Lady, it's not like war. Bandits give no quarter, and you don't offer it, you can't, because they've no honour. None. I wouldn't do it again, not for all the wine in Iberia."

While Gwladus packed, Hild turned her wrist, tilting the ring this way and that. This way, even in the overcast, the carved garnet pulsed like lifeblood. That way turned it dark as a scab. Light, dark. King's token, king's fist.

King's weight.

She checked her packets of healing herbs, tucked them into their pockets next to the bandages and needles, rolled the leather, and tied it.

When Gwladus put her own dress in the small pile by the leather saddlebags, Hild said, "No. You're not coming."

Gwladus stopped, looked at her. "Then who's to attend you?"

"No one. Pack enough for a month."

"A month? You can't—"

"You're not coming."

"But—"

"Enough. I don't want you."

Gwladus flinched.

She wasn't riding as Lady Hild, king's niece, king's seer. She was riding as Hild, king's fist. She doubted it would be as bad as old Bassus thought, but it was clear bandit-hunting was not a task that required well-dressed hair or clean clothes. She wouldn't ride with anyone who couldn't kill, nor anyone who might recall her to herself. She had to be the king's fist, a killer. She had asked for this task. It must be done.

She rode south into Elmet through the blazing heather, Morud running beside her, and Oeric and six gesiths arrayed in a jingling crescent about her: Gwrast and Cynan, Coelwyn and Eadric, and the brothers Berht.

She rode light, no spare clothes, just two slim saddlebags holding hard bread, mead, and her wound roll. She carried her tokens on her body: her beads, her seax, her cross, the cups Cian had carved, Begu's snakestone, and Edwin's ring. When the sun came out the stone on her thumb glowed, her carnelians burnt, and the gold on her belt and Ilfetu's headstall gleamed.

They camped the first night in the lee of a lichened rock: the moor's bones, poking from the thin soil. Apart from Oeric and Morud the men were used to the war trail and comfortable enough, though unhappy that she wanted them to take off their rings and wrap their horse gear in cloth.

"Even in the moonlight you'll glitter like barrow wights. They'll see you coming from a mile away."

"Good!" Coelwyn said. "We'll freeze their marrow."

"Would you want birds to know the net is there?"

"Birds? We're gesiths. We hunt fearsome beasts. We don't bother with small frightened things."

"You do now."

She took off her beads, coiled them in her hand, dropped them in the purse on her belt.

"If we let them run, they'll come back when we're gone. We're here to trap them, judge them, then settle or kill them."

They nodded. They'd all seen her kill, except Oeric.

It was as their lady, dealer of wyrd and woe, that she judged the miserable bandits they chased down, the children, women, and men hauled cower-ing in groups of six from bramble thickets, hiding by twos in an over-stood coppice, or snivelling alone over a half-eaten bird in the lee of a rock.

Children, weak and starveling, who could cry on command and, if you offered comfort, would poke your eye with a filthy finger and rip the pin from your cloak. That's what had happened to Coelwyn. He would most probably lose that eye, though she'd done what she could.

Women, lush as a water meadow but with no teeth. Women with broken knives hidden in both hands. It served Gwrast right, she told him every night when she changed his bandage. It would be a while before he could carry a shield—but he didn't need a shield to fight bandits.

Men, with muscles like steel bands and broken minds. Men who'd try to rape a nettle bush if it kept still.

Hild judged them all. She judged them as impersonally as a murrain or a bolt of lightning.

She sent children with milk teeth, even the wicked ones, to her mene wood, with Morud to guide and Coelwyn to guard. Morud brought back news that the beck glistened with eggs and flickered with flies; there would be a fine run of fish, sun or no sun. The mene would survive. Next year it might thrive. There would be plenty of work for healthy children. He also brought back two bow hunters and a netman; Rhin hoped the lady would return them by Blodmonath.

She was glad of the bow hunters: Bassus had been right about some things.

She rode from dawn to dusk, judging, settling, listening to the folk. Every steading had a story of a band of wolf's-heads, bandit fiends who raped and murdered and slaughtered the kine, burnt the fields, shat in the well from sheer wickedness. But like the Cait Sith these fiends always seemed to visit misery on someone else, someone over the hill or in the next valley.

She smashed the right elbows of two brothers they found stealing cattle from a widow and her sons at Brown Crag. Without use of their arms they would only survive if there were people who loved them well enough to feed them for a few weeks.

She settled one couple and nearly grown son, whom they'd caught holding nothing but a handful of stolen carrots, with a farmer just west of Rhin's old church. A week later, she led her band back to the farm hoping for an evening sleeping dry under a roof and a hot meal. They found the place smouldering, the farmwife raped and dead, and the husbandman's guts spilt in the straw of the byre where the bandits had cut off the milch cow's hind legs and tried to start a fire.

Hild looked at the dead couple, not skipping the gleam of bone and glisten of gut, the carefully mended shift now torn right across the wobbly weave. These people had taken the bandits in because she'd asked. Because she'd had mercy.

"Take what we can use, then finish what they started." She looked at her men one by one. Her gaze rested on Oeric longest. "Burn it well. May the smoke of the dead follow the wolf's-heads and carry their doom."

Oeric shivered, and swallowed, and hoped he wouldn't be sick. The bandit choked and his heels drummed on the turf; his shoes were more gap than leather, different shapes. Instead of hose he wore filthy wrappings from ankle to knee. The choking was the same sound Morud made when he hawked up phlegm before spitting, only the choking went on and on. Spitting made Gwladus angry. If Gwladus was here maybe then the lady would smile sometimes. Maybe she wouldn't be so pitiless.

It began to rain, a fat pattering summer rain, lifting the scent of earth and gorse flowers. Three ravens circled. From over the rise where the others waited, a horse whickered.

"The horses are getting cold," the lady said.

He had given an oath. Without that oath, without the lady, he'd be a farmer who bent the knee to any man with a sword. But men who carried swords must be able to use them. And it was just going to get worse. They were tracking a band, at least half a dozen, and now it looked as though the three from the farmstead had joined them. They would catch them soon. Tomorrow or the day after.

"Oeric."

He drew Clifer. Maybe the bandit would just die. Maybe the lady would hit him again and finish it. But she only leaned on her staff and watched him choke.

Those eyes saw everything. The green saw your heart, they said, the blue your mind, and the black . . . the black drank in wyrd and your woe so others might be safe. Killing was nothing to what those eyes had seen.

He swallowed again. He should stab the bandit through the throat, it was the surest thing, but he couldn't bear to look at what the heel of the lady's staff had done to it, oak driven hard and sure, with all her terrible strength. Since burning the farmstead the lady never hesitated. The lady never seemed unsure. Perhaps he wouldn't either once he had killed a man.

But this wasn't the hot glory of battle, the stuff scops sang of. This was like killing a wether with a broken leg. Only the wether didn't wear clothes, didn't laugh, didn't long for a swig of mead or the squeeze of a woman's thighs. A wether didn't try to kill your lady with a sickle.

His legs felt like wood. The hand wrapped around Clifer's hilt could have been a stranger's. The bandit stank.

"Don't shut your eyes," the lady said.

He lifted Clifer with both hands, plunged for the chest. Clifer jarred in his hands and skidded over the man's ribs. He stabbed again, again, again. Gore slapped him across the mouth.

Then he was on his knees, not sure how he'd got there. He lifted his face to the rain. It smelt musty.

"Make sure he's dead," she said.

Of course he was dead, he was hacked almost in two. But always be sure, she said. Always check.

"When you're done, clean your sword, then join us. Don't take too long."

The lady strode over the rise and it was just him and the dead man. A raven thumped into the turf.

The lady had said just yesterday, *An eyeless face discourages others*. He looked at that thick black beak and levered himself to his feet. He felt very tired.

By the fire, Eadric lent Oeric his bottle of linseed oil and Gwrast showed him how to use a chewed twig dipped in oil to work flecks of dried blood from under the wire wrapping on Clifer's hilt. Hild watched him. His smiles were jerky, his eyes shone too bright, and he blinked a great deal, but she didn't offer comfort. What he needed was the solace of ordinary companionship, of others like him.

Indigo drained from the predawn sky behind them. Flicks and flirts of wind ran over the sparsely grassed slope. Hild lay on her belly. Dew soaked slowly through her wool. She ignored it. To either side, her gesiths inched forward. She checked to the north and south: Both bow hunters were in place, bows strung, ready to block escape west with a rain of arrows.

Another flick of wind brought the smell of greasy ash, singed hair, smouldering hooves, and the thick stink of unwashed bandits. She counted the huddles around the remains of the fire below. Nine. Some were large enough for two. One was wrapped in a striped blanket that would be blue and green in daylight. The farmwife had been showing the bandit woman how to beat it clean the day Hild had ridden away feeling wise.

One of the lumps by the fire, she knew, was dead.

They'd tracked the family for four days, always heading north and west. On the second day they'd joined the band of wolf's-heads: hard, lean, and armed. Not poor folk getting by the best they could.

She'd listened to them last night, drinking whatever it was they'd stolen from some steading, then singing and laughing, and taking it in turns to fuck someone to death. From the sound she couldn't tell if it had been a woman or a stripling. Not a child. A child's screams would have been higher. While they fucked and roared and giggled, the last of the rancid cow leg thrown in the fire burnt. They must feel close to safety. There was no watch, and whatever they'd been drinking was potent.

Nothing stirred. Light leaked into the hollow, though not enough to change the greys to colour.

One of the bundles twitched, then unfolded to become a thin woman who tottered two paces before slumping into a squat with her shift around her waist.

Hild looked right and left. Nodded. The hunters nocked arrows. Gesiths loosened their blades and checked their spears. She tightened her grip on her stave and settled her seax. Gathered her feet under her. Lifted her stave. Bowmen drew, gesiths rose.

She drew her hand across her throat: no mercy. Strings thrummed, spears lofted. She ran.

She ran silent as a deer, muscles pumping, heels thudding on the turf. Straight for the squatting woman.

A spear thumped into the woman's foot and she started to shriek and turn, thin shit running down her leg. Hild was already swinging. Her stave took the woman in the throat. She felt the soft shock all the way to her shoulders, then she was leaping over the writhing ruin, lips skinned back, gaze fixed on the blanket.

"Death!" she howled. "Death!" And the dark hollow filled with men and spears and screams.

She stood on the brow of the rise, leaning on her staff, looking west and north to a great gap in the hills. They were twenty-five miles west of the Whinmoor. Those were the foothills of the backbone mountains. In the low sun the river running through the Gap glittered, and faint sheep tracks showed along the valley on either side. This was where the bandits had been heading: north, through the Gap, to Craven.

Cian was in Craven. It wasn't so very far. She could lead her men through the Gap and find out if Osric was such a poor ealdorman he didn't know about the bandits rooted on his land, or if he knew full well. Ealdorman Osric would have to kneel to her ring . . .

But perhaps Cian was already back in Sancton with Oswine. And the queen would be very nearly due. She had to be there for that.

Morud knelt and kept his eyes on the grass. "Lady, the iron's hot."

She followed him down into the hollow, past the row of bodies, to the youth struggling between the brothers Berht. Unlike Morud they were not afraid to meet her gaze. Their own was worshipful. A lady of wyrd, a lady who could kill. Skirt and sword.

A pile of goods for burning lay to one side of the dead fire. A much smaller pile lay on the green-and-blue blanket to the other. It was a good blanket. Rhin would be able to use it.

The stripling had curly brown hair, hazel eyes, and teeth still new enough to be straight. He went limp when he saw her, but he weighed so little the brothers didn't sag.

She nodded at the brothers and drew her seax. "Turn him to the light."

He struggled, but the brothers tightened their grip. She slit the tattered remnants of his tunic. Flea bites ran down his hairless chest. She shifted the seax to her left hand, laid her right palm against his breastbone. His heart beat wildly. She fixed her gaze on his eyes.

"What's your name?"

"Lady—"

"Your name."

"Tims, lady. Lady, I beg you—"

"Look at me." He did. His heart steadied, then slowed. "Tims, are you from Craven?"

His heart jumped. "Lady—"

"Sshh, sshh. No matter." His heart slowed again. "Tims, answer me now. Are you willing to do honest work?"

"Yes! Lady, I swear!" But his heart kicked like a hare, and his pupils shrank to dots.

She stepped back, sheathed her seax, and nodded to Coelwyn, who shoved a spear up through Tims's sunken belly and under his ribs. Tims screamed and writhed and Coelwyn shouted for the brothers to hold him still, still, you arseholes, and levered the spear to and fro, swearing until he found the big vein and Tims poured out, red on the bleached grass.

She toed through the pile on the blanket: a skin of mead, two good axes, a flawed beryl, a painted leather belt, and a bag of rust powder. She hooked up the mead skin, unstoppered it, sniffed. Mad honey. She poured it away.

Cynan and Gwrast hacked the heads and hands from bodies. Eadric carried them to the fire, where Oeric lifted the brand from the coals and burnt the wolf's-head onto every forehead and hand. He hated doing it, especially the women, but Hild had said, "I'm the king's fist and you're mine," and like the others he didn't dare argue with this new Hild, hard as iron. He was hers to command.

They hammered stakes across the Gap and impaled the bodies, the heads, the hands, in a long row facing Craven, all branded with the wolf's-head. That night, by firelight, her men limewashed their unused shields and painted a staked man and a wariangle in a glistening mix of blood, rust, and oil. Men of the butcher-bird.

Bandits would not trouble Elmet now for a while. She sent the bowmen back to her Menewood with the blanket and the axe heads. They were good blades, and the mene had no smith.

As she and her men rode north and east, the sky clouded and the ground turned soft. The sun hadn't shone here yet, but it would; she could smell the change of weather following them. It wasn't the only thing that followed them; but the Elmetsætne, instead of coming out to talk to her, stayed in the trees.

She told herself it was all to the good. The rumours were doing her work for her. But not far from the road a tremulous voice shrieked *Butcher-bird!* and a hazel tree shook as someone small scrambled out of reach.

She wanted to leap off her horse, climb the tree, back the child against the trunk, and shout, *It's how I keep us safe!*

But there was no *us*. Belonging was not a seer's wyrd. She held Ilfetu to a walk and didn't blink.

———

They returned to Sancton at midmorning under a tattered sky. Even as she reined in, she saw the looks that passed between the housefolk. She could have made her gesiths paint out their shields but it wouldn't have made a difference. Gesiths would tell their tales. *Fate goes ever as it must.*

She unhooked her saddlebags and tossed them to Morud. "Tell Gwladus to bring food to my room." The whispers left the byre before her, running through the vill like bracken fire: butcher-bird . . .

She strode to the hall. In the doorway, the low morning sun caught the carved boar on her thumb and struck fire from her carnelians. Gesiths paused in their games and stared, silent, at the enormous shadow with its stave, glittering around the edges like a wight. One was Oswine, playing knuckles with Lintlaf. But no king, no priests, no Cian. Had he been and gone again? She left without a word.

She found Edwin and Coelfrith, heads together by the gate in the east hedge where housefolk were gathering elm boughs. She hadn't seen anyone but wealh set elm aside since she was a child. The inner bark, when added to soups and stews of nettles, would thicken them enough to keep you alive, for a while.

Six gesiths, armed and armoured, stood to one side. Edwin gave no sign that he knew they were there, but they had an air of hurry about them, and their shields were on their arms, not their backs. When they dipped their heads to her ring they did not lower their eyes, and two did not bother to conceal the fact that they looked beyond her to see if she had brought her hounds: brothers who now wore shields painted with an emblem that was not the king's boar.

She stopped outside stave-reach of the king and bent her head. "Uncle."

He waited. She knelt.

He nodded. "Niece."

Coelfrith sighed and the tension left his knees. Hild felt herself split in two: the butcher-bird thinking, I could take him, and the seer, I serve the king. She leaned her staff in the crook of her arm and wrapped her fingers around the ring. Hesitated.

Now the king gave her an amused look: *Told you I'd want it back.* "Did you bring me anything worthwhile, Niece?"

She let go of the ring and pointed up. "The sun, Uncle."

"So we won't need these?" He waved at the housefolk with armsful of elm branches.

"Will Eadbald not trade his Kentish wheat?"

"Of course he'll trade. But why spend if I don't have to?"

She turned the ring on her thumb. "The sun's here to stay. You could plant a barley crop."

Coelfrith said to the king, "Why risk the seed? We should save it for next year."

"Don't look at me. She's the seer. Besides, she's still wearing the boar. Even from her knees she speaks for the king. So what should the king say, Niece?"

Hild understood why the king hated decisions. There were always so many of them. "Wheat and barley both from Eadbald?" she asked Coelfrith.

He nodded. "It's landed at Brough. It'll come by barge to York."

No risk of starvation, then, just silver. "Plant," she said.

"How much?"

"All of it. But plant today. Plant now."

"That's what I like," Edwin said. "Bold choice." He held out his hand for the ring. Coelfrith moved to go.

"Wait," she said. "Coelfrith, your brother. Coelwyn lost an eye. But he's hearty. He's strong. He fought well."

After a moment, Coelfrith said, "An eye. Well, he has another," because that was what gesiths were supposed to say. Just an eye, just an ear, just a finger. The gods gave us more than one. What will be, is.

He nodded to her, to the king, and walked back to the vill.

Edwin turned his hand over, palm down, pointing finger out. "Ring."

Hild pulled it off her thumb and slid it onto his finger.

He flexed his hand, rolled his shoulders.

"So. Staking them out. A strong statement for a few bandits."

"They came from Craven."

His eyes glittered. "You're sure?"

"You should ask Oswine."

"Ah, you've seen him, then. Oh, do get up. Very well, we'll ask Oswine. But don't upset him. Remember he's our honoured guest."

He had rolled the work from his, to theirs, to hers, slick as goose grease. She would remember that trick. She wanted to stretch but didn't want to seem too tall or too strong next to the king. "And our other honoured guest?"

"If, as you promised, the weather holds, your Boldcloak will be back from Rheged with Uinniau before the first leaves fall."

Her mother dropped the door of the weaving hut behind her and studied Hild. She nodded at her empty thumb. "It's left a mark."

Hild looked at the band of pale skin. She scratched it.

Breguswith put her hand under Hild's chin and turned her face this way and that. "The flesh is nearly burnt from your bones and the human from your heart. You're nothing but wyrd and ælf breath. Spend less time in the wind."

"Where is . . . everyone?"

"Begu attends the queen. It'll be soon. The Crow is no doubt hotfooting it back from his stone church in York. You've seen the king? He's been banishing people or whipping their feet raw. He's fretting about food."

"Not anymore."

Breguswith nodded. "You gave him good news, then. It's all he'll listen to. He drove the scop out, said if he had to listen to one more tale of luck and wyrd, he'd cut his throat and use his sinews for bowstrings."

She didn't care about the scop. "Where's—"

"Your bodywoman is no doubt making the housefolk miserable. Fear makes her vicious."

Fear. What did Gwladus know of fear?

Hild sat on the blanket. It was new: green-and-blue chevrons. She stood, paced. Unfastened her belt, slid off her seax and purse. Put them on the shelf by the bed. Sat. She was hungry.

She tried to turn the ring that wasn't there. She turned her beads, tolled through them. Penda. Cadwallon. Eanfrith, Oswald, Oswiu. And the yellow bead, the brightest. Christ, the most important of all. Whatever that meant.

She unfastened the beads, coiled them in her palm, weighed them. How mad was little Rhianmelldt now? What did Cian think of her? What would Cian think of the butcher-bird?

He'd come back with that bite on his jaw. He knew how it was.

She leaned over and put the beads next to her seax on the shelf.

Blue and green . . .

She felt the soft shock of stave on throat, the shriek of Tims as Coelwyn levered his spear up and down. She realised her lips were skinned back. She shook the memory out of her head. She was hungry, thirsty. More than hungry. Her clothes were filthy. She peeled them off, dropped them in a heap by the door. Sat down again.

What was keeping Gwladus?

She was so tired of waiting. Always waiting. She was the butcher-bird. She didn't have to wait; she could take.

The door rattled then swung open, framing Gwladus: holding a tray, hair unbound and freshly combed, smelling of flowers. An offering: herself; all she had.

Neither said anything.

A pot on the tray rattled as Gwladus lowered it to the table. Hild made no move towards it. Gwladus, very pale, took a breath, climbed onto the bed, lay on the blanket, and spread her bright hair over the pillow.

When Hild still said nothing, made no move, Gwladus took Hild's hand and laid it on her belly.

A thin linen dress. Nothing underneath. Hild let her hand lie there, feeling the heat and tremble through the light weave. Like Tims. She could tear it with one hand, tear Gwladus's heart out.

Who's to stop me, who in all the world?

She ached. She felt so alone. She wanted to feel Gwladus respond, rise under her, strong and fierce. Hers. She could take her, take her pleasure on her. This time Gwladus wouldn't try to stop her. She would pretend to cry out with need. She had to. She was a slave. With nowhere to go, no one to turn to. Hild had left her behind once. She had to please Hild or be thrown away, to gesiths like Lintlaf.

Who's to stop me?

She ran her hand up Gwladus's belly, touched her bare shoulder, pushed the dress down, cupped her breast—so pale against her dark hand, so plump, so soft. How would it be to lay her naked length against Gwladus, feel her tremble with need, not fear? Did it matter if it wasn't real? She swallowed. Rose to her knees, ran her hands down the pale ribs, bumping over them, one by one—so small—to her waist, her thighs, her hem. She lifted the hem, lifted the dress, pulled it with both hands, pulled it up, pulled it off. Left it draped over the pillow, over the spread hair. The vein at Gwladus's neck beat and fluttered like a trapped bird. Hers.

Gwladus closed her eyes.

Hild straddled naked cream and gold and ivory and breathed her flowery hair, her own sharp woman scent. She lifted the dress from the pillow, crushed it in her hands: so fine, so soft, nothing like the wobbly tabby of the farmwife.

Who in all the world?

On the shelf, her beads glittered.

Then I tell you truly, you must learn to stop yourself.

She hurled the dress at the floor. Gwladus flinched but did not move. Hild climbed off, muscles clenching, hands in fists. "Look at me!"

Gwladus opened her eyes.

"You're mine. You'll grow old in my household, die warm and well fed. You're my bodywoman. Some services I'll require, from time to time. But I won't . . . I won't."

Silence.

"Do you understand?"

Gwladus nodded.

Hild got off the bed, brought back the dress. "Then I will eat some cheese. And you may . . . comb my hair. And afterwards dress me in my lightest weave. The sun is here for a while."

With the sun came heat like a fist. The sky turned into a bronze-and-enamel bowl on which the sun beat until their world swelled and rang. The earth steamed. The people sweltered. The barley grew fast, green as grass, greener than the king's eyes.

The king toasted Hild in hall and tossed the empty cup at her to keep. The Crow looked as though he would prefer to throw a dagger. His priests crossed themselves if her shadow touched theirs. They had heard her gesiths' songs: wyrd dealer, miracle healer, butcher-bird. They all watched everything she did, watched everything she watched—and everyone. So she refused to see the men's strong jaws and women's soft skin, refused to notice the bright eyes, the clean limbs, and the swelling curves all around her. She would make do with Gwladus, for a while.

She made sure her cross hung on the outside of her dress, kept the impatience from her stride and command from her voice, and settled in to understand Oswine.

He spent his time with Lintlaf. She didn't approach them. She and Lintlaf might come to blows. The butcher-bird wanted that; Gwladus lay between them. And she might win. But then he'd be shamed, broken as chief gesith, and her uncle hated people to break his tools. Besides, she might lose. Lintlaf might kill her. Then her gesiths would try to kill him. Whoever won, men would die. She had sworn to be totem and token to her people, to light their path, not darken it. And she had the queen's impending birth to think about.

She sent for Morud—who seemed to sense that here she was Hild, his lady of the mene, the king's niece, not the awful butcher-bird—and set him to get close to Oswine's bodyman, find out what Oswine and his father knew about bandits.

"Dull as hammers," Morud said two days later. "Both him and his da. If either of them knows anything I'll eat that blanket."

"Does he think Osric plans to retake Deira one day?"

"Think?" Morud squinted, as he did when he was trying not to laugh. "He wants and he whines and he worries, but he doesn't think."

"What does he worry about?"

Morud shrugged. "That no one really likes him. That he's wearing the wrong brooch or fastens his jacket the wrong way. That the first time he's in a shield wall he'll get himself killed or, worse, make himself a laughingstock."

With the heat came the mosquitoes and flies. Cows lowed piteously and flicked their tails, men in the fields cursed and swatted, housefolk woke with swollen faces, and the cook swore she would kill anyone who left the door open again and let the flies in, she didn't care if the kitchens were hotter than the Satan's hell.

Begu worried about the queen. "She's due and past due. But at least she doesn't fret all the time now about the crops and omens. She was wearing her knees away, and it's not good for a woman that big to kneel so long. You came back just in time." Gwladus poured her beer. "And I must say, service has improved lately, too. How do you keep the beer cool in this heat, Gwladus?"

"By the power of her tongue," Morud said from the corner, then blushed strayberry red. "Her words, lady. Her words. She bullies people. It's for the lady Hild, she says. It's for the king's seer. Where do you think your bread is coming from this year? From the lady's word and wyrd, from her goodwill, so if there's only room in the cellar for one cask of beer, then that's the lady Hild's cask."

"What is wrong with him?" Begu said to Hild. "And what's wrong with you? Is it the heat?" But Hild saw the knowing glint in her eye.

Gwladus stepped back to the curtain, lifted it, and jerked her head at Morud.

When they'd gone, Begu stretched. "Well, I'm glad things are back to normal. Eat some more strayberries. You're still too thin."

Hild obeyed. "Gwladus tells me we have a new houseman."

Begu didn't even blush. "Swidhelm. Swid. He's a byre man, really. Good with colts. Strong."

"Cian will be back with Uinniau in autumn."

Begu smiled and bit a berry in half. "If it's a son, we'll need a scop to sing his praises, to bring his wyrd." For one heart-stopping moment, Hild thought Begu was with child. "Your mother will find one, she says, but I think she already has. I think she found him the day after the king banished the other one—the one who told the good story about the Geats and the dragon. You never know about babies, when they'll come. Even royal ones. Especially royal ones. You have to be ready anytime. I think the queen's dropped. She'll have her son soon. He'll be an Yffing . . ."

Begu believed in her powers completely; if Hild had said it would be a son, then it would be. When Begu was talking, Hild didn't worry that she might be wrong.

". . . the Crow will throw holy water on his head and burn incense and sing hymns, but an Yffing needs a song about his father and his father's father, and on and back, so everyone, not just Christ on his cloud, knows who the little ætheling is."

Christ on his cloud . . . A thought streaked across her mind but was gone so fast she couldn't catch it. Begu chattered on. If she used weapons the way she used words, no one would stand against her; they'd have no idea where the stroke would fall next.

But she trusted Begu on the matter of birth as completely as her gemæcce trusted her prophesying, so when the queen went into labour late that night, Hild was ready for the king's summons.

In the audience hall by the feast hall, with one silent attendant standing by the south wall, the king paced. "Tell me again how it will be."

This was a duel already begun. No backing away now. "The queen will have a son. Big and healthy. An Yffing with the strong hand and hard mind of his kin."

"And?"

"And autumn will be late coming. The barley will be brought in safely. We'll have barley bread this winter."

"And the men of the north?"

"The men of the north will truckle to the Anglisc."

"You don't say when." He scratched the welt on the back of his left hand, peered at it, rubbed it instead on his thigh and looked at her. "And you don't say to which Anglisc."

Hild wished there was a fire to crackle, even a fly to drone, something to fill the quiet, to stop her listening for a cry from Æthelburh. "What does Bishop Paulinus say?"

Edwin cracked his knuckles. "He can't see beyond that white shawl that he expects from the bishop of Rome with every ship." He paced again, back and forth. "Well, fuck the men of the north. Fuck Penda, bugger the West Saxons, and piss on Cadwallon."

Someone would, one day.

Back and forth. Back and forth. Scratch scratch scratch. "Your mother tells me you have a niece."

"Æthelwyn—"

A knock at the door. The king yanked it open before his attendant could get there. Wilnoð. A smear of blood on her sleeve. The king's gaze fixed upon it. Wilnoð bowed. Straightened. "May it please my lord King, you have a son."

Edwin swelled. Hild breathed out, but quietly.

"The queen is well. Your son is well. He's heavy. Big and strong."

Edwin clapped Hild on the shoulder. "You'll have his weight in silver! And a gift for your niece." Down the corridor, past Wilnoð, the air stirred then filled with striding priests: Paulinus and two attendants. "I have a son," Edwin said. "His name is Wuscfrea!"

Wuscfrea, the father of Yffi of long ago. A name announcing a claim and precedence.

When Breguswith brought the scop, Luftmaer, to the king's audience hall after breakfast, Hild saw immediately how it was. He was tall, young, wide-mouthed, and clean. He already wore an arm ring Hild had last seen in her mother's chest. The hands resting on his lyre case were long-fingered, his shoulders well-balanced.

The king told Coelfrith and Stephanus to come back with the accounts later, called for ale, and told the scop to sing the praise song he'd prepared for the feast.

Luftmaer unshipped his lyre with practiced hands, tuned the strings—though more out of habit, she thought, than need—and began. His peat-brown eyes filled with tears every other line, but none of them fell. His deep-grained voice drew and released verses, perfectly flighted. Along the side of the hall, gesiths began to beat out the rhythm with the flat of their hands. It was the kind of song they loved: blood and gold, never grow old, never feel cold, honey in the comb, hearth and home, glory and story, all topped, like foam on just-pulled milk, by the rousing, rhythmic chant of the forebears:

"Wuscfrea the son of Edwin king of the Anglisc, the son of Ælla, the son of Yffi, the son of Wuscfrea, the son of Wilgisl, the son of Westerfalca, the son of Sæfugl, the son of Sæbald, the son of Segegeat, the son of Swebdæg, the son of Sigegar, the son of Wædæg, the son of Woden, god of gods."

"King of the Anglisc, god of gods!" Edwin bellowed. "Again!"

Luftmaer obliged, eyes filling, fingers picking, voice drawing and releasing, exactly as before.

"Wuscfrea . . . king of the Anglisc . . . god of gods!" the gesiths sang.

"Wuscfrea!" the king shouted, and raised his cup. "My son!"

Everyone drank, and then the gesiths made boasts about how each would outdo the other to serve the young ætheling, the wounds they would endure, the fights they would relish, the gold they would win.

The gesiths had taken their singing outside, her mother had taken the scop away, and Hild half drowsed in the sunlight by the door while Edwin listened to Coelfrith give his accounting. With the better weather, trade had picked up. Two extra shipments of wheat had arrived from Eadbald . . .

She had a headache: partly the air, which was tightening and brooding though the sky was clear, partly too much beer that morning. It was good to not be worrying. Her neck itched. She scratched it. A mosquito bite. She wondered if there were mosquitoes in Rheged. She didn't remember any during the season she spent north of the wall, but it hadn't been hot like this. Which way would Cian bring Uinniau back? Ride the wall road, then Dere Street to York, or sail down the west coast, then ride east then south through Craven? But then he'd be bringing him through the Gap.

The staked bandits would be nothing but bones now, fallen and long picked over. She shook her mind free of that. Here she wasn't the butcherbird. Here she was the well-dressed seer wearing her cross. Tidy and clean. Tidy and listening. Tidy and restless.

The king was restless, too, twisting this way and that in his chair, tapping his ring on its gilded arm. She remembered the weight of it.

She turned her beads. They were tight around her hard muscle and big bones. Muscle, bone, skin sliding on skin . . . She shook her mind free of that, too, and thought instead of when she'd first got the beads from mad little Rhianmelldt. Back then, she could wrap the strand around her wrist four times. Now only three. Everything changes.

Christ, the most important of all . . . Again the glimpse of an idea was gone before she could grasp it, drowned in others' talk. This time Coelfrith saying two more stonemasons had come for the church, which now stood higher than a man's shoulder. And tithes from Craven were a little low. She would suggest to the king that they visit Osric in Craven, take the gesiths, claim the tithe in the form of hospitality. Maybe she should go. With the king's token.

Butcher-bird. Was that her wyrd?

She didn't want to think about it today. She closed her eyes. What did Æthelwyn look like? Like Hereswith or like Æthelric? Begu said sometimes children looked more like other kin than their parents: Perhaps little Æthelwyn would look like Hild. But even if she saw her niece, how would she know if Æthelwyn looked anything like she had when she was little? Perhaps when Cian got back they could visit the East Angles, and she could see for herself. If he got back before the autumn gales made it too risky to sail down the east coast.

Her mother could come, too—now Wuscfrea was born, cloth-making could be left to the queen. She didn't much like the idea of spending time with that scop on a boat, though. Then, too, maybe Cian wouldn't like being cooped up with her and Gwl—

The Crow was talking. She opened her eyes.

Paulinus stood with Stephanus before the king. "The ætheling Wuscfrea is to be baptised at the end of the week. Yet Father Stephanus tells me his praise song claims he's descended from Woden. It is blasphemy."

Edwin massaged the back of his neck. "Woden is my forefather."

"He's a false god. You may not name him."

Edwin gave Paulinus a long look. "May not?"

Hild would have liked nothing better than to see the Crow whipped around a tree, but *That man and his god are useful to me.* Paulinus was part of the plan to keep the kingdom safe, keep the Yffings safe. Keep her safe. Until she saw her wyrd more clearly.

She checked her cross, stood. "My king?"

Edwin nodded. She stepped forward.

"My lord Bishop. We Christians say that there is no god but Christ."

Paulinus looked at her down his nose, though he had to tip his head back to do so. She watched him test the assertion, looking for the trap. But he couldn't disagree. "There is no God but God, and Christ is His son."

"Then how can Woden be a god, false or otherwise? Woden is a man. A great man, a mighty man, the overking's forefather, but a man. It won't be blasphemy to name him so: honoured forefather of Wuscfrea. King of kings in his time. A man such as our new ætheling may hope one day to be."

"Ha!" said Edwin, with a beat of both palms on the arms of his chair. "Woden, king of kings! I'll hear no more of it."

The barley had grown heavy and golden. Wuscfrea thrived. Cian would be back soon with Uinniau.

Hild lay on her back in the hummocky grass, arms behind her head, alone on the moor. She had made it clear to her hounds that she liked to go away by herself. They had seen her kill. They knew she was a creature of the uncanny, so let her protect herself with wyrd and stave while she went to other worlds and communed with gods.

She smiled to herself and watched the sky, hearing nothing but wind feathered by the heather, seeing nothing, not a bird nor a bee nor a cloud, just endless sky. The empty blue worked itself between her and the world at her back, lifted, levered, pried her free, and then she was falling, up, up into the bottomless well . . .

An eagle sliced across a corner of the blue, and once again there was an up and a down, and she slid back into her body, right-way up, once more sheathed in muscle and skin.

The hummock under her back felt different, as though she'd been away a long time. She stretched and laughed to herself. It would make a good story: stolen by hobs and hidden in a fold of the world while the rest turned to dust. She would tell Cian.

She stood and dusted off her dress. The eagle began to rise. Round and round, higher and higher on its pillar of air, pinions flaring gold in the sun. What she must see . . .

As she walked her mind was with the eagle, soaring over the whole isle. North and east over the high moor to Onnen at the Bay of the Beacon where Mulstan tithed to Edwin and the ruined church crumbled into the cliff. Tilting north over hilly woodland to the wall, where Bryneich still talked of her prophecy of friendship forever. Still farther north to Yeavering and the strange talking stage, the totem now carved with a cross. Then arcing west over Rheged where mad little Rhianmelldt balanced at the crux of its future. Out over the heaving waters of the North Channel that divided the two lands of the Dál Riata. Back towards the mainland, the isle of Manau at her left wing tip. The northern mountains of Gwynedd, and Deganwy, the fort on the river that led to the sea, where Cadwallon held the warp of the Irish Sea trade and the web of shaved-forehead priests. Then south and east over the midland valleys and woodland of Penda's Mercia; Penda, unbaptised, who was pursuing unbaptised West Saxons south and west to Dyfneint towards an end no one knew. Turning again, rising east, Kent and the pope's overbishop out of sight, beyond her right wing. Over the fenland where Hereswith suckled her baby and listened to Fursey's advice. North again, over Lindsey where Coelgar oversaw the rich, tidy, newly Christian farmland . . .

Back at the vill the first person she saw was Swid, the byre man, leading two horses round the yard. Cian, she thought, and Uinniau. But they didn't look good enough for something a prince of Rheged might ride. "Been rode hard all day," Swid said. "From parts south."

The horses' withers were curded with sweat but there was no blood at the bit. Important, but not urgent. She would have time to change before the king called her.

Gwladus gave her the news as she dressed: Penda had caught the West Saxons at Cirencaester and thrashed them like washing, dashed Cynegils and Cwichelm's army to pieces. Cwichelm had fled—mortally wounded, said some, already dead, said others—and Penda had crowned Cynegils king and married him to his sister.

Penda now ruled the Mercians and the West Saxons, the whole middle of the isle and its southwestern toe.

The middle of the isle. The middle of the isle: Woden worshippers surrounded on all sides by baptised kings. Gwynedd, Kent, Rheged, Dyfneint, Dál Riata, Pictland, Northumbria, even the Idings. *Christ, the most important of all.* That was what Fursey meant. The Christ was everywhere, his priests were everywhere, advising every king, writing it all down. Penda was surrounded.

He must choose an ally. Cadwallon, in the west, with his shaved foreheads. Or Edwin, in the east, with his shaved crowns. Wealh or Roman. Whichever he chose, he would alter the great weave.

Penda was clever. He would choose Cadwallon because Cadwallon was weaker, more easily absorbed and overcome. But in the end it wouldn't matter. Even if Penda sided with Edwin, they would one day fight. Penda needed the Christ. Edwin needed the Christ. But only one could have the Christ's chief priest and the trade web allied with Rome.

21

✦

CIAN RETURNED FROM RHEGED with Uinniau. But Hild didn't see them much. They and Oswine were always riding out—the Bay of the Beacon, a visit to the Bryneich—at Edwin's suggestion, or so Hild persuaded herself. She hoped it was not that Cian could not bear to be near the butcher-bird.

The court moved to York. The longest Cian, Uinniau, and Oswine were with the household was at Yule, when they sat with the gesiths who were not Hild's hounds.

Spring came late to Yeavering that year. The court had been there a fortnight and still the top of Ad Gefrin was speckled with snow and the roe deer hadn't dropped their young. In the vill, the snow was gone, but a cold, wet wind blew without cease. In the king's hall the fires smoked. In the queen's hall, Eanflæd coughed until she turned red and wailed, and little Wuscfrea coughed himself pale and silent. All the children, wealh and Anglisc, visitor and local, sickened. The hall filled with mothers bringing children with sticky eyes and heaving chests to breathe the clearer air of the high women's hall and for Breguswith to tend. Begu and Gwladus helped. Hild did not. Hægtes, they called her. Freemartin. Butcher-bird.

Hild went out into the weather to find chickweed. It was too early in the year for full potency, but she gathered it anyway, gave it to Gwladus to put to steep in boiling water, and went back out to find more.

Uinniau, crouched in the lee of the hill to wash his bloody hands, paused, hands dripping. "What was that?"

Cian looked up from the doe he was butchering. Oswine dropped the twig he'd been feeding to the flickering flame.

"The fire!" Lintlaf said, as a gust of wind nearly snuffed it out. "Fuck."

"Sshh." Uinniau tried to listen past the bibble-babble of the water. "There's something out there."

He pulled his cloak tighter and peered into the windblown dusk. There were four of them, royal gesiths, no need to fear the dark. But the wind had been picking up, wuthering and moaning over the stones, like the orphans of Arawn pouring from the hollow hills, and they'd all heard the yowls of Cait Sith.

A pebble rattled into the wash upstream.

He drew his knife. Lintlaf picked up his spear.

He looked at Boldcloak; they all looked at him. But Boldcloak was looking only at the doe, as though it was the most interesting thing in the world.

"It's probably just a lost goat," Oswine said, but Uinniau didn't think so. He sniffed. Something . . .

The darkness tightened, curdled, and stepped forward. It was tall. Its hands trailed long fingers, too long, a wight's fingers . . .

"Look at its hands," Oswine said. "Look at its hands!"

"No farther," Uinniau said to the thing. "Show me your hands."

The tall figure said, "It's chickweed, Uinniau."

"It's the freemartin," Lintlaf said, and lowered his spear.

Uinniau stepped forward. "Lady?"

Hild said, "Yes. Your fire's about to go out."

Oswine fed it a twig. Lintlaf snorted. Uinniau glanced at Boldcloak again, but the doe seemed more interesting than ever.

Uinniau sheathed his knife. "Won't you join us, lady?"

The dark moved and glimmered. A headshake. "They need this back at the hall. The children."

"They're no better?"

"No. If you want to help, you can finish butchering that doe and search for more chickweed and some figwort."

The fire caught and flared, showing sad bundles of weeds held in scratched, filthy hands. He stepped back. Women's work.

She must have read his mind. Her laugh was flat. "Well. It's true mud and nettles can be terrifying at night. Enjoy the glory of the hunt, my lords."

She faded back into the gloom.

Uinniau looked at Cian. "You knew it was her."

Boldcloak wiped his knife on the turf. "Goats don't smell of jessamine." He dumped out the entrails and swore when they slopped on his foot.

Uinniau stared into the dark and crossed himself. He'd heard the songs. They all had. He'd kept expecting Boldcloak to defend her, but he'd stayed silent. He understood now. She was different. Cold, hard, uncanny. She'd been out there listening to them in the dark before she deliberately kicked that pebble. He shivered. Now he understood why her hounds spoke of her as they did: not human, more like a wall, a tide, the waxing of the moon. A force of nature. Implacable, untouchable.

Hild, cloak thrown back from her shoulders and face red from the wind, watched her mother cool the chickweed infusion by pouring it back and forth from one bowl to another.

Breguswith said, "You look like you've swallowed a thistle."

Hild didn't say anything. She rarely did now. Who wanted to listen to the hægtes, the wyrd woman, the butcher-bird? No one. No more than they wanted to be tended by her. A woman, but one who killed.

She turned and nodded for Begu to start bringing the children for Breguswith to dose. She stepped back.

Three-year-old Eanflæd was first. She shrieked at the taste; she had very powerful lungs. The chickweed was helping her throat, at least. Begu shepherded her back to the other toddlers. Eanflæd shrieked some more and punched one of the wealh children, who promptly wailed. Begu stroked Eanflæd's pink, sweaty forehead and murmured something Hild couldn't hear.

The queen carried Wuscfrea. Breguswith spooned warm liquid into his tiny mouth. He didn't swallow, just let the viscous stuff dribble from his mouth and laboured to breathe.

Breguswith wiped his mouth and nodded to Æthelburh, who tucked the soft brown blanket around his chin again. "Keep wiping his eyes."

They both watched the queen sit next to Wilnoð on the south hearth and settle into the same pose as a score of women in hall: children resting in left arms and laps, heads bent, cloaks sheltering them like tents.

At the east end of the hall, the older children played with a rag ball and wiped their noses on their shifts.

Hild said, "Is Wuscfrea all right?"

Breguswith hesitated, then nodded. "His lungs will clear, but I worry about his eyes. Did you find more figwort?"

Hild pointed to the hearth, where Gwladus stirred a brass pot. "Juice from the stems warming with honey. There isn't much." Blossoms were better, but it was too early in the year. "I think little Bassus is in most need."

Breguswith nodded, but Hild knew what she was thinking: Little Bassus wasn't the heir.

"I'll find some more." She pulled her cloak forward, reached for her hood.

On the way out she stopped by the hearth. Just to get warm.

Gwladus looked soft and rosy in the glow of the fire. Hild said, "Don't let it burn."

"Do I ever? Don't you stay out too long. That wind is as raw as a wash-woman's knuckle and swollen with wickedness."

They buried little Bassus with the horn spoon he'd teethed on, at the foot of the south slope of Ad Gefrin. "So he'll face the sun, at least," Wilnoð said. "If ever there is sun again."

They buried seven children, lying next to one another for company. Hild held a blanket over the grave to keep the rain from their faces while Stephanus gave his blessing and hurried back to the important business of the men's hall. Why were there no women priests?

The rain strengthened. An earthworm writhed on the side of the mound, pink against the dark dirt. Hild hoped none of the mothers had seen it. She folded the blanket then nodded to the housefolk standing by with wooden shovels.

As the housefolk sifted in the dirt, layer by layer, the women sang a lullaby, turned by the rain and the wind into a dirge, a drone of abandoned mothers, eyes blind with tears.

When the song was done, the housefolk tamped the earth gently with the backs of their shovels. Wilnoð clutched the queen's hand so hard Æthelburh's fingertips turned purple. Later, Hild knew, the housefolk would walk on the dirt, press it down, but not now, not while the mothers were here.

Her mother stood remote as a totem, as though she had never felt a thing in her life. Hild supposed she looked the same. But in their ways they had fought for every single life, fought as thin chests heaved and lips turned blue, fought as a dozen women prayed, frantically, feverishly, begging Christ and his mother, Mary, and all his saints to help, just this once. Never, they said aloud, careless of their secrets, I'll never do this, or that again. And God had listened to five of them, but Hild didn't know why; their prayers had sounded the same as the rest, and their guilty secrets.

She had fought and lost. And none of the secrets she had heard were useful.

At the foot of Ad Gefrin, the little shaggy cattle in the tithe stockade huddled close against the wind. Not as many of them as there should be, she noted, and all those of bad temperament, bad health, and bad luck. Men tried to underpay every year, but this felt different.

A band of local chiefs on their ponies, wrapped in cloaks, also huddled close. Several wore their cloaks with a hint of wealh style—a subtle check, old tribal colours, pinned here and there with an old-fashioned brooch. She thought she might even have glimpsed a torc—the thick, twisted kind usually found only in hoards, except when hauled out and worn for battle—gleaming from one old man's throat.

The north was turning, she could feel it. At night, when they rode in from the hills with their tithe of cattle, she could hear it: Not all of them spoke Anglisc all the time. The songs they sang were of old battles, of Coel Hen, only they weren't slow and sad and glorious, they were hard and bright and fierce. The men of the north tasted change in the wind and were remembering old slights, complaining of heavy tribute and ill omens.

They knew that Oswald Iding was marrying the niece of Beli of Alt Clut. They knew Eochaid Buide had died and been succeeded by Connad Cerr mac Connell, but that behind Connad waited Domnall Brecc, young and strong—and friend and champion of the Idings. They knew the north was beginning to ally against the Yffings, while to the south and mountainous west, Penda and Cadwallon rode horses to death in their eagerness to exchange messages. Edwin was not a lucky king, they said. The Christ was not a generous god.

She wondered what else they were saying now, in their little mounted huddle, but she made no attempt to approach and listen unnoticed. She was taller than any of them, and better dressed, and wearing more gold than an ætheling. They knew who she was. She was an ælf, a freemartin, a hægtes. She was an angel, a maid, a butcher-bird. She was rich, she was subtle, she could break your mind and read your heart. She had the ear of the king. The mouth of the gods. She could call the weather or sway a battle. She could speak any tongue of man and many of beasts. She would listen, she would feed you, and a gift from her hand had a way of multiplying. She walked in the night, invisible, said some, like Cait Sith. She could tell you where to plant or how to birth your cow. She could set a loom that would weave a cloak that would make you famous. She would hold your hand if you were dying, hold it like your sister might, or your mother. No doubt she would fuck your sister, or your mother, or your brother—maybe even your cow, for good measure. She could heal you or poison you, charm you, charm away your warts, charm the birds from the trees, fly up into a tree.

The rumours were inventive and always changing. "Bring me every word," she said to Morud, to Gwladus, to Oeric. "If I'm rumoured to turn into a frog and eat flies, I want to know."

They brought her rumours and gossip. The more she heard, the worse her dreams became.

Two nights after the burial, Begu woke her. "That's the second time you've kicked me. Why are you doing this to yourself?"

"They're afraid of me."

"Well, of course they are. You kill people. You save people. And you may as well be a carved totem for all the talking you do."

Begu bumped her forehead against Hild's shoulder, like a cat hoping for a stroke.

"You should talk to people. Ordinary people, about ordinary things. Like you used to with Cian."

Cian, who said nothing when others called her a freemartin.

". . . out hunting all the time, ever since you and— Well. I don't like the way Uinniau behaves when he's with them. So. People. You have to talk to them. And I don't mean freemen who only talk to other people who don't matter. I mean people like Lintlaf."

"He's not ordinary. He's the chief of the king's gesiths."

"You know what I mean. People listen to him."

"I don't want to talk to Lintlaf." She would rather kill him.

"You should try." She turned over and tugged at the blankets. "I'm going back to sleep."

"But what should I talk about?"

"Anything! Just open your mouth and let words fall out. But not to-night. Go to sleep."

And so Hild spent more time with people. She helped the kitchenfolk seek out fresh shoots for soups and stews. She consulted with the drovers on the state of the countryside they'd travelled, the turns of the weather. She let Wilnoð clutch her hand as she wept, and gave Bassus the Elder a small keg of white mead to share with the queen's other men, enough to drink until he sang through his tears and swore vengeance on the men of the north for bringing ill luck upon his house. Mead produced greater miracles than all the prayers in the world. Mead was the key to good fellowship. A better gift, sometimes, than gold. Her Menewood was good country for bees: She must remember to send word to Rhin for more mead as and when he could manage it. Or she could talk to the king about trading with the Franks for more. But then it would be the king's gift, the king's favour, not hers.

She attended Mass twice a week, bringing different of her gesiths each time, and eating with them afterwards, and dicing, or telling them to find a woman to patch their jackets, as suited each. She smiled at their jokes and offered opinions on their swordplay, which they accepted as they would advice from the king.

She consulted with the queen on an embroidery for Dagobert, newly king of Frankia, to remind him of their trade agreements. She sketched out a weave pattern she had thought of while watching wind in the grass at the edge of the ash coppice: a subtle ripple like ripe grain waving in the sun, like water as fish rose to feed, the flick and turn of bird flocks across a dawn sky. A spin-pattern weave that suggested ripe land and riches. On top would be an embroidery of royal blue, gold, and silver: wealth on wealth. She mentioned that, if it were possible, it might be good to make something, too, for Æthelric, prince of the Anglisc North Folk. He and the folk of the Gyrwe, south and north, were all that stood between an alliance of the middle and East Anglisc against their northern kin.

There was something about alliances she could not quite see, but the more she thought about it the less clear it became, so she set it aside for later.

She approached Cian just once. He was with Lintlaf and Oswine. They were cleaning their weapons by the fire: young lords, brothers of the shield wall, discussing the ætheling Eadfrith. They didn't see her in the shadow.

". . . heard he was talking to the East Angles and the Kentishmen."

"Talking," Cian said. He dipped his twig carefully in his bowl of oil. "He's good at talking."

Oswine slapped his sword. "This does my talking!"

Lintlaf and Cian exchanged glances, and Hild didn't like the amused contempt they shared for the hostage who thought he was a gesith.

She withdrew unseen.

Cian was better around Uinniau, but Uinniau spent as much time as he could with Begu. Hild didn't know who Cian's latest bed partner was. Perhaps he hadn't had a chance to find one while being princely with the two guests of the king and riding around as a shining example of wealh and Anglisc friendship. She didn't like princely Boldcloak much. She missed her Cian. Missed the Cian she might have told of misjudging bandits and what eagles saw.

She couldn't talk to Cian, she didn't want to talk to Lintlaf, and Uinniau's was busy with Begu. So when the young lords weren't riding around, she walked with Oswine and his dogs and listened to his worries over whether he was a hostage or a guest. He assured her his father was loyal to the overking. She mentioned the delights of Rheged. He agreed that, yes, no doubt it was lovely country, and he'd heard the stag hunting was good—but he seemed puzzled. Hild wondered if anyone could really be so dull. She tried not to feel the same contempt she'd seen from Lintlaf: Contempt for others, like a dog driven from the hall, always found its way back.

After Hild had spent four days talking to people, Breguswith drew her aside. "Stop it. You're making people anxious. The only person whose opinion counts is the king. Keep him happy, and you're safe."

Edwin was not happy. "It's slipping like yolk between my fingers!" he shouted at Coelfrith, whose latest tallies were not cheering: The northern cattle tithe was down, fewer men had come to bend the knee, and more of them brought complaints. More lords told of families selling themselves into their thegn's keeping because they could no longer feed themselves. Robbery and banditry were on the rise. There were rumours of murrain in the highlands and ague in the lowlands. Folk murmured about ill luck.

"My lord," Paulinus said, "if we have a good harvest this summer, all will be well."

Edwin looked at him. "And will Christ give us a good harvest, Bishop? Oh, I forgot, he doesn't speak to you of prophecy." He looked at Hild.

"Sick and hungry farmers don't harvest as much as those who are well and safe," she said.

"They will work for God," Paulinus said. "I will baptise them, and Christ will wash their hearts clean." Sometimes he sounded as though he believed what he said.

"And then they will gratefully pay a further portion in tithe," Stephanus said.

"With which we will beautify the church," Paulinus said. "And so fill their souls with awe."

"Awe will not give them back the seed you demand in tithe," Hild said. "Awe will not heal them of ague."

The gesiths around the room nodded: Nothing healed the ague, which came from the uncanny air stirred by the wings of mosquitoes.

"If they believe, Christ will heal them."

Edwin waved his hand: A few folk with ague were neither here nor there. "You promised Christ would bring luck and full coffers," he said. "But all he's brought is bad weather. He sent his luck to the Idings. They grow strong to the north, and Penda to the south. Pray harder, Bishop."

"With more souls to pray, Christ will listen."

"Then, by all means, go baptise. And you"—he turned to Lintlaf—"put a stop to the murmurings."

Hild knew how Lintlaf would go about that. To be token and totem, the light of the world, meant protecting people from more than blades and hunger. It meant shielding them from fear. One people at peace, content from sea to shining sea . . .

She slipped out and found Morud. "Delay Lord Lintlaf. I need to speak to Boldcloak."

She found Cian with Uinniau and Oswine. Cian would have seen that she wanted to talk alone and found a charming dismissal for his friends. Boldcloak saw it and didn't care. He gave her a flat look and didn't even stand.

She planted her staff before her. She had learnt to talk to others; she could learn to talk to this stranger. "Lintlaf is to be sent out to stop the murmurs," she said. "No doubt you'll ride with him."

"Sending me on another errand?" His tone was as flat as his expression.

Uinniau stood. "Come on, Os."

"But—"

"Come on."

When they'd gone, she said, "I'm not sending you. The king is. But I'd like to find you men. To ride under your orders."

"My orders?"

"Yours. Lintlaf . . . You know how Lintlaf is."

He neither agreed nor disagreed.

"The more men go, the faster the murmurs stop. It will make the king happy. If the king's happy, we're all safer." The Cian who had rubbed his lip might never have existed. "Say something."

He gave her that look and said, "You're a woman."

Her heart dropped into her belly.

"You could ask the queen for men."

She blinked. The queen. She should have thought of that. She turned her staff in her hands. "You'd lead them?"

After a long moment, he nodded once.

The queen smiled when she made her request. "Of course. Bassus would be glad to have something to do. I'm glad you came to me. I was beginning to wonder if I'd offended you in some way. We've missed you."

Hild wanted to believe her, but she had been different since Wuscfrea was so ill. At the best of times queens hid their true feelings; it was the way of the world. And Begu had spoken of her being on her knees to Christ all the time, terrified of the omens. Hild wondered how it must feel to have someone you didn't quite trust make prophecies about what mattered most to you in the world.

The brothers Berht were happy to go, along with Eadric and Grimhun. Oswine and Uinniau, of course, went wherever Boldcloak went.

"Listen," Hild said to the assembled gesiths. Half of them had a shine in their eyes she remembered from the field at Lindum, and the firelight as they painted their shields. For them, she didn't need a ring. "Heed me: honey, not vinegar. Nothing but good words about the generosity and strength of our king."

"For the bandits, steel, not words," Cian said.

She couldn't tell how he meant that. "Yes. For the bandits. For ordinary folk, food and kind words." She gave them sacks of bread and a small keg of mead each. "For the folk, not for you."

"Though we'll have to drink with them," Cian said to his men with a smile, and Uinniau hooted. They rode out, still hooting, horses high-stepping, glittering with gold and jewels.

Hild and Begu waved until they were lost to sight.

"Three princes," Begu said. "Like a hero song."

It was true. Cian carried himself like a prince, and Prince Uinniau looked up to him, as did Oswine, who would one day—if Edwin's plans worked—be ealdorman of Rheged. Everyone knew the tale of Ceredig king and the boy with the wooden sword. Cian Boldcloak: a far cry from the boy who almost wept at the thought of being in the same hall as the son of the son of the son of Owein, his sword blue and gleaming, his spurs of gold.

Paulinus rode out in even greater state with Stephanus and the new priest, Hrothmar, an oddly pale man with eyes the colour of water and white hair. It wasn't long before news trickled in to Hild of feverish mass baptisms on the River Glen, of men and women dragged from their homes and forcibly submerged in the fast, cold waters. *To save their souls. To save the Anglisc.*

She shared the news with the queen one afternoon as they compared the blue of their most recent dye batch to their standard, a loose skein and a swatch of fullered cloth kept in a tightly woven bag against the light.

"He'll turn the whole north against us," Æthelburh said. "How can we stop him?"

Hild rewound the new skein. She could never be certain of the queen's feelings, but perhaps on this they were of the same mind. "James the Deacon could help."

James arrived from York in a hurry of mud. Morud led him to the queen's chambers, where Hild waited.

"Your bishop has gone mad," Hild said, in Latin and quietly. Gwladus was at the door, but there was no point in taking chances. "He's baptising anything on two legs, willing or not. The whole north is murmuring. We have to stop him."

James stood there. Eventually he said, "It wasn't the queen who sent for me, was it?"

She poured wine. Rhenish, his favourite. "She's at meat with the king. She knows I'm here."

"You speak for her?"

"We share the same worry." She handed him a cup. After a moment he took it. They both sat. "The north is balanced on a sword edge. Your bishop could tip it the wrong way."

"What is it you want from me?"

"First, tell me exactly, tell me clearly, why he's forcing baptism."

"Boniface won't give him the pallium, won't make him archbishop of the north, until all the north is converted."

"But how will Boniface know? Does God keep count and drop tally sticks from heaven on the bishop of Rome's head?"

"Stephanus keeps the tally. He sends it to me. I compile the report that goes out under the bishop's name."

"If you wrote that we were all baptised, would Paulinus get his white wool shawl and leave us alone?"

"I can't lie to the pope!"

"Why?"

"Because." But she fixed him with her steady gaze. He sighed. "The pope is God's representative on earth. Lying to His Holiness would be like lying to God Himself. I'd go to Gehenna." The hot hell where you burnt like a pig on the spit, forever. "It would be a sin."

Sin: an oath-breaking, a straying from the path. She sipped her wine. "The Crow has to stop. The north will turn if he doesn't. The king could make him stop. But the king hears only what he wants to hear. Someone must persuade him the Crow is mistaken."

"Child—"

"Do you want the church in York to rise and your choir's voice to rise with it? Then the king must stay on his throne and ensure the church's tithe. He won't stay on the throne if the north turns. The north will turn unless your bishop is muzzled."

"How is that something the king will want to hear?"

"He'll hear if there's more than one voice. I'll speak. The queen will speak."

"The queen?" He looked into the distance, calculating the benefit. After a long moment he said, "It can't get back to the bishop."

She nodded. "Thank you."

"Thank me by pouring me another cup. In York they're very near with the wine when the king's away."

She wondered why he didn't ask his Christ to make wine out of water, but no doubt he'd have an answer for that, too. She poured, then excused herself to check with Gwladus, who told her that in hall the king had called for the scop; there was no hurry.

She went back to James. They drank steadily. He told her of the church in York: The Frankish stonemasons were skittish about every omen, fractious about the weather, finicky about the food. The choir, on the other hand, was beautiful, just wondrous, like heavenly angels.

His eyes glistened, his chin lifted. He stroked his carved cup. The wine made him happy. When you understood what made people happy, you understood them.

"Deacon," she said, "have you ever seen Paulinus happy?"

He ran a finger round the rim of his cup. "I have seen him uplifted in the service of God."

"Especially when it is in service to himself?"

He leaned back, hands behind his head. "That's not quite it. It's more that he's a man, though he likes to pretend otherwise."

She waited but he did not seem inclined to say more. "He doesn't think he's a man?"

"No, no. Simply that as a man he can persuade himself of ridiculous things in order to persuade others."

"I don't understand."

"Most of the time he believes he is truly saving all those hundreds of half-drowned baptisands." He mused for a moment. "And when he doubts himself, I'd say he banishes those doubts by banishing his bodily needs, denying his humanness."

Reminded, he eyed the wine jug. She nodded and gestured for him to go ahead. He poured and sipped.

"Ah. That's a truly lovely wine. But when it comes to the joys of the flesh, I am weak. No doubt because I'm a mere deacon. Paulinus, being a bishop, is made of sterner stuff."

"I've noticed that he doesn't care for food or wine."

"He thinks bodily joy—love of wine, of a handsome figure, of venison smothered in bilberries—a weakness, a sin."

"But you don't."

"God made our bodies. And God is love. Love is never wrong. And so love of bodily joy, I think the Christ would agree, is never wrong." He picked up his cup. "Except when it becomes greed. Which leads to gluttony. Which is most definitely a sin."

"How can you tell the difference?"

"That, dear child, is a mystery. For today, let us say five cups of wine is love, and six gluttony."

"Then you can have one more."

He beamed. "That's so."

"I have another question."

He waved a hand magnanimously.

"Why does God speak to some people and not others?"

She pretended to sip while he picked carefully through his thoughts. Next time she would suggest that the line between love and gluttony might be moved to eight cups.

"The only priests God speaks to, in my experience, are those who think they should be overbishop." He raised his eyebrows: Did she understand?

She nodded. All priests lie. Except to the pope. "But God does listen to some people. He listened to some of the mothers when their children were dying."

"Listening is not the same as speaking."

"He will speak to me. Tell me how."

"Oh, my dear. I wish we were sitting in the sunshine of Rome."

She frowned. "Does sunshine make a difference?"

"No, no. But Rome does. There are Greek texts . . . The Greeks thought about these things. You'd like them." He shook his head. "But I have none here. The bishop doesn't see the value. To tell you the truth, I don't think he reads it very well."

"Teach me how to talk to him. I want to ask something."

"Well, I don't think the bishop would disagree with me if I said that God helps those who help themselves."

She considered that. "So I can ask for something if I do something?" Give a gift, get an audience. That made sense. She had already arranged the alliance between deacon, queen, and seer. She would ask for an omen.

God sent an omen at dawn, tangled in a birder's net.

Hild stood in a shaft of light in the king's hall and held out the jay by its unnatural white legs. She shook it lightly. The king, the queen, even James stepped back.

"Look closely, my king."

But Edwin wouldn't come near it.

"White legs, white bill, white eyes. White as a ghost. But caught in a net, killed by hunters who already had full bags." She gestured at two men by the door, with nets and slings tucked in their wide leather belts and bloodstained game bags at their hips. They looked as though they would bolt, but for Gwrast on one side and Oeric on the other.

Edwin ignored them. "Tell me what it means."

"A warning about greed. Christ, they say, is often spoken of as a white bird." She looked at James, who nodded. Doves were white birds, after all. "The people ask: Why would I want to be baptised if my wyrd is to end strangled in a net? Others say: Greed is what killed the white bird, the hunter's greed. That sometimes the birds in the bag are enough. Greed and hurry, Edwin king."

"Ah. You're talking about the Crow. You want me to rein him in." He looked at Æthelburh, who nodded, and at James, who bowed his assent. Then at Hild. "I'll have to give him something to do," he said.

"There's Craven. We're to go in summer. The bishop could go ahead of us."

He thought about it. "Well, why not? Make him cousin Osric's problem. But not too much of a problem. We can't have more murmuring. The deacon here will go to keep an eye on him."

22

✦

AT THE BEGINNING OF SUMMER Edwin and his advisers joined Paulinus and James in Craven. They found Osric's household in disarray. Osric had taken apart the old fort of the kings of Craven and built himself a grand new hall, but, according to Gwladus and Morud, who had already winkled out the story from kitchen hands and byre boys, the new ealdorman gave contradictory orders, and the housefolk never knew from one day to the next whether they should be weaving a tapestry, sowing a field, or slaughtering sheep. The roof didn't leak, and there was food on the table and horsehair in the mattresses, but the atmosphere of the hall felt surly and nervous.

Edwin felt no need to impress Osric. He had allowed the queen—along with her ladies, including Begu and Breguswith—to go instead to Derventio. Osric had no wife, and his daughter was visiting her cousins in Arbeia. With few Anglisc women present, Osric's vill felt more like a travel camp than a high lord's hall: too much drinking and open rutting and men pissing in corners, while spitting and staring over their shoulders. Hild told Morud and Oeric to pass the word to the men of Craven that any who laid a hand on Gwladus would put his wyrd in the seer's hand. She told Gwladus to pin her braids close to her head and wear a thick old dress. "I mean it. No flaunting." But Gwladus was made as she was, and though she pinned her hair up, and though she wore an old dress and looked at the floor when she thought Hild would see, the looks she gave Osric's men brimmed with the knowledge of her power.

On the third day, when James asked Hild to walk with him, she was glad to get out of the hall.

The river roared and tumbled down falls and through weirs, teeming with salmon and roach, dace and minnow. Its steep green banks were streaked with otter slides, and hard-beaked kingfishers watched from every birch and alder.

James seemed a different man. His stride was longer, his face leaner. They walked for a while, until they came to a stand of graceful white birch on a high bank. Here the grass at the foot of a smooth boulder was broken and flattened. She was not surprised when they sat.

The air smelt like a newly unfurled leaf. Just breathing made her feel good: no scent of dung or charcoal or rotting thatch, only leaping fish and rushing water.

"Lovely, isn't it?" James said. "Fresh as the first day of creation. But dangerous. When it rains up in the hills, the water rises fast."

Hild said nothing, happy to wait.

"He's at it again. Baptisms. With no heed. I begged him to consider. Consider the will of the people. Consider the raging river itself. Last time we'd just finished—sixscore people in one baptism!—and waded to the bank when, *whoosh*, dead sheep swept by, bobbing and swollen. If we'd stayed in the water for one more immersion, just one, we'd have been washed away. Gone. Dead as the sheep."

Below, something, she couldn't tell what, swam against the current: a flash, a splash, and it was gone.

"As well as the baptisms, he's forcing people from their fields and pastures to help him build a new church from the stones at the old Roman fort."

"Osric has stoneworkers?"

"Dunod had one. Old now, but versed in the ways of tumbled Roman stone. So a new church is rising, and the bishop, in his zeal, will fill it with fresh souls. A new Rome, he says. Rome, in Craven! He's run mad."

Perhaps ambition drove everyone mad in the end. Power and ambition were two edges of the same sword, as she knew herself. She wanted to be powerful so she could protect her people; she had people because she was powerful. And there were different kinds of power: the still, pent power of the seer; the free, raging power of the butcher-bird. But did there have to be only one path?

James seemed to be walking a new path. "If you could choose, would you stay here or go back to York?" she said.

"I miss my choir," he said. "But I love it here. So wild and young and pure." And some steady yearning in his voice made her think of Uinniau when he spoke of Begu, and she knew James wasn't talking about the river.

She smiled. "Perhaps the bishop would be better advised to focus on his church in York and leave his deacon to supervise the new church of Catterick?" He straightened. "And perhaps the deacon might find a local man to help recruit labour through payment and persuasion rather than force."

"I have just the man. Quiet and strong, something of a leader in these parts."

"I'm happy to hear it. I'll speak to the king."

A kingfisher dove and missed.

"And you?" he said. "You're well?"

She nodded. "Though God hasn't told me anything yet." She kicked at her boulder, glanced up at him from under her brows. "Deacon . . . there's . . . It's said that God only listens to the pure of heart."

"Then he listens to no one. We're all sinners."

"Sin." She sighed. "I still don't understand sin."

"You don't need to understand it. You need to confess it, be absolved, and approach your prayer afresh."

She remembered Fursey's long, rambling opinions on the matter of confession. "But confession is an admission of guilt. A king or a seer . . . we can't just admit wrong. It's not . . ." She couldn't think what it was exactly. "Besides, what if we don't think what we've done is wrong?"

He watched the river. "I counsel my flock that, if in doubt, they should consider the ten commandments."

"Does Paulinus see it that way?"

"There are no commandments against love," he said.

She ran through them in her head. Not unless someone was married.

"God is love," he said. "Love is never wrong."

She was thinking of a different commandment. "But sometimes we do have to kill people."

"Then confess and be absolved."

"Also, for a priest or a seer what, exactly, counts as helping yourself so God will help you, and what counts as a lie?"

James burst out laughing. Hild had no idea what was so funny, but seeing his eyes turn to slits, his face turn red under the charcoal, and his greying curls bob as he bleated made her mouth stretch despite herself.

He wiped his eyes. " 'What counts as a lie?' You're as slippery as a bishop. If only women could take the vow!"

Hild said solemnly, "What, exactly, counts as a woman?" And this time she laughed, too.

They stayed in Craven for a month. Edwin seemed to enjoy eating his new ealdorman out of house and home.

She walked every day with James. She asked those she met about bandits, but no one knew anything. He introduced her to a farmer and part-time farrier called Druyen, who was indeed tall and quiet and strong. She practiced praying while walking, while lying down, while kneeling—that hurt, and worked no better than anything else—then tried confession.

"It's like picking out stepping-stones in the dark," she said.

"You're very good at it," he said.

At night, she composed a letter in her head to Fursey, about love and killing and confession, and in his imaginary reply, he told her to take care, take very great care, and not to fall in.

She went through another growth spurt, this time putting on muscle and curves. Gwladus shook her head and said she hoped Hild had a lot of silver put by, because when they got to Goodmanham, her lady mother, who now thought of little other than wool—apart, that is, from her scop— would charge an arm and a leg to clothe such a giant.

Cian also changed. He, too, put on muscle, and the bones in his face grew harder and bigger. His height increased a little; not nearly as much as his weight. His neck seemed to swell overnight, and his jaw looked clenched all the time, there was so much strength in it. Something more than his size changed, too. His laugh was harder, his words edged. Men began to back down more quickly when he disagreed with them.

He had a new woman, though Hild didn't know who. He disappeared at night and came back smelling of her in the morning. He still smiled, still told stories—to others. He had no time for walking, or riding, or sparring with her. No time even for talking. When he wasn't with the gesiths, he was hunting and drinking with Uinniau and Oswine.

———

And then Fursey sent her a real letter. Or part of one.

"Looks as though it's been eaten by a pig and shat out," Morud said when Gwladus let him into the room and he handed it to Hild. Indeed, the folded scrap was filthy and bedraggled, with half torn away.

She pulled her robe around her and ignored the looks Morud was giving Gwladus, whose hair was hanging loose.

She read it fast, or as fast as she could—some of the tiny lettering was blurred, as though rained on, or dropped in a puddle—then again more slowly. *S sent word to your sister's man that he arrives with arms and threescore men as soon as the weather is fair for war.*

Fair for war. In the south the first ship crossing from Frankia to East Anglia could have been a month ago or more. Sigebert and his threescore gesiths could be with Æthelric's war band already. How many men could Ricberht king-killer command?

She imagined her mother's cynical smile: As many as see advantage for themselves.

For ealdormen and thegns, advantage was tied to the web of trade and obligation woven over generations: Who could give them more power, more gold, more land, more influence? Sigebert and the Christian Franks, or Ricberht king-killer? For farmers, it was about food: the hams hanging from the ceiling, the honey in the crock, the grain in the sacks. If the weather in the south and east was good for the next two years, they wouldn't want anything to change; Ricberht would stay king.

Your sister is, by the way, with child again, though so is her husband's woman of the South Gyrwe. She—

But that was all. No matter how many times she read it, the rest was still torn away.

"Where's the priest who brought it?" Gwladus asked Morud. She'd repinned her braids. Beautiful hair. Hild loved the silky drag of it across her belly . . .

She missed Morud's reply.

"Find him," Gwladus said. "Put him somewhere out of the way, see that he's got food. What are you waiting for? Go."

Hild wished Gwladus hadn't tidied away her hair.

"You'll want to talk to the king after that priest?"

Hild nodded.

"I'll fetch your dress."

For most East Anglisc, the Christ was just the excuse. But underneath, baptism was the riptide dragging all boats off course. *Baptism is very much like a sword in this way: that the man whose hands the sword or the soul passes through adds his lustre.* Baptism added another pattern to the warp and weft of allegiance and obligation.

The murdered Eorpwald had been the godson of Edwin. Sigebert was of a different Christian lineage. He had spent his time across the narrow sea at the Frankish court of Clothar, and now Dagobert. If Sigebert was bringing threescore men, they would be Dagobert's. If he won with their help, he would be obliged to align himself with the Franks. What would that mean for Edwin? Where was Dagobert in relation to the growing alliances of the middle country and the west—Penda and Cadwallon—and the men of the north: Idings, Picts, Scots of Dál Riata, Alt Clut, perhaps Rheged?

Gwladus fastened Hild's sleeves, then began to dress her hair.

Cadwallon was the key, the thread between the Mercians of Penda, the Irish, and the men of the north. With Dagobert now added to the great weave, they needed to snip that thread, cut Cadwallon out. They had to do it now. Swift, sure, hard. War.

Was there time to call Osfrith from Tinamutha? No, he should remain with his household to watch the men of the north. But Eadfrith could be recalled. The time for talking was over, at least with Cadwallon—

"Lady?"

Oeric. Pale, dark-eyed, and hands working.

"News from Ireland of a battle at Fid Eoin. Connad Cerr is killed, and with him Osric Iding the Burnt. Domnall Brecc is now king of the Dál Riata and Oswald Iding his right hand."

So. It must be now. War. Real war. One king or another would die, and all his gesiths with him. Cian . . .

The yard stank of that sharp tang men give off when they want to fuck or kill. The smell of war.

The dogs knew it, they had been snarling since yesterday and the news of the battle of Fid Eoin. The horses knew it; those in the byre were kicking; outside, the stallions had to be corralled separately.

The men knew it most of all.

Hild, come from a bitter talk with the king, stood by the trough. She planted her staff before her, one hand wrapped around the other, and looked at Cian.

Where Lintlaf's shield had caught him between the ribs, a purple bruise, the colour of the loosestrife growing along the tumbled wall by Osric's byre, spread. But Lintlaf was bleeding from the scalp and sitting in the dirt. He held his jacket to his head, laughing, they were all laughing. War drove men mad.

She shouted, "Heroes!"

They turned. She uncovered her hand, the king's token burning red as blood.

"In the kitchens: a new barrel of beer and fresh bread!" The last fresh bread before they marched. The last some might ever eat. "Get it while it's hot!"

She wore the ring. It was not a suggestion.

She caught Cian's eye: *Wait*. He leaned his sword against the trough and sluiced himself with water as the gesiths left.

Blood thumped in his neck vein. A muscle jumped in his calf. She imagined how it might be: the muscle jumping in her own calf, her own blood flowing like a millrace, her muscle straining against bone to begin, to end this waiting, to sweep down on Cadwallon and crush the men of Gwynedd. Or be crushed. Real war.

He dropped the dipper, lifted his naked sword, tilted it to check along its length for nicks.

He looked at her. His chest rose and fell in rhythm with hers, his brows arched like hers, his hair, the same colour as hers, clung to his nape just as hers did. They were the same height. But his eyes were a sharper blue, and the bones of his face heavier. They were the two great timbers of a doorway, massive, matched.

She turned and walked from the vill.

He followed her without speaking to a flat grassy place by the racing river. The air still smelt like the first day of the world.

Remember this smell, she told herself, and stripped dress, hose, shoes, everything but the ring—the ring she was forbidden to take off until she gave it to the queen. She stood, stave at the ready, in only her shift. As she always had.

He hung his bloody jacket on a bush and kicked off his shoes. As he always had. He drew his sword with a slithering ring and tossed the sheath aside.

Hild saw the memory take him, as it took her: Derventio, his first fight with a king's gesith. He moved his left foot forward, right foot and arm back and waited. As though they had practiced it, she took Berhtred's stance of long ago: right foot and right arm forward, stave held out low.

Cian feinted, a fast jab with the point. As Berhtred had, she swung her weapon up, like a horizontal bar, but Cian's blade was already back, waiting, and she met only air. But she moved more lightly than Berhtred ever had, and she knew this dance, and she didn't teeter.

They circled, eyes bright, cheeks red, like the children they had once been. When she had the slanting morning sun in his eyes, Cian thrust. Once for the feint with the tip, to which she raised her stave only partway, then back and once more forward in a full stepping lunge, right foot leading now, and blade snaking over her weapon in a wrapping leftwise twist that would have flung Berhtred's sword up and into the grass.

But she was not Berhtred. She did not carry a sword. And when one end of her staff went whipping through the air she simply let the other end whip around in its turn and hit him, hard, left to right, across his bruise from Lintlaf.

Shock blanked the gleam in his eye, and she imagined that same look as a man of Cadwallon slid his sword into Cian's belly and she couldn't bear it, couldn't bear someone doing to him what she had done to the wolf's-heads.

"Wake up," she said. And hit him again, right to left, on the other side.

They bared their teeth—the same muscles, the same sinews, the same teeth—in the same wild grin. The same-shaped arms swung over the same strong rib cages. The same long feet moved over the grass. And now they laughed, like children. But they fought like dogs in a pit. They fought against fate.

They moved lickeringly fast, brutally hard, king's gesith and butcher-bird. The end of her staff split the skin on his shoulder. His blade sliced open her forearm: the same cut, the same place, as the first scar he had ever given her.

Her hands, slick with her own blood, began to slip on her stave.

She drove him back and back. He stepped on a thistle and she swept his legs out from under him. She lifted her stave.

He scissored her legs. She fell. He leapt on her.

Such weight. And, mixed with his wild scent, the smell of that woman. She shifted her grip.

"I can smell her on you," she said, and heaved him over her head. She landed astride him. "Who is she?"

"Not a slave," he said. "I don't need to own my women."

She hit him. The king's ring tore his nose. He threw her off. She landed on her face, and her lip burst. They faced each other on all fours, dripping.

She wiped her mouth. "At least mine doesn't stink."

"She does to me."

Hild blinked and when he punched her she was slow, and he hit between the breasts, a punch to the bone with a fist that could break a one-inch plank. Her heart stuttered and her lungs stopped, as though someone had filled them with milk. She couldn't see.

He scrambled around her, grabbed her from behind with arms like trees. Skin to skin, bone to bone; her shift was in tatters. He would crush her, snap her ribs like kindling. But he was holding her up. "You should have moved. You should have moved."

So many things they should have done. But now they never would. She turned in his arms, and they tripped, and in a confusion of scrabble and scramble, she was on top of him again, only she was leaning down and he was straining up, neck tendons taut, and they met.

She kissed him, hard, blood on blood. She lifted her head and looked down at his fallen body. She set her mouth against the line of muscle running like a thick rope, like the back of a salmon, from shoulder to nipple. She took the muscle and tendon between her teeth but didn't bite. She ran down the rope to the nipple, leaving a smear of red. Such a tiny thing, like a red currant.

He looked up at her. "King's fist," he said.

"King's gesith."

She folded down onto him like honey from the comb, slow and thick and gold. Cunt on his belly, belly on his breast, breast plump to his face. He closed his eyes and took her breast in his mouth, eyes closed, like the queen taking the host at Mass.

You can't have him.

She rolled away.

Startled, he got his legs under him to come after her.

"No!" she said harshly. He stayed where he was.

You can't have him. You don't understand. But you will.

She stood. A light breeze turned the wet hair between her legs cold. She looked down at him where he knelt, at his glistening prick poking through his hose, at the sun-dark chest, darker arms, white shins. The smear on his belly, the bruise on his ribs, the hurt in his eyes.

"No," she said again, and now her cheeks were cold and wet, too. She wiped them with the back of her hand. She wanted to touch his face, wanted to stand next to him, but didn't, couldn't.

Keeping him ignorant keeps him safe.

She picked up her clothes and stave.

"Cian." *I miss you.* "We are us," she said, and walked away.

She dressed herself, somehow, as she walked. Her throat ached.

The first person she saw in Osric's yard was Gwladus.

"There you are! The king has—"

"Shut up." The words ground over each other like millstones. "Follow me."

She walked fast, out of the yard, onto the hill path, not stopping to think or check that Gwladus was following. They walked up into the hills, along the river, down a track, to the shed where Druyen was hammering the last nail on a horse's shoe. He lifted the foot from his leather-aproned lap and set it back on the grass, straightened. "Lady?"

Hild nodded at Gwladus. "Cut her collar off."

Gwladus's hands flew to the collar. Her eyes turned black with shock, and her face white.

He came to Gwladus, lifting his big hand, slowly, deliberately, as he would with a horse, so no one would be startled, and reached out. Gwladus dropped her hands.

Druyen turned to Hild. "There's a stool in the forge. Fetch it, lady, before she falls down."

When she came back out with the three-legged stool, Druyen was rooting through a row of tools on the trestle by the trough. The gelding he'd been shoeing cropped a thin patch of grass.

He lifted a pair of what looked like shears, though oddly shaped: long black iron handles, tiny bright blades. "It's just the pin needs cutting," he said in British, to Gwladus. In Anglisc he said, "Lady, stand behind her, let her lean so she's steady."

Hild stood behind Gwladus, put her hands on her shoulders—so soft—and pulled her back so her head rested against Hild's bruised breastbone.

Gwladus trembled.

"Sshh," Hild said.

Druyen frowned, positioned the shears, held them with his left hand while he fiddled with the pin slotted through the iron-loop ends of the collar, nodded, put his right hand back on the shears, squeezed.

The bottom of the little pin fell to the dirt.

Druyen plucked the top half of the pin from the loop, bent and picked up the other half, nodded again, to both of them, and took his shears back to the bench.

Gwladus, shaking harder than ever, reached up and tried to unhinge the collar.

Hild came around to the front and did it for her. The hinge was stiff. She stepped back, let the collar dangle from her hand, like a dead hare. It felt cold and hard and ugly. She threw it as far from her as she could.

On the way back to Osric's hall Gwladus kept rubbing her neck. They both stumbled more than once but neither touched the other. Hild's legs felt the wrong size and made of wood. The muscles of her chest clutched and spasmed. Her mouth throbbed.

Morud was in Hild's room. His eyes went perfectly round when he saw them.

"Not a word," Gwladus said. "Light the fire. Then bring hot water, wine, food. The fire, Morud."

Hild sat on the bed while Morud got the fire going. She could hardly breathe, her chest hurt so much.

When he left, Gwladus said, "No sense spreading filth on the bed. Come stand by the fire. Let's get that dress off."

When Gwladus saw the bruises her face didn't change and her breath didn't catch, but her hands paused for a heartbeat then went on.

"You lost your drawers."

Hild hadn't noticed.

"Did you kill him?"

She started to shake her head, but that hurt her mouth too much.

"Shall I get Oeric?"

"No." She stopped Gwladus's hand with her own. "Will you leave me, too?"

Gwladus said nothing. She picked up a comb, worked on a knot. Threw the comb at the wall. Stood there, chest rising and falling.

"Clemen of Dyfneint would take you in," Hild said. "If I asked. You could— I owe, I'd give . . ." But words abandoned her. She began to shiver.

"Here." Gwladus dragged a blanket from the bed, draped it over Hild. "Where's that godfucked boy?"

23

✦

HILD TOOK WHAT HAD HAPPENED, put it in a box, wrapped it with a chain, and buried it deep. She wore the ring. She was the king's fist. She felt nothing, cared for no one.

She rode with James to York—Craven would have to wait—while Edwin and Paulinus took the war band to Elmet for the muster. Eadfrith would join him there, and Osric and his Craven thegns, and thegns from south Bernicia, Deira, and Elmet with their men. Gwynedd was the greatest kingdom of the British, rich with trade, strong with alliances in Ireland, the north and west, and Less Britain. Cadwallon would field many blades, and good ones. But Edwin would bring more, and better. This time Cadwallon's neck would meet Edwin's sword and Cadwallon's bishops would kiss the Crow's ring.

Hild and James arrived in York, where the queen and the infant heir, and all the queen's women, joined them from Derventio to lock themselves in the fortress. Hild, the king's niece, the king's seer, gave up the king's token to the queen and in exchange was given charge of the twoscore armed men. Men like Bassus and Oeric who had last stood in a shield wall a generation ago, or never.

But the walls were strong and the water sweet. If Eanfrith Iding brought his Picts down from the north, Osfrith and his men would stop him at the Tine. Oswald Iding was busy with the Irish. She wasn't worried about Penda: If he was as cunning as she thought, he'd be doing nothing, simply watching and waiting to see how the balance tipped between Edwin and Cadwallon.

The queen's women got back to work on the huge embroidery for Dagobert and the lesser one for Æthelric. The queen herself took up the reins of the wīc and the fortress. James reported to the queen, often with Breguswith and Hild at her shoulder, every middæg in the king's chamber—for life outside the walls went on as usual. Woodcutters and charcoal burners didn't make war. Wheat and barley grew untroubled except by weeds. Cows must be milked and butter churned in the cool of the morning.

Trade ships came and went with the tide. To the Franks, who brought wine and walnut oil in exchange for wool cloaks, it didn't matter that Domnall Brecc was now king of the Dál Riata, that with the death of Osric Iding in the defeat of the Ulaid, the tide of the other Idings now ran very high indeed. The Frisians, who traded glass and silver for jet and tunics, didn't care that Edwin had flung his army straight as a spear for the throat of Cadwallon to take Gwynedd before it could ally with Penda and form the solid anvil against which the Idings and the men of the north could hammer the Anglisc. The people of the Baltic, who brought amber for linen, were not interested in the grinding struggle between Sigebert and Ricberht for kingship of the East Anglisc. They cared only for the confluence of trade, the rich mix of goods from north and south, east and west.

The women grew snappish and the men surly. The army would be in Gwynedd now. Hild kept herself moving in the yard with the men, in the garth with the women, in the dairy, in the byre: If she kept moving, she didn't have to think. She didn't have to see into herself. If she kept moving, no one else could see into her, either. She was glad that it was easy to stay away from her mother in York.

She presented a smooth exterior, cool as enamel, to the world. She watched as the other women began to startle and clutch their crosses at every glimpse of a mail shirt turning a corner and every tramp of nailed war boots on stone, and refused to understand. Then one day, outside in the great yard watching the men try to form two shield walls, she heard the steel slither of blade from scabbard and began to turn, heart tripping, thinking Cian. She knew he was a hundred miles away, maybe lying with his guts fallen like a tangle of rope on the grass, or already dead, but for that moment she knew, just as certainly as she breathed, that it was Cian behind her.

That night she dreamt of them all dead, banners in the mud, bloodied men of Gwynedd gouging gold bosses from sword hilts and prying loose jewels; thin women stripping clothes and belts; vermin-riddled boys pulling boot nails, rummaging for blood-softened twice-baked bread. All night ravens croaked and thumped into the dream turf and flies boiled off the bodies.

The next evening, listening to the inferior scop who had been left behind, her throat tightened. He sang of war and glory and returning heroes, and Hild found herself remembering the parts Cian liked, how he sulked when she wouldn't play the firing of the furze. The box she had buried deep rattled in its chains.

On the ninth day, in her rooms to choose a gift ring from her box, she picked up instead the cunningly nested travel cups Cian had carved from the Elmet thorn. She touched the little hedgepig and she was there, at Aberford, wreathed in the scent of smoke, listening to Grimhun sing as Cian whittled, flick flick flick, the hairs at his wrist gleaming like bronze in the firelight. She was standing by her wagon in Elmet, holding the cups: *So we may drink to home wherever we are.*

"Drink it."

She blinked: Begu, sitting opposite, holding out the largest travel cup, now filled. Where had she come from?

"Drink it."

The mead was harsh. Hild drank it without blinking, not taking her eyes off the two smaller cups, still nested together, that Begu was turning over and over in her hands.

"—horrible mead. Not surprising with Gwladus tiptoeing around like a thief waiting to have her hand struck off. What's got into you? Oeric and Morud are half convinced you were possessed by an ælf in Craven or had your mind stolen by a river wight. It can't go on."

Hild didn't understand any of this. She slid the cup forward for more. After a moment, Begu refilled it, then she separated the two remaining cups and, with utmost care, filled those, too. She pushed Hild's towards her, picked up the medium-size cup, and raised it to the small one.

"To Cian. May he drink his portion with us soon."

Hild didn't realise she'd been crying until she started again.

"I thought so." Begu fished a handkerchief from her belt and mopped at Hild's face. "You're messier than Eanflæd. Though not as loud. Here. Blow your nose."

Hild obeyed.

"All done? Good. Because when you leave this room, you'll have your head high and a light in your eye. You're the lady Hild, the king's seer. We're at war. You'll wear a happy face."

She nudged Hild's cup until Hild picked it up again, and lifted her own.

"To Cian," Begu said again, deliberately, and nodded when Hild, dry-eyed, touched cups and tossed off the mead in one swallow. "Now. Listen. What's going on with Gwladus?"

"She's free."

Begu huffed. "I didn't think you'd cast a glamour and made the collar invisible. No. Look at me. Why are you being so mean to her? Anyone would think you were trying to drive her away. If that's what you're doing, you should just say so and put the poor woman out of her misery. Your mother would take her faster than that." Ringing snap of fingers. "But you need her, now more than ever."

"But she's free."

"Don't be such a child. Where should she go? She wouldn't last a day outside these walls. And working for you suits her. People step aside for her. She shines with your reflected wyrd. Like Oeric. Like Coelfrith with the king, or Stephanus with Paulinus. Why should it be any different for Gwladus just because she's free?" She sipped at her mead, pulled a face, took another sip anyway. "You'd have to pay her a little. Especially for the bed duties."

Hild shook her head. "No more of that."

Begu tilted her head. "Only Cian will do?"

"No!"

"So anyone will do?"

"I can't. Not with Cian."

"Well, no," Begu said. "He's not here."

"Not ever. You don't understand."

Begu laughed, but it was the same old hurt laugh she'd laughed a year ago over Ulnnlau. "I can recognise foals from the same stallion, even if I never met the stallion."

Hild stared at her.

"I'm not blind. And I'm not stupid. Though a lot of other people seem to be. But he's my foster-brother and you're my gemæcce. So, this once, we will speak of it."

Hild said nothing.

"So. Cian's father is your father. But if that was common knowledge, his life would be worth nothing next time the king gets nervous. Even Cian himself doesn't know, and you don't want him to because he'd give it away and get himself killed. Yes?"

Hild looked at nothing in particular for a while.

Begu sighed. "But I know, just from looking at him. Your mother knows, and Onnen, of course. And you. Who else?"

Eventually Hild said, "Fursey."

"That priest? Well." She tilted her head, thinking. "I think the queen wonders. And what the queen knows or suspects, so does Wilnoð."

"Bassus?"

Begu waved her free hand dismissively. "He's just her husband."

"The Crow."

"Ah. Yes. He's not stupid either, more's the pity."

Hild felt sick.

Begu nodded. "Too many people. One day it'll come out."

So many things to keep hidden. It would be easier to go to war, to charge with spear and shield, to fight in the open.

"Well, we can no more control that than we can control the birds. We can only control what we can control."

Control. Yes. Not of the thing itself but of the understanding of the thing. That's what she did. Nudge. Guide. Control.

". . . control yourself, at least. Me, I'll just continue to pretend I am both blind and stupid, and brightly say the things other people find foolish, and so make the truth foolish." She squeezed Hild's hand and let go. "Tidy your hair now, go talk to Gwladus, and set this house in order. Do rethink those bed duties. You'd only be punishing yourself and you can't be distracted. We're at war. You're the king's seer, the king's fist in all but name. Hold your head high and tell everyone it's going to be all right."

Silence.

"Hild, gemæcce, we all have men at war. So tell us it will be all right. Make us believe it. Please. Tell the queen. Tell your mother. Tell me."

Uinniau. Luftmaer the scop. The king himself. Every one of those thousand men had women waiting for news. But news would be a while. She would have to bridge the gap. She would have to do it alone. She was the king's seer. This was her path.

"Tomorrow," she said. "We'll feast."

———

It was a great feast. The fat of a fecund land at midsummer. Fruit, meat, bread, rich butter and sweet cream, fresh mead, the scent of roasting rosemary and thyme. At Hild's bidding, the scop sang only glad songs, songs of hearth and home, children and harvest.

Women wore their finest, children ran between benches, laughing, and if the dogs were too few and the din of conversation lacking the deep bass rumble of the war band, no one chose to notice.

The queen moved from bench to bench with the guest cup—not white mead but the gentler, sweeter yellow summer mead—offering it to traders and drovers, sailors and farmfolk who might never drink from such a thing again.

Hild had suggested to James that he give a blessing. He should wear bright robes, and speak only of grace and good fortune, speak simply and not at length; a hall was not a church, a feast not a Mass. James, more used to supervising fellow religious and attending to administrative detail, seemed thankful for the advice.

When he rose to give the blessing, the din quieted a little. His face seemed more ash than charcoal, his hair less bouncy than usual, and he tugged the collar of his robe from his neck; perhaps the thick embroidery itched. He lifted both hands, as Paulinus or Stephanus would but without the conviction.

Hild made a slight movement of her shoulders, a rolling, to draw his attention. When he looked at her, she lifted her cup and mouthed behind it *Food! Wine!* and nodded at the scop, who strummed a chord.

The din fell to a hum.

"Let us be thankful for our blessings!"

A few *Ayes!* and scattered thumps on the board set a muscle in his cheek twitching. Choirs didn't do that when he exhorted them. Hild smiled at him reassuringly.

"He brings us this food. He gives us this wine."

Then he seemed to lose the thread. Hild mouthed *Grace, good fortune, God's blessing.*

"And let us ask for His grace and favour for our army, whose cause is just."

Calls of agreement. *Short,* Hild mouthed. *Simple.*

"May His light shine upon them. In the name of the Father, and of the Son, and of the Holy Ghost. Amen."

"Amen!" Hild said loudly. *Amen,* said the queen and Breguswith. *Amen,* said the Gaulish stonemasons.

Amen, said the folk hesitantly. Then again, *Amen! Amen!*

James sat. Hild stood and spread both arms like an incantation.

"I had a dream!"

Silence settled into every corner of the hall. Every movement ceased. Every eye fixed on her.

"I had a dream. And in my dream the enemy gathered on a cold, wet heath. The men of Gwynedd tucked their helmets under their arms to listen to their treacherous king. But in my dream, they heard only the cawing of crows and ravens sitting wing to wing on a withered tree. Cadwallon Twister spoke but the men of Gwynedd heard nothing. For the crows rose like a black cloud and stooped on them. They flew and flapped about their bare heads, clutched at their skulls, and tugged at their hair. Black eyes, black beaks, black wings beating, beating. And when the enemy could look past the flurry of feathers, what did they see?"

Not a sound.

"The enemy saw, on the roof ridge of the hall, a raven with a red thread in its beak. And the enemy lost heart. For they knew, for we all know: They ride to disaster and ruin. The pulling of human hair means death. The perching on a withered tree means no food or drink. The red thread brings fire. I have seen it. Our enemies will starve in the saddle, they will fall before us, and behind them their homes will burn."

She lifted a hand and the drummer began a soft, slow beat.

"I say to you: The very trees and stones and sods of the earth will be against the men of Gwynedd. Every stream will run foul or hide its face from them. Their horses will stumble blind with terror and fall over shadows. Their army will scatter like birds before a thrown stone. Their bones will break, their wounds rot, and their children cry out. And with every cry, courage will leave them."

She looked at the women and men and children one by one. Up one bench. Down the next.

"But our men, oh, our fine men, every breath they draw will increase their courage. Every swing of the sword will multiply their strength. Every river will make itself known to them and its waters will be sweet."

The drumbeat quickened.

"No Anglisc spear will separate from its shaft, no sword break in battle. No spear will miss its cast, no shield fail. I say to you: Our men will reap the enemy like corn. I say to you: Our men will drive Gwynedd into the sea. It is their wyrd. I have seen it. Our gesiths, with their shining mail and inlaid helmets, with their swords and arm rings, with their bright cloaks and painted shields, our menfolk mounted on horses with glittering headstalls and chased-leather saddles, our husbands and sons and brothers will come home to us."

She looked at Æthelburh.

"Edwin Yffing, overking of the Anglisc, will return dark with sun and unscratched by anything but brambles."

She looked at Begu.

"Uinniau, prince of Rheged, will return wreathed in glory and glittering with spoil."

She looked at her mother.

"Luftmaer the scop will come home. He will come soon, with news that will make our faces split with smiling and our throats ache with song."

The housefolk began to move through the hall filling cups.

"So let us drink to our men, who will sit by us once again. To our men, who will be here for the corn harvest. To our men, oh, our shining men, who will sing with us at our next feast." She lifted the great guest cup. It still took two hands. "To our men!"

To our men! The hall bulged with their roar. They drank.

Hild smiled. Drank. Smiled again. Sat. The musicians played.

To Cian, she said to herself.

After the feast, people smiled at Hild when they passed. Gwladus stopped rubbing at her neck, and Hild began to treat her as she always had. Better: She fed her and clothed her as before, only now she gave her more presents, and now Gwladus didn't come to her room in the afternoon. It occurred to Hild that she would have to teach her to ride—only slaves were expected to run alongside the horses. She should probably teach Morud, as well. Morud, after all, had given his oath. Perhaps Gwladus would want to swear, too.

That first morning after the feast, Hild and the queen and the queen's women gathered in the little wooden chapel, now overshadowed by the half-built walls of the new church, to pray. They knelt silently. Hild tried to talk to the Christ, imagined casting her mind-voice up and up to fall into the sky. *Breathe upon them. Give them strength. Give them courage.* Silence. No one was listening. She thought instead of the pattern, of birds and foxes, the ripple of wind in the grass, the spreading ring of a salmon breaching in an Elmet pool . . .

On the second morning, a dozen housefolk joined them, standing quietly in the back. On the third, the chapel was full, and Hild felt their eyes on the back of her neck. *Soon*, she had said. *Soon, with news that will make our faces split with smiling and our throats ache with song.*

That night, lying naked next to Begu—it was too hot for a blanket— she half dreamt, half imagined a blue sky, bright with banners, and Cian looking at her, angry, rubbing his lip with a mailed fist. *You'll be sorry. I'll die wrapped in glory. The scops will sing of me for a thousand years, and boys with sticks will scream my name as they attack each other in the wood: Boldcloak!*

Angry. *Keeping him ignorant keeps him safe.* But angry was better than dead. Better than lying with his back broken across a ruined wall, with another man's ear between his teeth, mouth frozen in a snarl.

All the next day, and the next, the worry never left her. Cian shitting his bowels out in a ditch. Cian with a gaping head wound, not knowing his name. Cian with his eyes pecked out, buried with thirty others in a grave so shallow the dogs would dig him up as soon as the king rode on . . . On and on, like a cat licking her mind.

The flax was hacked and stacked and she was dressing a sickle cut when Morud ran into the yard shouting that two messengers had arrived: the scop and a priest, Hrothmar. The king had swept Gwynedd into the sea!

She stared at the split skin. Closed her eyes. *God, if you can hear me, let his skin be whole.*

Then she opened her eyes and finished the dressing.

Hrothmar was happy to let Luftmaer get the glory and play scop to the queen in her chambers. He was exhausted and filthy, too tired to stand up and too sore to sit comfortably. He slumped on a stool in the deacon's room, sipping beer, wishing the seer wasn't there. She took up all the air, like a smouldering fire. He couldn't breathe. And he didn't like the way she kept gripping the hilt of her seax and the muscle that jumped in her neck. He'd spent enough time with gesiths in the last three weeks to guess at her mood. He'd heard the songs. He just hoped the deacon could control her.

She loomed over him. "Tell me."

Just like the king in a bad mood. Oh, if only he'd never heard of the Christ. If only he'd fallen off his horse and died.

"Lady," said the deacon, "I think you're frightening the good father."

She turned on the deacon. She actually bared her teeth at him, like a hound lifting its lip. The world turned grey around the edges.

The deacon was saying something. "Don't faint, Hrothmar. Breathe. Heaven preserve us. Lady, please sit down. Over there, as far away as possible. Please don't make any sudden moves or he'll fall off his stool. Now, Hrothmar. Take a deep breath. Look at me. Tell us what happened, in your own words. The lady will sit quietly until you're finished."

Hrothmar doubted the lady would do any such thing.

The deacon sighed and stepped between them, blocking his view of her. "I'll ask questions, then. Answer them as you can."

He found that if he kept his eyes fixed on the deacon he could manage.

Yes, he said, they'd swept through Gwynedd, taken Deganwy. The king had driven the enemy into the sea. Right into the waves. Then they'd besieged Cadwallon on Glannauc, Puffin Island. But when they'd taken the fort on Glannauc—hard fighting, horrible, such noise, so many men wailing and weeping and bleeding on both sides, why did men do such things? Yes, yes. Thank you, just one more sip . . .

On Glannauc? Well, they'd found Cadwallon gone. Where, they weren't sure. The king was very angry. He'd ordered Luftmaer and him, miserable sinner that he was, to report the news to York without delay. Why him, he didn't know, perhaps . . . Why, yes, the bishop had given him a letter. Addressed to the deacon. A list of the dead.

"Give me the letter," the demon said in a voice as harsh as two boulders grinding together.

He shivered. He took the letter from his pouch and, trembling, held it out in the general direction of the deacon. If he met the demon's eyes he was lost.

The door slammed open.

"What's wrong with him?" Begu asked Hild while James fussed over the fainted priest. "He looks even whiter than usual. Did you hurt him? Well, never mind. I have a message! I have two. Luftmaer brought them. What's that?"

"A letter," Hild said, and broke the seal.

"Never mind that. I had a message from Cian."

The world sharpened. The weave on Begu's dress stood out as clear as knife cuts. The priest on the floor suddenly stank of horse.

"A message from Cian." Not dead. "To you?"

Begu nodded. "To 'Begu, my foster-sister.' "

"Give it to me, word for word."

" 'To Begu, my foster-sister, Mulstan's daughter, from Cian Boldcloak. Greetings. I am well. Uinniau is well.' That's it."

Hild stared at her. *I am well. Uinniau is well.*

"Uinniau sent a message, too. He said, well he said all sorts of things." Begu blushed. "But mainly he said he has a slash on his forearm, nothing really, and that he's bringing me a blue enamel bracelet. Just as you said! Decked with spoil! Oh, and he said Cian had a twisted knee. He's limping but fine."

Limping.

"So what's in it?"

Hild looked at the paper in her hand. "A list of the dead." She unrolled it. Tiny words. Long and dense and black. Many dead. But not Cian. Not Cian. "Lintlaf is dead." She sighed. She had liked the Lintlaf who made the ride to Tinamutha.

The priest moaned. James helped him back onto his stool. While Hild read the list, Begu found Hrothmar's beer cup and refilled it.

Gwrast, too, was dead. Brave Bryneich.

When Hild crossed the room the priest moved his head back, like a cat trying to avoid a hit in a fight. She pulled a ring off her finger and held it out. "Say a Mass for Gwrast. Say a Mass for every man. Say two Masses. One for those who are coming back, and one for those who are waiting for us beyond this life."

Hild kicked the stool by the window so hard it hit the other wall and fell on its side. "Don't even think about nagging me about giving away good rings," she snarled at Gwladus. "Limping. Limping! Poor thing. A message for Begu, 'his foster-sister.' I hope his bowels turn to water."

Gwladus righted the stool, tipped the jewels in the box onto the bed, started sorting through them. "Ah, the moss agate. Well, it'll be hard to replace that exact shade to match your earrings. But it could have been worse."

"I should never have freed you," Hild said.

"Oh, well," Gwladus said. She pondered the jewellery. "I'll have a word with the white priest. That ring's worth more than a pair of Masses."

"Why didn't he send me a message?" Hild said.

"His pride's hurt." Gwladus poured the rings back in the box. "And now your pride's hurt, I expect."

"I'm the king's seer. A gesith can't hurt my pride."

"No? Well, that's good then. Because men can be cruel when their pride hurts. Like Lintlaf. He was a fine boy, but then he was a man."

Cian was a boy; now he was a man. "Are you sorry he's dead?"

"The boy died long ago. We all die. Here." She held out a big ring of flawed jet. "Give this away next time."

Hild slid it onto her finger, felt its weight. It would leave a good bruise on Cian's cheek when he came back.

But Cian didn't come back. The king left Eadfrith at Deganwy to watch for Cadwallon and settle the countryside, and Cian stayed with him. Oswine came back, and Uinniau—bringing a bracelet fit for a princess for Begu, which she immediately slid onto her wrist, and a blue glass cup for Hild.

"There was a plate, too," he said, as he and Oswine ate with them in the sunny courtyard outside the women's wing. "But it broke."

Begu swatted him on the back of the head. "Glass does that, fool." He beamed at her. She poked him in the arm. Hild didn't know why they didn't just get down in the grass and go at it like dogs.

She looked from one to the other. "No message from Cian?"

Uinniau assumed the earnest face all men used when lying for their friends. "He said to say he was well. That he'd be back as soon as Gwynedd is settled."

We'll speak the truth, you and I. Boy, then man.

"That won't be long, surely," Begu said, stroking her bracelet, turning it this way and that in the sunlight. "Cadwallon's run away and his army's broken."

"It might be months," Oswine said. "Clemen in Dyfneint has heard rumours of Penda preparing to march. Eadfrith has taken half the remaining war band south to Caer Uisc to stiffen his resolve. Cian doesn't have as many men as he should. Gwynedd's army might be broken, but they're not dead." He realised Uinniau and Begu were both giving him looks. "What? It's true."

"Months," Hild said. "And he volunteered for this?"

"It's a great honour."

"You smell of horse," she said, and walked away.

The court moved to Derventio. Breguswith, who had been giving Hild speculative looks in York, was now busy once more with wool. The king, unhappy about Cadwallon still being alive somewhere, consoled himself with the thought of controlling all Gwynedd's trade with Ireland and Less Britain. He spent his time with the queen and her trade master, or plotting with Paulinus about how to extend their reach into Rheged. He didn't ask for Hild. Paulinus had been with him in Gwynedd; the campaign had gone well. Paulinus was now his sun and moon.

Hild knew Edwin would change his mind soon enough; it was his nature. She would be ready. Meanwhile, she spent her days with Begu. Begu was the only person who didn't make her angry. With Begu she didn't have to think.

They were making a new baldric for Uinniau, as they had long ago for Cian. This would be in a green-and-brown dart pattern. They were good at it now, after years of practice, and it was pleasant work: sitting in the sun, cooled by a light breeze, listening to the sound of housefolk not worried about war and fieldfolk pleased with the ripening corn, to birds singing and children who spent more time playing than chasing them off or pulling weeds. She could pretend it was enough to sit with a tablet weave between them, as women had for generations, and sometimes talk, sometimes fall into a half trance, mind floating free.

Begu hummed the gemæcce song to keep the rhythm of the back-and-forth: *One to hold and one to wind, one to talk and one to mind, one to beat and one to load, one to soothe and one to goad . . .*

A team, taking it in turns. Like her and Paulinus, though he didn't know it.

She followed the shuttle, back and forth, pondering her worth if Edwin didn't change his mind. Her worth as not-seer, as the king's niece. For Cadwallon or Penda, Eanflæd would be the great prize, but Eanflæd was too young. Lady Hild, the king's niece and seer, had kin ties almost as good. And her advice was gold.

But Edwin would rather die with his guts spread over three fields than see Cadwallon himself wed to an Yffing. Cadwallon's children, perhaps. Children were much more biddable. Cadwallon had two daughters by his first wife. She couldn't remember if they were marriageable but thought the eldest—Angharad? Antreth?—probably was. If Cadwallon had any wit, he'd be trying to marry the daughter to Penda.

Edwin couldn't allow an alliance between Gwynedd and Mercia. She couldn't allow it.

They are our enemies. We marry them.

And there it was. So simple. Her and Penda.

"Tighter," Begu said. Hild blinked. Begu nodded at the sagging weave, then more closely at Hild. "You look . . . I don't know. Are you too hot? Come on, we'll go inside. Wilnoð says Arddun found someone who knows of a patch of strayberries. You like those. I want to talk to your mother, anyway, about that brown cloth she got in from Aberford yesterday. It has a lovely hand, truly fine—better than that tunic the king got from the pope, I bet. Though not as lustrous; you need those foreign goats for that. But the colour would suit Uinniau, don't you think? Besides, if we're to be married, there's half a hundred things I need to be making."

Married. What would be, is. But there was no harm in being cautious and making sure of her fallbacks. And Cian's. What had happened between them had been a mistake born of her fear for his safety. Just fear. She could mend that.

"Ask Wilnoð to save some strayberries for me. I must speak to the king."

The king put his chin on his fist. "It seems we've been here before, Niece. If you're so in love with your bog, by all means go slog about in it."

"Thank you, Uncle."

The Crow never smiled, but she felt the intensity of his regard drop a notch. He was reassured by the king's indulgent tone. Rivals weren't indulged; counsellors weren't indulged. Nieces, mere maids and marriage counters, were indulged.

"Just try not to spike anyone important."

"Yes, Uncle."

"And if you should happen to hear or see anything interesting, I'd be happy for a message."

"Yes, Uncle. May I take some men along for the purpose?"

The Crow's gaze sharpened.

"There are men leaving tomorrow for Caer Loid and Aberford, as you well know."

"Yes, Uncle. But Pyr, I'm sure, will have a use for every one of them."

"Oh, very well, pick your usual faithful hounds. But you'll ride without my token."

The Crow's attention eased.

"Yes, Uncle." She would have refused the token if offered. The point of the visit was to find out what kind of token she did or didn't need.

She travelled with her household, a score of Edwin's men to bolster the garrisons at Caer Loid and Aberford, and a wagon of goods those garrisons—and her own Menewood—couldn't produce on their own. Some of the gesiths had recently healed wounds; she set an easy pace.

When they hit the old army street heading into Elmet, she turned in her saddle and said to Oeric, "Sing something! Something jaunty!" And so they marched into the cool wood singing about the Curly-Haired Cat from Caer Daun, who involved herself in an improbable number of adventures with an impressive variety of men.

When they left the shelter of the trees and crested the rise, she braced herself. But the new hall and tidy huts looked nothing like Ceredig's palace, nothing like the long ago with Cian. The orchards might never have been, and the great gouge where the thorn had been torn from the earth was grassed over and partly hidden by a stout stockade. The old oak was still there, but next to a new church. The smoke seeping from the eaves was wood smoke, not peat, and a cow lowed where the geese had cackled. This was a royal vill, thoroughly Anglisc.

Arrayed before it, spear blades glittering in the sun, a row of armed men drawn up to greet her. She smiled. Clearly it didn't matter to Pyr whether or not she bore a token.

Pyr and his new wife, the daughter of a local thegn, welcomed them with a feast, and every time Hild complimented him on a dish, he explained exactly where it came from and how he had made it possible. The swan? From the bywater north and east, which he knew about because of his careful survey last year. The salmon? Oh, yes, he'd not let the gesiths piss in the river east of the weir, so their breeding ground was clear. The medlar butter? Well, that was a lucky trade just this spring, though not really lucky because of course it was careful cultivation of the trade web the wealh—beg pardon, the Loides—had had since Ceredig was king. It had taken some patience to set up again, and careful negotiation . . .

Careful was his favourite word, and as she studied him from beneath half-lowered lids she wondered if he used it so often to counter the wealh reputation for recklessness and improvidence. What would it be like to grow up with that burden? But it was Pyr's wealhness that made it possible for him to be steward of such an important vill without the king worrying too much. Even if Edwin didn't visit often and mark it as his own, the local thegns wouldn't follow a wealh. At least not a common wealh.

Pyr's wife, Saxfryth, filled her cup anxiously. Hild reminded herself to guard her expression. They watched everything she did. She might not bear the token but they knew the songs, and she was still the king's niece and seer. No doubt they wanted to be reeve and steward to whomever Edwin named ealdorman, and her word carried weight. She smiled at the woman and said, "I know another woman called Saxfryth who lives south and east of Aberford. She's a fine weaver but could learn a thing or two from you when it comes to brewing. This is good mead."

The woman blushed.

"Pyr, you and your wife are stewarding the king's vill well. He'll hear that from me." Perhaps he blushed, too, but his skin was too sun-browned to tell.

She spent three days by the Aire, talking to everyone at the vill, spilling fulsome praise: for the sturdy stockade, the fine carving in the hall, the black earth and healthy coleworts in the kitchen garth, the strong hum of bees in the skeps along the garth's edge. She listened to the groom talk about pasture for horses and the unwillingness of the local thegns to part with the right feed. She discussed with Saxfryth the best way to recruit more women; the hall was still sadly lacking in fine linens. She suggested to Pyr's garthman that the place really did need an orchard and that, yes, she knew from experience apples and pears both would grow well just east of the stockade.

She talked and listened and sampled until the Caer Loid household began to relax. The king would be pleased, she said, over and over, but they still leapt to anticipate her needs, getting underfoot and irritating both her and Gwladus.

The nights were better. Hild reacquainted herself with Lweriadd and Sintiadd, both plumper than they had been but no less inclined to sly looks and slant comments. Sitting by the fire in the summer evening as Hild the daughter of the might-have-been king, not Hild the seer of the overking, speaking nothing but British, she felt her face setting in a new shape, happier, younger. But as she listened—to every joke, every complaint, every song, every tale of woe—she found that under their contentment ran a thin thread of unease, the sense of trouble a long, long way off. It took a while to tease out the thread: The thegns didn't come to the hall to gossip and catch up on news as often as the Loides thought they should; the Anglisc were suspicious.

Suspicious of what? That the Loides were in league with the Christ, and so with the wealh priest web, and so with the spies of the men who would overrun Elmet in their quest to bring down Edwin king.

Had they not heard that Edwin king had just won a great victory over the Welsh? she asked. Yes, yes indeed, Lweriadd said. She knew that; everyone who ate barley cake knew that. She knew that half the Christ priests around here were sons of priests who had inherited their books and couldn't spell more than their names. But the wheat-eating Anglisc were suspicious. Where was Cadwallon? they asked. Who was hiding him? Who was plotting with him? She knew that Cian Boldcloak had the Welsh king bottled up tight in one of his green valleys—set a king to catch a king, eh? and such a handsome one!—but the Anglisc thought all wealh were the same.

The next morning she told Pyr that instead of riding directly for Menewood she would personally escort the gesiths to their post at Aberford: In case Paulinus had any spies in hall, she told him the lady Breguswith would enjoy hearing how the weaving progressed there.

Morud guided them north and east to Brid's Dike, past Berewith, and on to Aberford.

She smelt Aberford before they rode over Becca Bank. She reined in, closed her eyes. Smoke, stale urine, lye, dung, and, sweetening it all, weld. "They've been busy," she said. "There must be a score of women working on cloth here."

The men sent as relief for the Aberford garrison glanced at one another, and one touched his breast where no doubt his amulet hung, but Oeric and the others exchanged knowing looks—except for Grimhun, who fidgeted with his arm ring and leaned forward in his saddle. Hild waved him on. "Go on," she said. "Go see what they've made of your walls."

He bent his head gratefully and kicked his horse into a canter.

The rest of them followed at a jingling trot.

Aberford was an oddly segregated settlement: gesiths in a long house by the banks to the west of the road, women in a series of huts on the east. The east was bright with swaths of yellow, green, brown, and smaller patches of red and blue and black: cloth drying on racks and lines. Goats were tethered—goats had a tendency to eat good wool—and children pulled weeds from plots of weld and other dye plants. A lost-looking duck paddled back and forth on a newly dug pond.

Hild stayed long enough to meet the garrison commander and Heiu, the woman Breguswith had put in charge of the cloth workers. Hild complimented her on her cloth—Begu was right, it was very fine—and promised that on her way back she would spend a little more time inspecting the weaving huts and talking about supplies.

Then she rode with Oeric, the brothers Berht, Morud, and Gwladus south and east over the high tussocky sheep land to the holding of Ceadwulf and the other Saxfryth.

The boy Ceadwin now had a little sister, Ceadfryth, in swaddling clothes. Saxfryth still wore Hild's yellow ring, but now she'd added a thin silver band inset with some muddy-looking blue stone Hild couldn't identify. The silverwork was fretted, not solid—but real silver.

The men and Ceadwin went to look at a horse Ceadwulf wanted their opinion on, and Gwladus disappeared into the kitchen to take the measure of the housefolk. Hild and Saxfryth sat with bread and cheese in the garth, with Ceadfryth in a wooden cradle at Saxfryth's left hand.

"Good cheese," Hild said. She smiled at the sleeping baby. "She looks strong, well fed. And Ceadwin must be three hands higher now."

Saxfryth beamed, as women did when you praised their children and housekeeping. "The gods have been kind." She sighed and rolled her shoulders. "And you, lady? Have the gods been kind to you?"

"Well enough, though now it's the Christ that the king and his household look to."

"The Christ." Saxfryth sucked her lip, leaned over the sleeping child, and brushed away a fly that wasn't there.

"He's a god like any other," Hild said. "With priests who are men and subject to men's fancies. I know some good priests, wealh and Anglisc alike."

"Gesiths came through here last year, hunting wealh priests. Spies, they said. And then Anglisc priests came, but they were more like reeve's men than priests. You could see it in their eyes, feeling the backs of sheep for the wool, tasting the beer, peering at the cows and the hay in the rick. Weighing in their minds, totting it all up, and making marks on those slates of theirs."

If Paulinus wasn't careful, his zeal would drive a wedge between the Elmetsætne, returning them to Loid and Angle. If she were Cadwallon she could make something of that. "A woman should judge priests for herself, as she would any other man. When they make demands you think unfair, speak to the king's man at Caer Loid."

"He's half wealh himself, they say."

"He is. And a fine king's man."

"The gesith you were here with last time, Boldcloak, he's wealh, too, they say. Son of a king."

Hild nodded blandly.

"I liked him," Saxfryth said.

"Yes. He liked your buttered mushrooms."

"He remembers!" Saxfryth gave her an arch look. "So he's not with you?"

"He's in Gwynedd. The king's right hand."

"Well! A wealh."

"Another wealh," Hild reminded her. "Just like Pyr. A trusted man. And worth getting to know." Saxfryth nodded. "Aberford. You find it a good market for your wool?"

"It is, lady. Though uncommon picky. Our neighbour had half her weight turned down. Short-fibred, they said." She smiled complacently. "But my sheep give the best wool. Ceadwulf knows how to breed them."

Hild smiled and nodded. "A good market for good wool, then. More than enough to balance out the king's tithe?"

Like all good traders, Saxfryth hunted for a way to dodge praising the seller's goods, or at least hedge that praise, but Hild caught her gaze and held it. "Yes, lady. More than enough."

Hild nodded, ate a piece of cheese, tilted her head back to watch a hawk circling against the blue sky.

"Lady? Ceadwin is seven now."

Hild closed her eyes briefly. "If he came with me, he would have no foster-brothers or foster-sisters."

"At least not yet."

"And he'd have to be baptised."

"Christ's a god like any other," Saxfryth said. "As you say."

"I travel a lot."

"Even so. Lady, you promised. He'll be no trouble. Besides, having a child at your knee will soon make you bear children of your own, everyone knows that. And Boldcloak won't stay in Gwynedd forever."

Hild stood. "I'll send for him in spring."

They rode in a glittering, jingling column, past adders sunning themselves on south-facing rocks and knots of red campion. The sky was as blue as the heart of a cornflower and the furze flamed yellow.

They rode down the slope to the ancient track for a mile or so, until they were moving parallel to the low hills to the north.

Hild watched the right-hand edge of the ancient track closely. At her heel—unlike Gwladus, he still preferred his feet to a horse—Morud said, "You won't see a path. I used a different way each time. That way it stays secret like."

"Secret."

"You never said, but I thought you might want it that way."

Hild was glad, fiercely glad. Secret. Yes. "Morud, I'll give you a new knife for this. Two knives."

Hild had fallen in love with what Menewood could be. Now she fell in love with what it was becoming: a thriving settlement in a fertile, half-secret valley of bogs and becks and ponds and meadow.

Four dozen souls less one, Rhin told her, with fields of clover and oats, barley and colewort. He showed her tally sticks for everything from folk able to wield a sickle, to pigs, to skeps, to milch cows. They toured the byre, made of good oak; the tiny new forge; and a dairy laid in dry stone. He showed her the cleared millrace, the great gritstone grindstones from over the Whinmoor, and the almost finished elm mill wheel. He took her round to the mix of huts and homesteads, some timber, some wattle, some with stone foundations and reed roofs. And everywhere men and women knelt to her and kissed her hand. She was not just the king's seer, the king's niece, she was their dryhten, their lord. They lived and breathed at her pleasure and the efficiency of the land's management.

Hild touched the children under the chin so she could look into their eyes, and held the hands of old folk long enough to feel the size of their bones. The dull-eyed ones, Rhin said, were lately come to the mene. They would soon fill out, soon shine. And Hild's heart filled until she could hardly breathe: her people.

The first fortnight she spent every morning and most afternoons with Rhin, walking, talking, pointing, running grain through her fingers, listening to the hum of bees. He had taken her at her word and in the spring had set all the children to searching the countryside for hives, giving a reward for every one discovered. They had two beekeepers, though one was mostly plaiting skeps, and those skeps hummed and dripped with honey.

She walked in the evening through her domain, as aware of it as of her own body. The dragonflies and damselflies zooming over the water; the gush and rush and mineral bite of the millrace compared to the softer babble of the beck. The clatter of reeds by the pond, scented with green secrets; the chatter of wrens and goldcrest flocks, squabbling with each other like rival gangs of children.

Everywhere she looked, she thought of things she must tell Rhin: Set aside much of the mead for white mead this winter; thin the coppice and make sure they made more charcoal this autumn, for next year when Penda made his move there would be war, long hard war, and war meant iron, and there was no smelting without charcoal. Breed more goats, especially the long-haired kind. Graze them in that overstood beech coppice— pollard the standards and let the goats trim the rest or cut them for firewood and tree hay.

So she fell in love with the mene, and the mene fell in love with her. She felt buoyed by her people, her land. Everything tasted round and ripe. The air was as rich and sweet as cider. Just breathing fed some part of her. She spent half the nights lying by the pond listening to the bullrushes and the frogs. At dawn she rode Cygnet along the ridge and looked forward to the next month when she might see the peregrines returning.

Mine, she thought, looking down at the low woods with the water glinting through the green. *Mine*, when the men and women formed their line to start sickling the barley. *Mine*, when she smelt the wild garlic in a just-cut glade of coppiced hazel. *Mine, mine, mine.*

She ignored the rattle of the box buried at her heart, and the whisper of *Penda* . . . Not now. Not yet. Here, now, this was hers. Secret. Hidden.

Sometimes she found letters in the hollow pollard oak to the south of the mene, left by some priest or other for Rhin, but more often the priest web was a thing of tired-looking men arriving at night and huddling with Rhin to share rumours of the isle before moving on north or west or east to the coast and a boat to Less Britain.

Sometimes at night she stayed up with Rhin, drinking the last of the heather beer and discussing the news. The Picts had sent some kind of embassy to Rheged and been rebuffed. Yes, he'd try to find out more. Cadwallon, they said, was in Ireland. He was enough of a nuisance that Domnall Brecc had sent a war band, led by Oswald Iding, to subdue the troublemakers. Good news for Edwin, they agreed, two enemies off squabbling with each other.

Good news, too, for Cian Boldcloak: His time in Gwynedd would be much easier without rumours of a king to stir up opposition. Perhaps he would come home soon.

She couldn't sleep that night and instead walked into the woods and lay on her stomach by the garlic in the coppiced glade, cheek on her hands, sighting along the tips of the grass stems, dull as lead in the moonlight. Was Cian sitting under the moon in Deganwy? Perhaps it was raining. Perhaps he was sitting, chin in one hand, drinking horn dangling from the other, listening to stirring Welsh song, half drunk, half dreaming of glory. Though he had glory in plenty now. Perhaps he was listening to a song about himself. With Eadfrith still in Dyfneint, he was the most important Angle in Gwynedd, and scops and Welsh bards were not stupid.

There were songs in plenty about Penda, too. He was cunning, and young, and strong. But Penda was a decision for another time. She found herself wondering, instead, if Cadwallon would stay in Ireland. He was as wily as a fox, and his hatred ran deep. There was nothing for him in Ireland. He'd find his way back to Gwynedd in the end. Cian needed to come home. He'd be safer. And she could tell him all the things she had seen, the things she'd learnt, the people she was helping. She would show him the mene, tell him of her plans. They could mend what had broken between them. They could ignore it. It hadn't happened.

A hedgepig wheezed and puffed at the edge of the clearing, nosing in the grass for snails and worms. *So we may drink to home wherever we are.*

The barley was cut and drying. After a report of bandits, Hild and her gesiths rode out to the Whinmoor.

It was a fine day, sound as a late plum. They rode from flock to flock, copse to copse, but found nothing. As they turned back for the mene, Hild told herself she was glad; she didn't want to see the light go out in anyone's eyes. Nonetheless Cygnet was skittish. She wasn't the only one. Oeric's mount pranced and snorted.

She caught Oeric's eye, then Berhtnoth's. She grinned. "A ring to the first back!" She kicked Cygnet into a gallop. With whoops and whistles, the men raced after her.

And so her blood was singing under her skin and Cygnet hot under her thighs when she saw the birds flying from the old ivy-covered oak just north of the beck, where it flowed west to east before turning south for the mene. She touched Cygnet into a tight, hard curve, slowed to a canter, then a trot, and reined in.

Part of her registered her gesiths shouting and making their own turns to follow her, but she was focused on the tree, unsure of what she'd seen, only that it had made her pay attention.

There. A starling with a worm still wriggling in its beak, disappearing into the deep V of the top boughs about three times her height from the ground. Then, yes, a dove, with a fly. Her heart thundered from the ride, and Cygnet was blowing hard, but gradually they both settled. After a little while, first the dove then the starling flew away from the oak.

She swung off Cygnet. Thick ivy made the climb easy. By the time Oeric jumped down from his snorting mount, she was perched on the right-hand bough, peering into the cleft. She stripped a twig and used it to bend the ivy to one side.

A nest. Four chicks. When the twig poked through the ivy they sat up, peeping, and flapped their tiny wings and opened outsize beaks to show red, red mouths.

Two starlings and two doves.

"Lady?" Oeric called from the base of the tree.

"Doves and starlings," she said, amazed. "Sharing the same nest."

"Doves and starlings?"

"Doves and starlings." She laughed. "Starlings and doves!"

Oeric was looking nervous, but she didn't care. She laughed again, as chains burst in the dark and a box shattered to splinters. "It's an omen, Oeric. An omen!" His horse was good, and Grimhun's, and Berhtnoth's. Good for hours. "Omens must be spread!"

That evening she drank beer with Rhin. She felt as bright as the first morning of the world. "I sent them galloping to every corner of Elmet—to Caer Loid, to Aberford, to Saxfryth, to the south river, even back to the Whinmoor. Doves and starlings sharing a nest, like Loides and Anglisc sharing Elmet." An omen that would persuade even Edwin. "It is possible. It's all possible."

He was smiling at her. "Of course, lady. Because of you. Have some of these currants. Our latest visitor picked them on the way in this morning and your woman said you were fond of berries."

Hild ate a handful, bursting them with her tongue against her teeth, one by one, tart-sweet pops of deep red juice. Doves and starlings. Starlings and doves. She only had to think how to couch it to Edwin, and for Cian to come home.

"Sadly, our visitor won't tell anyone where the patch is; his to know, he says, ours to be grateful. But he did bring news. A rumour of Cadwallon. He's in Less Britain, they say."

Less Britain. Cadwallon was lining up the Britons-over-the-sea against the Anglisc. Oh, yes, Edwin would have to listen. Elmet needed Cian. It would work. Doves and starlings. Starlings and doves.

"Just a rumour, less than a rumour, a whisper. Though no doubt it will please Boldcloak, now that he's taken up with that Welsh princess."

Hild swallowed carefully. "Welsh princess?"

"It's the latest news. Cadwallon's daughter."

Her tongue felt like wood. "Another wild rumour, no doubt."

"Oh, no. This one's true. I've heard it twice."

"A bastard daughter?"

"No. His eldest by his first wife. Angeth, his treasure. A rare beauty by all accounts, ripe as a June strayberry and twice as subtle. Now playing lady and hostess to Boldcloak's lord and host in the king's hall at Deganwy. Boldcloak's to be Edwin's underking there, do you think?"

This must be what it was like to be fighting, to be winning, to lift your arm for the triumphant blow, only to blink, to sway, to look down and see a thick snake in the grass, but it's not a snake, it's your arm, staff still in its hand. Between one blink and the next your arm is no longer your arm. There it is, it's just not yours. Stupid, stupid Cian.

"Lady?"

She watched her hand—it looked so strange—reach for the currants, pick the reddest, the plumpest, put it in her mouth, and deliberately burst it against her teeth.

The world was easier to understand when choices fell away. It was like understanding a tree when all the leaves dropped: There it was, the pattern of the boughs, the tree itself.

She saw patterns everywhere. Where before she had seen flowers humming and rippling with bees, now she saw that bees liked red flowers best. Red and striped.

"Plant more phlox," she told Rhin. "Phlox, red clover, campion." She didn't bother to explain. She didn't repeat herself. More red meant more honey, which meant more mead, and therefore more people willing to listen. She was going to need people to listen, or Cian would die and Elmet with him. Edwin would not like this news. She needed time to think, to plan, before Edwin heard it.

As the days cooled the colours around her did, too. Bright red flowers were replaced by dark red berries. The sun set earlier. The berries now were tinged with blue. Perhaps it was warmth that made the colour. Red meant life. Blue meant the blue lips of harsh breathing and death. The end of things.

She rode out often on her own, or walked, from dawn to dusk, watching everything. Cows, she noticed, stood broadside to the sun on a cool day, but nose into the wind, and otherwise, when sleeping, when chewing, pointed their head or tail south.

Then she realised deer also lined up north to south.

There were patterns everywhere. She saw it in the tiny yellow clusters of a late daisy, and they reminded her of the seeds on a strayberry. There was an order there, she could almost taste it, but she couldn't articulate it. If she just kept looking it would all come clear.

Migrant peregrines began to arrive. The young, first. Brown and buff. Females followed by smaller males. Why were young birds so dull? It was always the same, no matter what kind of bird. The adults, which followed days later, were much more definite: blue-black on top, whitish barred with grey beneath. Did that mean something?

The sky turned grey. Grass bleached. Leaves fell. More rumours came from Gwynedd: Cadwallon was readying ships in Less Britain. Eadfrith ætheling was planning to stay in Caer Uisc with Clemen for Yule. Bold-cloak's woman was with child.

When Morud brought the message from Caer Loid that the king wanted his seer in York, Gwladus was already packing.

Hild stood before Edwin still in her travel cloak. The queen was with him, and Paulinus and Coelfrith, but no others, not even the endlessly scratch-scratch-scratching Stephanus.

Edwin's eyes were red-rimmed. "What the fuck is Boldcloak doing?"

Killing us all. But the habit of protection was too strong.

She flicked dirt off a fold of her cloak. "Being a man, my king."

"With the Twister's own daughter?" Paulinus said.

"With all of them, no doubt."

Silence.

"He is young," said Æthelburh. "And he feels like a conqueror."

"I'm the conqueror."

"Yes, my lord," said Paulinus. "He's a gesith getting above himself."

"He's thinking with his breeches, lord King," Hild said. "As young men do."

"I never did."

And Hild, surprised, realised he was right. She had never seen him take a woman after a battle. "You're a king, lord. Cian is a king's man. Your loyal man."

"But to get her with child!"

Hild bent her head. Cian had been stupid.

"Perhaps it'll bring Cadwallon back," Æthelburh said.

"It's too late in the year for a ship to cross from Frankia," the Crow said dismissively.

Hild wondered at that. Frankia, not Less Britain? She wondered, too, why the queen didn't have the Crow flayed for such a tone. But the Crow was right, it didn't matter for now: No one could cross the sea, whether from Frankia or Less Britain, until spring. And there were other things to worry about.

"Cadwallon has two daughters," she said.

"Oh, by the Christ! Don't tell me he's taken the other one, too."

"No, King. In my worst dreams, she's in Penda's bed."

Edwin's eyes swarmed green and black, but he turned his gaze not to her but to his queen and reeve and priest. "Just why didn't any of you think to mention this before?" He swung back to Hild. "And where the fuck have you *been*?"

The winter was mild. To Hild it seemed as though every woman in hall was swelling with child. Except Æthelburh, who smiled relentlessly at other women's bellies. The queen seemed truly happy only when James arrived for the twelve days of Yule and led a new choir for the Christ Mass. When he went back to Craven, the queen went back to smiling and keeping her own counsel. It occurred to Hild that for a royal woman it must be like living as a hostage in an armed camp. Paulinus was her go-between. Was this how it was for Hereswith, how it had been for her own mother?

She tried to talk to her mother about it, but Breguswith—like Begu—was spending most of her time with her man. She seemed impatient: no armies were moving, no messages could cross the winter seas, no one could do anything about anything until spring. Why didn't Hild stop thinking and just enjoy herself? Hild wondered if her mother had been possessed by an ælf or if this was just how it was with a man in your life. She could no more stop thinking than stop breathing.

She thought about marrying Penda. Edwin would like it. One of the conditions for the marriage would be Penda's conversion. Edwin would be his godfather and therefore Penda's overking. Overking of all the Anglisc.

Paulinus would like it. With all the Anglisc converted, he'd get his pallium at last. He could die happy, knowing that as overbishop he'd sit in heaven at the right hand of the pope.

Penda would like it. Her kin ties were strong, her advice better than gold. She was young and strong. She could manage a household—she could manage a kingdom.

Would she like it? If Penda was as cunning as she thought, she might like him well enough. She could take Begu with her. And her household.

One day when Uinniau was out hunting with Oswine, she asked Begu how she thought Uinniau would like to be her chief gesith. When she got married.

"Who are you marrying?"

"I don't know yet."

"Because the queen hasn't said anything. And I thought the king didn't want to let you go. You're his seer. Oh, have you annoyed the Crow again?"

"No. Uinniau. Would he like it?"

"Why wouldn't he like it? I'd like it, anyway. I don't want him going off to war anymore. He's done enough now so that Luftmaer can write a song or two for our children. Only I suppose it wouldn't be Luftmaer who'd be doing the singing, would it?"

Everything would be different. Everybody.

"Do you suppose he'd get fat, like Bassus? Sitting at home safe and sound while everyone went off to war with your husband king. And, oh, Oeric would be cross."

"Oeric could never be a queen's chief gesith."

"You do have someone in mind. I knew it. Or is this just one of your endless plots? It's winter. You really should just drink some more and find someone to play with. You spend too much time in your head. I wish you'd take Gwladus to your bed again. If you won't do that, at least climb a tree or something. You'll start looking like the Crow, nothing but bones and a beaky nose."

That evening Hild watched Paulinus at meat, eating little, covering his cup with his hand. He was a foreigner, like Æthelburh, a long way from home. But unmarried. A bit like a seer. Did his god talk to him? Did it make him feel the way she did when she felt the pattern looking out at her from every blade of grass, every leaf, every beetle's wing? Had he watched beetles when he was a boy, at home? She found she couldn't imagine him as a boy. Couldn't imagine him at home, belonging. He had always looked like this: planed and hollowed, eyes hooded, lost to the world of men, honed to nothing but patterns and plans.

When Gwladus brought her wash water the next morning she sat and stared at herself. She lifted her hair from her face. Planes and hollows, eyes hooded . . .

Gwladus's face appeared over her shoulder. They looked at each other in the water: Gwladus so soft and pliant, Hild hard and clear.

"I'm not pretty."

"You don't need to be pretty. You're like lightning. Like a tide. Like a blizzard."

"Something to run from."

"Something to get caught up in. Something to remember for the rest of your life."

As Penda tightened his hold on the middle country, he swept the roads clear of bandits. He appeared to have no quarrel with priests; the web hummed. Hild wondered if this was because he didn't know about the web or because he wanted it to flourish for his own purposes. He seemed like a canny king. But kings always fell in the end. It was the way of the world.

That night she dreamt Fursey was talking to Hereswith. *It's what women do: weave the web, pull the strings, herd into the corner. It's their only power.* Then she was inside Hereswith, and Fursey was talking to her. *Unless they're seers. Your mother has built you a place where you can speak your word openly.*

She lay looking at the elm of her ceiling for a long time. Power. Place. Marriage. She did not see how they fit together. Perhaps Fursey would.

She woke Gwladus to stir the fire and light candles and then wrote Fursey a long letter, using the codes they each hoped the other understood:

S for Sigebert, P for Penda, R for Ricberht, Uncle for Edwin, Sister for Hereswith, Æ for Æthelric . . .

In the morning she took the letter, along with a ham, to Linnet's house, where a priest would call soon and carry it by a circuitous route to Rhin, who would see it safely to its destination.

Winter passed. Messages flowed freely. Sigebert was still fighting Ricberht in East Anglia. Eadfrith and Clemen were still in Caer Uisc. Still no clear sign of Cadwallon. She pondered Less Britain. Long ago, its kings were the sworn men of Gwynedd. Did that oath hold?

She didn't share her thoughts about Cadwallon with anyone. She didn't mention Penda. She didn't tell anyone of her Elmet omen. For the first time, she could not see her path. She would wait.

24

✦

SOLMONATH AT BEBBANBURG, and the world shimmered with light and salt. White-grey sky, grey-white sand dunes, silver driftwood, walls weathered to the colour of limestone. The light, sourceless and bright, seeped into every corner and crevice; it was like living inside a hollow pearl. Many women were huge with child.

Hrethmonath, when they should have been hunched down tight in their wind-lashed fist of stone, isolated. The seas were unnaturally calm and shipping was already creeping along the coast: from Kent to Gipswīc, to Brough, to the Bay of the Beacon, to Tinamutha, to Bebbanburg. It was the first time anyone could remember getting easy news while the seals sang and the guillemots dived.

Edwin grew restless and shouted at his counsellors. Where was Cadwallon? What good were a seer and a priest if they never brought him information? What if that nithing king, heading a fleet of Frankish ships groaning with Frankish gesiths, was floating up the Humber to York?

Hild said nothing.

Her web hummed: letters from Fursey and Hereswith, and gossip from Onnen in Mulstanton, all funnelled through Rhin in Menewood, then forwarded to the farmstead of Rathlaf and Cille, who held the letters in exchange for mead and, when there was any, soft white bread. She rode out every week or so and accepted with great ceremony any letter they had, along with a bowl of something by the fire. After the third time, they stopped asking after Boldcloak.

One day there were two letters from Fursey. The first read:

As to your question about a union with P, remember that the
baptism of the high is wound about with worldly as well as
heavenly obligation. Whosoever stands as godfather to another
adopts him in religion but this adoption spreads like a smile, like a
blessing, into the affairs of the world of men. The son in Christ
inherits very much of the godfather's mantle.

Very much. Fursey never emphasised words. He thought it vulgar. What
was he trying to say?

Cille brought her a bowl of sour ale and settled in the corner to watch
Hild read. It seemed to fascinate her.

Hild cracked the seal of the second letter. Long. And much more like
Fursey. She sipped the ale and let his soft Irish voice unfurl in her head:

Your ever-fruitful sister has provided her husband with a son,
named in Christ Ealdwulf. If volume were to be equated with
strength he will in time, no doubt, prove capable of lifting the
earth. Æ, with an heir to sharpen his edge, is now swinging most
heartily for S. If S, a most Godly man, should prevail over R—and,
Christ willing, I now don't doubt it—then your nephew will be
his eventual heir. Your sister is twice-happy because although her
husband's woman also had a child, sadly for both mother and
child the issue is female. Howsomever, your sister is less happy at
the name chosen for this by-blow: Balthild. It is an offence against
her dignity, she believes, that this babe should share even part of
her sister's noble name.

That, at least, seemed clear enough: Sigebert was winning. He would
be king of the East Angles, and Æthelric his heir.

She rolled up the parchment, tucked it in her belt. A sound thread of
news she would share with the king—when it would work to her advantage.

She sipped the ale.

Hereswith now had a daughter and a son, heir to the East Anglisc king.
Did that make her feel safe? In a strange hall, what made a wife belong? It
was different for men. They stayed in their hall, the women came to

them. Except Cian, who was in Angeth's hall. What did she look like? Did he feel at home there?

She didn't want to think about Cian. She was sick of thinking about Cian. She swallowed the last sour mouthful of ale. She stood, produced the bottle of mead Cille had been hoping for, and solemnly accepted four dwarfish winter coleworts in return. It took more effort than it should have to put them in her saddlebags; Cygnet kept sidling and dancing. The mare hadn't been ridden enough. Like Hild, she needed a run.

Instead of heading south over the fields and back to the fort, she rode north angling towards the beach. She'd forgotten how stony it was. Cygnet's hooves slid and clattered on the pebbles. The vegetable-heavy bags flapped and bounced and Cygnet rolled her eyes.

"Steady down." But Cygnet snorted and fought the bit. Hild thumped her withers. "What's wrong with you?"

Then she smelt it, a solid rancid stink. Seal. She reined in, swung a leg over the mare's neck, and slid off. She led, one hand on her seax.

The hut tucked into the lee of a dune was familiar but she couldn't remember whose it was. A wisp of smoke curled from the crude stone-weighted driftwood roof.

"Hello!"

Nothing but the hiss of sea through pebbles and the mewl of gulls.

She lifted the leather door curtain. The reek nearly overpowered her. Now she remembered. Heah and Din. She'd visited them once with Cian. She hung the curtain over the twist of wood jammed in the doorframe and peered into the gloom. Empty, but the fire was unbanked, and a pot of sea stew still steamed on the hearth: recently lifted from the coals. The sound of a horse had no doubt frightened them. They'd be back.

She sat in some dune grass and got out Fursey's first letter again. *Whosoever stands as godfather to another adopts him in religion.*

She read it over and over until the light began to die and the grass hissed in the rising wind.

Something growled behind the dune. A dog? She stood, hand on seax. "Come out. Heah, Din, I won't hurt—"

"Don't say their names!" A woman's voice. A woman in a sealskin cloak, whirling a sling, lit by the setting sun. "Don't say their names, wight!"

A woman with supple hands and a mouth like plums. Gode. Cian's woman.

"Why shouldn't I say . . . their names?"

Gode came sideways down the dune, sling still in her hand but not swinging. "They're dead."

"I'm sorry."

Gode ignored her. "Put that down."

"Put—? Oh." She rolled the letter, stowed it in her purse.

Gode's shoulders relaxed. "I thought you were him. You're as like to him as a pea in a pod. But you're not him." She walked around Hild, sniffing. "Are you an ælf?"

An ælf? "I remember you." Like a goddess of the sea, Cian had said. Like a river, like a wave.

Gode's belly growled.

"I'm Hild." Her belly rumbled, too.

"You're hungry." Gode tipped the pebble from her sling, tucked the leather in her belt. "Come with me. If you like."

Inside, Gode shrugged off her sealskin cloak, dropped it by the fire, added driftwood, and set the stew bubbling. Hild unclasped her cloak.

"Lay it over mine. Protect your nice dress."

They sat hip to hip on the fine blue cloak and ate from the same bowl. Gode held it. Every now and again she nudged Hild to take a spoonful.

"The lord liked to look at me, too," she said. She took the bowl from Hild, put it to one side. She unfastened the neck of her shift. "He sang me songs. He sang to me of my white throat and supple hands. He sang of my plump breasts and mouth dark as plums."

Hild swallowed. "I don't sing."

"What would you like to do?" She kept unfastening her shift.

Do? She gazed into the interesting swell and shadow.

Gode made a throaty sound that Hild thought might be a laugh and pushed the smock from her shoulders. "Come here." She opened her arms.

It was an astonishment, a blessing, a gift. To feel a nipple swell in your mouth, to not know whose breast was plump on whose palm, to feel the thing pour back and forth between you, her breath harsh as a hound on your shoulder, her eyes turning black. The strength in her shudders.

And she was strong. They were both strong. They held each other down, let each other up. Like drowning, like swimming, like breathing.

Afterwards, they lay together under Hild's fine blue cloak. "It's different with a woman," Gode said. "But not so different." She stroked the soft cloak.

"Why did you think I was an ælf?"

Gode, fingering the dense weave, said, "Because you're taller than the world. Because I watched you sit and open a spell."

Hild hitched herself up on her elbow. "A spell?"

"You opened it and it leapt into you and possessed you. You didn't move for an age."

"Oh. No. That's a letter. A message. Words from someone far away."

Gode nodded. "Magic."

"No." But it was magic, in a way.

"And you looked so like him, but you weren't him, not quite. And you smell like flowers, like someone from the land of summer who finds herself in winter."

The jessamine. "But you invited me in."

"Your belly growled, and I saw the way you looked at me. Besides, this cloak wasn't made by ælfs."

"I'll send you one." But not in royal blue. She lay back and folded her arms behind her head. "Have you ever seen an omen?"

"Everything's an omen. The cry of a seal. The colour of a cloud's belly at sunset. But everyone disagrees about what they mean. My ma and da disagreed. They drowned."

"I'm sorry."

"You said that. People die. Omens lie."

"Not always."

Gode shrugged. "When you don't know if they're lying or not, it's best not to listen."

"I'm never wrong."

"Never?"

"Never. Only . . . I don't know how to make this one come true."

"Where there's a will, there's a way. That's what Ma always said."

But Hild knew there was no way for this. Never.

"There again, she's dead. Da said the trick was to know what you want, exactly. He's dead, too."

Hild knew Gode wasn't really listening to her and wouldn't understand even if she were. But she had to tell someone, before she let it all go forever. And so, as the firelight turned from yellow to orange to red, she told this woman she would never see again about the nest, and the doves and starlings, and how Cian had ruined it all, just thrown it away. "My whole life, wherever I've been, I've known where he was, and part of me has pointed towards him, the way cows and deer point south when they chew. I thought he pointed to me, too. *We are us.* Whatever I did, I thought about how I'd tell him about it, how I'd explain what it means. If I could make him understand, then it was real. Even when I was angry with him, even when I thought he was stupid, I was angry with *him*. And I've been angry. So angry. Thinking about how I'll fight him when he gets back, how I'll shout, how I'll *make* him understand."

But he wasn't coming back. Not to her. And now her anger was running out of her like the tide, leaving her empty.

"You didn't eat a thing tonight," Begu said when they undressed for bed. "Was it that song about Branwen?"

"Um?"

"I told Oeric a fortnight ago to bribe Luftmaer so he didn't sing any of those maudlin things, especially the ones Cian used to sing. But I forgot to remind him. Besides, I thought you were getting better, until today."

Begu turned down the cover.

"Anger always spends itself in the end. I thought I'd be glad when you weren't angry anymore, but I'm not. I don't like this look. Like a calf standing by its dead dam, too forlorn even to bawl."

They climbed into bed.

"You're the king's seer. You can't go around with a face like that. I think you frightened Luftmaer so much he forgot himself."

"Listen," Hild said. "The seals are singing."

Begu said nothing, but she stretched out her arm. "Come here. Don't argue."

Slowly, carefully, like an orphaned foal folding itself down on the straw by a cat and her litter, Hild tucked herself alongside Begu and laid her head on her shoulder.

"You smell of seals," Begu said.

Silence.

"Hild, gemæcce, talk to me. You're frightening me."

"I did something today. It was . . . No one even knows she exists. But it was stupid. She and Cian used— I thought, is this what it's like for him? Does she look like the Welsh princess? Well, that wasn't why. But it was part of it."

"Did you kill something?"

"In a way."

"I don't understand."

"Pick people who don't matter, my mother said. But people who don't matter aren't equals. We pick them up, play with them, then put them down."

"Not if you get married."

"I'd have to leave here. Marry an enemy. Or at best be like Æthelburh. Never quite belonging. Careful. Always careful."

"But you are now."

"But I hoped. I thought one day . . . Tonight, I looked at the men singing. I looked at their belts. I wondered what it would be like to hold on to one of them, to stand next to a man and think, We are us. Do you think I could ever do that with Penda?"

"So it's Penda?"

"Today I understood: It's real. All of this. I was angry: He ruined everything, all my plans, even the ones I hid from myself."

"Penda?"

"Forget Penda." She would never marry Penda. She knew that now. She pressed her cheek into Begu's arm. "A princess of Gwynedd is not a dairymaid at Mulstanton or a sealer's daughter on the beach. A princess of Gwynedd isn't a passing fancy. She's a knife in the table, there for all to see. He's made his choice: That's his place, she's his path."

They listened to the wind and the waves.

"But what's my path? I'm the light of the world. The king's seer. And I can taste it in the wind, I can feel it in every move Penda makes, every threat from Cadwallon and battle fought by Idings . . ." But she couldn't say it aloud, not even to Begu: The Yffings would fall.

At meetings of the king and his counsellors—Paulinus, Coelfrith, and Æthelburh, and Stephanus scratching at his wax tablet—she stood hard and plain as a spear. No one spoke without glancing at her. Even the dogs watched her. She listened to everything everyone said, and weighed it against her own choices, and kept silent.

Paulinus had news that Ricberht was winning.

"No," she said. "Sigebert will win. Ricberht will die."

Paulinus's gaze fastened on hers.

"God made me a seer," she said. "Listen or not."

The Yffings would fall, and Paulinus with them. But she was going to live. She would find a way.

A letter came to her from Rhin: The king of Less Britain had given Cadwallon three ships and the men to crew them. Three ships: sixty men, seventy-five at most. Not enough to retake Gwynedd. She said nothing.

A message came to the king from Eadfrith: He had left Clemen of Dyfneint in Caer Uisc and would wend a lazy, meet-the-people route back to Deganwy, where Cian Boldcloak held the fort.

Three days later, Penda besieged Caer Uisc.

"Send the prince Eadfrith back," Paulinus said. "We will ride down to meet him with the cross on our banners and save Dyfneint from the pagans. Penda will flee and Dyfneint will kneel before God and his rightful representative."

"No," Hild said to Edwin. "Let Clemen fall. Let Eadfrith rejoin Bold-cloak at Deganwy as fast as he can. Faster than fast." Three ships from Less Britain. "Cadwallon is coming."

She sat in her room with Gwladus and listened to the screams of two women giving birth at once. One wailed and moaned, the other cursed. Both voices planed along the iron-hard walls and floors of the fortress, echoing until they seemed to come from everywhere at once.

"You're wan as a wight," Gwladus said. "You should eat."

"I'm not hungry."

"Eat anyway."

They ate cheese and wrinkled apples. Gwladus, as she always did, sniffed at her apple before she bit it, and smiled, as at some memory.

"Do you miss Dyfneint?"

"I miss the smell of cider in autumn. There's nothing like it: The air tastes sticky, sweet with that tang like copper. And the buzz of wasps. Wasps everywhere during cider season. But it was long ago and far away."

Home was never far away. "Do you mind that I said we shouldn't rescue Clemen?"

"What do I care for kings? He doesn't know me. I don't know him."

Late the next morning a ship beached on the white sand of the hythe, and a frightened, filthy messenger made his way to the counsellors: Cadwallon, with a retinue of men from Less Britain, had joined Penda at Caer Uisc and slaughtered Clemen. Two days ago. Petroc Splinter Spear had fled west.

Silence. Then Edwin said, "Who the fuck is Petroc Splinter Spear?"

"Clemen's heir," Hild said. A king with no country, king now of western rock cliffs and a burnt and broken city. All kings fall. *Fate goes ever as it must.* And, oh, she had been stupid.

"You're turning grey," Edwin said.

"Women worry," Paulinus said.

Her rib cage was too small. She couldn't breathe.

"At least the prince Eadfrith wasn't caught there, my lord," Coelfrith said.

"And now we know where that nithing is," Edwin said with some satisfaction.

"With Penda," Hild said. "With *Penda.* They broke Caer Uisc and now have a port for more ships to join them from Less Britain. Any day. They won't need to keep many men there. So they can strike north together. North to retake Gwynedd."

Gwynedd, where, in the absence of Eadfrith, Cian was playing at prince with Cadwallon's daughter. Lord of the hall. Men at his command. At ease. At home. No longer wearing armour at meat. Sitting with Angeth on his lap, twirling her dark hair around his finger, eyes shining at some song when armed men burst through the door, men with swords already bloody from the slaughter of his guards at the stockade. He would have time to drop his ale—sudden sharp scent under the peat smoke—and draw his sword. Then they'd be on him, bright and brutal, grunting, sharp steel shoving through soft skin.

No, it wouldn't happen that fast. She knew the songs. The Welsh liked their punishments slow and public. They would beat the woman, hack off Cian's hands, stake him out on the mountain for children to throw stones at in the morning, ravens to blind in the afternoon, and wolves to tear into by night.

She closed her eyes, willing her vision to rise from the blood-spattered green mountainside.

In her mind's eye, she rose like a hawk turning on a pillar of air, rising, widening, taking in the whole isle. She marked boundaries and vills, roads and ditches. Nodded to herself. Yes, if she were Penda, that's what she'd do. Gwynedd's ports, and Caer Uisc, and the middle of the country . . .

Penda was remaking the great weave.

"Yes," she said, and her voice was thin and keen, the cry of a hawk on a clear morning. She opened her eyes. "They will strike for Gwynedd. No doubt. None. How many men does Eadfrith have?"

Coelfrith said, "Fourscore under his command. Some with him, some with Boldcloak."

"Penda?"

"Four hundred."

She turned to Edwin. "Even if Clemen fought hard and killed like a hero, they outnumber your son five to one."

Silence. Behind her lids, Hild watched armies move. Bebbanburg was a long, long way from Gwynedd.

"Lord King," Paulinus said, "I will pray. I will hold a Mass tonight, and vigils."

"We need to do more than pray, Bishop." Toenails scratched the stone floor as the dogs stirred; they recognised the tone. *We'll eat the horse.* "Coelfrith."

"Lord King?"

"When can the war band ride?"

"Two days."

Hild's mind soared over the isle, seeing, weighing, judging. Not soon enough. Even today wouldn't be soon enough. From Bebbanburg to Deganwy was half again the distance as from Caer Uisc. If Penda had left immediately, he had probably arrived before the messenger's ship had passed Tinamutha.

If Eadfrith and Cian were still alive, they'd be running for their lives. No, not they. Eadfrith was ætheling. Cian would stay and fight a rearguard action while his prince escaped north. But Cian would gradually be forced north, too. If he lived.

If he was dead, there was nothing she could do, so she wouldn't consider it. He was alive. Alive and running north, one step behind Eadfrith. Who would give chase, and how many?

An army needed food. Food wagons travelled slowly. Penda could march his men north through Gwynedd on what they could carry, but then he would have to wait for their wagons to catch up before heading north. And after a siege, Penda's wagons would be empty.

But Cadwallon was fresh. And Cadwallon was a madman who wanted to wipe Edwin and all his kin from the face of the earth. If Eadfrith were known to be running, the Welsh king would give chase, even to Bebbanburg.

Then, in her hawk's eye, she saw clearly how it would be. Elmet. It had always been Elmet.

Begu stared at her as though she'd lost her mind. "You can't," she said. "Gwladus, tell her she can't!"

But Hild hardly heard her. She was calculating miles, days, rations . . . She tightened her heavy travel belt and said to Oeric, who was clammy and pale, "Tell Bassus an extra five men might make the difference for the ætheling's life. The queen is safe as the sun here in Bebbanburg." To Morud: "Reckon on Bassus's men. Food for five days, not a sackful more." If they lived, Elmet would feed them. To Gwladus: "We leave an hour before æfen, ready or not."

They hurried away.

"It's madness!" Begu said. "Why not ride with the king's men? What can you do with only a score of raggle-taggle gesiths? And why Elmet?" Hild tied her seax tightly into its sheath. "At least wait for morning."

"The king doesn't see," Hild said.

"Then make him."

Hild shook her head.

There was no time. Penda would have Gwynedd by now, would stay in Gwynedd. What was needed was not a well-supplied army marching deliberately to meet the Mercians but a small band to race south, to fling itself like a shield between the remaining Northumbrians and the chasing Cadwallon until Edwin's war band rolled in. But Edwin was in no hurry. His son would have sped safely away while Boldcloak guarded his back. Edwin was no doubt half expecting to hear word from York that the ætheling was there and safe even before the royal war band set out from Bebbanburg. What was Boldcloak to him? A half-wealh gesith who had reached too far. Edwin's main aim was to trap Cadwallon outside his homeland and crush him so finely he would never rise again. Besides, as he saw it, Boldcloak was probably dead. But she knew, as surely as if the Christ whispered it in her ear: Cian was fighting, furlong by furlong, north, to Elmet, to home. And Cadwallon's Welsh and Breton wolves were following. And no one would stand between the mad king and Pyr and Lweriadd in Caer Loid, Saxfryth and Ceadwulf, Grimhun in Aberford, Rhin and the folk of Menewood.

"Tell my mother: They are my people. They are my path. It's where I belong. She'll understand."

She whirled her cloak onto her shoulders, picked up her stave with one hand, and pulled Begu to her with the other. She squeezed Begu tight, and left.

She drove them at a killing pace. Nineteen horses and their cloaked riders. They could rest if they lived. She lay down at night, as they all did; she ate when food was put in front of her; she heard the talk around her, even sometimes answered, but her whole attention was focused on her target. She was falling, stooping to the kill, wings folded back, wind whistling past her pinions, eyes fixed on her prey. Waking and sleeping alike were a thing of hollowing air and falling.

They ran south along the old army road that turned in a great curve on the eastern flank of the Bernician upland. Thundered across three rivers. Tore through Corabrig on the wall, where they shed a messenger east for Tinamutha. Then the long, straight Dere Street—canter, trot, canter, trot—until the fork just north and west of York, where they shed another messenger, this time for York, then on to the west and south road, gaining speed, homing in, hurtling for Caer Loid.

Just before the road split into west, southwest, and south, Hild swerved to one side and looked out over the high moor.

Rain blurred the air. The moor smelt of that turn from winter to spring. Silence, but for blowing horses and champing bits: no birdsong, no rustle in the tussocky grass—they'd frightened everything for miles with their hurry.

To the west: road running over empty moorland. South: the great river valley, where the forest grew in a tangle of bare branches, grey and black and brown. She thought she saw the glint of the river. South and east: Caer Loid, hidden by a series of low rises. East: where the wood had gathered close to what was left of Ermine Street—London to Lindum to Brough, through Aberford, to York—birds lifted in a cloud thicker than smoke.

Hild pointed. They wheeled.

Bare branches dripped. On either side of Hild, behind ferns and a line of mossy, fallen trunks along the edge of a natural clearing, her men crouched behind their shields, swords in hand, breathing through their mouths. Five of the shields were newly painted. In the wet, the red wariangle ran and stretched into a gaunt nightmare bird. Behind them, a horse stirred, trying to rub the unfamiliar baffling from its bit. Hild turned her head slightly, but Gwladus was already offering the horse a sliver of dried apple and stroking its nose. Her gleaming hair was hidden by a grey cloth.

Hild stood sideways behind an elm in the centre of her line: seven men on one side, seven on the other, stave upright in both hands. She was no longer falling.

She listened. They were coming, straight for them: a small group, trying to hurry quietly through the tangled undergrowth, trying to escape. And behind them, shouts, the ringing clash of steel; the main group of Northumbrians fighting, slowing down pursuit.

Her men had exact orders. She waited.

She heard everything: the drip, the creak as one man eased his position, the sudden rattle of branches in a sough of late-afternoon wind, and closer, closer now the harsh breath of men tired beyond endurance and mindless with running.

There: three of them. No, four. Two men with Anglisc swords, carrying a rough litter, grunting with effort as they ran across the clearing, and a woman running alongside, knife in one hand, eyes starting in every direction. Her torc was Welsh. She was ripe with child.

Hild caught Oeric's eye, held up four fingers, waited til he touched the shoulders of the brothers Berht and Eadric the Brown, who all turned to her and readied themselves as she mouthed, *One, two, three!*

Men with big hands, men with the strength of desperation and the advantage of surprise: They grabbed each of the little group, one arm around the waist, one hand over nose and mouth, and heaved them past the tree line. Before the snatched could begin to struggle they faced a thicket of swords and the tallest woman they had ever seen, with one finger at her lips then pointing at the boar insignia on Eadric's helmet—the boar that matched the banner lying beneath the battered man on the litter. Eadfrith.

The two gesiths lowered their hands, away from their sword hilts, and the Welsh princess blinked, nodded, and crouched behind the nearest fern.

As though it had been a signal, the clearing filled with the noise and stink of men shouting, straining; the flash and clash of steel; bright blood.

Wait, Hild signalled, *wait*, and she let her mind float free, judging the wind on her cheek, the pace of the fighting men, their strength, the speed with which her men might step over the trunk . . .

"Now!"

And fourteen men slid neatly between pursuer and pursued, and locked their shields.

But these men hadn't worked together as a shield wall before, and instead of one interlocked line, they formed two pieces. And the Welsh—a hundred of them, it seemed to Hild—filled the clearing with blades and sweat, and three fleeing Northumbrians were caught on the wrong side of the shields.

Hild howled and hurled her stave like a spear at the chest of the wealh swinging an axe at a man wearing a filthy cloak that might once have been red and black. The axeman fell. She saw the pale blur of Cian's face, then her world dissolved into a whirl of grappling and kicking.

She was squeezing a man around the throat with her big hands, squeezing, kicking, kneeing, stamping, spitting in his eye. His sword was useless. He dropped it, clawed at her. She squeezed, squeezed.

Then he was gone, and she was running at the Welsh, seax-first, hacking, hacking at the men before her.

Then the men before her were nothing but backs, disappearing into the trees.

Her hands hurt. She lifted them. They were red.

She fumbled for her sheath.

"No," he said. "You must wipe the blade first."

Cian, holding out the corner of his bold cloak of red and black. *To hide the mud and blood.*

"Angeth?" he said. "Eadfrith?"

"Safe."

"The others?"

Her head rang. Everything seemed rimmed with light. "Others?"

"Edwin king. The war band."

"Three days north."

They sat on their cloaks under the dripping trees, chewing twice-baked bread dipped in beer. Three women. Twenty-four men. One broken prince. One body.

Angeth tended Eadfrith, who was half-conscious but unaware. She wasn't pale and dark-haired, nothing like the seal hunter's daughter. She was brown and cream and tawny, like a lynx.

Hild sat knee to knee with Cian, alone in the centre. Not woman and man but commanders of men.

Hild chewed carefully. She'd bitten her tongue; she wasn't sure how. Perhaps when she'd been hit by whatever made her jaw swollen. She wiped one hand absently on the moss, but the blood was dried on now, and the moss wasn't wet enough to help.

She felt very calm. She looked at the body, the butcher-bird shield covering the worst wounds. "Poor Cynan."

"He always lost at knucklebones," Cian said.

He had a ragged cut under his chin, and was thinner and harder, yet more like the boy who took his wooden sword from Ceredig king than the thegn's foster-son and then king's gesith she had known. He belonged here, like this.

"You're not surprised to see me," she said.

"Elmet always has you in it."

And though she was hurt and they might die, though they were damp and cold, though he had a wife who was with child, though he was a fool who had ruined everything, it was all right.

He dunked more bread, chewed. "And then, too, you are a seer."

She laughed, and a score of pale faces turned her way. She waved off their attention. "They think I'm mad."

"Perhaps you are."

They spoke easily, as though they were children in the wood, poking the water with a stick after a quarrel. She wanted to sit closer, the way children do, or puppies. She didn't move. "How many men has Cadwallon?"

"Fewer than he had."

"Tell me."

Cadwallon and Penda had caught Eadfrith and his men at Long Mountain. Eadfrith took a sword cut across the ribs, and six of his men had ridden with him to Deganwy, to Cian and his fifteen men.

"He escaped only with six? Out of sixty?"

"He left the rest at the head of the valley, to slow Penda and Cadwallon."

Hild turned to look at the man murmuring to himself under the trees. He had left his men. "Perhaps he didn't know what he was doing."

"He knew." Cian's face changed, and Hild knew he was thinking in British, thinking bitter thoughts. He rearranged it with an effort. He said sternly, more to himself than to Hild, "He is ætheling and eldest. He was hurt. He couldn't have won."

Hild kept her face still. It was done. She gestured for him to go on.

Between them, Eadfrith and Cian escaped with twenty-one men and Angeth. Penda didn't give chase, but Cadwallon did, with more than fifty Welshmen and Bretons. Eadfrith couldn't ride well with his wound. Cadwallon caught them crossing the Kelder. He had bowmen. They shot their horses out from under them. That was when Cian had lost his shield. Five men were killed and Eadfrith was injured again, this time kicked in the head and half drowned when he was trampled underfoot in the river.

"He's been wandering in his wits since. And coughing."

Hild nodded. Now was not the time to think of that. "Cadwallon. You said less men than he had."

"We set traps along the way. He has less than forty now. Perhaps three dozen."

"Your plans?"

"To get to Aberford."

She nodded. That might have made sense, before Cadwallon caught them a second time. "Cadwallon's?"

"To kill."

"He'd kill his own daughter?"

"He hates Edwin, hates the north Angles. His hatred has made him mad."

He was in Anglisc territory with just forty men, some of them only on loan from the king of Less Britain. He must know Edwin would be coming in force. Mad. Yes. But how mad? "Will he run now?"

"First he'll kill and rape and burn, throw Anglisc babies on the fire. Caer Loid's only . . . eight miles?"

"They have a stout stockade and a dozen gesiths to guard it. And I sent a message. He won't get in. Not with three dozen men."

"Then he'll burn and kill outside."

Menewood was most likely safe; it was hidden. But Lweriadd and Sintiadd and, beyond them, Saxfryth and Ceadwulf . . .

She stood and crossed to Angeth, who was crouched by the murmuring ætheling. The tawny woman stood. They regarded each other a moment, then turned to the man, who, though tied to his litter, moved ceaselessly. "How is he?"

"With a warm room and a dry bed I don't doubt he'd live." Her Anglisc had the up-and-down of the Welsh hills, with a skirl of wind and a hint of brook.

"May I?"

Angeth stepped aside. Hild knelt. Felt the back of his neck: hot but not raging. Pressed an ear to his chest: congested but no worse than a child with a snotty nose. Lifted the edge of the rough bandage on his ribs and sniffed: not going bad. "Hold his head."

Angeth knelt at his head and gripped the back of his head with both hands.

Hild felt the clotted lump above his temple. Soft with swelling. She pressed gently. He moaned. She pressed harder, to be sure, but nothing moved under her hand. Nothing broken. She peeled both eyelids back. The right pupil tightened more slowly than the left. She'd seen that before: a woodcutter hit by a branch of a falling tree. He'd recovered, but it had taken a fortnight, and he'd had dizzy spells for a month and a headache for half a year.

"Thank you," she said. She went back to Cian and sat.

"Too much more jogging about might kill him. His litter must go by road. Or it must not go at all."

"We should stay here?"

Lweriadd, Sintiadd. "It's your job to guard your prince. And Angeth. Mine to guard my people."

"But we're stronger together."

She nodded at Eadfrith. "We can't stay together."

"The king's coming—"

"And men, perhaps, from Aberford before then. Perhaps as early as tomorrow. But he can kill a lot of people before tomorrow."

Eadfrith murmured. The trees dripped. Daylight was seeping away.

She stood. "We have one spare horse. Come with us."

He stood, too. "No."

"No?"

"I go after Cadwallon. My men on your horses. You and Gwladus stay here with Angeth and Eadfrith, with Oeric and your men."

Silence.

"I know Cadwallon. I know his tricks. And your men couldn't make a shield wall."

She thought of Oeric coming to her with his old battered sword, Oeric who had wanted to look away when he killed his bandit. Bassus and his men who had guarded the queen for years and who had to add longer leather laces to their mail shirts to fasten them.

"When we fought in the wood, my stick was just a stick. For you it was always a sword. This is your path."

Her people, but his path.

She turned and walked to Cynan's body, lifted the butcher-bird shield. She held it out. "Don't drop it."

25

✦

OUTSIDE CAER LOID, with his seer at his shoulder, his eldest son safe in a dry bed in a warm room, and his war band ranged around him, Edwin watched the Elmetsætne who had come to pay tribute to their king kneel first to Cian, who stood young and glittering with his wife, and call him lord.

"Lord," said the thick-chested man with four daughters. "Thank you for saving my farm." "Lord," said the old woman who kissed the hem of his cloak, "for the chickens and the ewes and my son's babby, may Christ set a flower upon your head." "Lord, Lady," said the brothers who made charcoal in the woods, "let the gods smile on you and your children."

Edwin crooked his finger to Hild. She bent to listen.

"How far gone is she?"

"Perhaps six months."

"He'd better pray it's not a boy."

"He's loyal, body and soul. He saved the ætheling."

"He saved me from Eamer. But a man changes his ambitions when he has a son. And his son, they say, would be a mix of Ceredig and Cadwallon, an heir to Elmet and Gwynedd. It doesn't take a seer to foresee the north dreaming of Coel Hen come again and making trouble for the Yffings for all time. No, I want Cadwallon's line stamped out, quenched forever. When it's time."

Cadwallon had escaped back to Wales, and Edwin would not follow. They did not know how strong the Mercian and Gwynedd alliance was.

Penda hadn't followed Cadwallon to Elmet, to Northumbria, and now was not the time to provoke him.

Edwin was looking at her with particular intensity. "Quenched forever," he said again. "When it's time." He leaned back. "Though, as you say, Boldcloak did save the ætheling. He should have something for that." He smiled, slitty-eyed. "Yes, he shall have something for that."

Hild's belly clenched with dread.

At York, the new church loomed huge and hollow and half-built around the tiny wooden shelter where they'd been baptised, dwarfing even the full war band glittering and gaudy in their gold. Their newly painted shields seemed childish and defiant against the cold stone; their arm rings and finger rings and looted torcs didn't shimmer in the shadow. They rubbed their wrist guards and jewelled hilts against their cloaks, trying to coax an extra gleam or two, but they stayed sullen and dull. Some touched their crosses. Many more, their hidden amulets.

It felt all wrong. James had suggested to Paulinus that for this ceremony, perhaps the gesiths' training yard would be best, but Paulinus had insisted—Christ's house for Christ's warrior—and when Hild had raised it with the king, Edwin, still slitty-eyed and unfathomable, had said that in matters of godness, he would let his chief priest decide.

After the Mass, James's choir did their best, but without a roof to reflect and multiply their note, the rising hymns felt like loaves with their tops sliced off: flat and strange and thin.

It was strange, too, to watch a man take an oath on his knees.

But when Edwin raised him and faced his war band, and Hild, and the very pregnant Angeth, and pronounced Cian Boldcloak his right hand, his chief gesith, they beat their shields and roared: Boldcloak! Boldcloak! And Cian glowed like Owein come again. He glowed for Angeth.

Hild watched her. Three months.

James poured her more wine, and said, "You look as though your burdens are heavy on you, child."

"I'm marriageable age, three hands taller than you, and I helped save the ætheling. I'm not a child."

James sipped without comment, and Hild sighed.

"I'm sorry. Yes. They're heavy. And part of me wishes I were a child." Had she ever been? Perhaps in Elmet, before her father died.

"Do you wish to confess?"

"No." Flat and hard. She sipped her own wine: sour. "This is sorry stuff."

"I'm spending less time here than I did. And sometimes my stores . . . Well, let's just say sometimes my stores appear to evaporate in my absence."

Thou shalt not steal. If Christians truly believed they would go to a fiery hell for breaking commandments, how come so many of them did? "How is Catterick?"

"Osric scowls and schemes, but he's all wind."

For now. But Osric was like everyone else, waiting, watching for the misstep: hers, Edwin's, Paulinus's. Waiting to see which way Penda cast. "The church?"

"Almost finished. And it feels . . . blessed."

"This morning I had news you might find interesting. Felix, a Burgundian bishop, has arrived in Canterbury."

"Burgundian? That is interesting. What is Dagobert up to?" He tapped his fingers against his lips and hummed, a mannerism that no longer quite suited him. "Didn't you say that Dagobert is backing Sigebert?"

She nodded.

"Penda and Cadwallon, Cadwallon and Less Britain, Dagobert and Sigebert . . ." He shook his head. His hair was shorter: his curls no longer bounced. "I do hope it doesn't turn into another interesting year. I think we've had enough excitement."

But Cadwallon stayed in Gwynedd. Penda went back to his Mercian stronghold at Tomeworthig, and his West Saxon subking took charge of Dyfneint. Eadfrith recovered, and took a hundred gesiths to Craven to remind Osric of Edwin's strength, and then on up to Tinamutha for the summer, to reinforce Osfrith in case of Pictish raids: There were rumours of bad weather north of the Tweed.

The court moved to Sancton. Every other woman in the place seemed to be giving birth, every other gesith beaming through his whiskers or getting drunk in despair, according to his situation. Breguswith and Begu were so busy that eventually the mothers asked Hild to help. The rumour began that the seer's touch was a blessing: The babies came faster, more easily, and with less pain.

"She doesn't do anything different from me," Begu said, scrubbing her arms over a bucket, while Breguswith sat on the stool, showing her age for once, and Gwladus, muttering about Hild's sleeves, untied Hild's bloodied apron for the cold tub. "It's not fair."

"She's the seer," Breguswith said tiredly. "She tells them, 'You'll give birth right now and you won't feel a thing,' and they're too frightened to do otherwise."

Gwladus snorted.

Begu stood there dripping. "Well, how can I learn to do that?"

"Start by growing half an ell."

And have a mother who prophesied the light of the world and fought for it to be true, Hild thought. A mother who left her home not once but twice to make a place for her children. She poured a cup of the new ale and took it to her mother. She touched the familiar cheek. Breguswith blinked and tilted her head. Hild smiled and shook her head. She sat on the bed. She watched her mother, and Begu, and Gwladus, and felt, for the first time in an age, at home and ordinary.

"Just two left," Begu said, wiping her arms dry.

"Arddun's due any hour," Breguswith said. "But if I'm any judge hers'll slip out like an eel." She paused. "Then there's Angeth. But she's not due for weeks. We'll be at Derventio by then."

Gwladus shook her head.

"What?" Begu said. She looked at Hild. "What is it? Is something wrong with Angeth?"

Leaves unfurled. Hedgepigs woke and siffsaffs flew anxiously, endlessly, back and forth from their nest in the nettles with food for the fledglings. Ewes swelled like the fluffy white clouds in the cornflower-blue sky.

After the king dismissed his counsellors, Hild caught up with Cian outside the hall. "My lord Boldcloak!"

He turned. "My lady seer. The king wants us back?"

She shook her head. They stood more than a pace apart. His hair gleamed chestnut in the sun. He wore it differently now, shorter. Perhaps Angeth liked it that way. "Walk with me," she said.

They walked without speaking along the path they knew well, west, to the elm wood, where once they had sparred. She had her staff. He wore his sword. She knew they wouldn't use them, might never use them with each other again.

Finches sang. A bittern boomed.

"Do you remember the morning I got baptised?"

"I do. You wet your head. You had a bite on your jaw. You have the mark of it still, when you burn dark in summer."

He touched his chin.

They came to the clearing.

"Oh," he said. There, on the old stump, was a robin. "Not the same one, surely!"

"His son, perhaps." It turned its head, looking at them with one eye, then the other, then flew away. "Angeth," she said. "Is she quite well?"

He came alert as a dog at the scent. "She was sick yesterday. But women with child do that. Don't they?"

Not usually past the fourth month. "And has she gained weight?"

"They do that, too, surely?"

"Send her to me."

The robin sang from the trees.

"Cian."

"She might not come," he said. "I . . . I spoke harshly of you in De-ganwy. At first."

She looked him in the eye, the eyes she'd seen wide with lust, wet with tears, shining with joy. "I'm sorry. That day . . . I am sorry. Do you believe me?"

"Yes."

"Then send her to me. Make her come."

Hild pulled her stool next to Angeth's and took her hand. She pressed it gently with her thumb. Her thumb mark filled out slowly.

"It's not usually that bad," Angeth said. Her face was puffy, too, no longer the smooth tawny health of Elmet.

"Have you been having headaches?"

"Yes, but that could be anything. The sick headaches and lights, anyone can have those."

"You had the sick headache as a girl?"

"No."

"And you've been throwing up?"

"It could be anything! If every woman who—"

"And the belly pain, right here." She touched Angeth at the crease of her baby bulge, right under the ribs. It wasn't a question. And now she knew this was not her mother's doing.

Angeth shook her head. "No. No."

Hild wanted to stroke her, soothe her like a horse, but she knew Angeth would shy away. "We have to know." She stood, stuck her head through the curtain. "Gwladus. Bring the piss bucket."

When the bucket came, with two inches of water in the bottom, Angeth shook her head again. "No. No. Not now, not today. My bladder's empty."

"Then we'll fill it." Hild got up again. "Gwladus! Small beer. Lots of it." She sat down. "Tell me a story of Gwynedd." Silence. "Or not. I could offer you yarn to spin instead."

After a while, Angeth said, "You're so young." Hild said nothing. "They say you're a witch."

"Your husband knows better."

Silence. "You're very like," she said eventually. "Now I see why you might have quarrelled. Like to like don't always agree." Her hazel eyes were small in the swollen face, but not dull. "So very like. In the wood, when you grabbed me, I thought you were him, just for a heartbeat. Him, or a devil taking his form. When I told him that, he laughed. He laughs a lot with me."

"Yes," Hild said. "He chose you."

And then the beer came, and they drank, and they talked peaceably of gesiths and how sometimes they had no more sense than sheep. Of trade from Deganwy to Manau to Ireland. Of the gold route from Tintagel. Of how it was to leave one's father's house. And Hild found she liked Angeth, princess of Gwynedd.

When it came time, Angeth pissed in the bucket and let Hild take it and tilt it towards the light.

"It's foamy," she said. "But there's no blood." Not yet. "We have time."

Angeth cupped her belly with both hands.

"You could have another."

She shook her head. "I could pray."

"Christ doesn't always listen. Angeth, please. We have time, but not much."

Angeth shook her head. "There's always hope."

"I've seen this before. And there's nothing anyone can do to stop it.

You'll puff up like a fungus. Your muscles will start to ache. Your piss will turn pink. You'll have fits. You'll fall unconscious. You'll die. There's a tea."

"I want my baby."

"It's wise not to wait."

"You want it dead. You all want it dead." She sounded more tired than angry. Then she bent suddenly, head in her hands. "It hurts so."

Hild put a hand on her shoulder. The shoulder hardened to iron. Angeth straightened. A princess of Gwynedd.

"Can you say there is no hope, not one jot or tittle? No. Only God is infallible. Can you say you have never been wrong? Can you swear it? Can you swear that I'd live?"

"It's not—"

"Can you swear it?"

She had no power over life and death. "No."

"Then I won't take your tea."

Seven weeks later, in Derventio, Hild found Cian kneeling in the church. It was splendid now, nothing like the plain stone of long ago. Carved and painted wall panels glimmered with gilding. Candles burnt against the violet dusk.

He lifted his face from his hands. His pupils were dark with despair, like holes scorched in wood. "I didn't believe you when you told me they'd put glass up there. But there it is." The wick on one of the candles flickered and spat. "She had a fit. She can't see. You must save her."

"I'll try."

"You must."

"I'll do everything I can."

"Swear to me." He gripped her arm. Strong hand on strong arm. "I'm sorry, for everything that's passed. I'm sorry. Swear you'll do what you can, for both of them. Swear to me." The grain of his face was taut and twisted, knotted as a burr, hard as iron.

Hild looked at his hand. A match with her own. "I swear."

And she tried. While the rain drummed outside and Cian drank steadily in hall, she and her mother fought like dogs to save Angeth and her baby. To drive the shadows from Angeth's chamber they lit candles as though beeswax cost nothing. After her water broke they walked the semiconscious Angeth back and forth. They sang to her.

A cup of pennyroyal tea two months ago and it would all have been over. The baby dead but the mother alive. Pennyroyal now might bring the baby fast enough for it to survive, but it would kill Angeth. And though she couldn't see, she could smell, and nothing would hide the minty scent of pennyroyal. And she was mad with fear.

"We should make her comfortable," Breguswith said, meaning dose her insensible and let her die in peace.

Can you swear? Angeth had asked. Hild shook her head.

"It's cruel," Breguswith said.

"I swore," Hild said. "Help me."

They did what they could. They stripped her naked and bathed her with scented rosemary when she was hot, wrapped her in blankets when she shivered. They tried to get her to drink parsley broth. They massaged her belly with goose grease, felt the shiver and squeeze, counted.

Angeth seemed to think she was a girl again, on the mountainside, falling over, bruising her belly on a stone, crying about the pain. Hild hoped she stayed there. The green grass of Gwynedd was a better way to end than blind agony in a dark, close room.

Hild measured Angeth's hand across the knuckles, then measured the same distance above her inner ankle and rubbed the shin. Felt her belly, counted. Too slow.

Angeth passed out again. They flipped her over. While Breguswith held her face free, so she could breathe, Hild tried to find the dimple by the spine, above the bottom, but Angeth was so swollen she wasn't sure if she was rubbing the right place.

They turned her over, propped her up. She shuddered, half conscious. Breguswith laid her hand on her belly, counted, shook her head.

Angeth moaned like a child. Then shrieked, hard and sudden, and fainted again. After a moment, she writhed. Her arms and legs shot out, stiff and straight.

"Hold her!"

It was like trying to hold a greased pig.

"It's coming!" Breguswith said, and there it was, crowning. "Push. Push."

Angeth couldn't hear them. Hild pressed on the quaking belly, timing it to the ripple of muscle under her hands.

Angeth jerked and thrashed. Breguswith hung on to a foot, grunting like a man in a tug-of-war. Hild, half tangled in the blanket, held the belly down with both arms.

Angeth foamed at the mouth. Hild tried to wipe it away.

"Just push!" her mother shouted.

And the baby slid out, slick and blue and still. Breguswith whipped it, her, into a blanket. Hild lifted Angeth's head, floppy now. Her eyes were rolled up, blank as eggs.

Her mother had the baby. She focused on Angeth. She cradled her in her arms—perhaps she would feel like Cian—and whispered, "It's a little girl. Breathe, Angeth."

And Angeth did. She opened her eyes, smiled. "I smell rosemary, love." And died.

Hild picked up the blanket.

"Wait," her mother said. She laid the tiny wrapped baby next to her. The baby was still blue. In the swaying candlelight, Hild thought she moved, but it was just shadow.

"You can tell Cian you did your best. Wash the blood from your face, change your dress. Go. I'll wash them. Send Begu to help."

When Cian saw Hild, his face emptied. "You took time to wash," he said. "She's in no hurry, then?"

"No."

"Then neither am I." He drained his cup, poured more. "I don't want to see her."

"Them. The baby was a girl. She had black hair."

He didn't seem to be listening. "She was never going to live, was she?"

She wanted to shake him. *I tried!*

But she did nothing, said nothing. For the first time, she was afraid of Cian. His face was as smooth as sand, his voice bleached and light as driftwood. His tide had gone out. She dreaded what it might bring back.

The court moved to Goodmanham. Then Brough. On the surface, Cian's waters were still, but the undertow was vicious. He never raised his voice, never got drunk, but every week Breguswith had to splint some gesith's arm or leg after sparring. The only time he seemed alive, the only time he smiled, was with children. He took to spending time with Eanflæd and Wuscfrea. Æthelburh, his godmother, allowed it.

Eanflæd now was as sturdy as a small oak and bossy; Wuscfrea toddled determinedly. Cian made him a tiny blunt spear. Wuscfrea threw it at everything, including his father.

"That's my little man," Edwin said, when Wuscfrea flung the stick at the table where his closest counsellors were talking idly after sorting the business of the day.

A houseman wiped up the spilled beer. Hild poured more, nearly spilled it afresh when she saw what Edwin was staring at: son and chief gesith sitting on the floor, head to head, torchlight glinting from chestnut hair.

"He likes you," Edwin said. A dog whined. "Anyone might think you were his uncle."

Hild's skin felt too tight. But Cian just ruffled Wuscfrea's hair and smiled. *Keeping him ignorant keeps him safe.* But she didn't know if his obvious innocence would be enough.

As summer turned to autumn she hardly dared lift her gaze from the king's face. He gave no sign, but her dreams rang and echoed with danger.

At the Christ Mass in the still-unfinished church of York, Paulinus asked God's blessing for the fruit of the royal loins, and Æthelburh was observed to leave the church to vomit. She was too unwell to attend the feast.

Hild carried the guest cup the length of the board. Hereswith wasn't there, or Osfrith and Eadfrith. Lilla and Lintlaf and Dunod were long dead. But it looked the same: silver and gold and rich colours, but for the Crow's black. It sounded the same: the boom and roll of laughter of people glad to be alive, stitched through with the sinewy plink of the lyre. It smelt the same: roast meat, unwashed men, fruit paste, and sharp white mead. Light of the world. This was what she knew. This was who she was. Her wyrd had been born before she was. She chose this path, this place, because she had always chosen.

She raised the cup to Edwin and wondered how much longer she could help him stay king.

26

✦

THE WORLD TURNED. They moved to Bebbanburg, to Yeavering, to Derventio. It was a warm spring, a warmer summer. The queen swelled.

At Goodmanham, dogs panted in the shade and every day the heat
thickened. Fleeces piled in the woodshed stank. Milk curdled. Æthelburh,
big as a cow, leaned on her women and sweated and did not always attend
the king's counsels.

Cian made Wuscfrea a tiny bow with blunted arrows, and Eanflæd
borrowed it and nearly blinded her brother. The queen, who knew of her
godson's troubles, did not forbid him her children. Instead, she asked Hild
to watch over them until she herself could do so again.

So Hild took to bringing berries and small beer to the yard where Cian
played with the children, and then would sit and spin while they ate in the
shade of the great elm. Sometimes she and Cian talked a little, idly, of the
weather, or of Eanflæd's fearlessness, or of Æthelburh's health. Sometimes
he would float away while still sitting there, and Hild, who knew him so
well, heard the wash and lap of his thoughts as though they were her own.
*My daughter also would have been fearless; my daughter would have been crawling by now; my
daughter might have taken her first step today.*

As far as she knew, he had not wept.

One day, over strayberries, while Eanflæd played with her new toy—a
cunningly carved dog—and Wuscfrea piled dirt, they began to talk about
the news they'd discussed in council with the king: a contagion in the
south, sweeping through Kent, and the death in East Anglia of Ricberht.

"Hereswith's husband, Æthelric, is Sigebert's heir," she said.

"So. And, after him, your nephew Ealdwulf?"

She nodded, but he had already drifted away, though this time, when he came back, he spoke aloud. "They would have been of an age."

"Yes," she said, and gave him the reddest strayberry in the bowl. A strayberry for a daughter. But it was all she had.

Hereswith had also written, in part:

For my wedding present you foretold my husband's death as king.
Pray that it is not soon.

Pray, not for her to be wrong—kings fell—but that it would not be soon.

Eanflæd shrieked: Wuscfrea had snapped the tail off her dog. After she had been persuaded to stop trying to make him eat it, Hild and Cian talked of other things.

The queen got bigger. Goodmanham sweltered.

News came to the counsellors from Osfrith at Tinamutha: Clotrude, his wife, had died in childbirth. For the rest of the morning, Cian was drawn and distant. As they left Edwin's council, he asked Hild how the queen did.

"She's well," Hild said. "But it's too hot to carry such weight in public with grace."

The heat did not ease. Tempers frayed. Hallfolk and housefolk alike slept outside, and talked late, and drank too much, and were up at dawn, looking to the south and west, hoping for cloud. The sky stayed blue. The midden heaps reeked.

"We should go to Elmet," her mother said. "Or north to the Bay of the Beacon. A bit of sea air would do us all good."

"You could go," Hild said. "Take Luftmaer."

The queen came to the next meeting of counsellors and their hangers-on. Hild relayed her latest news from Fursey: the Burgundian bishop, Felix, had moved from Canterbury to Rendlesham. Perhaps to escape the contagion. More likely at the behest of Sigebert.

Edwin looked at Paulinus. "A Frankish bishop at the court of a Frankish puppet king of the East Angles. Where is your pope in this? And where else is Dagobert dabbling his long Frankish fingers?"

Hild looked at Æthelburh, who was herself from the Frankish-influenced court of Kent. There again, so was her own mother. But her mother thought now only of herself and her children.

Æthelburh said, "Your son's son is half Frankish."

Paulinus said, "And Osfrith has no wife now. What if he chooses a Kentishwoman or one of the East Anglisc, builds ties with those Frankish-leaning kingdoms? What if he has plans?"

Æthelburh wanted her son to be heir. Paulinus also saw advantage in that. Between them, they knew all Edwin's fears: Osfrith was well liked, and, at the cusp of Deira and Bernicia, well-placed. And he had given his heir a dynastic name.

"Bring the child to court, my lord," Paulinus said. "An honoured guest."

A hostage for good behaviour of kin, like Oswine for Osric.

"Yffi's very young," Edwin said. But Hild could see he was thinking about it. "And what of the rest of the north? What of Rheged?"

"We're grooming Oswine for Rhianmelldt," she said, and glanced at Æthelburh. The queen's eyes glimmered, but Hild had no notion what she was thinking. Would she raise the old idea of marrying the mad maid to Cian? But Æthelburh said nothing. "Meanwhile we have Uinniau."

"A nephew," Paulinus said. "Any king would sacrifice a nephew." Any king would sacrifice anyone, but no one thought it prudent to say so.

"Then send Eadfrith to charm Rhoedd," Hild said. "He could talk the birds from the trees." And he was no use at the head of an army; gesiths no longer quite trusted him. Perhaps he could even be married to Rhian-melldt. It would flatter Rhoedd, and suit Æthelburh . . .

"Lord King," Cian said, and everyone turned. Boldcloak rarely spoke on matters other than war. "Lord Eadfrith might be better sent to Penda. To counter Cadwallon's sway. Penda is Gwynedd's friend, yes, but perhaps not yet wholly our enemy."

"You're thinking marriage?" Hild said. "I don't think Penda has an-other sister. Or a daughter."

Paulinus bent his gaze on Hild. "Perhaps the king of Mercia has a spare son."

"He doesn't," she said.

"Pity," Edwin said.

"But what of Penda himself?" Paulinus said to Edwin. "Your niece is of age."

Now they all turned to look at her: woman, not seer. Future queen of Mercia. But she watched the queen, whose smooth face hid something.

"You would stand as Penda's godfather at his baptism," Paulinus said. "He would acknowledge you as overking."

Overking of all the Anglisc. But marriage to Penda was not her path, had never been her path.

Hild did her best to sound bored. "My king, a priest once told me, 'Whosoever stands as godfather to another adopts him in religion.' Penda would be as your adopted son. He would expect to inherit your mantle as overking. My lord bishop is a priest. He forgets how much a man wants for his sons."

Counsellors murmured agreement and cast sidelong glances at the foreign man in the black skirts. Hild turned back to Æthelburh, expecting gratitude for protecting Wuscfrea's inheritance, but met, instead, a polished, impenetrable queen.

Edwin sent a messenger to Eadfrith in Tinamutha: Bring Yffi to me, then go to Mercia to charm Penda.

Paulinus, thwarted, began to nag Edwin. About Elmet. About more money for the church in York, to hasten the building. About bringing Rheged firmly into the fold. Paulinus was feeling his age, Hild realised. He wanted his pallium before some old-man's illness swept him to heaven.

The heat built. Æthelburh no longer attended the council. Housefolk and hall folk were irritable and sleepless. In council Paulinus raised the subject of Woden's enclosure.

"It's an affront to God on our very doorstep, a monument to pagan practice. We must tear it down."

"The people won't like it," Hild said. "They're already uneasy."

"The people must do as the king directs," Paulinus said. "God is on our side."

Hild bent her head to her uncle. "My king, not yet. In autumn, perhaps, or when the weather breaks. But not yet."

He raised his eyebrows.

"It's empty of its god. It has no power. But last night ravens and jays were calling after the owl was abroad." A murmur went round the room. "Housefolk say: ravens and jays in conversation with the restless dead."

"Superstition," Paulinus said.

Ten years ago, Edwin would have smiled and said, *Don't spit.* But he was getting older, too. He had called his son Wuscfrea. He was as desperate as Paulinus to make his mark. He said nothing.

"You need a husband," Paulinus said.

Edwin studied her, then turned to Paulinus. "Burn it."

The day they tore down Woden's totem, lightning cracked the sky open and spilled thick, cold rain. Cool wind gushed through the hall. That night, as the rotting timbers burnt, Æthelburh, attended by Begu, gave birth to twins, quickly, easily, like popping peas.

In counsel the next morning, Paulinus smiled at Hild triumphantly: the heathen totem was destroyed, the weather had broken, the queen was well and the twins healthy. He would baptise them on Sunday.

But on Friday, Hild was woken by Gwladus before dawn. "Wilnoð says come. The twins are hot as fire."

Their cheeks were red, their eyes dull, their lungs full. "They're going to die," the queen said. "I know it. They're going to die."

"No," Hild said. "Not if we rub their chests til they cough out the phlegm, and then keep them warm when they start sweating."

Æthelburh didn't seem to hear her. "They're going to die."

Hild laid the back of her hand across Æthelburh's forehead. "You're hot." She looked at Wilnoð. "Has she been coughing?"

Wilnoð nodded.

"Well, nothing to worry about," Hild said. "I'll give you some tea."

"You wanted to give Angeth tea," Æthelburh said.

"This is a different tea."

"We have to baptise them," Æthelburh said.

"No, lady," Hild said. "That's not what they need. They need—"

"You were going to marry Penda and steal the overkingship from my son."

"Lady, that was the Crow's idea."

"You put it in his head. You've put demons in my babies." She clutched her cross. "Get back, hægtes! I won't listen to you."

Hild shook her head, hurt. She said to Wilnoð, "She's raving. Why didn't you call me earlier?"

Æthelburh shouted, "Don't listen to her! Is she the queen? I'm the queen! Bring me the bishop!"

Wilnoð, with an apologetic look at Hild, left the room. Hild wished her mother was there. She murmured to Gwladus, "Find Begu." She was probably with Uinniau. "If you can't find her, get Cian, and tell Arddun to bring Eanflæd and Wuscfrea."

Æthelburh would see that Cian loved her children, all of them, like his own. He was her godson. If he said baptism could kill them, she'd listen to him, surely.

But she didn't. And in the middle of the shouting and pleading and Eanflæd's wailing, Paulinus and Stephanus arrived, breasting the night in their robes like ships in full sail, unstoppable. "Keep trying," she said to Cian. "Do what you can. I'll talk to the king."

But it was no use. Edwin pointed out that the totem had come down, the weather had broken, and Paulinus was his chief priest. The queen was the queen. If she thought the babies should be baptised, then they would be.

Cian, who had tried til the end to change the queen's mind, came to find her under the daymark elms. "They're dead," he said. "Both of them. Still in their baptismal robes. The girl had black hair."

He didn't even sway, just folded down on his knees, thump, like a butchered bullock, and for a moment Hild saw blood, red as a mummer's sheet, falling from his throat and running over the grass.

She folded him in her arms, as she had Angeth, as though he were small enough to carry, and he shook, and she stroked his hair, over and over. His arms crept around her. He wept.

He wept for an hour. He wept as the elms shivered and the shadow changed and her back began to ache, but she didn't let go.

27

✦

AUTUMN IN ELMET. At Caer Loid and then Aberford, Edwin watched
while the Elmetsætne bent the knee and brought their children to the
lady seer and Prince Boldcloak for blessing. Then it was Christ Mass in York,
the turning of winter to spring in Bebbanburg, and the wind-whipped
grass of Yeavering while the chief men gathered and brought their tribute.

Æthelburh had not apologised for calling Hild hægtes; queens never
did. Instead she gave her presents—oil of jessamine, blue silk the colour of
periwinkles on a dark day, a beautiful string of pearls and moss agate that
would buy three warhorses—and gifted Begu and Uinniau, and Breguswith and Luftmaer as well. Small things, mostly, combs and pretty eating
knives. More precious, she included them in all she did: her weaving circle, her Masses, apportioning the yarn, and consulting on supplies. She
discussed sending Breguswith to Arbeia to sort out the cloth trade flowing
through the Tine valley. She had in mind a place called Redcrag, not far
from Tinamutha. Perhaps Breguswith could find Osfrith a nice wife while
she was at it. Some northern princess. If the Picts and Irish got restless, it
would be good to have the Gododdin and Alt Clut bound to the Yffings.

Begu and Uinniau could not be promised in marriage until the Rheged
situation was settled, but they behaved as though they were and lived as
part of Hild's household.

One afternoon Begu spooled the last of the yarn into her skein, twisted
it neatly. "I wish Rhoedd would marry Rhianmelldt off to someone. Anyone. I don't care. I want Uinny. I want him safe. When will that be?"

"I don't know."

"Well, I want it settled before there's another war. Just tell me there won't be war for a while. Tell me Eadfrith is charming that horrible Penda."

"I'm sure he's doing all he can," Hild said. She reached for another heap of yarn. War with Penda would come, one day. The Yffings would fall, one day. She would make sure it was not soon. But Mercia was strong and getting stronger, and Edwin, instead of spending time giving away gold and attracting gesiths, was letting the Crow fill his head with nonsense about God and divine kingship and true marriage.

"What?" Begu said, pausing mid-spool. "Is there going to be war?"

Hild shook her head. "It's not that." Edwin was planning something. She just didn't know what.

Spring at Yeavering. They cantered into the wind at the top of Ad Gefrin: Hild on Cygnet, Eanflæd on a dun pony she called Nettle, and Cian on Acærn, cloak streaming behind him, with little Wuscfrea tucked in the crook of his right arm. He galloped with his head thrown back, laughing, and Wuscfrea crowed at the wind.

Eanflæd rode ferociously, fearlessly, as though she were twenty feet tall and her mount straddled the world. She hated Hild to get ahead. She wanted to be first. Today Hild indulged her.

In hall, the king watched them. Paulinus watched them. She thought perhaps the queen watched them, but more subtly. She took care to wear her gold cross prominently outside her dress, took care that her every public word supported her uncle. Care, always care. Meanwhile, she sent a message to Fursey: *Get someone inside Mercia. Tell me who leads, Penda or Cadwallon.* But Penda's hall was not Christian. She sent a message to Rhin: *Get someone inside Gwynedd. Get someone to Rheged. Get me information.*

Cian had a woman in Yeavering, the sister of the goatherd he had taken up with before. He'd had one in Bebbanburg and, before that, York. She had smelt her on him as he'd laughed and swung Eanflæd around in the rain by the great hedge. She'd smiled, gone to Linnet's, helped her wring the neck of three chickens, and told herself she was glad he was healing. That night, when she held out her wrist for Gwladus to unfasten the carnelians, Gwladus stroked her hand and stood, breasts forward, mouth parted, and Hild understood she was offering herself: a gift, a solace. Hild swallowed and didn't move, didn't touch.

She hadn't touched anyone. Every day the chief men arrived in Yeavering with their proud young sons and daughters: soft skin, hard muscles, challenging eyes. Every day, Hild found a way to step to one side of her yearning. It was too dangerous. Every day, Paulinus and his priests watched her. Every day, the king watched her.

Sometimes she rode with some laughing girl or strong young man. She drank with them, she played tug-of-war, she sat hip to hip with them on spread cloaks to watch the mummers perform by roaring bonfires while cattle lowed, and she knew what it meant when sometimes one of them took that extra breath or held her eye for that extra heartbeat, but she turned them aside with a smile. And with Cian she always remembered to turn in time to hide that same look in her own eyes; grew practiced in dropping her shoulders when he leaned past her for beer and she smelt another woman on him; learnt to pretend she didn't notice when he sometimes paused and looked at her, puzzled, then turned away.

She stepped to one side of her yearning but didn't step outside herself, didn't close down. She simply pruned those parts that might reach out, that could damage her. Like pollarding an oak. One day, she would no longer need to train her growth, one day she would be free to spread as she wanted. Then she would grow very like the others, very like: though, as with all pollards, with the marks there for those who knew to look. For now, she was the light of the world. She wanted to keep the Yffings in power for a while, keep herself—and Cian and Begu and her mother—safe until she could find another way. She sent a second, longer message to Rhin: *Here is silver. Have your man sow discord between Rhoedd and Cadwallon.* Discord would weaken the British, perhaps make the west look ripe for Penda to pluck instead of allying with them. War between the Mercians and the British would weaken them both and delay the clash of stags.

In the south, plague spread. In East Anglia, Bishop Felix began a great abbey for Sigebert. In the west, Cadwallon quarrelled with Rheged and Alt Clut. Hild smiled.

Eadfrith sent a messenger with news of gifts sent to York from Penda.

"What gifts?" Hild asked.

"Gold," the messenger said. "Eadfrith weighed it at a stone, exactly."

"What kind of gold?" Why would he send tribute? It didn't make sense.

"Hackgold."

"Describe it."

"Pommels," he said. "Strap ends. Hilts."

Cian was coming alert now. "War gear!"

Hild nodded, said to the king, "These aren't gifts. They're taunts. Probably stripped from the gesiths he killed in Gwynedd." Penda was feeling stronger.

Edwin flushed and something moved behind his eyes. Some decision.

The high wooden sides of Edwin's Romish talking stage sheltered the thegns from the wind. The chief men assembled on the benches were glad to fling off their cloaks and soak up the sun.

The Yffing totem, recarved with a cross and repainted in crimson, blue, and green, with the boar in bronze and gold, gleamed. Paulinus stood before it, on the platform, the other king's counsellors, including Hild and Cian, ranged behind him. Hild was the only woman. The queen sat with her women, including Begu and Breguswith, on the side benches.

Paulinus spoke of the great church rising in York, the church in Craven, the Christian king of the East Angles and their king-to-be, the king's great-nephew.

"What do we care?" one man called. Hunric.

Paulinus kept talking: "The gesiths who now flocked to Christ's banner—"

"Aye, and got the shit kicked out of them in Gwynedd!"

"—the king's heir, Wuscfrea, there, to the king's right, born into a marriage blessed by God."

"He's still sucking his thumb!" shouted a man behind Hunric. Some of the thegns laughed, but more nodded. Hild had told her uncle it was madness to let Paulinus speak—did he not remember last time? But Edwin had smiled that smile with too many teeth and said didn't she see the world was changing? Besides, the Crow was chief priest of the Yffings and entitled to speak.

Hunric stood. Paulinus's cheeks mottled, but before he could start foaming, Edwin shouted cheerfully, "Bishop, let the thegn speak! Haven't you learnt anything yet? Sit down. Let him have his say."

Paulinus sat down just a little too quickly.

Hild glanced about her: Cian, as surprised as she was. Paulinus, angry, yes—a bishop of Rome to be interrupted by a barbarian!—but underneath that a glint of . . . satisfaction? Then Coelfrith, face showing nothing; not surprised. The queen, her face composed.

This was planned. Hild's heart moved from a walk to a trot.

Hunric bent his head. Straightened. "He looks like a fine boy, King. Strong, lusty. But a boy. We have Idings in the north, Rheged and Gwynedd to the west, and Penda to the south. We need a strong man in Elmet. We need Cadwallon crushed. Will you call your grown sons to you?"

Hild's gaze locked on Æthelburh. The queen was examining her cuff. She looked at Begu, who was frowning slightly, puzzled. At her mother, who wore her usual enigmatic expression.

Edwin didn't even bother to stand. "I hear you, good Hunric. You are wise, as always. I will think on it. Come to the feast tonight and hear my word."

The hall was packed. The mead flowed. Hild, wearing her best clothes and jewels, didn't drink a drop. She couldn't eat. She kept smiling, kept raising her cup, kept meat in her hand, and when no one was looking, tossed it to the dogs. No one noticed. Noise rose like the tide.

Hild's ears rang. Something was coming.

Speeches. Toasts. Songs. It passed like a dream, or like the charge into battle. Unreal. And in the centre of it all, Edwin, her uncle, sitting, chin in one hand, smiling, eyes half-lidded, watching, in no hurry. Her mind whirred, but this time her lathe was blunt, and the world simply spun and made no sense. This time, all the people she loved were here, in a row, at the king's board. This time her mother didn't have her back to anyone. She was laughing with Cian.

This time there was no Osric, staring about him with beetled brow. This time it was just her, searching face after face, trying to understand.

Her mother caught her glance and smiled. That smile she had smiled when Hild was seven years old and preparing to carry the great gold welcome cup: *Be brave, be strong.*

Then she saw Coelfrith stand and leave the hall, nod to the scop on the way out. She caught Edwin's gaze, and he smiled that smile with too many teeth. For her.

Gwladus leaned in, filled her cup unnecessarily, murmured, "Pinch your cheeks. You've gone white as milk."

Hild wasn't listening. She was watching Coelfrith come back into the hall with two men, one bearing a sack made not of hemp but of fine white linen, one a keg of polished oak, bound with copper.

She was vaguely aware of Gwladus on one side, Begu on the other, but she couldn't pay attention. She was caught in what felt like a dream, one of those endless dreams that turned on itself, one she couldn't escape. It unfurled with dreadful lack of surprise. It had all happened before.

Edwin stood.

The scop played a dramatic chord.

Edwin took his time catching the gaze of all his people: the beady black of the Crow, Uinniau's open hazel, Breguswith's bright, bright blue, Cian's darker blue, and her own moss agate.

She felt the weight of gold around her neck, the wink of carnelians at her wrist, the seax at her waist, the fine dress with stiffly worked gold borders. A sacrificial cow.

Edwin poured the white mead with his own hand. Smiled at her again. Then he turned to Cian, held out the cup.

Cian rose. Hild, still in a dream, half expected to hear the hiss of surf, see Mulstan grinning and holding out a sword. But it was Edwin, with a cup.

Cian took the cup.

"Cian Boldcloak. Hero of Gwynedd. Chief gesith. Queen's godson. Son, so it is said, of Ceredig, king of Elmet."

Cian's hand began to shake.

"Hunric has said we need a strong man at our border. A loyal man. Hunric is wise. Cian Boldcloak, you have proved your oath beyond doubt. You saved my life. You saved the ætheling's life. You love our son. You are brave in battle. You're strong. You're baptised. You are royal through your father. Your father whom I bested in fierce and honourable battle." Men began to beat on the benches. Cian looked as though he were facing a strong wind. Edwin raised his hand. "Cian Boldcloak, will you and your lady wife take Elmet? Will you hold it as ealdorman until Wuscfrea comes of age?"

Cian blinked, said, "Lady wife?"

"My niece, the lady Hild."

Every head in hall turned. Hild felt the weight of their regard. Like a gold crown. She regarded them back.

"Don't faint," her mother murmured, one hand under her elbow. Where had she come from? "Take a breath. Take another. Stand." The ground was a long way down, and heaving. "Breathe. Straighten your back. Smile. Step forward. Step now, child."

She walked with her mother at her elbow. Palms beating on tables followed her like surf.

Then she was standing with Cian before the small oak table carved and inlaid with Edwin's emblem. The red-gold boar's head flickered and swam in the torchlight as though it was running. Coelfrith's men placed the sack and the keg on the table, opened the sack to spill a handful of hazelnuts over the oak. Mead and hazelnuts. Fruit of Elmet.

"Bishop," Edwin said, and Paulinus stepped forward with the white cloth in his hand.

Edwin smiled at her, that spreading, lard-melt smile of a king roping his subject, harnessing her to his purpose. Paulinus smiled at her. Cian smiled at her and held out his left hand.

Cian, with his chestnut hair. Cian, with his bold cloak. Cian who didn't know the truth. *You can't have him.*

His hand was still out. Cian, the six-year-old with the stick, the fourteen-year-old with the boy's sword, the gesith with the ringed sword.

You can't have him. But now she must. The Yffings would fall. She'd seen the pattern. And now, at last, she also saw a way, when that time came, to keep them both safe. To keep her people safe.

She put her hand in his.

They put their hands on the table. Edwin and Æthelburh laid theirs on top, and the Crow draped the cloth over all.

Paulinus spoke for a long time—of loyalty, of a marriage to be witnessed before God in Elmet, of sacred oaths—but Hild hardly heard him. All she could see was the triumph on his face, the satisfied articulation of his lips: Sinner, his mouth said, doomed sinner and no more my rival. He knew the truth. Æthelburh knew. And Edwin. But now the lie, *Cian, son of Ceredig king,* would be sealed over the truth. Edwin thought the lie would make him safe without having to call in the sons Æthelburh wanted to keep far away. Without having to let his seer go.

But that was like a tiny piece of grit in a loaf of pure white bread. It was nothing. It didn't matter. What mattered was the truth, rising like birdsong, like the scent of flowers opening to the sun, of her wyrd. Cian's hand beneath hers. It always had been so. It had always been meant to be so. *Fate goes ever as it must.*

On the slow journey from Yeavering to Elmet, during the day, riding one on either side, Cian and Hild talked to Edwin of revenues and tithes, of plans and obligations; of how Edwin would bring Wuscfrea to learn the land and how often seer and ealdorman would visit the court. At night they separated, Cian to the fireside among his gesiths, Hild to her wagon, with her mother and Begu and Gwladus.

Her mother spoke to her alone just once. "This keeps you safe, both of you. It keeps us all safe. We think it's for the best."

We. Æthelburh and her mother, protecting their children.

As they rode south the weather softened to full spring. James the Deacon joined them outside York with his choristers. At Caer Loid, the night before the wedding, he heard her confession.

"There can never be too much love in the world," he said. "You do it to save two lives. More than two. God blesses you. God blesses your land. Pray, every day, and find peace." Then he smiled and looked around the small, plain church. "Also, give the place a bit of gilding. A beautiful house makes God happy."

The small church was packed: Paulinus and Stephanus officiated, embroidered robes swinging as stiff as dragonfly wings through the incense smoke, jewels winking in the bright candlelight—white wax candles, lots of them. Lots of wax from lots of bees; her bees; her church; her people. James and his two choristers sang, though the wooden church packed with people was not the best sound board he could have chosen. The Latin flowed over her like smoke.

The front was packed with those who would leave soon: Edwin and Æthelburh, Wuscfrea and Eanflæd, Wilnoð and Bassus, Breguswith and Luftmaer. She would never live with them again. She would never follow the court to Bebbanburg and Yeavering, Derventio and Goodmanham, Sancton and Brough and York. She would only visit. At the end of the second bench, Begu and Uinniau. Strange, to think she was marrying before Begu.

The back rows were dense with her people: Oeric and Hild's gesiths—a formal gift now, from the king. Pyr and Saxfryth. And behind them Morud and Gwladus, Lweriadd and Sintiadd, Rhin and a knot of Menewood folk.

Onnen wasn't there. There had been no time. But perhaps they could visit the bay after the harvest. She shied away from that, the world where she was married. Not yet. Not just yet. She gripped her seax for courage. Now she knew how Hereswith had felt. She wished Hereswith were there. But there were scores of people. Elmetsætne. Her people. Faces she didn't know, not yet. But she would. She would know them all.

She looked left and right. She couldn't see as much as she'd like; the unfamiliar veil got in the way. No doubt she'd learn how to manage that, how to use it to her advantage, as her mother did.

Paulinus droned on. James sang some more.

And then Paulinus was giving them the blessing, ". . . Son, and the Holy Ghost. Amen."

Blessed by God. *You can't have him.* She had to. *God blesses you.*

The church bulged with the people's *Amen.* Cian was beaming. Beaming at Paulinus, the king, the people. Her.

This was the sum of all his dreams. Greater than his dreams. This was honour, respect, riches. Belonging. Ealdorman was not so different from king, and he was to be ealdorman in his very own Elmet wood, ealdorman for a strong king. For a while.

She took his hand.

Beef and mutton, salmon and eel. Good bread and mead, an astonishing quantity of mead.

Gwladus filled her cup often. Cian filled her cup. She filled Cian's. They drank a lot and didn't talk much. The space between them slowly filled with awareness, like a honeycomb, thick, dense, holding them in their place.

No one noticed. Wedding feasts were for the guests, not the newlyweds.

Night was for the newlyweds.

Hild sat on the borrowed blanket on the borrowed bed in the bower, wearing nothing but her thinnest, finest undershift, while Gwladus hung her overdress and veil in the nook and pondered where to hang the belt and seax.

"Here, over the corner post," Hild said.

Gwladus looked at the slaughter seax, then at Hild. "It's a wedding night, lady, not a war."

"I'm used to it. He's used to it. It's just a knife."

Gwladus sighed, hung the belt over the post, and carried the bucket of soapy water through the curtain. When she came back she brought a tiny bottle and a gold comb from Hild's box. She dabbed a drop of jessamine on her little finger, ran it over the comb's teeth, and combed Hild's hair. Hild closed her eyes, enjoying the pressure of the hand on her crown, the tug of the comb, the firm strokes.

"There." Gwladus tipped Hild's chin up, examined her critically, tucked a fall of hair behind Hild's left ear. Nodded. She put the comb and bottle away, then spent a while fussing with the placement of the taper, trying the table, then the niche, back to the table, the windowsill. Hild couldn't see what difference it made.

Eventually Gwladus settled on the table by the corner.

Hild picked at the blanket. Gwladus cleared her throat. "So. I beat the mattress. The sheets are clean and warmed. That is, they were warm, and I've no doubt you'll warm them up again soon enough. And I found some dried lavender for your pillows. There's water in this pitcher, beer in this, and cheese here under the cover."

"Gwladus . . ."

Gwladus ignored her. "I won't be outside the curtain, not tonight, but I'll be in Begu's room next door. If you need me. Not that you'll need me."

"Gwladus . . ." She heard voices outside.

Gwladus stood before her, close enough for Hild to smell. Hild didn't look up. If she did, she would pull Gwladus close and never let her go. "Enjoy him, lady. I can hear them outside now. I'll send him in. Only him."

The curtain swished. The door beyond opened. Raucous laughter. Hild reached for her belt, arranged the seax so its handle would be towards the bed, an easy draw.

"No," Gwladus said clearly from the other room. "No, I mean it. You, and you. Not a foot past this door or the lady will turn you into a toad. A prickless toad. That's right, you clutch at it while it's still there." More laughter. Muffled comments. "Now, my lord. This way. I'll run these oafs off."

The door closed. She stared at her knees. The curtain swished.

He sat on the bed next to her.

She stared at his knees. Blinked. Looked up at his face. "You're wearing your cloak. Are you cold?" It came out as a challenge.

Even in the shadowed light, she saw his pupils tighten to pinpricks. "You've got your seax to hand. Are you frightened?"

Silence. Voices outside slowly faded. She tried again. "Really, are you cold? I am."

He jumped up, flung out his left arm, and settled back down with his arm and cloak around her. Around her shoulder. They sat stiffly. The thin linen between her breasts trembled. Was she scared? This was Cian. She had knocked him down half a hundred times.

She touched her cheek to his. It prickled, a little. A muscle in his jaw jumped. He had knocked her down half a hundred times. But his jaw still jumped. She reached around his waist. Closed her eyes.

Silence. She breathed, in and out, in and out. He breathed, as fast as she did. She felt the muscles sliding over his ribs. He smelt of thyme and mead and that iron-and-salt tang that made her nostrils flare.

She knew what he looked like. Knew how his prick bobbed free, that his nipples looked like red currants. Knew the feel of his tongue. Knew him alive and alert and ready. But she didn't know this man.

She put her other hand on his belly. Hit his buckle. She pulled back. "That buckle!" The knife buckle.

He blushed.

"Take it off. Take your cloak off. Take it all off."

"Not until you throw your knife in the corner."

They sounded like six-year-olds. "I won't throw it."

She stood and carried it carefully to the nearest corner, by the table. Turned. Saw how his gaze fastened on her as she stood outlined by candle-light. Trust Gwladus. She let him look. It was a very thin undershift. He could probably see right through it, right to her. Her nipples sharpened.

He took off his cloak. She folded it carefully while he pulled off his shoes, then his belt, then his tunic. She laid them in a pile on the cloak, then carried it to the corner, next to her knife, out of reach. She turned, looked deliberately at him, at the lines of tight muscle under his hose. The baggy part, tented now. Growing, pointing a little to the left.

They both swallowed.

"I don't know what to do," he said.

That made no sense. "But you've had lots of women."

"I know what to do with women. I don't know what to do with you. No, I don't mean— You're not housefolk. You're highfolk. And Anglisc."

She didn't know what to say.

"And I don't know if you want me. I don't know why you didn't want me before."

She took his hand, laid it on her breast. She knew how that would feel, knew the line of fire that would run to his belly, to his loins. "Of course I want you. I've put my hand on your belt since I could say my name. I've shown you magic, I've made magic for you. Drop your shield now, and we'll give each other magic."

She stepped against him, so his nose touched the arch of her ribs, so he could smell her, smell that earth and honeysuckle and sharp sap of woman running out of her. She put a hand on his shoulder—the fillet of muscle running from his neck to the bone at the point—and one on the back of his head. And it leapt between them, like the understanding between gesiths locked in combat, like the awareness running between a school of fish, a flock of birds, a herd of horses: *We are us.*

She did want him. She wanted all of him, everything, wanted to fill herself with him until she couldn't breathe. Wanted to pull him through her from the outside, to pull his skin through her skin, his muscle to hers, his bone to her bone. She could squeeze him, crush him to her, flex, strain, and reach, fight without blood, without bruises.

And she did.

She closed tight around him, tight as a fist, tighter, and his eyes were the bluest blue she had ever seen, bluer than the sky, bigger than the sky, wide, endless, the horizon of home.

On the day after her wedding she lay at the edge of the hazel coppice, one cheek pressed to the moss that smelt of worm cast and the last of the sun, listening: to the wind in the elms, rushing away from the day, to the jackdaws changing their calls from "Outward! Outward!" to "Home now! Home!" In a while she would follow.

Author's Note

✦

Hild was real. She was born fourteen hundred years ago in Anglo-Saxon England. Everything we know about her comes from the Venerable Bede's *Ecclesiastical History of the English Nation*, the foundational text of English history.* The first half of her life can be summed up in one short paragraph:

She was born circa 614, after her mother, Breguswith, had a dream about her unborn child being a jewel that brings light to the land. Hild's father, Hereric, of the royal house of Deira, was poisoned while in exile at the court of Ceredig, king of Elmet. Her older sister, Hereswith, married a nephew of Rædwald, king of East Anglia. Hild, along with much of Edwin's household, was baptised by Paulinus circa 627, in York. She then disappeared from the record until 647, when she reappeared in East Anglia about to take ship for Gaul to join her sister—at which point she was recruited to the church by Bishop Aidan.

We don't know exactly where Hild was born and when her father died—or her mother. We have no idea what she looked like, what she was good at, whether she married or had children. But clearly she was extraordinary. In a time of warlords and kings, when might was right, she began as the second daughter of a homeless widow, probably without much in the way of material resources and certainly in an illiterate culture, and ended up a powerful adviser to statesmen-kings and teacher of five bishops. Today she is revered as Saint Hilda.

So how did Hild ride this cultural transformation of petty kingdoms into sophisticated,

---

* Read a translation, by Professor Roy M. Liuzza (Joseph Black et al., eds., *Broadview Anthology of British Literature,Volume 1:The Medieval Period*. Peterborough, Ont: Broadview Press, 2006; hosted and linked to with permission of the translator), of the relevant passages here: http://nicolagriffith .com/Bede_on_Hild.pdf.

literate states? We don't know. I wrote this book to find out. I learnt what I could of the late sixth and early seventh centuries: ethnography, archaeology, poetry, numismatics, jewellery, textiles, languages, food production, weapons, and more. And then I re-created that world and its known historical incidents, put Hild inside the world, and watched, fascinated, as she grew up, influenced and influencing. (The deeper I go, the more certain I become that I've caught a tiger by the tail. I'm writing the next part of her story now.)

While people in Hild's time may have understood their world a little differently from how we understand ours, they were still people—as human as we are. Their dreams, fears, political machinations, fights, loves, and hesitations were shaped by circumstance and temperament, as are ours. Hild, though singular, was singular within the constraints of her time. Her time was occasionally brutal.

I don't pretend to be an historian. Although I did my utmost not to contravene what is known about the early seventh-century material culture, languages, natural world, power politics, and individuals of the British Isles, this is a novel. I made it up.

A NOTE ON PRONUNCIATION

Hild would have encountered at least four languages on a regular basis: Old Irish (Irish), Ancient British (Brythonic), Latin, and Old English (Anglisc).

I won't attempt to codify the pronunciation of Old Irish; it's defeated better than me.

Ancient British is easier. If you think of it in the same terms as modern Welsh, you'll get a sense of how to proceed. Every letter is sounded, c is pronounced k, dd as th, ff as v, rh as hr, and u, g, and w can be . . . mercurial. So:

Cian: KEE-an
Gwladus: OO-la-doose
Arddun: AR-thun
Rhroedd: HRO-eth
Urien: IRRI-yen
Uinniau: oo-IN-NI-eye (the short form sounds very like Winny)

Latin sounds much as it looks with the exception of v, which sounds like w. Consonants are hard (g as in go, and c as k).

Old English is a particular and deliberate tongue, with every consonant and vowel sounded, r's trilled, and dipthongs accented on the first element. Some simplified rules include pronouncing:

æ: like the a in cat
sc: sh, as in ship
g: sometimes y, as in yes
īc: usually as itch
f: sometimes as v, as in very
ð: th, as in then

So:
Gipswīc: Yips-witch
gesith: yeh-SEETH
gemæcce: yeh-MATCH-eh
thegn: thayn
ætheling: ATH-ell-ing
scop: SHOW-p
Anglisc: ANG-glish
Eanflæd: AY-on-vlad
seax: sax
Yffi: IFF-y
Hereric: herr-EHR-itch
Wilnoð: oo-ILL-noth

Glossary

✦

æfen: six to nine in the evening
ætheling: male youth in the line of succession, prince
Anglisc: pertaining to Angles (the people, the language)
Arawn: British (wealh) underworld
baldric: wide belt for weapons worn crosswise over the shoulder
basilica: main hall of old Roman administration building
Belenos: British god
Beli Mawr: legendary British figure
Blodmonath: November
Cait Sith: black cat of British legends
ceorl: freeman
chape: tip of a scabbard, usually metal, often highly decorated
Coel Hen: fifth-century British king
cyrtel: loose, long-sleeved dress; informal
dryhten: absolute lord
ealdorman: high lord (similar to viceroy)
ell: about thirty inches
Elmetsætne: the people of Elmet
Eorðe: Anglisc goddess
etin: giant
freemartin: female calf masculinised in the womb by male twin
gemæcce: formal female friendship or partnership; one of a pair
gesith: member of a king's personal war band; elite warrior
Gewisse: people of Upper Thames area; West Saxons
hægtes: supernatural figure; witch

Hel: Anglisc for hell, a cold place

Hrethmonath: March

Hwicce: people of the area around Worcester; Saxons

hythe: landing place or harbour

Idings: royal dynasty of Bernicia

league: about three miles

Loides: ruling tribe of British Elmet

Lyr: legendary British god

mene: valley

middæg: middle of the day, noon to three o'clock

morgen: six to nine in the morning

nithing: oath-breaker; one who is shunned

Northumbria: Bernicia and Deira

Œstremonath: April

Oiscingas: royal dynasty of Kent

pace: two strides, about five feet

principia: old Roman administrative building

redcrest: Roman

rhyne: ditch, canal

scop: Anglisc bard

seax: knife with a large, single-edged blade

selkie: mythical creature who lives as a seal in the sea but becomes
    human on land

sidsa: magic

Sigel: Anglisc god

Sirona: Romano-British goddess

snakesteel: pattern-welded steel

snakestone: ammonite (fossil)

Solmonath: February

thegn: lord

thung: poisonous flowers (e.g., wolfsbane)

Thunor: Anglisc god

tree hay: chopped-up brush, used as winter fodder

tufa: king's standard

undern: nine in the morning to noon

vill: royal estate

wariangle: butcher-bird, or strike

wealh: Anglisc for "stranger" and root word of current "Welsh"

Weodmonath: August

wīc: king's trading settlement, usually a port

wight: supernatural figure, ghost

Winterfylleth: October

Witganmot: assembly of notables, usually annual

Woden: Anglisc god
Wuffings: East Anglian royal dynasty
wyrd: fate
Yffings: Deiran royal dynasty
Yr Hen Ogledd: the Old North; kingdoms of northern England
and southern Scotland

Acknowledgements

✦

I've been thinking about this book for a long time. The list of people to whom I'd like to offer acknowledgement and thanks is correspondingly long:

To my editor, Sean McDonald, and everyone at Farrar, Straus and Giroux: Jonathan Galassi, Andrew Mandel, Jeff Seroy, Kathy Daneman, Spenser Lee, Devon Mazzone, Emily Bell, Taylor Sperry, Nick Courage, Charlotte Strick, Abby Kagan, and all those who have worked hard and intelligently on behalf of this book. I also want to thank Karla Eoff, my copy editor.

To my agent, Stephanie Cabot, and Anna Worrall and all at the Gernert Company. It's a privilege working with such a team.

To the Society of Authors, in the United Kingdom, who gave me a grant for travel and research at a critical juncture.

To the medieval bloggers, academic and otherwise—Michelle of Heavenfield, Jonathan Jarret, Magistra et Mater, Tim Clarkson, Sally Wilde, Guy Halsall, Carla Naylund, Reverend Brenda Warren—who have helped me, some unwittingly but most with deliberate effort and patience. Thanks also to Lisa Spangenberg and Wendy Pearson for input on various things, and to Dennis King, and David Burke and John Clay, for fixing my Old Irish. All mistakes are, of course, my own.

To all composers, compilers, translators and enthusiasts of Old English poetry. Rædwald's elegy on pages 141–42 is how I imagined part of the first draft of *Beowulf* might have looked if it were written just before the Age of Conversion rather than a little later (as most scholars agree is most likely the case). I used a variety of translations as the basis of my linguistic retro-engineering project and then much poetic license. Again all errors are my own.

To my friends, for practical assistance, patience, encouragement, wine, and more: Angélique Corthals, Liliana Dávalos, Maria Dahvana Headley, Liz Butcher, Guillermo

Castro, Ginny Gilder, Lynn Slaughter, Dorothy Allison, Val McDermid, Robert Schenkkan, Karen Joy Fowler, Matt Ruff, Karina Meléndez, Jennifer Durham, and Vicki Platts-Brown.

To my family, in the United Kingdom and the United States. Thank you.

To Steve Swartz, who appears here as Stephanus the Black because he contributed enough money to the African Well Fund to bring potable water to hundreds if not thousands of people.

To Roger Deakin, Robert Macfarlane, and Richard Mabey, for their wonderful books about Britain and its wild and wooded ways. And to Thomas H. Nelson, author of *The Birds of Yorkshire*, published in 1907 and long out of print, for writing about the miracle of doves and starlings in the same nest.

To my community of readers, everywhere, for following me to strange places (sometimes literally).

To the U.K. rugby fans of my youth who introduced me to several scabrous ditties. The song on page 211 is based on one of them. Some of you will know the tune . . .

To the experts who (mostly) have never heard of me but who nevertheless helped in ways that one day I hope to pay forward: Sarah Foot, Nicholas Higham, Robin Fleming, Chris Wickham, Barbara Yorke, Richard Underwood, Alex Woolf, D. P. Kirby, Edward James, Kevin Crossley-Holland, Alaric Hall, Rosamond McKitterick, Sally Crawford, Clare Lees and Gillian Overing, Penelope Walton Rogers, John Blair, Peter Hunter Blair, every contributor to *The Heroic Age*, and, naturally, the two who got me started, Trevelyan and Stenton.

To Hild herself, of course, for changing the world, which is what it takes, sometimes, for me to pay attention.

And finally, above all, to Kelley, always Kelley, for not, ever, letting me do less than my best. After all these years, I still want to impress her.